WIT'CH GATE

Book Four of

The Banned and the Banished

JAMES CLEMENS

orbit

www.orbitbooks.co.uk

D0514690

ORBIT

First published by The Ballantine Publishing Group, 2001
First published in Great Britain by Orbit 2003
Reprinted 2003, 2004, 2005, 2006

A CIP catalogue record for this book is available from
the British Library.

ISBN-13: 978-84149-197-4
ISBN-10: 1-84149-197-7

Printed and bound in Great Britain by
Mackays of Chatham plc, Chatham, Kent

Orbit
An imprint of
Little, Brown Book Group
Brettenham House
Lancaster Place
London WC2E 7EN

A member of the Hatchette Livre Group of Companies

www.littlebrown.co.uk

James Clemens was born in Chicago, Illinois in 1961. He now has a veterinary practice in Sacramento, California, where he shares his home with two Dalmations, a stray German Shepherd and a love-sick parrot named Igor.

Find out more about James Clemens and other Orbit authors by registering for the free monthly newsletter at www.orbitbooks.co.uk

By James Clemens

The Banned and the Banished
WIT'CH FIRE
WIT'CH STORM
WIT'CH WAR
WIT'CH GATE
WIT'CH STAR

The Godslayer Series
SHADOWFALL

Look out for
HINTERLAND

ACKNOWLEDGMENTS

Thanks to all the friends and family who have helped polish and hone this book into its present form, especially my personal group of work junkies: Chris Crowe, Michael Gallowglas, Lee Garrett, Dennis Grayson, Penny Hill, Debbie Nelson, Dave Meek, Jane O'Riva, Chris "the little" Smith, Judy and Steve Prey, Carolyn McCray, and Caroline Williams. Additionally, a special thanks to the four people who remain my best critics and most loyal supporters: my editors, Steve Saffel and Veronica Chapman, and my agents, here and abroad, Russ Galen and Danny Baror.

FOREWORD TO
WIT'CH GATE
by
Proctor Sensa Dela,
Chairman and President of
University Press

Treach.er.y, trech´ ə.rē, n. (1) breach of allegiance, faith, or
confidence (2) an act against the Commonwealth (3) dispar-
agement of the Law by word or print (synonyms: *betrayal,*
knavery, double-cross, villainy, treason, Scroll-kissed)
— *Encyclopedia of Common Usage,* Fifth Edition

READ AGAIN THE DEFINITION ABOVE; THEN LOOK AROUND THE
classroom, a chamber once filled with bright-eyed, eager scholars.
How many students still remain after the study of the first three
Kelvish Scrolls?

See the empty seats.

By this point, statistically, two-thirds of each year's students
fail to pass the rigorous psychological examinations following
their study of the Scrolls. As you know, those who were found
wanting were shipped to the sanitariums of Da Borau, where
they await the painful surgeries to dull their minds and remove
their tongues. But I am not here to speak of the fallen ones, those
slack-jawed unfortunates dubbed the "Scroll-kissed." Instead,
I write this foreword for those of you who have successfully
passed these tests and have been deemed of sufficient constitu-
tion to read and study the fourth of these banned texts.

This warning is for you.

In the past, many students have grown haughty after succeeding this far in their course of study, but now is not the time to
lift toasts to one another—for ahead lie pitfalls that may yet capture the unwary. Herein lies the path to *treachery.*

The forewords to the other texts admonished you about the
nefarious nature of the Scrolls' author, declaring the madman
of Kell to be a liar and a deceiver—a snake in the grass, if you

will. Now it is my turn to expand upon the dangers that yet await you.

In the past years of study, you have experienced the hiss of the snake. You have carried the beast in your hands, in your school bags. You have fallen asleep with it at your bedside. But do not be lulled by its pleasant caress or its pleasing colors. They mask the hidden poison of the beast.

Only now, while you are dulled to the danger, will the snake begin to show its true demeanor. In this book, while you look elsewhere, the snake will raise up and strike! That is what I've come to warn you: This book has *fangs*.

So beware its bite!

Even as I write these words, I can hear the whispered scoffing. Do you doubt me? Look around your hall once again. Not at each other, but at the empty seats. Already the Scrolls have claimed many of your fellow classmates.

In this fourth volume, the author will continue his assault upon your sanity, to try to win you to his will, to spread his poison throughout your body. But I hope to give you the antidote to this toxin.

A cure in two simple words: knowledge and guidance.

To attempt to read these cursed Scrolls on your own would be like pressing a viper to your breast, inviting death. Scholars of the past have devised this course of study to keep the poison from your minds, so be mindful of your lessons.

It is imperative that you listen to your instructors. Obey their every order, complete every assignment, and most important of all, do *not* read ahead on your own. Therein lies your only hope. Even a single page could corrupt the ill-prepared. So do not stray from the path of instruction, a track well-worn by the heels of previous scholars. Without this guidance, you would surely be lost among the weeds and tall grasses—where the snakes are waiting.

So be forewarned one last time: *There is poison in these pages.*

Poi.son, poi´ zon, n. v. (1) a substance that taints, corrupts, or destroys (2) the act of administering a toxin, venom, or deadly draught (3) to alter one's perception of right and wrong (i.e., "to poison another's mind") (synonyms: *corruption, perversion, venom, bane, miasma, contagion, disease*)
        —*Encyclopedia of Common Usage,* Fifth Edition

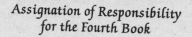

Assignation of Responsibility
for the Fourth Book

This copy is being assigned to you and is your sole responsibility. Its loss, alteration, or destruction will result in severe penalties (as stated in your local ordinances). Any transmission, copying, or even oral reading in the presence of a nonclassmate is strictly forbidden. By signing below and placing your fingerprint, you accept all responsibility and release the university from any damage the text may cause you (or those around you) by its perusal.

_____

Signature   Date

Place inked print of the fourth
finger of your right hand here:

*** WARNING ***

If you should perchance come upon this text outside of proper
university channels, please close this book now and alert the
proper authorities for safe retrieval. Failure to do so can lead to
your immediate arrest and incarceration.

YOU HAVE BEEN WARNED.

WIT'CH GATE

Sung in ice but born in thunder,
So the Land was torn asunder.

I FIND MYSELF GROWING RESTLESS AGAIN. LATELY, THE WIT'CH HAS been calling to me in my dreams to complete her tale; she whispers in my ear as I walk about the city. At times, I swear I feel her breath on my skin, like the itch of a rash. Nowadays, as I go about my errands, I hardly see the streets and avenues of my home. I picture other places, other sights: the sun-seared ruins of Tular, the broken granite shield of the Northwall. I find myself living in the shadowy half-world between past and present.

I've begun to wonder: *If I write again, will I be forever lost in the past?* Will this land constructed of letters and ink become more real than the air I breathe? Will I become mired in memories, doomed for eternity to relive old terrors and rare triumphs?

Though I know the risk must be taken, I find I cannot write. I know it is the only way to lift her curse of immortality. Only by completing her tale will I finally be allowed the balm of death. Yet, in the past moons, I've begun to doubt her promise. What if her ancient words were a trick, a final act of malice on the part of the wit'ch?

So for too long a time, I have sat frozen, hovering between terror and salvation.

That is, until this morning—when she sent me a sign!

As I woke with the crowing of a cock and splashed cold water on my face, I discovered a miracle in the mirror above my washstand. Nestled within my dark locks rested a single gray hair. My heart clenched at the sight; tears blurred the miracle. As the morning's fog melted in the rays of the rising sun, I refused to move. I dared not even finger that single strand, afraid it might be an illusion. I could not face such cruelty. Not now, not after so long.

3

In that moment, I felt something long dead in my heart spring to life—*hope!*

I fell to the floor, knees too weak to hold me up any longer. I sobbed for what seemed like days. It was a sign, a harbinger of old age, a promise of death.

Once I regained control of my limbs, I rose and touched the strand of gray. It was real! The wit'ch had not lied.

This realization shattered the impasse. Without eating, I gathered the tools of my craft—pen and scroll—and set to work. I must finish her tale.

Outside, the winter days have grown muted, as if all color has been bled from the world. People huddle down drab streets, wrapped from head to toe in the browns and grays of heavy woolens. Beyond the city walls, the snowy hills are stained with ash and soot from the hundred smoking chimneys of Kell. It is a landscape done in shades of gray and black. Even the skies overhead are cloaked by flat, featureless clouds—a massive blank slate.

Midwinter.

It is a storyteller's season, a bare canvas that awaits the stroke of a pen to bring life and substance back into the world. It is a time when folks crowd around hearths, awaiting tales full of brightness and sharp colors. It is the season when inns fill up, and minstrels sing bawdy stories of other lands, of fire and sunlight. In other seasons, stories are bought with coppers—but not in winter. In this season of dull skies and somber hearts, even a poor storyteller could find his pot blessed with silver and gold. Such is the hunger for tales in winter.

But, of course, with this tale, I seek not gold, but something more valuable, something all men are granted at birth but that was stolen from me by a wit'ch. I seek only death.

So as the world huddles in the quiet of a winter's cloak, I once again begin Elena's tale. I ask you to close your eyes and listen. Beyond this season of whispers, angry voices are raised. Can you hear them? Men using words like swords, hacking and parrying one another . . . And there sits one lone woman, caught in the midst of their fury.

Book One

THE WEIR

1

ELENA FOUND HER THRONE AN UNCOMFORTABLE SEAT. IT WAS A chair meant for someone harder and more age-worn than she. Its high, straight back was carved in twining roses, the thorns of which could be felt through her silk robe and dress. Even its seat was flat and unforgiving, polished ironwood with no pillow to soften its hard surface. For ages past, it had been the seat of power for A'loa Glen. Both kings and praetors had sat here in judgment, sea-hardened men who scowled at the comforts of life.

Even its size was intimidating. Elena felt like a child in the wide and tall chair. There were not even armrests. Elena did not know what to do with her hands, so she ended up simply folding them in her lap.

One step below her, though it might have been a league away for as much as they paid her any attention, was a long table crowded with representatives from every faction willing to fight the Gul'gotha. Elena knew what the majority here in the Great Hall thought of her. All they saw was a slim woman with pale skin and fiery hair. None noticed the pain in her eyes, nor the fearful knowledge of her own dread power. To them, she was a pretty bird on a perch.

Elena brushed aside a strand of hair from her face.

All along the length, voices cried to be heard in languages both familiar and strange. Two men on the far end were close to coming to blows.

Among the throng, there were those Elena knew well, those who had helped wrest the island of A'loa Glen from the evil rooted here. The high keel of the Dre'rendi Fleet, still bearing his bandages from the recent war, bellowed his demands. Beside

7

him, the elv'in queen, Meric's mother, sat stiffly, her long silver locks reflecting the torches' radiance, a figure of ice and fire. At her elbow, Master Edyll, an elder of the sea-dwelling mer'ai, tried continually to force peace and decorum amid the frequently raucous discourse.

But for every familiar face, there were scores of others Elena knew only by title. She glanced down the long table of strangers—countless figureheads and foreign representatives, all demanding to be heard, all claiming to know what was best for the war to come with the Gul'gotha.

Some argued for scorching the island and leaving for the coast; others wanted to fortify the island and let the Dark Lord destroy his armies on their walls; and still others wanted to take the fight to Blackhall itself, to take advantage of the victory here and destroy the Gul'gothal stronghold before the enemy could regather its scattered forces. The heated arguments and fervid debates had waged now for close to a moon.

Elena glanced sidelong to Er'ril. Her sworn liegeman stood to the right of her seat, arms crossed, face a stern, unreadable mask. He was a carved statue of Standish iron. His black hair had been oiled and slicked back, as was custom along the coast. His wintry eyes, the gray of early morning, studied the table. None could guess his thoughts. He had not added one word to the countless debates.

But Elena noticed the tightness at the corners of his eyes as he stared. He could not fool her. He was growing as irritated as she at the bickering around the table. In over a fortnight, nothing had been decided. Since the victory of A'loa Glen, no consensus had been reached on the next step. While they argued, the days disappeared, one after the other. And still Er'ril waited, a knight at her side. With the Blood Diary in her hands, he had no other position. His role as leader and guide had ended.

Elena sighed softly and glanced to her gloved hands. The victory celebration a moon ago now seemed like another time, another place. Yet as she sat upon her thorny throne, she remembered that long dance with Er'ril atop her tower. She remembered his touch, the warmth of his palm through her silk dress, the whisper of his breath, the scuff of beard on her cheek. But that had been their only dance. From that night onward, though Er'ril had never been far from her side, they had scarcely shared a word. Just endless meetings from sunrise till sundown.

But no longer!

Slowly, as the others argued, Elena peeled back her lambskin gloves. Fresh and untouched, the marks of the Rose were as rich as spilt blood upon her hands: one birthed in moonlight, one born in sunlight. Wit'chfire and coldfire—and between them lay stormfire. She stared at her hands. Eddies of power swirled in whorls of ruby hues across her fingers and palm.

"Elena?" Er'ril stirred by her side. He leaned close to her, his eyes on her hands. "What are you doing?"

"I tire of these arguments." From a filigreed sheath in the sash of her evergreen dress, she slipped free a silver-bladed dagger. The ebony hilt, carved in the shape of a rose, fit easily in her palm, as if it had always been meant for her. She shoved aside memories of her Uncle Bol, the one who had christened the knife in her own blood. She remembered his words. *It is now a wit'ch's dagger.*

"Elena . . ." Er'ril's voice was stern with caution.

Ignoring him, she stood. Without so much as a word, she drew the sharp tip across her right palm. The pain was but the bite of a wasp. A single drop of blood welled from the slice and fell upon her silk dress. Still Elena continued only to stare down the long table, silent.

None of the council members even glanced her way. They were too involved voicing their causes, challenging others, and pounding rough fists on the ironwood surface of the table.

Elena sighed and reached to her heart, to the font of wild magicks pent up inside. Cautiously, she unfurled slim threads of power, fiery wisps of blood magicks that sang through her veins, reaching her bloody palm. A small glow arose around her hand as the power filled it. Elena clenched her fist, and the glow deepened, a ruby lantern now. She raised her fist high.

The first to spot her display was the aged elder of the mer'ai. Master Edyll must have caught the glow's reflection off his silver goblet. As the elder turned, the wine spilled like blood from his cup. He dropped the goblet with a clatter to the tabletop.

Drawn by the noise, others glanced to the spreading stain of wine. Gaze after gaze swung to the head of the table. A wave of stunned silence spread across those gathered around the table.

Elena met their eyes, unflinching. So many had died to bring her here to this island: Uncle Bol, her parents, Flint, Moris . . .

And she would speak with their voices this day. She would not let their sacrifices be dwindled away by this endless sniping. If Alasea was to have a future, if the Gul'gothal rule was to be challenged, it was time to move forward, and there was only one way to do this. Someone had to draw a line in the sand.

"I have heard enough," Elena said softly into the stretch of quiet. From her glowing fists, fiery filaments crawled down her arm, living threads of reddish gold. "I thank you for your kind counsel these past days. This night I will ponder your words, and in the morning I will give you my answer on the course we will pursue."

Down the table, the representative from the coastal township of Penryn stood up. Symon Feraoud, a portly fellow with a black mustache that draped below his chin, spoke loudly. "Lass, I mean no insult, but the matter here does not await your answer."

Several heads nodded at his words.

Elena let the man speak, standing silent as fine threads of wit'ch fire traced fiery trails down her arm, splitting into smaller and smaller filaments, spreading across her bosom and down to the sash of her dress.

"The course ahead of us must be agreed by all," Symon Feraoud continued, bolstered by the silent agreement of those around him. "We've only just begun to debate the matter at hand. The best means to deal with the Gul'gothal threat is not a matter to be decided over a single night."

"A single night?" Elena lowered her arm slightly and descended the single step to stand before the head of the table. "Thirty nights have passed since the revelries of our victory here. And your debates have served no other purpose but to fracture us, to spread dissent and disagreement when we must be at our most united."

Symon opened his mouth to argue, but Elena stared hard at him, and his mouth slowly shut.

"This evening the moon will again rise full," Elena continued. "The Blood Diary will open once more. I will take your counsel here and then consult the book. By morning, I will bring a final plan to this table."

Master Edyll cleared his throat. "For debate?"

Elena shook her head. "For all your agreements."

Silence again descended over the assembly. But this was not the stunned quiet of before; it was a brewing tempest—and Elena would not let that squall strike.

Before even a grumble could arise, Elena raised her glowing fist over the table. "I will brook no further debate. By dawn's light tomorrow, I will make my decision." She splayed open her hand; flames flickered from her fingers. Lowering her hand, she burned her print into the ironwood table. Smoke curled up her wrist. She leaned on her arm as she studied each face. Flames licked between her fingers. "Tomorrow we forge our future. A future where we burn the Black Heart from this land."

Elena lifted her palm from the table. Her handprint was burned deep into the ironwood, smoldering and coal red, like her own palm. Elena stepped away. "Anyone who objects should leave A'loa Glen before the sun rises. For anyone left on this island who will not abide by my decision will not see that day's sun set."

Frowns marred most every face, except for the high keel of the Dre'rendi, who wore a hard, satisfied grin, and Queen Tratal of the elv'in, whose face was a mask of stoic ice.

"It is time we stopped being a hundred causes and become one," Elena declared. "Tomorrow Alasea will be reborn on this island. It will be one mind, one heart. So I ask you all to look to your hearts this night. Make your decisions. Either join us or leave. That is *all* that is left to debate."

Elena scanned their faces, keeping her own as cold and hard as her words. Finally, she bowed slightly. "We all have much to decide, so I bid you a good night to seek counsel where you will."

Turning on a heel, she swung from the table where her print still smoldered, a reminder of who she was and the power she held. She prayed the display was enough. Stepping around the Rosethorn Throne, her skirts brushed softly on the rush-covered flagstone. In the heavy hush, time seemed to slow. The heat of the assembly's gazes on her back felt like a roaring hearth. She crossed slowly toward Er'ril, forcing her limbs to move calmly.

The swordsman still stood stiff and stoic by the seat. Only his gray eyes followed Elena as she neared him. Though his face was hard, his eyes shone with pride. Ignoring the plainsman's reaction, she stalked past him and toward the side door nearby.

Er'ril moved ahead to open the heavy door for her.

Once beyond the threshold, Er'ril stepped to her side, closing the door behind him. "Well done, Elena. It was time someone shook them up. I didn't know how much longer I could stomach their endless—"

Free of the hall, Elena stumbled, her legs suddenly going weak.

Er'ril caught her elbow and kept her upright. "Elena?"

She leaned heavily on her liegeman. "Just hold me, Er'ril," she said shakily, her limbs trembling under her. "Keep me from falling."

He tightened his grip and stepped nearer. "Always," he whispered.

Elena touched his hand with her bare fingers. Though she appeared a grown woman in body, in truth, her bewit'ched form hid a frightened girl from the Highlands. "Sweet Mother, what have I done?" she moaned softly.

Er'ril turned her slightly and held her at arm's length. He leaned closer, catching her gaze with his storm-gray eyes. "You've shown them all what they were waiting to see."

She glanced down to her toes. "And what is that? A mad wit'ch bent on power?"

Er'ril lifted her chin with a single finger. "No, you've shown them the true face of Alasea's future."

Elena met Er'ril's gaze for a breath, then sighed. "I pray you're right. But how many will still be at that table when the sun rises tomorrow?"

"The number who stand at the table doesn't matter. What is important is the strength and resolve of those hearts."

"But—"

Er'ril silenced her with a shake of his head. Still holding her arm, he urged her down the hall. "We've licked our wounds here long enough after the War of the Isles. Your instinct is right. It is time to separate the grain from the chaff. Those who remain at the table at sunrise will be those ready to confront the Black Heart himself."

Elena leaned into the plainsman's support as she walked. The halls through this region of the sprawling castle ran narrow and dark, the torches few and far between. "I hope you're right," Elena finally said.

"Trust me."

They continued in silence. Elena quickly regained her legs, pondering Er'ril's words. *Alasea's future.* But what did it hold? Elena frowned. Who could know for sure? But whatever path lay ahead, it would have to be tread.

Suddenly, Elena's arm was jerked backward. She was yanked to a stop as Er'ril stepped in front of her. "What are you—?" she started to blurt.

"Hush!" Er'ril's sword was already out and pointed toward the shadows ahead.

From out of the darkness, a figure stepped forth.

"Stand back," Er'ril barked. "Who goes there?"

Ignoring the plainsman's brandished weapon, the figure moved another stride forward, into the torchlight. He stood a full head shorter than Er'ril and was waspishly thin. Wearing only a pair of knee-length canvas breeches, his dark skin shown like carved ebony in the flame's glow. The white scar on his forehead blazed, the rune of an opening eye.

Elena pushed Er'ril's sword down and stepped nearer. It was one of the zo'ol, the tiny warriors who hailed from the jungles that fringed the Southern Wastes. They had fought bravely at her side aboard the *Pale Stallion.*

The dark man bowed his partially bald head. His single long braid of black hair, adorned with bits of conch shells and feathers, lay draped over his shoulder.

"What are you doing skulking in these halls?" Er'ril asked brusquely, keeping his sword unsheathed.

The man raised his eyes toward Elena. They glowed with pain and anguish.

Elena moved a step forward and was surprised to feel Er'ril's grip tighten in warning. Would the plainsman's suspicions never end? She shook free of his hand and approached the small shaman. "What's wrong?"

As answer, the man lifted his arm and opened his hand. Resting on his palm was a tarnished silver coin imprinted with the image of a snow leopard.

"I don't understand," Elena said. She knew from talking with her brother Joach that this small man was considered to be a shaman of his people, what they called a tribal *wizen*. She had also learned that the man had some ability to use talismans to speak across vast distances. He had done so with Joach in the past.

The small man raised his coin higher, as if this was explanation enough.

Misunderstanding, Elena reached for the coin, but the man's fingers closed, keeping her from touching it. He dropped his hand. "He calls," the shaman said, backing up a step. "Death draws near to all of them."

Er'ril moved to Elena's side. "Who? Who calls?"

The small man's eyes flicked toward the plainsman, then back to Elena. He struggled with the common tongue. "Master Tyrus, the man who rescued my people from the slavers."

Er'ril glanced to Elena. "He must mean Lord Tyrus, captain of Port Rawl's pirates and heir to the throne of Castle Mryl."

Elena nodded. Tyrus was the man who had lured off Mycelle and a trio of her old companions: Kral, Mogweed, and Fardale. For two moons now, Elena had heard no word of the party, except that they sought to regain Castle Mryl and the Northwall from the Dark Lord's forces. "What do you know of them?"

The shaman bowed his head, struggling again with the common tongue. "I hear a whisper. Pain. Fear. A call for help."

Elena turned to Er'ril. "They're in trouble."

Er'ril's lips tightened to a hard frown. "Perhaps, but if so, I don't see what we can do. They could be anywhere by now, lost deep among the endless forests of the Western Reaches."

"But there must be a way," she mumbled. She swung to the zo'ol warrior. "Did you learn anything else?"

The shaman shook his head. "I hear only one other word. I no understand. A curse, I think."

"What was it?"

The small man's dark face scrunched with thought. "Gr-graff-on."

Elena's brows pinched together. She frowned. What did that mean? It was nonsense.

Then Er'ril jolted beside her. "Griffin!" He stepped nearer the small man. "Did you say 'griffin'?"

The shaman brightened, nodding vigorously. "Yes. Graff-on! Yes, yes!" His eyes were wide, clearly hoping this was significant.

"I still don't understand," Elena said.

Er'ril stood silent, gäze turned inward, brooding on some past event. His voice was soft when he spoke, breathless. "A Weirgate."

The single word drew a gasp from Elena. *Weirgate.* The word froze her heart. She remembered the massive statue of a monstrous black bird, a mythical wyvern. But it was more than just a loathsome sculpture. Carved of ebon'stone, it was a foul construct of power, a portal to a well of dark magicks called the Weir. Elena recalled her mind's brief brush with the evil inside the statue. Her skin prickled with just the memory. She had almost lost Er'ril to that evil.

Er'ril continued to speak. "Back when I freed the book, the darkmage Greshym told me of the other Gates. He said there were four. The wyvern we had already encountered, but also three more: a manticore, a basilisk, and—" Er'ril's gaze fixed back on Elena. "—and a griffin."

Elena choked on her own words. "But . . . but a Weirgate in the Western Reaches? Why? What is it doing out there?"

"I don't know. Greshym hinted at some plan of the Gul'gotha. Something to do with positioning Weirgates at key sites around Alasea."

"Like at Winter's Eyrie," Elena added. She remembered that that had been the ultimate destination of the Wyvern Gate before they had stopped it. "What could the Dark Lord be planning?"

"Even Greshym didn't know," Er'ril answered, but he nodded toward the zo'ol shaman. "But obviously, whatever the Black Heart's plan, it poses a danger to the others out there."

Elena studied the small warrior. "Can you reach Lord Tyrus? Find out more?"

He raised the coin again. "I try many times. The coin has gone cold. Empty. A very bad omen."

Elena straightened. "Then what do we do? We can't just ignore this message."

Er'ril finally sheathed his sword with a sharp snap. "It was their choice to venture into the western wilds. We cannot spare any forces on a futile search."

"But—"

"You have your own battles to fight, Elena. And a night to consult with the Blood Diary and decide on a plan for the war council tomorrow. You have burned your commitment into the ironwood of the table. You must honor your word."

"But how can I? If Aunt My is in danger—"

"Mycelle is a skilled swordswoman and now a full shapeshifter again," Er'ril interrupted sternly. "Like the others, she must face the threat with her own strength and skill."

Elena's consternation could not be hidden.

Er'ril gripped her shoulders. "I will check with the Brotherhood's library here. See what I can find out about these Weirgates. But you must remain focused. You've a long night ahead of you. I suggest you rest, sleep. Put aside these worries for this one night."

"How can I?" she whispered softly and pulled away. "How do you shut out your heart?"

"By knowing there is nothing your worrying will do to help Mycelle and the others. If you take on their burden and your own, both will suffer."

Elena nodded, her shoulders slumping. Er'ril was right. She had made a commitment to point the various factions in one unifying direction. She had asked the leaders around the long table to look to their own hearts and be ready to put aside all distractions. *Could I do any less now?*

She raised her face to Er'ril and hardened her countenance. "I will do as you say."

Er'ril nodded, satisfied. "Then let's get you to your room. I will wake you just before moonrise."

She nodded and moved forward, suddenly very tired. She touched the zo'ol shaman's shoulder as she passed him. He still wore a worried, sick expression. Whatever he had felt from Lord Tyrus had shaken the man deeply. "We will learn what we can this day," she promised him. "Fear not. If there is something we can do, we will."

The shaman bowed his head, pressing the back of his fist to his scarred brow.

Elena moved on down the hall, her thoughts still on her lost friends. Silently, she prayed them safe, but in her heart, dread settled like a thick mist inside her chest. And within this fog of worry, another emotion flared brighter: a growing sense of urgency.

Something was wrong out there.

She knew it as surely as she knew the moon would rise full tonight. And if she was to be honest with herself, this dread was not new to this moment. For the past two days, everything had seemed wrong to her: sunlight had seemed sallow, voices had become strident, food bland, her skin had even seemed to itch constantly. Since this morning, Elena had felt as if the walls of the castle were closing around her.

In truth, this cloying sense, more than anything else, had driven her to stand before the council and demand an accounting of them. Er'ril may think her brave and bold, but honestly, it was only exasperation and worry. She had acted because time was narrowing for her—for them all. She had been unable to sit quiet any longer.

Elena glanced behind her, searching for the small figure of the zo'ol wizen. But the man was gone, swallowed in shadow.

If only her fears would disappear as easily.

FROM THE HEIGHTS OF THE EASTERNMOST TOWER OF THE KEEP, Tol'chuk watched the salvage work among the docks and through the maze of half-submerged towers below. Crouched amid the tumbled blocks of granite and volcanic stone of the ruined tower parapet, he was alone with his thoughts. Ever since the elv'in warships had destroyed the tower, none dared risk the unstable ruins—except Tol'chuk. It was his haven.

As he stared, voices from the docks reached up to him. Men called to one another—some in barked orders, some in comradely song. At the sea's edge, nets and ropes worked at dredging masts and sections of hull from the tangle of debris caught among the avenues and streets of the sunken section of A'loa Glen.

It was a daily chore. With each morning's tide, the dregs of the last moon's slaughter washed ashore. It was as if the Great Deep sought to expel the pain and bloodshed from its salty depths. And not only broken ships floated and rolled in the stagnant waters, but also the bloated corpses of men, dragons, and tentacled monsters. The stench in the morning drew scores of seabirds to the feast.

Like marauders in the night, the men and women laboring below wore scraps of cloth across their mouths and noses. But the rotting reek did not bother Tol'chuk. To him, the smell was somehow fitting. Even before the war had started, Tol'chuk had been unable to cleanse the stench of death from his nose.

Turning his back on the sea, Tol'chuk fished out the chunk of crimson heartstone from his thigh pouch. Here in the shadows cast by the western section of the castle, his stone glowed with its own inner light. Where once it had blazed like a ruby sun, it now only shone with a feeble, almost sickly glimmer. Tol'chuk held the crystal toward the points of the compass: north, east, south, west. Nothing. He felt no familiar tug on his heart. The crystal that had once guided him did so no longer.

He lifted the crystal toward the evening glow. Deep within the facets, he stared at the shadow at its heart: the Bane, the shadow in the stone, a curse laid upon his people by the Land itself for an atrocity committed by one of his great ancestors, the Oath-breaker. Tol'chuk had been assigned to correct his ancestor's crime by the ancients of his own tribe. He had been gifted with the stone, a vessel for his people's deceased spirits, as a guide. But the Bane had nearly completed its curse. It had grown as it fed on his tribe's spirits inside the crystal. When Tol'chuk had begun his quest, the tiny worm had been difficult to see through the thousand facets of the crystal, but it was now plainly evident, well fed. It was changing, too. Like a caterpillar transforming into a butterfly, the Bane had grown into a shadowy creature, curled and lurking inside a ruby cocoon. But what was it? What was it becoming?

Tol'chuk lowered the large gem.

In truth, what did it matter? The spirits of his ancestors were almost gone, eaten away. Tol'chuk leaned over the dark stone. Why had the Heart of his tribe led him to this wit'ch? Was there a clue hidden in this fact? By helping her, would he be helped? He had no way of knowing. But what other course lay open to him?

Tol'chuk fingered open his pouch as he stared again at the scavengers below. He watched the birds wheeling in the sky, crying and cawing over the feast on the beach. He saw sharks fighting over a netted corpse. He turned away. *Life always feeds on death,* he thought morosely.

Struggling to force the heartstone back into its pouch, he grumbled and fought the straps. Then the stone, as if angry at his tussling, flared bright. Tol'chuk gasped. The stone rolled from his clawed fingers to rattle across the floor of the tower. It settled to a stop beside a toppled pillar. Yet it continued to shine like a star.

Tol'chuk squinted, eyes tearing from both the pain of the brightness and from relief. The Heart had come alive again.

He crawled to his feet, leaning on a knuckled arm. His other hand shaded his eyes from the glare. Then a shadow appeared from the very heart of the intense ruby sheen. It grew larger with each thunderous heartbeat in Tol'chuk's ears. The darkness swirled up from out of the brightness. Fear froze Tol'chuk in place.

The Bane. It had come to claim him.

Still, Tol'chuk did not move. In fact, he straightened from his crouch. If death came for him this day, he was ready. The ruby brightness was all but eaten away by the swirling blackness. Then the shadows grew denser; the crimson brightness an aura around it. Still the brightness stung, like the halo of an eclipsed sun.

The swirling cloud of shadows coalesced on itself, a form taking shape. Even with the glare, Tol'chuk's eyes grew wide at the sight. Soon the image of an og're, sculpted of shadows, grew before him. Hunched, bent-backed, it knuckled on an arm the size of a tree trunk, a bristle of spiny fur trailing down its bare back. Large eyes, swirls of dark clouds, stared back at Tol'chuk. It could have been a dark mirror image of himself—and in some ways it was.

He stepped forward, tears blurring the miracle. "Father?"

The shadowy figure still did not move, but a crinkle of amusement seemed to mark its face. Eyes traveled over Tol'chuk's upright form. "He-who-walks-like-a-man."

Tol'chuk glanced down at his posture, then bent to knuckle on his clawed fist.

"No," the figure said, its voice sounding both like a whisper in his ear and a call from far away. It spoke in the native og're tongue. "Don't. The Triad named you truly."

"But, Father—?"

A shake of shadowy head. "I don't have much time. I must speak quickly."

"But the Heart? It glows again!"

"Only for the moment." The dark og're raised his eyes toward his son. "I am the last of the spirits in the stone. It is our blood ties that have kept me from the Bane for this long. But as the sun sets, I will be gone."

"No!"

An angry grumble flowed. "Stones fall from heights, and water runs downhill. Even an og're cannot fight these things. And you are an og're, Son. Accept my fate as I do."

"But—?"

"I come at my end with a single guidance for you. As the Bane nears, I sense the path you must take next. But from here you must walk without the spirits. You must walk alone."

"But why? If the Bane empties the stone, why continue?"

"All is not lost, my son. There is still a way to destroy the Bane, to revive the Heart of our people."

"I don't understand."

The details of the figure began to fade, as did the radiant crimson glow. Even the voice began to fray. "Take the stone . . . to where it was first quarried."

"Where?"

The answer was a brush of wind in his ear. Tol'chuk staggered back. He gasped. "No." But he knew he had not heard falsely.

The image faded back to shadows. "Do as you are bid . . . for your father's memory."

Tol'chuk clenched both fists. What he asked was impossible, but still Tol'chuk nodded. "I will try, Father."

The shadows receded into the brilliance. A last whisper reached him. "I see your mother in you." The glow faded back into the stone. "I go happily, knowing we both live on in you, my son."

Then only the dull stone remained on the cold granite.

Tol'chuk could not move. There was not even a glimmer left in the crystal. Finally, he crossed over and gathered it in his clawed hands and sank to his knees, cradling the Heart of his people in his lap.

Tol'chuk sat until the sun lowered beyond the western horizon, unmoving, except for the roll of an occasional tear down a cheek. Finally, as his tower was swallowed by darkness, Tol'chuk lifted the stone to his lips and kissed the faceted surface. "Good-bye, Father."

*   *   *

Joach hurried down the abandoned hallways, praying to escape. His breath was ragged, and his fine clothes dusty from racing through these unused corridors. He paused and listened for a moment. He heard no sounds of pursuit. Satisfied, he slowed his pace and removed a handkerchief to wipe his brow. *That had been too close!*

He came upon a small winding stair on his left and took it. The walls brushed his shoulders on either side. Clearly here was an old servants' stair, too narrow for regular traffic. He took the steps two at a time. If he could reach the main floor of the Great Edifice, he knew the way by heart to the kitchens. His belly growled its complaint at the thought of a loaf of bread and a bowl of barley stew. His narrow escape had cost him his dinner—but it was a small price to pay.

Joach clambered down the last of the stairs and pushed through the narrow doorway. He was instantly assaulted with the clamor of the kitchens: pots banging, fat sizzling, and the roar of the head cook over the organized chaos. The double-wide kitchen doors opened to his immediate left. Firelight from the row of hearths flickered like sunset on the walls. From this haven, the aromas of roasting rabbits struck his nostrils. Bread, fresh from the ovens, flavored the air with the resins of rye and onions. Joach was drawn toward the smell, enthralled as if still under the darkmage's spell. Forgetting his frantic flight a moment ago, his limbs moved of their own accord toward the noise and scents.

He entered the kitchens, bumping into a young scullion girl with her hair pulled back in a single tawny braid under a stained handkerchief. She kicked at him, clearly thinking him one of the other kitchen workers trying to grab more than a loaf of bread. "Och! Get off me, you oaf! I'm no tavern wench."

Joach took an elbow blow to the midriff before he could grab her arm and gain her attention. "Hold on!"

She turned, finally seeing him. Her skin was dark, a deep bronze that matched her rich golden hair. Her eyes traveled up from his black boots, over his fine gray breeches, to his emerald silk shirt with a gray formal cloak over his right shoulder. Her gaze settled on his face.

Panicked, she dropped to her knees. "Lord Joach!" Her cry

drew many other eyes. The clamor of the kitchens died around him.

Joach's face reddened to match his fiery hair. He reached and pulled the young girl to her feet, but the muscles of her legs seemed to have vanished. She was like a limp doll. He had to hold her steady. "I am no lord," he said. "I've worked in these same kitchens."

"Aye, he did!" a rough voice called out. A large man pushed through the gawking kitchen help. He wore a stained apron over his swollen belly. His cheeks were still ruddy from the flames. It was the head cook. Joach recognized the man from the time when Joach had been enthralled to Greshym. The large man swung his wooden ladle toward the head of a thin potscrubber. "And if you all don't get back to your chores, I'll tan your arses but good."

The crowd dispersed around them both, except for the girl. She took a step back but no farther. Her eyes were huge.

The cook tapped his large spoon into his other meaty paw. "I don't figure you're down here to fetch someone's supper."

Joach turned his attention to the rotund man. "I can't believe you're still here. How did you survive the darkmage's siege of the island?"

"Aye, even monsters and darkmages need to eat." He fingered a leather patch over his left eye. This feature was new. Joach saw a small purplish scar trailing from the man's forehead to disappear under the patch. "Of course, you'd better make sure you don't overcook their meat, if you get what I mean." A glimmer of old horror flashed in the man's one good eye, but then vanished to be replaced with good humor. "Now what can I do for my little lord?"

"I am no lord," Joach repeated with a tired frown.

"That's not what I hear tell. I heard you're a royal prince of those flying boat people."

Joach sighed. "So they claim," he muttered. The elv'in seemed to think he and his sister Elena were the last descendants of their ancient king. "All I know was that I was born an orchard farmer, and I claim no more."

"A tree picker!" The cook brayed like an amused mule and clapped him on the shoulder, almost throwing Joach to his knees. "Now that I'd believe. You're a lanky one, all right!" The cook guided him, none too gently, toward an oaken work table. He kicked a chair forward. "So I'm guessing from the way you came in here with your nose sniffing in the air that you're looking for a bit of nibblings."

"In truth, I . . . I haven't eaten."

The cook placed him in a seat. "How come? I've filled that cursed banquet hall to the rafters. They kin't have eaten their bellies through all my fare so soon."

Joach shifted in his seat. "I chose not to eat up there this night."

"Och, I don't blame you. All that prattling and yammering." The cook waved to his kitchen help, directing them with no more than a point of his ladle and a firm frown. Soon the table was filling with loaves of bread, thick slabs of cheese, platters of berries. A small lad carried a bowl as big as his head and slid it in front of Joach. It contained a stew of rabbit with potatoes and carrots.

The cook tossed him a spoon. "Eat up, Lord Joach. It may be plain, but you'll find no better fare even in that banquet hall." Then he was gone to attend his hearths.

The scullion maid Joach had bumped earlier swept up to the table with a flagon of ale. She filled his mug, splashing more out than in with her nervousness. "Sorry, sorry, sorry," she intoned like a litany.

Joach reached and steadied her hand. The cup was promptly filled. "Thank you," he said. He found himself staring at her.

Her eyes, which he had thought from a distance to be a deep brown, maybe even black, were actually the color of a twilight sky, an indigo blue. Joach found himself caught in their pools for a breath. His hand still held hers, though his mug was already full. "Th-thank you," he repeated.

She stared back at him, unblinking, then slowly withdrew her fingers from his. Her eyes lingered a moment on his gloved hand. He wore a custom-tailored lambskin glove to hide the healing scar of his right hand. Two fingers and half his palm were missing, eaten away by an ill'guard demon during the taking of the castle. Her eyes returned to his, unfazed by his disfigurement. She gave the smallest curtsy and backed away.

Joach's arm was still held out toward her. "What's your name?" he asked in a hurry, before she could flee.

She curtsied again, a bit deeper this time. She did not meet his gaze, which Joach regretted. "Marta, my lord."

"But—" Before he could finish denying his heritage or say another word, she was already gone in a swirl of rough-spun dress, flying away on swift feet.

Sighing, Joach returned to his meal. He found his gnawing appetite had somehow vanished. But he picked up his spoon and sampled the stew. The cook had not lied. The broth was rich in spices, and the rabbit meat so tender it melted on his tongue. He had not tasted such a stew since back on his family's farm. It reminded him of home, of his mother's care at preparing a winter's meal. Joach found his hunger again. But as wonderful as the meal tasted, Joach could not shake from his mind the image of the scullion's twilight eyes.

Lost in reverie and the spread of food, Joach was not aware of the newcomer to the kitchen until he heard a voice behind him.

"There you are!"

Joach did not need to turn to know who stood at the door. It was Master Richald, the elv'in brother to Meric. He groaned inwardly. His escape had not been far enough.

"It is not fitting that a prince of the Blood break bread with commoners," the elv'in lord said with clear distaste, striding to the table.

Joach turned, cheeks reddening from both embarrassment at the man's rudeness and simple anger. Richald stood stiffly beside the table, eyes above all the clamor, refusing even to see the hard work being done here. He had the bearing of all the elv'in: aloof, cold, dismissive of all those around them. His pale features were similar to his brother Meric, but much sharper, as if cut from a finer knife. His hair was the same bright silver, except for a streak of copper over the left ear.

Pushing off the stool, Joach faced the elv'in, though the man stood a hand taller than Joach. "I will not have you disparage these folks' hard work with your rudeness, Master Richald."

The man's frosted blue eyes lowered slowly to meet his gaze. There was only ice and disinterest in those eyes. "My rudeness? My sister had gone through great efforts to bring her six cousins to the banquet to meet you. You could show them the courtesy of more than just a terse greeting and vanishing."

"And I did not ask to be assaulted at dinner by a flock of elv'in virgins."

Richald's brows rose slightly, a supremely shocked response for an elv'in. "Watch your tongue. Prince or not, I will not have my family dishonored by a half-Blood."

Joach suppressed a satisfied grin. So he had finally managed to crack that stoic shell—to reveal this man's true disdain for him, of all the elv'in's disdain: *half-Blood.* Half elv'in and half human.

For the past moon, Joach had been flattered by all the attention of the elv'in. Every silver-haired man or woman with a daughter or niece had vied for his eye. He had been introduced to countless women, some younger than their first bleed, some older than his own mother. But after a time, he had begun to sense something behind all this attention—an underlying distaste that would only show through cracks, in whispered words and hard glances. Though he shared the blood of an elv'in king, to their eyes, he was still tainted. For all their attention and the countless daughters and nieces presented to him, the elv'in as a whole found Joach distasteful. He was a mere vessel of the ancient king's blood, a stallion to impregnate one of their pure stock and return the bloodline to their people. Once done, Joach imagined he would be tossed aside, a spent coin of no value.

It was this cold ritual that he had sought to escape this night. He was tired of this artificial dance. It would end now.

Joach stared up at Richald. "How I must gall one of your stature, the son of the queen," he whispered up at the taller man. "How it must make your blood race with fire to see the best of the elv'in breeding stock fawning over a half-Blood like myself, while you're ignored."

By now, Richald's limbs were trembling with rage. He couldn't speak; his thin lips had disappeared to taut lines.

Joach brushed past him, heading toward the door. "Tell your aunts, tell all your people, that this half-Blood is no longer on parade."

Richald made no move to stop him as he headed toward the kitchen exit. Out of the corner of his eye, Joach spotted a pair of scullion girls huddled by the door to one of the cupboards. A pair of eyes followed his path across the room. *Marta.* She had removed the handkerchief from her head and loosened the tail of her tawny hair, a drape all of bronzes and golds.

Joach tripped over the kitchen door's threshold.

His misstep raised the ghost of a smile on the girl's lips. Joach straightened his cloak over his shoulder and returned her grin. She bowed her head shyly and withdrew into the shadows of the cupboard.

Joach watched her disappear, then crossed out of the kitchen's warmth. He was finished with the ice of the elv'in. It had finally taken the kitchen hearths to melt their hold. Joach glanced back at the open doors. In truth, it had not been just the heat—it had also been a shy girl named Marta.

After a moon of fawning, the simple truth in her eyes had shamed him. Love should not be bartered and contracted. It should start with a glance that reached the heart, then grow from there.

Joach turned his back on the kitchens, but he promised to return.

Both for the wonderful food and to see what else would grow in the glow of the kitchen's hearths.

WITH THE SUN JUST SET, MERIC SAT NEAR THE PROW OF THE *PALE Stallion*, leaning his back against the rail, legs extended. He fingered the lute in his lap and plucked a few stray notes. The sound carried over the open waters around where the *Stallion* lay anchored. Meric's gaze followed the notes across the seas and skies.

The moon had yet to rise; the stars were a jeweled blanket overhead. In the distance, around the isle of A'loa Glen, the spread of stars ended, blotted out by the sleek windships hanging over the castle like gilded clouds. The Thunderclouds, the warships of his elv'in people. Even from here, their magickal iron keels glowed softly in the night, an inner elemental fire holding the ships aloft.

Meric frowned at the sight. He knew his mother, Queen Tratal, was up there somewhere, probably wondering why her son spent more time aboard the *Stallion* than on her own flagship, the *Sunchaser*. Even after a moon among these people, she still did not understand his attraction to and affection for those who were not of his Blood. She had listened patiently to the stories of his adventures on these shores, but her face had never warmed. The elv'in, creatures of the wind and clouds, had little interest in what went on below the keels of their boats. Even with the tales, his mother could not understand her son's feelings for these land-bound peoples.

Meric drew a hand across his scalp. What was once burnt stubble after his tortures below Shadowbrook was now a rich field of new silver growth. The length of his hair tickled his ears and the back of his neck. But this growth could not hide all his scars. A long trail of pinched, pale skin marred the smoothness of his left cheek.

"Play something," a voice said near a barrel tied to the starboard rail. The boy Tok sat bundled in a thick woolen blanket, lost within its folds. Only his ruffled, sandy-haired head protruded from his cocoon. The nights now grew cold much faster as autumn gripped the Archipelago. But the chill was refreshing to Meric. It helped clear his mind.

"What would you have me play, Tok?" The boy always joined Meric when he played Nee'lahn's lute. It was a private time the two shared together, and Meric had come to enjoy both the boy's company and their mutual appreciation of music. Some nights even Tok would strum nail on string and practice a song. But it had been almost a fortnight since Meric had last played.

"Don't much matter," Tok said. "Just play."

Meric knew what the boy meant. It didn't matter what song was strummed. It was the sound of the lute itself that was most appreciated by both. The wooden lute had been carved from the dying heart of a koa'kona tree, a tree whose spirit had been bonded to the nymph Nee'lahn. Elemental magick still sang in the rich vibrations of the whorled-grained wood. It sang of lost homes and hope.

Bending over the instrument like a lover, Meric fingered the neck and stroked the strings. A cascade of chords sang from the lute like a long sigh, as if the lute had held its breath and could now finally sing again. Meric smiled and sighed, too. He had put off playing for too long. He had forgotten how just the voice of the lute calmed his heart.

As he reached for the strings once again, a long crash echoed nearby, a hatch banging open. Voices interrupted the quiet of the night. "How many?" a rough voice barked.

Two figures appeared from belowdecks and crossed to the rail not far from Meric. Holding the neck of the lute, Meric stood, so as not to appear to be eavesdropping. "What's the matter?" he asked.

The taller of the two glanced his way. It was Kast. The broad-shouldered Bloodrider nodded to him. Kast's long, dark hair was a braided mane down his back. The tattoo of a winged dragon shadowed his cheek and neck. "We've just heard word from the council," Kast said brusquely, barely able to suppress his anger. "Did you hear?"

Meric shook his head.

The slim woman standing beside Kast slipped her small hand into the larger man's. Meric noted how Kast squeezed her palm and ran his thumb along the tender web between her thumb and finger. A casual gesture. Probably neither was even aware of the small signal of affection and support between them.

Sy-wen nodded her chin out to sea. "My mother sent an emissary. It seems Elena has forced the council to make a stand."

Meric stared over the seas. In the far distance, he could barely make out the humped shadow of the Leviathan, one of the living behemoths that housed the mer'ai while they traveled under the seas.

"She gave them a choice," Sy-wen continued. "Agree with her plan or leave this night."

Meric's brows rose and he was unable to suppress a shocked grin. It seemed Elena was growing into her role as leader and wit'ch. In her veins ran the blood of ancient elv'in kings. It seemed their colors were finally shining forth.

"The high keel had already given his support," Kast said. "The Dre'rendi Fleet will stay."

"As will the mer'ai," Sy-wen said. "Master Edyll convinced my mother that, with the assault on the island, there was no further hiding for the mer'ai."

"But what of the others?" Meric asked. He wondered what his own mother's decision would be. "I had better return to the *Sunchaser* and ensure the elv'in fleet will not abandon the cause."

"No need," Kast said. "I heard from Hunt, the high keel's son, that the elv'in will stay. It seems they mean to keep your ancient king's bloodline safe, whatever her decision."

Meric nodded, but a part of him was suspicious of his own mother's quick decision. Had his stories reached some part of her heart? Or was there another agenda hidden behind Queen Tratal's generosity? "What of the others?"

Kast frowned. "May the Mother curse them all for their cowardice," he spat.

Sy-wen touched the large man's shoulder. "Before even the sun set, practically the entire delegation from the coastal townships left. I imagine most who yet remain will wait to hear Elena out in the morning, but who can say for sure?" She pointed out to a flotilla of sails, lanterns in the rigging. The ships were drifting away from the island. "Like them, more may flee during the night."

Meric frowned. Bloodriders, mer'ai, elv'in—all outsiders to the lands of Alasea and the only ones willing to fight alongside a wit'ch. No wonder these lands were conquered five centuries ago.

"What now?" Meric asked.

Kast shook his head. "We wait until dawn." The Bloodrider's hard gaze surveyed the seas, as if daring anyone else to abandon the island. Sy-wen leaned into the man's embrace, tempering his hardness with her softness. Together, they watched the seas.

Meric drifted a few steps back to his post by the ship's prow. Nearby, Tok's bright eyes reflected the glow of the moon just now rising. Meric had promised the boy a song, and he would not disappoint.

Still standing, leaning against the rail, Meric swung the lute up and settled the instrument against his belly. He drew his nails across the strings. The music seemed so loud against the quiet backdrop of the softly creaking boat and the gentle lap of water against the hull. Meric frowned slightly. Even this brief scatter of notes sounded unusually strident, almost scolding.

Tok sat up straighter in his blanket, also noting the change in the lute's character. Meric felt the gazes of Sy-wen and Kast swing in his direction.

Meric positioned his fingers and began playing, trying to recapture its usual bittersweet song. But all that sang forth were strident chords, discordant and frantic. Meric continued, trying to discern an answer to the strange music.

His strumming became more vigorous, not of his own accord,

but because the music demanded it of him. Behind the hard music, it was almost as if he could hear the beat of the drum and the strike of steel on steel. What was this strange song? Meric found his skin heating as he played. Sweat beaded his forehead on this cool evening.

"Meric?" Kast mumbled.

Meric barely heard him. His fingers danced along the long neck of the lute; his nails thrashed the strings. Then from behind the music a whispery voice arose. "I have waited for so long . . ."

Startled, Meric almost dropped the lute, but it would not let him. He continued to play. It was as if he were unconnected to his own body: He could not control his fingers or limbs. The lute had somehow cast a spell over him. The voice continued, stronger now, familiar, "Come to me . . ."

"Who is that?" Kast said, reaching for the lute, seeming to sense Meric's distress.

"No!" Meric barked out. "Not yet!"

The speaker now all but sang through the notes of the lute, a bell among reeds now, as clear as if the speaker was standing on the planks with them. "Bring me the lute. All will be lost without it."

Meric's eyes grew wide as he recognized the singer behind the notes, but it was impossible. He had helped bury her himself. "N-Nee'lahn?"

"Bring me my lute, elv'in. It is the only hope against the Grim."

"Where are you?" Meric gasped out.

"Western Reaches . . . the Stone of Tor. Come quickly . . ." The voice began to fade. Meric's fingers began to slow. He tried to force his fingers to quicken again, but Meric could sense the spell weakening.

"Nee'lahn!" Meric called out, struggling with his fingers. The chords began crashing apart, strident notes becoming chaos.

One last message strangled through the noise. "Break the Gates! Or all will be lost!"

Then Meric's fingers spasmed. The lute fell from his fingers. But Tok dove forward and caught the instrument in his blanket before it struck the planks. Meric sagged to his knees, weak.

Kast and Sy-wen approached him slowly. Sy-wen reached toward him, but didn't touch him. "Are you all right?"

Meric nodded.

"Who was that?" Kast asked.

Meric ignored the question. He was not ready to answer that yet, not even to himself. He turned to stare up at them. "Can you get me to the castle? I must speak to Elena. Now."

Sy-wen glanced to Kast. The Bloodrider nodded. The two backed to the center of the deck. Kast stripped out of his boots, breeches, and shirt. Soon he was standing, bare chested, wearing only a loincloth.

As Sy-wen neatly folded the Bloodrider's clothes on the planks, Meric drew himself up and retrieved the lute from Tok. He watched Sy-wen approach and stand before Kast. The Bloodrider leaned down and deeply kissed Sy-wen. It was a kiss of good-bye.

After a long moment, they broke apart. Meric saw the glint of tears on Sy-wen's cheeks. She reached toward Kast's cheek and touched the dragon tattoo on his neck. "I have need of you," she mumbled softly.

Kast jerked under her touch; then the two of them were lost in a dark explosion of black scale, silver claw, and wing. A trumpet of triumph flowed from the whirling flesh. Soon a massive black seadragon crouched atop the deck, silver claws dug deep into the planks. Its neck was stretched toward the skies, silver fangs glinting as long as a man's forearm. Its triumphant roar filled the skies.

Tok gasped beside Meric. The boy had never seen Kast transform into the dragon Ragnar'k before.

Atop the beast's back, Sy-wen sat perched. She held out a hand toward Meric as the dragon rolled a single black eye toward him.

"Grab Kast's garments," she said. "Let us be off."

2

ER'RIL CLIMBED DOWN THE LONG LADDER FROM THE OBSERVATORY loft to the library floor. He bore a satchel of books over one shoulder and a small oil lamp with a short taper. He had fled the immense stacks of the library for the solitary quiet of the Edifice's observatory. Amid the old brass scopes and prismed lenses once used to study the stars, Er'ril had pored through the ancient texts. But the reward for his strained eyes was meager. He had found no mention of the Weirgates in any book or scroll. All he could find was an obscure reference to the mythic Weir itself.

But what did it mean? He was no scholar. He knew swords, horses, and little else. Still, he did not want to fail Elena. He had seen her eyes shine with determination when she had heard of the danger faced by her Aunt Mycelle and the others. A new Weirgate, somewhere near Castle Mryl in the north. Why up there? Er'ril had hoped for some answer in these dusty shelves, some way to help guide Elena on the best course. But he found only more mystery.

The *Weir*.

The single reference mentioned the elemental energy inherent in the Land. The ancient writing theorized this elemental energy could not exist without an opposite in nature. All the natural world had two sides. Reflections, one of another. Mirror images. The sun had the moon. Fire and ice. Light and dark. Even the twin magickal spirits, Chi and Cho, were reflections of each other: male and female, a duality that produced a balance in all things. The text imagined an opposite to the Land's power. Where elemental magicks encompassed all facets of nature, this other power would reflect all that was *un*natural. The scholar named this mythic power the *Weir*.

32

Er'ril stepped from the ladder to the library floor with a shudder. Personal experience had proved the Weir to be anything but myth. He had been drawn into the ebon'stone statue of the Wyvern Weirgate, into the Weir itself. Though he remembered nothing of the experience, he knew the memory was buried there somewhere—but his mind had walled it away for his own sanity. Er'ril did not fight this. He suspected that if light should ever illuminate that corner of his mind, he would be lost forever.

Striding the long length of the narrow library, Er'ril placed his oil lamp and satchel of books beside the white-robed Brother who had helped him research the Weir.

With spectacles perched on the tip of his nose, the old scholar looked up. "Were the volumes of any use?"

"I'm not yet sure, Brother Ryn. I need to dwell on what I've read."

The shaven-headed man nodded his understanding. "Only in that way is wisdom ever attained." The elderly Brother returned to the crumbling scroll atop the table. "The other scholars and I will continue to peruse the shelves and see what else we can learn for you."

"Thank you, Brother Ryn." Er'ril bowed and made ready to depart.

But the scholar spoke again, stopping him. "These Weirgates . . . You described them as lodestones of magick, capable not only of drawing magick into them, but persons of magick, too."

"So the darkmage Greshym explained them to me."

"Hmm . . ." the Brother said. "And the Weir is also the well from which the Dark Lord draws his power."

Er'ril nodded. It was a secret he had managed to drag out of Greshym when last they had met.

"And are these Gates the only way to access the Weir?"

"Greshym seemed to think so. He said the four ebon'stone statues were somehow linked together, creating a portal to the Weir."

Brother Ryn glanced up at Er'ril, removing his spectacles. The man's eyes were hoary with age, but a sharp intelligence shone through his cloudy orbs. "Then it would seem prudent to find these four Gates and destroy them before confronting the Dark Lord directly."

Er'ril stared back at the old scholar. What the old man asked sounded so simple and plain, but in fact was impossible. He pictured the Wyvern Gate flying off from the tower heights. It had been headed back to Blackhall with his brother, Shorkan. But what of the other three? No one knew where they were hidden, and even if they could be found, how did you destroy such monstrous creations?

The scholar returned to his reading. "Knowledge is the answer, Er'ril of Standi," he mumbled, as if reading the plainsman's mind.

Er'ril nodded and turned to leave.

Brother Ryn, though, had one final word. "You are simply missing the key."

Er'ril glanced over his shoulder. "What's that?"

"For the past fortnight, I have sensed that a piece of this puzzle is still missing. Discover that and I suspect a way will open."

"What piece? What do you mean?"

"The unifying element. Some fact to bring the Gates, the Weir, and this font of the Dark Lord's power into one clear picture. We are looking at individual pieces, while the whole portrait still remains blank to us. If you can find this last piece, all will come clear."

"That's easier spoken than done, Brother Ryn."

"As is the path to all wisdom," the old scholar said and waved him away, as if dismissing a student. "The moon rises. Go to your wit'ch."

Er'ril bowed one last time and strode toward the doors to the library. His hand came to rest on the hilt of his sword. He'd had enough mysteries for one evening. It was time to be a simple liegeman again. Elena had a long night ahead, and he would be at her side when she opened the Blood Diary.

Casting aside his worries, Er'ril strode through the halls and stairs of the Edifice to the westernmost tower, the Wit'ch's Dagger. He mounted the stairs two at a time and climbed toward the tower chamber where Elena rested.

As he marched, he felt a small twinge build in his right leg, where he had borne the thrust of a goblin's poisoned blade while protecting Elena. The ache remained like a sour memory. Halfway up the tower, Er'ril was forced to slow his pace to single steps as the pain grew.

It was at these times that Er'ril felt his mortality. With the book bequeathed to Elena, its gift of immortality had been transferred to her. With the spell gone from his own body, Er'ril had expected his hair to grow quickly gray and his limbs to become ricketed with arthritis. Instead, he aged at a normal pace, a pace which no man could see when studied day by day; it could only be perceived upon reflection over winters. But here and now, with his leg aching, he felt the march of time more sharply. Er'ril continued on with a sigh. Finally, he reached the top of the stairs, his lips in a tight grimace. He could hardly hide his limp from the two guards stationed to either side of the iron-bound oaken doors.

The guards straightened their stances as he approached.

"How fares Elena?" he asked.

The guard on the right answered. "The old healer has been watching over her. She gave the wit'ch a draught of dreamweed to help her rest until moonrise."

Er'ril nodded and strode toward the door. The guard on the left knocked softly, then pushed the door open for the plainsman.

The room beyond was dimly lit. Only a scatter of thick white candles flickered on the mantel above a hearth glowing with the coals from a tiny fire. The only other illumination came from the row of tower windows. Long and wide, they revealed the western night skies and the flow of bright stars. In one window, the edge of the moon could be seen cresting from the sea.

In the dimness, the clearing of a throat drew Er'ril's attention to a cushioned chair by the hearth. An old woman dressed in a dark shawl and robe rested with a book in her lap. Her hair, braided and wound like a nest atop her head, matched the gray of her robe. She smiled softly at Er'ril as he turned. "She rests in the next room," Mama Freda whispered. "I was about to rouse her, as I see the moon rises."

"It does, but let her sleep a few moments more. The moon has yet to grow full in the skies. She has a long night ahead and a hard morning tomorrow."

"So I've heard. The fate of Alasea rests on her decision." This statement brought a broader smile to the woman's burnished features, as if the idea amused her. "Such small shoulders to carry the world."

"She'll manage," Er'ril said sternly.

Her smile turned wry. "Oh, with you at her side, I don't doubt it."

Er'ril found himself rankling slightly at the attitude of the healer. "Elena is strong," he said, as if ending the discussion.

Mama Freda shifted in her chair, settling deeper into the cushions. The movement triggered a squeak of protest from the animal perched on her shoulder. It was Tikal, the golden-maned tamrink from her native jungles. Its tail, ringed in black-and-copper fur, was wrapped around the woman's neck. Its tiny bare face, framed in a fiery mane, was filled by its two large black eyes. "Elena is strong . . . strong . . ." it chittered, mimicking Er'ril.

The woman calmed the beast with a touch and a scratch behind an ear. The animal doubled as both companion and eyes to the old healer. Born without eyes herself, she had been bonded to the tamrink long ago and saw only with the beast's vision. Right now, Tikal's attention remained with Er'ril. "Strong, you say?" Mama Freda mocked. "You did not help the lass to her bed or double the dosage of dreamweed just to get her to slumber. She bears a great burden."

"I'm well aware—"

"Are you now? Then a little more support than just a curt word or nod might ease her heart a little."

Er'ril sagged slightly under the accusation. In truth, ever since the dance atop this very tower, he had tried to keep his relationship with Elena at arm's length. He could not keep his true heart from showing. Elena did not need that burden.

"Did you know that tomorrow is also Elena's birthingday?" Mama Freda asked.

"What?" Er'ril could not hide the shock in his voice.

Mama Freda nodded. "I heard it from her brother."

"But why didn't she—?"

"Because she's trying to be so strong," Mama Freda said, standing up. "Wit'ches don't celebrate their birthingdays with pastries and well-wishes." The old healer brushed past Er'ril on the way toward a side door. "Come. It is time we waked her."

Er'ril had to force his feet to follow. He felt the fool. After five hundred winters, would he ever understand the female heart? He sighed as he crossed toward the door.

When it came to women, even the impossible riddle of the Weirgates paled.

ELENA WOKE WHEN SHE HEARD VOICES IN THE MAIN CHAMBER OF her tower rooms. Though she could not make out the words, she recognized Mama Freda's accent and the clipped cadence of Er'ril's native Standish. Elena closed her eyes and stretched her limbs. She had been dreaming of home, of her mother's singing as she baked in the kitchen, and her father's laughter as he came in after a long day in the orchards. She kept her eyes squeezed shut. How she wished to return to that dream, instead of to this world of blood magicks and demon armies.

As the voices drew nearer, Elena forced her eyes open. Her bedchamber was windowless and dark, giving no sense of how much time had passed. But if Er'ril was here, then the moon must have risen. He must have come to wake her.

She scooted up slightly. The darkness of her chamber was not complete. In a corner, upon a pedestal of silvery Tauesian marble, rested a tattered black book with a burgundy rose etched in gilt on its cover.

The Blood Diary. Elena's talisman, birthright . . . and burden.

From the cover of the tome, the gilt rose glowed softly now, an azure hue not unlike moonlight itself. The moon was calling for the book. Elena knew that as the moon ripened and rose to its zenith, the glow would deepen to an inner fire. Then the book could be opened, and the path to the stars bridged once again.

A soft knock on her door announced the others. Elena shifted up in the bed. "Come," she called out.

The door opened. "Did you sleep well?" Mama Freda asked as she peeped her head inside.

"Yes, thank you."

"Good, good." Mama Freda pushed the door fully open and crossed to the bedside table, bearing a long, flaming taper in one hand. The old woman lit the single lantern as Er'ril entered.

Elena eyed the plainsman. She noticed the slight way he favored his right leg and how his eyelids narrowed as he bore weight on the limb. Though he hid it well, his leg still pained him from the dagger wound. As he approached, she saw he had changed from the finery of the Great Hall to his usual Standish riding clothes: black boots, worn brown breeches, and a green leather jerkin over a rough-spun beige shirt. He had even tied his raven hair back with a strip of red leather.

For some reason, the familiar clothes eased Elena's heart. Here was the Er'ril she knew and trusted.

Elena pushed back her sheets. She still wore her bedclothes. As she slid from the sheets, the lantern flared brighter. Elena caught a glimpse of herself in the mirror above the washbasin. Again she felt that twinge of shock. Who was that stranger in the mirror? She touched her face. Her hair spread to her shoulders in a fall of gentle, fiery curls. Her eyes, still the green of the young girl, were now flecked with gold in the lantern light. A spell cast aboard the *Seaswift* had stolen four winters from her, maturing her prematurely. Her hand traced from her face down the curves of her new body. Though she had grown accustomed to this physique, moments like now still occasionally surprised her.

"The moon is almost risen full," Er'ril said. "We'd best prepare."

She nodded. "I thought we'd go atop the tower here." She quickly pulled a thick woolen robe over her bedclothes, sashing it in place, and pushed her feet into a pair of warm slippers.

Once dressed, she crossed to the Blood Diary and reached for it. The glow of the rose had grown richer in just the short time. Her fingers hovered a breath before touching the tome. From this night forward, nothing would be the same. She sensed the shift of worlds under her feet. But there was no turning back. Taking a firming breath, she took the book in her two ruby hands. Raising the tome, she turned. "I'm ready."

"Then let us go." Er'ril led the way out of the bedchamber to the main room. He crossed to a wall and swept back a tapestry to reveal a hidden door to a short staircase that led to the roof. With Er'ril ahead of her and Mama Freda behind, Elena climbed the stairs. The evening's chill reached her, blowing down from the open roof. As they stepped free of the staircase, a breeze flapped the edges of her robe. She drew the sash tighter around her, then clutched the book to her chest.

Behind her, the old healer's pet squeaked at the cold and buried itself tighter against Mama Freda. "Are you warm enough, child?" Mama Freda asked Elena, holding up the lantern.

"Yes, but there is no doubt that winter nears."

"We can still return to the rooms below," Er'ril said. "The book can be opened anywhere."

Elena shook her head and crossed to the stones of the parapet. The circle of the moon had climbed fully from the sea. "No. I would like to open it here, in the face of the moon." She lifted the book. From its cover, the rose glowed brightly.

Er'ril and Mama Freda retreated to give her room.

She was reaching for the cover when the roar of a dragon shattered the night's quiet. Elena cringed down over the book, protecting it, but she quickly recognized the trumpeting voice. It was Ragnar'k.

Elena straightened, and the trio moved to the parapet's edge. "Something must be wrong," Er'ril said as he stared out over the city of A'loa Glen.

Suddenly a black shape shot across the silver of the rising moon and dove across the towers, aiming for them. Mama Freda raised her lantern high while Tikal mumbled, "Big bird, big, big, bird."

The dragon glided over the thousand spires of the ancient city, drawn like a moth to the light. Once near, it circled on a wingtip overhead. A small voice called out from the beast's back, but the rider's words were lost in the winds. Er'ril stepped to the side and waved an arm for Ragnar'k to land.

Roaring, the dragon dove to the far side of the roof, and with a sweep of its massive scaled wings, it alighted on the distant parapet. Silver nails dug deep into the stone, holding its perch. Black eyes, aglow with starlight and moonlight, studied them coldly.

Two figures were saddled on its back. Elena recognized them both: Meric and Sy-wen.

The elv'in prince slid from his perch and landed on the parapet stones, dancing a moment to keep his feet. He seemed oblivious of the long drop behind him. Being a creature of the wind and air, heights were not something he noticed. Meric hopped from the stones to cross toward the gathered trio. He dropped to a knee before Elena, head bowed. "Princess of the Blood," he said breathlessly.

Elena found her cheeks growing heated even with the cold. "Get up, Meric. Enough of this nonsense. What has brought you here so urgently?" Elena nodded toward the dragon and Sy-wen.

Meric held up a hand, still out of breath from his flight.

Behind Meric, Sy-wen slid down the beast's neck and climbed off her mount. The mer'ai woman rubbed the dragon's snout and leaned her forehead against his scales, clearly sharing some inner thought with the great beast. Elena noted the sad smile on Sy-wen's face as she lifted her hand away.

Scale, bone, and wing whirled in on themselves until a naked man stood on the parapet ledge. *Kast.* Elena glanced away as Sy-wen helped him down and passed a bundle of clothes to him.

Meric finally seemed to have caught his breath. Still kneeling, he slipped a bag from his shoulder and opened it. He pulled free a lute. The rich umber and gold of the polished wood almost glowed in the starlight. Elena knew the instrument. A twinge of sorrow lanced her heart.

It was Nee'lahn's lute.

"What's wrong, elv'in?" Er'ril said gruffly.

Meric climbed to his feet and only acknowledged Er'ril with a scowl. "I have news," he said to Elena. "A message from . . . from . . . Oh, Sweet Mother, this is going to sound mad."

Elena reached and touched Meric's hand. "From whom?"

Meric met her gaze with his bright blue eyes. "From Nee'lahn."

Elena's hand fell from Meric's. She could not suppress a gasp of shock.

"That's impossible," Er'ril said.

"Don't you think I know that?" Meric glanced around at the others.

By now, Sy-wen and Kast had joined them. Kast's graveled voice spoke slowly. "The elv'in does not lie. We all heard it: a voice behind the strings of the lute."

"What are you talking about?" Er'ril asked, frowning deeply.

Meric related what had happened aboard the *Pale Stallion.* "I know it was her voice," he finished. "She commands me to bring the lute to the Western Reaches. Something is threatening the forest."

"But she's dead."

"Maybe . . . maybe not," Meric said. "Nee'lahn is nyphai. She is a creature of root and loam, even less human than I."

Er'ril opened his mouth to argue, but Elena stopped him with a raised arm. She stepped nearer Meric. "Alive or not, what threat did Nee'lahn sense?" Elena recalled the urgent message from the zo'ol shaman. Danger in the Western Reaches. Weirgates.

Meric shook his head, glancing away. "I'm not sure. A threat to the forest." He shrugged. "The last of her message did not even make any sense, but she was so urgent." Meric raised his eyes. " 'Break the Gates or all will be lost.' "

Shocked, Elena turned to Er'ril. Neither spoke, but each knew the other's thoughts. Weirgates. A second warning in less than a day. "We cannot ignore this," Elena whispered to him.

Er'ril nodded his chin slightly, but he left the decision to her.

Meric spoke up. "I'd like your permission to take one of the elv'in ships and search out Nee'lahn or her spirit. Return the lute to her."

After a moment's hesitation, Elena glanced to Er'ril, but spoke to Meric. "This is not the first word of warning we've heard coming out from the west." Elena touched Er'ril on the shoulder. "Tell Meric about the zo'ol shaman's warning."

Nodding, Er'ril rapidly related the dire message from Lord Tyrus.

When he was done, Elena continued. "Mycelle and her party are bound for Castle Mryl. If you should go, I would ask that you take the zo'ol tribesman with you. His ability to farspeak may aid your search. I suspect the two warnings are, in fact, one. There is a Weirgate out there, threatening us all. It must be destroyed."

"We're overlooking something," Er'ril said.

All eyes turned to him.

"What?" Elena asked.

"Nee'lahn warned us to break *all* the Gates, not just the one. All of them: Wyvern, Basilisk, Griffin, and Manticore. Earlier today, someone else warned me to do the same. The four Weirgates are the portal to the Weir, the font of the Black Heart's power. If we destroy the Gates, we destroy his power."

Elena clutched the Blood Diary in her hands. Was that the answer she had been seeking? Could that be their next step in their assault upon the Gul'gotha? Kast stepped forward and asked the question plaguing her. "But where do we find these others?"

"I don't know," Er'ril said. "Shorkan took the wyvern back to the Gul'gotha at Blackhall, but the others could be anywhere."

"But why the Western Reaches? Why put a Weirgate way out there?" Elena wondered aloud. She faced Er'ril. "Did you discover any answer in the castle's library?"

Er'ril shook his head with a scowl. "Brother Ryn and the other scholars will continue to search the library's books."

Elena crossed to the center of the parapet. She lifted the Blood Diary. "Here is another book that may hold an answer." She nodded toward the rising moon. By now, its silver circle had climbed high in the night sky. "It is time we seek another's guidance."

Before anyone could object or her heart could falter, Elena opened the book. A wash of scintillation wafted out from the open tome, silvery fireflies on the wind. A whisper of crystal chimes followed, blown quickly away by the evening's chill breeze.

Elena held her breath and glanced into the book. Instead of white pages of parchment, she found a window open on a starry sky, as if she held a mirror in her hands, reflecting the heavens above. But it was not the skies of her world in the book. Through the portal, vaporous clouds, painted in rainbow hues, flowed between densely packed stars. Strange ice-ringed moons circled past the window, cold and dispassionate. Elena sensed the Void within the book. She felt she could easily fall within these pages and lose herself forever.

But this path was not hers. From the Void, a wispy form of light and crackling energy flowed up through the covers of the Diary to swell into the night.

The faces of those gathered on the roof followed the sight, lit from above by the glow. Overhead, the apparition spread limbs of woven light, arms and legs of carved moonstone. It stretched as if waking from a long slumber. As the figure slowly spun, the ghostly form gained substance, taking on a familiar shape. The visitor studied the ripe moon in Elena's sky, then settled to the stones of the tower roof.

Elena knew the shape of this spirit. It was as warm and familiar to her as her own palm: the stern countenance; the thin lips set hard with duty; the small, upturned nose; even the braided hair tucked under a bonnet to keep stray strands from the flame of the baking hearths. Elena noticed the ghostly figure even wore an old, frayed apron.

"Aunt Fila?"

The eyes of the figure turned toward her, and Elena instantly knew this resemblance was a ruse. Distant stars shone behind those cold eyes, and ancient suns burned to cinder in its gaze. It was as if the Void in the book had been given form and substance. The visage was not Aunt Fila, but something foreign that wore her shape, something that had never walked under a normal sky.

"Cho?" Elena whispered, naming the spirit inside, a creature of magick and power, light and energy: the being who had granted Elena her gift of blood magicks.

The figure ignored Elena and swept its gaze over those gathered atop the tower roof. No one else spoke, but neither did they retreat.

This show of strength helped Elena find her tongue. "The moon is again full. I ask that you share your wisdom with us. We seek guidance."

The cold eyes again settled on Elena. *"I speak now."* Behind the simple words, the Void could be heard in echoes of ice and timelessness. The figure lifted its arms to study its moonstone limbs, head cocking slightly. *"I have shared with the one named Fila, the one who is the Spirit Bridge to your world. She has taught me of your lands."*

Elena stood straighter. "Then you know our need. A great evil has taken hold here. We seek a way to stop it, so we might seek Chi without interference."

"Chi . . ." For a moment, the coldness of the figure seemed to melt slightly. The voice grew a trace warmer. *"I feel him all around me."*

Elena bowed her head. She did not fully understand the relationship between Chi and Cho. They were opposite, yet paired: brother and sister, wife and husband. But the bond was not exactly a familial one either. It was broader than that. Almost something natural, like the sun and the moon.

Elena raised her face. "We still search for clues to the whereabouts of your . . . of your . . ." Elena could not complete her statement. What was Chi?

The spirit must have read Elena's mind. The warmth still hovered at the edges of the Void. *"Brother . . . Call him my brother."* Their gazes met. Elena felt the momentary flash of sadness in the other's eyes. Though this entity moved between stars and lived unlike any creature that walked the lands, this hurt was too familiar: mourning and loss. The emotions took Elena back to her own, on the streets of Winterfell when her brother Joach had been stolen away. Though Elena did not understand this spirit, she knew this pain because it had once been her own.

"We have many scholars and wise men searching for the whereabouts of your brother," Elena consoled. "We will find him, but this world is choked by an evil that keeps us chained and hiding. Once free of this evil, we will be free to search for—"

"No!" The ice returned to both form and words. *"This evil is of no importance! You will find Chi."*

"We're trying, but—"

"No! I can feel my brother's pain. It eats at me, calls to me." A coldness spread out from the moonstone figure. The stones of the parapet cracked with frost. *"Chi must be found! Now!"*

The cracks in the stone spread like spiderwebs from the toes of the spirit. Elena sensed Er'ril draw near to her, ready to whisk her to safety, but she held her ground.

"I know your pain, Cho," she said calmly. "But what you ask is not easy. We have no idea where to begin even searching. And if we run blindly, the evil of this land will try to thwart our every step. It cannot be ignored." Elena stared into the Void that was the spirit's eyes. She did not balk from the sight.

The spiderweb of cracks reached toward Elena. "We are trying our best," Elena continued quietly, unmoving. The frigid magick flowed from the figure and reached toward Elena's toes. At her feet, granite stones shattered with ice.

Still, Elena stood, back straight. "It is all we can do."

Across the damaged stone roof, the figure's shoulders fell. Silence descended like a physical weight upon the rooftop. When words were spoken again, they were free of frost. *"But he cries out for me,"* Cho whispered. From eyes that opened upon the Void, tears now flowed, as human as any. *"His pain is worse than if it had been my own."*

Elena slowly worked across the terrain of broken stone until she stood beside Cho. "A pain shared can lighten a heart." Elena lifted a ruby hand and touched the edge of the figure. She was surprised to find substance there. She reached up and touched the face that was both so familiar yet at the same time so foreign.

"We are here for you. You have given us the power to fight and free our lands. We owe you our lives and our freedom. We will not fail you."

Cho leaned into her touch. It was as if Elena cupped a statue of ice, but she did not flinch. Instead she willed the magick in her heart to fill her hand. A ruby glow slowly grew, swelling out to warm the cold cheek in her hand. *"I will not fail you, Cho. This I swear. We will find your brother."*

For the first time, a sad smile formed on the moonstone lips. *"The one called Fila has told me much of you, Elena,"* Cho said. *"It seems she was not mistaken."* The figure straightened and stepped away. Her eyes grew glazed as if staring somewhere other than here. *"She wishes to speak to you."*

"Aunt Fila?"

Cho nodded. *"But I have heard you, Elena. For now, I will give you your lead. Fight this evil as you see best, but take my pain as your own. Find Chi. Find my brother."*

Elena bowed her head. "I will."

Though the ghostly figure remained as solid as ever, the voice faded, as if drifting down a bottomless well. *"I will give you power, Elena . . . and magicks never seen before . . ."*

Elena shivered at these last words. What did Cho mean? In the moonlight, Elena glanced to her two hands, bloodred and ripe with power. *Magicks never seen before.* Elena's hands trembled as they held the Blood Diary.

Then a voice drew her back to the rooftop. It was like a warm hug on a cold day. "Elena, child, it seems you've grown into the woman whose body you now wear."

Elena glanced up. All traces of the Void were gone from the apparition. What was once carved moonstone had become a warm memory of home. Elena could not stop the tears. "Aunt Fila!"

"Child, dry those tears," her aunt said brusquely, but her warmth and love could not be masked. Eyes that once held the Void now only shone with bemusement and concern. "Have you rested well since last we talked?"

"Yes, Aunt Fila," Elena said, but from the stern tightening of her aunt's lips, Elena knew she was not believed. Elena spoke quickly. "The lands ready for war. With the taking of the island, all look here for what we do next."

"And what is that?"

Elena glanced over to Er'ril. The plainsman moved to her side. "So far, mostly arguing," Er'ril answered sourly.

"Just like men," Fila muttered. "Their tongues are always bolder than their arms."

Er'ril ignored this rebuke. "But Elena has called them to task. She is to bring a plan to the war council tomorrow—a plan all will obey."

Elena quickly added, "I sought your counsel here before making any decision. I know Cho wishes us to cease our fight against the Gul'gotha while we search for her brother Chi, but all will be lost if we ignore the Dark Lord."

"I agree," Aunt Fila said. "But sometimes two causes can become one."

Elena nodded. She had said about the same thing to Meric just a moment ago. "But we've learned nothing of Chi. All our research suggests the spirit vanished from this world five centuries ago, when Alasea fell."

"He did not vanish," Aunt Fila said firmly. "My spirit mingles with Cho's now. I sense what she senses, and I've felt the whispers of her twin brother. I have heard his cries echoing through the Void. He is here."

"But where?" Er'ril said. "How do we even begin to look?"

Aunt Fila's features grew thoughtful. "I have tried to trace Chi's cries, but to no avail. All I perceive is pained emanations and an occasional snatch of tattered dreams—nightmares really. Strange beasts attacking and tearing at Chi. Creatures of twisted form and shape. A lion's head on an eagle's body. An og're with a scorpion's tail." Aunt Fila shook her head. "Just nonsense. Nightmares."

Er'ril moved forward, almost faltering a step. "A lion on an eagle's body? A winged lion." Er'ril glanced back at Elena. "A griffin!"

Elena gasped, eyes wide.

Er'ril turned to the apparition of moonstone. "Do you recall among these nightmares a large black bird, a winged lizard with a hooked beak?"

Aunt Fila's brows drew together. "Y-yes. It was one of the strange beasts holding and ravaging Chi in his dreams."

"Mother above, it was no dream." Er'ril covered his face with his hands. "The answer's been in front of me all the time."

"What?" both Elena and Fila asked together.

Er'ril lowered his palms and faced them both. "The words of the darkmage Greshym, when he told me of the nature of the ebon'stone Gates."

"What are these Gates you speak of?" Fila asked.

"Weirgates," Elena said. "Portals of power." She waved for Er'ril to elaborate.

He nodded. "The Dark Lord, with the aid of d'warves, sculpted four monstrous talismans. They were anointed in blood and had the power to draw magick inside them, willing or not. They could even draw in a person if his spirit held enough magick. One day, according to Greshym, something strange fell into one of the Gates, but it was too large to be held by a single statue. So it spread to all four, both trapping itself and fusing the Gates together. Thus the Weir was created, the well of the Dark Lord's power." Er'ril squeezed his eyes closed, his face lined in agony. "It all makes sense now. The loss of Chi here in Alasea, and the rise in power of the Gul'gotha. We have been so blind."

"What are you saying, Er'ril?" Elena asked.

Er'ril opened his eyes and stared in horror at her. "The Weir *is* Chi. They are one in the same. He fell in the Gates and was trapped. Now the Dark Lord draws upon Chi's power like some foul leech."

Elena felt the bones of her legs grow soft. "The Dark Lord's black magick has been Chi all along?"

"Yes." Er'ril could not keep the despair from his voice.

Too shocked to speak any further, Elena took a step away. The Blood Diary was still clutched in her fingers. She stared into the endless Void inside the pages of the tome. She could almost sense the tides of fate shifting under her. "Then it is clear what we must do," she mumbled.

Er'ril moved to her side. She met his gaze and felt the eyes of the others upon her. But it was nothing compared to the tides of fate flowing around the book in her hand.

"It seems the two paths have truly become one," she said. "To defeat the Dark Lord, Chi must be rescued."

"But how do we accomplish this, Elena?" Er'ril asked.

"By doing what Nee'lahn asked," she answered, turning to

face the moon. "We find and break the cursed Gates." She glanced over her shoulder at Er'ril. *"All of them."*

THE CLOAKED FIGURE CROUCHED MOTIONLESS IN THE MURK OF THE keep's courtyard. Her slender form was but another shadow amid the piled rubble of stone and twisted iron. She had been waiting, motionless, since midnight, spying on the play of lights atop the wit'ch's tower. She had watched the dragon alight on the stones of the parapet and vanish. Still she had not moved. Even when the glow of moonlight had faded from the tower heights, she remained frozen in her hiding place. Patience had been taught to her by her master. Those trained in the deadly arts knew that victory lay in the silence between battles. So she had remained throughout the night.

By now, drops of morning dew collected in the folds of her midnight green cloak. A cricket crawled across the back of her hand as her palm rested in the dirt. While she watched the castle battlements, she felt the small insect scratch its hind legs together, heard a whisper of cricket song. The promise of dawn. Now was the time. She moved smoothly to her feet as if she had only paused to pick a flower from the newly planted garden. Her motion was so swift and smooth that the cricket remained on the back of her steady hand, still playing his last song of the night.

She raised the hand to her lips and blew the surprised insect from its perch. If only her current prey were so unsuspecting.

Without pausing, she moved from her cubby of fallen stones and fled swiftly across the courtyard. None would know she had passed. She had been trained to run the desert sands without disturbing a single grain. The main doors to the central castle were guarded. She could see the backs of the guards through the stained glass windows. But doors were for the invited.

As she ran, she flicked her wrist, and a thin rope shot out from her fingers and flew toward the barred windows of the third landing. The trio of hooked trisling teeth, fastened to the end of her rope, wrapped around the bars. Without stopping, she tugged on the rope and tightened her grappling. The rope was strong, woven of braided spider's silk. It would hold her. She flew to the wall and up it. No one watching would have even suspected she was using her rope. The ancient stone was full of pocks and old battle scars; climbing was as easy for her as scaling a steep stair.

Without even raising a sweat on her brow, she reached the barred window of the third floor. From a pocket appeared a vial of blackfire. She smeared the oil on three bars, top and bottom. The stench of scorched iron wafted briefly, but no glow marked the work of the blackfire oil. *Nothing must draw the eye:* one of the first lessons taught apprentices.

She ticked off the time. At the count of ten, she grabbed the bars and yanked them free. The blackfire oil had eaten fully through. Carefully, she rested the freed iron rods on the window's granite sill. She couldn't risk someone hearing the clatter of iron on stone if she merely dropped them.

Reaching through the opening, she flicked her wrist, and a thin steel blade appeared in her fingers. She passed it through the window's casement and slipped the latch. She tested the old window hinges. An immediate rasp told her this particular window had not been opened in ages. Frowning at even this tiny noise, she reached into a pocket and oiled each hinge.

Satisfied, she pushed the window a finger-breadth wide and used the polished surface of her steel blade to study the reflection of the hall. Empty. Without waiting, she squeezed through the narrow opening and rolled into the hall. She was on her feet and in the shadows within a single heartbeat.

Still she did not pause. She raced down the passage and slid down two staircases, never even leaving a footprint in the dust. Within a short time, she had reached her goal—the doors to the Grand Court. She crouched. A dance of tools and the lock was open. She cracked the door just enough to squeeze her lithe form past the threshold. At least these hinges were already well oiled.

Once inside, she hurried to the long ironwood table. At its head was a tall chair on a raised step. Its high back was carved with twining roses. As she approached, a trace of misgiving threaded through her veins. Here was where the wit'ch sat. Her feet slowed as she worked down the long length of the table and neared the seat of power. She could almost sense the eyes of the wit'ch upon her. She knew such thoughts were nonsense, but still she shivered.

Cringing slightly, she sidled around the table's edge and stood at its head. With her back to the tall chair, she reached inside her cloak and withdrew her weapon. In the dimness of the hall, the long black blade almost glowed. Her hand trembled slightly as she held it. "Don't make me do this," she whispered to the empty hall.

But there was no retreat now. She had come too far, given up too much. If there was to be any chance, this cowardly deed must be done.

Raising the long black dagger high in both fists, she prayed for forgiveness and drove the dagger down into the table. Its sharp point pierced smoothly through the ironwood, as if it were only warmed butter. Still a shock spiked up her arms as the hilt hit the table. Gasping loudly, she pulled her hands free and ground her palms on her cloak, trying to escape the feeling.

She stared at the impaled blade. Its hilt protruded from the center of the handprint burned into the table—the handprint of a wit'ch.

As she watched, crimson blood welled up from the wood, spreading along the table's surface. The pool ran over the table's edge and flowed in rivulets to the stone floor. But that was not the worst. As she stood frozen, a distant cry of pain and shock rose from the spreading pool.

Raising a fist to her throat, the cloaked figure backed away. *What have I done?*

Turning on a heel, she fled out the door and into the maze of halls. But even the shadows could not hide her from the echoing cry of a wounded wit'ch. *Gods above, forgive me!*

3

WRITHING IN A TANGLE OF BEDSHEETS, ELENA CLUTCHED HER hand to her chest. Her palm felt as if it were on fire. Through the red haze of agony, she barely registered the loud pounding on her chamber door.

"Elena!" It was Er'ril.

His yell gave her an anchor to focus upon. She freed her hand from her sheets, expecting to see it wounded and raw. But in the room's predawn gloom, her hand appeared unharmed. As the pain slowly waned, Elena rolled from her bed and staggered toward the door.

The pounding continued. A board in the door cracked as Er'ril increased his assault. "Elena! Answer me!"

Trembling, Elena unhooked the door's latch and swung open the door. She found Er'ril disheveled and red faced. Over his shoulder, she spotted his blanket tossed and rumpled in the chair by the hearth. Last night, the plainsman had fallen asleep by the fire as the discussions of Weirgates and Chi had dragged well past midnight. Mama Freda had encouraged Elena to let Er'ril sleep where he sat. "Are you hurt?" he asked desperately, sword in hand.

With the pain now no more than a dull ache, Elena could finally think again. "I'm all right," she said, but the tremor in her voice betrayed her.

"What happened?" Er'ril asked, his eyes wandering from her toes to her head.

Elena remembered she was only dressed in a long linen shift. Suddenly aware, she backed from the door to her wardrobe and slipped into her robe. "I don't know," she said. "I awoke with my hand burning in pain." She shoved her arm through the robe's sleeve to show Er'ril.

As her hand popped from the cuff, Elena gasped at the sight. With the light from the main room's torches now illuminating her bedchamber, Elena saw her hand was not as unaffected as she had first thought.

Er'ril moved nearer, taking her hand in his. He inspected her palm and fingers. "I see no wound." He met her eyes. "But what happened to your Rose?"

Elena shook her head. She had no answer. Freeing her hand from Er'ril's grip, she lifted it higher in the flame's light. It was as pale and white as the rest of her arm. The ruby hue had vanished. Her hand no longer bore the mark of the Rose.

Er'ril stepped more fully into her room, glancing all around.

"I don't understand," Elena said. "I cast no spells. Especially nothing so strong as to drain my magicks." With her eyes, she urged him to trust her.

"I believe you. You'd have had to torch the entire tower heights to expel that much wit'chfire." He stared up at the glow of dawn through the chamber's high windows. "But when the sun rises fully, you'd best renew quickly."

Elena nodded, confused and worried. She wandered from her room toward the red coals of the main room's hearth, drawn by the warmth. She held her palms toward the soothing heat. Her left hand was still the crimson red of the Rose, but her right was milky white. What had happened? "Have you heard of anything like this, Er'ril?" she asked. "Of a mage's power just vanishing?"

Sheathing his sword, he approached the fireplace and picked up his woolen blanket from the floor. "No. Even when Chi disappeared, a mage only lost his power as his stored magick was spent." He folded the blanket. "I've never seen this happen before."

She turned from the coals, unable to hide the fear in her eyes. "Could it be a trick of the Dark Lord? Has he found a way to steal the magick from me?"

Er'ril's face grew clouded. "I don't know. But whatever happened this morning was not natural. I suspect deceit."

Before either could speak further, a knocking on the door intruded. Er'ril glanced to Elena and slid his sword out once again. "Stay behind me," the plainsman whispered.

He crossed to the door. "Who is it?" he yelled through the barred door.

"It's Joach! I've been sent by the castle's chamberlain. There's something Elena must see."

Frowning, Er'ril shoved his sword away and hauled the length of fire-hardened oak from the brackets. He yanked open the door.

Elena stood at Er'ril's shoulder. Her brother wore his usual finery, but he must have dressed in a hurry. His shirt was untucked, and he had missed buttoning his breeches properly. "What is it?" Elena asked.

Joach glanced between Er'ril and Elena, his eyebrows rising slightly in surprise at the sight of the two of them together so early. Elena glanced to her own bed robe and bare feet. She blushed slightly at what her brother must be imagining.

After clearing his throat, Joach said, "I . . . I think you should see this for yourselves. Others have already congregated at the Great Hall, and the lower halls are all abuzz with rumor. I had the chamberlain chase everyone out of the main hall and post guards at the door."

"Why? What is going on?"

Joach shook his head. "El, you'd better get dressed. If nothing else, you need to make an appearance down there. All sorts of rumors are starting to grow."

"What happened?" she asked.

Waving away her question, Joach pushed into the room. "Probably nothing. Just some drunken rouser making a bold statement about your diplomacy."

"Speak clearly, Joach," Er'ril growled, drawing the young man's eyes. The plainsman moved to Elena's side and lifted the cuff of her robe. He exposed her white hand. "Elena's magick was stolen from her. Something foul is afoot, and I tire of your little game of mysteries."

Joach stared in shock at Elena's white hand. "Sweet Mother . . . Then it wasn't just a prank," he mumbled.

"What?" she asked irritably, pulling her arm from Er'ril.

"Somebody—nobody saw who—jabbed a long knife in the palm print you burned in the Great Hall's table." Joach could not take his eyes off her hand. "I'd figured it was simply a gesture meant to insult."

Elena rubbed her palm with the fingers of her other hand. She glanced to Er'ril.

"Joach was right earlier," the plainsman said angrily. "We'd best see this for ourselves."

"What do you make of all this?" Joach asked.

Er'ril's gruff voice filled with anger. "It means we've been too lax, too trusting in our supposed allies. There's a traitor amongst us—someone who's been plying the dark arts in our very midst." Er'ril stalked toward the door. "Let us go."

Elena remained standing. "Wait." She turned toward her bedroom door. "I have something I must do first."

ER'RIL SHOVED BRUSQUELY THROUGH THE CROWD GATHERED OUT-side the doors to the Great Hall. Elena strode in his wake, flanked by guards and dressed in a plain but efficient riding outfit of brown calfskin boots, black pants, and matching jacket. Her hair had been tied back in a severe braid that made the gold flecks in her green eyes stand out. To hide the change in her hands, she also wore a pair of brown calfskin riding gloves.

Reaching the doors, Er'ril glanced approvingly at Elena. Back at the tower, she had been wise to ask for a moment to change. She had insisted that she present a commanding image, rather than her usual delicate wear. "If there is a traitor here," she had explained, "I want them to wonder if his deceit worked. And even if the renegade has fled, it would be best to present a hard front to those who remain."

Er'ril held the door, then followed her into the nearly empty hall. The only occupants were the most trusted leaders of her allies: Kast stood with the high keel of the Bloodriders; Sy-wen stood beside her mer'ai elder, Master Edyll; and Meric stood with his mother, Queen Tratal of the elv'in. Elena strode to the head of the table, Er'ril in step beside her.

The gathered folk remained silent, wearing worried expressions. Elena glanced to Er'ril, then bent to study the knife.

The long hilt of the knife thrust up from the table. Elena leaned closer, studying the sculpted hilt. Er'ril knelt down and peered under the table. The blade of the knife jutted from the underside. It was the same material as the hilt. Er'ril straightened. "This dagger is carved from a single black stone," he mumbled.

Elena reached tentatively toward it, but Er'ril stopped her with a touch to her elbow. "For now, we'd best leave it be until we know more about it."

"Is it ebon'stone?" Meric asked, approaching the table.

Elena shook her head. "No. The stone here is translucent, almost like a black crystal."

Er'ril moved around Elena to get his own view of the carving. Perched atop the hilt was a wingless dragon or lizard, its long tail wrapped along the length of the hilt, holding it in place. A fanged mouth was open in a hiss. Er'ril leaned closer. He could just make out the tiny collar of feathers around its neck. "Sweet Mother . . ." Er'ril groaned.

Eyes swung toward him until the high keel strode forward and spoke. "I know this crystal," he said gruffly.

Er'ril straightened and faced the broad-shouldered man. "What is it?"

"The fleets of the Dre'rendi have traded in treasures from all the lands of Alasea. It is nightglass. Very prized. Shards of it trade for a mighty price. Something of this size and sculpted with such artistry could be bartered for a small ship."

"But where does it come from?"

The large man scratched his head. "If I remember right, it comes from the desert of the Southern Wastes. Mined from the Scoured Sands around the Ruins of Tular."

"Tular?" Elena asked.

Er'ril answered, unable to keep the strain from his voice. "An ancient keep, abandoned for ages, so old no one knew its history even in my time. Its crumbled rooms and halls hide in the shadow of the Southwall itself."

Elena's eyes grew wide at the mention of the Southwall.

Er'ril could read the suspicion in her gaze. First a danger arising near the Northwall, and now omens from the Southwall. "That's not all," Er'ril mumbled to her.

"What?"

He nodded toward the lizard carved on the hilt. "There lies the ancient crest of Tular. I'd forgotten until now."

"What is it?"

Er'ril stared at her, unflinching. "A basilisk."

Elena gasped, stumbling back from the table.

By now, the other leaders had gathered closer. "What is the meaning of this?" Queen Tratal asked, storm winds sounding behind her stern words.

Er'ril turned to Elena.

She nodded. "Tell them. I was going to make the announcement soon anyway."

Bowing his acknowledgment, Er'ril explained the portents from the night, of the Weirgates and their significance.

Queen Tratal turned to Meric. "So, my son, you intend to take a ship and search for this Weirgate in the north."

He nodded. "Yes. With your approval, I would like to leave before the sun sets this evening."

Queen Tratal turned to Elena and Er'ril. "I will allow it. But what of this?" She waved long fingers toward the imbedded dagger.

Elena took a deep breath, composing herself. "I think the signs are too clear to ignore. If the Dark Lord positioned a Weirgate near the Northwall, there is a certain symmetry that he'd position another at the Southwall." She indicated the dagger's hilt. "We cannot dismiss this omen—a basilisk like one of the four Gates. It must be investigated."

"I can spare one other ship to aid you in your quests," the elv'in queen stated coldly. "No more."

"But the Southern Wastes are vast and endless," Er'ril argued. "With more ships involved in the search—"

"No," Queen Tratal said, her silver hair crackling with elemental energy. "I cannot weaken our fleet."

Er'ril frowned, but from the ice in the woman's gaze, he knew she would not budge.

"Then I would go with them," Kast said, lifting his head from where he had been whispering with Sy-wen. He drew the others' attentions. "The dragon Ragnar'k can add his keen eyes to this search." Kast put his arm around Sy-wen. "We will accompany the elv'in ship."

Er'ril nodded, satisfied.

The high keel wore a broad grin, puffing with pride. "If Kast goes, I would like my son, Hunt, to accompany them. The Dre'rendi will help in this search."

"Thank you," Elena said. "Thank you all."

Master Edyll spoke for the first time. "If the griffin is hidden somewhere in the north, the basilisk perhaps in the south, and the wyvern has been taken to the volcanic lair of the Dark Lord by the darkmage Shorkan—" Edyll eyed them all with his wise gaze. "—then where is this fourth gate? This Manticore Gate."

No one answered.

"What do we know of it?" Edyll asked. The elderly mer'ai leaned on his cane, but mostly for effect. He had been free of the sea for almost a full moon and hardly needed the cane to walk on hard land.

Er'ril shook his head. "The spirit of the book mentioned it. An og're with a scorpion's tail."

"Nothing else? No other clue?"

Elena began to admit their ignorance when the creak of hinges from a side door interrupted. Their faces all turned. A guard, spear in hand, stepped forth cautiously. With clear nervousness, his eyes took in the assembled crowd.

"What is it?" Er'ril asked.

The man's eyes drifted to the plainsman. "I . . . I came to announce . . ." He waved his free hand toward the opening.

A large shape climbed awkwardly through the narrow doorway. Hunched, the massive og're pulled himself up to face the others. His large amber eyes, slitted like a cat's, studied them.

"Tol'chuk?" Er'ril said, brows pinched. Lately, the og're had made himself scarce, retreating to deserted sections of the castle. From his expression now, clearly something was troubling him. His craggy features were a carving of hopelessness and despair.

"What's the matter?" Elena said, stepping beside Er'ril. "What's wrong?"

As answer, the og're moved near them and raised a clawed fist. In his grip was the chunk of precious heartstone, the Heart of his Tribe. The torchlight glinted off its facets, but its usual glow was absent. "They be gone," Tol'chuk grumbled, struggling with the common tongue of Alasea. A large tear rolled down one cheek. "All my people's spirits. The Bane has consumed them. The Heart be dead."

Elena crossed toward the large creature. She reached and touched his hand with her gloved fingers. "Oh, Tol'chuk, I'm so sorry."

Er'ril also moved forward to console him, but Tol'chuk pulled free of Elena and turned slightly away, hunching his back toward them. "I don't deserve your words of peace. I have failed my people." He seemed to hunch even farther in on himself. "And now I must fail you all, too, my friends and brothers."

"What is this nonsense?" Er'ril asked, not unkindly. He reached and gripped the thick shoulder of the og're.

Tol'chuk flinched at his touch. "I must leave you."

"What?" Elena gasped. "What do you mean?"

Er'ril understood the girl's shock. The og're had been their companion since the very beginning.

"The shade of my father appeared to me," Tol'chuk mumbled gruffly. "He has given me one last task—a way to revive the Heart."

"How?" Er'ril asked softly.

Tol'chuk would still not turn. "I must return the heartstone to where it be first mined."

"Back to the mountains of the Teeth?" Er'ril asked.

"No." Tol'chuk turned and faced him, his face a mask of pain. "To Gul'gotha."

Elena backed a step away. The others were too stunned to speak.

Tol'chuk's shoulders hunched farther. "I cannot refuse my father."

Er'ril glanced around. First Meric called by Nee'lahn, and now Tol'chuk sent a message by the shade of his father. Both companions called away by the words of the dead. Er'ril frowned at the coincidence.

Master Edyll noted another coincidence. "The og're is summoned to another shore. Does anyone else find this significant?"

"What do you mean?" Elena asked.

"We seek the hiding place of the fourth Gate—a gate sculpted like an og're with a scorpion's tail. And now comes an og're with a calling to cross the Great Ocean to the lands of Gul'gotha. Could this be the sign we were looking for?"

"I do not understand what you speak," Tol'chuk answered. "I go at the bidding of my father, to find a way to free my people's spirits from the Bane."

"And what is this Bane?" Master Edyll said. He held up his hand when Tol'chuk began to answer. "I have heard your tale, Master Tol'chuk. What I mean is what exactly is this creature in the heartstone?"

Tol'chuk held the stone up toward the light. "I don't know. It has changed, grown as it's fed on the last spirits."

"May I see it?" Master Edyll said.

Tol'chuk glanced to Er'ril and Elena. Elena nodded, her face curious.

Tentatively, the og're relinquished the chunk of heartstone to Master Edyll. The elder had to hold the large stone in both hands. He moved to one of the torches in a wall sconce. Straining slightly with the weight of the stone, Edyll held the crystal up to the flame, peering inside. The Heart glowed brightly with the firelight. The old mer'ai leaned closer, grimacing slightly. "Hmm . . ."

"What?" Er'ril asked.

"Just as I thought." Master Edyll stepped to the side, still holding the crystal near the torch. He nodded to the far wall.

Er'ril and the others all turned. The refracted firelight spread to the distant wall, bathing it with a ruby glow. But at the center was a darkness. It was the shadow of the Bane cast on the wall for all to see.

Gasps spread all around. Er'ril took a step nearer.

As they watched, the shadow shifted, uncurling, as if it sensed their gazes. Black claws spread out, scrabbling on the wall. A spiked tail rose from the heart of the shadow, poised in threat.

"A black scorpion," Elena said, a clenched fist at her throat. She turned to Tol'chuk. "The Bane is a scorpion."

JOACH WOUND HIS WAY DOWN TO THE LOWEST LEVEL OF THE CASTLE. His stomach growled in complaint at his missed morning meal. Elena had rescheduled the war council meeting for midday. After the revelation of the scorpion, she had said she needed to ponder all she had learned. Before she left, Joach had watched Elena bow her head with Er'ril's, whispering something to him. The plainsman's expression had darkened at her words; then the two had whisked out together, wearing almost matching stern expressions. Neither had bothered to include him in their plans.

With the remaining folk in the Hall talking within their own groups, Joach had found himself ignored. With no one to talk to, he had quickly become aware of his empty stomach. Seeking food, Joach had left the Hall and now worked his way down the last staircase toward the castle's kitchen.

In truth, it was not just his stomach that urged him toward the kitchens. In his mind, he pictured a serving girl with eyes the color of twilight and hair the color of spun gold. His lips breathlessly formed her name: *Marta*.

Joach's feet sped faster down the steps. Again, as he entered the lower level, he was instantly assaulted with the rich odors and cheery sounds of the kitchens. Joach glanced down at himself and straightened the lay of his jacket and shirt, then marched with forced casualness into the kitchen heat. He would not let his feet betray his heart.

As soon as he entered, his eyes quickly scanned the bustling servants and kitchen help. So intent was he on peering through the crowd that he failed to see the discarded ladle on the floor.

His heel struck it with a loud clang, and his leg went out from under him. Eyes turned his way.

Flailing, Joach fell forward. Grabbing for a table's edge to keep from falling, he missed, and his palm struck the edge of a large bowl of corn porridge. He twisted just before hitting the floor, taking the brunt of the impact on his shoulder. With the breath knocked from his lungs, he gasped and rolled to his back—just in time to see the large bowl of porridge topple over the table's edge and dump its contents over his head.

The warm corn porridge splattered him from crown to shoulder, blinding him, filling his open mouth. Thank the Mother, it was just the remains from the morning meal, left cooling on the table. If it had been steaming hot, he could have suffered a severe burn. Even so, his cheeks were aflame with embarrassment. Sputtering and pushing to his elbows, Joach spat out a mouthful of porridge, choking.

"Watch it, you fool!" a voice scolded.

Joach felt a cool, wet rag begin to wipe his face, first his lips and nose so he could breathe. Embarrassment made his voice meek. "I'm sorry . . . I didn't see . . . I tripped . . ."

The cool rag moved to wipe the porridge from his eyes. Joach, humiliated enough, sat straighter and took the rag in his own hand. "I can manage," he muttered, heat entering his words.

He wiped brusquely at his eyes and face. Finally, he could see again. He glanced up to thank his benefactor and found himself staring into midnight blue eyes. Framed in golden hair, her bronze skin shone in the heat of the kitchen's hearths. "Marta," he gasped.

With his face now almost cleaned, Joach saw Marta's eyes grow equally as wide as his. She bowed her head quickly. "Prince Joach," she mumbled.

Joach had noticed the trace of panic and fear in her eyes just before she had turned away. "It's all right, Marta. It was my fault. I wasn't watching where I was stepping." He did not want her sharing any guilt for his own clumsiness.

"I'll get you more rags," she muttered. "You'd best give me your jacket. I'll soak it in cold water before any stain sets in the wool."

Joach wiped the rest of his face clean. "No need. I can manage on my own. But thank you all the same."

He stood and finally noticed the entire kitchen crew gaping at them. Joach's cheeks grew hot. He raised a hand and found his hair coated thickly with porridge. Frowning, he stepped to a washbasin and shrugged off his jacket. Before cleaning his clothes, Joach dunked his entire head into the deep washbasin. For a moment, he thought of drowning himself to escape his embarrassment. But he could not stop a small smile from forming on his lips as he worked the porridge from his hair. So much for his casual entrance.

Pushing up from the basin, he shook his hair free of the water. He found Marta at his side, a clean towel in hand. Joach accepted it with a shy grin. He was surprised to see a matching expression on the young woman's face. "I came down here for a quick breakfast," he said as he toweled his head. "But I didn't expect it that quick."

Marta smiled at his attempt at a joke. "I'll get you a proper meal." She nodded him to a table and waved another servant to take his jacket. "Take a seat, Prince Joach. The head cook is at the Great Hall arranging for the midday repast, but I'll find something for you to eat."

"Just not porridge," he said as she stepped away.

She glanced over his shoulder. "Don't worry. I'll make you something special."

He watched her move confidently through the kitchen, ordering the younger help around. One of the other servant girls whispered something in Marta's ear, then darted away when Marta snapped a rag at her. The girl ran giggling away, but not before giving Joach a knowing wink.

Joach shook his head and hid his grin as he used the damp towel to wipe his shirt down and clean behind his ears. Before he had even finished, Marta returned with a stoneware plate and a fork. The plate steamed with a mix of braised meat over a bed of shredded potatoes. As she set the plate down, Joach smelled rich spices unlike any he had ever smelled before. The odor slightly burned his nostrils.

"It's a morning dish of my people," she said. "It is made to wake the tongue to the morning's sun."

Joach forked a piece and brought it to his lips as she spoke. As he tasted it, his brows rose in appreciation. A full and rich spice accented the meat perfectly. "What is this?" he asked, lifting a second chunk of meat.

"Sand shark," she said meekly, "A delicacy from the Southern Wastes—my homeland." She poured him a mug of cold ale. "You'll need this."

It was just then that the spices took full hold of his mouth. They bloomed with a fiery heat on his tongue. "Sweet Mother!" he choked out. His fingers scrabbled for his mug. He doused the fire with a generous wash of ale. The burn quickly faded. Joach sighed. "That is the way your people greet the morning sun?"

"It is, when you live in the desert," she said with a small smile. "Burning tongue for the burning sun."

"I see," he said. He forked up another piece of meat. Regardless of the spicy burn, it had tasted wonderful—but more importantly, he did not want to appear a milk-fed calf in front of Marta. "Why don't you join me?" he added, nodding toward another seat.

She bowed her head. "Thank you for the consideration, Prince Joach, but I've work to do here in the kitchen." She raised her head, a sly grin on her face. "Besides, this dish is meant only for men of my tribe."

As she turned away, Joach studied her, drinking in her beauty as much as he had the ale a moment ago. But this draught did not soothe the burn in his spirit. He reached out and touched her elbow.

"Thank you," he said.

She stopped and glanced over her shoulder at him. Smiling, she drew back a fall of her hair to see him better. "It is an honor to serve a prince of the Blood."

Joach suddenly could not breathe. With the firelight playing across her cheek, Marta's beauty held him enthralled as surely as any dark spell. Then her silken hair fell back over her face, breaking the spell as she moved away and returned to her duties.

"I'm no prince," he muttered as she disappeared inside a pantry.

ELENA FOLLOWED ER'RIL DOWN THE DARK, NARROW STAIRS. Farther ahead, a thick-bellied guard led the way with a torch held high. As Elena continued, the brush of a spiderweb whispered across a cheek. Scowling, she wiped the sticky strands away with a gloved hand. This section of the Great Edifice had seen little improvement since their victory here.

"I still don't see why we need to consult them," Er'ril argued again.

Elena answered in a tired voice. "If Tol'chuk means to journey to Gul'gotha, then I mean to give him as much guidance as possible. You saw the scorpion in the stone. It has to be a sign that the Manticore Gate lies at the end of Tol'chuk's path."

"But what do you hope to gain here in the dungeons?"

Elena sighed. "Hopefully an ally."

The guard stopped ahead at a thick iron-bound door. He pounded a thick fist on the oaken frame. "Open up, Gost!"

The only reply was a coarse grunt, but the grate of old latches sounded. The door creaked open with a cry of pained hinges. A half-naked man stood at the threshold with a lantern raised. In his other hand was a thick ironwood club. It was the dungeon keep. His one good eye grew wide at the sight of Elena and Er'ril. The other half of his face was a frozen storm of scars.

Their guide nodded to the dungeon keep. "This is Gost. He'll take you from here. But don't expect no cheery banter from the poor grunt." Their guide snickered. "He had his tongue cut out when he himself was a guest here of the Dark Lord."

Gost clearly heard the guard's words. After bowing toward them, he turned his face from the torch's flame. The movement reminded Elena of Jaston, the scarred swamp man, hiding his scars from the brightness and light of the sun. Elena's heart went out to the broken man. So much goodness had been butchered by the Gul'gothal tyrants.

Their guide stepped aside to let Er'ril pass. Elena followed more slowly.

Beyond the door, the passage ahead narrowed even farther. They were forced to continue in single file. The only illumination came from Gost's lantern. As they walked in silence, Elena sensed they were slowly winding deeper under the castle. The air smelled more damp, with a hint of brine. To either side, the walls of the hallway changed from quarried stone blocks to passages carved in raw rock.

At last, a dim glow appeared ahead: the guardroom to the dungeons. Gost led them into the chamber and crossed to a ring of iron keys hanging on a hook. Elena glanced around the room. A small hearth glowed in one wall, the rock edges around it stained black from the smoke of countless centuries of fires. Four beds rested at the corners of the rooms, but three had their thin mattresses rolled up atop them, unused and dusty.

Gost must man these dungeons by himself, Elena realized.

While waiting for the guard to find the right key, she noticed the touches of a man who had made his home here under the castle. Small personal objects hung on the wall above the single dressed bed. An oil painting, no bigger than her palm, depicted a smiling woman astride a handsome chestnut stallion. Draped around the picture was a fine set of bridles and reins. The leathers shone in the feeble light, clearly well maintained. The metal of the bridle sparked brilliantly. *Silver,* Elena imagined. She studied these pieces. Here was a reflection of a different life, a life before the coming of the Gul'gotha, before the time of scars and mutilations. For the thousandth time, Elena promised herself she would end such pain. Alasea had suffered enough.

Finally, a grunt drew her attention back to Gost. The scarred man held up a long key. With a satisfied nod, the guard led them to a door on the far side of the room. He opened the way— lantern in one hand, ring of keys in the other.

Beyond the door was a hallway with a long row of short doors. Er'ril's face darkened at the sight. He even stumbled a step. Elena remembered that Er'ril himself had recently been imprisoned in these very cells. Most of the doors now lay open. The dungeons had been emptied after their victory. Sadly, many of the victims of the Dark Lord's attentions here had had to be destroyed. Strange, twisted creatures had been discovered howling, cowering in their own filth. Once men, but no longer, their minds had been ground away by dark magicks.

Thankfully, Gost led them past these cells to a branching hallway. Here there were larger cells, meant to hold multiple captives, with doors composed of iron bars as thick as a man's wrist.

Gost led them to the centermost cell, the largest, as big as a small ballroom. The prisoners here, the only occupants in all the dungeon, had insisted on being housed together. Elena had agreed to their request. How could she refuse? She had not even wanted them imprisoned. After the war, they had sworn allegiance and fealty to her. But her allies, including Er'ril, were still mistrustful of these former enemies and had insisted they be incarcerated in the dungeons.

Elena stepped to the doorway. She was glad to find the area clean. Even iron braziers had been moved into the cell to warm the damp from the air and offer a bit of light and cheer. Clearly, Gost proved a fair innkeeper.

Amid the braziers, thick-bodied forms huddled, some wrapped in blankets and snoring, some whispering among themselves. They stood no taller than Elena's shoulder but weighed threefold, all muscle and bone. Faces turned in Elena's direction as her footsteps stopped at the cell's door. Under heavy brows, narrowed eyes stared at her.

"Oath or not," Er'ril muttered, "I do not trust any d'warf."

Elena stepped nearer the door. "When do you trust anyone?" she answered glibly.

The leader of the d'warves, an ancient with an old scar running from crown to jaw, came forward to the bars, then quickly dropped to one knee. He was bald but bore a long gray mustache that drooped below his chin. "Mistress Elena," he said, bowing his head farther, "how may I serve you?"

Elena's cheeks grew hot with shame at their imprisonment. His position reminded her of a similar display when she had first encountered the warriors. Wennar's battalion, bearing heavy axes and protected by impenetrable spellcast armor, had fallen to its knees—not for her, but for the sacred talisman she bore. The *Try'sil*, the rune-carved Hammer of Thunder. The sight of the magickal talisman had succeeded in breaking the Dark Lord's hold on these fierce warriors.

She waved to Gost. "Could you open the gate please?"

Gost was quick to obey. His keys rattled in the barred door's lock.

"Is this wise?" Er'ril said, and moved to Elena's shoulder, hand resting on the hilt of his sword.

As answer, she glared at the plainsman.

Once the gate swung open, she moved closer to the kneeling d'warf. "Please rise, Wennar," she said, using the leader's name. "I come to ask your aid."

The d'warf was slow to climb to his feet. He kept his eyes downcast. "You have but to ask. We are yours to command."

By now, all the d'warves were intent on their conversation. Even those slumbering had been shaken awake.

Elena inclined her head in acknowledgment to Wennar's statement. "Thank you. I have a request of all of you."

Wennar nodded, waiting, eyes downcast.

"You know Tol'chuk, I believe."

The d'warf leader nodded again. "The og're."

"He prepares to embark on a dangerous quest."

Wennar glanced slightly up, his gaze narrowed in confusion.

"To Gul'gotha," Elena finished.

The d'warf's eyes grew large. Murmuring arose from those gathered behind Wennar. "He must not go there," their leader mumbled. "The very ground is poisoned by the Nameless One. Only death lies there for the untainted."

"He must go. Both at the behest of his father's spirit and in the hope of aiding our battle against the Gul'gotha."

Wennar turned his back slightly. "No good will be found on those shores."

Elena glanced at Er'ril. The plainsman acted as if he expected no other response.

"What would you have of us?" Wennar asked, his gaze focused on a glowing brazier nearby.

"I would have you go with Tol'chuk. Those are your lands. You know them and can help."

Wennar's shoulders trembled with her words. "We swore an oath to you, but what you ask is not possible."

"Why?"

"Centuries of winters have passed since any d'warf has set toe on Gul'gothal soil. Our homeland is dead to us. We would know it no better than the og're."

"But surely you've seen old maps, know something of—"

Wennar swung back toward Elena, moving more swiftly than she imagined he could move. Er'ril yanked his sword from his sheath at the sudden movement, but no harm was intended by the d'warf leader. "Our homeland is dead to us!" Wennar wailed. Tears ran from the corners of his eyes. Anguish was etched in stone on his old face. "It is forbidden."

Er'ril spoke for the first time. "I told you coming here would prove a waste."

Wennar slunk back around. "I'm sorry, Mistress Elena."

Elena was not ready to admit defeat. "And what if you bore the Try'sil on this journey?"

Wennar tensed.

"I promised Cassa Dar," Elena continued, "that I'd one day return your sacred talisman to its homelands, to the mines of Gul'gotha, and fulfill the ancient prophecy."

"The Hammer of Thunder," he mumbled.

"It is foretold that the return of the hammer would herald the rebirth of your homeland."

Wennar still would not turn. He drew even tighter inward. "It is not a d'warf hand that must carry the Try'sil."

"Then Tol'chuk will," Elena said.

"No." Wennar slowly turned. "Did the d'warf mistress of the swamps not explain this to you? The legend is exact. Only the one who freed the Hammer can bring the Try'sil home." Wennar raised his eyes and met hers squarely for the first time. "Only you can free our lands."

Er'ril slammed his sword back to its sheath. "Elena cannot go to Gul'gotha. She is needed here."

Elena's immediate reaction was the same as the plainsman's. They had fought so hard and lost so many lives to bring the wit'ch to A'loa Glen. How could she think of venturing on this side journey when the larger war loomed? But once she heard the plainsman speak it, Elena considered this thought more deeply. She remembered sitting on the Rosethorn Throne, all but forgotten by the others. Was it truly so vital she be here? The war was not fought to bring the wit'ch to the island, but Elena to the book. And with that accomplished, was she needed here? Did she plan to hide in safety while her friends scattered throughout the lands in search of the cursed Weirgates? Should she not bear her magick and power in pursuit of the Gates' destruction? Elena clenched her fist. Still, dare she consider leaving the safety of this fortified island? She had no answer—but one last question had to be asked aloud.

"If I go," she said, "will you come as guides?"

"Elena!" Er'ril blurted. "You can't think to—"

Elena held up a hand to silence him. She kept her eyes on Wennar's.

Slowly he fell to his knees and bowed his head to the floor.

The other d'warves did the same. "We would be yours to command," Wennar said, his voice swelling with hope. "We would die to keep you safe."

Elena nodded. "Very well. I will consider this."

"You will *not*!" Er'ril said in rattled shock.

Elena did not even glance his way, but turned on a heel and led the way back out of the dungeons.

Er'ril chased after her as Gost locked up the cell behind them. "Elena, you can't truly be thinking of going to Gul'gotha. You can't risk yourself this way. You're safe here. You have armies from many lands protecting you."

Elena did not stop her march back toward the castle proper. "Safe?" she asked. She slipped the glove from her left hand, exposing her pale flesh. "There are assassins within these very walls. The Dark Lord knows that I hide here and will try again and again to destroy me. I am a sitting target, just awaiting his next arrow."

"But—?"

They had reached the dungeon keep's domicile. The light here was much brighter. Elena turned to Er'ril. "I have made no final decision, Er'ril. I only said I would consider it."

"Then I would ask you to consider this, Elena. By going, perhaps you would be playing into the Dark Lord's hands. Maybe the assassin was not meant to kill you, but to scare you, to chase you from the island, so he might snare you when you are less protected."

Elena sighed and stopped. Her eyes settled on Gost's portrait of a smiling woman on a handsome horse. "No one can know what game the Dark Lord is playing. To guess his next move is the path to fear and indecision. I've heard enough of that in the Great Hall over the past moon. All I can do is follow what my heart tells me." Elena turned and met Er'ril's eyes. "Can you trust that? Can you trust my decision?"

Er'ril closed his eyes and slowly nodded. His words were a bare whisper. "Always. I am your liegeman."

KAST STOOD AT THE PROW OF THE DOUBLE-MASTED ELV'IN WINDship, the *Eagle's Fury*, and glanced below to the dock. Men bustled with crates and supplies among the thick ropes tethering ship to land. Winches creaked and draft horses whinnied as they fought the pulleyed ropes to haul gear to the elv'in warship floating two stories above their heads. Open hatches on the underbelly of the ship awaited their cargo.

Scowling, Kast turned his back on the sight. Outfitting the ship for the journey to the Southern Wastes would have gone much faster if the ship had docked like any normal seagoing vessel. But the captain of the *Eagle's Fury*—Meric's brother, Richald—had refused to let his ship settle into the sea for loading. "No Thundercloud has ever touched the world's surface," Richald had stated coldly. "It would taint the *Eagle's Fury*, and auger ill for our journey."

Kast had not argued. It was not his ship. On this expedition, he was a mere passenger. He stared up at the masts with their furled sails and at the thin, waspish fellows climbing lithely among the ropes and rigging. As much as he found this mode of travel distasteful, Kast could not fault the skill of Richald's crew. They walked the ropes as well as any man walked the planks of a normal vessel.

Sighing, he glanced away. On the far side of the dock, the twin to this boat floated two stories above the water. It was Meric's own ship, the *Stormwing*. Its magic-wrought iron keel glowed like warm coal, its elemental power keeping the ship afloat in the air. Men bustled under its hull, too, as it was being outfitted and readied for its flight to the northern stretches of Alasea. From here, Kast spotted the elv'in lord among his own crew atop the deck, including the trio of dark-skinned zo'ol tribesman who would accompany Meric on the search for Elena's companions.

There was a certain symmetry here. Two brothers, two ships, two tasks. One headed to the north, one to the south. But how would each fare? Twin victories or twin defeats?

The scrape of bare heel on wood drew his attention from his reverie of the future. Dressed in mottled sharkskin, Sy-wen might as well have been naked. From the swell of her breasts to the curves of her thighs, nothing was hidden by the thin material. She smiled as their eyes met, oblivious to the immodesty of her dress.

But others were not so blind. At her side strode the captain of the ship, Richald. Kast noticed how the elv'in kept trying to avert his eyes from Sy-wen's form, but failed. A slight blush glowed on the captain's pale cheeks as his eyes flickered toward her periodically. It seemed the blood of elv'in princes did not entirely flow with ice.

Sy-wen slipped easily under Kast's arm as she neared him, giving him a quick brush of her lips on his cheek. Kast firmed his grip around her waist, making it clear who lay claim to her heart.

Richald cleared his throat and glanced off to the empty skies. "We are on schedule. We'll be off with the first light."

Kast nodded. "It seems Meric fares just as well."

This triggered a hardening of Richald's countenance. His eyes narrowed as he glanced toward the *Stormwing*. "Luckily my brother's crew has been trained well." It seemed Richald was not about to give Meric any credit for leadership in this matter.

"Ah, but a crew is only as good as their captain," Kast mumbled.

Richald's fist clenched. "That is yet to be seen. My brother has been too long on solid ground. Let us see how he fares in the wilds of the empty skies."

"I'm sure your brother will do well," Sy-wen said, pulling slightly away. She squeezed Kast's arm, scolding him silently for goading Richald. "But I must be off. Mother is expecting me."

"You're going now?" Kast said, surprised. "What about Elena's council meeting?"

"I am not needed. Master Edyll represents our people." She nodded toward the two masts of the *Eagle's Fury*. "Besides, it is clear where we are headed next. And if we are to leave at dawn, I have little time to say good-bye to Mother." She stepped toward the railing. "I will return by nightfall."

Kast refused to let her leave so easily. Catching her wrist, he pulled her back, drawing her to his chest and staring down into her eyes. "I expect you back before the sun's last light," he whispered, then leaned near her ear so his words were private. "We have a new bed to bless this night."

His words brought a blush to her cheeks. He leaned for a kiss and found her lips as warm as her cheeks. With lips still touching, she breathed a promise. "Fear not. I'll be here, my dragon." A finger traced his chin as she pulled away, outlining the edge of his tattoo. Her touch was like fire on his flesh.

Then she stepped away again.

In the distance, the blare of trumpets sounded from the castle heights. The council was being summoned.

"I must be off," she said.

Kast had no words left in him. He only raised a hand in farewell.

Sy-wen crossed to the ship's leeward side, climbed over the railing, and without a glance back, dove smoothly over the side.

Kast strode to the rail and leaned out. Far below, the barest trickle of bubbles marked where she had entered the water. The sea had welcomed back its own.

4

As THE ASSEMBLY GATHERED, ER'RIL STOOD AT ELENA'S SIDE BEside the Rosethorn Throne. Er'ril noted how half the council seats remained empty. During the night, the faint-hearted and the profiteers had clearly packed and fled, wanting no part of any real action against the Gul'gotha.

Er'ril turned. Elena wore a deep frown as she also stared around the assembly. Few members spoke as they settled into their places, eyes flicking toward the empty chairs.

From beyond the chamber, a trumpet blew a final note, announcing the start of the war council.

At this signal, Elena stood. She still wore her leather riding outfit but had abandoned the pair of matching lambskin gloves. The Rose was bright again on both hands. Earlier the assassin's dagger had been carefully extracted from the table and given to the scholars in the library for study. With her handprint free of the magickal talisman, Elena had found she could easily renew in the light of the sun, returning the gift of wit'ch fire to her right fist. She kept her hands bared now to dismiss any rumor of weakness.

Though Er'ril was relieved no permanent harm had resulted from the mysterious attack, he felt a twinge of misgiving. He stared at the wounded handprint, as did others around the table.

What did this assault mean? Why go through so much trouble for so little result?

As he stood guard, hand on sword hilt, Elena lifted her right fist for all to see. In the torchlight, the crimson hues whorled over her flesh. To the less observant, it seemed a twin to her left, but Er'ril recognized the slight fade to the Rose of her raised fist, a sign of magick spent. But the drain was no trick from the magickal dagger. After Elena had renewed, Er'ril had insisted she practice manipulating her magick to test whether her gift had somehow been tainted. Elena had lit a series of candles from ten paces away, her control so precise that not even a single drop of wax had melted. It seemed the attack had had no lasting damage.

And this fact bothered him more than anything.

He studied the tabletop. Just what had been the purpose of this assault? Why so much stealth and secrecy? The lack of any reasonable answer kept Er'ril on edge. He kept a wary eye on the faces along the table. Was the traitor still here, or had he fled with the night?

As if feeling his hard gaze, the crowd finally settled to full silence.

Elena took a step forward and clenched her raised fist tighter. A glow blew forth from her hand. But when she spoke, her voice was quiet. "This past night, we have seen the result of a wavering heart. While we've sat and argued, dark forces have grown in our midst, like poison in stagnant waters. Well, no longer. From this moment onward, we will be a rushing river, a torrent of determined force that no petty thief in the night can taint." As she spoke, fire grew in her voice, and the glow of her Rose flared brighter.

Er'ril had a difficult time keeping a watch upon the table and surroundings, his gaze drawn to her like a moth to flame. Slowly, Elena lowered her fist.

"I thank you all for showing your true hearts here this day," she continued. "Though our numbers are fewer, we are stronger, steel forged from iron. And before another winter passes, I promise we will bring this new blade to the throat of the Black Heart himself."

A fist pounded rhythmically on the table. It was the high keel.

His eyes were bright with the promise of war. "Let the oceans run red until our lands are free!" the high keel growled. Others murmured, and more fists added their support along the iron-wood table.

Elena lifted a palm to silence the rising response. "War will come. There is no way to avoid it. But before we cast our bodies upon the shoals of Blackhall, we must be ready."

"We are ready!" the high keel declared boldly, ignoring the bandages still peeking from under his clothes.

Elena smiled. "I'm sure you are. The Dre'rendi are not ones to shun a battle, even when the numbers are against them."

The high keel nodded, chest swelling.

"But for now, another path lies ahead of us."

"And what might that be?" These words were from a familiar dissenter, Symon Feraoud, the portly representative from Penryn. He blew out his black mustaches as he huffed his skepticism. Er'ril had been surprised to see the man take a seat at the meeting. He would have laid odds on Feraoud being the first to ship back to his coastal home last night.

Elena nodded to the question raised by the thick-bellied fellow. "As you all know, I have taken the night to consult the spirits of the Blood Diary and have studied the words coming from far places. We now know the source of the Dark Lord's magicks. It is a set of four ebon'stone Gates that contain the font of his black powers. Before we take our war to the shores of Blackhall, we must first discover these Gates and destroy them, stripping the Dark Lord of his magick. Therein lies our only chance at victory."

Er'ril noticed Elena was careful not to mention what she had truly discerned from the Blood Diary—that the imprisoned spirit of *Chi* was the true well of power. Such news would not have been well received.

"And how will you attempt the destruction of these Gates?" Symon asked.

"We will not just *attempt* this," Elena said coldly. "We will do it. Already elv'in ships are being readied to search them out."

A new murmuring grew around the table.

Master Edyll of the mer'ai spoke up. "Tell us your full plan."

Elena bowed her head to the elder, then answered. "We know of four Gates: the Wyvern, the Basilisk, the Griffin, and the

Manticore. One we cannot reach. The wyvern statue has been taken by Shorkan to Blackhall. We will leave that Gate until we are ready to take the battle to Blackhall itself. But words and signs point to where the other three might lie."

Elena continued to explain about the twin journeys: one to the north led by Meric, one to the south led by Prince Richard and accompanied by Sy-wen and Kast.

"And the Manticore Gate?" Master Edyll asked.

Elena grew silent for a few moments, then finally spoke. "The og're, Tol'chuk, will search to the east, across the seas to Gul'gotha."

This announcement stunned most of the members, except the handful who had been in the hall earlier.

"That is a most dangerous journey," Edyll countered. "None who have attempted to seek out that distant shore have ever returned."

Elena nodded. "That is why I have enlisted the aid of guides."

Her answer lifted the brows of the mer'ai elder. "Guides?"

"The d'warf captives in the dungeons below. It is their ancient homeland."

At the mention of the d'warves, faces grew stern and angry.

"Even if such guides should prove faithful," Master Edyll said, his voice thick with doubt, "this journey still is the most dangerous of all and the most likely to fail."

"Not if I go with them," Elena said simply.

Her answer had the entire assembly on its feet. Even Er'ril took a step toward Elena, but he restrained himself. He had sworn an oath to her. He would abide by her decision.

But that did not mean the others would.

The high keel's face was as red as a bloodied bandage. "You cannot mean to travel to that cursed land! It is certain death."

Er'ril could not stop his own head from nodding when others shouted their dissent. It was absolute folly.

Elena bore the brunt of their outburst, a rock beaten by waves.

Queen Tratal spoke for the first time. Her face, usually unreadable, was a mask of rage. "I will not allow this!"

Elena turned slowly to the elv'in queen. "I am going."

The two women stared at one another. Tiny spats of lightning sparked among the silver strands of Queen Tratal's hair, raising a slight nimbus around her head like a silver crown. Still Elena met the woman's ice with her own. The hall quieted as the two faced each other down. The scent of the room grew to that of a brewing storm, and time seemed to slow to an excruciating length.

Finally, Queen Tratal clenched her fists once and settled back. "So it seems the blood of kings does run in your veins." Lightning died around her—but her eyes remained narrowed, cold and brittle as shards of winter's ice. "But if you mean to cross the Great Ocean, it will be aboard my ship."

Elena bowed her head in acquiescence, clearly growing into a diplomat as much as a wit'ch. "I would be honored."

The high keel, however, was not so easily swayed. "If Elena goes, then we go, too. The Dre'rendi have sworn blood oaths to protect you."

Elena turned to the leader of the Bloodriders with a warm smile. "I appreciate your loyalty, High Keel of the Dre'rendi. I am doubly honored, but A'loa Glen must also be protected. I would ask the Dre'rendi and the mer'ai to keep the island safe while we are gone on our journeys. If we succeed, there must be a rallying point to which we can return. And I would prefer not to wage another War of the Isles to regain it."

The high keel grumbled, but the winds seemed to die in his sails.

"And more importantly," Elena continued forcefully, "this small island is the seed from which a new Alasea, a free Alasea, must grow. I will not have it fall again under the shadow of the Dark Lord."

The high keel bowed deeply, fist raised to throat. "On the blood of every Dre'rendi, such a curse will never happen."

Elena crossed her arms across her chest in the typical Dre'rendi fashion. An oath accepted. She then lowered her arms and faced the assembled council. "Are we agreed?" she asked simply.

The question need not have been asked.

Er'ril turned from the council as they pounded their assent upon the ironwood. He stared at Elena as she stood at the end of the table. The words of Queen Tratal echoed in his head: *The blood of kings runs in your veins.*

There was no doubt.

* * *

IN AN ABANDONED SECTION OF THE CASTLE, A CLOAKED FIGURE huddled in the deeper shadows of a shallow alcove. She waited for the signal with only spiders and dust beetles for company. Then she heard it, echoing down through the halls of the Great Edifice: a trumpet's blast. The council meeting had begun. The wit'ch and her companions would be occupied for a stretch of time. Straightening her lithe form, she slid smoothly from her alcove, not even disturbing the drape of spiderwebs overhead. She stepped through the parade of dust beetles without squashing a single insect. Her master had taught her not to leave behind even a single clue of her presence.

Around her, the halls were empty, as she imagined even the more populated sections of the castle were at this time. The entire castle held its breath at the outcome of the meeting in the Great Hall. But such matters of politics and intrigue were not her concern. She had accomplished half of her task. All that remained was a final act and her escape.

Running silently on feet padded in the thinnest leather, she left no footprint upon the floor's thick dust. She ran the halls, winding her way toward the upper floors of the castle. Dashing down a last passage, she quickly came upon the door she sought. She tested its latch. It did not budge. She silently sighed in relief. It was locked, suggesting no one was inside. Allowing herself a tight grin, she sank to one knee. Tools slipped easily into hand. Deft fingers played the slim lengths of steel into the door's lock and searched for the releases.

The tumble of the lock's mechanism rewarded her efforts. She stood and tested the latch once again. It gave way easily.

Not pausing to appreciate her handiwork, she pushed the door open only wide enough for her slim form to slip past the threshold. She leaned on the door and let it snap closed behind her, thumbing the lock back in place.

The room was dim; only a single small lantern glowed atop a table in the far corner, its wick trimmed to the smallest flame. She frowned at the sight. Why was a lamp left burning, even as low as it was? Had one of the scholars been forgetful? She hurried deeper into the room. She could not trust such a thought. None of the scholars would risk an untended flame, especially here.

To either side, shelf after shelf of books and scrolls stood guard over the room. The rows towered three times her height with a scattering of ladders between them to aid the library's staff in finding the proper text among the highest shelves. She crossed to the far side of the room, where desks, chairs, and tables were spread before a tall hearth. She glanced quickly around, ensuring herself that no one skulked in some shadowed corner. She neared the hearth and raised a palm toward a mantel stone. Still warm. The hearth had only recently died.

Biting a lip with worry, she hurried about her task. She had listened to the rumors among the castle help and knew where she needed to search. She crossed to the largest of the many desks. It was a huge oaken monstrosity with scrolled edges and so thickly cluttered that not a single space was bare atop it. Stacks of books were stationed at every corner, and parchment lay scattered amid a handful of open texts and inkwells. There was even a trio of scrolls splayed wide atop the desk, held open with small lead weights in the shapes of woodland animals.

She ignored all the determined research and went to the centermost drawer of the thick desk. She tested the drawer and was surprised to find it unlocked. Could she be mistaken? Fearing the worst, she yanked the drawer open with a loud squeak of wood.

She closed her eyes briefly with relief. It was still here! Opening her eyes, she reached into the drawer. Her fingers hesitated only a breath before touching the crystal dagger's sculpted hilt. The carving of the basilisk, the ancient symbol of the ghouls of Tular, sickened her. Still, she lifted the blade from the drawer and examined the long shard of razor-sharp nightglass. Holding it up to the light, she saw the length of the blade's core now glowed with a fiery brightness that had nothing to do with the lamp's tiny flame.

Her master had not been mistaken!

She was so stunned that it took her half a moment to recognize the telltale sound of a key in a lock. She froze as voices rose from behind the door. Someone was coming!

Sliding the dagger into the sheath sewn into her cloak, she sped to the nearest row of bookshelves and flew up them without the use of any of the library's ladders. She pulled herself atop the bookshelf and stood on the narrow strip of wood, balancing, praying it would hold her weight and not topple.

Across the room, the door swung open and a pair of robed scholars entered the room, one young, one old. They bore platters of bread and cheeses as they talked.

Not waiting, she ran for deeper shadows, where the row met the library wall. None noticed her motions or the dance of her shadow on the ceiling overhead. Her master had taught her the value of heights as a means of flight. Most men looked forward and down, but seldom up. This proved true now.

Carefully, as the scholars continued toward their desks, the cloaked figure jumped from row to row, retreating back toward the doors.

Below, as they passed, the older scholar urged the younger one. "I'm sorry to disturb your meal, Brother Ungher. But my eyes are not as keen as they once were. I would have you see this for yourself."

"It is never a bother to help you, Brother Ryn. I know your study of the dagger is of the utmost importance."

"I just need you to study this blade with your younger eyes. There is an odd glow. I can't discern if it's just a reflection or something born inside the nightglass."

The scholars' exchange almost made the escaping thief miss a step. She came near to slipping from atop the last stack. Waving an arm for balance, she steadied herself and crouched to calm her heart. They meant to examine the dagger. Any hope of escaping the castle before the theft was noted was disappearing rapidly. Silently, she crept down the shelf back to the stone floor.

The murmur of voices had dropped below her ability to pick out words. She peeked around the edge of the bookshelf. The two scholars had paused to rest their trays atop one of the smaller tables.

The younger one's voice rang clearer as he straightened. "Would you like me to relight the hearth, Brother Ryn?"

"No, no, this won't take long. Come see the dagger."

The two robed figures disappeared out of view.

With her heart in her throat, she slipped to the door, undid the latch, and prayed the hinges remained silent as she pulled the door open just enough for her to pass.

She backed into the hall just as she heard a startled outburst from inside. Her theft had been discovered! She quickly pulled the door shut and imagined ways to jam the lock to trap the two scholars. In this lonely section of the castle, it might be a long time until someone heard their yells for help. With a sudden idea, she backed a step and ran into a person standing silently behind her.

Before she could react, strong hands grabbed her elbows and yanked her arms painfully behind her. She gasped at the sudden attack and attempted to writhe out her assailant's grip. She stamped a heel on the attacker's toes.

Now it was his turn to gasp and jump, but his grip and twist on her arms did not let up.

She was shoved hard into the library door, smashing her forehead hard enough to see lights dance before her eyes.

"What are you doing skulking about here?" the attacker yelled, shoving her again and pinning her against the door. "Answer me!" he hissed in her ear.

She tasted blood from a split lip. She had no words in her. *So close,* she moaned only to herself. *So close.*

Suddenly the door at her face opened. The two tumbled past the threshold to land in a tangle of limbs at the foot of the younger scholar. She struggled to take advantage of the surprise and loose herself. But her attacker was no fool. As she fought and kicked, he took the assault with grunts and spats of swearing, but kept his grip. Twisting savagely, she attempted to tear free but only succeeded in ripping her cloak. The dagger fell free and skittered across the stone floor. She shot a hand out toward it, but the scholar reached it first, retrieving the weapon.

"We have our thief!" the young Brother called out, triumphant.

With the dagger lost from her possession, she found her strength vanish with it. She was again pinned under the attacker's weight and groaned in despair. *So close . . .*

She did not resist when she was wrenched from her belly to her back, still held tight by her attacker. Through a blur of tears, she saw who had captured her: his fiery red hair, his angry green eyes. The brother of the wit'ch. "Lord Joach," she moaned.

Joach reached and pulled at the cloak's hood. She tried feebly to stop him. *No, not this, too.*

Stronger, his fingers ripped back her hood, exposing her face for all to see. She stared back at him, tears on her cheeks. She saw his eyes grow wide as he recognized her. The anger in his face drained to pain. She closed her eyes against his hurt.

But she could not shut out the heartbreak in his voice. "Marta?"

AS THE MEETING DISPERSED, ELENA LEFT THE GREAT HALL, followed closely by her eternal shadow, Er'ril. She felt the storm cloud brewing over her shoulder as he kept pace. She knew the plainsman wanted to vent his rage at her decision to go to Gul'gotha, yet he remained silent, keeping his word to support her. But in some ways, this was even worse. His silence was brooding. The stiffness of his back and the white-knuckled grip on his sword hilt announced his dissent as loudly as words.

Once free of the crowds, she slowed so Er'ril could walk abreast of her. This matter had best be settled before the journey began. "Er'ril," she said, "I must go to Gul'gotha."

"I am your liegeman," he answered dutifully. "You are free to pursue the path you believe best. I will follow you anywhere. So I've sworn."

Elena sighed. "I do not make this decision rashly, Er'ril. If Tol'chuk is to succeed in his journey, if the Manticore Gate is to be discovered, he will need my power."

"I understand your desire to help, to not sit idle. Even I—"

"It's not just that." Elena struggled to find the words to explain herself better. "Portents and signs all point to the east, to Gul'gotha: the scorpion in the stone, the spirit message from Tol'chuk's father, the d'warf legend of the Try'sil's return. I sense . . . I sense I must voyage there. For too long, the lands of Gul'gotha have been tainted by the Dark Lord. If we ever hope to free our land, theirs must be freed, too." She stopped Er'ril with a touch and turned to him. "Can you understand this? Support this? Not just from your oath bond as liegeman, but as a . . . friend."

The plainsman's hard stance slowly melted. He lowered his head with a sigh. "After we talked with the d'warves, I knew you'd make this decision. But I hoped otherwise."

"I'm sorry—"

"No, I spent the time before the meeting pondering what the d'warves said . . . what you said. Perhaps a journey to Gul'gotha is not such folly. It is from those distant lands that the Black Heart himself arose. Perhaps once there, we can learn more of the Gul'gothal lord. Even after five centuries, we know so little about the tyrant's true nature. And where but his own birthplace could we perhaps discover more, maybe even discern a weakness in his armor?"

Elena felt her heart lighten with his words. His support of her decision lifted the burden from her lone shoulders. "So you agree with my going?"

He lifted his face; his eyes were full of agony. "I wish I could lock you away and keep you from pursuing such a dangerous path." He turned away. "But in my heart, I know there is no safe place anywhere any longer. Not Gul'gotha, not here."

Elena stared at the plainsman, hesitant, then reached and took his hand. "Yes, there is, Er'ril. There is one place where I am forever safe."

He glanced to her hand and did not pull away. "Where is that?" His voice was hushed, almost choked. "Tell me and I'll take you there."

"No need." She gently squeezed his hand and leaned in closer to him. "I'm already there."

He tensed with her words. Had she spoken too boldly, shown her heart too clearly? He would not meet her eyes—but neither did he free his hand. "Elena . . ." he whispered. "I . . . I . . ."

A commotion ahead drew their attention forward. Elena felt Er'ril's fingers slip from hers as Joach and a robed scholar stalked around the next corner. They were followed by two guards hauling a trussed-up girl.

Joach's eyes widened as he spotted them, and he hurried forward. "We've found your attacker," he said, breathless. He nodded toward the guards.

"What?" Er'ril asked, shocked, moving forward to protect Elena.

Joach lifted his hands, revealing the long, black dagger. "She tried to steal it and was caught." He stepped aside so Elena could see her attacker.

The girl was thrust roughly forward, falling to her knees. She made no sound as she struck the hard stone. She just hung her head, hair draping her face. Her clothes, a cloak over loose shirt and leggings, were torn to rags. Clearly she had been roughly searched by the guards, her pockets ripped and rifled through.

"She had posed as a scullion," Joach explained, voice tight.

"And that is not all," the scholar, an old man in a rough-spun umber robe, said. Elena recognized him as Brother Ryn, caretaker of the castle's library. He moved toward the girl and reached to her nape. "Most interesting . . . most interesting . . . I thought them disbanded long ago and vanished."

"Brother Ryn, what is it?" Er'ril asked.

"Something we found when we searched her." The elderly Brother reached and gently brushed the girl's tawny hair back from behind an ear. "Do you know this symbol, Er'ril?"

Er'ril moved nearer, and Elena followed. He bent closer as Elena peered over his shoulder. Behind the girl's ear was a tiny tattoo: a small dagger entwined by a snake. "A guild mark . . . the Assassins' Guild," Er'ril said, straightening with a frown.

"Like Cassa Dar?" Elena asked, remembering a similar tattoo hidden behind the ear of the swamp wit'ch. "But I thought she said her guild ended with the fall of Castle Drakk, their stronghold."

"It seems some of the seeds cast after the fall found fertile soil to grow again," Er'ril said sourly. "But why attack you?"

Elena knelt before the girl and reached a hand to her attacker's chin. She lifted the girl's face. Elena was immediately struck by two things: the deep indigo hue to her eyes and the hopelessness found therein. "Who sent you?" Elena asked softly.

The woman stared back, silent.

"She refuses to speak," Joach said. "We've asked the same of her already."

From the bruise on the girl's cheek and her split lip, the first interrogation had been none too gentle. Elena frowned. She sensed no enmity from the girl, only a profound despair. Narrowing her eyes, Elena continued quietly. "What is your name? Surely that is not forbidden for you to disclose."

Confusion crept into the other's face.

Joach interrupted. "Her name is Marta."

Elena glanced up to her brother, but a meek voice drew her back to the roped girl. "No, my true name is Kesla."

"Kesla?" Elena asked.

The girl nodded and spoke rapidly, pleading. "I beg that you let me go. Return my dagger, and I will vanish from these shores forever."

Er'ril snorted harshly. "Not likely, assassin. It's into our dungeons you'll be vanishing."

Kesla ignored the plainsman, keeping her eyes on Elena. "I meant you no harm . . . at least, no lasting harm. My war is not with you."

"Then who is it with?"

The girl studied the stones at her knees and mumbled. "The master of the guild has sworn my tongue against speaking of such matters."

Elena sighed and stood. "My tower is near. Perhaps we should continue this discussion in my chambers."

"I see no reason to continue it at all," Er'ril countered. "Leave her to the dungeons. We've much planning ahead this day if we are to be ready in time."

Elena saw Joach help the prisoner to her feet. Kesla glanced up at Joach and quickly away. Joach swallowed hard and left her to the guards. Elena sensed more to the story between them than had been spoken aloud. "I would still like to question her further," Elena said to Er'ril, stepping around him to lead the way back to her tower.

Er'ril grumbled something under his breath, but followed. The others shadowed after them. Once the tower was reached, Brother Ryn excused himself to return to his library, and the remaining group continued the long climb in silence.

Elena rubbed her right hand with her left as she led the way. She remembered the intense pain as the magick was wrenched from her flesh. What manner of assault had that been? She pondered the mystery. Another member of the Assassins' Guild, Cassa Dar, had once strangled her power with a spellcast swamp weed, luring Elena into the bogs and swamps of the Drowned Lands for a cure. But what did the guild want with her now? Before she left this coast, she needed an answer.

At last, they reached the top of the long stairs. A pair of posted guards snapped to stiff attention, spears in hand at her appearance. She nodded to them; one of the pair stepped aside and opened the thick iron-and-oak door.

Elena entered first and waved for Er'ril to light the lamps, while Joach started a fire in the hearth. At the doorway, Elena took the prisoner by the elbow. "I will take her from here," she said to the guards. "You may return to your duties."

After a moment's hesitation, the leader bowed his head and backed away. Elena closed the door, then led Kesla to a chair by the fire that Joach had quickly stoked.

Once all were settled, Er'ril stood to the left of the girl's chair, hand on his sword hilt, wearing a deep frown. Nearby, Joach leaned on the mantel, a hearth iron in hand. He stared into the fire.

Elena knelt by Kesla's chair. "Tell us about yourself. Where do you come from?"

The girl glanced down and away.

"She comes from a village in the Southern Wastes," Joach answered, then added more bitterly, "unless that was a lie, too."

"It was *no* lie," Kesla said, her voice heated.

Elena, her brows pinched together, glanced up to Er'ril. The Southern Wastes? Could this be another sign pointing toward one of the gates in the far south?

Er'ril guessed the questions in her eyes and shrugged.

The girl spoke again, her words almost a moan of despair. "I must have the nightglass dagger."

Elena turned. "Why? If you meant us no harm, then why can't you tell us your need for it?"

"My oath . . . It is forbidden . . ."

Elena sighed and leaned back on her heels as she knelt. She thought in silence for a few moments.

"If you want any answers from her," Er'ril said, "there are many tools of torture in the dungeons, left over from the time of the Dark Lord's armies."

Shocked, Elena glanced up at Er'ril. But from behind the girl's shoulder, he gave his head a slight shake. He had no intention of ever using such devices, but the prisoner did not know this.

Elena calmed her reaction and spoke more slowly, taking the more passive role. "I'm sure that won't be necessary, Er'ril . . . at least not yet."

Kesla stiffened in her seat at their words.

"Now, Kesla," Elena began, "though we mean you no true harm, we can't ignore this attack upon us. You must understand this."

The girl's lips drew taut.

"Let's start again. If you can't tell us the reason for this assault, then tell us about yourself. How did you come to be in the Assassins' Guild? Where were you trained?"

Kesla lowered her head. "I don't know how I came to Alcazar, the sandstone citadel of the guild. I was told the master found me ten winters ago, just a small child lost in the deserts of the Wastes, but I don't know if this was the truth or not."

Er'ril spoke up, his voice brittle with feigned anger. "And what of your designation? Your tattoo? The assassin's dagger wrapped by a snake."

Elena recalled Cassa Dar's tattoo: a dagger wrapped in nightshade vine. It had marked her as an assassin who specialized in poisons.

Kesla spoke meekly. "I was trained in the arts of hidden moves: to enter unseen, to leave undetected. The snake is an assassin's symbol of stealth."

"Just a thief, in other words." Er'ril snorted derisively.

Kesla jerked in her bonds, twisting to stare at Er'ril. "I am *no* common thief! I trained for ten winters in the assassin's methods."

"But have you ever killed?" Er'ril asked with clear scorn.

Kesla sank back around. "A bloody hand does not make an assassin."

Er'ril glanced over the top of Kesla's head at Elena. He nodded for her to continue again.

Elena took a more conciliatory tone. "So you came all the way from Alcazar in the Southern Wastes, disguised yourself as a scullion maid, and slipped your way past the many armies guarding this island. Impressive. You must have been trained well."

"I was," she said proudly. "Master Belgan is one of the finest guild members."

"And so, like a snake, you slipped into our midst undetected, waiting for the proper moment."

Kesla nodded with Elena's words.

Er'ril spoke again, almost yelling. "And then when the moment was ripe, you took your dagger and brutally stabbed it into Elena's mark, ripping away her power, torturing her!"

Kesla shied from his words. "I . . . I did not think . . . I didn't mean . . ." Tears welled in her eyes.

draw her magick inside it. Only then could there be any hope of defeating the beast of Tular."

Elena rubbed her palm on a knee, remembering the burning drain of her magick. The dagger had absorbed her wit'ch fire. "Tell us of this beast."

Kesla shuddered. "Only one person has seen the monster: the man who leads the children to their doom. He told all who would hear about the horrible beast hidden in the ancient fortress." Kesla's voice cracked with fear. "It was the Ghoul of Tular reborn after ageless centuries, come to life once again to destroy our lands."

"The Ghoul of Tular?"

Kesla turned once again to Joach. "The beast who once guarded Tular. Its image entwines the dagger's hilt."

Joach slipped the weapon free and held the dagger up. A feathered serpent lay curled around the hilt, its beaked mouth open in a silent, fanged hiss. The basilisk, the ancient totem of Tular.

Elena stood abruptly and crossed to Er'ril. "It must be the Weirgate."

He nodded.

"And the children . . . Ebon'stone always craves blood." Elena paled with the thought. All those sacrifices.

Kesla spoke up. "That is all I know. I have a boat waiting to take me back to Alcazar. The dagger must be returned to Master Belgan."

"And it will be," Elena said, turning back to her.

Kesla sat up straighter. "You'll let me free?"

"Yes, but I'll send you back to Alcazar more swiftly than any boat or horse can carry you. Tomorrow morning, one of the elv'in windships is set to fly to the Southern Wastes, to seek out and destroy the very beast that plagues your people."

Kesla's eyes grew wide.

"For your freedom, I ask that you swear a new oath to me: to lead this ship to Alcazar and let us aid your guild in ridding your people of this curse. Can you promise me this?"

Kesla bowed her head. "I can only promise to lead the way to Alcazar. I cannot speak for Master Belgan. He must decide for the guild."

"Fair enough." Elena nodded to Joach. "Free her and take her to the *Eagle's Fury*. Introduce her to Prince Richard and let him know my wishes. Er'ril and I will join him later to go over the plans in detail."

Joach hurriedly untied Kesla's bonds. She stood, rubbing her wrists. But when Kesla reached for the dagger at his belt, Joach twisted away. "I think I'll keep this for now," he said. "For safe-keeping. It seems there are many thieves in this castle." He stared hard into Kesla's eyes.

The girl's cheeks reddened at his accusation. "I'm sorry for lying to you, Lord Joach."

"I am not a *lord*," he said in a tired voice. "I wish you'd quit calling me that."

"Then quit calling me a *thief*," Kesla countered, swinging away.

"Fine, you're an assassin. That's so much better." Joach rolled his eyes and crossed to Elena, pulling her aside. "El, I have a re-quest of you."

"What is it?"

He clutched the dagger's hilt. "I'd like to go with the *Eagle's Fury* on this journey."

"What? Why?"

Joach glanced a moment back at Kesla. "Since I rescued the knife, I think I should still watch over it."

"Why?"

Now it was Joach's turn to redden. "It's just that . . . Well, I mean . . . I don't think its just coincidence that the dagger should fall into my hands." Joach sighed in exasperation. "It's hard to explain. I just think I need to go."

Elena remembered making the same vague argument with Er'ril just a few moments before. It seemed the fates were align-ing to draw them all apart, to scatter them across the face of the world. "You are old enough to make your own decisions, Joach. If you feel this is a path you must follow, I will not stop you."

A grin appeared on his face, and he stepped over and hugged her. "Thanks, El. I knew you'd understand."

"Actually, I don't understand," she said in his ear. "I would rather you stay here." In her heart, she did not want Joach to go, but how could she refuse him when she herself was planning to leave soon? She returned Joach's embrace, wrapping her arms tightly around him as if she could hold him forever safe. But she knew that was impossible. "Just make sure you come back."

Joach broke their embrace. "Don't worry. I will."

He turned away, but Er'ril grabbed him by the shoulder. "Joach, I would have a word before you leave."

Joach's brow crinkled. "What is it?"

Er'ril nodded toward Kesla, who waited near the doorway. "Watch her."

"What?"

"I saw the way you looked at her, the relief in your eyes when she told her tale. Do not let your heart cloud your judgment."

"I don't—"

Er'ril squeezed his shoulder tighter. "Once you thought me a creature of the Dark Lord. Now you accept this story from a confessed assassin without a second thought. Here could be another trap."

Joach's face crumbled into confusion.

Elena leaned forward, intending to argue against Er'ril's suspicions. She sensed no menace in this girl, only honest fear for her people. But Elena held her tongue, withdrawing slightly. Perhaps simple caution was warranted.

Joach glanced toward Elena and saw the agreement in her eyes. He sighed, and his face hardened. "I will be wary—both in heart and action." With those words, he backed away, gave a final nod toward Er'ril and Elena, then crossed to Kesla and departed.

Elena watched them leave, her chest already aching for her brother.

Only Er'ril remained in the room. He stepped beside her, reading her heart. "It is not easy seeing someone you love walking willingly into danger, is it?" he said quietly.

She leaned into Er'ril, too tired and pained for words.

LEAGUES AWAY, IN A CAVE HIDDEN DEEP WITHIN THE STONE FOREST of the northern coast, a lone figure crouched over a shallow hole dug into the granite floor. Intoning words of power, he slowly poured quicksilver from a bowl into the hole, filling the cavity to its rim. In the meager light cast by the clouded skies outside the cave, the surface of the quicksilver pool shone like a mirror, reflecting the hooded figure's face.

Scowling and squinting with milky eyes, the figure bent

closer and studied his own reflection. A crooked finger rose to trace the ancient ruin of a face. He pulled back his hood to reveal a scalp bare of all but a few gray hairs. "Soon . . ." he mumbled.

A scrape at the cave's threshold drew his attention. Silhouetted against the light stood the thick form of his servant. The creature stood no higher than his waist but was all gnarled bone and muscle. It was a stump gnome, one of the few creatures that could live for long in the poisoned forest outside. A simple twining spell had tied its will to his.

"Come closer, Rukh," he ordered sharply.

It grunted. Gnomes had little more intelligence than a trained hog, but they were strong and single-minded. It shambled into the cave. Closer now, its face was also similar to a pig's. It was as if someone had smashed its muzzle with a club. Under eyes the size of polished black pebbles, its face was all flattened nose. Two peaked ears sprouted like afterthoughts on either side of its leathery skull.

"Do you have what I asked?"

Rukh forced his thick tongue to form words, fangs glinting yellow and rotted. "Yes, M-master Gr-greshym."

The stink of the beast reached the darkmage in the close quarters. *Like a barn of wet goats,* Greshym thought, wrinkling his nose at the stench. "Then leave it and be gone!" he snapped.

With the heave of a thick shoulder, Rukh tossed his dead quarry at his master's feet. The doe's neck lay twisted the wrong way, recently strangled by the hard hands of the stump gnome. Greshym nodded his approval. His servant must have traveled far to find such an untainted animal.

Rukh backed from the cave, slather drooling from his jowls at the scent of the abandoned meat. Greshym could only imagine the torture it must have been for the stupid creature to resist tearing into the doe. Slipping free a long dagger with a rose-carved hilt, Greshym set about the task of removing the doe's heart. By the time he was done, his robed arms were drenched in blood. He heaved the warm organ from the defiled chest and waved the stump of his other hand for Rukh to clear away the rest. Greshym had what he needed.

The gnome dashed into the cave; his claws quickly sank into the flesh. Rukh dragged his prize away. "G-good meat," he rumbled.

Greshym ignored the sounds of snapping bones and feasting from outside the cavern. He turned back to the pool of quicksilver.

Raising the doe's heart, he carefully drizzled the blood across the quicksilver pool. The blood spread, blurring the silvery reflection. Once done, he touched the pool with a finger and spoke a single word, a name. "Shorkan."

The blur upon the pool swirled, and an image formed, a window on another place. He watched the silent tableau. Within the pool, the view of a white-robed man appeared. He stood on the shore of a black sand beach and stared to the south. Shorkan's lips moved, but no sound was heard. In the background rose the volcanic cone of Blackhall, cored and hollowed into a thousand-room warren. Beneath it, Greshym knew, lay the dungeons and crèche of the Dark Lord himself, while above, a black smudge rose from the cone to stain the sky with a perpetual plume. It was not just volcanic forces that created the stream of smoke and ash, but also the poisonous forges at the heart of the mountain, furnaces of dark magick.

Shifting, Greshym glanced back out of the cave. Even from here, though leagues from the sea, he spotted the black plume on the horizon. Winds from the south continually blew the smoke and ash over this forest, making it all but unlivable except for the poisoned creatures who had migrated here to skulk in its shadows, like his servant Rukh. But this land had not always been like this. Long ago, before the volcanic cone had first erupted, this had been a living forest. But the torturous, fiery birth of Blackhall had blasted the landscape with heat and ash, petrifying the entire woodlands in a single night and killing all within it.

Greshym had chosen this place to hide because of the residual magick that fell with the ash from Blackhall's plume. It had helped resuscitate the darkmage after his battles a moon ago. Weak and drained, he had limped and crawled into this toxic bower. For days, he had wandered through the forest, near blind, near dead, absorbing the trace magicks cast off from Blackhall, regaining his strength.

Finally, he was ready to leave this exile—and exact his revenge.

In the quicksilver pool, the image of his fellow darkmage suddenly turned from his study of the coastline to peer directly back at Greshym. Cringing, Greshym waved a hand and wiped away the image. That had been too close. Shorkan must have sensed his spying and had almost caught him. But at least Greshym knew where one of his enemies lay—at Blackhall.

"So, Shorkan, you're still licking your wounds," Greshym whispered with grim satisfaction. Greshym had noted the black burns and pale healing flesh that marked the once handsome face of Shorkan. It seemed even the Dark Lord's pet had not escaped unscathed from the battles of A'loa Glen.

"Good . . ." Greshym allowed a smile to form on his lips. For too long, Shorkan had mocked him with his handsome, youthful face. Though both had been granted eternal life by an ancient spell, something had gone wrong for Greshym. While Shorkan never aged, Greshym's flesh had continued to wrinkle and decay like any man's; only death was kept from him. He smiled wider, a dry cackle flowing from his thin throat. *Now Shorkan knows what it's like to be disfigured!*

Retrieving the doe's heart, Greshym again cast his spell. This time he dipped his finger into the quicksilver and spoke another name. "Elena."

The blood blurred again, and a new image formed. Greshym crinkled his brows, momentarily confused by the view. The fiery-haired wit'ch stood at the rails of a mighty ship; three masts towered behind her. But the seas were nowhere to be found. Then Greshym realized she must be aboard one of the elv'in windships. He noted the position of the sun. The ship was heading away from the setting sun. East? Away from Alasea? A single tear rolled down the woman's cheek as she stood at the stern of the boat. He smiled again. Was she trying to flee? Leaving Alasea?

He adjusted the mirror's view. Far away, past the peaks and spires of the island city, two other windships sailed for the far horizons—one north, one south. Greshym noted how the wit'ch seemed to be staring at the ship fleeing southward. He watched as her lips moved. Though no sound came, he knew whose name she formed: *Joach!*

Greshym's fist clenched. The brother of the wit'ch! The cursed boy who had thwarted Greshym twice, even destroying his staff in their last confrontation. *So brother and sister are separating,* he thought as he studied the mirror closer. *Trying to escape the backlash of the Gul'gotha.*

Leaning over his pool of quicksilver, Greshym stared at the tiny windship retreating south. He followed its path as the magick faded, and the image dissolved back into a blur of blood. After several breaths, Greshym leaned back. He could try the spell a third time and find out more of Joach's exact destination, but he dared not risk draining more of his energy in such spying. Not when he had yet another complex spell to cast.

Standing with a creak and crack of old bones, Greshym reached to the wall of the cave and retrieved his new staff. He lifted the weapon. Mined from the heart of one of the poisoned stone trees of the forest here, it was grained like an ash tree, but it was no longer wood. He ran his hands over its stone surface, impregnated from centuries of toxic ash and magickal waste. His fingers tingled with the touch. Bound with spells, the stone of the staff was as light as oak. In many ways, this new staff was superior to his ancient poi'wood one. Perhaps he should thank Joach for ridding him of the original.

He crossed to the threshold of the cave and into the hazy light. "To my side, Rukh."

The stump gnome pulled his bloody mouth from the deer carcass. He wiped his lips with the back of one wrist and glanced longingly at the half-eaten remains. Hunger marked his posture and expression, but he knew better than to disobey his master. Rukh shambled over.

With his staff, Greshym dragged a circle around the both of them. One more spell to cast. He let his lids droop lower and spoke the portal spell. Under both their feet, the ground turned as black as oil. Greshym ignored the gnome's terror and glanced to the south. He squinted as if peering far away. Then, satisfied, he nodded and lifted his staff. He tapped it once. A black portal opened at their feet, and both gnome and mage fell away.

As Greshym vanished, only one desire burned in his mind: *vengeance.*

Book Two

CASTLE MRYL

5

IN THE MURK OF PREDAWN, MYCELLE KNELT BY THE RIVER, BLOODY and sore. Her gelding, Grisson, kept to her side, his flanks heaving, sweat thick on his golden coat from their long, hurried flight. He bent to drink from the river, but Mycelle yanked at his lead. She did not want her tired horse to stove up from drinking the stream's cold water when he was so overheated. With the camp still leagues away, she could not risk compromising her mount.

Cocking her head, she listened for sounds of pursuit. Somewhere deeper in the dark wood, a horn sounded. She sighed in relief. It was far off to the north still. As she stood, the snap of a twig on her left twirled her around, her twin swords unsheathed in silent pulls. With her steel glinting in the reflected moonlight from the river, she stood steady.

Then from beyond a fringe of an elderberry bush, a pair of amber eyes glowed back at her. Images flashed across her mind's eye: *Two tired wolves greeting one another on a trail, noses touching, a lick on an ear*.

"Thank the Sweet Mother," she said, sheathing her swords. She recognized this familiar touch on her mind and returned the welcome in the silent tongue of the si'lura. *Greetings, Fardale*.

As answer, a sleek figure flowed through the bushes, so silent that not even a leaf whispered. The snap of a twig a moment ago had been done on purpose, to alert her of the newcomer's presence.

The huge treewolf, though free of the bushes now, still remained indistinct in the gloom of the forest's eaves. His dark pelt, speckled in golds and coppers, blended with the dappled shadows, seeming more spirit than substance. But his bright

97

eyes were as hard as granite. She and Fardale had been lucky to survive this night.

"I had thought you lost for sure when we were attacked," Mycelle said.

Fardale glanced at her and gave her a wolfish shrug, retreating to the river's edge to lap gently at the water. But he no more than wet his tongue—even he knew better than to drink after a long run. The wolf settled to his haunches, ears pricked for sounds echoing over the water.

"They're far off," Mycelle said. "I think we lost them."

Fardale glanced her way, making eye contact so he could speak. Images formed: *A brutish, bruised-skinned beast snuffling along a woodland trail.* Fardale was right. The hunt for them would continue. Their best chance was to reach their camp below the Stone of Tor and seek another path to Castle Mryl. The woods ahead were too dangerous.

Three nights ago, she and Fardale had left the others to scout the territory north of the Ice River, but they had run afoul of a troop of d'warf raiders. The two had barely escaped with their lives. It was only luck that the raiders had borne none of the Grim among their party. If the twisted creatures of the Dire Fell had been among them, neither wolf nor rider would have escaped.

For the past moon, Lord Tyrus had set them a hard pace north through the forests of the Western Reaches, camping at last by the Stone of Tor, a pinnacle marking where the Ice River joined the Willowrush. According to reports from the trappers and hunters, the forests north of the Ice River were no longer safe for man or beast. Tales were whispered around campfires, of strange lights that baffled and led the unwary to their deaths, of keening wails that drove strong men to their knees with fear, of trees found twisted and gnarled, as if tortured to death.

Mycelle and Tyrus both knew what these portents suggested. The Grim wraiths from the northern forest of the Dire Fell had truly spread into the Western Reaches. If left unchecked, the entire length and breadth of the mighty forest would be corrupted by their touch.

Even now, Mycelle tightened a fist. She would not let that happen. But their only hope lay in reaching Castle Mryl and repairing the damaged Northwall, restoring the barrier between the diseased Dire Fell and the expanse of virgin woodlands. Mycelle stared back over the flow of the Ice River, toward the dark forest beyond. Another path must be found to the castle.

Suddenly Fardale was at her side, appearing as if from mist. A low growl rumbled at the back of his throat—a warning.

Mycelle did not wait. She swung out her swords from the crossed scabbards on her back. "What is it, Fardale?" she hissed. The wolf's senses were keener than hers.

At her forearm, she felt a stirring and the slide of scale on flesh. She risked a glance. A tiny rainbow-colored snake lay wrapped around her arm. It squirmed in a slow dance around its perch. Even the paka'golo, the healing snake of Mama Freda, sensed something was amiss.

Mycelle concentrated on the forest. Fardale stood tensed at her side, hackles raised and wary.

They did not wait long. A rising wind soughed through the forest's eaves. Leaves shook overhead, and a flurry of dry pine needles skittered in small whirlwinds. But it was another sound, a hollow moaning, that ate through flesh and bone. Mycelle's swords shook in her grip. It was no natural wind that moved through the forest toward them.

"Flee!" Mycelle yelled, giving up any pretense of hiding. "Make for camp!"

Fardale hesitated, but Mycelle swung up onto Grisson. "Flight is our only hope!"

Already the moaning rose in pitch to a piercing cry.

"A Grim wraith!" Mycelle screamed above the growing wail. "Flee! They cannot be fought!" Mycelle tugged Grisson around. The horse's eyes rolled white with fright. Froth spattered from around his bit. Mycelle dug her heels into him, but the gelding only trembled, too terrified to move. She struck Grisson's rump with the flat of her hand; still the horse only cowered.

Fardale, who had sped several paces away, turned back toward where Mycelle struggled with Grisson. Images flickered rapidly before her mind's eye: *A deer freezing at the appearance of a wolf. A human falling to all fours and changing into a snowy-maned wolf and racing away.*

Mycelle groaned and kicked at her mount again, but the horse only tossed its head and whinnied its terror. Fardale was right.

Grisson was already lost to the cry of the wraith. She slid from the saddle. Her only hope was flight. But how could she?

She turned to touch Grisson's nose, to will her mount back to calmness, but teeth snapped at her fingers. Her horse was too mad with fear to know better. There was no hope. Mycelle reached toward her saddlebags, but a low growl from Fardale warned her away.

She pulled her hand back. What was she thinking? She had taken human form for too long, become too grounded into their way of thinking. From here, she could carry neither bag nor sword. She swung back to the treewolf. "Run," she said and willed the change.

Beneath her leathers and undergarments, flesh melted and flowed, bones twisted and bowed. Shrugging and writhing out of her human clothes, she fell to her hands and knees. With a final prickling tremor, snowy fur burst forth from her skin, claws sprouted, and a long narrow snout stretched to sample the air. New eyes opened on a world much brighter. She sniffed the air and discovered paths unseen, marked in spoor and musk.

Tufted ears pricked at the wail of the Grim wraith. It was almost upon them. Mycelle glanced one last time at Grisson, then at the pile of shed clothes with the crossed scabbards resting atop it. She felt a deep sense of loss, as if she was abandoning a part of herself, but now was not the time to mourn. All she could carry was the small snake nestled in the fur of her forelimb. The paka'golo was one item she must never lose. It had helped resurrect her in Port Rawl, and now its magickal bite was still necessary to sustain her.

Turning on a paw, she flashed past Fardale and dashed away. He joined her, two shadows fleeing, now just two wolves of the wood.

Behind them, a sudden scream of terror rose from Grisson, the cry unlike any Mycelle had heard from a horse before. She glanced back in time to see a dark shape sweep over her loyal mount. It was as if a shredded piece of shadow had torn loose from the world and attacked Grisson.

Mycelle's keen nose caught the coppery scent of the horse's panic. She slowed her pace, turning slightly. *Flee,* she willed Grisson.

Whether hearing her or merely finally sensing the true peril,

Grisson broke for the cover of the wood. But as the horse brushed under the limbs of a black pine, the shadowy wraith flew through the same tree's branches, and a tangle of roots suddenly shot up and snagged the horse's limbs. Grisson squealed again, a cry of death and defeat.

The wraith descended on its trapped prey. As it draped over its meal, the nearby trunk of the black pine twisted; overhead, its branches scrabbled and writhed into torturous tangles. It was as much a prey as the horse. As the Grim wraith fed, life drained from both wood and flesh. Green pine needles yellowed and showered down; the flesh of her mount sank to bone. It was as if their very essences were being sucked away. Soon all that would be left was a pile of bones under a twisted grave marker. That was all the Grim ever left behind.

Mycelle swung around as her horse's cries grew strangled. She could delay no further. They had best be far away before the forest wraith finished its meal and sought more nourishment. No one knew how to defeat a wraith. It was rumored they could be held off with silver, but such claims were just myth. At Castle Mryl, she had been taught that the only guard against the Grim was continual vigilance. Their deathly moans always preceded an attack. A keen ear and a swift retreat were the best defense.

Acknowledging this adage, she raced after Fardale, following his scent as surely as a well-marked trail. For the better part of the long night, the two wolves fled through the forest, splashing along brooks and streams to confound any trackers, constantly alert for the telltale wail of a Grim wraith. But the night remained quiet, almost hushed.

They stopped only to feed briefly on the steaming remains of a small hare caught by Fardale. To her wolfish tongue, the blood and raw meat tasted like the finest wine and roasted loin. Despite the terror and hardship of the long night, Mycelle could not suppress a tremble of exhilaration. It had been so long since she had run free and sampled life in a new form.

Fardale must have sensed her elation. His eyes shone at her over the bloody remains. An image formed: *A lone wolf, tired and pad-sore, rejoining its pack after a long night's hunt.*

She growled her assent. It was like coming home again.

With the small bones eaten and the pelt buried in a hole to hide the scent of their meal, the pair took off once again, ready for the last leg of their journey back to camp. The leagues seemed to disappear under her paws. She and Fardale settled into a pace both swift and steady. Mycelle thought she could run like this forever.

Still, as the sun finally rose over the distant mountains to the east, the glow of dawn found Mycelle beginning to stumble and trip. Her inexhaustible energy seemed finally to be waning. Even Fardale moved with a slight limp, his tongue lolling as he panted away the heat of their night-long run.

At last, ahead, a pinnacle of granite rose from the wood, piercing the canopy of trees to thrust up at the sky. Morning sunlight had already reached its highest ramparts to glow brightly and announce the approaching day. It was the Stone of Tor.

Delighted at the sight of their destination, both wolves found renewed strength to race the last distance to the camp. So excited were they to return to the others that neither noticed the acrid reek to the air until they were only a few paces from the clearing.

Fardale pulled to a stop. Mycelle crept beside him. Her ears were pricked for any noise from the camp ahead. She heard nothing. Even if the camp was still asleep, she should hear some sign of life. She slinked forward, Fardale beside her. What was that smell in the air?

She cautiously pushed her face through the last of the underbrush to view the camp and tensed at the sight that awaited them.

Ahead, the camp lay in ruins, tents and bedding shredded, horses dead in fetid pools of blood. A flock of carrion birds raised bloody beaks at her approach. A few angry squawks tried to drive her away, but Mycelle ignored them.

She worked her way forward.

With the Stone of Tor looming to the east, the camp remained in shadow. Amid the gloom, Mycelle and Fardale searched for signs of the living. Had anyone escaped this attack? She came upon an ax with a short handle. It was slick with blood. She nosed it. The scent of d'warf still lay heavy upon it.

Straightening, she willed her body to change. If she was to investigate further, she would need hands. Though it was a strain to shift twice in one day, she forced her flesh to melt and the snowy fur to retreat away. She rose from a crouch and stretched back into her familiar form. Naked of both fur and clothing, she noticed the morning chill to the air. She wrapped her arms around herself for warmth.

"Search for any signs of the others," she ordered Fardale.

With a whip of his tail, the wolf sped off. Mycelle watched him a moment, with a twinge of worry. His sendings had grown coarser and less frequent. Fardale grew close to losing himself to the wolf. He was already beginning to settle into this form. If the curse wasn't lifted soon, the wolf would claim him forever.

As she continued into the camp, these worries were overwhelmed by the horror at hand. Past the remains of a dappled mare, she found the body of one of the Dro warriors who had guarded Lord Tyrus. The woman's blond braids were fouled with blood and mud. She lay on her side, her bowels draped across the ground from a savage rip in her belly. Mycelle stepped farther into camp and discovered the other two Dro warriors, sisters to the first. Each had died horribly.

As she searched, she discovered no sign of any of the others: Lord Tyrus, Kral, Mogweed, Nee'lahn. Frowning, Mycelle returned to one of the Dro women.

Praying for all their spirits, Mycelle stripped one and donned her leathers, fixing a new set of crossed scabbards to her back. Though exhausted, she did manage to adjust her form enough to fit the new garments. "I will avenge you," she promised as she slid the two swords into place.

Fardale had wandered farther to the west. A growling drew Mycelle's attention. She crossed to the wolf's side.

Even without the keener wolf's senses, she noticed the acrid reek grew stronger as she approached Fardale. Before the wolf, an area of the clearing's floor had been blackened and burned in a perfect circle. She knelt and fingered the region. Even the dirt had been blasted to form a glassy crust.

With a heavy heart, she stood and surveyed the ruins of the camp.

Where were the others? What had happened here?

As she stood, the sun finally broke around the looming pinnacle of rock. The ravaged camp became bathed in the new dawn's light. Mycelle began to turn away, but her gaze was caught by a sharp glint in the blasted circle. Frowning, she stepped cautiously into the ring. The forest floor was deeply burned; it was like walking on granite. She crossed to the source of the reflection and knelt on one knee.

Leaning closer, she discovered a silver coin. She tried to pick it up, but it was imbedded in the blasted surface. She had to tug hard to yank it free.

Standing, she studied the coin, flipping it back and forth in her fingers. On one side was stamped a familiar face, old King Ry, father to Prince Tyrus. And on the other was the sigil of their family—a snow leopard, crouched to strike. Clutching the silver piece, she studied the burned circle. Lord Tyrus could not have survived.

Fardale sank to his haunches beside her. Images flashed at her. He had discovered no sign of the others in the camp.

She shoved the coin into a pocket. "Then we will find them."

BOUND TIGHT, MOGWEED LAY SLUMPED ON HIS SIDE IN THE WAGON, feigning sleep. Each bump of the wagon's wheels as they passed along the old rutted forest track jarred his spine. He had to bite back a gasp as the wagon popped over an exceptionally large root. Mogweed flew several handspans above the buckboard and landed with a thud. He heard a groan to his left and carefully moved his neck to view the large form of the mountain man, Kral, who lay behind him.

In the dawn's light piercing through the tiny barred window of the enclosed wagon, Mogweed could just make out Kral's thick black beard, still damp with blood. He prayed the larger man remained unconscious, fearing further abuse from the d'warf guards if Kral should try to free himself. Mogweed glanced surreptitiously around the cramped space. Only the four of them remained. They were too few to fight the score of armored d'warves that still marched outside the enclosed wagon.

If only I had remained awake at my post . . . Mogweed thought with a twinge of guilt. Then he bit his lip in anger. No! He would not accept blame for this. Even if he had been awake and could have alerted the camp in time, they all would surely have been caught anyway. There was no safe path through the forests north of the Stone. He had begged them all repeatedly to abandon this journey to Castle Mryl, but none had listened. It was their own fault they had been captured.

I should have left when I had the chance, he thought sourly.

But in his heart, he knew such an option was not a real one. He tugged his arms and tested the ropes for the thousandth time. His efforts only succeeded in tightening the knots further. In truth, he was bound to these others as surely as these ropes bound him now—bound by a whisper of hope.

Lord Tyrus, former pirate and prince of Mryl, had lured him and his brother with words of prophecy, a chance to finally free themselves of the curse that trapped the two shape-shifting twins into their current forms, man and wolf. The prince's words echoed to him now: *Two will come frozen; one will leave whole.*

Now even this thin hope was vanquished. With Fardale lost in the deep wood somewhere, how could their curse ever be lifted?

Mogweed rolled over as the wagon hit another stubborn root. He lay on his other side now, staring at the prone form of Lord Tyrus. The man showed no signs of life. He lay as limp as a dead eel, head lolling with the wagon's motion, blood dribbling from both nose and mouth. From here, Mogweed could not tell if the man still breathed.

But what did it matter? For all their fighting and swordplay, what had it won them? The three Dro women slain and the others beaten to within a life's breath. Foolish men. During the melee, Mogweed had remained hidden. Once the fighting had passed him, he had crawled to one of the women's corpses and smeared his brow with her cooling blood, then lay sprawled at her side, pretending to be knocked out.

As Mogweed recalled his subterfuge, he became lost in the memory of screaming horses and the grunting barks of the d'warf raiders. While feigning injury, Mogweed had watched between narrowed eyelids as Lord Tyrus, shielded by the last of his Dro bodyguards, had defended himself with a flashing blur of his ancient family sword. It was a dance of death that none who neared had survived.

Farther back in the camp, the mountain man had attacked the d'warves with ax and teeth. Even now, a chill ran down Mogweed's back at this memory. It was as if Kral had become more beast than warrior. But no one could question his results. D'warves had died all around the large man.

For that single moment, Mogweed had entertained thoughts of their victory—but even the strongest bear is eventually brought down by enough wolves.

Kral fell first, swamped by six massive d'warves. On the other side, Lord Tyrus continued his bloody dance. He seemed to grow more invincible with the loss of Kral, sustaining not even a scratch as his bodyguards died around him. Hope of victory still burned in the strength of the prince's steel.

Then a thunderous crack split the night, and a monstrous shadow appeared behind Tyrus. Though the clearing was lit only by a single campfire, Mogweed had no trouble making out the shape of the new attacker.

Darker than oiled pitch, it stood out starkly in the gloom. Towering on clawed hind limbs, its shape was that of a thick-maned cat. But the spread of wings to either side of its muscled shoulders belied this image.

Tyrus named it at that moment. "The griffin!" he yelled.

In horror, Mogweed buried his face in the mud. During their trek north to the Stone, refugees fleeing to the south had told rumors of such a monster: a beast so repellent that the mere sight of it could kill a man. Taking no chances, Mogweed squeezed his eyes tightly closed. His last view was of Lord Tyrus backing away, a silver coin falling from the prince's fingers.

Then a roar shattered through the clearing, so loud it seemed to suck at Mogweed's mind, trying to draw his will away. For a brief moment, Mogweed passed out in truth, overwhelmed by the griffin's scream. When next he became aware, the camp was as silent as a tomb. A peek revealed the griffin gone and Lord Tyrus sprawled and bloodied in a circle of burned soil.

Around the camp, the remaining d'warves had slowly stirred and began to collect the survivors. Mogweed had had no trouble feigning unconsciousness, his limbs already weak and boneless from fear. Tossed into the enclosed wagon like a sack of oats, Mogweed had kept his wits about him. Through slats in the wagon's walls, he had watched which way they were being taken: *north,* the very direction they had sought themselves.

Even now, the flash of bright leaves through the slats was beginning to change to the darker needles of black pines as they entered the northernmost fringes of the Western Reaches. Mogweed estimated them only a day's journey from the Northwall itself.

Suddenly the wagon struck another rut in the road, jarring Mogweed back around. From out of the wagon's gloom, he found a pair of eyes staring back, studying him. They seemed almost to glow in the meager light cast through the small opening.

It was the fourth and last member of the camp to survive the attack. Like Mogweed, she had neither fought nor offered resistance. In the filtered sunlight, the honey-colored hair of the slender figure shone brightly. Mogweed whispered her name. "Nee'lahn?"

He expected no answer. Since they had discovered the nyphai woman almost a moon ago at the edge of the Western Reaches, she had not spoken a single word. Questions were ignored, conversations shunned. She hovered at the periphery of the camp, often wandering the forest paths alone, eyes dreamy and lost. The other members of the party tolerated her, but her behavior was much debated—as was her purpose in joining them.

Mogweed, Fardale, and Kral had all witnessed her death in the foothills of the Teeth, victim to an ill'guard monster. In private, they wondered if this silent figure was their dead companion reborn or simply some trick of forest magick. How could it truly be Nee'lahn? It was impossible.

"Fear not, Mogweed. It is I."

The words were spoken plainly, but Mogweed gasped in shock. After so long, the ghost in their midst had finally spoken. He shoved away from her. "H-how could . . . I saw you . . . The spider creature killed you!"

Nee'lahn interrupted his babble. "Do not be deceived, Mogweed. I am not human, any more than you are. I am nyphai, a creature of root and loam. This body is mere dust and water given life by my bonded koa'kona spirit. Though the shoot might be trampled, as long as the root lives, I cannot die."

Mogweed struggled for sense. "B-but then why wait so long to be reborn?"

"It is not an easy transition. I needed the strength of this mighty forest. The treesong of the Western Reaches was necessary to revive me. After my old body was destroyed, Elena blessed my grave with an old oak's seed."

Mogweed nodded, remembering the black acorn he had given Elena.

"I sent my spirit into this tiny seed, hiding inside it until I could grow strong enough to move. In spirit form, I brought the seed to your brother, hoping you'd eventually return to your homeland, to these great woodlands. Only here was the elemental magick of root and loam strong enough to pull me from the seed and give me substance and form again."

"Why have you not explained this earlier? Why have you remained so silent?"

"It has taken me until now to draw my spirit fully into this new form. After an entire winter in spirit only, I found it difficult to separate from the treesong all around me. It took all my concentration to withdraw myself from the endless music of the forest. But when the monster appeared and attacked this man—" She pointed to Lord Tyrus. "—it ripped the treesong for leagues around. It jolted my spirit fully back into this body, finally making me whole again."

Mogweed slumped against the wagon's wall. "A small blessing there. You're whole again, just in time to be tortured and killed by our captors."

"Perhaps. But I have sent out a call—a plea for help. I saw a glimmer of another place: sails and sea. And the elv'in Meric . . . He still retains my lute, protecting the heart of my spirit tree. As long as the lute remains, there is hope."

"For you, maybe. If I die, I don't come back."

Nee'lahn didn't seem to hear his words. She continued, eyes adrift, "The trees of the forest whisper of the winged black beast that attacked the camp. It lives in a stone gateway somewhere near the Northwall. I even hear whispers of a twin evil far to the south, another black beast near the Southwall. The trees scream from its mere presence." Nee'lahn's eyes focused on Mogweed. "These Gates must be destroyed."

"Why?" Mogweed asked tiredly.

Nee'lahn glanced away. "I-I'm not sure. But they threaten the very Land itself. They have the power to choke the world."

Mogweed shivered at her words. "What can we hope to do?"

Nee'lahn seemed to withdraw into herself again. "There is only one hope."

"What is that?"

"The Grim of Dire Fell."

Mogweed sat up straighter. "The blood wraiths? The shadow spirits of that black, twisted forest? Are you mad? How can those savage creatures be of help?"

"I must convince them."

"Why? How? They serve the Dark Lord."

Nee'lahn shook her head. "No. They are wild creatures whose lusts merely aid the Black Heart's needs. No one controls the Grim wraiths."

"Then what hope do you have of enlisting them?"

Nee'lahn grew quiet for a long stretch. "They will listen to me," she finally said, pain clear in her words.

Mogweed was not satisfied with this answer. "Why?"

"Because the Land is a cruel mistress" was all she whispered back. Nee'lahn turned her back on him, ending their discourse, as silent again as when they had first found her.

NEAR MIDDAY, MYCELLE STOOD BESIDE THE THREE MOUNDS OF freshly turned soil. She leaned on the spade with which she had dug the trio of graves. The ruined camp was not a safe place to tarry—already vultures circled overhead, calling all to the feast that lay below. Other predators would soon gather. Mycelle could not leave her three sword-sisters to the ravages of fang and claw. She shared an oath with them.

Mycelle stared as the sun began its decline toward the western horizon. She still had time to be well away from here before night set in. Tossing the shovel away, she sank to one knee before the graves. The odor of fresh loam almost masked the reek of offal and blood from the slaughtered horses around her. She bowed her head. "I'm sorry, Sisters. Be at peace. Go and seek out your lord, King Ry. Tell him I will avenge the death of his son."

Tears welled in her eyes. She had failed her oaths a second time. First, in not hearing the call when Castle Mryl had been under attack, and now in leading the last prince of the Wall to his death.

She reached into a pocket of her borrowed leathers and slipped free the silver coin. The image of the snow leopard seemed to glare out at her. She clenched the coin firmly. "I will hunt down your killers and burn their corpses so the scent of my revenge will reach you all. This I swear."

Then a tingle at the back of her mind alerted her to another's presence. She turned to discover Fardale standing at the forest's edge. She had sent him to search for signs of the attackers while she had dug the graves. His eyes glowed like molten amber. An image appeared of a forest track only a quarter league away, and a pair of fresh wagon ruts driving northward. Fardale's imagery focused on the deepness of the wheel's imprints in the damp soil. The wagon was heavily laden—with prisoners, perhaps.

Had any of the others survived? She allowed herself a glimmer of hope.

A new image ended Fardale's sending: *Two wolves—one snowy, one dark—following the trail.*

Mycelle nodded and stood. The attackers had a half day's lead on them, but the wolves could move more swiftly through the forest than a troop of d'warves. But to travel as a wolf would leave her naked and weaponless. She fingered one of the sword hilts at her shoulder. Without blades, how could she hope to free the others? Still she would not forsake them.

If there is any chance . . .

"We must hurry." She eyed the coin in her hand and vowed not to fail again. She lifted the silver piece to her lips and kissed the cold surface, planning to leave the Mrylian coin as a grave marker, a token of a promise sworn. But as her lips touched the surface of the coin, the silver grew warm in her hand. The skin of her arm prickled as if from a sudden chill.

The paka'golo stirred from its perch on her forearm, clearly sensing something odd. The tiny snake lifted its head and hissed with a flicker of red tongue.

Mycelle lowered the bit of silver and studied it closer. What was this strangeness?

As if in answer to her thoughts, words formed in her head, not unlike a sending from one shape-shifter to another. But here the words were a whisper in the wind. *"I hear you. The sorrow in your heart calls to me through the coin."*

She glanced around the clearing, then down at the coin. "Wh-who are you?"

"I give you my name freely. I am Xin, of the zo'ol. Friend to Tyrus. Share your name so I might forge this link more strongly."

Mycelle did not understand any of this. She remembered the prince mentioning the black-skinned tribesmen, ex-slaves he had freed. He had hinted at some magick in their leader. In fact, a few days past, after their group's first skirmish with a d'warf scouting party, Lord Tyrus had sat by the campfire, clutching this same coin. He had claimed he could send word out to the east, to warn of the danger and to spread the rumors of the griffin beast. But afterward, he had pocketed the silver with a frown, unsure if anyone had heard him. "Too far," he had mumbled, and would speak no more of it.

But apparently someone *had* heard him. She clenched the coin and spoke her name. "I am Mycelle."

"I accept your name, Mycelle of the Dro," the voice responded solemnly. *"I know you well from the words of others. We come even now to seek you out. Speak where we might find you. Your link is strong, so you must not be far."*

She frowned. How was that possible? The last time she had seen the zo'ol tribesmen they were leaving with Tol'chuk and Meric to find Elena—out in the distant Archipelago, thousands of leagues from here. "No, I am too far," she answered. "I am lost deep in the Western Reaches."

"This we know. We already fly over the great green sea. Tell us where."

Mycelle stared up at the sun, her mind awhirl with confusion. "H-how?"

"Meric of the elv'in. We fly his ship of the wind."

She gasped. "Meric?" A sudden memory of the wounded elv'in, scarred from battle with a minion of the Dark Lord, flashed across her vision.

"He is here," the voice continued. *"Tell us how we might find you. I tire quickly and cannot maintain this link much longer."*

These last words were clearly the truth. The whisper from the coin faded rapidly. Mycelle had to lean closer and clutch the silver more tightly. She glanced to the east, to the wall of stone that thrust up into the day's sky. "The Stone of Tor!" she yelled, fearing she would not be heard as the coin grew colder in her palm. "I will meet you atop the Stone of Tor!"

She waited for a response, some acknowledgment. But the coin remained silent, cold again in her palm, just plain silver. She clamped her fingers around it, trying to will back the magick.

Fardale nosed her fist, startling her. She glanced down to the wolf, and in the silent tongue of the si'lura, she explained the strange contact.

The wolf's response was skeptical: *A mother wolf nosing a dead pup, trying to wish it back to life.*

"You may be right," she answered aloud. "I don't know."

She turned to study the straight peak of granite jutting up past the tallest trees. Its distant heights glowed in clear sunlight. Across the spread of forest, the protruding stone would be a clear mooring spot. None could miss it. Still, her face remained grim. Had she been heard? And what was coming? What had she called forth from the coin?

She lifted her fist to her chest. There was only one way to find out. From the camp, a thin trail could be seen winding from the base of the steep peak to its summit, a darker trail against the black stone. "Let's go," she said, leading the way. "Let us discover if a dead man's coin holds any true magick."

AS THE SUN NEARED THE WESTERN HORIZON, MERIC STOOD AT THE prow of the *Stormwing*. Dressed in a loose linen shirt and billowed leggings, he sensed every current in the air. Normally his silver hair was kept long and loose, free to the winds, connecting the elv'in even more intimately to his skies. But no longer. Meric passed his palm over his ravaged scalp. Though his silver hair had grown long enough to comb, his locks were not long enough to appreciate the breezes, to extend his connection to the winds.

He lowered his hand. He should not complain. His intimate connection with the ship more than compensated for this loss. Though Meric had been gone from her planks for over two winters, the *Stormwing* already felt like an extension of his own body again. Only an elemental of sufficient strength had the power to fuel these ships of the clouds and keep them aloft. And it was through this elemental contact that ship and captain became one. As he stood at the prow, Meric sensed every screw and nail in the ship, felt the snap of sailcloth as if it were his own shirt. Each creak of the hull reverberated like the aching joints of his own limbs.

Aboard the *Stormwing*, it was as if he were whole again. The tortures and brutalities in the cellars of Shadowbrook dimmed to a distant memory. He could almost imagine such horrors had happened to someone else. Here, flying among the clouds, Meric felt immune from the evil in this land.

But in his heart, he knew such security was as insubstantial as the thin clouds they scudded through. Not even the skies were safe from the corrupting touch of the Dark Lord. During his journeys, Meric had learned firsthand how the land, the sea, and the sky were all interconnected. The elemental energies of the world were an infinite web, overlapping, woven, twisted and tied together. One element could not be tainted without affecting another.

He had tried to explain this to his mother, Queen Tratal, but he feared such ideas had fallen on infertile soil. Such were the ways of the elv'in. For too long, they had been absent from the lands, thinking themselves free of such bonds. Meric knew better. To defeat this evil would require the unification of all elementals. If left divided, all would fall.

He would not let that happen.

Gripping the rail firmly, Meric scanned the sea of foliage skimming a quarter league below his hull. Earlier the zo'ol shaman, Xin, had brought him word of his link to Mycelle. Though he didn't understand it fully, clearly a message had been shared. The swordswoman had indicated a location at which to rendezvous: *the Stone of Tor*. Meric and Xin had pored over maps of the Western Reaches and discovered such a place, a peak at the confluence of two rivers.

Even now they followed a silver thread through the dense greenery. It was a narrow river, named the Willowrush, that delved through the heart of the forest. The place where this flow met the Ice River of the north was their destination.

Meric lifted his gaze to the horizon, instinctively making slight corrections to follow the river's course. Near the horizon, a shadow appeared, a single black thunder cloud rising above the forest's edge.

"Is that the place?" a voice said at his shoulder. It was Tok, his eternal shadow. He had forgotten about the lad sitting on a cask of oil nearby.

"I believe so," Meric said, his tongue thick as he was pulled back from the skies to the planks of the ship. He lifted a hand and signaled the men in the rigging. Sails were adjusted. "We should be there at dusk."

"Should I tell Master Xin?" Tok hopped from his perch with a scuff of heel on plank.

Meric felt the movement like an itch on his own skin. "Yes, he rests in his cabin with his two tribesmen." The brief discourse with Mycelle had drained Xin's energies. When he had brought

Meric word, the man had been weaving on his feet, eyes blood-shot and hooded. "If he is able, the shaman must try to reach the others again."

Tok gave a nod and trotted away. Alone, Meric watched the shadow on the horizon slowly grow substantial. Limned by the setting sun, the pinnacle of rock was an upthrust finger, its cliffs sheer and straight. Withdrawing his magick slightly from the spellcast iron keel, he let the ship sink toward the trees as they approached the distant peak.

Meric concentrated on the delicate dance of magick and wind. As he did so, he felt, more than heard, the approach of the three zo'ol and Tok.

"They were already on their way here," Tok said as introduction. "But I told 'em what you wanted."

Meric turned and nodded his head in greeting. The small black-skinned shaman returned the acknowledgment. The pale scar on the man's forehead, a rune of an opening eye, almost glowed. His true eyes were as bright. It seemed his energies had returned. "Were you able to reach Mycelle again?"

Xin shook his head and crossed to the rail. The man's expression seemed distracted. "No. To speak, she must hold the coin and wish it," he said dismissively. "All remains silent."

Meric felt a twinge of misgiving at his words. He turned back to the study of the horizon. The Stone of Tor had grown substantially in just the brief distraction. Meric willed further adjustments before returning to the others. "We will arrive shortly. We'd best be ready."

"It will be too late." Xin turned to Meric, his gaze fearful. "I have been a fool. Too weak to hear until now."

"What do you mean?" Meric's misgivings flared.

The shaman touched the scar on his forehead. "I sense other eyes out there. Angry, wicked, twisted minds whose desires shudder the heart."

Meric frowned. "Where?"

"They ignore us. But they too travel toward the tall stone. I sense them swirling toward the peak as quickly as we fly."

Meric studied the expressionless expanse of forest. He saw nothing but did not doubt the shaman's ability to pierce the canopy and sense the feelings of what lay below. Xin had proven his abilities in the past. "Will we make it in time?" Meric asked.

Xin turned to Meric, gaze narrowed with concern. "We must fly faster."

Meric trusted the zo'ol shaman. "I will try."

Turning back to the rail, Meric sent out a whisper of magick—not to the ship, but to the skies around them. He strove to draw the winds to his sails. But with his attention split between the ship and the skies, it was a strain on even his significant skills. He felt the crackles of blue energies dancing on his skin—or was that the ship's hull? He became lost somewhere between.

He gathered the energy trapped in the clouds and stray winds around him, tying them into a tighter weaving. He pulled and drew upon this energy, creating a conduit for power.

Come to me, he thought urgently.

Then, like a push at his back, he felt the first tug upon his ship. Overhead, the sails slowly stretched, ropes strained. Fresh winds whistled past his ears, past the hull. Quicker and quicker, the *Stormwing* surged ahead. Meric adjusted the magick in the ship itself. Like a striking hawk, the ship dove down and across the forest. He used the weight of the ship to add speed to his sails.

Vaguely, Meric was aware of the others around him grabbing for handholds, stumbling under the sudden flight. Beads of cold sweat formed on Meric's forehead as he maintained the winds. "Wh-what do you sense?" he spat out between clenched teeth.

"I'm sorry. The shadow creatures move too swiftly." Doom trembled in the wizen's voice. "We are too late."

MYCELLE CLIMBED THE LAST FEW STEPS TO THE SUMMIT OF THE peak. Exposed atop the pinnacle, she shivered as the winds seemed to pick up. Ahead, the trail ended at a small, carved altar. Mycelle approached the sacred site. Though none knew who originally carved the altar, the site itself was still used for rituals to the Mother on solstices and equinoxes.

At her side, Fardale sniffed around the altar's edges, nosing the strange beasts carved on its stone side. He nosed one particular beast on the north face of the altar and growled. Mycelle glanced down at the image. It was a winged lion with clawed paws raised. Mycelle frowned. A griffin, just like the rumors they had been hearing from the refugees. Was this some clue?

Mycelle circled the altar. On its south face was a monstrous rooster with the body of a snake. On the other two sides were a reptilian bird and some bullish figure with a scorpion's tail. Mycelle turned away. She had heard nothing of these other beasts, but worry settled coldly in her chest. What did this mean? Was there some connection?

Unable to answer these mysteries, she crossed to the edge of the summit and turned her attention to the skies around her.

The blue expanse appeared empty of all but a few low clouds and a rising mist from the forest. There was no sign of any ship, flying or otherwise. Standing at the cliff's edge, she pulled the silver coin from her pocket. She clutched it. Had the journey been for naught? Had they wasted half a day pursuing phantoms? Even now she wondered if it all had been a dream. It did not seem real.

Suddenly the coin grew warm in her fist again. An urgent voice entered her head. *"They come! Beware the forest!"*

She raised the coin, relief mixed with fear. She had not imagined the voice after all. "Who? Who comes?"

"Twisted creatures with diseased thoughts. They surround the Stone even now!"

Mycelle glanced back at the altar and peered over the edge at the woods below. *Creatures?* She saw nothing amiss. "We're already at the summit," she said. "I don't see anything."

"They are there. But we come swiftly."

She lifted her eyes to the heavens. Still she saw nothing.

"To the east," the voice urged, as if sensing her desire to see the ship. *"Above the Willowrush."*

Mycelle swung slightly around. She squinted her eyes. Nothing.

Then the barest glint of sunlight reflected off something hanging above the trees near the horizon. As she watched, it slowly grew in size. She could just make out a flurry of sails. She stared in wonder. A flying ship! Could it be?

Fardale whined at her side. He must have spotted the strange vessel, too. She glanced briefly down to her fellow si'luran, but the wolf's keen eyes were not on the skies. Fardale studied the darkening woods below. Though the peak's height was aglow as the sun set, the forest below was already lost in dusk and mist.

Mycelle followed the path of his gaze. "What is it, Fardale?"

His only answer was a low growl.

"Tell me what—" she started to say. Then she heard it, too. It came not from coin or wolf, but from the forest itself.

A cry rose with the wind from the woods below. The wind itself? Mycelle knew better. She stared harder. Near the base of the peak, trees began to twist and curl, tortured by something unseen in the shadows below. Mycelle now knew what the speaker from the coin warned against. *Twisted creatures.* Not the mythical beasts from the altar, but something worse.

It was the Grim!

Mycelle stepped along the summit's edge. All around, trees writhed and limbs flailed, leaves grew brown and drifted on the twilight breezes. It was as if the cry from below was the scream of the tortured trees themselves. But Mycelle knew it came from the wraiths—hundreds of them!

From here, she spotted shadows shifting among the misshapen trunks. She did not understand this strange gathering. The wraiths were generally solitary creatures, seldom found in more than a pair. What had drawn them all here? And what stayed their hands now? Below, they simply milled and churned. As swiftly as they moved, they could be atop the summit in only a few moments. But they tarried in the forest below, contorting the trees in which they roosted. What kept them at bay?

Mycelle glanced back to the altar. Was there some ancient magick here? For the thousandth time since beginning this journey, she wished she still retained her seeking skill, an ability to read the magick around her. She felt as if a vital sense had been stolen from her.

She lifted the coin and spoke. "I see the creatures, but they hold back for now. Hurry, before their numbers give them the courage to assault the peak."

A fading whisper came. *"We hurry . . . Be ready . . ."*

She turned and found Fardale's eyes upon hers. Images formed: *A snowy-feathered bird taking wing from the peak and flying high into the sky, away from the twisted forest.*

"No," she answered him aloud. "I will not abandon you."

Fardale shrugged and turned away, as stoic as a real wolf.

Mycelle returned to studying the forest and sky. The wail of the Grim echoed off the cliffs. There were so many. Suddenly the ground shook under her feet. She fell to her knees to keep from tumbling over the edge. Crawling closer, she peered below.

Around the pinnacle, hundreds of trees had uprooted themselves, many of them thousand-year-old giants. In packs, they attacked the Stone's base with their gigantic roots, digging into cracks in the granite.

Mother above! The forest was attacking the Stone of Tor, trying to tear it down.

In the branches of these twisted trees, Mycelle spotted the reason for the assault. The shredded shadows of the Grim perched in those warped branches. The wraiths rode the attacking trees like riders on horses. The ancient trees dug and attacked the rock, yanking chunks with shuddering blows from the side of the pinnacle. As she stared, she suddenly understood how the Northwall had been sundered. Even that ancient shield wall, also of granite, could not have sustained such an attack for long.

Mycelle, on hands and knees, backed away from the edge. She eyed the skies. With the sun setting behind her, the expanse was still bright. She could easily spot the ship's sails now. It lay no more than a league away. In the darkening sky, its keel glowed like a dull coal, ruddy and bright. Even without her seeking ability, Mycelle could almost smell the magick. It was this glowing energy that kept the vessel afloat in the air.

She clenched the coin. "Hurry," she urged.

No answer came, but in truth, what words could make any difference? Either the ship would arrive in time or not.

Mycelle crouched upon the altar as the rock shook under her. For a moment, she entertained Fardale's idea: to shift into the shape of a large bird and wing away from the danger. It was tempting. She did not want to die. She had done so once before and cared not to repeat it. But even a shape-shifter had limits. Most could only summon enough energy for a major shift once a day. And she had already shifted twice this day—from woman to wolf and back again. She had no energy for another change.

She stared at the large treewolf as he steadied himself on wide-placed paws and maintained his vigil on the assault below. Even if she could shift and fly away, she would not. She could not abandon her last companion. She had failed too many others, and that pain was worse than any fear of death.

Biting her lip, Mycelle turned her attention to another matter of the wraiths. What had drawn the Grim here like moths to a flame? If she had that answer . . .

The ground lurched again. The whole peak tilted. Mycelle grabbed the altar's edge to keep from rolling.

Nearby, Fardale dug in claws and scrabbled to keep his footing, but he was losing his battle and slipping toward the edge.

The Stone was toppling under them!

"Fardale!" She thrust out an arm, reaching from where she clutched the altar. Fardale slipped farther away from her hand, his hindquarters tumbling over the edge. "No!"

She willed the flesh of her arm to meld and stretch. She had no energy for a full change, but maybe this small shift . . .

She concentrated, straining. Slowly the burn of melting bone answered her silent plea. Her arm thinned and lengthened. Her fingers crawled across the rock.

Fardale's eyes went wild with desperation as he struggled to keep his precarious perch. Then he lost the battle and slid away.

"No!" She lunged with her flowing arm. Her fingers clamped on the wolf's forelimb as he slipped over the edge. "Hold on!" she urged between tight lips.

She fed some of her torso's bulk into her thinly stretched arm, building muscle to aid her grip. In her mind's eye, she became just two arms—one gripping rock, one gripping her friend's flesh. Nothing else mattered. She fed her will with all her strength, her heart thundering in her ears. How long she struggled like that, she did not know, but slowly she forced her flesh to pull back to its original form. She maintained her grip on Fardale's leg as her arm shortened, dragging the wolf back over the edge and to her side.

Once near enough, she shifted her grip, pulling Fardale tight under her arm. Exhausted, she finally realized that the Stone had ceased its topple and rested dangerously askew, the summit tilted at a steep angle. A lucky reprieve, but for how long?

Already the wail of the wraiths rose again from below.

Mycelle could not worry about that. With her eyes squeezed closed, she fought to keep her position on the slippery granite. If she lost her grip on the altar's edge, they would both be lost.

As she concentrated on the muscles and fibers of her limbs, she felt loose hairs, those not braided in place, rise over her head. The smell of the air changed, as after a summer's thunder shower. Energy! Mycelle opened her eyes and cried out in a mix of shock and relief.

Overhead, the sky was gone, consumed by a vast wooden hull and a shining iron keel. As she watched, a hatch opened on its underside. A long rope snaked out, the end of which fell to hang tantalizingly close above her. If she stood, she could easily grab the rope. But that was impossible. If she shifted even a single muscle, she feared tumbling away.

The rock under her, as if to remind and scold, shook again. The pinnacle tilted farther.

Sweet Mother . . . So close!

A thin figure appeared in the hatch's opening, clearly an elv'in. The slender man had the rope looped around his belly. He dove from the hatch and rolled down the rope, using the loop's friction to slow his descent. Still, as fast as he fell, Mycelle was sure he would tumble from the rope's end and fall to his death. But at the last moment, the agile elv'in sailor hooked a twist of rope around his knee and ankle and dropped to a stop, hanging upside down from the rope's end by only one leg.

Long-fingered hands grabbed the leather of her jacket. "Don't struggle," the man warned with little warmth. "And keep hold of that dog."

As soon as he had her gripped, the length of hemp began reeling back into the hatch above, dragging the elv'in and his wards upward.

Mycelle was afraid to trust both their weights to the thin sailor. But what choice did she have? She reluctantly released her grip on the altar and hugged the large treewolf to her chest with her two arms. They were drawn slowly upward.

As her heels lifted free of the rock, a massive crack exploded from below. She gasped at the sudden noise, almost losing her hold on Fardale.

Under her toes, the pinnacle toppled away, falling at first slowly, then more rapidly, like a felled tree. Time seemed to slow as the length of stone crashed into the forest. A muffled roar accompanied the collision. Leaves and bits of shattered trunk blew into the sky as high as the flying ship itself. Water exploded far into the air as the felled pinnacle crashed across the Willowrush, damming the river and diverting its flow.

Tilting her neck, she eyed the opening of the hatch. It seemed a league away. The tackle and pulley that strung the rope from the hatch slowly turned, and she found the eyes of the elv'in sailor meeting hers. He seemed unconcerned about the destruction or danger, his expression bland as if he were merely hauling dry goods to a shop. But Mycelle noticed the sheen of sweat on his forehead from the strain of their weights.

But there was nothing she could do to help, so Mycelle glanced back down. The view was lost in a cloud of debris and mist. She saw no sign of the wraiths. Again she wondered what had drawn so many of them to this peak. Were they after her? Fardale? The ancient altar? Somehow Mycelle sensed it was none of these. Something else had drawn them here. But what? What were they after? What had driven the wraiths to such odd behavior?

Staring up again, she saw they neared the hatch. Hands grabbed them as they were hauled inside. At last, Mycelle found firm decking under her heels. She set Fardale down. Their elv'in rescuer clambered free of the rope and landed deftly on his feet. He gave them a cold bow of his head and strode away, as if their salvation were of no significance.

Mycelle shook her head at the strangeness of the elv'in and stared below one last time as the hatch was closed and sealed.

There was a mystery to the Grim that had yet to be answered, and she was sure the path to winning here in the north lay within that riddle. But such answers must wait on another day. For now, she was free, safe, and with new allies.

"Well met, Mycelle," a voice said behind her.

She turned toward a familiar lanky form standing in a doorway. Relief flooded through her. "Meric!" She crossed over and hugged the elv'in tightly.

"It seems we've much to discuss," Meric said as he was finally let free. He gave Fardale a pat of greeting, then searched around the crowded hold.

With an eyebrow raised, he faced Mycelle. "But where are the others?"

6

KRAL AWOKE TO CHAOS. WINDS SCREAMED, THUNDER UNLIKE ANY he had heard before shook the ground. He jerked awake, snapping up, banging his head into the roof of the rocking cart. A growl escaped his throat. He reached to his waist, but found his ax gone. Then his memories returned in a flood of light and screams. The attack by d'warf raiders . . .

He twisted around and spotted Mogweed, a tiny mouse of a man, huddled in the corner.

"Where are we?" Kral asked gruffly. "What is going on?" His eyes quickly attuned to the darkness. Though his iron ax with its ebon'stone heart was missing, Legion still lived inside Kral, caged in this human form. His nostrils flared, sniffing the air with the senses of this inner beast. His ax was near, still sheathed in the pelt of a snow leopard. With the pelt in place, Kral had access to the leopard's form and nature, but he dared not reveal his shape-shifting abilities—at least not yet.

Nearby, Nee'lahn lifted her face, pushing aside a fall of honey-colored hair. On her knees, she leaned over the still form of Lord Tyrus, her expression pained. "We've been captured and travel north."

Kral frowned. A mix of conflicting feelings jangled through him as the nyphai's violet eyes pierced to his bones. Her beauty stunned him. Her lips were a blooming rose on virgin snow. Her form was all curves and valleys. His senses drank her in, but he kept his face and voice stone. "What caused the ground to quake?"

Already the splintery roar was echoing away, and the tremble under the wagon's wheels calmed.

Nee'lahn cocked her head and remained silent for a few moments. "I . . . I hear mourning in the woodsong, but can tell nothing more. Broken trees, drowning waters." She shook her head. "Some disaster. I don't know its meaning."

A whip cracked overhead, and the cart jolted forward, moving faster. Off balance, Nee'lahn toppled into Kral's side. He caught and gently righted her. She straightened the cloak about her shoulders, nodding in thanks.

Her scent filled Kral's nose: musky loam and honeysuckle. His rocky countenance threatened to shatter. He turned away.

Lord Tyrus groaned where he lay at Nee'lahn's knees.

"How fares the prince?" Kral asked, turning his attention.

Nee'lahn touched the wounded man's shoulder. "He lives but swims in sick dreams. He won't wake."

"Yet he's always crying out," Mogweed added, edging closer to them. "Bloodcurdling wails." The man shivered, hugging his thin arms around his chest.

Kral eyed his two conscious companions. They were too few for him to lead an assault on their captors, even if he could break out of the wagon. Had the prince been hale, Kral would have attempted it. He had seen the man fight, a flurry of steel. Tyrus was surely his father's son. Ten generations ago, it had been an ancient king of Castle Mryl who had helped Kral's clans escape during the D'warf Wars. A blood debt was owed to the Mrylian royal family. So even though Kral was bound to the Black Heart, he had not refused the prince's call for arms at Port Rawl's docks. How could he?

Though the Dark Lord might have opened his eyes to the beauty of raw flesh and fear, he had not totally burned away Kral's honor. A lesser man might have been vanquished fully, enslaved completely. But in Kral's veins ran the magick of deep, underground passages, of gray granite and black basalt, whorled agate and glassy obsidian, the bones of the world. Though the Black Beast of Gul'gotha had branded Kral's spirit, the Rock had protected Kral's deeper self. He was scarred by darkfire but not shattered.

"How long have we been traveling?" he growled.

Nee'lahn settled back, sinking into her cloak. "Almost a full day. Night nears."

Kral moved to the plank walls of their prison. He tried to peer out between the slats, but he could discern little in the meager light. He closed his eyes, extending the senses of his inner beast. He listened to the tromp of hoof and boot, the rattle of short sword and ax. He counted the thudding heartbeats of his captors. Over a score of the cursed creatures—*d'warves,* the blood enemy of his people.

In ages past, the d'warves had wrested Kral's clans from their ancestral home, the mighty mountain Citadel above the blue lake of Tor Amon. The slaughter—monstrous beasts, foul magicks, horrible sacrifices—was sung in ballads and woeful odes around the flames of clan hearths. Out of a people that had numbered in the tens of thousands, only a hundred had escaped, including Kral's great ancestors, the last of the Senta Flame, the royal house. It had been his great-great ancestor who had last sat on the Ice Throne of the Citadel. The same man had led the ragged bands out of the mountains, abandoning their homelands to become wandering nomads. Kral clenched his fists, nails drawing blood from his palm. No longer would they wander! He would regain his birthright—the Ice Throne—and call his people home. He would restore honor to the Senta Flame. This he swore!

Lost in the past, he sat frozen as the wagon trundled farther and farther north. He became stone, unmoving. Two days passed him by. Food was shoved through a slit in the door: moldy bread and a meatless gruel. Kral ignored it. To the side, Nee'lahn tended to the prince, dribbling water over Tyrus' lips. At night, the cold drew the other three to huddle together, but not Kral. He remained fixed, a boulder of granite—waiting, patient. Occasionally the prince would cry out, drawing his eye. Behind his screams, Kral heard the mindless terror and the gibber of the mad. He turned away, dismissing the man. Lord Tyrus' body might live, but surely his mind was gone.

So the days passed by.

Only on the third day did Kral stir. Night had fully descended, and a bright moon hung high overhead, glimpsed through cracks in the roof. The wagon slowed, and the guttural chatter of the raiders grew raucous amid coarse laughter.

"We must be nearing this evening's camp," Nee'lahn whispered.

"I don't know," Mogweed mumbled, his face pressed to the forward wall, one eye peering out. "I see torches ahead, through the trees."

"It is no temporary camp," Kral warned. He felt the vibration in his blood. Tuned to the world's bones, Kral knew what they neared. He gritted his teeth. He could not believe the others were deaf to the roaring in his head. It was as if they approached the shore of some storm-swept ocean, waves pounding on rock.

The wagon continued to slow. New noises intruded: the clash of steel, the whinnying cry of horses, the blare of horns. Kral inhaled deeply: smoke and pine, blood and sun-cured meat, the stink of trench latrines. They were approaching a major encampment. Between the wooden planks of the wagon, a fiery light grew. Calls were exchanged between their captors and outer sentries.

As the wagon rolled into the encampment, the noises enveloped them. Fists occasionally pounded on the sides of the wagon, applauding the raiders' success. But still the wagon rolled.

"Where are we?" Mogweed asked, his eyes wide with fright.

Kral kept his silence. The wagon finally ground to a halt. No one breathed. Only Lord Tyrus stirred. He writhed in an unending nightmare, worse than ever.

Nee'lahn remained at the prince's side. "What's wrong with him?"

Tyrus' eyelids suddenly flickered open. Fingers clawed the air. "The Wall . . ." Though his eyes were open and bright, there was no consciousness. "The Land's voice . . . the pain . . ."

Nee'lahn tried to console him, holding his hands.

A jangle of keys drew Kral's attention. It sounded from the rear of the wagon. He turned, fists clenching. With a loud clanking, a lock and chain fell away. Oak scraped oak as a bar was shoved free.

Kral braced himself. He touched the dark magick in his bones—the magick of Legion, his secret self tied to the chunk of ebon'stone in the iron heart of his ax. He sensed his weapon nearby, felt the leopard trapped under his skin, ready to burst free, teeth and claws sheathed in this human form. Still, he held back. There was power in secrets.

Hinged at the bottom, the rear door of the wagon crashed down, becoming a ramp to freedom. Beyond, the flames from fires and torches were blinding. Kral squeezed his eyelids to slits. After three days locked up in the dark wagon, the brightness stung.

A voice barked at them, coarse, in the common tongue. "Get your arses out here! Now!"

The speaker, a d'warf lieutenant, stood flanked by a half score of his comrades, all armored and bristling with weapons. The guards bore axes in one hand and spiked hammers in the other. Kral knew from experience that the squat creatures were skilled with both weapons, unnaturally dexterous with either limb. It was not a fight he could hope to win, not without the aid of weapons or the beast nested within his flesh.

Kral crawled first from the wagon, climbing down the ramp. Mogweed followed with Nee'lahn, the prince's limp form slung between them.

The guards stared at the small party, wary. No one sheathed a weapon. Rumors of the battle under the Stone of Tor had reached these ears. No chances were taken. The lieutenant stepped toward Nee'lahn and Mogweed, but his eyes were on the unconscious form of the prince.

"He's of no use," the d'warf leader said. "Cut his throat and feed him to the sniffers."

Kral noted a pen of purple-skinned beasts nearby, chained and tethered, like living pieces of twilight. Rows of fangs glinted. *Sniffers.* The most fearsome predators of the woodlands. Kral had once run the streets of Port Rawl as such a beast. Hunger and lust flared at the memory. Tender flesh, the spurt of hot blood . . .

One of the guards stepped toward the limp form of the prince. Nee'lahn backed away with Tyrus. Mogweed abandoned the man completely, leaving the tiny nyphai bent under the prince's weight.

Kral stepped between guard and prisoner. "No. I'll not let you harm him."

The guard raised his weapon. Kral stared at the d'warf; a low growl flowed from his throat. Kral let the beast inside shine forth. His vision grew more acute; his senses bloomed outward. He heard the d'warf's twin heartbeats quicken.

The guard held his weapon, faltering a step.

The lieutenant raised his short sword and moved to the guard's side. "The beasts are hungry. Mayhap we should feed you *both* to our pets." The d'warf leader glanced up and down Kral's large form. "Or maybe not. It has been a long time since my men and I have tasted the flesh of the mountain people. We'd make several good steaks and roasts out of you."

Kral felt his control of the beast inside weakening. He kept his fists clenched, hiding the daggered claws of the leopard sprouting from the tips of his fingers.

The lieutenant raised his sword. "So make your choice. Move aside or die!"

Kral remained where he stood. "You'll not harm the prince." As the leopard within writhed, fur sprouted under Kral's leathers. His pupils grew slitted.

The d'warf leader balked, clearly sensing a dark current here. Touched by the Black Heart himself, had this d'warf recognized the kindred spirit before him? The sword remained poised.

A new voice intruded. "Leave the captives be, Lieutenant!"

All eyes swung to the right. Another d'warf approached. He was wider in form and heavier in bulk, twice the mass of the already large lieutenant. Atop his melon-size head was a black cap with a silver insignia. Kral recognized the rank marking. The guards grew stiffer. Kral smelled their nervousness.

The lieutenant retreated a half step. "But, Captain Brytton, the man hanging in the woman's arms is clearly too weak to work in the mines. I thought not to waste his meat. The sniffers—"

"Quiet, Lieutenant." The captain moved toward Nee'lahn, who cringed back from him. "The mountain man is correct. No harm must come to this man. The griffin has marked him."

"Sir?"

Captain Brytton waved to the guards. "Take them to the castle dungeons. All of them."

Kral was baffled by the turn in events. The beast inside quieted. What was going on? He strode to Nee'lahn's side and collected Tyrus up in his arms, unburdening her. As a group, they were led around the wagon.

Mogweed gasped as he turned, his gaze rising high into the air.

Kral understood his shock. Two hundred strides away, the world ended. The black granite shield wall known as the Northwall rose before them. Stretching a league into the sky, its surface was as polished as a piece of sculpture, reflecting the firelight and the moon and stars. It was too high for the mind to grasp. It was said that the air at its summit was so thin that none could breathe it and not pass out.

The great wall marked the northernmost boundary of the Western Reaches; beyond it lay the Dire Fell. It had been here for as long as histories were spoken, thrust up by the Land itself to stop the evil of the Grim from ever passing into the woods of the Reaches. Eventually, the Wall had become the birthright of Tyrus' people, the Dro, who kept vigil here.

"Castle Mryl," Nee'lahn said softly, pointing to the west, toward where they were heading with the captain and guards.

Kral nodded, spotting the structure.

Limned in firelight, the granite castle was hard to miss, growing like a boil out of the Northwall and sprouting forth with ramparts, turrets, and towers, all formed of flowing black stone. The massive castle climbed the shield wall in countless granite terraces, merging so smoothly that it was hard to say where one started and the other ended. And in truth, there was no distinction. Castle Mryl was a part of the wall, a flowing construct grown by the Land to house the wall's chosen, the Dro.

Kral craned his neck up. Beyond the reach of the camp's firelight, tiny windows glowed like stars against a black firmament, openings into high rooms and chambers in the wall itself. Tales spoke of passages and secret chambers that ran the length of the wall's thousand leagues, like the arteries and veins of a living being.

And in actuality, the wall was no dead rock. An ocean of elemental energies flowed through the stone. Even now, Kral heard the magick's call, and if Kral allowed it, he could be lost in that song. It vibrated through him. In his arms, Tyrus stirred again, writhing and moaning. The prince, too, heard the call and struggled to answer it.

Kral held the man to his chest. These lands had always been rich in rock magicks. Like the Dro, Kral's people had lived in these mountainous lands, becoming imbued and blood-tied to these magicks. And though centuries had passed since any of his clansmen had returned here, the magick had never left Kral's people. It was one of the chief reasons the clans had remained in the mountains of the Teeth: to be forever close to the granite spirit of the Land.

Kral felt heat on his cheeks; his vision clouded. He could not stop the tears. For the barest moment, he remembered himself fully. The darkness receded from his blood. He stumbled to a stop, a cry on his lips. Horror at what he had done, at what he had become, flared sharply, cut him deeply. Then the dark energies surged again in his heart, feeding off the raw power flowing here. Doubt and guilt faded.

"Are you all right, mountain man?" Nee'lahn asked, dropping back beside him as they marched toward the castle.

Kral closed his eyes, touching the beast inside, reassuring himself that all was in order. "I'm fine."

Nee'lahn looked little convinced, but she remained quiet.

As a group, they were herded to the main gate of the castle. Broken gates lay open to the south. Along the walls overhead, mounted on iron spikes, were the heads of the castle's previous wards. Bleached by the sun, scavenged by ravens and crows, the decapitated heads were little more than white bone. As Kral stared with his keen vision, he spotted more of the castle's decorations. All the walls, terrace after terrace, were mounted by these trophies of the dead. Thousands upon thousands.

Kral turned away. The great cat inside him stirred, scenting the bloodshed and terror. Kral reined in the beast with a promise. One day, he would replace each skull with a d'warf's.

Kral followed the others through the gate and across the stone courtyard, carrying the prince of the castle back into his home.

Across the yard stood the main keep. Its stone doors lay cracked and toppled. Scorch marks and pocked holes marred the polished surfaces of the yard, clear evidence of foul magicks and fierce fighting.

Captain Brytton halted before the stairs leading into the keep. He pointed to the side, to an open doorway with steps leading down into the ground. "Take the prisoners below. Lock them away."

The lieutenant nodded and drew them away at swordpoint.

The passage down into the castle's dungeons was narrow, barely wide enough for Kral's shoulders. As the mountain man bent and climbed down the stairs, the granite walls swallowed him up. Though he was being led to his imprisonment, Kral could not escape the sense of coming home. The magick in the stone swelled through him, reminding him of hearth and clan. Even

Tyrus grew quieter in his arms, seeming to slip into true slumber rather than the endless nightmare that had consumed him.

The long stairs opened into a large guardroom. Five d'warves sat around a hewn pine table, scraps of a meal spread before them. Kral spotted a human leg bone, well gnawed. A part of him turned away in disgust, while deeper inside another part growled with hunger.

The lieutenant grumbled in his native tongue, and one of the d'warves stood and grabbed up a ring of keys. The group was led past a stout oaken door and into a long passage of barred cells. The passage reeked of excrement, urine, charred flesh, and blood.

Nee'lahn wrinkled her nose in distaste.

As they were led down the way, the occupants of the cells glanced up, eyes dull with defeat. In one cage, a bruised and battered man hung from chains on the walls. He had no legs, only burned stumps. One of the d'warves leading them laughed and nudged his companion, licking his lips. Kral pictured the leg bone on the dinner table and shuddered.

He and the others were led all the way to the end of the passage, to the largest cell. Its door was opened, and they were shoved inside. With a clang, the door slammed shut and was locked.

The lieutenant leaned close to the bars as Kral settled Tyrus to the straw-covered stone floor. "Do not think yourself safe, man of the mountains. I mean to taste your blood."

Kral, his arms freed, lashed backward with a fist, leopard swift. The lieutenant failed to move fast enough. Bones crunched under Kral's knuckles; hot blood spurted over his wrist.

The lieutenant cried out, falling back.

Kral slowly turned to face him. Without a word, he lifted his fist and licked the lieutenant's blood from his wrist.

Regaining his feet, the lieutenant lunged at the bars, his nose a crooked ruin. "I'll eat your heart, mountain man! Do you hear me?"

Kral licked his wrist again, then swung around, ignoring the man's screeches. He found the others' eyes on him. Mogweed's mouth was hanging open.

The lieutenant was dragged away by his fellow guards.

"Was that wise, Kral?" Nee'lahn asked. "What does it gain to provoke them?"

He shrugged.

Further discussion was forestalled by a loud groan from the prince. Nee'lahn knelt beside him, taking his hand. The man's other arm rose, his fingers brushing over his face like a blind man struggling to recognize a stranger. Another groan escaped his lips.

"Lord Tyrus," Nee'lahn whispered.

Eyelids slowly pulled open. His pupils rolled for a few breaths, then settled on Nee'lahn. He reached to her face with his free hand and touched her cheek, as if firming in his mind that she was real and not another figment of fevered dreams. He tried to speak, but all that came out was a rasp.

"Hush," Nee'lahn said.

Tyrus pushed up on his elbows, weak. Kral stooped and helped the prince sit up. "Do you know where you are?" he asked.

The prince nodded and rasped an answer. "Home."

"You've been unconscious for almost three days," Mogweed said, coming forward to join them.

Tyrus held a palm against his forehead. "I heard the Wall. It helped me find my way back."

"Where were you?" Nee'lahn asked. "What happened?"

Tyrus closed his eyes and shuddered. "I . . . I don't remember. All I recall is a shadow falling over me while I fought the d'warves. Its touch numbed the marrow of my bones. I felt my mind pulled from my body, leaving me unmoored and unable to find my way back."

"It was the griffin," Nee'lahn said. "I saw it. A monstrous statue made of shadows and fire. It attacked you."

Tyrus slowly shook his head. "I don't remember. I became lost in nightmares, surrounded by strange, twisted beasts, and fiery eyes that burned into me."

"Fiery eyes?" Kral mumbled, shifting uncomfortably. He remembered his own branding by the Black Heart. He sniffed at Tyrus. He sensed no corruption and was secretly relieved. The blood debt to the kings of Castle Mryl was ingrained in Kral like a vein of quartz in granite. Even darkfire could not burn away this bit of ancient obligation. He was glad to discover the prince untainted.

Nee'lahn spoke up. "The d'warf captain seemed especially interested in you, Lord Tyrus. He called you 'marked by the griffin,' suggesting some importance in your capture."

Tyrus sat straighter, his strength slowly returning. "I can imagine. As the last living prince of the Wall, my magick would be a boon to the raiders."

"Magick?" Nee'lahn asked.

"Scrying," Tyrus explained. "Tellings of the future. The Wall speaks with the will and knowledge of all the Land." Tyrus attempted to stand but needed Kral's help. He limped to the rear wall of their cell and laid a palm on the glassy surface—black granite, like all the castle. "I will not let them have me. I'll not let the Land's gift to my family be twisted."

"We'll protect you," Kral said.

Tyrus smiled, cracked lips splitting and bleeding fresh. "I don't doubt your honor, Kral, but honor can be outnumbered— as was proven on the battlefield three days ago."

"So what do you propose?"

"To vanish."

"How?" Mogweed asked.

"There's a magick in the Northwall that is known only to members of the royal family—something more than scrying." Tyrus glanced at them.

Kral's eyes narrowed with suspicion. "What?"

Tyrus paused, then took a deep breath and spoke softly. "As Castle Mryl is a part of the Wall, so are its kings and princes. Granite runs in our blood. We are as much the Wall as the castle itself."

"I don't understand," Kral grumbled.

"Then watch." Tyrus turned and placed both palms on the Wall. He closed his eyes.

Kral felt the flow of the Wall's energy shift, like a river changing course. The rumble of elemental magick swept down upon the cell, swirling through the walls in torrents.

At his side, Nee'lahn gasped.

Kral's attention returned fully to the prince. The man's pale hands slowly blackened, matching the granite. As Kral watched, the transformation flowed up the prince's arms, turning limbs to stone, polished and smooth. And still the magick spread, consuming chest and legs, swamping over the man's head. In a matter of breaths, his entire form had become living granite.

Stone lips moved. "We are not called the Blood of the Wall for no reason. We are one with the Land's heart. It is our *true* home."

Tyrus stepped forward, merging into the stone wall. He stopped—half in, half out. He turned to them. "Fear not. I'll watch over you. But in the Wall, I can walk the castle unseen and learn the foul purpose of those who roost here."

Nee'lahn reached and touched the man's cheek. "Be careful. Even the strongest stone can shatter."

"So I have learned." He sank deeper into the wall, his clothes ripping and falling to the straw. Soon there was no sign of the prince, only bare wall.

Mogweed touched the stone, disbelieving his eyes.

Lord Tyrus' face reappeared above Mogweed's fingers, growing into a stone mask hanging on the wall. Torchlight glinted off his glossy eyes. Granite lips smiled mischievously. "Be ready."

Then he was gone.

As dawn rose, Meric stared over the bowsprit of the *Stormwing*. Overhead, the morning breezes swelled the sails, ropes snapping taut. This close to the colossal wall, the winds blew in cold gusts, threatening to toss the ship against the looming cliff of granite. It took all Meric's skill to keep the ship gliding beside the Northwall, edging along the misty heights, hiding from the hostile eyes far below.

Meric stood bundled in a thick-furred cloak. At this height, ice frosted the smooth rock, and the air was almost too thin to breathe. He craned his neck. Even from the deck of the *Stormwing*, Meric could not spy the Northwall's summit. It was too tall, higher than even the *Stormwing* could fly.

After rescuing Mycelle and Fardale from atop the Stone of Tor, Meric had flown his ship directly north, pursuing the trail discovered by the wolf's keen nose. There was no doubt where their captured friends were being taken—to Castle Mryl.

By air, it had taken only a day to reach the Northwall. Once here, they were forced to wait, well out of sight of the castle. Only at night did they dare risk drifting nearer, spying upon the encampment around the castle. A pair of elv'in sailors had drifted on long lines below the keel, bearing spyglasses. Maps were quickly drawn of the castle grounds and surrounding forces. But so far, there was no sign of the others. As Meric and Mycelle waited, worry had begun to worm into their talks. What if they were wrong? What if the captives weren't being taken here?

Something bumped Meric's knee. He glanced down and found Fardale settling to his haunches. He touched the wolf's flank in reassurance. "We'll find your brother and the others. If they're out there, we won't leave without them."

Fardale leaned a bit against the elv'in's leg, silently thanking him.

Together, the pair watched the sun rise over the mountains of the Teeth. As the first rays reflected off the upper heights of the Northwall, Meric tacked the *Stormwing* slowly backward, putting distance between them and the castle. He slipped back along the Northwall to sit out another long day—another day of interminable waiting and worry.

Fardale whined at his side. The wolf's nose was pointed toward the cliff of granite. At first, Meric failed to see anything, then spotted movement. Something swept toward them, a shadow on the rock. Clutching the rail, Meric leaned out, eyes squinted.

A great bird shot along the cliff face, diving from heights higher than the *Stormwing* could fly. Meric stepped back as the creature arced toward the deck of the ship. The elv'in, his blood tied to all things of the air, recognized the bird: a great roc. The huge black bird swept toward their ship. Its wings were wider than Meric was tall. With a piercing cry, it tucked its wings and dove toward the deck, a deadly black bolt.

Meric stood his ground. When the beast was a span from the deck, its wings snapped open, braking its fall. Talons dug into the deck as the bird landed. It held its wings wide, a crown of feathers flaring up. Its beak stretched open as it panted from its flight. Glowing amber eyes stared back at him.

Fardale padded up to the bird, sniffing at it.

Meric spoke to the majestic beast. "What have you learned?"

As answer, the bird drew its wings down, ruffling its feathers with a shake. Black pinions withdrew back into pale flesh. Bones stretched. Blond hair sprouted to replace black feather, and wings rejointed into arms. In a matter of moments, bird became woman. The only feature shared between the two forms were the deep amber eyes.

Naked, Mycelle pushed up from her crouch, gasping slightly, still out of breath. "Th-they arrived during the night. They've been taken to the dungeons."

Meric slipped off his fur-lined cloak and draped it over her bare shoulders. "All of them?"

She snugged the cloak tight, shivering against the cold. "All of them. But Lord Tyrus appeared unconscious. Kral was carrying him. I could not judge the extent of his injuries from where I was perched."

"Then we proceed as planned," Meric said.

She nodded. "Tonight. Under the cover of darkness."

"Will they be safe for that long?"

"They'll have to be. Our only hope is stealth. There'll be no victory without the advantage of surprise."

Meric guided her toward the hatch. "Then you'll need to warm up and rest. With winter nearing, the days are shorter."

Mycelle scowled. "Not short enough." She stared at Fardale, eyes growing briefly brighter as the two shared private thoughts. Afterward, the wolf nodded his head once, then swung away.

Meric followed the pair. At last, the waiting was over.

As the others disappeared through the hatch, Meric closed the doors, remaining on deck. He returned to his post by the bowsprit, shivering in the thin air. Mycelle still had his cloak. Ahead, the high mists thinned.

A quarter league beyond the bowsprit, the sheer face of the granite cliff lay shattered and broken. Distracted by Mycelle's reappearance, he had let the *Stormwing* drift farther than he had intended. He slowed the winds in his sails. It was the first time the *Stormwing* neared the place where the great wall had been sundered. Meric had considered it too dangerous.

But now, with the wound in sight, he found himself drawn to it. Boulders the size of small villages lay tumbled into the meadows and forests of the Western Reaches. The trough of devastation stretched leagues to the south: gouged tracks, acres of broken trees, shattered hillsides. The horrendous fall of the Stone of Tor was a broken twig compared to the devastation here.

Meric extended his sight toward the Northwall. From summit to base, the wall was split completely. But as the ship drifted nearer, Meric saw the breach itself was quite narrow, no more than a hundred steps. It was as if a giant ax had cleaved the wall.

Both curious and appalled, Meric allowed his ship to sweep forward. As the *Stormwing* glided over the destruction below, Meric's eyes remained fixed on the sundered cliff face. He held his breath as the view beyond the wall opened up. A thin slice of the dark forest appeared.

The *Dire Fell*. The twisted home of the wrathful Grim.

Meric stared. The trees of the Fell were nothing like the pines and aspens of the northern Reaches. These trees were *monsters*. The giants reached as high as the summit of the Northwall itself, their upper branches crowned with ice. The boles were as thick around as farmhouses, each mounted atop a tangle of knotted roots. But worst of all, their branches, rather than sprouting straight, were twisted and curled upon themselves, appearing more like vines than tree limbs. Adding to this appearance was the lack of leaves. Not a single green tuft of foliage marked this skeletal forest.

Staring, not breathing, Meric shuddered. It was as if the word *tortured* were given living form in these behemoth trees.

He tore his eyes away, glancing below. Extending from the forest into the breach, a tangle of roots slowly writhed. Blind, woody worms shuffled and dug at the edge of the wound. To be seen from this height, Meric knew each root had to be thicker than a horse's flank, powerful enough to chew into stone. Meric knew he was looking at the cause of the wall's sundering. As at the Stone of Tor, the Grim must have directed their enslaved trees to tear this breach in the granite.

But *why*? What control did the Dark Lord exert over these wraiths? What had caused them to break free after countless centuries and leave their own trees to hunt the Western Reaches?

Over the past two days, Meric had learned the wraiths' patterns. Only at night did the Grim flow out of the Fell to hunt the forests of the Reaches, creating an unnatural barrier around Castle Mryl, protecting the encamped d'warves. But again—*why*? What dread pact had been forged between the mindless wraiths and the furtive d'warves?

Meric had no answer. He swung the *Stormwing* around. Tears froze on his cheek. Though there was so much unknown, Meric knew one truth, one secret. Something he had not shared with anyone, not even his own men.

He turned his back on the Fell. "Oh, Nee'lahn . . . maybe it would've been better if you'd stayed dead."

"YOU DON'T LOOK WELL," MOGWEED SAID.

Nee'lahn opened her eyes. She leaned against the cold wall of the cell, huddled in her cloak. Mogweed crouched before her. "I'm fine," she lied, turning away and pulling the hood of her cloak higher.

The mousy-haired man settled beside her. He picked a strand of long blond hair from the shoulder of her cloak. "What's wrong?"

Nee'lahn remained silent. Though she strove to hide it, this crypt of stone threatened her rebirth. While in the vast Western Reaches, the woodsong had helped sustain her, but now, cut off, surrounded by spans of hard granite, she could barely hear a whisper of the endless song of the great forest.

"You need your lute, don't you?" Mogweed whispered, keenly perceptive. "A nyphai cannot be far from her bonded tree spirit."

"No more than a hundred steps," she answered quietly. Years ago, as the last koa'kona tree of her ancestral grove, Lok'ai'hera, had succumbed to the Blight, a skilled woodcutter had carved Nee'lahn a magnificent lute from the heart of her tree, freeing the tree's spirit, preserving it. With lute in hand, Nee'lahn had been able to travel across the lands of Alasea to search for a cure, to return vitality to what was now Blighted.

But no longer. She did not have her lute, and in its absence, she needed the strength of the vast forests of the Reach to keep her from unraveling. And now, imprisoned in granite, cut off from the forest, Nee'lahn felt herself weakening, fraying around the edges. Her lips were dry and cracked, and no amount of water could quench her thirst. Her hair hung limp, and strands fell like autumn leaves.

"How long can you hold out?" Mogweed asked with concern.

"Not long. Maybe a day." Closing her eyes, Nee'lahn reached outward, concentrating on the whispers of song wending down through the passages and stairs. As she strained, she heard another song, a darker melody. It came not from before her, but from behind, from the Fell. She knew that black song.

splayed nose and wide lips made him appear some squat toad perched before a lake. "All is in readiness. The shaft under the Citadel has been mined and the chamber completed under the lake of Tor Amon."

"And what of the griffin statue, Captain Brytton?" The speaker floated in the hot waters of the tub. It was hard to make out any features through the steam, but the voice sounded distinctly feminine, lilting and sweet, but with a deeper undercurrent of menace. "What of the Weirgate?"

"It has been returned to its roost at the Citadel. We await only the next full moon to finish the last step."

"Good." The figure settled deeper in the tub. "I thought it foolish of the Dark Lord's lieutenant to mount the griffin and hunt a few stray elementals lost in the wood, especially at this critical time."

"As the hour approaches, the Black Heart grows especially wary."

"Or at least the one named *Shorkan* does. That burned fiend watches all the Gates, popping between them like some scalded rat, keeping an eye on everything. With my brethren on guard, there is nothing to fear in the north. Our site is secure." The figure sighed. "Still, the discovery of the prince of the Wall was a fortuitous boon. And with the griffin returned to its roost, we remain on schedule. Nothing lost, everything gained."

"But the prince remains mindless."

"Then we must pray his will is strong enough to withstand his brush with the Weir. If the prince could be broken to our cause, his skill at augury would serve our master well."

"Aye, but what of his companions in the dungeon?"

The figure shifted in the tub. "They'll be kindling for our fire. We shall use their tortures to help forge the young prince. We will not lose him as we did his father." The bather slid deep into the tub. "Though in truth, even that matter did not end entirely without gain; this body I wear has grown quite comfortable. I had forgotten the delights of the physical flesh. Like this bath . . . and fine wine." A hand, barely discernable through the steamy mists, reached for a glass as red as blood. The bather sipped at the wine, savoring it, then lowered the glass and stood.

The sudden motion stirred the steam in whorled eddies.

"When the prince wakes, we'll break him to our will. Where we failed with the father, we'll succeed with the son."

The mists parted as the figure stepped from the bath, naked. The snowy beard that trailed over the broad chest belied the feminine voice.

Tyrus gasped, reaching out of the wall, unmindful of exposing himself. "Father!"

The room's two occupants turned in his direction, startled.

Before he was spotted, Tyrus yanked his arms back inside the granite.

"Did you hear something just then?"

The d'warf nodded, his long ears twitching. "A muffled outburst. Maybe from the next room."

"Go search!"

The d'warf captain fled.

The naked figure strode to the wall, standing before it. Hands rose to explore the surface. Tyrus hovered frozen in the stone, half an arm's length away. He searched his father's face, seeing a man he had spent a decade mourning. His arms ached to reach out and hold his father in his arms, but Tyrus knew King Ry was no longer there. The eyes before him were cold and glowed with cruel fires.

Fists clenching, Tyrus bit back a scream of rage.

The squat captain returned, ax in hand. "The rooms are empty."

The figure turned savagely, his voice ice. "Check on our prisoners."

"Aye, my lord." Captain Brytton bowed out of the room.

Now only father and son remained—along with something foul wearing King Ry's form. "I can smell you," the demon whispered to the empty air. "The scent of blood in the walls."

The figure moved back to the bath, voice raising, the feminine lilt growing hard and frosted. "I don't know what trick of magick this is, but I'll find whoever you are and twist you to our end. This I promise!"

As Tyrus watched, a darkness exuded from his father's body, flowing from every pore. Tendrils of dark smoke probed the mists, hunting for him.

Tyrus dared not risk capture—not when the others were counting on him. He sank down the wall, dropping away. The movement must have been sensed. The demon sprang toward his hiding spot, clawed nails bared.

But Tyrus was already gone, sunken into the lower depths of the castle, wending his way back toward the main wall.

As he moved, tears flowed down his granite cheeks.

Father!

7

AS THE MOON CLIMBED THE NIGHT SKY, MYCELLE HURRIED DOWN the woodland trail toward the glow of the encampment around Castle Mryl. She did not bother trying to hide. The trail ended at the forest's edge. The Northwall and Castle Mryl loomed before her, a hundred paces away.

Taking a deep breath, Mycelle stepped out into the open and strode toward the sentry line of the outer camp. Around her upper arm, under her thick leather jerkin, the paka'golo snake curled in agitation. *It must smell the magick given off by the Wall.* Once Mycelle herself could have sensed the great well of power here; her ability as a seeker had been keen. But no longer. Risen from the dead by the small snake's magick, she had traded one ability for another—*seeking* for *shape-shifting.*

Mycelle walked up to one of the outer sentries and lifted an arm in greeting. He just nodded at her, bored, leaning on a pike. She hurried past, eyes down.

Her deception had held. Earlier, Mycelle's group had waylaid a trio of d'warf hunters. It had not been hard. Meric had lowered the *Stormwing* and dropped four of his kin into the trees, armed with poisoned crossbows. They had quickly dispatched the thick-bodied hunters, then signaled the all clear. After the attack, Mycelle had joined the archers. Choosing carefully, she had rolled the smallest of the dead d'warves, a female, on its back. Leaning over the slack form, she had studied the body and face, then shaped her own physique to match. Once satisfied with her appearance, she had quickly donned the target's clothes and cinched her own weapons in place, hidden under an outer furred cloak.

The elv'in bowmen then clambered back up the ropes to the waiting ship, leaving Mycelle to traverse the trails alone back to Castle Mryl. Her goal: to reach the upper heights of the castle and eliminate any stray eyes so the *Stormwing* could moor.

"How was the night's hunting?" a squat guard asked in the d'warvish tongue as she passed. He sat on a stool, honing his ax.

Mycelle swung around, quickly translating the words in her head. She shoved aside a cloak and revealed a trio of skinned hares hanging from her belt. "The Grim have left us little to hunt."

The guard nodded, concentrating on his ax. "Damned ghouls. Shrieking and wailing all the time. Makes my skin twitch."

Mycelle grunted and continued down the rows of tents and billets. She adjusted her cloak, nervous as she worked her way through the wide camp. With most of the host asleep in their tents, no others accosted her.

She soon reached the gates in the outer curtain wall of Castle Mryl. Two guards were posted. They straightened as she neared, pikes shifting in their grips.

Mycelle bit back a curse and kept her head down as she marched up to them. She did not want her amber eyes betraying her true heritage.

A long pike tipped with a steel blade lowered across her path, blocking the way. "What manner of business do you have here at this time of night?"

Mycelle again parted her cloak, revealing the trio of hares. "Late-night meal for the captain of the guards. He asked I bring him something tasty." She let her cloak open farther to reveal her figure's ample bosom, shape-shifting slightly to swell the fullness even more. "Are these tasty enough to pass inspection?" she asked with a lascivious grin, tilting one hip to make the rabbits sway.

Neither guard noticed the hares.

With a single finger, Mycelle reached and slid aside the pike. "If you'll excuse me, I've heard the captain's grown quite hungry."

There was no resistance as she sauntered past, only a mumbled protest. "That damn captain gets all the best—"

"—rabbits," his partner finished.

Both guards guffawed and settled back to their posts.

Mycelle continued across the central keep. Though the night had grown cold, sweat pebbled her brow. Her limbs threatened to shake. She had to concentrate on walking slowly.

Climbing the stairs toward the main entrance to the castle, Mycelle found the way thankfully unguarded. It seemed the marauding force had grown complacent, content with the security of the entrenched encampment and the legions of Grim loose in the surrounding forest.

She moved through the broken stone doors and sped deeper into the keep. She strode with more assurance, knowing her way from here. Decades ago, she had trained in these very walls, learning the way of the sword, and once done, she had sworn fealty to King Ry in the great feasting hall. But as she climbed the twining stairs and sped along the dusty passages, she barely recognized the place. The once neat and bright hallways were now dark and fouled. Broken furniture and refuse lay scattered. At the top of one stairway, she found the old bones of a defender tumbled in a corner, bits of leather and cloth still clinging to them. She turned her face away and hurried on, chased by ghosts, while rats and other vermin scurried from her path.

This was not the castle she remembered.

Still, though the insides had been defiled, the structure was the same. Mycelle followed the last of the winding staircases to the topmost level. She marched toward the terrace's open parapet. At the door, she paused to check her weapons.

According to last night's reconnoitering, there were two guards.

Leaning against the door, she braced herself. No alarm must be raised. She slipped out her pair of throwing daggers and palmed them, testing their weight. Satisfied, she pulled the door's latch and rolled through. One of the guards swung around at the squeak of hinges. She flew toward them.

"What are you—?" The first d'warf's words were sliced from his throat by the dagger now protruding from under his chin. Blood spouted as he coughed and bumped backward.

His companion was a moment too slow in recognizing his fellow guardsman's distress. Before he could turn, Mycelle was there, jamming her second dagger into the soft spot where the spine met the skull. She slammed the heel of her hand against the pommel, driving its point deep into the brain. His body spasmed, his wide mouth opening and closing, silently gasping. Then his muscles gave out, and he slumped to the stone.

Mycelle did not witness the end of her handiwork. The first d'warf had ripped the dagger from his own throat and tossed it aside. In his other hand appeared a long-hafted ax. He tried to sound the alarm, but all that came out was a gurgle, his voice box a bloody ruin.

Backing a step, Mycelle took in the situation. The advantage of surprise was gone. The soldier spun his ax skillfully, fire and hate in his eyes. She did not like her odds. Twin-hearted, d'warves were hard to kill, and she wore an unfamiliar form—but she had neither time nor magickal reserve to shift.

The d'warf attacked.

Mycelle whipped out her twin swords, caught the ax's haft in her crossed blades, and turned it away. The axhead struck the granite floor, casting sparks at her heels. Mycelle danced, spinning and thrusting her sword deep into her attacker's belly.

With a growl, the d'warf heaved around, dragging the hilt from Mycelle's hand.

Mycelle backed, reduced to one weapon. She cursed her current form. It was too slow, too thick-fingered.

The d'warf, her sword hilt showing under his rib cage, swung on Mycelle. Blood frothed his thick lips. The impaled blade had not fazed the creature, no more than a thorn in his side. His ax spun again.

The next strike aimed for Mycelle's head. With no hope of deflecting the heavy weapon, she didn't even try. Instead she lunged toward her attacker, bringing herself under his guard. The oak haft struck her shoulder, driving her to her knees. Using both hands, she drove her second sword up into his belly, then rolled away.

Shoving to her feet, she twisted around.

The d'warf had dropped to one knee, now impaled with two blades, the last of Mycelle's weapons. Using his ax as a crutch, he pushed himself up and glared at her. He glanced to her empty hands, and a bloody sneer formed as he straightened.

Now what? Mycelle thought. She found her back against the

parapet wall. Her left arm was almost limp, numbed by the blow to her shoulder.

With a muted roar of victory, he rushed her, ax raised high.

Reacting on pure instinct, Mycelle dropped to the stone floor, legs sliding out from under her, her back striking the granite hard. She ignored the blade aiming for her face and lifted her feet. She caught the d'warf in the belly.

He let out a loud *oof*, blood spraying from his lips—but still his ax fell.

She kicked out with her feet, driving his bulk a single step back. Thrown off balance, the ax struck the stone of the parapet just to the side of Mycelle's head. She felt the jar of the impact in her legs.

Reaching past her knees, she grabbed the hilts of her twin swords. In a clean sweep, she unsheathed them from the guard's belly.

He groaned and fell toward her, meaning to pin her.

Mycelle let him. In a flash of blades, she crossed her swords before her and kicked the guard's legs out from under him, accelerating his fall atop her.

Surprised, he tumbled, his neck falling squarely between the crossed blades. The weight of his fall against the twin razored blades finished the work started by the first dagger. His neck was sliced all the way to his spine. He landed atop Mycelle, bleeding a hot lake across her face and upper chest.

Mycelle strained to move him, but he was too heavy. Blood filled her mouth and nose. She spat and choked on it, coughing, close to drowning. Then the twin pumps in his chest ceased their chugging beats, and the flow slowed enough for her to catch her breath.

Still, she was trapped. He was too massive, too wide. Giving up, she fumbled into a pocket and pulled free a silver coin, the prince's coin: on one side, a leaping snow leopard, on the other, the visage of the prince's father, King Ry.

She kissed the elder's face, thanking him for her training, then closed her eyes. *Xin,* she silently willed. *Xin, hear me.*

Almost immediately, the coin grew warm in her hand. *"I hear you."*

She signed in relief. Earlier, it had been decided to use the coin to signal the ship, a silent dispatch. Xin had been awaiting her call.

"The way is clear," she said. "Bring the ship in."

"It will be done. We come now."

Mycelle pulled the coin close to her lips. "Hurry . . ."

KRAL STARED ACROSS THE CELL AT LORD TYRUS. THE PRINCE WAS curled on a pile of straw. Ever since the man's journey through the stone, Tyrus had grown ashen and sullen. Kral matched his mood.

Last night, the prince had popped back through the cell's wall, startling them all. Grabbing up the shreds of his clothes, he had hurriedly draped his naked form and hissed for them to remain quiet, warning that Captain Brytton was on his way down to check on them. Settling to the floor, Tyrus feigned to be still lost in a mindless nightmare, while the others sprawled about the cell, looking tired and hopeless.

The prince's warning quickly proved true.

Moments later, the squat captain had shouted his way down the row of cells, stopping at their cage. He had stared between the bars, studying each for any subterfuge. Satisfied that his prisoners were still secured, he had grunted angrily and swung away.

Later, Tyrus had explained what he overheard in the royal chambers—a foul plot unfolding in the north. He had also reported how his father's body had been possessed by a demon. Since then, Tyrus had remained distant.

Hearing the news, Kral also withdrew. So the Dark Lord seeded some plot in the north—at the Citadel. He cringed at the thought. Whether he was a servant or not, Kral could not stomach his ancestral home being tainted and possibly corrupted by black magicks. Conflicting loyalties twisted inside his chest: one forged in darkfire, the other formed of stone. As the day wore on, the answer slowly dawned in Kral. He had already defied the Dark Lord by coming here, abandoning the hunt for the wit'ch. Having started down this path, he would see it to the end. The Citadel would be his people's again, even if it meant thwarting his master's plan here.

Mogweed spoke up from across the cell, drawing Kral back to the present, where he sensed that night had again fallen. Mogweed nudged Tyrus. "I still don't see why you can't just walk through the walls and get the keys. Free us. Why are we rotting here in these dungeons?"

Tyrus, his eyes shadowed with circles, shook his head. "And what then? There are over a legion of d'warves camped at the castle's gates. We'd be recaptured, and my secret would be revealed. As long as I feign unconsciousness, it'll buy us time. I'll hunt again this night when the guard here is lighter and see if I can learn more, something to free us."

Mogweed slumped back against the wall. "I hate this waiting."

"You'd hate more being in a d'warf's stew pot," Nee'lahn snapped irritably. It was the first time the nyphai had spoken all day. She looked sickly. Her skin was blotched, her lips dried and shrunken. Her hair hung lifeless to her shoulders.

Tyrus pushed to one elbow. "Enough squabbling. I'll go search again. If the dungeon guard is light enough, I can try taking them out, giving you all a chance to escape, but I'm staying here."

Kral grumbled. "If you stay, so do I."

"And I," Nee'lahn whispered hoarsely.

All their eyes turned to Mogweed. He sighed dramatically. "I'm *not* going by myself."

Kral nodded. "Then it's decided. Tyrus, you search for any means for us to leave here. I've heard tales of secret passages that run the length of the Northwall. What if we could make it to one of those?"

Tyrus frowned. "The passages are just myth. They don't exist. There is only one secret path, a secret means of escape in case of attack. But I don't think we want to tread that path."

"Where does it lead?" Kral asked.

"To the Dire Fell, the dark wood beyond the Wall, to the forest of the wraiths. But there is no salvation in that wood. None may walk it safely. It would be better to die in battle than be a meal for the Grim. Growing up here, I never understood why this secret exit was even built."

"I know," Nee'lahn said in a dry rasp.

Tyrus glanced at her in surprise. "Why?"

She shook her head. "It no longer matters. You're right. That path now only leads to a doom worse than death."

The prince's eyes narrowed with suspicion. She met his gaze, unblinking.

Kral broke the silence. "The night is full. Mayhap it would be best if you traveled the Wall again. See what you can learn. I wager our captors' patience wears thin. I've seen how the passing guards have eyed our cell with hunger."

Tyrus nodded and scooted up. "You're right, mountain man. I fear how long the demoness wearing my father's flesh will wait for me to wake." He stood and shrugged out of his torn clothes, showing no shame at his nakedness. He moved to the Wall and placed his palms on the stone, calling up the magick.

Kral sensed the shift in energies. Soon Tyrus was sinking into the wall, vanishing away. The beast inside Kral sniffed for a sign of the prince, but came up empty. Not even a heartbeat.

Granite had absorbed granite.

MERIC LEFT THE *STORMWING* UNDER THE CHARGE OF HIS SECOND cousin. The ship floated a hundred spans above the highest terrace of Castle Mryl, hidden in the icy mists that cloaked the upper Northwall. Meric craned his neck as he moved across the stone floor. His ship was indiscernible, the only sign of it the long trailing rope linking the hidden vessel to its mooring point on the parapet.

He crossed to the others gathered in the shadows. Mycelle looked truly ghastly. Still formed in the shape of a d'warf, her toadish body dripped with blood and gore. So shocked was he by her appearance, Meric's left boot slid from under him. He cartwheeled his arms for balance and righted himself, scowling at the slick pool of blood that had betrayed his footing. The entire narrow open terrace was treacherous with blood and the bodies of the dead.

Meric straightened the lay of his dark cloak and repositioned the pack on his back, careful of its delicate contents. "Are we ready?" he asked as he joined the others.

Standing beside Mycelle were two of the elv'in sailors, the most skilled with bow and dagger. Around them prowled the wolf Fardale, who had been lowered in a basket. His keen nose would come in handy in the search. Left aboard the *Stormwing* were the remaining crew, including Xin and the boy Tok. Xin's ability to farspeak would allow the rescue team to keep in contact with the ship above.

"We're ready. Make haste," Mycelle said, wrapping a clean cloak over her bloody clothes. "I know the way to the dungeons, but I had best go first to make sure the halls are free of any prying eyes."

Meric nodded. "Then let's go. Silent and swift."

Mycelle led the way, followed closely by Fardale. Meric and his two crewmates, the elv'in twins Pyllac and Syllac, kept up the rear guard. No one said a word as they worked their way down the flights of stairs and hallways. Mycelle would hurry ahead, then signal them with hand gestures to proceed or hold.

By this late in the evening, the upper tiers were deserted, and they made quick progress. But once they neared the lowermost levels, servants and sleepy-eyed guards wandered across their paths, and care had to be taken.

Fardale slunk ahead of Meric, sticking to shadows. Mycelle slipped around a corner, then waved a halt. She continued forward alone. Meric and Fardale crept to the corner and peeked past it. The hall ahead was quite wide. Halfway down the passage, a dozen d'warves lounged around a game of bones-and-cups. There was no way around them.

Mycelle approached, sauntering casually. Words were exchanged, but they were in the d'warvish tongue. Mycelle seemed to be arguing with them, clearly trying to get the group to shove off, but she was not succeeding. Finally she leaned against the wall, one hand signaling behind her back.

Be ready to fight. Wait for my signal.

Meric shrugged out of his bulky pack and set it down with care. Next he slipped free his blade. Ready, he fed magick into his limbs. An elv'in could move with blinding speed for short bursts. Meric remembered his sword battle with Kral in the underground warrens of the rock'goblins. It seemed a lifetime ago.

Behind him, his elv'in companions set quarrels into their crossbows, while Fardale crouched, teeth bared.

Down the hall, Mycelle shoved off the wall, two swords appearing in her fists as if from thin air. She drove them through the throats of the nearest two and twisted. Blood sprayed the wall.

The d'warf band sat stunned a moment, then reacted with a roar.

Mycelle abandoned her swords and rolled away. Daggers appeared in her fingers, flashing in the torchlight. She tossed one into the eye of a d'warf holding a handful of coins. Bits of copper and silver showered into the air as he fell backward, dead before his head hit the stone. She threw her second dagger just as surely. Another dropped, a hide cup rolling from his dead fingers.

Meric was impressed. Four dead in the span of a moment. Clearly she was growing accustomed to fighting in her bulky form.

But now the advantage of surprise was over; the other eight d'warves drew weapons and sprang to their feet. Mycelle danced away down the hall, drawing their attention to her. Empty-handed, she signaled Meric.

With the d'warves' backs turned, Meric led the charge, sword raised. He flashed down the hall, a ghost in silver. Two dropped quickly to the poisoned bolts of the twins' crossbows, and a third died upon the lightning-quick blade of Meric—two jabs, piercing both hearts, and a slice across the throat. Meric kicked the body over, toppling it across the spread of tossed bones.

Now the hall was littered with bodies, and the true melee began—five against five.

Fardale knocked over a thick-limbed d'warf and ripped teeth into his throat. Meric looked away.

The two twins nocked up two more quarrels, but the fighting was fierce. Working as a team, they swung on a d'warf that sprinted down the hall, attempting to flee and raise the alarm. Two feathered barbs sprouted in his back. He continued to run until his pumping hearts fed the poison throughout his body and he stumbled to his knees, skidding, then fell face first.

Meric ducked an ax swing. The blade whistled over the crown of his head. He bounced back up, sword tip leading. The blade pierced the d'warf's groin and drove upward. Moving faster than the average eye could follow, Meric dragged his hilt up, splitting the d'warf's belly from stem to stern. A slather of intestines and organs spilled across the stone floor.

Meric leaped away. The d'warf, still alive, stumbled after the elv'in, ax raised. But his own bowels betrayed him. He slipped on the blood and the loops of gut, and crashed to the floor. He writhed, but could not rise.

Swinging around, Meric saw Fardale rip into the hamstring of another d'warf, bringing the squat creature toppling down. The elv'in twins were already there, abandoning their crossbows in such close fighting and attacking the downed d'warf with their long daggers.

Meric spun again. Down the hall, he saw the last and largest d'warf closing in on the weaponless Mycelle. She backed against the far wall, hands raised, ready to fight bare fist against iron ax.

Meric touched his magick but felt the leaden pull of his limbs. He had no reserve of lightning speed.

"Mycelle!" he called to her.

MYCELLE CROUCHED, LOOKING FOR SOME WEAKNESS IN THE other's defense. Her eyes flicked over her opponent. He handled his ax expertly, balanced evenly. From the top of his ax, a sharp spike of iron protruded long enough to impale a small adversary. A wicked weapon.

She clenched a fist. If she could hold him off long enough, perhaps the others could come to her aid.

As she studied him, a swordbreaker appeared in his other hand. The long dagger was deeply notched, meant to trap and break an opponent's blade. But this night, there was no sword to break; its sharp point and single-edged blade would do enough damage. The d'warf rolled the small weapon in his large grip, moving it as comfortably as a baker would a spoon.

Unlike the guard on the terrace, this d'warf was not about to underestimate her. He moved in for a swift but cautious kill.

Mycelle heard Meric call from down the hall, but she knew no aid could come from that quarter fast enough.

"Prepare to die, traitor," he grumbled at her as if he were chewing rocks.

Mycelle's eyes narrowed, readying herself. But she knew the battle was lost. Not only was she weaponless, she was exhausted and shaky from the long night of fighting.

The d'warf lunged, swiping in with both ax and dagger. She moved a step forward, twisting sideways, attempting to duck under his guard, but her attacker was not so easily fooled. The point of the dagger skimmed her side, forcing her back into the path of the descending ax blade. Encircled by blades, Mycelle knew her doom.

Ducking away, she prepared to take the ax blow to the shoulder, praying for a glancing blow—but the strike never happened.

Iron rang on stone.

Mycelle glanced up and saw an arm sprouted out of the wall—*an arm of granite!* Stone fingers were latched to the haft of the ax, stopping its descent.

A voice whispered in her ear—from the wall. "Move aside, Mycelle, unless you wish your death."

She recognized the taunting, sarcastic voice. "Tyrus?"

"Move, shape-shifter!"

Though she did not understand this miracle, she ducked and rolled from beneath the imprisoned ax.

Her d'warf attacker, too stunned to respond, let her escape.

A few steps away, she twisted back around. The d'warf tugged on his weapon, trying to free its from Tyrus' stone grip. He failed. Instead, as he pulled, Tyrus was drawn forth from the wall, stepping forth as a figure of granite.

The d'warf jabbed around Tyrus' torso with his dagger, meaning to puncture a kidney, but the blade shattered against the stone. Tyrus smiled and dragged his other arm from the wall. In its grip was a long sword, a sliver of granite formed from the substance of the wall itself.

His smile hardened to a sneer. He swung the blade and impaled the d'warf. "This is for Castle Mryl!" He yanked out his weapon and plunged it in again. "And this is for my people!"

Free of the wall, the magick faded from his skin, and granite flesh became pale skin again. Naked, Tyrus pulled his blade from the bloody d'warf. The ax fell from the creature's thick fingers. Tyrus took his granite sword in both hands and swung from the hip, twisting his body with all the muscle of his taut form. The blade ran clean through the d'warf's neck, slicing through both flesh and bone. The large pumpkin head went flying, striking a wall and bouncing off.

Tyrus straightened, sword still held in both hands. "And that was for my father," he said to the decapitated figure as it fell backward.

Mycelle approached the prince with caution. His body shook with pain and fury. "Tyrus . . ."

He glanced up at her, the rage dying in his eyes. "What are you doing here?"

She kept her eyes diverted from his nakedness. He was the son of the man to whom she had sworn fealty. "We came to rescue you."

"Who?"

Mycelle nodded at the approach of the others. "I think you remember Meric from the docks of Port Rawl."

"One of the allies of the wit'ch. The burned one."

"I've mended from my injuries," Meric said, sheathing his sword and introducing his elv'in compatriots.

Tyrus patted the wolf on the shoulder as he came nosing forward. "Good to see you again, too, Fardale." He then turned to those gathered around him and bowed slightly. "Welcome to my home. Welcome to Castle Mryl."

Mycelle was surprised at the amount of dignity the man could assume even when naked as a newborn. Meric met his bow and explained briefly about the *Stormwing* while Mycelle marched back to the dead and sifted through the bodies for her weapons. Once returned, she asked, "What of the others? Mogweed, Kral, Nee'lahn."

Tyrus shook free a cloak from the dead and wrapped it about himself. "In the dungeons. I'll take you to them. With the ship above, we now have a means of escape." He began to lead the way.

Mycelle glanced to the blank wall from which he had stepped.

Tyrus noticed her attention. "An extra gift of the Wall to the royal family."

She nodded, though she scarcely understood. Explanations would have to wait another day.

As a group, they continued down the halls. With Tyrus' ability to meld into the wall and sneak upon the unwary, it was not long until the group moved past the guardroom and into the dungeons.

Mycelle unlocked the cell.

Kral was the first out. His eyes were wide upon the newcomers. "Meric?"

The elv'in lord nodded in greeting. "It's been a long time, mountain man."

Mogweed followed next, supporting Nee'lahn under an arm. Fardale nosed his twin brother, whining a greeting. Mogweed briefly acknowledged his brother, but groaned under the thin weight of the nyphai. "She weakens," he said. "We must return her to the forest. Leave this sick place to the d'warves."

"No," Mycelle said. "Not until we discover the whereabouts of the Griffin Weirgate."

Tyrus frowned. "Weirgate? I know nothing of such a thing, but I do know the griffin beast has returned to some roost in the north."

"At the Citadel," Kral added. "We must go there!"

Mycelle nodded. "We will. We must. Come. I'll explain on the way up to the *Stormwing*. The Griffin Gate must be destroyed."

"Wait," Meric said, his eyes wide upon the resurrected nyphai. He fumbled with his bulky, oversized pack and fished inside. He removed a velvet-wrapped object. Lifting it, he peeled back the covers to reveal the small musical instrument protected inside. The lute's heartwood shone with such luster that it seemed to glow warmly with its own inner light. As he offered the tiny instrument to Nee'lahn, the dark-grained whorls churned with gold.

"I think this is yours," Meric whispered on bended knee.

HER FINGERS TREMBLING, NEE'LAHN ACCEPTED HER LOST LUTE. It was as if a severed limb were returned to her. She sighed as the warm wood met her skin, the touch of sunlight after an endless night. She stroked the instrument's skin, sensing the trace of spirit in the wood. She brought it to her lips and kissed it gently. *Beloved,* she whispered silently, a brush of breath upon the wood.

Her eyes brimmed with tears as she looked up at Meric. "Thank you." Already vitality infused her limbs. She was able to stand on her own—two halves made whole.

"We must be off," Tyrus interrupted. "The dead will soon be discovered. We must be gone before the castle rouses."

They quickly freed the other prisoners in the neighboring cells: two unlucky woodsmen who had been captured by the raiders, food for the pot. Unfortunately, the man with the burned stumps for legs was found dead in his cell. He had chewed through his own tongue, drowning and choking himself to death.

"Poor man," Nee'lahn said sadly.

No one spoke from there, but simply moved on, backtracking through to the guardroom and up into the central keep. Tyrus and Mycelle led the way, Meric and Nee'lahn next. The rest trailed with Kral in the rear. The mountain man found their stolen gear and supplies in the guardroom. He had his ax in hand again, and Tyrus his family's sword.

In a long thin parade, the group trod up the many stairs and through many twists and turns. Tyrus knew the castle well and guided them quickly and steadily, ducking through rooms and out into other halls. It was a winding path through a granite maze.

Nee'lahn barely noticed at first. Her only concern was the lute in her arms, hugged to her chest. Its warmth seeped into her core, spreading through her limbs. Her sight became sharper, her senses more acute. It was as if she were waking after a long dream.

At the top of a winding staircase, Tyrus paused, letting the line of stragglers along the stairs close ranks. "It's not much farther," he called down, encouraging them. "Another four levels."

Next, Tyrus led them off the stairs and into a lofty side chamber, a desolate ballroom with frescoed walls.

As Nee'lahn stepped from the stairs and into the room, she felt a pluck on the magick inside her—a vibration that shook her limbs. She stumbled to a stop at the doorway. "Something . . . *something* comes."

With the words just out of her mouth, a scream arose from down the stairs. Mycelle and Tyrus returned to Nee'lahn's side.

"What is it?" Meric asked, unsheathing a long, thin blade.

The answer came soon enough. Mogweed and Fardale flew up out of the darkness of the lower stairwell. "D'warves! Scores of them!" Mogweed skidded to a stop at the entrance to the ballroom. "Kral is holding them off as he retreats, but arrows took out the two woodsmen. And one of the elv'in twins took an arrow through the shoulder."

Tyrus barked commands. "Get everyone inside!" He waved at the ballroom. "We can bar this door, slow them enough for us to reach the ship." Tyrus pulled one of the thick double doors closed. Mycelle moved to the others.

In moments, the elv'in archers came limping up the steps. One leaned heavily on his twin, his shoulder a bloody wound with a feathered shaft protruding from it. The sounds of combat—roars of rage and clash of iron on iron—echoed up the staircase.

"Close the door!" Mogweed cried out, retreating from the threshold.

Mycelle held the second door cracked open. "Not until Kral gets here!"

Tyrus was ready with the bar. Meric looked after his kinsmen and helped the pair deeper into the ballroom.

Suddenly, Kral burst through the doorway, wild-eyed, chest heaving, covered head to foot with blood and gore.

Nee'lahn gasped, stumbling a few steps away. It took her a moment to recognize their companion. For a flickering moment, she had seen a monster instead of the mountain man. She blinked away the image as Mycelle slammed the door and Tyrus slid in the thick bar.

"Quickly!" the prince of the castle called out. "Out the far door."

Meric took the lead with the injured.

As Nee'lahn stepped to follow, she realized the strange welling sensation in her chest had not abated. In fact, it had grown worse. Strange vibrations strummed through her. "Wait!" she yelled sharply, drawing all their eyes.

Meric turned. The elv'in twins bumbled on ahead toward the distant door. "What is—?"

The far stone portals burst open behind Meric, casting shards into the room, throwing the elv'in prince to the floor. His two kinsmen were not as lucky. The wounded one took a blow to the face, falling backward, nose smashed. His brother was struck by a flying shard to the leg, breaking the thin bones and crumpling him to the floor.

Meric rolled to his feet, meaning to go to their aid. Mycelle and Tyrus ran with weapons in hand. Kral and Fardale guarded the barred door, along with Nee'lahn and Mogweed.

"No!" Nee'lahn warned from behind the mountain man's shoulder.

Through smoke tainted with sulfurous brimstone, two figures strode into the room. Nee'lahn recognized them both: Captain Brytton, the d'warf leader, and an old familiar face, King Ry.

But when the latter spoke, it was clear that the king was here only in body, not spirit. "It seems the dance is about to begin," the bearded figure said in a high, sibilant voice, so unlike the hard shape it wore. The demon-possessed figure waved a hand around the ballroom. "But where are the minstrels and song-birds? Where are the courtly dancers?"

"It's your father!" Mycelle gasped, lowering her sword.

"No," Tyrus said, raising his weapon higher. "No longer."

"So the princeling has woken, I see." The figure of King Ry spread his arms. "Come to me, my son." The voice rang with high-pitched laughter.

Tyrus spat. His spittle arced across the space, striking the possessed in the face.

The demoness did not bother to wipe the spittle away as it dripped into the snowy beard. "Is that any way to greet your elder?" The creature strode forward, now exuding an oily dark-ness, revealing its true form. It stepped between the two fallen elv'in brothers. Black tendrils wafted out from the king's finger-tips, like curling ebony serpents.

Nee'lahn's inner magick thrummed to the energies in the room, recognizing it. *Sweet Mother . . . no!* She knew what manner of beast possessed good King Ry.

The snaking bits of darkness lashed out to either side, biting into the prone elv'in twins. As the darkness touched them, their bodies racked with agony, mouths open in silent screams.

Tyrus and Mycelle rushed forward, but a second legion of d'warves flooded into the room, bristling with weapons, ward-ing them away.

On the floor, the elv'in twins continued to writhe. Slowly, their skin was drawn to bone; their bodies curled in on them-selves, bones twisting, as the life force of the brothers was sucked into the darkness. In moments, only dried husks remained on the stone floor.

The face of King Ry was ripe with pleasure, eyes aglow with a dark light.

Mycelle tugged Tyrus back as the figure stepped toward them. "I know this creature. It's one of the Grim, the wraiths of Dire Fell."

Before them all, the darkness continued to pour forth, fed with blood, seeking more. Soon the true guise of the possessor took shape around the body of the king—a shred of night, all darkness and blood lust.

Nee'lahn knew she had to act lest they all be destroyed. She stepped around the broad back of the mountain man. "Let us pass!" she called out to the apparition.

A disdainful face turned her way. "Who seeks to order in such a sweet voice?"

Nee'lahn stepped more fully forward and raised her lute, letting it settle easily into her hands. A fingernail touched a single string, and the weak note pierced across the room with devastating effect.

The figure of King Ry crumbled backward, its living shadow reeling as if from a mighty gust of wind. A shriek arose from the darkness: the familiar wail of the Grim.

"You know who I am, don't you?" Nee'lahn plucked a second string. "You know the magick in the wood, the power of woodsong."

The demoness swung on the captain of the d'warves. "You've brought a nyphai here! How could you, you fool?"

Captain Brytton shook his head. "Impossible. The nyphai are all dead."

"Not all of them! One yet lives!" A finger was pointed at Nee'lahn. "You fool!"

Nee'lahn continued to step forward, fingers now moving brightly across the lute. Chords and notes echoed off the wall.

The wraith wailed again.

"I don't know who you are," Nee'lahn said. "But you serve the wrong master. Have you forgotten the song of the True Glen?" Her fingers danced across the strings, conjuring up memories of green life and purple blossoms, fairy lights and hummingbirds.

"No!" The wraith pulled free of its possessed body and retreated. King Ry's body, now an empty shell, collapsed to the floor.

"Remember!" Nee'lahn urged, following the creature. "Remember who you are!"

"No!" The wraith screamed in a high-pitched child's voice and flew back into the ranks of the d'warves. Where it passed, it left behind a path of destruction. D'warves fell dead on the spot. Others fled, breaking ranks and running from the ballroom.

"I command thee to remember!" Nee'lahn called, singing, adding her voice to the chorus of the lute's woodsong.

The wailing died away. A smaller, scared voice rose from

the shred of living darkness as it paused by the door. "I . . . I cannot . . ."

Then the Grim fled, leaving an echoing cry behind it.

Clearly wary of the magick here, Captain Brytton called a retreat and backed out of the ballroom, regrouping his damaged troops.

Mycelle ran forward and checked the hall. "They've gathered just around the bend. We must move out *now* before they grow bold again."

The sharp sound of steel on stone drew Nee'lahn's attention back to the ballroom. Tyrus leaned over his father's body, sword in hand. His father's head lay cleaved from its neck. "I will not give the demon a place to roost. At least, not in my father."

Mogweed and Fardale joined Mycelle by the door. "Let's go," Mogweed urged.

Kral helped move Tyrus from his father's side. "There'll be time for burials and prayers later."

"There's no blood," Tyrus said dully, pointing with his sword.

Nee'lahn stepped to the prince's other side. "He was long dead. An empty vessel for the . . . for the . . ."

Tyrus swung on her, eyes hard as the black granite. "What? You know more than you say!"

Nee'lahn clasped her lute across her chest protectively.

Meric came to her aid. "Leave her, Lord Tyrus. Such matters are best discussed well away from here."

Mycelle agreed and ordered them to follow. She ducked out the door and raced down the hall, opposite where the d'warf host regathered. In a tangled group, they fled.

"I know the way from here!" Mycelle called back. She fumbled a coin from a pocket and clutched it to her lips. *"Xin, hear me!"*

Nee'lahn heard no answer, but in a few steps, Mycelle stumbled to a stop, pausing at the entrance to another winding staircase. After a few hushed heartbeats, Mycelle lowered the coin, fingers white-knuckled around it.

She turned to them. "Trouble. The *Stormwing* had to break its mooring and flee. They had been discovered. The top terrace now crawls with d'warves. Another trap."

Meric's thin lips frowned deeply. "What are we to do? We can't go up. We can't go back."

They all remained silent.

Finally, Nee'lahn answered. "We go down." She pointed toward the stairs that wound back into the depths of the castle. She turned to Lord Tyrus. "The secret tunnel you mentioned in the cell. Take us there."

"But it only leads to the Dire Fell. Even you said that path is death."

"No longer." Nee'lahn held up the lute. "A way opens."

"How?"

She shook her head. "Lead us."

Tyrus bit his lip in indecision, eyes narrowed with suspicion of her.

Behind them, a roar arose from Captain Brytton's forces.

"They come!" Mycelle said.

Tyrus scowled and hurried forward. "This way then." He raced down the steps, taking them two at a time.

MERIC FOLLOWED BEHIND NEE'LAHN. IT DID NOT TAKE MAGICK TO sense the tension flowing from the small nyphai. Her arms hugged the lute to her chest, her face—when he glimpsed it—was pale. Tyrus led the way down at a furious pace as the booming calls of the d'warves gave chase. Nee'lahn stumbled to keep up.

Moving to her side, Meric gripped her elbow, supporting her. "You don't have to do this," he whispered, careful to keep their words private.

"We have no other choice."

"It's not too late. We could try to forge a path through the encircled encampment. If we could reach the forests of the Western—"

"There is no going back. You saw what lurked in King Ry."

"One of the Grim."

Nee'lahn glanced hard at him. "Both of us know better than that."

Meric lowered his face. "Can you control them? Will the lute's song enchant the wraiths long enough for us to pass through the Dire Fell?"

"I believe so. Memories hold great power. They will either flee or become enthralled. Either way, they should leave us safe."

"But what of the one who possessed King Ry? Where was her

madness? Though clearly bent to the Dark Lord, she was lucid, calculating."

Nee'lahn shook her head. "The Gul'gothal demon must have found a way to untwist the damage. But I don't know why she serves the Black Beast."

Sudden insight dawned in Meric. He recalled his own darkfire trial in the cellars under the ancient keep of Shadowbrook. "She must have been forged, changed into an ill'guard."

Nee'lahn frowned at him, not understanding.

Meric explained. "If the Black Heart can use his dark magicks to enslave an elemental, bend the pure magick and spirit to his will, then perhaps, while forging this spirit, the Dark Lord's fiery process unwound what was twisted, allowing this one's sanity to return, warped though it may be."

Nee'lahn seemed to grow paler. "If he could do it to one . . ."

"He could do it to the entire host."

Nee'lahn began to tremble. "That must not happen. I'd rather them all destroyed, than turned against the world."

Meric pulled the nyphai under his arm. "We'll not let it happen."

She leaned into his arms.

Below, Tyrus came to a halt between floors. He placed his hands on the neighboring wall, eyes drifting closed. Then he shoved, and a section of blank wall swung open—a secret door. He grabbed a torch from a sconce. "This way! It's not much farther."

The prince ducked through the threshold and closed it after them, then continued on.

Meric and Nee'lahn followed. Beyond the door was a long, narrow passage. It ran straight. They followed the flickering torch as Tyrus ran. It seemed like forever until the end was reached. The passage ended at a blank wall of granite—a dead end.

As the others gathered, Tyrus knelt and picked up something glittering from the floor. He turned with it in his hand. It was a simple circlet of gold, unadorned except for a thumb-size inset of polished black granite shaped like a small star. Tyrus' fingers shook as he held it.

Mycelle identified the discarded object. "The crown," she said in a hushed voice. "The crown of Castle Mryl."

"My father's crown," Tyrus said. He stared back at the blank wall. "He came this way."

"After the fall, he must have attempted to escape. One last desperate act." Mycelle shook her head sadly.

Tears filled the prince's eyes. He clutched the crown in one hand and moved to the blank wall and touched it with his free hand. "And he failed." Tyrus turned to Nee'lahn. "Beyond here lies the Dire Fell. You said before that you knew why this secret passage had been built. I want to know why. My father took this path, and it led to his death . . . and worse. Why should we trust your word now?"

Nee'lahn glanced to the floor.

Meric gripped her elbow. "Tell him."

"Open the door, and I'll tell you all."

Mogweed scooted nearer. "Is it safe?"

"As long as I have the lute, no harm will come."

Tyrus hesitated, then turned to the wall and placed a hand on its surface. In moments, his hand grew as black as the granite and sank into its depths. Meric watched the prince concentrate, his arm moving as if his sunken fingers were manipulating something inside the rock.

A loud crack sounded. Tyrus gasped and pulled his hand from the rock. "The lock was very old" was all he said.

Using his shoulder, Tyrus pushed, and a door opened in the wall, swinging outward. Lifting his torch, Tyrus ducked through the portal and out into the night.

The others followed, stepping from stone to soft loam.

Ahead, the dark forest of the Dire Fell opened before them. Monstrous trunks climbed high into a sky obscured by twisted and leafless branches. Massive roots, knobbed and protruding, created a woody maze of barked arches and colonnades. Beneath it all huddled an underbrush of sallow ferns and prickly bushes.

The forest lay silent. Not a bird twittered; not an insect whirred.

Tyrus turned to Nee'lahn. "What secret do you know of the Dire Fell?"

"I know all its secrets," Nee'lahn said softly. She stepped forward, staring into the forest, tears on her cheeks. Then she turned and faced the others and lifted an arm to encompass the entire wood. "This is my home. This is Lok'ai'hera."

No one spoke for several moments, too stunned.

"Your home?" Mycelle asked with stunned disbelief.

Nee'lahn nodded.

"And what of the wraiths?" Tyrus asked coldly. "The Grim?"

Nee'lahn glanced to her toes. "They are the last of my people."

Tyrus stepped toward her, murder in his eyes, but Mycelle stopped him. "Let her speak."

"Ages ago," Nee'lahn said dully, not looking up, "long before the coming of man to these shores, the forests of Lok'ai'hera spread from coast to coast. In our arrogance, we tried to reshape the Land, bringing down mountains so more trees could be seeded. But one day, a great Blight was cast on the wind. Trees began to die, twisting on themselves, leaves falling dead. The nyphai tied to these trees were not left unchanged. As the wood-song of their bonded trees was warped, so were my sister's spirits, ripping them from the flesh and changing them into the mad wraiths—the Grim."

"But why did this happen?" Mycelle asked. "Where did this Blight come from?"

Nee'lahn glanced apologetically at Meric. "In our continued arrogance, we blamed the elv'in, thinking they had betrayed us. But now I know better. It was the Land itself, warring against our attempt to thwart the natural order. We had grown too haughty and were punished for it. The disease ate away our forests until there was only this small grove here at the northern edge."

"And the rest of the blighted forest?" Mycelle asked softly. "Where did it go?"

Nee'lahn's voice choked. "We burned it. By our own hand, we torched the diseased trees, hoping to burn away the sickness before it threatened this last section of the woods. During the great conflagration, ash clouds hid the sun for many moons."

Nee'lahn wiped at her eyes. "But eventually new growth took root in the razed lands, and green shoots grew forth from ash. As this new forest took shape, the Northwall and the Southwall formed, thrusting up and encircling the Western Reaches, giving form to the Land's will that this burgeoning forest be protected and cherished. And over the centuries, the Western Reaches was born, birthed from our fires."

"And your own glen?"

"Our efforts had failed. We did not escape the Blight. Trapped beyond the wall, our trees continued to die until only the smallest grove at its heart survived. By this time, man had come to inhabit the lands of Alasea. The magick of the Chyric mages helped sustain us. This new magick held off the Blight and kept the surrounding Grim at bay. But with the fall of Chi, we became defenseless again. The Blight returned to threaten the last of our trees. The Grim grew stronger. The Northwall became home to the Dro, human allies of the Land charged with keeping the Grim from penetrating the Western Reaches. The last of my sisters joined the Dro and their kings in this cause." Nee'lahn glanced to Tyrus. "Hence, the secret passage through the wall: an unspoken pact between our two peoples."

Nee'lahn turned to the forest. "But eventually there was just my lone tree, the sole survivor. The lute was carved from its heart, and using the last dregs of Chyric magick, my bonded's spirit was moved into the lute's wood, preserving it from the Blight and allowing me to search the lands of Alasea for a cure."

Mycelle moved and touched the nyphai's shoulder. "I'm sorry, Nee'lahn."

Tyrus seemed little swayed by her story. His eyes remained dark. "And these wraiths, these blighted spirits of your people—they'll allow us just to pass?"

Nee'lahn raised the lute. "The pure woodsong will keep them at bay."

Meric stepped forward. "Like it drove away the Grim that possessed your father, Tyrus."

"The wraiths of my people cannot stand to hear the old songs, to remember the True Glen. It forces them to face memories that are too painful. They will not come near us. This I promise."

Tyrus' face remained hard as he closed the secret door. "Then let us go," he said, stepping away from the Wall and toward the forest. "Let us seek out this griffin beast and return the north to its peoples."

This earned a growled assent from Kral.

Nee'lahn stepped to the prince's side and touched his elbow. "I'm sorry for your father, Lord Tyrus. Fifteen winters ago, it was King Ry who opened this very door to allow me passage into the south. He knew terrible times were coming, and an even greater darkness than the Grim was taking root in the far north. He was a good man."

Tyrus grumbled something under his breath, but his shoulders were less tight, less angry.

Nee'lahn bowed her head.

Meric joined her, walking in silence as they entered the edge of the dark forest. "I know that was hard," he consoled her. "But in these times, secrets are as dangerous as magick. Only truth will set us free."

"Thank you, Meric," she said with a tired smile.

Distantly, a single wail echoed through the forest, full of hunger and fraught with madness.

Mogweed edged closer with Fardale at his side. His words were full of sourness and spite. "Welcome home, Nee'lahn."

Meric scowled at the bitter-tongued shape-shifter.

But Nee'lahn seemed not to have heard him. Instead, she raised her lute and began to strum a slow melody, the notes as haunted as the deep forest. She slipped ahead of the rest, leading the way into the darkness of the Dire Fell.

Book Three

BURNING SANDS

8

ATOP THE DECK OF THE *EAGLE'S FURY*, JOACH STUDIED THE SUR-
rounding lands far below. The sun beat mercilessly, and the heat
could not be escaped. Taught by the elv'in sailors, Joach wore a
bit of folded tartan atop his head, keeping the sun from his face
and neck. Standing middeck, he stared out past the rails.

The terrain below was a broken waste of sand and rock. Sun-
blasted mesas and deep canyons crisscrossed the landscape
under the keel of the mighty windship. The region, known as the
Crumbling Mounds, was where the southern end of the mountainous Teeth waned down into dry foothills before disappearing
completely into the endless sands of the Southern Wastes. Few
lived among the scrabbled cliffs and flinty scarps. At night, occasional camps could be seen by their campfires, most likely silk
caravans crossing the harsh land. The only true inhabitants were
the thick-browed giants who roamed these lands, living in deep
caves away from the sun, coming out only to hunt at night.

Behind him, Joach heard a delighted giggle. He turned. Under
the shade of the sails, the assassin Kesla was playing a game
with a tiny child. The pair knelt over a tumble of thin sticks, carefully attempting to remove each piece of wood without disturbing the others.

Kesla bent with her nose almost touching the pile, her fingers
teasing free a sliver of wood. Suddenly her hand jerked, and the
pile of sticks crumbled.

On the other side, the small child clapped her hands with delight, laughing brightly. "I win! I win!"

Kesla straightened up. "You're too good at this, little flower."

The child clambered to her feet and dove at the assassin,
giving her a firm hug.

Kesla returned the affection, squeezing her tightly, and slid smoothly to her feet, pulling the girl up into her arms. Turning, she found Joach staring at her. The slim smile on her face hardened.

With a final squeeze, Kesla lowered the child to the planks and patted her on the backside. "Sheeshon, why don't you find Hunt? Get him to fetch you a treat for winning."

The girl bobbed her head vigorously and ran off, all legs and a flag of black hair.

Wearing a frown, Joach watched her disappear down the aft hatch. Though the girl had been born among the Dre'rendi, she bore the likeness of the mer'ai: webbed fingers and toes, glassy inner eyelids. Joach was still not comfortable with a youngster of just six winters joining them on this risky venture. But the child, Sheeshon, had come aboard with Hunt, the high keel's son. The odd pair shared some strange bond, tied to magicks and old oaths. "She is my charge," Hunt had said firmly as he boarded. "I swore a blood oath to her grandfather to watch over her."

Kesla knelt back down and began to collect the sticks from the deck.

Joach stepped to her side. They had been en route toward the Southwall for almost a quarter moon, and he had spoken barely a word to her. She glanced up at him. Her deep violet eyes flashed in the bright light, cutting to his heart.

Swallowing hard, he turned away. He still had trouble reconciling the kitchen scullion named Marta with this smooth assassin. How easily his heart had been tricked.

Kesla cleared her throat. "Why don't you come try your hand at this game? It's not as easy as it appears."

"I have no time for games," he said coldly, but his legs refused to move.

"Yes, you looked so busy there standing by the rail. Besides, it's not just a game. It's a guild exercise tool, used to train apprentices in the subtle movements of fingers and hand."

Joach scowled. "An assassin's game. Then I'll have nothing to do with it."

" 'Fraid I'll win?"

He turned and found her staring up at him with one eyebrow raised coyly. He hesitated, feeling his neck growing red, then swung to the far side of the pile and collapsed to his knees. "Throw the sticks."

She collected the remaining bits of wood, tapped them into order in both her fists, then tossed them into a thick pile, like a tumbled deadfall in the deep wood. "You have to choose carefully. Pluck a twig without moving any others."

"I know how to play."

"So you've been spying on us."

Joach glanced up. She cocked her head. Her amber hair, braided into a tail, hung over one shoulder. "It's a simple enough game," he answered.

"Sometimes the simplest games are the most tricky. Pick a stick."

Joach chose carefully. A stick from the top of the pile. A deft pluck should leave those under it undisturbed. He used his left hand, since his right was missing two fingers. As he reached, concentrating, his fingers trembled. He pulled back, clenched a fist, then reached again. This time he tweezed the small sliver of wood and removed it cleanly. He sat back up. "Done!"

"Very good," Kesla whispered, and bent over the pile. She studied it with narrowed eyes. First from the right, then the left. From top to bottom. Finally, she chose a stick near the very bottom—a risky move with the other sticks piled atop it. Her fingers darted forward, almost too fast for the eye to follow, and the stick appeared in her hand. "Done," she said, placing her token near her bare knee.

Joach stared at the pile. *How had she done that?* He reached for another stick from the top and removed it without disturbing the rest.

She nodded and took another twig from the middle of the pile.

After six more exchanges—Joach plucking from the top and Kesla removing slivers from the bottom—Joach's brow was beaded with sweat. His palms were damp. She moved with such assurance, lightning quick. Joach knew he was outmatched and that Kesla had let Sheeshon win the earlier games.

His fingers reached again, trembling. He felt her eyes drilling into him. He could hear her breathing, smell her pleasant scent. *Lavender.* Distracted, he glanced up at her.

She nodded to the pile. "Your move."

Joach bit his lower lip and leaned close to the pile, beetling his brow with concentration. He reached for a twig balanced on the top. An easy target. Across the pile, Kesla made a chirping noise deep in her throat, warning him away.

Joach scowled. He would not be tricked. His fingers steadied. He reached and plucked the stick without disturbing any of the others. He held it up proudly. "Done. Now it's your—"

Kesla pointed to the pile. It trembled and collapsed in upon itself.

Joach stared, stunned, suspecting some trickery. "How . . . ?"

"Sometimes a wall is only as strong as its roof."

Joach's mouth hung open. He knew he had not only been outplayed, but outfoxed, too. She had skillfully hollowed out the support in such a way that by his lessening the weight on top, the underlying structure could no longer stand and had collapsed.

"Loser picks up the sticks," Kesla said, standing and moving to the rail.

Joach watched her step away: her slender figure, the swell of her breast, the tilt of her hip as she stood, the way the wind played with stray bits of unbraided hair. He was suddenly glad he had to pick up the sticks. He was not ready to stand, not in these tight breeches. He concentrated on his work, moving slowly, trying to find his way back to his anger for the woman—but he found he could not.

With the stray bits of wood collected, he composed himself and shoved to his feet. Perhaps it was time they finally talked—really talked.

As he moved to her side, standing close, she lifted an arm and pointed. "The dragon returns."

Joach searched the skies and saw nothing at first. Then, against the backdrop of the blinding sun, a black shape dropped out of the glare and swept toward them. It was Sy-wen and Ragnar'k.

The pair had left at dawn to search the country ahead as the ship approached the western edge of the Crumbling Mounds. They had not been expected back until dusk.

As he watched, Joach saw the dragon lurch, tumbling down toward the broken landscape. He gasped, clutching the rail. Then the wings sprang wide, catching an updraft. The plummeting fall evened out into a long swoop, shooting upward, back toward the ship. "Something's wrong," Joach said. "Fetch Hunt and Richald!"

He glanced to his side but found Kesla already gone. Turning farther, he saw her ducking through a hatch, a call for help already being sounded. Joach returned to his study of the sky.

What could be wrong?

SY-WEN HUGGED TIGHT TO THE MIGHTY DRAGON, HER FEET CLAMPED tight in the ridge folds at base of his neck. "You can do it, Ragnar'k. It's not much farther."

The dragon's voice whispered in her head, so unlike his usual brass voice. *No fear, my bonded. My heart is strong as sky and sea together.*

"I know, my great dragon." She ran her webbed fingers along his scales. "I never doubted it."

A throaty growl of pride sounded from his long neck. He swept his black wings and struck for the higher skies. To the east, the *Eagle's Fury* hung even higher. It would be a difficult climb.

Sy-wen tried to straighten in her seat, but her link to Ragnar'k meant she felt his pain. The skin of her belly and legs burned with a phantom fire. She bit back a cry. She could only imagine how much worse it must be for Ragnar'k. The attack had flayed his entire underside, searing it, blistering it.

Bonded . . . ?

"I'm fine, Ragnar'k." She gasped between clenched teeth. "You need to catch another updraft. We'll need more height to reach our roost."

I try. His muscles bunched under him, and he beat his wings, scrabbling upward, straining.

Sy-wen leaned back down over her friend. Agony spread down her arms as he fought for more sky. Tears ran down her face. "Higher, my sweet beast . . ." She tilted her head and saw a miracle.

The sleek windship dove toward them, sweeping in a graceful arc to intercept. They had been spotted, their distress noted.

"The ship comes. Hold out a little longer."

For you . . . forever.

Behind the beast's thoughts, she sensed Kast. Ever since the trials of the War of the Isles, the two had not been so separated. She sensed the man behind the beast. She pressed a palm to the dragon's scaled flank and, closing her eyes, sent out her love to both hearts buried deep—dragon and man.

Ragnar'k shifted under her. Without opening her eyes, Sy-wen sensed the approach of the ship and felt her mount prepare to alight on its aft deck. She clung tight as he tucked his wings. "Careful," she whispered.

She need not have worried. The landing was sure. She opened her eyes and saw Richald, the captain of the *Eagle's Fury*, climb up the ladder from the middeck. She raised an arm in greeting as the dragon under her collapsed to the planks.

"Ragnar'k!"

Tired . . . sleep now.

Sy-wen rolled from his back, keeping one hand on the beast to maintain the magick. His chest heaved, and the breath from his wide nostrils was ragged. Her feet slipped a bit on the deck as she edged forward. Glancing to the wet deck, she realized it was blood—from Ragnar'k. "Oh, no . . ." She swung to the elv'in captain. "I need dragon's blood—*now!*"

Richald nodded. The copper streak in his silver hair glowed like a streak of fire. "It comes." He pointed back to the ladder where Hunt climbed the rungs, a large cask balanced on his shoulder.

"Hurry!" Sy-wen urged. She felt her own breath growing short, gasping, but it was only her shared senses with the dragon.

Richald whisked over to the Bloodrider's side and relieved him of the barrel. The elv'in captain rushed to the dragon's snout.

Sy-wen maneuvered to join him, fingers trailing along the scales. "Drink, my sweet giant," she urged.

Richald struggled with the cask's lid, face growing red with the effort. Then Hunt was there, a short ax in hand. He cleaved into the lid and ripped the cracked planks with his fingers.

"How is he?" a voice asked behind Sy-wen. It was Joach. He and the girl Kesla climbed to the deck.

Sy-wen waved away his inquiry and leaned her forehead against Ragnar'k's neck. "Smell the blood. Drink."

Near her elbow, the cavernous nostrils twitched. She felt muscles strain, but he was unable to raise his head. Bending, using her shoulder, she struggled to lift his head. "H-help me!"

On either side, the group lifted the beast's snout. Hunt shoved the barrel closer. A long, snaking tongue slid out and tasted its thick contents. The others strained under the bulk. The tongue lashed out again and scooped up a large draught.

Good . . . the dragon sent to her weakly.

"Keep drinking."

"I think he's doing better," Joach said at her side.

Muscles moved under the thick scales, and Ragnar'k ducked his nose into the cracked barrel, snuffling and drinking. In moments, the group was able to step back as the dragon began supporting himself. Ragnar'k slurped at the thick blood of his brethren, strength returning as he healed.

Once the cask was empty, Ragnar'k flipped it over the far rail with a toss of his nose, trumpeting his satisfaction.

Sy-wen hugged his thick neck. "Now you can rest, my giant."

Have large . . . *big heart* . . . he echoed.

"As big as the sea and sky together."

A gentle feeling of pride and contentment overwhelmed her, coming from the dragon like the purr of a kitten on a lap.

"Sleep now," she said softly, and stepped back.

As her fingers left his scales, the transformation reversed. Scale and wing exploded outward in a spinning whirlwind of bone and claw. The sails nearby flapped, caught in the edge of the maelstrom. Then the storm of scale collapsed in on itself, winding down and around, forming at last into the large frame of man lying on the planks belly down, naked.

"Kast?" she asked tentatively. She always worried that sometime the transformation would fail to return the man she loved.

The tall Bloodrider groaned and rolled over onto his back. His belly and the tops of his legs were seared red, raw and blistered.

Sy-wen covered her mouth fearfully and dropped to her knees beside him. But as she reached out a hand, the healing of the dragon's blood continued its magick. Yellowed blisters sank. Red skin grew pink, then pale. Singed hair across his broad chest grew back into familiar landscapes. She touched his cheek as his eyes fluttered open.

"We made it?" he asked, thick-tongued and dazed.

She nodded. "Back on the *Eagle's Fury*. Do you know what happened?"

He nodded. "The more times I become Ragnar'k, the more

the dragon's memories merge with mine." He struggled to sit up but winced in pain.

Joach flipped off his own cloak and drew it over Kast's shoulder. He and Sy-wen helped lift the big man to his feet.

"He needs to rest," Joach said. "Let's get him to your cabin."

"No," Kast said with returning strength. He ran a hand over his chest. "We must prepare."

"I can tell them what we've seen," Sy-wen argued. "You rest."

Kast struggled from their grips. "I'm fine." But his next step toppled him back toward the planks. Joach caught him and held him up. Kast groaned. "Perhaps . . . a *short* rest."

As a group, they assisted Kast to his cabin belowdecks, then returned to the large galley to discuss the events of Sy-wen's journey. Everyone gathered around a long wooden table; the cook prepared a platter of fruits and cheeses and a pitcher of thin ale.

"What happened?" Hunt asked.

Sy-wen chewed on the edge of a dry biscuit. "We flew away from the sun in a direct course, following a dry riverbed as a landmark. About forty leagues from here, we spotted a wide lake stretching north and south and went down to investigate. We figured it might be a good place to restore our water supplies for the desert journey. But as we neared it, we saw it was not water that reflected the sun so invitingly, but a field of flowers whose petals were silvered blue and reflected the sun's light."

Kesla gasped. "Narcissus vine. But it doesn't grow among the Mounds, only in the deep deserts, near the Southwall."

"You've seen this flower before?"

Kesla shook her head. "No. Only a few blademen, those who hunt the deep wilds of the Blasted Fringe, have seen the vine and lived."

"What sort of plant is it?" Hunt asked.

The assassin hesitated. "Some say it was born from the blood of the ghouls that once haunted the ruins of Tular. As I said before, the vine usually grows only along the sandstone cliffs of the Southwall. Rootless, it's able to crawl along the wall's length, hunting its prey. All who approach too near the Southwall must be wary of its path. A single bloom by itself is harmless, but the vine, as it stretches across the sand or drapes along the sandstone cliffs of the Southwall, will produce hundreds, thousands, of palm-sized blossoms. Each is able to collect the sun's heat in its shiny petals and reflect it back on an enemy. Multiply this by a thousand and it can produce a blaze as hot as the sun itself, capable of burning a man down to a smoking skeleton in mere heartbeats." She gaped at Sy-wen. "You were lucky to have survived."

"We almost didn't. But Ragnar'k's scales are as hard as stone. He shielded me and took the brunt of the attack on his belly. Yet even his scales could not protect him from the flames."

"So what are we to do?" Richald asked. "I can't take the *Eagle's Fury* across there."

"We'll have to go around it," Kesla said. "It'll delay us reaching Alcazar, but it's better than burning to cinders."

"Time runs short already," Joach mumbled, then turned to Kesla. "How many days until the next tithing of children is demanded by the demons of Tular?"

Kesla frowned. "Half a moon."

"So any delays could lead to more deaths," Joach said. "How about if we just crossed the field at night? After the sun has set?"

"It won't help. At sunset, the petals close, storing the day's sunlight. The vine uses this stored heat to hunt prey at night. I've seen their lights from far across the desert—flashes along the wall as the vine attacked mice and lizards. Night is no haven from the narcissus."

Everyone grew quiet.

"Then we go around," Richald said. "Find another way to reach Alcazar."

Sy-wen sighed. "It'll be a long way. Even Ragnar'k could not see where the fields ended. It is a solid barrier for endless leagues." She turned back to Kesla, searching for some other answer. "There must be a weakness. When the vines attack at night, is their heat as intense?"

"I . . . I'm not sure. But I've heard tales that once a bloom casts its heat, it won't be able to renew until the next dawn."

Sy-wen leaned back in her chair, thinking. "So it can only shoot one burning volley; then it's harmless."

Kesla nodded. "That's according to old stories. But I'm not sure if it's true or not. So little is known about the narcissus."

Hunt stood up. "So either we add days to our journey, searching for a break in the weed, or we take our chances on a nighttime flight across the fields."

Richald frowned. "I will not risk my ship."

Sy-wen stared across at the elv'in lord. "You may not have to."

As THE SUN SET, GRESHYM SHAMBLED OUT OF THE LAST CANYON and into the empty sands. He was wrapped from head to toe in flows of linen and rough-spun cotton. As darkness spread and stars began to shine, Greshym hardly noticed the change in heat or the drop in light. He had a small spell cast around his body, keeping him cool and his sight keen. As he walked, he clutched his staff of petrified wood in his left hand. The magick trapped in its crystalline structure throbbed dully with his own pulse. Its energy was weak.

Free of the canyons, Greshym glanced skyward, calculating his bearings. He still had far to go.

Rocks skittered down a slope to his right. Slowing to a stop, Greshym cocked his head, extending his senses. It was Rukh returning. The stump gnome hopped down a slope of boulders, his split hooves moving with goatlike skill. At the bottom, he fell to his knees before Greshym.

"M-master . . ."

"Did you do as I asked?"

"Y-yes, Master." Rukh's porcine face groveled in the rough sand. He held up his claws, dripping with blood. Clenched in each grip was a bloody heart.

"The children of the caravan leader?"

"Yes."

The darkmage noted the dried blood around the creature's fanged muzzle. "You've fed?"

Rukh ground his face into the sand at the tone of reprimand. "Hungry . . . much hungry."

Greshym lifted his staff threateningly, then lowered it back to the sand with a sigh. He could not blame the gnome. The journey through the Crumbling Mounds had been a long one, and they still had far to go.

Glancing to the stars, he wished he could have used his

magick to bring himself directly to his target, but he dared not. When he had transported from his cave in the Stone Forest, he had sensed the vortex of energies swirling near the Southwall and knew it best to keep his magick to a whisper in its shadow. He could not risk any eyes turning in his direction.

So he had untied his magick and brought himself and his servant into the dry wastes of the neighboring Mounds. He had spent the past half moon hiking and climbing through this sunseared terrain, using the barest touches of magick to bring strength to his decrepit body and to draw water up from the rocks. Then, two days ago, he had run into an even worse challenge than the stubborn landscape—a field of deadly narcissus blooms blocking his way. Casting out his senses, he was able to divine that the infernal weed circled the entire region, a barrier protecting the foulness germinating at its heart. Determined not to turn back, he was forced to use more magick to cloak Rukh and himself so they could pass the weed unharmed. It had been a risk to cast such a strong spell, but he had no other choice—not if his gambit was to succeed.

Luckily, nothing seemed to notice his flare of magick. In fact, shortly after passing the weed, Greshym encountered a caravan, a mix of silk traders and ragged families carrying all they owned on their backs. The group had been attempting to flee the Wastes, but they had been turned back by the narcissus. Greshym had joined them, gladly accepting their hospitality and water, preserving his waning magick. He traveled in comfort with the group while Rukh tracked the caravan from a league away.

Then earlier this afternoon, with the open desert of the Wastes in sight, Greshym had cast the caravan into a sleep spell. He had no further use for his new companions. Upon leaving, he ordered Rukh to slay them and collect the hearts of the leader's two girl children. Both were virgins, untouched, rich in the power that surges just before their first bleed.

"Enough groveling, Rukh. Hold the hearts higher for me."

The beast's long ears twitched in relief. He rose from the sands, sitting back on his heels, and held out the pair of hearts at arm's length.

Greshym reached out with the heel of his staff, touching one of the hearts, then the other. With its touch, the two lumps of flesh began to beat anew, throbbing, squirting blood into the sands. Rising from the twin hearts, a distant wail could be heard. The spirits still trapped in the hearts cried for release.

"Patience, my two little ones . . . Patience."

Greshym lowered his staff to the sand and leaned on it as he bent over the two hearts. He brought his lips to the throbbing bits of muscle and kissed them gently, inhaling as he did so. He felt their spirits and energy flow into him. Their magick of burgeoning womanhood drew into him, becoming part of him as tiny screams of horror filled his ears.

He straightened, feeling vastly renewed and invigorated.

In the claws of the stump gnome, the two hearts were now just dried and wrinkled chunks of meat, like grapes gone to raisins in the sun. Greshym grinned and wiped the blood from his lips. "That was refreshing," he whispered contentedly.

He patted the leathery skull of his servant as he thumped on past with his staff in hand. Suffused with fresh magick, he knew nothing could stop him from reaching his destination.

Alcazar, the desert guild of the assassins.

In its tunneled and sculpted halls, he would lay the trap for his prey. As he moved into the desert, he spoke to the stars and empty sands. "I'll be waiting for you, Joach."

JOACH STOOD AT THE BOWSPRIT OF THE *EAGLE'S FURY.* HE SHIVERED and wrapped his cloak tighter around his shoulders, unable to escape an uneasy edginess. He glanced behind as if expecting an enemy to attack. No one was there.

In the rigging, elv'in sailors climbed the masts and worked the sails. Richald was a figure in silver on the stern deck, hands in the air, drawing on the magick of the winds, ready to propel them swiftly across the deadly fields. Already stray gusts and wild flurries spat around the ship as energies gathered.

Kesla popped her head by the ladder. "Sy-wen and Kast are ready. Did you want to see them off?"

He nodded, unable to shake off his misgivings. Joach had been blessed with the gift of prophetic dreams, and though he was awake, he could not dismiss his growing sense of catastrophe.

He crossed to the ladder and clambered down. On the middeck, Sy-wen and Kast held each other's hands. The Bloodrider looked fully healed and rested. He would need to be. Sy-wen leaned on the man's arm. The two would risk much to bring the ship swiftly over the fields of burning flowers.

As Joach stepped up to them, he heard Kast grumble, "The winds smell bad, like smoke in the air."

Joach's eyes narrowed. Was the large man feeling the same misgivings he had felt? "It's not too late to change course," he offered. "We could still circle around the field."

Sy-wen shook her head. "No. The vine's field extends to the northern and southern horizons. There will be no way around the vine, only through it."

Kast hugged the mer'ai woman closer to his side. "She's right. We must attempt this."

Joach reached out and shook the larger man's hand. "Be careful."

"And *swift*," Kesla added at Joach's side.

"Ragnar'k has never failed me," Sy-wen answered them, then glanced up into Kast's eyes. "Not when fueled with two strong hearts."

The Bloodrider leaned down and kissed her fully on the mouth, passionately. Arms reached to pull each other tight. Sy-wen was lifted off her feet.

Joach glanced away, giving them a moment of privacy.

Then Richald called from the stern deck. "The winds come! We must be off!" The sails overhead snapped with more vigor.

Sy-wen and Kast broke their embrace, fire still in their eyes. "Are you ready?" she asked the tall Bloodrider.

He nodded.

Together, they moved to the starboard rail. The landscape below was limned in silver from the moon and stars.

"Safe journey," Kesla whispered.

Kast nodded and shrugged out of his robe, standing naked. With a nod to Joach, he picked up Sy-wen in his arms again and toppled over the rail.

Joach leaned and watched them tumble through the air. "They're off!"

In response, the ship lurched forward as a fierce gust swelled the sails and sped the ship toward the fields. Kesla, off guard, slid into Joach's side. He caught her under an arm and held her steady. Together the two searched below the keel of the windship.

Kast and Sy-wen were gone.

SY-WEN CLUTCHED KAST TIGHT AS THEY PLUMMETED THROUGH THE darkness toward the broken terrain below. They needed as much momentum as possible for their mission to succeed. Her green hair whipped like sea snakes about her head.

"Now, Sy-wen!" Kast yelled. His lips nuzzled her ear, but the wind almost ripped the words away. Still, she could hear his thrill and excitement, a Bloodrider at heart.

She shifted her fingers from his shoulder to his neck, then up to his cheek. As her skin met his tattooed flesh, her fingertips warmed. Kast stiffened under her, arms squeezing tight; then she spoke the words. "I have need of you."

With these words, the ancient magick ignited. The world vanished around her into a whirlwind of roaring. Clouds of magick burst forth. Scaled flesh spread apart her legs and slowed her fall, taking her weight. She squeezed her thighs, holding tight. In another heartbeat, Sy-wen was no longer falling, but riding the back of the great black dragon, sweeping at amazing speeds.

Ragnar'k trumpeted his rebirth with an echoing cry. *Bonded!*

Despite the tension, Sy-wen smiled. She heard the same excitement in the dragon's voice as she had in Kast's words a moment ago.

"Do not slow. We must forge a path through the burning blooms," Sy-wen instructed, then silently added additional directions to her mount.

Though he remained quiet, she sensed his confusion.

"At night, the weed can only shoot at us once. We must get the flowers to unleash their fury upon us, opening a safe passage for the ship that follows."

Ragnar'k swept toward the fields, using the momentum of their plummeting fall to increase his speed. *Danger. Risk to bonded.*

"I know, my brave heart. But this time we will not be caught by surprise. We *know* the danger. We must be swift, cunning. You must fly better than you've ever flown before!"

The equivalent of a dragon chuckle filled her mind. *Bonded has heart as big as dragon!*

Sy-wen thumped the side of his neck. "It's not bravery! I just know my dragon! I trust *his* heart and wings!"

Dragon laughter trailed behind them as he dove steeply toward the blooms, spinning in a curving arc.

Sy-wen leaned over his neck, hugging him tight. She felt the flare of wind under wing, sensed the dizzying spin of the landscape below. Instead of terror, she felt delight, sharing not only her dragon's thrill but that of the man buried deeper, all three spirits merging in this common goal.

As the dragon roared, Sy-wen added her own voice, yelling her challenge into the wind.

FROM THE BOW RAIL, JOACH WATCHED THE VINE'S FIERY ATTACK begin. A quarter league away, the night was shattered by spears of brilliance blasting skyward. Some shot straight up, others striking at angles from the side. The lances of searing energy were so bright it hurt to stare at them directly. "Can you see the dragon?" he asked, grimacing.

Kesla stood at his side, a spyglass fixed to her right eye. "I . . . I'm not sure. I spotted a flicker of movement, a spark of reflection, but it moved faster than I could follow."

"It must be them," Joach said.

"I'd guess so, too." She lowered the spyglass. "The vine is certainly hunting something."

As Joach watched, the sprout of bright spears traced farther away, deeper into the wide valley. Closer, the near edge of the field died back to dark, the blooms spent by their attack upon the dragon.

Joach half turned, lifting an arm. "Now, Richald! Steer a straight course!"

Both the elv'in lord and Hunt stood ready at the stern. The Bloodrider raised a hand in acknowledgment, but Richald showed no sign of hearing his call. The elv'in lord stood stiff, his head thrown back, cascades of crackling energy coursing over his body, his mind lost to the winds.

Just as Joach wondered if he had been heard, the gales grew worse around the ship. Overhead, the rigging and ropes groaned, strained by the sails stretching even farther. The ship sped faster, its bow rising for a moment, then settling into an even flight.

Turning, Joach gripped the bow rail. Below, the ship's keel crested over the deadly fields. He waited, holding his breath. Were they right? Had the blooms emptied their energies pursuing the dragon? Was it safe to cross?

He glanced up. The fiery display drifted even farther away. The dragon still fled, a lightning rod for the field's energy, hopefully leaving a swath through which they could fly. Joach stared back down, leaning far over the rail.

The fields beneath the ship remained dark.

He let out a long sigh, allowing hope to grow.

"Oh, no . . ." Kesla said at his side.

He straightened back up.

"Look," Kesla said. She pointed to either side of the ship. In the distance, a weak glow flowed toward their position—from both the north and the south.

"What is it?"

Kesla passed him the spyglass. Joach pointed it toward the strange sight. Magnified, the continuous glow broke into a thousand gleaming snakes winding under the leaves and flowers, converging toward them.

"The field is one continuous vine," Kesla said. "Its stalks are sucking energy from blooms elsewhere, siphoning power to fill this void, like roots moving water up a trunk."

"Mother above . . ." Joach's stomach tightened.

"Once it reaches here, the blooms will be able to attack again. We'll be snared."

Joach dropped the spyglass and swung around. By now, they were thick in the fields. It was too late to swing the ship and retreat.

Turning back forward, Joach stared. Distantly, across the fields, the fiery display slowly died away. Sy-wen and Ragnar'k must have reached the far side. Joach estimated the distance. *At least another two leagues.* He glanced north and south. The glow sped rapidly toward their position.

He shook his head. They would not make it in time.

Joach pushed away from the rails.

"Where are you going?" Kesla yelled.

"To warn Richald! We need more speed!" Joach fought to

keep his footing in the gale blowing from the stern. He leaned into the wind.

"Let me!" Kesla argued. She danced from the rail, as if the wind didn't exist, and sped forward, racing sure-footed across the rocking deck. Reaching the ladder to the middeck, she waved him back to the bow rail. "Keep a watch!" Then she vanished down the ladder.

In a heartbeat, Joach spotted her again, running across the middeck toward the raised stern. He stared dumstruck after her. The girl was not only quick-limbed, but she had the balance of a jungle cat. Relenting, Joach allowed himself to be blown back to his position at the bow rail.

To either side, the snakes of bright energy twisted and slithered toward them. A single bloom shot a spear of light off the starboard side. It angled toward them, splashing against the ship's side. Though bright, the one flower did not have enough power to burn—but soon there would be more. As the glow swept under the ship's keel, new pillars of light blasted into the skies on both sides, creating a forest of blazing trunks.

As Joach watched, more and more blooms ignited.

SY-WEN GUIDED HER DRAGON TO A FLAT-TOPPED PINNACLE OF SANDstone. Ragnar'k settled to the rocky perch, with a heaving sigh from his chest.

As he dug in his claws, Sy-wen rubbed her right arm, wincing, but the stinging burn would not subside. She glanced to the dragon's wing. Ragnar'k held it slightly out to the side, like a gull with a wound or a broken bone. The edge still smoked. The reek of burned dragon scale filled the night.

Thankfully it had been only a glancing strike. They had been lucky to escape with so little damage. The vine had fought fiercely, stabbing at them, chasing them to and fro across the sky. As they had flown, the vine had even seemed to grow wise to their evasive tactics, anticipating their moves. Luckily, they had reached the field's end before the vine had grown too skilled at hunting dragons.

Ship comes, Ragnar'k said.

Sy-wen twisted in her seat. Across the field, she spotted the *Eagle's Fury* in the skies. The slower ship was under attack.

"Sweet Mother . . ."

Lances of light streaked across the skies. As she watched, a sail caught flame and flared like an oiled torch.

"We must go help them," Sy-wen said.

Cannot, my bonded. Ragnar'k tried to extend his wing. She felt the agony shoot up her own arm. *Too far . . .*

Sy-wen gasped with the pain. The burning strike had been worse than she had initially thought.

I have failed you, my bonded. The agony in his heart was worse than his wing.

She leaned down and rubbed his neck. "Never, my sweet dragon. Never." She stared out at the beleaguered ship, a flaming cloud in the night sky, and prayed for them. It was all she could do.

As THE *EAGLE'S FURY* FOUNDERED ABOVE THE BLAZING FLOWERS, Joach raced to where the others were gathered atop the stern deck. Overhead, the burning foresail was cut free, and it flapped away. In the rigging, a chain of elv'in sailors passed buckets, hand to hand, to drench ropes and stanch the smoldering of the foremast.

Joach climbed the stern ladder. Smoke began to rise all around the ship. Its planked sides were etched and burned from swiping passes of the fiery lances. Pulling himself up, Joach called to Hunt and Richald. "We need more height! We need to keep the keel between us and the blooms!"

"Richald is trying," Hunt said. "But he is tied to the ship; each strike weakens him."

As Joach neared, he heard the elv'in lord groan, his face a mask of pain. Kesla hovered around the tall figure. "We have to find a way to help him."

Joach searched the skies for an answer, wishing his sister were here. They needed Elena's magick. Coldfire or wit'ch fire— either would be welcome now. Anything to fight this weed!

A ripping explosion sounded behind him. The ship's deck bucked, tossing him to the planks. Joach rolled around. Sprouting from the middle of the ship, a spear of light shot into the sky, thrusting right through the belly of the ship. Bits of burning planks flew high, spinning away. The mainsail burst into flame.

A pair of the elv'in sailors, caught in the blaze, tumbled from the rigging and over the ship's side. Another was incinerated where he stood on the deck, his seared bones standing for a moment, then toppling down.

As quickly as it had struck, the spear blinked off. The blooms that had generated the intense spike had exhausted their energy. But for how long? The vine was growing cunning, learning to coordinate its efforts.

"Joach! Help me!"

Half blind from the radiance, Joach turned and saw Kesla struggling to hold Richald up. The elv'in's face was lined with horror and agony. "My ship . . ."

Hunt was already on his feet. "Help the captain. The fires need to be doused before they spread!" The Bloodrider vaulted over the rail to the middeck. He joined the dwindling crew of sailors in putting out these new flames.

Joach half crawled over to Richald and Kesla. Under him, the ship lurched, drifting down toward the deadly fields. Joach grabbed the elv'in lord's other shoulder. "You must keep fighting!" he urged. "Don't give up!"

"The *Fury* . . . I can't . . ."

Joach shouldered the man to his feet with Kesla's help. "Yes, you can. Or are you all *wind* and no substance? Prove your worth, prince of the Blood!"

Richald's eyes flicked toward Joach. A flash of anger flared past the hopeless pain.

"You still have a ship! You still have sails! You're supposed to be the heart of this vessel. Act like it, Richald! Meric wouldn't give up like this and weep like a child!"

Anger changed to prideful fury. The man shook free of Joach's grip and shoved Kesla away. Richald glared at Joach, then turned his eyes to the skies. He lifted his arms, and elemental magick bloomed in crackling spurts along his raised limbs.

The gales resumed. The foundering ship pushed forward, edging upward again. Drawn by its movement, new flares of light attacked. Smoke and flames encircled the ship.

Off the port side, Joach saw several spears joining together, attempting to fuse into another dread spike. The ship could not take a second such coordinated attack. Something had to be done. He leaned over the rail as wind whipped his lank red hair. He held the locks from his eyes—then snapped upright, a sudden idea coming to him.

Why hadn't he thought of this earlier?

He swung back to the elv'in lord. "Richald! We're pointing the wind the wrong way! Drive it into the weeds! Lash the flowers with your gale. Don't let them hone in on the *Fury*!"

Richald's eyes slowly focused from the sky back to Joach.

Kesla straightened. "Sweet Mother, he's right! Caught in the winds, the flowers won't be able to focus!"

Richald slowly nodded, too strained to speak. Overhead, the remaining few sails began to sag as some wind was stolen from them and diverted.

Joach returned to his watch by the port rail. The river of winds split, and a whirling tributary swept down upon the vine. As the winds shook petals and rattled stalks, the beams of fiery light were blown out like candles. Nearby, the growing spike of coordinated energy was driven into disarray.

"It's working!" Kesla yelled. "They can't aim!"

Joach leaned and searched forward. They were only a quarter league from the end of the fields. Around them, the burning lances of light wobbled and spat sporadically. With luck, they might make it.

Hunt yelled from the middeck, his voice booming with command. "Get back, everyone! Its no use! She's lost!"

Joach had concentrated so fully on the fields that he had forgotten about the more immediate risk. He turned and saw the main mast explode into a flaming torch, catching another sail in its blaze. Other flames raced along ropes and rigging. Elv'in sailors leaped from their perches to the deck.

Hunt suddenly appeared, flying up the ladder to join them. He carried the girl Sheeshon in his arms. His face was blackened with smears of soot. "The fire's in the lower holds. It's burning from the inside out. The ship is doomed."

With his words, the winds ebbed. Behind them, Richald sagged, lowering his arms. "We can't win."

Joach strode up to the elv'in prince and struck him hard across the cheek. "Don't ever say that!"

Richald's eyes flew wide. He touched his bloodied lip as rage flared bright. "No one strikes—"

"Fly this ship, Richald!" Joach screamed. "As long as we live, there's always hope! You'll drive this ship until it burns out from under you."

Richald stepped toward Joach.

"Enough!" Kesla said, stepping between them. "Use your anger to fuel the winds! We're almost through the fields. The open sands lie not much further."

"I have only the one sail."

"Then you must prove your skills, elv'in," Kesla said.

Richald stared at her, then set his face to stone. He lifted his arms, and the winds grew sharp again. "We'll never reach the sands."

"What does it hurt to try?" she challenged.

Around them, smoke billowed as the ship limped forward. The heat from the growing fires became a roaring hearth. Occasional lances of light chased after them, but the straggling winds kept the vine cowed.

No one spoke. Everyone held their breaths, clinging to handholds.

Joach searched beyond the rail, an arm across his nose and mouth, choking. Below the ship, the smoke parted. Under the keel, a broken terrain of dark canyons and sand-swept mesas appeared. He leaned closer, blinking the smoke and tears from his eyes.

No vines, no flowers!

Joach spun around, yelling, "We're clear of the fields!"

Faces turned in his direction, a glimmer of hope—then an explosion blasted. A middeck hatch blew high into the air. Flames licked upward from the ship's bowel, roaring like a netherworld demon. Under Joach's feet, the entire ship shook and began to list. He grabbed the rail as the ship rolled.

Behind him, he heard Kesla call out. "Don't falter, Richald."

"Too weak . . ." the elv'in captain gasped.

The ship tilted, canting at a steep angle. Joach's legs went out from under him. He hugged the rail with both arms.

"Hang on!" Kesla screamed.

The *Eagle's Fury* slipped into a steep dive, a flaming stone crashing from the skies.

9

It took until dawn for Sy-wen to reach the wreck of the *Eagle's Fury*. Her mount's injured wing had limited their flights to short, feeble hops. Ragnar'k struggled for longer jaunts, but Sy-wen forced the dragon to proceed slowly. Sharing his spirit, she sensed his pain. Her right arm felt as if it had been thrust into fire, and when in flight, the agony almost overwhelmed her. Despite their injuries, they worked themselves across the scrabbled landscape of the Crumbling Mounds, following the path where the flaming ship had passed overhead.

As the sun crested the eastern horizon, Sy-wen and Ragnar'k finally reached the open sands and dunes of the great Southern Wastes. Sy-wen hung limp atop her mount—weak and thirsty. A thick column of smoke marked their goal.

Without being told, Ragnar'k shoved off the spur of rock that he had lighted upon and took wing, gliding low over the tall dunes. Sy-wen leaned on his neck and stared at the desert below. *Like a great ocean of sand,* she thought dully. It seemed endless, welling up into smooth waves, its constancy interrupted only by occasional rocky shoals.

As she clung to her mount, Ragnar'k crested over a tall dune and swept up in a wide circle. *Bonded . . . the ship . . .*

Sy-wen straightened. A gouged trail of destruction led forward. Dunes lay blasted; hunks of wood flanked the path; a broken mast stood impaled in a shallow slope of sand.

Ragnar'k rose higher on a thermal.

*   In a deep valley ahead, Sy-wen spotted the bulk of the ship. It lay beached up against a dune, its hull cracked. Small fires still glowed and smoldered from its broken belly. Tiny figures moved

190

around and over the husk of the ship. Rescued crates and supplies stood piled off to one side.

"Some still live," Sy-wen said, pointing an arm. She silently directed her mount to land.

Ragnar'k circled the smoky column and spiraled to the sand.

Eyes watched them land. As the dragon settled with a loud huff of relief, figures moved toward them. Sy-wen spotted Joach and the Bloodrider Hunt. She slid from her seat and lifted an arm.

Joach approached, his clothes torn, a large bruise on his cheek. "You survived," he said, exhaustion heavy in his voice.

She nodded. "But Ragnar'k is wounded. He'll need a draught of dragon's blood to heal. I don't think he can fly any farther."

Hunt shook his head. The large man was covered from crown to foot with soot. "I'm sorry. The casks were burned or shattered. The little that survived was used to help those injured by the crash. There's not a drop left."

Sy-wen groaned and turned, still resting a hand on the dragon. "We'll manage."

Ragnar'k swung his head around and snuffled at her hair. *Strong heart . . . will heal.*

"I know you will," she said, "but perhaps you should sleep. We can mend the wounds easier as Kast."

Man . . . not as big heart. He pouted.

She smiled tiredly. "But he has smaller wings."

Ragnar'k nuzzled her again, sending a silent but reluctant consent. She hugged him and willed him her love and thanks, then stepped back. The ancient spell reversed, and scale and claw wound back down to bare legs and arms.

As Kast stumbled forward out of the spell, he clutched his arm to his chest. His forearm was seared and blistered, but he kept his face stoic. "How many survived?" he asked, ignoring his own injury.

Joach offered the naked man his cloak, torn and soot-stained. As Kast tied it around his waist, Joach answered his question. "Besides us, not many." He pointed to the piled supplies. "The girl Sheeshon and the assassin Kesla were bruised and shaken up, but they're doing well."

Sy-wen spotted the young woman rocking the girl in her lap.

Joach continued. "Richald survived the crash, but he shattered his leg and now won't speak. He keeps with the other elv'in. More than his broken leg, I think it's the loss of his ship that has truly crippled him."

"What of his crew?" Kast asked.

"Three survived. Four died in the crash."

Kast surveyed the broken and smoldering wreck. "What now?"

"We continue on foot. Kesla says Alcazar lies about seven leagues from here—a hard trek but manageable. This day, we'll gather what we can, then rest. After the sun goes down, we'll load a litter and travel by night."

Sy-wen stared up at the pillar of smoke. "Will it be safe until then? Eyes—not all of them friendly, I imagine—are sure to see this and investigate."

Kesla suddenly appeared at her elbow, startling Sy-wen. The assassin moved so silently. Turning, Sy-wen saw that not a single footstep marred the smooth sand.

Kesla answered her question. "Sy-wen is correct. It's not safe. Not only will eyes see the smoke, but the sands of the Wastes hide even worse beasts. They'll be attracted to the blood. We should build a pyre and burn the bodies. Leave no trail and leave as soon as possible."

Joach shook his head. "We have no water. We're all exhausted. It'll be cooler to walk the night."

"And more deadly," Kesla argued sternly.

Sy-wen watched Kesla and Joach stare each other down. Clearly the friction between them was piqued by more than just their current situation.

Kast spoke up. "I think we should heed Kesla's guidance. She knows the Wastes better than any of us. These are her homelands."

"I agree," Sy-wen said.

Joach stared a moment longer, then turned on a heel. "Fine. I'll let the elv'in know."

Kesla stared at his back, then sighed. "I should get Sheeshon ready."

"I'll help you," Hunt said, following after her.

Alone, Sy-wen turned to Kast. She stared up at him with a weary smile, glad to have him back at her side. "How's your arm?"

"I'll live."

"You'd better." She leaned into him, careful of his burns.

He put his good arm around her and pulled her tight. "We've a long journey ahead of us. Perhaps we should find a bit of shade and rest while we can."

She trailed a finger down his chest. "Rest?"

Kast stared down into her eyes. "Did you have something else in mind?"

She reached up with her lips and spoke huskily. "I have need of you."

A ghost of a smile shadowed his face as he leaned down to meet her mouth—but before their lips could touch, a scream arose from near the shipwreck.

GUILDMASTER BELGAN KNELT WITH THE SHAMAN IN THE DARKENED private courtyard. Though the morning sun climbed the blue sky, it had yet to rise above the heights of Alcazar to shine down into the tall, narrow yard. In shadows, the pair crouched beside the tiled mouth of a small well. Around them, flowering bushes dotted the small garden amid bits of sandstone statuary.

Atop the red paving stones, Shaman Parthus tossed a set of bleached bones: tiny vertebrae, knobbed knuckles, lizard skulls, and other bits of bird bones. The bones danced and clattered, then settled to a scattered pattern. The shaman's head cocked as he studied the bits of white bone against the red stone.

Belgan brushed back his white hair and tried to peer at the bones himself, but they made no sense. He did not have the gift. "What does it show?"

Parthus held up a hand that was just withered bones itself, wrapped in sun-cured leather. The old shaman leaned and sniffed at the scrying bones, eyeing the pattern with one eye then the other, like a bird studying an intriguing beetle. His long nose and sharp features added to the hawkish image.

Belgan sat back on his heels, waiting impatiently. Both men were wrapped in red desert cloaks, their hoods tossed back—but it was their only common feature. Where the shaman was bald, all bones and leather, Belgan was large boned, pale of skin, with long, flowing white hair. Belgan had been nicknamed the "Ghost of Alcazar," both for his skill at moving unseen and for his pale form.

Though so dissimilar in appearance, the two men shared a common purpose. For the past two moons, the pair had come each morning to toss the bones, to search for some sign of hope. In only ten days, the next tithing would be demanded. More children would be led to their doom.

As the master of the Assassins' Guild, Belgan had accepted the charge to free the Wastes of the corruption that now roosted in Tular. He, in turn, had put the fates of the desert people into the small hands of a young girl, an assassin trained in the arts of stealth—one of his best students. Before she left, her blood had been dribbled on the bones, allowing them to track her progress. For the past two moons, the shaman had discerned vague clues to her whereabouts. Then, half a moon ago, the bones went silent, no sign nor clue, as if the girl had vanished completely from the lands.

Belgan wrung his hands together. As each morning passed with no further word, his hopes for success dimmed. If there were no answers by tomorrow, Belgan would have to send word to the tribes to gather their children, to again choose who would live and who would die. They had no other option. The demand for blood would have to be answered.

Across the tossed bones, the shaman's eyes narrowed. His head jerked up. "I see her."

Belgan froze, afraid he had heard him wrong.

Parthus growled. "She is near. Already in the sands."

"Kesla? Are you sure?"

He nodded.

Belgan gasped with relief. The girl had made it back to the Wastes! "Thank the Sweet Mother. I knew she was a strong one."

The shaman held up a hand of warning. "Before you rejoice. The bones also warn of a danger surrounding her."

"What danger?"

"The bones are not clear. Blood and smoke . . . teeth and torn flesh."

"Will she survive? Will she make it back here?"

Parthus frowned. He reached and shifted the slivered jawbone of a desert rat. "Not even the bones can answer that."

UNDER THE MAKESHIFT AWNING, KESLA HELD UP A RUMPLED blanket as a scream echoed over the sands. It was a child's cry of terror, coming from the far side of the smoldering wreck.

Hunt, a few steps away, called out, "Sheeshon!"

Kesla dropped the blanket and ran toward the ship. "I left the child there, napping."

Hunt followed. Even with his longer legs, she kept well ahead of him, moving swiftly across the sand. The pair raced around the broken stern of the wreck. Others were converging from all around.

First to round the hull, Kesla immediately saw the danger. The elv'in, in respect for their dead, had built a small shelter on the leeward side of the ship. It shadowed the four dead bodies from the blistering sun.

As she watched, one of the bodies was dragged from the shelter and drawn under the sand. The thief could be seen by its thin white fin and muscled tail protruding from the sand. It thrashed, throwing sand high into the air. Thin elv'in bones cracked, and the body disappeared along with the predator into the cooler depths of the sand. All that remained was a bloody stain.

Another scream arose.

"There she is!" Hunt said, coming around the ship and pointing.

Sheeshon stood atop a spit of sandstone, balanced precariously, a look of terror on her tiny face.

Hunt moved toward her as others rushed up behind them.

"No," Kesla said, pulling him back by an arm, holding the others in place, too. "Don't move."

Hunt began to protest, but a pair of fins rose ominously from the sand and circled the rock, sweeping up and around the bank of a dune.

"Sand sharks," Kesla said. "They're drawn by the blood of the dead."

Sheeshon had spotted them by now. She reached her arms out, pleadingly, tears running down her face. "I need you!" she called out, eyes staring straight at Hunt.

The tall Bloodrider suddenly stiffened beside Kesla and broke her grip. He plodded toward the stranded girl.

"No!" Kesla yelled. "Stand still! Besides blood, they're attracted by movement!"

Hunt seemed deaf and continued onward.

"It's the spell," Sy-wen said. "Between mer'ai and Bloodrider. He's enthralled."

Kast whipped off his cloak, naked again, and rushed forward. He tossed the wrap over Hunt's head, breaking contact between the girl and the tall Bloodrider. Hunt sagged as if a string had been cut between him and the girl. Confused, he tried to rip away the cloak, but Kast restrained him. "Keep your tattoo covered, Hunt."

Nodding his understanding, Hunt slid the cloak down to his shoulders and wore it as a scarf over the tattoo around his neck.

"No one move!" Kesla ordered.

Other fins surfaced, over a dozen.

At the shelter, two more elv'in bodies were dragged under the sands. Another was torn between two of the predators fighting for meat. Bloody gobbets were tossed, only to be consumed by smaller sharks darting up and snagging the bits with a flash of serrated white teeth.

"Will they attack us?" Joach asked.

"They're mostly scavengers. They seldom attack the living. But in a feeding frenzy, they've been known to attack anything that moves. Just stand still. They should leave once they've fed."

Kesla sensed the tension in the others. It was difficult to stand frozen with the girl sobbing and crying for help. But they had no choice. To move would draw the attention of the bloody jaws under the sand.

As they waited, the sun climbed the sky.

With the bodies now devoured and gone, the fins sank back into the sands with swishes of powerful tails until there was only one remaining. Kesla watched the last fin through narrowed eyes. It was the tallest of the group—the bull shark. It led and herded the others. Its fin circled the bloody sand, clearly scenting for any traces of remaining meat. It swept up the far dune bank, sinking away, then was gone.

She allowed the breath trapped in her chest to slowly escape. They had survived.

The child began to clamber off the stone. Hunt moved toward her.

Then Kesla saw a ripple in the bank of sand, something drifting just under the surface. *Hiding.*

"No!" she yelled. "Get back!"

But she was too late. The small girl had reached the sand and ran toward the tall Bloodrider, arms raised to be picked up.

Neither noticed the tall fin rise again from the sand and surge toward them.

The others screamed warnings, too.

Turning, Hunt finally recognized the approaching danger. He darted forward and snatched up the girl, diving to the side as the fin swept up and passed by him, missing his heels by a hairbreadth. Cut off from both the spit of sandstone and the ship, he twisted around and struggled to climb the neighboring dune. But the loose sand fought him. The fin of the bull shark swept toward him in pursuit.

Other fins arose, hungry, circling, cutting off any means of rescue.

Kesla jerked Joach around. "The nightglass dagger! Give it to me!"

Joach's brows knit suspiciously.

"It's the only thing to fight sand beasts. Trust me!"

Joach hesitated—then a scream arose from Sheeshon. He yanked the dagger from its sheath under his cloak and thrust it at her. She grabbed the cold handle, wrapping fingers around the coiled basilisk.

Kesla glanced to the group, her voice as sharp as the blade's edge. "No one move until I tell you!" She ran forward as even more fins rose from the depths, cutting and crisscrossing each other in a hunting pattern. Kesla danced up and through the thrashing tangle. Trained as an assassin, she knew how to run the sands without disturbing a single grain. None of the predators noticed her passage through their territory.

Past the smaller fins, Kesla raced to the far dune. "I'll draw it off!" she yelled up to Hunt. "But you have to stop moving!"

Hunt tried to stop, but his feet slid in the loose sand. Sheeshon clutched his neck. The fin aimed straight for them. Kesla recognized the rising panic in the tall Bloodrider's eyes as death swept in, but he fought to obey her orders. He slid to a stop, teetering, up to his shins in the loose sand.

Kesla angled away from them, trotting up the dune's face. This time she did not try to hide her steps but used her skill to accentuate them: pounding the sand with the flats of her feet, slapping with each footstep.

As she did this, she watched over her shoulder.

The fin continued to sweep toward Hunt and Sheeshon—but it slowed, coming to a stop only a step from the Bloodrider's legs.

Kesla slowed also, stopping and pounding one foot harder. "Hear me," she pleaded between clenched teeth. The fin did not move. It needed more coaxing. She drew the nightglass dagger across her palm, the blade so sharp she hardly felt its bite. Blood welled up, creating a dark pool in her palm. Turning her hand, she squeezed her fist and dribbled blood into the dry sand.

Near Hunt, the fin sank a bit. Then, in a burst of sand, the sand shark heaved itself around, its tail thrashing. Hunt was knocked backward, landing on his backside in the sand, cradling Sheeshon. But the bull shark seemed not to notice, fixed on the scent of fresh blood. The fin aimed toward Kesla.

Kesla backed up the dune, still walking flat-footed, ensuring her steps echoed deep into the sand, dribbling blood at the same time. At the peak of the dune, she paused. "C'mon, hunter. Prove your hunger."

In the valley below, she saw her companions staring up at her, worried expressions fixed on their faces. Around them, the other smaller sharks continued to circle, not interfering with their leader.

Kesla crouched, ready.

The fin angled toward her position, sweeping up the face of the dune. Kesla waited until the beast was only two steps away— then ran directly at the fin. This close, the beast sensed its prey and surged up out of the sand, a maw of teeth and black throat. Kesla leaped, rolling through the air, and landed atop the fin. Raising her dagger high, she plunged its full length deep into the beast's back.

Impaled, the beast bucked under her. It bulged up from the sand, its tail whipping viciously. She rode the shark, her fingers clenched to the fin's edge. One hand reached out and yanked the dagger free. Black blood poured over the sand and down the dune's face. As the shark thrashed, she plunged the dagger in again, more to anchor her perch than as a true attack.

The shark attempted to flee, diving back into the sandy deep. Kesla was almost dragged down with it, but at the last moment, she tugged free her weapon and vaulted clear, rolling down the dune.

At the bottom, she slid to her feet, blade raised against any further attack. The smaller sharks circled a moment more, then slipped back under the sand, following their wounded bull. She signaled her companions to remain where they were. She wanted the pod of sand sharks well away from the area before anyone moved.

She wrapped her sliced palm into the edge of her cloak. She did not want her blood attracting stragglers. As she stood, she saw movement among her companions gathered on the valley floor.

It was Joach. His arm shot up, his mouth opening . . . The tiny hairs on Kesla's nape quivered. Joach was pointing to the slope behind her.

Spinning on a heel, Kesla dropped.

"Watch out!" Joach's scream echoed behind her.

From the bank of the dune, a huge shape leaped forth, a monstrous wall of muscle and teeth. The bull shark, blind with anger and blood lust, flew its full length out of the sand, hurtling through the air toward Kesla. Its fleshy mouth stretched wide, baring rows of razored teeth. Kesla could have walked upright between its open jaws.

Instead, while still crouched, she dove forward—low, under the beast's maw. As the shark flew over her, she thrust her dagger high. The magick-fed nightglass cut cleanly, as if through air.

As the monster's bulk hurtled by, the dagger sliced its belly from end to end. But the tip of its tail clipped Kesla's shoulder, throwing her hard to the sand. The blow knocked the dagger from her hand and sent it twirling away.

Weaponless, she rolled to her belly, tiny lights dancing before her eyes. The bull shark crashed to the valley floor, landing on its side. Intestines and blood spilled from its gutted belly. Writhing, its cavernous mouth gnashed at the sand. The others backed away warily. But its twitching quickly grew still. Blood spread in a widening lake.

Kesla pushed to her feet. "We should be safe for the moment," she gasped out, bruised, the air knocked from her lungs. "The bull's blood will drive away its brethren. But there are other predators. We must keep moving."

Joach collected the dagger and came to her side, offering his arm for support. "What you did . . . Your speed . . ."

She smiled weakly. "So you've finally found a use for an assassin's skills."

Hunt came up on her other side, Sheeshon still in his arms. Tears and sand stained the girl's face. She scowled at the shark's corpse. "Big bad fish," she scolded in childish anger, holding her nose against the rising smell.

Kesla reached up to touch the girl's cheek, but her legs wobbled with sudden exhaustion. She stumbled back toward the sand.

"I've got you," Joach said, catching her.

Kesla stared up into his eyes. "Thanks."

He slid the nightglass dagger into her belt. "I think you should keep this. You've earned it."

Kesla glanced down at this clear token of trust. She turned away to hide her welling tears and cleared her throat. "We . . . we should head out as soon as possible." She straightened and stared at the dead bulk of the shark. "The tribes have an old adage: 'In the sands, only the dead stop moving.' "

"Then let's break camp," Kast said, and stepped ahead with Sy-wen, leading the way back to the smoldering wreck of the *Eagle's Fury.*

Joach kept near to Kesla's side. She noticed his gaze on her as she followed the others. Instead of his usual smoldering anger, she sensed something else—something she hadn't felt since back at the kitchens of A'loa Glen, when she had posed as a scullion maid.

She glanced out of the corner of an eye. Joach shuffled beside her, biting his lower lip, eyes thoughtful. Turning, she kept her face hidden and allowed a small smile to shine.

BELGAN STOOD AT HIS HIGH WINDOW AND STUDIED THE SPREAD OF deserts around Alcazar. A moon, near to full, climbed the skies and cast the sands, dunes, and rocks in silver. It was so bright that he could see far into the distance.

"Where are you, Kesla?" he whispered to the desert. Worry kept him far from sleep this night. The shaman's scrying bones were mixed with omens, both glad and dire. Kesla had reached the desert—but she was far from safe.

After reading the bones, the shaman had left Alcazar. He would send some of his tribesmen out into the desert to watch for the girl. Belgan prayed they would find her safe, prayed she had succeeded in priming the ancient dagger in wit'ch blood. So much depended on someone so young.

But he knew Kesla was more than she appeared. He was the one who had found her a decade ago, walking the desert sands. She'd been naked, less than five winters of age, with no knowledge of her family or past—but he had known right away that she was special. The harsh sun had not marked her. Her tawny hair was long, dragging in the sand behind her as if its strands had never been sheared. She had walked into his night camp as if birthed by the desert itself. For one so lost and alone, she appeared unnaturally calm, though she could not speak. He had first believed her addled, but she had learned quickly: speaking within the year, reading the next, quickly mastering any and every skill and challenge posed her.

There was something special about Kesla. It shone from her. When the task came to wet the nightglass dagger in wit'ch blood, there was no other choice. Even if the shaman's bones had pointed another way, Belgan would have chosen Kesla. To him, she was the desert's best hope.

A knock sounded behind him.

He turned, wondering who could be disturbing him at this late hour. "Enter," he called out.

The door to his room opened, and an apprentice bowed into the room. "Master Belgan. I apologize for disturbing you so late."

"What is it, Seth?"

"There comes to the gate a wanderer, someone begging entrance to Alcazar."

"Is he alone?"

"Yes."

Belgan frowned. To walk the desert alone was the act of a fool. The dangers were too plentiful for a single pair of eyes to guard against. And at this late hour, he did not have the patience to tolerate fools. "What does this wanderer want?"

"That's why I disturbed you. He wishes to speak to you. He says that he comes with a warning."

Belgan sighed. He had better investigate. Plucking his cloak from its peg, he drew its red folds around his pale form. "Have you let him inside?"

"No, Master. He waits outside the gate."

He nodded. Good. With the dangers and diseased creatures loose in the desert, the gates were ordered locked at twilight and were not to be opened until dawn. "Take me to him."

Seth held the door open for his master, then scurried ahead, leading the way down the stairs and through the sandstone halls.

Ages ago, the keep of Alcazar had been hollowed and sculpted from a tall outcropping of sandstone. Approached from the desert, Alcazar appeared to be a plain pinnacle of stone, but a natural vertical crack in its northern face led into an inner central courtyyard, open to the sky above. The keep itself had been carved from this yard's surrounding cliffs, sculpted into straight towers, corkscrewing spires, and gigantic sculptures of ancient kings. It was a castle encased in a shell of sandstone, the private keep and hold of the Assassins' Guild.

Seth pushed through a thick ash door and held it open. Belgan stepped out of his tower and onto the paving stones of the central yard. From here, Belgan continued ahead, Seth trailing at his heels.

As he crossed the yards, the moon hung high overhead, shining down into the heart of Alcazar. To the right, the stables housing the desert malluks whispered with their mewls and chuffing. The usually stoic beasts were clearly agitated, frightened. Even the stablemaster had been roused. Belgan saw Humph, dressed only in his nightclothes, hauling the door open to check on his charges.

As he stared, a stray breeze wound under Belgan's cloak and shivered his skin. He wrapped his garment tighter to his thin shoulders, hugging his sides. *Strange omens ride this night.*

Seth caught up and passed him. "This way, Master Belgan."

On the far side of the yard, the crack in the sandstone cliff led out to the open desert, but it had been sealed from top to bottom with a crosshatch of iron bars, each as thick as a man's wrist. Spikes of poisoned barbs festooned the far side, discouraging any thief from attempting to climb the construction. The only opening in its iron face was a portcullis that could be raised or lowered by winches and counterbalances.

Seth led the way to the closed gate. In the dimness beyond the portal, Belgan spotted a shadowed lump.

As he neared, two apprentices stood to either side, spears in hand: the night's sentries. Belgan nodded to the pair, then slipped a flaming brand from a sconce and approached the gate.

The desert wanderer glanced up from where he knelt at the door.

Belgan gasped and fell back. The face under the cloak's hood was all wrinkles and milky eyes. It was as if an ancient mummified corpse stood at his portal. But this was no dead man. Leaning on a length of grayish wood, the stranger dragged to his feet. Hoary joints popped and creaked.

Belgan composed himself. "How . . . How may I help you, old man?"

The figure revealed a stumped wrist and shoved down his hood. The man's staff swiped before his wrinkled face as if waving away a biting fly. Now that the stranger was standing and fully exposed to view, Belgan realized his first impression of the wanderer had been mistaken, a trick of flickering torchlight. Certainly the man was old, but not as corrupted as he had first thought.

Belgan cast aside his initial trepidation. There was nothing to fear.

The wanderer's voice, when he spoke, was rich and deep, though coarse with age around the edges. "I come not seeking *your* help, Master Belgan, but to offer you *my* assistance."

"How so? Who are you? Where do you come from?"

"I have many names, but you may call me Dismarum. I am a nomad, wandering the many lands of Alasea."

The staff again waved before the man's face as he shifted his tired limbs. The old face suddenly reminded Belgan of his grandfather. He felt a twinge of guilt at his own lack of hospitality—but he kept his tone even. "Why have you come to my gates?"

"To warn of an enemy coming this way."

Belgan lifted one eyebrow. "What enemy might that be?"

"A boy cloaked in black magicks. He goes by the name Joach."

"And what makes you think he might be coming here?"

Dismarum leaned heavily on his staff, clearly weak and hungry. "He's the brother of a wit'ch."

Belgan jerked with these last words, shocked. "How did you . . . a wit'ch?"

"I've heard rumors on the road. He comes seeking to avenge the death of his sister."

Belgan felt the blood drain out of his limbs. The torch trembled. What had Kesla done?

"I would tell you more, but the desert has worn me, drained me." The visitor's words seemed to worm into Belgan's skull. "I would beg a boon. *Let me in.*"

Belgan's suspicions flared, but the man's staff waved again. Belgan blinked, staring back at the guileless old man. How could he distrust this wanderer who had risked so much to bring him news? Guilt at his rudeness surged again. He stepped back. "Raise the gate," he instructed Seth.

"Master?"

Belgan noticed the worried look on the apprentice's face. "We'll offer this desert wanderer a drink and a warm meal. Now open these gates."

Seth hesitated, glancing past the gate's bars with disgust.

Belgan remembered with shame his own initial revulsion of Dismarum and scowled at Seth. "Do as I say!"

Seth's eyes widened as he rushed over to the winch.

Belgan touched his forehead, surprised at his own outburst. He never raised his voice. It must be the lack of sleep, the days of worry for Kesla. His eyes drifted back to the old man behind the gates. Dismarum lifted the staff, rolling it in his palm—and all Belgan's concerns vanished. What was he thinking? He must treat this elder with the utmost compassion. Perhaps he should even offer him his own room for the night, compensation for his lack of hospitality so far.

Gears cranked, and iron groaned. Slowly the portcullis rose, its speared lower tips drawn from the sandstone. Soon the way lay open.

Belgan hurried forward and offered Dismarum his arm. The man smiled gratefully, all warmth and friendship. Belgan smiled back, content that he had pleased his guest. He led Dismarum under the gate and into the central yard.

For just a moment, Belgan thought he saw movement out of the corner of his eye. A blur of something hulking, a glimpse of claw and cloven hoof. Then it was gone, leaving the scent of goats in the air.

Belgan slowed, his brow furrowing. In his chest, his heart beat faster, panicked. Something was wrong, dreadfully wrong. His feet tripped.

Then the old man was there, catching him up, brushing him with his staff. With its touch, Belgan sighed with relief, all fears gone.

He shook his head at his own foolishness and continued toward the sculpted towers and spires. His ears ignored the burst of panicked nickering rising from the stables as he passed with his guest.

Instead, he patted the old man's arm. "Welcome, Dismarum. Welcome to Alcazar."

10

ON THE SECOND DAY OF TREKKING THROUGH THE DESERT, JOACH marched beside the litter bearing the broken-limbed Richald. They were the last in the line of marchers. Kesla led. Hunt walked beside her, bearing Sheeshon in his arms. Ahead of Joach, Kast and Sy-wen strode side by side, wrapped head to toe in drapes of cloak and cloth. The only skin exposed to the sun were their two hands, fingers interlocked as they crossed the sands.

Joach glanced skyward, squinting. He shaded his eyes. The sun touched the western horizon. Soon they would need to seek another campsite for the night—and it could not come quick enough. The entire party was hot, sunburned, and thirsty.

Last night, Kesla had led them to a site amid a tumble of rocks. Off the sands, the risk of attack from the desert's nighttime prowlers was less. As they had set up camp, she had also directed them to prop up sections of the singed sails. "To collect the night's dew," she had explained.

It proved a wise move. By morning, the cups and pans positioned under the lower edge of the canopies were filled with fresh water. It was not enough to wash the sand and dried sweat from their bodies, but it did allow them each to drink a small amount and to fill leather flasks for the day's journey.

But now, as the sun lowered to the west, Joach's small water supply had long been used up. His lips were cracked, and his tongue felt like a sticky piece of hide. Kesla had shown him how to keep a pebble in his cheek to help stave off thirst and moisten his mouth, but he had spat it out long ago. As he walked, every joint and crevice in his body was chafed raw by the sand. Joach's eyes ached from the blinding reflection of the sun off the surrounding dunes. It seemed as if they had been marching for moons instead of days. Even Joach's dreams had been of sand and of endless, empty skies.

And he was not alone in his suffering. Each member of the party slogged through the desert, head hanging, beaten down by the sun. The litter bearers bore the worst, carrying Richald slung between thin poles. The elv'in prince used traces of his magick to lighten his body and make his burden less for them, but the desert sun sapped everyone's energy. At times, Richald would allow his bearers to rest and would limp with a crutch across the sands, his stoic face lined with pain. But he could not do this for long and would have to return to the litter.

"Joach?" A hoarse whisper rose from the litter's rumple of cloths and sails.

Turning, Joach shifted the scarf of cloth from his face to stare at Richald. It was the first word the elv'in prince had spoken since the crash of the *Eagle's Fury*. "What is it, Richald?"

Richald shifted to one elbow. "I'm sorry."

"For what?"

"I failed you all."

Joach crinkled his brow. "How so?"

"I should not have lost the *Fury*. It brings shame to my family."

Joach sighed. He recognized the pain in the other's eyes. Living among the clouds, Richald had seldom been so seriously challenged as he had been two nights ago. The experience had taken the winds out of his haughty sails.

Reaching up, Joach touched the other's wrist. Richald tried to pull away, but Joach tightened his fingers, gripping the man's arm. "I'm sorry you lost your ship, Richald. Truly I am. But you sailed us through the narcissus fields and made it possible to continue our journey here. You have not shamed your name or family."

"But the *Fury* . . ."

"It was just wood and sail. As long as you live, another ship can be built. *You* are the true *Fury*."

Richald's wounded face softened a few degrees. He stared at Joach for a moment, then pulled his arm free. "Thank you," he whispered, then rolled away.

From ahead, Kesla lifted an arm. "We'll camp just over the next rise."

Joach groaned with relief, glad this long day was over. According to Kesla, they should reach Alcazar by midday tomorrow.

As Joach trudged forward, he found renewed strength. The entire group increased its pace with the end of the day's trek in sight. The last slope was a monstrous dune, sweeping up to the height of a steep foothill. The team climbed the ridge of sand, passing back and forth in ascending switchbacks.

At long last, as the sun sank into the western horizons and shadows stretched into a twilight gloom, they reached the summit. Joach, last in line behind the litter, saw the party stop with gasps of surprise on their lips. He trudged the final distance and stared into the next valley.

"Sweet Mother!"

Below was a wonderland. A small grove of tall, thin trees crowned with canopied leaves lay in the valley. The twilight gloom was even thicker in the deep trough, but there was no mistaking the glint of water—a wide pond! Beside the water, tiny lanterns glowed, illuminating a scatter of tents. The tinkling whisper of some stringed instrument floated up to them.

"The oasis of Oo'shal," Kesla said with delight. She swept back her hood. The last rays of sunlight lit her cascade of tawny curls into strands of gold.

"Why didn't you tell us you were heading here?" Kast asked, mildly irritated. The same question was on Joach's mind, too.

"I could not. It is taboo to speak of an oasis until you are at it. The desert tribes believe that to waste the moisture of one's breath to name or speak of an oasis will offend the gods of this land. As punishment, they might drain the waters back into the sand or hide it from your path." Kesla searched their faces with a trace of a smile. "And you wouldn't want that to have happened, would you?"

Hunt answered. "Not for all the gold in the sea." He began to hurry down the slope.

Four masked men suddenly rose from the sand, stepping out of hiding behind small boulders and slipping from under camouflaged flaps of cloth. In their hands were long, sickle-shaped blades.

Kesla stepped forward, empty palms raised. *"Naato o'shi ryt,"* she said calmly to the guards.

The lead swordsman's eyes grew large when he spotted her. He swept back his own desert hood and mask. "Kesla?"

She grinned and bowed. "It is good to see you again, Innsu."

The man sheathed his sword and ran up the slope. Joach noticed how tall and broad-shouldered the young man was. His skin was darkly complexioned, and he had deep, penetrating black eyes and a small, neatly trimmed beard and mustache. The dome of his head was shaved bald, as were all the other guards'.

Reaching Kesla, he picked her up in his arms and swung her around. "We've been watching for you."

"Watching for me?" Kesla asked, breathless from the greeting as he set her back on her feet.

"Shaman Parthus is down at the camp." Innsu nodded to the collection of low tents. "His bones warned of danger along your path through the desert. We came searching for you. I knew you'd come here to Oo'shal."

Her grin broadened. "You know me so well."

"And why wouldn't I? How many times have we been out here training? I couldn't keep you away from the water." As Innsu turned, Joach spotted a small daggered tattoo behind the man's left ear marking him as another assassin.

"How's Master Belgan?" she asked.

The tall young man rolled his eyes. "Worried, as usual."

This raised a bit of laughter from Kesla.

Joach frowned, irritated by the man's familiarity with the tawny-haired girl.

As if sensing his emotions, Kesla glanced back to him. "We've had a long day's trek, Innsu. Perhaps we'd better get these folks cleaned, fed, and settled. Then we can catch up."

He sobered. "Of course." Straightening, he addressed the rest of them formally. "Be welcome to Oo'shal. Come share our waters." It was clearly a common greeting, spoken rotely without true emotion.

Innsu turned and spoke in the desert tongue to his companions. One darted away and ran down the slope toward the valley, evidently to spread the word of their arrival.

Kesla waved them all down toward the trees and waters. "Come. We've all traveled through hardship, and I imagine the road will grow even harder from here. But this night, let us honor the gods of the Wastes and enjoy the hospitality of Oo'shal without worry or fear." She led them with Innsu at her side.

Joach glanced behind him. The other two guards vanished into the sand, returning to guard the valley.

Turning back around, he found Kesla's eyes upon him again. Her violet eyes matched the deep twilight waters below. Joach's breath caught in his throat. She slowed her pace to come abreast of him and touch his elbow, leaning close. "We'll be safe tonight. There'll be nothing to fear."

He nodded, noticing the hard, studied look Innsu gave him from behind Kesla's shoulder. *A desert eagle studying a scurrying mouse.*

Joach met his gaze, unblinking. An unspoken challenge passed between them.

With a slight narrowing of his eyes, Innsu turned away.

Kesla, seemingly oblivious to the exchange, continued to speak. "Oo'shal is a desert name. It means 'jewel of the sand.' "

"A jewel indeed," Sy-wen said, holding Kast's hand. "It's beautiful."

The small pond's color deepened to a midnight blue as they worked down the slope and into the shadows. It stood in sharp contrast to the red sand and green trees. After the unending landscape of wind-sculpted dunes and jutting rock, the oasis seemed a paradise of splendor and color.

As they neared the outskirts of the oasis, the noises of the camp grew in volume. Voices called across the valley in ululating echoes, sounding the arrival of the newcomers and the return of Kesla from her journey. The single stringed instrument was joined by the strike and beat of scintillating cymbals, a much merrier tune than the previous melancholy one.

Stepping under the fronds of the tall, narrow trees, Joach stared up. Pendulous gourds of a purplish hue hung from the high canopy.

Kesla caught his gaze. "Gre'nesh fruit. Its flesh is very succulent and sweet. The tribesmen make a potent ale from its mashed and strained seeds, while shamans chew the seed whole to walk the dream desert."

Joach's ears pricked up. "To walk the dream desert? What do you mean?"

"It's a shaman's ritual. In truth, I never fully understood it."

Joach was disappointed. Since his loss of Flint and Meric, he'd had no one to instruct him in his own talent of *dream-weaving*. After his near-disastrous misinterpretation of one of his dreams, Joach had grown to consider his talent more a threat than a gift. Over the past moon, he had sensed the occasional twinge of magick attempting to infuse his dreams, but Joach had shunned it like an unwanted guest.

A voice spoke out the shadows ahead. "You ask of the dream desert. Maybe I can explain it better after you've rested." A thin figure stepped across their path. He was gaunt, all worn bone and gristle, with skin burned to a deep bronze. Only his eyes seemed fresh and bright, almost aglow in the twilight murk.

"Shaman Parthus!" Kesla exclaimed, rushing forward to hug the old man. She quickly made introductions.

"Come," the shaman finished. "We've healers to help the injured, and food and drink—but first I imagine you'd all like to wash the sand from your feet."

"And hair, and mouth, and ears, and arse," Kast said.

This earned a small smile. "Fear not, Oo'shal will cleanse your body and spirit. Innsu will lead the men to their bathing pool; Kesla will take the girl child and woman. In the meantime, I'll guide the injured to the healer's tent." Parthus waved a hand, and a group of tribesmen led Richald and his litter bearers down a side path.

Kesla scooped up Sheeshon, whose eyes were wide at the new surroundings. "This way."

Sy-wen kissed Kast on the cheek and followed the lithe assassin.

The remaining men were led down another path toward the waters.

Joach noticed the shaman's eyes following him as he left. Caught staring, the shaman nodded knowingly. The shaman's lips moved in words meant only for Joach, and though the man was a distance away, Joach heard him as clearly as if he had whispered in his ear. "We'll speak after the moon sets," the old man said.

Still pondering the shaman's strange words, Joach found himself at the edge of the pool. As the sun finished setting, stars began to appear in the sky, mirrored in the waters here. As Joach stared, he was surprised by the size of the pool. From this shore, the far bank was almost indiscernible, more a small lake than a pond.

Kast tugged off one boot and reached a foot into the water. "It's nice and cool."

Innsu explained, arms crossed over his chest. "Oo'shal is fed from underground springs deep beneath the desert."

Kast nodded and pulled his other boot off, then quickly shed his garments. Joach and Hunt did not hesitate, stripping off their sandy and sweat-stained cloaks and undergarments. Kast ran and dove into the waters, Hunt and Joach at his heels. Their whoops of delight must have been heard far across desert.

Innsu just stood on the bank, arms still crossed, face stoic as stone.

After rubbing the sand and grime from their bodies, the trio floated and swam. None of them wanted to leave the balm of the cool lake. But eventually Innsu waved them back to the shore. Climbing from the waters, they found clean, loose robes to don.

"Your clothes will be washed tonight," Innsu said. "Now we must hurry. A small feast is being prepared."

Joach quickly learned that *small* was a subjective term. In a clearing at the center of the low tents, a large woven blanket had been spread. Bright sitting pillows interwoven with thin strands of silver dotted the edges, but it was the platters and bowls of fruits and roasted meats and the flagons of ale that drew Joach's eyes. His mouth watered at the sight. And the rich scent of spices and sizzling roasts almost made him swoon on his feet.

Sy-wen, Sheeshon, and Kesla were already seated, waiting with clear impatience. "It's high time you men showed up," Sy-wen said, wearing a scolding smile. "It seems these desert tribesmen have the odd custom of allowing their men to eat first."

Kast crossed and settled onto a pillow next to his mate. "Sounds like a fitting rule to me."

His statement earned him an elbow jabbed in his side. He laughed as Joach and Hunt took pillows on the far side of the spread of food.

Innsu bowed. "I must return to my watch. I bid thee a good meal."

Kesla smiled up at her fellow assassin. "Thank you, Innsu."

Before he left, he glanced to Joach, his face again stone, unreadable. Then he swung away. The other tribesmen also gave them privacy to enjoy their meal, retreating to their tents, though somewhere a pair of musicians continued to ply the night with soft chords and the tinkle of bells.

Now settled, Kesla showed them how to partake of the meal. There were no plates, knives, forks, or spoons. All that rested before each pillow was a short spear, about as long as Joach's forearm. Kesla demonstrated how to use the tool to jab a morsel and bring it to one's lips.

She did not eat what she speared but nodded to Joach. "Men must eat first."

Joach smiled and speared a chunk of sizzling meat.

"Roasted owl," Kesla explained.

Joach brought it to his lips. His eyes closed with satisfaction as his teeth sank through the charred skin to the tender meat. He sighed with appreciation, tasting the sweet juices used in the marinade. He had never experienced anything so wonderful.

Noises of appreciation arose from the others. With the men having sampled the fare, the women began to spear and jab at the feast. As the night wore on and the moon climbed high in the sky, laughter and ale flowed, easing residual tensions and aches. Joach could almost forget that he sat in the middle of the Southern Wastes, one of Alasea's harshest lands. Finally, his stomach full, he groaned with pleasure and put down his spear.

"More?" Kesla teased.

Joach shook his head. "I couldn't stand another morsel of your people's hospitality—Not without bursting like an overripe pumpkin."

The group shared his views. Sy-wen and Kast were soon retreating to their assigned tent, arms locked around each other. Hunt stirred, too. "I should get Sheeshon to bed." The child leaned against the Bloodrider's side, gently snoring. She had fallen asleep long ago. He picked her small form up under one arm and stood. Sheeshon did not even stir. Weaving slightly from the ale, Hunt strode toward the tents.

"Sleep well," Kesla called after him.

He lifted an arm in acknowledgment, then disappeared into a tent.

Turning, Kesla's eyes found Joach's. They were alone now. She glanced shyly away. "I told Shaman Parthus about the night-glass dagger. He'll join us on the journey to Alcazar tomorrow."

"That's good," Joach mumbled, suddenly awkward. He rolled his feet under him, pushing up. "I guess I should find my tent."

Cross-legged, Kesla stared at her toes. "Already?"

Joach felt his heart jump. He shuffled his feet. "Well, I . . . I'm actually not that sleepy."

She slid smoothly to her feet. "It's good to walk a bit after a large meal. Better for the digestion."

"So I've heard. But walk where?"

She finally lifted her eyes back to his face. "I'll show you." Kesla waved him to a trail between a dense grove of trees. "There's something you should see."

Kesla led, but Joach quickly stepped beside her. "Where are we going?" he asked.

"You'll see."

In silence, they wound through the trees. Small bats roosting in the canopies took flight at their approach. But soon the trees were behind them, and they were climbing a path up the face of a dune. Joach's feet kept slipping in the sand, but Kesla moved lightly up the slope. She reached back and helped him.

Her hand was an ember in his palm.

"If you walk with the inner edge of your feet, you'll not need to fight the sand as much."

Joach did as she instructed and discovered she was right. But though he moved more easily, she never released his hand. He did not object. In fact, he moved closer to her side. He could smell the water of Oo'shal in her hair, and the soft scent of her skin.

All too soon, they reached the crest of the dune.

The desert, etched in silver by the bright moon, stretched forever. "It's beautiful," he mumbled.

She leaned closer to him and pointed her free arm. "Do you see that spear of rock near the horizon?"

Joach squinted. He could just make out a lone mountain in the distance, its slopes limned in moonlight. "What is it?"

"It's Alcazar. My home."

Joach stared down at her. Her eyes brimmed with tears. He let go of her hand and draped his arm around her shoulders, pulling her to his side, hugging and holding her.

The cold assassin melted into his side, now just a woman.

RICHALD LAY ATOP THE THIN BLANKET, THE SAND BENEATH sculpted to his contours. The camp had long gone quiet, but sleep escaped him. The tribe's healer had given him medicines to dull his pain, but the ache in his broken leg still nagged. His remaining crew lay around the wide tent, curled in slumber; a whistling chorus of snores surrounded him.

He closed his eyes. He could still sense his ship, even from leagues away. During his life, he had seldom left its planked decks. To lose the *Fury* was like losing a part of himself. He felt naked, vulnerable.

He remembered his distraught words to Joach. *Foolish,* he thought to himself. It was not proper for a prince of the Blood to show weakness, to ask for forgiveness, especially from a half-breed like Joach.

But in his heart, he knew he needed the comfort of the young man's counsel. As much as he sniped at Joach, Richald had grown to respect the man. He had proven his royal blood, both in the past and even on this journey. It had been Joach who had goaded him into finding that last bit of strength necessary to guide his ship over the vine's fields. If it hadn't been for the boy, they all might have died. Joach had given Richald the strength to find his honor, to ply his elemental skills to their fullest.

And as much as the loss of his ship was a wound in his heart, Richald relished that final flight: the rush of wind, the snap of sailcloth, the dance of flames, even the overwhelming pain as the ship broke apart under him. At that moment, he had never felt more alive and vigorous. Lives had depended on him. His skill was all that had stood between life and death.

Tears filled his eyes. He owed the experience to Joach.

Richald shifted his hip, triggering a flash of agony up his leg. The pain helped focus his thoughts. Injured, he was more a burden than an asset to the mission here in the deserts. The plan was for him to recuperate at Alcazar while the others continued in their efforts to destroy the Basilisk Gate. And this rankled him—it was the true reason sleep escaped him this night. He owed Joach a debt, and he meant to honor it.

But how? How could he be of use in his current broken state?

Richald stared at the tent's roof. If there ever was a way to repay Joach, he would.

"This I swear on the blood of my family," he muttered softly.

Content with his spoken promise, Richald rolled to his side, guarding his leg, and knew he could finally sleep.

IN THE THICK OF THE NIGHT, JOACH WOKE WITH A START, AS IF someone had called his name in the dark. He sat up, his heart pounding harshly. He stared around the small tent. It was empty— some stored rolls and bags, but nothing more. He tossed aside his blanket and rolled from the thin bed, naked except for a pair of cotton breeches. The cool desert night chilled his bare flesh. His ears strained for what had startled him awake.

The only noise outside was the soft whisper of tree fronds wafting in the gentle night breezes. Still, Joach shivered.

Stepping to the tent flap, he pushed a corner open and peeked outside. The night had grown darker than when he had climbed into his bedroll after his walk with Kesla.

Beyond the tent, past a few trees, Joach spotted the central clearing. As his eyes adjusted to the dark, he spotted a shadowy figure standing out there. The stranger waved an arm, indicating Joach should approach.

Glancing right and left, Joach hesitated. Not a single light glowed anywhere around the oasis. But he knew guards had been posted around the valley. No intruder should have been able to enter the area without raising an alarm.

Joach bit his lower lip and slipped through the tent flap. Out of the shelter, the night breeze chilled him to the bone. He wrapped his arms around his bare chest.

Ahead, the dark figure waited, unmoving.

Joach stepped forward, swallowing back his fear. Once closer, the features of the lurker grew clearer: his bald head, his burnt-copper skin, and his piercing eyes that glowed as bright as the moon. Joach recognized the tribe's shaman.

He strode more confidently forward. "Shaman Parthus."

"Joach Morin'stal." The shaman's voice rasped like flowing sand.

"How may I help you?" Joach asked hesitantly, not fully able to shake his nervousness.

The shaman did not answer. He simply waved Joach to sit with him in the sand. The old man folded to the ground, cross-legged.

Joach felt uncomfortable looming over the elder, so he settled to the sand, too. Only then did he spot a small bone bowl resting before the shaman's knees. It was filled with thumb-sized nuts.

Parthus noticed his attention. "Gre'nesh seeds."

Joach remembered Kesla's description of the fruit's seed. Diluted, it made a strong, intoxicating ale, but when taken whole, it supposedly helped the shamans of the tribes in some mysterious ways.

Parthus picked up the bowl and offered its contents to Joach. The young man took one of the offered seeds, as did the shaman.

"I don't understand," Joach mumbled.

"You are a shaman. I spotted it in your eyes when you first came to Oo'shal."

Joach shook his head. "I have the gift of dreamweaving, nothing more. I am no shaman."

Parthus stared at Joach with those intense bright eyes. "That will be seen." The shaman popped a gre'nesh seed into his mouth. A loud crack sounded as his teeth bit into the nut. Parthus nodded for Joach to do the same.

He hesitated, then did as instructed. He popped the seed between his molars and crunched down on it. Almost instantly, a bitter taste filled his mouth. He swallowed back a gag.

"Do not fight it," the shaman said, but his voice was dreamy, almost as if he were drifting away.

Joach stared across the small space, eye to eye. His mouth filled with saliva as his tongue fought the bitterness, trying to wash away the taste. With his fingers clenched on his knees, Joach swallowed hard. For a moment, he felt nothing, just relief to get the foulness off his tongue.

With a nod, the shaman spit out the empty husk of his seed; Joach did the same.

Joach coughed on the residual bitterness. "What now? Is there some—" Then the world dissolved around him. Trees and tents, water and sky—all washed away. All that remained were two things: the endless sand and the lone figure of Parthus still seated across from him.

Joach craned his neck. Overhead, the night sky was empty—no stars, just an endless blank expanse that spread to all horizons. Yet instead of finding this strange landscape dark, Joach had to squint against the brightness. All the sands around them glowed with the same shine found in the shaman's eyes.

Joach gawked at the landscape. As strange as this all was, Joach felt a twinge of familiarity. He had been here before. Last night, as he slept, he had dreamed of this place. In the morning, he had thought the sandy dream a mere reflection of the day's arduous trek. But here he was again.

Parthus rose smoothly to his feet and held out a hand. "Come. It is time you walked the dream desert."

Joach, his mouth still hanging open, accepted the man's firm grip and allowed himself to be pulled to his feet. "Where exactly are we? What is this dream desert?"

"The gre'nesh seed freed our spirits from our bodies. Once untethered, those attuned to the elemental energy of sand are drawn into the desert's endless dream."

"But I have no skill in sand magick."

Parthus nodded. "I know this. But you thrum to all things dreaming. You were drawn not by the sand, but by the *dream* itself."

Joach frowned and stared around him. Not a creature stirred, not a wind blew. But even though it was quiet, he sensed a great pressure all around him, as if he were submerged deep under the sea and something large were examining him for dinner. He wrapped his arms around his bare chest and wished he had thought to don a shirt. Turning back to the shaman he asked, "But where exactly are we? Why did you bring me here?"

"Follow me." Parthus swept his cloak around his thin shoulders and struck out across the smooth landscape.

Joach matched his stride. As they walked, Joach sensed great distances were crossed with each step. "Where are you taking me?"

"To the heart of the dreaming . . . To the Southwall itself."

Joach cringed. "Is it safe?"

"As long as you stay at my side. Don't wander off."

Joach studied the landscape of empty glowing sands and emptier skies. Where could he go?

As if reading his thoughts, Parthus spoke. "To walk alone here can threaten your very spirit. Occasionally other dreams will intersect with this plane and bring nightmares to the sands. Here they have the strength of real beasts. They can kill or worse."

"Worse?"

"Sometimes as you engage another's night figment, you can become drawn out of this landscape and into the dreamer's mind. If that happens, you will be lost forever."

Joach's belly became queasy. He studied the sands more closely. Was that a flicker of movement at the corner of his eye? His gaze darted all around him.

"Do not search too closely. It gives the figments power, sapping your own spirit through your attention. Instead, focus on your own goal. Do not be distracted."

Joach nodded, but his eyes spotted a shimmer to his left. He looked. A handsome silvery woman appeared from the sands wrapped in diaphanous silks, barely hiding a lithe body of long legs and inviting curves. Joach stared.

The figure noticed his gaze and smiled. Joach found his own lips curling to match her expression. She raised a slender arm and, with a single red-nailed finger, motioned for him to come nearer.

Joach stepped away from the shaman—but a bony grip clenched his elbow. The shaman held him tight. "Look closer, boy," Parthus hissed in his ear.

Blinking, Joach opened his mouth to protest, but the shaman's words cast the glamor from his eyes. The slender woman still stood in the sands, inviting, alluring—but from the waist down, Joach realized her body was that of a monstrous coiled snake, writhing in the sands.

Joach jumped away, bumping into the shaman behind him.

The nightmare hissed, lips parting to reveal silvered fangs.

"Keep moving," the shaman said, shoving Joach forward. "It's nothing. A figment. But a moment longer, and your attention would have pulled it fully from the sands."

Joach swallowed the terror down into his belly, suddenly sick.

The shaman steadied him with a hand on his shoulder. "Take deep breaths. The figment drew some of your energy. It'll take a moment for you to gain it back."

Joach nodded and kept marching. He drew great gasps into his chest, and after a few moments, the queasiness did indeed fade away. "I'm feeling better," he mumbled as Parthus drew beside him.

"Good, because we're almost to the Wall."

Joach frowned. Ahead the desert stretched just as featureless as usual. "Where?"

The shaman motioned him to silence. "No further words from here." He reached and took Joach's hand.

Together, they walked across the desert. Again Joach was struck by the odd sensation of great distances being traveled, but soon this feeling waned. Though they walked at the same pace, Joach felt as if they were slowing, less distance being crossed with each step.

At last, Joach noted a slight ripple in the sand ahead. He squinted, but it was too far away. They continued on in silence. Slowly details emerged as they approached. Movement—the ripple grew into a silver river cutting across their path, with only a slight meander to its course.

As they neared, Joach saw it was not water that flowed along this channel but what looked like molten silver. Parthus drew Joach up to the nearest bank. He could feel the power here, like a pressure in his ears. The sand led at a gentle slope to the silver's edge. Parthus pointed into its depths.

Leaning over the river, Joach saw his own reflected face, as clear as in any looking glass—but that was not all! He bit back a gasp, covering his mouth with a hand. Reflected in the silver was the night sky filled with stars and a massive wall towering behind Joach. He glanced over his shoulder but saw nothing—just the endless smooth desert. He returned to his study of the reflection. Glancing to the left and right, he saw the wall's length was reflected along the silver river's entire course.

"The Southwall," Parthus whispered. "The desert dreams of it here."

Joach's eyes widened in wonder.

Before he could comment, Parthus hushed him and led the way along the bank's edge, heading to the left. Joach followed. He found it hard for his eyes to leave the river. Along the silver channel, he watched their images striding along the length of the Southwall. *Amazing*.

But after a bit of time, the reflection in the river began to fade, growing darker. It was a subtle change, but with each step, the silver seemed to lose its luster. Joach also noticed that the constant pressure of power wavered, too. He glanced questioningly to the shaman.

The elder held a finger to his lips. He led the way over a slight slope. The river swept around the sandy hill in a gentle curve. As they crested over the low mound, Joach cringed at what came into view.

A short distance ahead, the river swept around the slope and into a cauldron of blackness, where it was swallowed away. The sick flow churned in on itself, forming a swirling vortex, a whirlpool of disease. Beyond this cauldron, Joach spotted a trace of the silver river continuing deeper into the desert, winding toward the endless horizon. But even from the distance, Joach could tell the flow was feeble, weakened and corrupted by its passage through this black stain.

Joach returned his attention to the vortex of corrupted energy. He saw that the stain was not limited to the river's course, but tendrils ran under the sandy banks and spread into the desert, shadowy veins that burrowed far, dimming the glow of the dream sand.

Joach shuddered. He remembered Kesla's description of a spreading poison that tainted the Southern Wastes. He knew he was staring at the cause.

At his side, Parthus raised an arm and pointed to the black cauldron of swirling corruption. A single word formed on his lips, a name. "Tular."

With this revelation, the shaman drew Joach back down the slope and away from the river, heading back the way they had come. Joach marched in silence, stunned by what he had just been shown. The evil at Tular was feeding off a vein of the Land's energy, twisting this font of power to its own fetid purposes.

As he walked, Joach recalled the manner by which the ill'guard were forged, how certain elementals' energies were corrupted and bent to the Black Heart's cause. The same was going on here— only on a grander scale. Horror ran like ice through Joach's veins. Could the Dark Lord twist the Land itself into an ill'guard slave? Was such a thing possible? If it came to be, if the Land itself turned against their side, no one would be able to withstand the Gul'gotha—not even Elena.

Joach's hands formed tight fists. That must not happen.

Joach was tugged to a stop. His eyes refocused back to the dream desert.

"We've returned," the shaman said, folding his legs and sitting. He indicated for Joach to do the same.

Joach settled to the sand, too shocked to resist, and asked the question foremost in his mind. "Why did you show me this?"

The shaman closed his eyes and raised his hands, holding two fistfuls of sand. He tossed the glowing grains high into the air, sweeping it over both men. As the sand fell, it drew back the real world, like drawing down a curtain. Trees and tents reappeared around them. Over the shoulder of the shaman, the waters of Oo'shal again reflected the starlight.

Parthus opened his eyes. In them, Joach recognized the glow of the dream desert. After a lifetime of communing on the dream plane, the shaman now shone outwardly with its magick.

"Why did I reveal this to you?" the elder repeated. "Why you?"

"Y-yes."

"Because you are strong, yet do not know your full strength."

Joach frowned.

"You are no ordinary dreamweaver, a mere prophet of dreams. Has no one mentioned how infinitely deep your dreaming power runs?"

Joach remembered Brother Flint's statement of long ago: how the old mage had claimed Joach was one of the strongest elementals in dream magick. He shook his head. "I still don't understand the significance."

"Most dreamweavers are just passive bystanders, reading the writing on the wall, watching things happen from a distance. But you, Joach, have the ability to do so much more. The dream plane is your canvas. Rather than be a passive player, you can be a participant. You can be a dream *sculptor*, someone with the ability to craft elements from the land of dreams and bring them into the real world."

Joach made a scoffing noise. "I've never heard of such a thing."

"Because you're the first sculptor to appear in countless generations. It was an art thought forever lost. But we sand shamans have never forgotten. It is seared into our most secret histories."

"I don't understand. What histories?"

Parthus sighed. "The histories of Tular."

Joach blinked with shock. The image of the black vortex flashed across his vision. "Tular?"

"Long ago, when the Southwall was new, the Land drew certain desert people to its sandstone walls. It grew the castle of Tular to house these special guardians and gifted them with a part of the desert's dreaming magick. They ruled the Southern Wastes with honor and justice. During this time, the desert flourished, and the tribes grew in number. It was a wonderful age."

"So what happened?"

The shaman's face darkened. "Slowly the power began to corrupt the leaders of Tular. Guardians became ghouls. They learned to bring demons and beasts from the dreamscape to terrorize the Wastes. One of their most fearsome was the great basilisk, a feathered serpent with an undying thirst for blood. For centuries, the ghouls of Tular ruled with an iron fist. Until one day, the Wit'ch of Spirit and Stone came to our aid."

"Sisa'kofa?"

Parthus nodded. "She rallied our people and used her own blood to create weapons that could slay the dream beasts. The ghouls were torn from their roosts and the misshapen beasts destroyed. Tular was left empty and abandoned. And the magick of dream sculpting died with it." The shaman eyed Joach. "That is, until now."

Joach licked his lips nervously. "How can you be so sure I have this power?"

The shaman studied Joach hard and long. "I don't know if you're ready for that answer. Can you simply trust that I know?"

Joach's eyes narrowed. "Tell me why you suspect such a thing."

"I do not just suspect—I *know*."

"How can you be so certain?"

"Because Kesla found you and brought you here."

Joach waved away his answer. "She found me because she needed to prime the nightglass dagger with my sister's blood. Nothing more."

Parthus frowned. He took out a small pouch, opened it, and poured tiny white bones into his palm. "I use these to study the unseen paths in life. But not all roads are clearly marked. Kesla was sent with the dagger, but was it solely to wet its blade in wit'ch blood—or was there another reason? A path to another end?" Parthus glanced up at Joach.

"What? To find me? To bring me here?"

He slowly nodded, rolling the bones from one hand to the other. "Many paths twine and wind. It is often hard to say which is the truest path."

Joach sighed. "I still don't see the significance. So I came here. So I'm strongly gifted in dream magicks. How does any of this make me one of these dream sculptors?"

The shaman closed his eyes, his face pained. "Because as soon as the two of you walked into the oasis, I could read your hearts, see the ties that bound you two together. She loves you like she has loved no other." The shaman opened his eyes. "And I suspect the same could be said of you toward her."

Joach's cheeks grew warm with a fierce blush. He attempted to rebut the shaman's words, but all that came out was a nonsensical stammer.

"Do not deny your heart, boy," Parthus spat angrily. "I will hear no lies spoken in Oo'shal."

Joach swallowed back any further protest. Cowed, he nodded for the shaman to continue.

With a grumble, Parthus calmed his voice. "Before Kesla left on the journey to A'loa Glen, her blood was dribbled over these bones. It is a trick shamans use to keep track of a person from afar." He rattled the bits in his fist. "But on the first tossing, I learned much more. The bones spoke Kesla's true name and from where she had come."

Joach crinkled his brow. Kesla had claimed she had been found wandering in the desert by the head of the Assassins' Guild, then fostered at Alcazar and trained in the guild's ways. Was there more she hadn't revealed? "What did you learn?"

"It is difficult to speak aloud. I have told no one, not even Guildmaster Belgan." The shaman dropped the bones into the sand and stood.

Joach stared at the spread of the fallen bones, then up at the thin shaman. "What did they reveal about Kesla?"

"It is late," Parthus said, partially turning away. "We have a hard trek to reach Alcazar tomorrow."

Joach stood up quickly, kicking sand over the bones. He grabbed for the shaman's elbow, but the man moved beyond his reach.

Parthus turned. "One last time—do you truly want the truth? About Kesla, about her connection to you? Why she marks you as a sculptor?"

Joach felt a momentary twinge of doubt, fearful of the answer. But a part of him had to know this secret, could not be satisfied with mere faith. Not trusting his voice, Joach nodded.

"No," Parthus said. "I want to hear it in your own voice."

Joach cleared his throat with great difficulty. "Tell me," he croaked out.

"You must swear to tell no others. Not your friends, not even Kesla."

"I swear."

Parthus sighed, his body sagging. "The girl you love, Kesla— she is not what she appears."

"I don't understand."

Parthus turned away. "Kesla is a dream, a figment sculpted by the desert and given form and substance to walk this world. As she has chosen you, so the desert has also chosen. It has drawn a sculptor back to the sands of the Wastes, to call you back to guardianship, marking you as the one to rid the deserts of the pestilence that festers in Tular." The shaman moved away, leaving Joach standing stunned. "But Kesla, the girl—she is not real."

Joach stood in the clearing, frozen. The shaman's words bound him in place as surely as any ropes. Trembling, Joach pictured Kesla's tawny hair, her crooked smile, the way she tilted on a hip when joking, how her hand fit so snugly into his palm. As he stood, a thick tear rolled down his cheek—while deep inside, something shattered into a thousand sharp and brittle pieces.

His pained voice whispered over the waters of Oo'shal. "Kesla . . ."

11

WITH THE SUN DIRECTLY OVERHEAD, KESLA CLIMBED THE RIDGE ahead of the slower caravan. She wanted to be the first to glimpse Alcazar, to share a moment of private homecoming. She cast off her sweep of silk scarf from her face and shook loose the hood of her desert cloak.

Half a league away, the red sandstone cliff of Alcazar thrust sheer from the desert, a solitary behemoth, a great ship in the sand. Its sweeping bluffs glowed in the sunlight, its dense silicate crystals sparkling like jewels. It took a keen eye to discern that this mountain of wind-sculpted rock harbored a castle in its heart. But Kesla knew the hulking rock as well as her own face. Alcazar was the only home she had ever known, and to her, its secrets could never be hidden in shadow and stone. From the dune's ridge, she spotted small crevices and cracks high up the cliffs that masked windows and spy holes. She imagined eyes staring back at her, sentries alert to the approach of others.

She lifted an arm to these unseen watchers, a salute of welcome.

As she waited, no acknowledgment came, not even the customary flash of a signal mirror. Kesla lowered her arm with a frown. At dawn, Shaman Parthus had sent ahead two sand runners to carry advance word to Master Belgan. Surely they had arrived a quarter of a day ahead of them.

Kesla sighed and glanced over a shoulder. Her companions

worked up the last of the switchbacks toward her position. She shifted her feet, impatient to continue ahead. With Alcazar in sight, she could hardly constrain herself. It had been so many moons since she had last seen her friends and caretakers: Shargyll, the rotund matron who had trained Kesla in her scullion's skills; Humph, the long-eared stablemaster and his herd of ornery malluks; and Crannus, the master of poisons who told the most vile jokes. But most of all she missed Master Belgan—her teacher, her counselor, her confessor. In many ways, he was the father she had never known.

This last thought made her melancholy. She stared at the great spread of the Wastes. Where had she come from? Where in this sand-blown landscape was her true home? Her gaze settled back on the great rock of Alcazar. She knew the answer: there stood her home.

Sighing, she turned again as the caravan of desert tribesmen and her fellow companions worked their way up to the ridge. Joach was the first to join her. His eyes were instantly drawn to the cliffs and sandy ledges of Alcazar.

"It's so large," he said, craning for a better view.

She nodded with a shy smile. "It houses over four hundred apprentices, journeymen, and masters of the guild."

"You can't even tell anyone resides there."

"That was done purposefully. Five centuries ago, when the keep of Alcazar was first carved from the rock, the guild was fleeing from the sinking of Castle Drakk in southern Alasea. They wanted privacy, a secure place away from prying eyes and their Gul'gothal pursuers, a strong citadel in which to regroup and rebuild the Assassins' Guild."

"I see," Joach mumbled.

Kesla moved a step closer, but Joach shifted away from her. She noticed how he seemed to sink deeper into his cloak. From the corner of her eye, she watched him. All day he had been distant like this: refusing to meet her gaze, communicating with terse words, always seeming to be too busy to talk. Though his attitude was not as rude and distrustful as it had been on the journey from A'loa Glen, it was markedly more cold than the warmth they had shared under the desert stars.

"Joach . . ." she began softly, gently trying to coax some answers.

But he twisted away as the litter bearing Richald neared. "I should help them." He hurried to lend his shoulder with the elv'in in lifting their captain up and over the ridge. Behind them, Hunt trudged up the last slope with Sheeshon riding his shoulders.

"Lookie, Kesla!" Sheeshon called to her. "Hunt's a malluk."

Kesla smiled. "He certainly is." The girl had been enchanted by the desert's beasts of burden, plaguing the drovers as they loaded and prepared the shaggy creatures for the journey.

Hunt rolled his eyes as he moved past Kesla's post. "After trekking here, I must smell like a malluk, too." The large Blood-rider continued over the ridge, following after the litter.

Slowly the rest of the caravan trundled past. Sy-wen and Kast climbed over the ridge, only pausing to share a sip from a water-skin. From the way Kast had to squeeze the leathery malluk bladder, it was the last of their share. As he drank, Kesla noted that the wide-shouldered man's singed arm was slathered in yellowish serpent tongue oil, a potent healing balm. Already Kast's arm looked much less red, the blistering subsiding. If there was one thing desert healers knew how to mend, it was skin burns; the sun of the Southern Wastes was merciless.

As the two lovers moved down the slope toward Alcazar, the desert tribesmen with their drovers and laden malluks swept past. The malluks, as usual, were unfazed by the trek, shambling along with their riders half dozing in their saddles. The beasts towered twice the height of an ordinary man and had a thick insulating coat of sandy-red hair that blended almost perfectly with the desert. Their wide, flat-splayed feet padded across the loose sand, and their large brown eyes studied Kesla as they passed. One of the beasts leaned toward her and snuffled at her, checking to see if she had something good to eat. She gently but firmly nudged him away.

Soon the caravan was past, and Kesla stood with Shaman Parthus at the ridgeline.

The leathery elder leaned on a length of sandalwood. "Are you glad to be almost home, child?"

"I will be happy to see Master Belgan again."

He offered his elbow to her. "Then let's not keep him waiting."

Together the pair worked down the slope.

"I talked to the young man with the red hair last night." The shaman's words were spoken casually, but it was clearly forced. Parthus wanted to tell her something. His feet also moved slower as he feigned disability, leaning on her arm and on his staff. The rest of the caravan moved farther and farther ahead.

"You spoke to Joach?"

"Yes. We shared the fruit of the gre'nesh."

Kesla now slowed their pace even more, surprise hobbling her feet. She had never heard of any shaman sharing the magick of the desert fruit with someone uninitiated into their brotherhood. "What happened?"

He shrugged. "The man is quite rich in the dreaming magicks. He will be a strong ally in the coming assault against the ghouls of Tular."

Kesla touched the hilt of her sheathed weapon. "All I need is the nightglass dagger. If its blade is sharp enough to kill the basilisk, I will not fail. I can be in and out of Tular before any of their minions grow wise."

"I do not doubt your skill, Kesla. But I believe the true battle against Tular will prove more of a challenge."

"You tossed the bones?"

"I did." Frowning, he eyed the windblown heights of Alcazar. "But it does not always take prophecy to see the future. One simply has to open one's eyes and look."

Kesla found her gaze following the shaman's. The heights remained as empty as when she had been atop the ridge. By now, the front of the caravan was winding into the black crack that led into the rock's interior. She listened but heard no horn announcing their return. No one moved on the sentry ledges. She squinted her eyes, trying to spot the camouflaged guards at their high rocky posts. Either they were well hidden, or no one was there.

Twinges of unease skittered across her skin like the tickle of spiders in the dark, but ahead, the last of the caravan was swallowed into the narrow canyon with no signs of distress.

Kesla glanced over at the shaman. He continued to amble after the others, apparently unconcerned, but why then had he spoken to her? Why hint at something wrong but not voice it?

"A test," he mumbled, seeming to read her heart. "A rite of passage."

"For me?"

He shrugged. "The young man must learn the depths of his own power and strength."

"Joach?"

Again the shrug.

Panic welled up inside her. Wide-eyed, she stared at the towering rock. The sun cast its cliffs in shadows and flows of reds, like blood running down its flanks.

"I must help him!" She moved to race ahead but found her arm locked in the shaman's hold.

"It is his test, Kesla. You cannot take it for him."

Wild with fear and concern, Kesla used her skills to break the shaman's grip and raced forward. But even as her feet flew across the sands, she did not need the shaman's prophetic words to know she would be too late.

JOACH WAS THE FIRST THROUGH THE IRON GATES OF ALCAZAR. THE litter bearing Richald followed behind. Two things struck him immediately.

First was the castle's beauty. As he stepped under the gates and into the central yard, the keep of the assassins opened before him. He craned his neck. Impossibly thin towers, twisting spires, and slender statues climbed the cliff faces, carved from the very heart of this great block. It was a small city encased in sandstone.

But as the others joined him in the yard, his second impression overwhelmed his wonder of this place. Hunt voiced it aloud, settling Sheeshon to her feet. "Where is everyone?"

The keep was deserted. No one manned the gate. No one greeted them. Joach was unaware of the custom here, but it seemed strange to leave the gates unguarded.

Kast stepped to Joach's other side, Sy-wen in his shadow. "I don't like this," the tall Bloodrider grumbled.

To punctuate his statement, the gates to Alcazar fell closed behind them. The spiked portcullis crashed into place with a clang of finality.

Joach spun around. Iron bars now separated them from the desert tribesmen, who through the bars looked just as confused as Joach was. Only Innsu, the tall bronzed assassin, stood trapped on this side of the gate, along with two of his men.

"Something's wrong," Innsu said, turning and sweeping back his cloak. His sickle-shaped sword flashed in the bright sunlight of the open yard.

"It's a trap," Sy-wen said.

Kast already had his own sword in hand. The elv'in bearers lowered Richald's litter to the paving stones of the yard, and crossbows appeared from under their cloaks. Hunt pushed Sheeshon behind him, freeing a short ax from his belt.

Joach reached for the nightglass dagger but found his belt empty. Defenseless, there was nothing he could do but scan the heights around him and wait for their attackers to reveal themselves.

Across the yard, a set of thick double doors burst open, thrown wide by more than just the strength of arm. The wooden portals crashed against the stone, ripping from their iron hinges and falling away. Two figures walked out of the castle's darkness and into the sunny yard.

The first was tall, striking, dressed in a sweeping red desert cloak. His pale face and snowy hair were strange in this land of dark men. But it was his eyes, sparking red with anger, that held their attention. He eyed them all. "I see our doom. I see a boy who brings destruction upon people of the Wastes."

"Master Belgan?" Innsu said, stepping forward and lowering his sword. "You misunderstand them. They mean us no harm. Shaman Parthus says—"

"Silence!" the pale figure snapped.

Joach noticed how shocked the young assassin was by his master's outburst. What was going on here?

The second figure hobbled around the taller man, fully hidden in folds of cloak and silk. He leaned upon a staff and moved closer to Belgan. "Do not listen to the young fool," the bent-backed man whispered. "He is clearly enthralled by the dire magicks of the wit'ch's brother."

As these soft words reached Joach's ears, he froze, ice forming in his veins. Even whispered, Joach knew that rasped voice. It had been in his head for over half a winter. He could never forget. He knew who stood at the guildmaster's right side—the murderer of his mother and father. The one who had ripped him from his sister's side and used him like a puppet.

The darkmage *Greshym*.

The bent figure shifted his grip on his staff. Belgan's eyes seemed to shine momentarily stronger with the false brightness of a fever. Joach recognized a spell of influence, one of Greshym's favorite magicks. But Belgan clearly fought this possession, trying to struggle through the fog of deceptions.

Now alerted, Joach could almost smell the dark energies here. He had once dabbled in the black arts himself when he had stolen the darkmage's staff. Squinting, Joach studied the monster's new stave. Greenish crystals laced its length, shining sickly like dripping pustules on the gray wood. This new staff appeared even more deadly than the old poi'wood one. Joach's blood rang with its proximity. Attuned to the dark magicks, he sensed the power welling through the staff and into the enfeebled figure.

Strong emotions flared in Joach: rage, fear, hatred, loathing. But as he stared at the staff, his heart burned with both disgust and desire. A part of him was drawn to the energy emanating from the sick length of gray wood.

His hands formed twin fists. He stepped forward, unable to control himself.

Greshym's gaze flicked in his direction. Milky eyes in an age-ravaged face stared back at Joach, amused, triumphant. From the doorway behind Greshym, a crooked, hulking creature clambered down the three steps on cloven hoofs. It groveled at the edge of the darkmage's robe. From a flat-muzzled face, piggish eyes glared at Joach. Its pointed ears were held back against its skull in clear aggression.

"Do you like my new pet, Joach?" Greshym whispered. "I needed someone to be my dog after you left me."

Before Joach could respond, the darkmage flicked his staff and touched the guildmaster's shoulder.

Belgan's arm sprang up like a tweaked marionette. A signal. All around the yard—at windows, ledges, and doors—scores of armed men and women appeared. Weapons bristled: bows and arrows, swords and axes.

Joach retreated toward his companions.

The staff moved again, and the guildmaster's arm swept down, like an ax cleaving wood.

"Kill them!" Belgan yelled. "Slay them all!"

*   *   *

KESLA REACHED THE CANYON THAT LED INTO ALCAZAR'S HEART as Belgan's order echoed out to the sands. She froze. *What is happening?*

A malluk, eyes rolled to white in panic, burst out of the chasm's gloom and galloped toward her. Kesla dodged to the side, almost trampled into the sand as it raced from the canyon and out into the open desert, packs and gear flying from its back. Its drover was not far behind, a shout on his lips, a whip raised in his hand. The man's forehead was bloody. He must have been thrown by the beast.

Kesla stopped him as he ran past. "What's wrong?"

Already the clash of steel on steel rang out to her. Men shouted deeper in the canyon.

The tribesman shook his head and spoke rapidly in the desert tongue. "An ambush. The master of Alcazar has gone mad. He's closed the gates to the castle and seeks to murder the outlanders."

"Why?"

The man shook his head and ran after his panicked mount, leaving Kesla alone at the entrance to the canyon. She tried to grasp meaning behind the drover's words. It made no sense.

Turning from the entrance, she raced back into the desert and ran along the edge of the great rock, circling its base. When she was younger, she and Innsu used to sneak out of Alcazar. Both trained in the assassin ways of the snake, and there were few walls they could not scale. Flying past a tumble of sandstone boulders, Kesla came upon a section of cliff face that seemed sheer.

She shrugged her cloak aside and, with a flick of her wrist, shot a grappling rope up to a small outcropping high overhead. With a skilled tug, she set the trisling hooks and scrambled up the thin rope of braided spider's silk. Her toes in their soft boots found easy purchase. Once high enough, she used her weight to swing the rope, her feet racing along the wall. At the right moment, she shoved with all her strength and swung up and out to a small ledge. She let go of the rope with one hand and snatched a hold on the ledge's lip. Hanging precariously, she caught a loop of the rope around an ankle so as not to lose it, then freed her other hand and grabbed the ledge. Quickly, she pulled herself up onto the narrow shelf. Rolling, she retrieved the slack rope, snapped its length to free the trisling hooks, and wound the rope back to her hip.

She repeated her efforts twice more to scale the sheer face until far above the desert floor. At its top was a lookout's post, long deserted and mostly forgotten. She and Innsu had discovered it in their youth. Pulling up onto the stone platform, she crossed to the tiny tunnel that burrowed into Alcazar. The passage was no more than a long crawlway. On hands and knees, Kesla scurried down its length.

In the narrow space, the panic in her heart welled up. Why was Belgan attacking her companions?

Dusty and abraded, Kesla finally reached the tunnel's end. She used a spy mirror to examine the small storeroom. Nothing but crates and an old rolled rug propped in the corner. She crawled out, senses straining for any sign of others. Once up, she slipped to the door, pressed an ear to the wood, then tested its hinges. A whispered creak sounded as she twisted the latch and edged the door open.

Beyond was a deserted servant's hall. The air smelled little disturbed; dust lay thick. Kesla did not hesitate. She had been taught the wisdom of when to sit still and when to hurry, skills learned from the masters of this very house.

In a few swift steps, she reached the stairs leading from the heights to the more-occupied lower sections. As she flew down the steps, the sounds of battle grew around her: screams, shouts, clashes of steel.

When she reached the fifth level of the keep, she darted from the stairwell and headed toward the windows and balconies that opened onto the central yard. She did not have to go far before she collided into one of her fellow students, five years her junior, running back from the open window.

He had a bow slung over a shoulder, and his quiver was empty. His eyes flew wide as he recognized Kesla.

She grabbed him by his shoulder before he could flee from her. "What is going on, Symion? Why are you attacking the outlanders?"

The younger boy cowered a bit. "Master Belgan says they come to destroy us all, minions of the wit'ch you killed."

"Killed? What are you talking about?"

"You're bewit'ched! You've brought death back to Alcazar!" Symion tried to break free of her grip, attempting to use the cinch-knot technique, but Kesla easily countered it and held him in place.

"Nonsense," she hissed at him. "I'm not under any spell. The wit'ch still lives and has freely offered to aid us in our battle against Tular."

In Symion's eyes, suspicion shone.

"It's true, Symion. This fighting must be stopped, or all hope for saving the Wastes will be lost. You must take me to someone who will listen."

"But the wit'ch's brother—"

"Joach?"

Symion frowned. "A wanderer came from the desert. He holed up with the guildmaster in his rooms for half a day. When Belgan came out, he was convinced the wit'ch's brother was a danger to all the Wastes, bent to avenge his sister."

Kesla was shocked. Master Belgan was not one to believe rumors and innuendos. What had convinced Belgan that Joach and the others were a threat? Again it made no sense. Belgan would not move without serious proof. For a moment, she began to doubt herself. Could it be possible? Could she have been somehow deceived?

She shook her head. There was no way. "Master Belgan must have been deceived," she mumbled, though such a thought shook Kesla to her foundations.

Distracted, she allowed the boy to wriggle free of her hold and dance out of her reach.

"You are the one deceived!" Symion yelled back at her and raced down a side corridor before she could stop him. She heard his voice raised in alarm, announcing her presence.

Kesla hurried away, toward the windows and balconies. She had to see what was happening. She had to find a way to stop this madness that had infiltrated her home.

She turned a corner, and sunlight flared up ahead, flowing through a set of doors thrown wide open. She hurried forward to the balcony. It was abandoned, most likely Symion's post during the ambush. She recalled his bow and empty quiver. He must have run out of arrows and gone to fetch more.

Stepping into the bright light of the midday sun, she crossed to the balcony's balustrade. The sounds of battle swelled. She leaned over the rail to view the central yard.

Below, chaos reigned. The paving stones flowed with blood. Bodies lay sprawled across the yard. The clash of steel rang loudly, as did the cries of rage and screams of pain.

Amidst the fighting, Kesla easily spotted her friends.

Kast and Hunt fought with axes in one hand and swords in the other. They were twin whirlwinds of death, laying waste to all that neared. The two guarded both Sy-wen and little Sheeshon. They would let no one come close.

Not far from them, in the thick of the melee, Innsu twirled, bringing the quick death of the striking snake. He spun and twisted his curved sword, while two other tribesmen fought to guard his flanks. Even from her high perch, Kesla recognized the mask of pain fixed on Innsu's face as he slew those he knew by name.

From the far wall, a volley of arrows arced toward the outlanders and their allies, but rather than raining down upon them, a sudden gust turned the flight aside. Below, Kesla spotted the reason for the sudden fortuitous breeze.

Richald sat upon his broken litter, an arm held high, scintillating with energy. Around him, his fellow elv'in danced with crossbows and thin silver swords, guarding their captain. They flew like flittering moths, almost too fast to see, bringing death both near and far. Richald suddenly flicked his wrist, and the deadly volley of arrows swung to pepper down upon the attackers themselves.

Men and women fell. Kesla watched one girl, no older than eight winters, take a bolt through the eye and fall, twitching upon the stone.

Kesla knew her name. *Lisl.*

Tears of frustration and anger blurred Kesla's vision. Master Belgan would never allow someone so young to fight. He would never allow *any* of this to happen—not if he was in his right mind.

The fighting continued.

Off to the right, someone screamed and fell from a balcony, crashing broken-limbed to the pavement below, an elv'in bolt through his neck.

Death had truly come to Alcazar—but not for the reason

Master Belgan had claimed. It was not vengeance that fueled this battle. It was delusion. Two allies had been set against one another. But why? And more importantly by *whom*?

Kesla searched the bloody yard. Finally, leaning far over the rail, she saw her answer directly below her. Master Belgan stood at the main entrance to the keep, his red cloak and flowing white hair easy to spot.

At his side stood a bent-backed figure, leaning on a long staff. Kesla had never seen him before, but she could guess who he was—the wanderer Symion had mentioned.

From her vantage point, she watched in disgust as a misshapen creature pranced about the pair of men. It was clearly being driven wild by its blood lust, gnashing at the air, claws ripping at the edge of Master Belgan's cloak. But Kesla's teacher seemed oblivious to the horrid creature's antics and braying cries. Watching this, Kesla cast aside any lingering doubts. The guildmaster was possessed by some geis or spell.

The cloaked figure lifted a stumped wrist and pointed. The motion drew Kesla's attention from the strange beast. Belgan stepped aside, and Kesla saw to where the bent figure pointed.

At the foot of the stairs, a figure was forced to his knees. An arrow protruded from the prisoner's shoulder. He was held in place by two journeymen assassins: Dryll and Ynyian, masters of the hunt.

Belgan waved a hand, and the figure's hood was ripped away. The prisoner glared up at the two men.

Kesla gasped, a fist at her throat.

It was Joach.

JOACH GLOWERED AT GRESHYM, THEN SPAT AT HIS ENEMY, HIS aim true.

The darkmage merely smiled at his display, not even bothering to wipe the spittle dripping from his chin.

The response from his captors was more dramatic. Joach's head was yanked cruelly backward by a fist twisted in his hair. One of the assassins leaned to his ear. "Do not again insult a guest of Alcazar."

On his other side, the second guard grabbed the arrow imbedded in his shoulder and ground the shaft in farther. Joach's shoulder exploded with fire. He tried not to cry out, but the pain was too great, too sudden. A scream ripped from his throat. Tears rose in his eyes.

Moments ago, he had been knocked off his feet by the hunter's arrow. He had been stunned, unable to move, even when the tides of battle had flowed away from him. Cut off from his companions, he had been easily captured by the pair of hunters.

His head was released, and Joach sagged to the paving stones. Behind him, cries and the strike of steel grew dim as agony threatened to overwhelm him. Movement drew his eyes back forward. Greshym leaned toward him. A leathery beast capered at the darkmage's ankles, snuffling at Joach's blood. Greshym nudged it aside and reached toward Joach with the butt of his staff.

Joach struggled to pull away, but he was restrained by his captors. The sick, corpse-gray stave wavered before his eyes.

"You can smell the magick in here, can't you?" Greshym said. "You've tasted the blackness. It marks you, Joach."

"Never," he gasped out. But in truth, he *could* sense the energy thrilling through the foul wood. Its greenish crystalline surface glowed and pulsed with power. Joach had a hard time looking away. It was darkly beautiful. His blood remembered wielding the dread magick of balefire.

Unbidden, a hand—his half hand, two fingers lost to the sick magick of an ill'guard in the catacombs under A'loa Glen— reached to the wood. It was the hand that had once held Greshym's stolen staff. It drew to the length of wood like lodestone to iron. Blood dribbled from his fingertips—blood that had trailed down his arm from his impaled shoulder.

Greshym's wrinkled smile spread wider.

A part of Joach knew he'd be lost if he touched the staff. It would claim his spirit forever—but he could not resist. Bloody fingers stretched to the gray wood, drawn by its power. Deep in his heart, a scream bubbled up. He knew he was a moment away from total annihilation. A simple touch, and all would be lost.

A savage howl erupted. It cut through the dark enchantment. Joach's eyes flicked to the side. The beast at Greshym's feet lunged forward. It snapped at Joach's bloody fingers, crazed by blood lust and hunger, unable to resist the flesh dangling so near. The creature's wide maw swallowed his hand to the wrist; razored teeth tore into flesh, crushing through bone.

Joach fell back, but his arm was caught by the creature. It shook his limb like a dog fighting for a bone.

"No, Rukh!" Greshym screeched with thwarted rage. He struck the creature backhanded with his staff. The beast flew high, striking the wall hard and landing in a curled ball. It mewled and writhed on the stones, its flesh smoking where the staff had touched.

Joach was thrown backward by the flare of magick, colliding with his captors. On his knees, Joach raised his arm. Blood fountained from the severed stump of his wrist. His hand was gone.

One of his captors quickly twisted a length of binding cord around his upper arm, cinching it tight, squeezing off his blood. Joach swooned on his knees, falling on his face toward the stones. Before he hit, he was jerked slightly and landed on his good shoulder. He rolled enough to see the fighting in the yard: blood, steel, screams, sprawled bodies, and crawling wounded.

In the middle of the chaos, a black blur grew, spreading wide. Joach tried to focus on it through his pain and shock. A smoky cloud. Then the darkness formed a great winged dragon crouched in the center of the yard. It bellowed with rage.

Ragnar'k . . .

"Grab the boy!" Greshym ordered savagely. "Bring him into the castle!"

His captors hesitated. Joach turned his head. Greshym motioned to the tall pale figure, who had remained a statue the entire time. The figure turned to the hunters. "Take the boy!" he croaked out, clearly a puppet whose strings had been pulled.

"Yes, Master Belgan."

Joach was jerked to his feet and slung between the two tall men. Greshym led the way through the open doors and into the castle's darkness. The beaten creature followed, groveling at its master's heels.

Passing through the threshold, Joach craned back around and watched Ragnar'k rip into the defenders of Alcazar, tearing through them, forging forward.

But it was too late for Joach. His limp form was hauled farther into the depths of the castle. Ahead, Greshym lifted his staff, aglow in the murk. Behind them, the castle's broken doors swept back into place, slamming shut with the finality of a coffin's lid.

*   *   *

SY-WEN SAT ATOP HER DRAGON. THOUGH THE GREAT BEAST WAS NOT able to fly out of this confined space with his injured wing, he was able to defend their rapidly weakening companions. Up to now, they had managed to hold off the ambush through magick and strength of limb, but neither was an indefatigable resource. Against so many, it was only a matter of time until the sheer numbers attacking them overran the smaller party.

As such, Sy-wen had no choice but to call forth the dragon. They had delayed up to now, hoping for some sense to come to the denizens of Alcazar. Once the black dragon was released, it would be hard to convince the castle's defenders that their group was not some minion of the Black Heart. And this concern proved rapidly true. The sudden appearance of the dragon triggered a general panic. People fled. Some of the slower were trampled under the feet of others. Those that remained, the bravest and most skilled, fought even harder. From here, there was little chance of gaining the trust of Alcazar. Their best hope lay in escape. They would have to take their chances in the open desert.

Using wing, claw, and fang, Ragnar'k cleared a space between the attackers and the defenders. Behind the large dragon, the others gathered in a corner of the yard, not far from the gates. A temporary lull settled over the courtyard as both sides regrouped. The northerners needed a way out of here.

Sy-wen pointed to the iron barrier. "Can you rip out those bars?"

A dismissive snort sounded. *Small cage not hold Ragnar'k.*

As the creature turned, Richald called from his broken litter, his weak voice carried on winds of magick to her perch. "Joach . . . I don't see the boy anywhere here."

Sy-wen twisted in her seat and searched the small corner. The elv'in was right. Joach was missing. In the confusion of fighting, he must have been separated. She searched the wide yard but saw nothing.

She stood slightly on the dragon's back and yelled, "Joach!"

No answer. An arrow whistled past her ear. She sank back closer to Ragnar'k, under the shield of his half-raised wings. A small voice shouted from the far side of the yard. Sy-wen squinted and spotted Kesla standing at an upper balcony. How had she gotten up there?

"Joach was captured!" Kesla shouted, her words as shrill as an eagle's cry. "He was taken inside! I will try to find him, but some dark magick has taken root here. Make for the desert! Join with Shaman Parthus! I will join you with Joach if I can!"

Sy-wen lifted an arm, acknowledging that Kesla had been heard.

Hunt spoke near the dragon's wing. "It could be a trick. It was Kesla that led us into this ambush. How do we know she does not mean Joach harm?"

Innsu, the young assassin, heard his words and responded hotly. "Kesla is no traitor."

Sy-wen considered both their words—but she also remembered the way Kesla had stared at Joach on the journey here. It was not hard to read the young girl's heart. It took a woman to recognize love in another's eyes. Sy-wen straightened in her seat. "She will not betray Joach," she said firmly, and turned away. With a silent thought, she urged Ragnar'k to attack the gate.

With a grunt of assent, his neck twisted; fangs as long Sy-wen's forearm grabbed the bars. She felt the dragon's muscles tense and bulge with the strain of the stubborn iron. His silver claws dug deep into the paving stones.

One of the assassins used the moment of distraction to race forward, ax raised. But Hunt ducked under the dragon's wing and blocked the cloaked man. Ax rang on ax. Both men were skilled masters of their weapons—but Hunt was not as fresh. His heel slipped in a pool of blood, and he missed a parry. The wood handle of his opponent's ax cracked across the Bloodrider's face. He fell backward.

The opponent lunged forward, his ax sweeping down in death stroke.

"Ragnar'k!" Sy-wen yelled.

I see, my bonded . . .

The dragon twitched his wing, slamming its edge into the attacker's side. From her perch, Sy-wen heard ribs crack, and the man went sailing across the yard. Hunt, dazed, lumbered to his feet and wiped blood from his lips. He spat out a single tooth that skittered across the stones, then glared at the row of attackers, daring another to approach.

No one did. It seemed they were only too happy to let the outlanders leave.

The groan of iron and rasp of stone drew Sy-wen's attention. Glancing back to the gate, she saw the portcullis and a section of the barrier above pull free. With a final tug, Ragnar'k ripped it away and tossed it across the yard. It clanged and bounced across the bloody paving stones.

With the way now open, Sy-wen waved the group forward. She and Ragnar'k would defend their rear.

Outside the gate, a group of desert tribesmen, those who had accompanied them from Oo'shal, helped the injured. One of the party stepped forward, eyeing the dragon warily. "Shaman Parthus waits for you in the desert."

Sy-wen nodded. "Hurry," she urged her friends.

Innsu helped one of his injured comrades, while Hunt carried Sheeshon, who was clearly terrified. With the litter broken, Richald was hauled between two of the cloaked desert men. The other elv'in were too weak from fighting to assist. Limping, the worn and bloodied party retreated into the chasm.

Once the others were safely under way, Ragnar'k backed into the canyon, keeping a watchful eye on any last attack. It never came. No one was willing to challenge the beast, especially when it was clearly leaving.

Sy-wen glanced across the fouled yard. Blood stained the red stones black. Bodies lay twisted. The very air reeked of death. She glanced to the castle beyond. Though the fighting in the yard had ended, somewhere in the keep's shadowed halls, the battle still awaited a final act. Two of their party had yet to escape this ambush.

Sy-wen willed them her strength. "May the Sweet Mother protect you both."

KESLA FLED THROUGH THE HALLS, MOVING LIGHTLY ON HER TOES, ears pricked for any noise. She had to find where they were taking Joach. She had seen the ravenous beast's attack. Joach needed a healer's attention as soon as possible. But she had to be cautious. Clearly the cloaked stranger wielded black magicks.

Wending down stairs and gliding silently along passages, Kesla came at last to the first level of the keep. She stepped into the great meeting hall and pulled her cloak's hood over her head, hiding her face in shadow. She studied the room. People crowded here, some helping the wounded, some walking dead-eyed. All were shocked and bone-tired. Among them, servants bustled with hot water, bandages, medicinal herbs, and salves.

Kesla kept her face down as she strode purposefully across the room. Groans and cries of pain echoed around her, and she cringed. As she walked along one of the walls toward the far side, familiar voices caught her attention. Her feet slowed.

"I can't believe Master Belgan did not at least try talking to these outlanders." It was Humph, Alcazar's stablemaster. There was no mistaking his short, stout body and muscled arms. "It is so unlike Belgan to strike without council."

"And that desert wanderer . . ." Kesla recognized Humph's companion: Mistress Shargyll, matron of the kitchens. The large woman wiped her hands on her stained apron. "He crossed near me as I prepared the morning's meal. My skin crawled with his mere presence. There is something wrong about that man."

"I agree. Master Belgan takes this stranger's advisement too easily. During the attack, I saw young Innsu fighting alongside the outlanders. And when the group left, I overheard a tribesman say they were being taken to the desert, to join Shaman Parthus." Humph blew out a rude noise, sounding not unlike a disgruntled malluk. "None of this makes sense."

Kesla paused, hearing her own sentiments in the stablemaster's words. Could she trust these two to help her? Joach's chances were best with more allies. Kesla stepped to Mistress Shargyll's side.

The large woman glanced over to her, sensing her presence. "What is it, child?"

Kesla lifted her face and saw the shock in the kitchen matron's eyes. "I need your help," Kesla whispered.

Mistress Shargyll stared, stunned. Humph leaned over and blinked in surprise.

Kesla did not know how they would act from here. She pleaded with her eyes—then Shargyll reached a thick arm and scooped her to her side, pulling her between them. "You should not be seen here, little Kes. There is murder in the air. Many think you've betrayed Alcazar."

Kesla nodded. "I ran into Symion. I know the lies that have been seeded here and that took root in Master Belgan. These outlanders came at my bidding, with Master Parthus' blessing. They are strong allies; they come to help us, not harm us."

"I knew it!" Humph exclaimed a little too loudly.

Others glanced their way. Shargyll moved her wide bulk to hide the smaller girl and tugged Kesla's hood a bit farther over her face.

"Master Belgan is under some dark enchantment," Kesla said. "He and the stranger have taken a prisoner, a friend. I must find where they have imprisoned him. According to Shaman Parthus, the future of the Wastes lies in this man's blood. He must be freed."

"I saw the lad you mentioned," Humph whispered. "Gravely wounded. He should have been taken to the healers. Even a prisoner deserves having his wounds dressed. That callousness alone made me question Master Belgan's spirit."

"Do you know where he was taken?" Kesla asked.

Mistress Shargyll answered. "I overheard Ynyian and Dryll when they came down for a flagon of ale. They have the boy bound in Master Belgan's chambers."

"I must go there."

"How can we help?" Humph said.

Kesla had been taught in the assassin's way of the snake: to move unseen, to enter hidden places, to strike swiftly. But here she would need help. She glanced to her two old friends. "It will be dangerous."

GRESHYM'S BLOOD RAGED. HE CLUMPED ANGRILY BACK AND FORTH across the small chamber whose windows had been curtained against the sun. His plan had come so close to fruition. He glowered at the misshapen beast cowering in a corner. If not for the untimely attack by the stump gnome, Joach would have been lost to the black magicks by now, his spirit tainted forever. With the boy bent, it would have been a simple thing then to complete the one final act necessary to return youth to Greshym's decayed body.

So close . . .

Leaning on his staff, Greshym studied Joach. The boy was tied to the bed, naked, spread-eagled. Blood from his severed wrist seeped into the bedding, even with the tourniquet. His skin was pale from shock and blood loss. Joach's eyes remained dazed, as he waxed into and out of consciousness.

Greshym scowled and crossed back to Joach. The boy must

not die. In his young body, so rich in magicks, lay the hope of freeing Greshym of his own decrepit one. Greshym lifted his staff and touched Joach's stumped wrist. He whispered a quick spell. Slowly, severed veins and arteries closed; then flesh sealed over the exposed bone. Soon the ragged tear was replaced by a smooth stump. Satisfied, Greshym repaired the arrow wound just as effortlessly.

Greshym saw the boy's body relax, his breathing deepen. Death had been staved off for the moment.

Though still lost, Joach's eyes slowly refocused.

Good. Greshym leaned away. He could now continue what had been interrupted. He leaned his staff against the bed, then held out his hand to the room's only other occupant.

Belgan passed him a long, crooked dagger.

Greshym's fingers closed over its hilt. There was another way to break this boy. It would take only a little more work.

JOACH WALKED THE DREAM DESERT AGAIN. HE STOOD NAKED UNDER the starless sky. Blood trailed his feeble steps across the sand. He teetered, weak. Then a wave of coolness swept over his body. It was as if he dove again into the refreshing waters of Oo'shal. The soothing energy spread through his body, centering upon his burning wrist and inflamed shoulder, a balm that washed away pain. He sighed in relief, lifting his arm to watch rent flesh seal to a smooth stump.

"Magick," he mumbled to the empty desert.

The desert answered. "Dark magick. Can you tell one from the other?"

Joach turned and found a familiar figure standing at his side. "Shaman Parthus?"

The elder was dressed in his usual red desert cloak, the hood tossed back. His eyes shone brightly. "It is time you accepted your heritage."

"What do you mean?"

"You are a shaper. A dream sculptor. If you are to live, you must accept your gift."

"I don't under—" Joach suddenly gasped, folding over as pain again struck him, ripping into his chest.

The shaman did not move to aid him, but simply stood silently.

Joach lifted his hand from his chest. Blood dripped from his fingers. He stared down to his bare skin and saw a rune slowly form, carved in fiery lines of pain. Glancing back up, he saw a new world overlap the dream desert. A small chamber appeared as a ghostly image. In this other world, his body was bound to a bed. He watched as Greshym, bent over his body, dragged a dagger along his chest, drawing the rune in his flesh.

Greshym seemed to sense Joach's attention and glanced up. "So you wake, Joach? Good. I want you to watch this."

In the desert, Joach turned to Shaman Parthus. The tribesman and desert had grown just as insubstantial as the room. "What is happening?"

"You are twixt the dream and the real, Joach, where only a sculptor can walk. I can't follow you there."

Greshym also seemed to have heard Joach's question. "You ask what's happening, my boy? Isn't it obvious?" He lifted the bloody dagger. "What won't be given willingly, I'll take by force. I mean to steal your spirit and twist it past any undoing. You will be mine forever."

As the darkmage returned to his work, Joach stared back at Shaman Parthus. "Help me," he pleaded.

The image of the shaman faded further. "I can't walk your path, Joach. Only you can do this." Parthus lifted an arm and pointed to the bloody trail he had left in the sand.

Joach stared at the bright stain.

"Remember what I taught you," Parthus said. "In the dream desert, what is figment can be given substance by your attention. Use this knowledge; tap into the power of your blood."

"I don't know how to—"

"The dreaming desert has called you. It is time you answered." The shaman's form slowly dissipated. "You go now where I can't follow."

Joach gazed around him. The dream desert seemed to glow brighter. Simultaneously, the room beyond grew more substantial. He watched as Greshym handed the dagger to the tall, pale figure of Master Belgan. In the corner, he spotted the crouched beast, licking its burned flank.

Even in his nose, the two worlds commingled: the dry stillness of the glowing desert mixed with the hint of burning tallow from the bedside candles. But one smell was shared by both worlds—the red scent of Joach's own spilled blood.

He stared again at the bloody sand. With the two worlds overlapped, the red trail seemed in both planes: dribbled both on the sand and across the floor of the chamber. A connection between the two worlds. Though he did not fully understand, he remembered the shaman's words. He concentrated upon the blood, trying to make it more real. As he did so, he felt a bit of his spirit and strength drain out and fill the blood. The stain grew brighter and more substantial, the connection between the two worlds stronger. Joach began to sense the flows of power here. He could almost see the threads of magick twining out from his blood and into the sand. And as he stared further, these thin strands grew more substantial. But what did it mean?

Before he could ponder the mystery, a loud knock drew his attention back into the castle chamber. Someone pounded on the room's door.

At his bedside, Greshym waved his hand, and Belgan called out gruffly. "What do you want? Who disturbs us?"

The room's door creaked open, and a short, stocky man bowed his way into the room. "I've come to report that the outlanders have been chased off. They're retreating deep into the desert."

Belgan nodded. "Thank you, Humph."

The man's eyes flicked toward Joach strapped to the bed. Greshym noticed his attention. "Persuasion to make the young man reveal his secrets."

Humph nodded, wearing a sick expression. His eyes narrowed briefly as he turned away. He waved a hand, and a portly woman stepped into the room. She carried a wide tray in her arms, burdened with tankards of ale and plates of sliced meats and breads.

"I thought you and your guest might like some food," Humph said. "Mistress Shargyll has prepared a small dinner."

From the corner, the hunched beast lifted its head at the smell of roasted meats, still warm from the kitchens' ovens. It shambled closer, snuffling.

The woman glanced to the creature, suddenly seeing it. Her eyes flew wide, and she shrieked, throwing her platter into the air. Food and ale flew high. She pulled out a small dagger and warded off the beast.

"There is nothing to fear," Greshym said with thick irritation.

The woman glanced to the darkmage, all panic gone from her face, leaving only cunning. "Yes, there is." The dagger flew from her fingers and pierced Greshym's left eye.

A long leather whip appeared in Humph's hand. As Greshym stumbled back from the dagger strike, Humph snapped his whip, wrapping its tip around the darkmage's staff, and with a tug, ripped it from his fingers. The stave flew across the room to clatter against the far wall.

It had all happened in a heartbeat. Beside the bed, Master Belgan sagged, like a marionette with its strings cut. "Wh-what is going on?" he asked blearily.

Hope surged in Joach—but it did not last long.

Greshym straightened. He raised his hand, and the stolen staff flew back into his fingers. Energy surged along the gray wood's length. Joach recognized the spell. *Balefire.*

"Run!" he croaked out—but he was caught between two worlds, unable to help those who had come to his aid.

Greshym pointed his staff, its end flaring with black flames.

"No . . ." Joach moaned.

Then, from the curtain behind Greshym's back, a small figure glided out, moving so silently that not even the drapery rustled. It was Kesla. Joach caught a brief glimpse of an open window behind the curtain and a trailing rope outside. She ran with a dagger in each hand. Before Greshym could react, she struck him from behind, driving both daggers into his neck. Black blood surged from the wounds.

Kesla danced back, a cry on her lips. Her hands smoked where the darkmage's blood had touched her skin.

Greshym whirled around, sweeping his staff toward Kesla. Dread energies coursed its length. Humph attacked with his whip, but when its leather touched the wood this time, its length was set aflame. Humph grunted in surprise, tossing his weapon aside as it burned to ash.

Joach watched in horror as the end of Greshym's staff bloomed into a black rose of darkfire. The daggers piercing the darkmage's flesh fell away harmlessly. "You will pay for that!" Greshym screeched.

Kesla backed to the wall, her hands curled painfully to her chest.

Fire flared from the staff's end.

No! Without thought, Joach struck out instinctively, grabbing the threads of power in his veins. From the bloodstained sands of the dream desert, a colossal fist of sculpted sand shot upward, passing from this world to the next.

As balefire shot out of Greshym's staff, sandy fingers opened, and the large palm blocked the spew of deadly energies, absorbing it, growing more substantial. Its flow stanched, the sudden backlash of power threw the darkmage across the room.

Kesla, shocked and confused, remained sheltered behind the sculpted hand.

Greshym shared her expression as he rose from the floor. He slid along the wall until he was near his beastly pet. The darkmage's single milky eye studied Joach, seeming to read the flows of power in the room, sensing the source. "You are full of surprises, boy."

Joach, still twined to his power, birthed another fist of sand. He swept it toward Greshym and his foul pet, meaning to swat them from this world. But before it reached them, Greshym struck his staff on the stone floor—and the beast and darkmage vanished in a whirl of oily blackness.

Words and laughter echoed out. "This is not over, boy!"

The dream fist slammed into the empty wall and blew into a shower of sand. The first hand, however, remained where it stood, now a sculpture in sandstone, sheltering Kesla.

Belgan collapsed toward the floor, no longer supported by magick. Humph and Shargyll rushed to his side while Kesla retrieved a dagger and sliced Joach's bonds.

She touched his cheek, her fingers cool on his hot skin.

"You must get the boy out of here," Shargyll said. "Join Parthus in the desert with the others."

"How is Master Belgan?" Kesla asked.

"He lives but has been cruelly used. It will take time to return him to his wits. Until then you and the boy must not be found here."

Kesla nodded, her expression worried.

Humph stood, eyeballing the sandstone sculpture. "We'll go to the stables. I'll saddle up one of the malluks so you can travel swiftly."

Kesla gently wrapped Joach in the bed's blanket. "I'll need help with him. He's still dazed."

Humph leaned over the bed and scooped up Joach and the blanket in strong arms. "We must not tarry."

Kesla checked Joach and tugged up a corner of the blanket, but before drawing it over his face, she quickly leaned down. "Thank you," she whispered in his ear, then kissed him on the cheek.

With the touch of her lips, Joach lost his hold on the real world. Consciousness faded. He drifted deeper into the dream desert again. As he did so, the sands grew brighter. The figure of Shaman Parthus reappeared in the sands at his side.

"You've done well, Joach," the elder said with a quiet smile of satisfaction. "Now sleep."

"But—"

"Sleep. The road from here leads to the Southwall . . . to Tular. You must be rested. So sleep, sculptor."

Given permission, Joach let loose his control. The dream desert and the shaman faded around him. He fell into a deep slumber, where even dreams did not exist. Still, one memory swirled down with him into the bottomless depths of his spirit: *the brush of soft lips on his skin.*

Book Four

STORM CASTLE

12

FROM THE DECK OF THE *SUNCHASER*, ELENA STARED AS THE COAST-line appeared like an apparition out of the mists. A light rain fell, but she stood under an awning set up on the foredeck and was dressed warmly in a calfskin leather jacket trimmed in rabbit fur. Overhead, the weeping sky was a featureless gray that stretched forever, as it had for the past six days, covering both sun and stars. During these last days of the long journey over the Great Ocean, the only difference between day and night was a slight brightening in the gloom.

But at last their flight was almost at an end.

Ahead, the skies blew against a steep coastline, bunching up into dark thunderheads. Lightning crackled, but the storm was too distant for them to hear any thunder.

Still, the forks of lightning lit up the mist-shrouded cliffs of Gul'gotha. It was a formidable sight. Jagged rock faces were beset with an angry white surf, while cracked boulders churned in the waters like clashing seabeasts. No ship dared approach this place, let alone try to make landfall.

Earlier in the day, Elena had studied the map of Gul'gotha with the others. Along this coastline there was only one safe port, far to the south: Banal, a trading port that made Port Rawl seem like a well-kept, civilized haven. But they would not be going there. With the elv'in windship, they could land any-where. Wennar, the d'warf battalion's leader, had placed a thick finger on a mountainous region of the map, a good hundred leagues from the coast. "We should go here," he had stated.

"Why?" Er'ril had asked with his usual sharp suspicion.

The thick-browed d'warf had grunted. "It's our homeland—

and the birthplace of the Dark Lord's reign. If you seek something of the blackest evil, it will be found there."

Without any better idea where to begin their search for the Manticore Gate, they had agreed to start there. As Elena stared out at the storm-besieged cliffs, she remembered Cassa Dar's old story of the Dark Lord's appearance among the d'warves:

Five centuries ago, a troupe of deep miners discovered a vein of ore, leagues under our mountains. They had never seen such a stone: blacker than the darkest tunnel and impervious to any tool. Undaunted and determined to mine this vein, they used the kingdom's strongest hammer to attack the stone. They employed the Try'sil, the Hammer of Thunder. Its magick-wrought iron was said to shatter any stone. And this claim proved true. The stone was mined and given the name ebon'stone by its discoverers. At first, it was greatly treasured: every D'warf Lord lusted to work a piece, to prove his skill at fashioning the new ore. Bowls, cups, plates, swords, even statues were carved from the material. But then the stone began to warp and bind the d'warves in ways they did not understand. The lands, too, began to sicken and poison. Volcanoes grew, and the ground constantly shook. Gases and ash soured the skies. Poisonous beasts, the mul'gothra and skal'tum, began to appear from pits deep under the mountains. The Dark Lord arose among our people, almost as if out of the bowels of the land. Some said the Black Heart was a d'warf, succumbed to the stone's black magick, while others said he came from the stone itself, released by our miners from an ebon'stone tomb. No one knew for sure.

Though dressed warmly in leathers and woolens, Elena shivered at the thought of where they must travel next—into the heart of Gul'gotha, into the heart of this ancient mystery. Who was the Dark Lord of the Gul'gotha? Where had the demon truly come from? Cassa Dar's final words echoed in her head: *No one knew for sure . . .*

As Elena frowned at the broken coastline, a voice spoke behind her. "You should go below. We will be upon the storm soon."

Glancing over her shoulder, she saw Tol'chuk crouched

nearby. How long had he been there? For such a hulking creature, he could move as silently as a mouse sometimes. He leaned
on one knuckle of his thick right arm, bent to peer under the
awning. In the open, the rain had soaked the ridge of fur along
his bowed back and dripped down the thousand crevices of his
face and body. He appeared like a weathered mountain worn
down by the rain. The only part of him that did not seem carved
of rock was his large eyes, glowing a warm amber in concern
for her.

She smiled at his worry and touched his damp shoulder with a
gloved hand. When they had first met, his monstrous appearance
had frightened her, but over time, she could no longer see the
monster, just the large heart and undying loyalty. "I think the
storm is the least of our concerns in the days ahead," she said
softly. "But I appreciate your worry. I'll go down below in a moment. I just wanted to see Gul'gotha with my own eyes."

He nodded, peering over her shoulder. "It be not a welcome
sight."

Elena saw Tol'chuk touch his thigh pouch that hid the jeweled
Heart of his people. She moved a step closer to him, bringing her
arm around his thicker one. "We will not leave here until *both*
our missions are finished. This I promise. If there's a Gate here,
we'll destroy it. And if there's a way to rid your people of the
Bane, we'll find it."

A deep rumble flowed from the giant. Though it was wordless,
Elena heard the thanks in his tone. They stood silently for a few
moments more, then Tol'chuk spoke. "I don't think it be mere
luck that our paths go the same way now."

"What do you mean?"

"The Heart first guided me to you. I believe both our paths
will end at the same place." He stared out toward Gul'gotha.
"Wherever the Manticore Gate be hidden, it be there that all answers will come."

Elena nodded. "I believe you're right." She frowned once
more toward the coming storm. Thunder finally rumbled out to
them, as if trying to ward them off. She wished she could mind
the storm's warning but knew she could not. She turned from the
sight. "I'm ready to return below. Let's keep warm while we
still can."

Tol'chuk grunted and swung around. He led the way, sheltering her somewhat from the sting of the cold rain.

As Elena followed, she pondered the twining lines of fate. The Bane, the Weirgate, the birthplace of the Black Heart, the homeland of the d'warves—how did they all weave together?

Once again, Cassa Dar's words echoed to her.

No one knew for sure . . .

Elena glanced briefly over a shoulder before ducking through the hatch held open by Tol'chuk. On this path, answers to these mysteries would be discovered—of this she was sure. But she shivered as a bigger question loomed: *Would they be strong enough to face those answers?*

QUEEN TRATAL WATCHED THE FIERY-HAIRED WOMAN DESCEND INTO the bowels of the *Sunchaser*. Neither the woman nor her large companion had been aware of the queen's presence. Aboard the ship, Tratal could move unseen whenever and wherever she wanted. Wisps of energy still traced her figure, casting a heavy mist that hid her from others' eyes without clouding her own vision. She walked from her position by the stern rail. One hand trailed along the wood, caressing it like a lover brushing a sweetheart's cheek.

Alone, except for a lone sentry in the crow's nest atop the central mast, Tratal extended her senses into the ship. She made sure the woman was gone, feeling Elena's footsteps on a lower deck ladder. The wit'ch soon joined the others gathered in the galley.

Good . . .

She dropped her cloak of mists and stared ahead, past the ship's bow. No one had seemed to sense the falseness to the tempest hovering at the coastline. She signaled the elv'in sailor in the crow's nest. He nodded back to her.

All was in readiness.

Tratal faced forward. Along the bow of the ship, elemental energies crackled brightly as she tapped into the power of the storm ahead. A nimbus of silver-white hair plumed about her slender face as the magicks swelled in her. She lifted her arms, sighing in the play of wind and power. Sails swelled. Tratal aimed for the heart of the storm, a hard smile fixed on her face. In the gray light, her skin was carved ice, her eyes imbedded jewels of azure.

"Show yourself," she wind-spoke to the heavy clouds that hung above the storm-lashed cliffs ahead. "It is time!" Her words were borne on gusts of winds.

Near the coast, the mists slowly blew apart and a bank of angry clouds opened. A fleet of a dozen small sky-cutters broke free and swept forward like a flight of angry bees. Energy crackled along their black keels, stabbing downward in dazzling bolts of lightning. The swift warships split into two waves, diving to circle the larger flagship.

Whispers in the wind carried greetings and acknowledgment from each of the cutters' elv'in captains. They sounded their readiness.

"Then let it begin," Queen Tratal commanded. She sent more energies out into the false storm.

The black length of cloud swirled, and a passage opened through the middle of the storm. The small cutters, now flanking the larger ship, escorted it toward the roiling tunnel in the tempest. Far ahead, buried in the clouds and lit by flickers of lightning, she spotted familiar fortresses and battlements.

Queen Tratal smiled. For the past moon, Elena had refused to abandon this petty war and accept her true heritage and bloodline. Even her own son Meric had foolishly been swayed to the passions of these mud dwellers. But Queen Tratal was not so easily persuaded. She knew her duties to the past and future of her people. The bloodline of their lost king would not be lost again. It would be returned to its rightful place. What did the squabbling of land-bound nations concern the elv'in? They had flown above such fighting and wars for countless centuries.

Still, her attempts at convincing Elena had been another matter. The wit'ch had proven to be obstinate and headstrong. But there were other ways to turn a stubborn wind. If Elena would not travel willingly to the elv'in kingdom, then the kingdom would be brought to her.

The *Sunchaser* swept down into the long stormy tunnel, flanked by the cutters that assisted her in keeping the tempest at bay. Lightning flared in bright glows along the passage's walls. Ahead, at the end of the tunnel, massive wooden gates swung open. Bright, clear sunlight flowed out into the passage from the heart of the elv'in's sky fortress.

As they neared the open gates, the lead cutter's captain announced the return of their queen. Almost lost in the rumbling thunder of the storm, trumpets blared. Tratal's keen ears picked up the triumphant greeting. The head captain turned his attention back to the *Sunchaser*. His words were bold on the winds. "Welcome, Queen Tratal. Welcome back to Stormhaven."

As the city in the sky opened before her, she smiled, like ice finally breaking with the coming spring. It was good to be home again.

Stormhaven.

The elv'in citadel floated atop this unnatural storm, hidden from below, open to the bare sky above. For centuries, the city had flown over the world's seas and islands, oceans and lands— just an unexpected gale passing overhead. None were aware of what rode atop this tempest. For an endless time, none but the elv'in had ever set eyes upon the ancient citadel.

Until now.

Upon first learning of Elena's intent to leave A'loa Glen, Tratal had sent word by hawk to Stormhaven, ordering the citadel's keepers to fly the fortress to the monstrous cliffs of Gul'gotha. All was going as she had ordered. Before any of the others grew wise, the *Sunchaser* would be docked at Stormhaven—and at long last, the ancient king's bloodline would be rejoined to her own.

Queen Tratal whispered her own greeting to the girl below. "Welcome home, Elena. Welcome to your true home."

ER'RIL BARELY NOTICED AS THE RUMBLING THUNDER GREW WORSE. The planks under his feet trembled with each roar. Ignoring the storm, he remained intent on the map spread atop the galley table. He had borrowed the browned and weathered parchment from the libraries back at A'loa Glen. His eyes ran over the old names, many unreadable, the colored inks faded to blurs by age.

The lands of Gul'gotha.

Across from him, the captain of the d'warves, Wennar, hunched just as raptly. The craggy-faced d'warf poked a thick finger at a mountain. "We can land on the slopes of the southern side of Mount Gallmanor. There is an old trail that winds around its flank and into our homeland valleys. It should allow us to approach the region in secret."

"Why could we not just fly directly into your lands?" Elena asked. She stood by the hearth, warming her hands. Her hair still dripped and clung to her face. "I thought the mines and townships of your people were long abandoned."

Wennar glanced to her from under heavy brows. "They were abandoned by *d'warves*. But they are not uninhabited. I've heard tales of the diseased creatures and awful rites that are still performed there, fouling our lands. To explore, we must move swiftly and attract no unwanted attention." He tapped the map. "This is an old hunting trail. Few should be watching it."

Er'ril nodded. As much as he distrusted this d'warf, he could not fault his plan. It seemed sound. If anything lurked in the mines and valleys of the d'warf homelands, a more cautious approach was warranted. "I think we should consider Wennar's plan. In fact—"

Rrrippp . . .

Er'ril turned to see the little tamrink, Tikal, snatch up a torn corner of the map and pop it into his mouth. The furry beast chewed its stolen prize with much gusto. Er'ril swung a backhand at it, but Tikal went hopping away. It dodged around the crouched figure of Tol'chuk and scrambled toward its keeper.

"Tikal!" Mama Freda scolded with a snort. The old woman, who had been drowsing in the chair, pushed up. She scooped the fiery-furred tamrink and settled it into the crook of her arm. Her sightless face turned to Er'ril. "I'm sorry. He's unduly agitated right now."

An explosion of thunder rattled through the ship's bones.

"I'm not surprised," Elena said, her eyes glinting with worry. "The storm along the coast is piled high and dark."

Er'ril returned to his study of the map. "Queen Tratal will get us through safely. She said the storm is of no concern."

Mama Freda cleared her throat as Tikal whined in her arms. "I don't know." She cocked her head. Tikal mimicked her. "Something sounds wrong with this storm."

"What do you mean?" Er'ril grumbled, instantly suspicious.

The old healer simply shook her head.

Tol'chuk stirred, eyes slowly opening. "I should go and check."

"No need," Mama Freda said. "Tikal is faster." She bowed her face toward her pet, and Tikal jumped from her lap. The tiny tamrink scrambled out the door, running on all fours, a flash of fur.

Er'ril straightened from the map table. The others stood silently.

Mama Freda tugged her black shawl tighter about her shoulders. "Tikal has reached the middeck." Her lips pursed as she concentrated. "The winds are strong. Angry black clouds surround the ship on all sides. The sky is afire with lightning."

To punctuate her words, a new volley of rumbling thunder echoed through the ship.

"But . . . but the light is wrong. It's too bright. Tikal is climbing the rigging to get a better view. I see Queen Tratal. She's at the stern, full of power and crackling energy. She stretches for the sky, her toes barely touching the planks."

Mama Freda suddenly sat up straighter.

"What is it?" Elena asked.

"Other ships . . . I see smaller boats flanking ours."

Er'ril moved forward, a hand shifting to the hilt of his silver sword. "Attackers?"

"I don't think so. With Tikal's keen eyes, I can spot elv'in in the other ships' riggings."

"Elv'in?" Er'ril scowled. "From where?"

Mama Freda frowned, holding up a hand. "The light . . . Sweet Mother, there's sunlight ahead!" She burst to her feet, wobbling in her blindness, her vision fixed elsewhere. Elena hurried forward to steady the eyeless healer. "A city! There's a city in the storm!"

Er'ril unsheathed his sword and moved toward the door. "We've been betrayed!" Elena made a move to follow him, but he placed a restraining hand on her arm. "Stay here with Mama Freda. Tol'chuk and I will go and investigate." He turned to the blind elder. "Mama Freda, keep your pet's eyes atop the deck. Watch and be ready if there's trouble."

Elena yanked off one of her gloves, then grabbed her wit'ch dagger. The small blade flashed in the lamplight.

Er'ril blocked her dagger. "Be cautious with your magick. Even you can't fly if the boat is burned out from under you."

She slipped her hand free of his, then flicked her blade across each fingertip. "Don't worry, Er'ril." Blood turned to tendrils of fire, rising from her fingers. He watched as she wove the flames into a rose burning in her palm. She stared tightly at him, her eyes bright with power. "The ship won't burn."

Er'ril's eyebrows rose at Elena's mastery of her magick. With a nod, he swung to Tol'chuk, who waited at the doorway.

Behind him, Mama Freda spoke urgently. "We fly toward the city's gates. Hurry."

Er'ril raced up the steps, taking them two at a time. Tol'chuk followed. Er'ril burst out the door to the middeck, sword raised. The shock of the sight awaiting him stumbled his feet.

Catching himself, he gaped at the spectacle. All about the ship, angry black clouds roiled, lit from within by flashes of lightning. Thunder rolled everywhere, and distantly he thought he heard the blare of hundreds of trumpets. But all this was nothing compared to the sight beyond the *Sunchaser*'s bow.

Massive gates of wood towered a quarter league high into the sky. They lay open on a wondrous sight. Beyond the gates lay a vast sunlit city, resting atop the storm itself. Above the roofs and towers, the late afternoon sun hung clear, shining down upon this city in the clouds.

Just beyond the walls lay a wide open space, a sheltered bay, where wooden docks and piers protruded into the air above roiling storm clouds. Er'ril spotted other ships moored there, of all shapes and sizes: sleek cutters, thick-bellied supply ships, even fanciful boats shaped like swans and eagles. Beyond the port's docks, wooden buildings and shops climbed the clouds, spreading to the horizon. Some had chimneys leaking thin streams of smoke; others had small faces peering from windows. But all were brightly colored, like the plumage of a peacock. Instead of stone streets or muddy tracks, complex bridges and wooden spans connected the buildings together in a maze of rope and wood. Higher on the cloudy slopes, larger homes, towers, and steeples poked toward the sunny skies as the city spread far and wide.

But all this was d'warfed by the lofty castle in the city's center, its walls of solid iron glowing bright with the energy of the storm below. Beyond the wall, the central keep's score of towers climbed to impossible heights. Clustered tight together, they appeared not unlike a gathered bunch of reeds.

Tol'chuk stepped to Er'ril's side, neck stretched as he gawked at the wonder. By now, elv'in sailors appeared from hatches and doors. Ignoring Er'ril and Tol'chuk, they swarmed up into the rigging and began to reef the sails.

Er'ril turned away. He could guess the name of the sky city they approached: *Stormhaven*. In the past, he had heard Meric speak of the elv'in citadel in the sky. But what he did not understand was what the city was doing here, and why they were flying through its gates. Er'ril's face hardened to granite. He knew one person who held these answers.

"Come on," Er'ril ordered. He led the way to the ladder up to the stern deck. Mama Freda had mentioned seeing Queen Tratal near the stern rail. The old woman was not wrong. As Er'ril clambered to the deck, he spotted the elv'in queen framed in crackles of blue energies, her arms raised high. Her silver-white hair was an angry cloud about her upturned face.

"Tratal!" Er'ril barked. "What deceit is this?"

The woman's gaze slowly lowered from the skies. Her eyes flashed with lightning. "I will take the wit'ch to her true throne. Her blood will unite the elv'in's past with its future. It is time Elena put aside her mud-wallowing, to accept her true heritage."

Er'ril kept his sword in hand. "I won't allow you to kidnap her."

Queen Tratal's heels settled to the planks as she lowered her hands. "And what do you think you can do?" She waved an arm as the *Sunchaser* swept through the gates, flanked by its escorts. "Our home flies leagues above the world. Beyond our walls lies only death. There is no escape."

Er'ril considered her words. In truth, there was no way down from the clouds without the cooperation of the elv'in. They were all dependent on their host's good graces. Still, over the centuries, Er'ril had learned that another's cooperation could often be bought at the point of a sword. He stepped forward, sword raised. With a queen as hostage . . .

Tratal snapped her fingers, and a small bolt of lightning lanced from the energies about the ship. The blinding bolt struck Er'ril's sword and burned it from his hand.

Er'ril gasped and shook away the burn. His sword clattered at his feet. Tol'chuk rumbled in menace, but Er'ril held him back.

Queen Tratal remained as still as ice. "Retrieve your sword, plainsman." She turned her back on him, unconcerned by any threat he could offer. "It is time you accepted your fate as well."

Er'ril collected his sword. He held it a moment, then shoved it back into its sheath. "Elena will never cooperate with you."

Tratal swung around, leaning against the rail, oblivious to the energies racing along the wood. "She will when the fate of her dear friends is held hostage against her goodwill. She is a smart girl. Here all the wild magick in the world will not free her, it will only get you all killed."

Er'ril opened his mouth to argue, but he found no words. Elena would fight this imprisonment—but not at the cost of all their lives. Tratal was most correct. They were caught snugly in her icy web.

Cursing his blind trust, Er'ril stared at the spread of Stormhaven as the flagship swept toward the docks. The vast elv'in city glowed under the golden sunlight. Already hundreds of residents flowed along bridges and appeared waving at windows. All had come to cheer the return of their queen. Trumpets blared, and drums began to beat cheerily. Several banners waved, bearing the sigil of an azure eagle against a silver background.

Behind them, the mighty gates swung slowly closed, shutting out the storm beyond, cutting off any means of escape.

"A handsome city, is it not?" Queen Tratal asked airily.

Er'ril frowned at the bright citadel. "It's as pretty a prison as I've ever seen."

ELENA FOLLOWED THE OTHERS ALONG THE WIDE BRIDGE SPANNING the length of Stormhaven. Queen Tratal led the way, borne in a draped litter floating above the bridge. Energy crackled along the small vessel's iron runners. The lithe woman lifted an arm and waved to her people as flower petals floated and swirled in the air, tossed from windows and doorways, scenting the thin air in sweet fragrances. Voices were raised in welcoming cheers, well-wishes, and song. Tratal acknowledged them all, nodding and waving.

Elena scowled at the spectacle. Upon disembarking the *Sunchaser*, Tratal had invited Elena to accompany her aboard the cushioned litter, but Elena had refused. "I'll walk with the other prisoners," she had said coldly. Tratal had merely shrugged and climbed into the high seat.

Upon first hearing of her imprisonment, Elena's initial instinct had been to strike out, ripe with coldfire and wit'chfire.

Who dared stand in her way? But Er'ril had talked her down from her sharp fury. Hers was a power of destruction and the laying of waste. Here, her magick would only lead to a tumbling death. Mama Freda had agreed with Er'ril, insisting that time and wise words might win, where sword and fiery magick failed. Elena had finally forced her bright anger down to a tight-lipped glower. With no other choice, she accepted her fate—for now. But as the parade led to the royal keep, Elena silently promised herself to find a way out of this gilded birdcage. The fate of Alasea depended on it.

Er'ril marched at her side, keeping a watch on windows and doorways as they passed. Wennar and Mama Freda marched behind, flanked by a half dozen elv'in swordsmen. Tol'chuk and the other six d'warves of their party remained imprisoned aboard the *Sunchaser*, ransomed against their good behavior.

So the group marched sullenly toward the spired citadel across the vast city. To either side, carefully crafted homes and shops lined the way. Lintels and beams were ornately carved. Windows were filled with colored glass. Everywhere Elena looked, the skills of the elv'in artisans were evident. The city was one extensive work of sculpted art. As much as her kidnapping rankled, she could not dismiss the wonder of the place.

Children, barefoot and dressed in motley colors, danced on the ropes and thin spans bridging the skies. They raced and launched kites in various shapes and sizes, all creatures of the air, their shapes and colors both real and fanciful: sharp-eyed eagles, black-winged crows, osprey, terns, bats, butterflies, even colored clouds. The hues and shimmers flared in the bright sky, shining as brightly as the children's songs and laughter.

Unbidden, a smile came to Elena's lips. One bold child ran up to her, dodging easily around Er'ril's attempt to wave him off; he could be no older than five winters. He ran beside her, matching her stride, staring up at her with large blue eyes, his hair an unkempt gale of white-blond hair. "You don't look like a king," he said with a small frown. "Papa says you're a king. Kings are supposed to be boys."

"I'm not a king, little one," she said with an amused grin. "Just the grandchild of your ancient king."

He studied her with narrowed eyes, his mouth crooked as he

pondered her words. "You still don't look like no king," he finally concluded, but he offered her his hand to take anyway.

She accepted it. How could she refuse?

He leaned a bit toward her, his eyes peeking past to Er'ril. "Papa says when I turn six, he's gonna get me a sword for my birthingday party. Then I'll guard you instead of him."

"I would be honored, little knight."

He nodded, satisfied with his future assignment. After a bit, he waved her down closer and kissed her quickly on the cheek. With his prize won, he ran away on light feet, singing at the top of his lungs. "I kissed the king! I kissed the king!"

Smiling, Elena watched other children converge on him to hear his exciting tale. It seemed young ones were the same the world 'round. By now her mood had greatly improved. Still, she only had to look down to be reminded of her prison.

Underfoot, the bridge was composed of slats of white ash. Each iron bolt in the wood glowed with the magick of the elv'in—magick keeping it afloat above the endless fall. Elena could smell the magick thick in the air—or was it just the scent of lightning? Below, between the slats, the storm roiled like a raging torrent. Lightning flared deep in its heart, thunder a constant rumble.

Wennar moved up to her side. "Gul'gotha lies below."

"How do you know?" she asked.

Wennar pointed to the north. Elena turned. Between a slate-roofed cobbler's shop and a two-story chandlery, the view of the skies opened to the storm beyond the city's towering walls. Thunderclouds churned and swirled. But this was not the sight that the d'warf leader indicated. Up from the whorling bank of black clouds, a solitary peak protruded, an island of steep cliffs and flinty outcrops riding an angry sea.

"The Anvil," Wennar said. "It's a sacred mountain to our people. It is said in our histories that upon this peak, the first of our people were forged by the gods' hammers."

Elena nodded. The peak's flat summit did indeed appear like a giant's blacksmith anvil. She watched as the storm swept up its slopes, the clouds trying to swamp the island in the sky. "We're adrift," Elena mumbled. She sensed no movement, but as she stared, the storm rode past the giant mountain. Stormhaven was on the move, passing over Gul'gotha.

Er'ril moved closer. "How far are we from the coast?"

"A half dozen leagues, I'd say."

"And how far from your homeland valley?"

"A ten-day march. Fifty leagues or so."

As they continued following the queen's litter, the view vanished behind a blue house trimmed in silver. Six leagues from the coast? The storm moved swiftly.

Er'ril grumbled. "Then we'll be over your valleys by morning."

"And well beyond after that," Wennar added quietly.

Er'ril glanced to Elena, his expression hard. She understood what was left unspoken. *They must escape this very night, or they would be lost forever.*

Elena, her chest tight with worry, stared down between her boots. Deep in the whirling darkness, lightning lit the heart of the storm. How did one escape a prison in the sky? For the hundredth time, she wished she could consult her Aunt Fila and Cho. But the Blood Diary had been confiscated along with the Try'sil, the Hammer of Thunder. Not that the book would be any help. The moon would not grow full for several days. She would find only blank pages if she opened it now.

As Wennar slipped back behind, Mama Freda took his place at Elena's side. "I heard what the d'warf said," the old healer whispered. "It leaves us little time to sway these cold-blooded sky dwellers."

"If we can't sway them," Elena said hotly, "I'll burn their city from the sky."

Mama Freda glanced over at her. Though the lack of eyes made the woman's expression difficult to read at times, now the healer's shock was etched in every wrinkle. "You'd kill the boy who came a moment ago stealing a kiss."

Elena lowered her face with shame.

Er'ril answered. "Elv'in only respect strength. Innocents are often killed in war."

"Perhaps." Mama Freda's next words were for Elena. "But can you slay them with your own hand, not accidentally, but willfully and with forethought?"

Elena tightened her fingers into frustrated fists. "No," she finally sighed. "No, I can't."

"Good. I feared perhaps that I was aiding the wrong side in this war."

"It was just my anger speaking."

Mama Freda nodded and touched Elena's shoulder. "Then heed me a moment, lass. There are ways to play this that don't require fire and death."

"What do you mean?"

"Tikal allows me to see and hear much that others would not wish known."

Er'ril stepped closer to Elena's side, half huddling. "What have you learned?"

"As we were off-loading from the *Sunchaser*, I overheard some sailors speaking privately. Rumors say that Elena will be forced to wed an elv'in prince as the moon rises tonight. Her bridemate will be announced at a feast with the sun's setting."

Elena was aghast. Married? "I will never! I'll refuse."

Mama Freda nodded. "I suspect that our lives and continued comfort will depend upon you acquiescing. Even words of marriage spoken under duress are recognized by the elv'in."

Elena's feet stumbled.

"And this very night, they will take your maidenhead upon your marriage bed—by force if necessary."

Elena grew cold. Though she had already flowered as a woman and her moon's blood marked her old enough to be wedded, the thought of lying with a man terrified her more than any ill'guard demon. With her body's spellcast maturation, she understood the needs of a woman. And her own mother had explained the ways of men and women when she was much younger. In fact, she had once practiced kissing with a farmhand from the Nickleburry ranch. But to bed a man? Someone she did not know? A stranger?

"I will not allow this," Er'ril said with an icy menace.

Mama Freda nodded. "I didn't expect you would. But these elv'in mean to reclaim their ancient king's lineage, to rejoin the royal lines."

Elena found her voice again, but her words cracked. "Y-you hinted of a way out of this trap."

"As I was saying, these sailors were talkative, and their blood was up with their return to Stormhaven. It seems your looks and charms have not gone unnoticed by the men in the rigging.

One of the sailors seemed especially captivated by you. With a coarse laugh, he suggested challenging your bridemate by rite of *ry'th lor*."

"What is that?" Er'ril asked.

"I asked my cabin boy as he was helping me from my room. *Ry'th lor* translates as 'heart's blood' in the high elv'in tongue. A suitor for a woman's hand can be challenged by another. A trial by combat. The victor wins the hand and no other can contest it."

Er'ril touched his sword hilt. "Then I will challenge this queen's man."

"It is not as easy as that. The challenger must fight the potential suitor with his bare hands. The suitor is under no such restraint. He will be armed with a ceremonial sword and dagger."

The plainsman's expression hardened. "I will still challenge."

"Of course you will . . . and most likely die."

Elena shook her head. "You must not, Er'ril."

"And even if you succeed, you will be forced to take your suitor's place. You must marry Elena within the day of the challenge."

Er'ril and Elena glanced at each other. Even in the chill air, her face flushed warmly. His own eyes seemed a mix of confused emotions.

Er'ril cleared his throat. "If I must, I must."

"I . . . I still don't see how this will help us," Elena mumbled.

"Upon your marriage kiss, Er'ril can make one request of the suitor's family. A dowry, so to speak, for the stolen bride." Mama Freda glanced significantly at them. "It cannot be refused."

Elena understood almost immediately. "Er'ril could ask that we be let go."

"Exactly. What cannot be won in war can be gained by love."

"But would they honor this tradition?" Er'ril grumbled.

"I believe so. Even though they'd take Elena by force to gain her bloodline, they are still a people of tradition and strict law. If the challenge is made, it must be honored. If they broke their code in order to father a king's child from Elena, the Blood would be tainted—no more than a bastard child. No, I believe they must bow to the challenge of *ry'th lor*."

Elena turned to Er'ril. "Then it must be attempted."

She glanced up to her knight. Deep inside her, something

more than hope swelled in her heart. She fought tears, remembering a dance atop a tower roof, arm in arm, the brush of his cheek on hers. No words had been shared during that long night—but it did not always take words to speak one's heart.

"It will be a hard fight," Mama Freda warned.

"I will succeed." The plainsman's gray eyes never left hers. His words were hushed. "I will win Elena."

Mama Freda nodded. "Then there is only one other item you must know."

"What?"

"Before the suitor's family honors your request, you must prove your marriage."

"Prove our marriage?" Elena broke her gaze from Er'ril. "What does that mean?"

Mama Freda stared forward, her expression unreadable. "Before we are freed, Er'ril must take your maidenhood himself."

13

ER'RIL STARED AS ELENA WAS LED INTO THE FEAST HALL. SHE WAS a beauty in green velvet. Her gown flowed in draperies and trains, held aloft by a pair of young girls in matching velvet as she stepped down the stairs and into the hall. Her hair was woven into a sweep atop her head, held in place by a fine net of silver filigree, fiery with diamonds. At her appearance, polite applause rose from the nobles gathered to either side of the hall.

She was led into the room by the queen herself. Queen Tratal was a cloud of silk laced with gold filaments. In her arms rested a scepter of red iron shaped like a lightning bolt, as stark and unforgiving as the one who cradled it. As she moved, traceries of azure energies danced along the scepter's length.

Queen Tratal crossed the great hall. To either side, tables were decorated with rose petals amid settings of crystal and porcelain. Overhead, the vaulted beams were festooned with flowering vines. Serving staff waited in doorways laden with wine bottles and trays. Smells of the kitchens wafted up from the hearths below. The hall held its breath for the feast and celebration to begin.

On the room's far side, atop a raised dais, Er'ril stood with Mama Freda and Wennar at the main table. Each of them had also been bathed, perfumed, and dressed in fineries. As Er'ril stood, waiting for the long procession of courtiers to file in after Elena and the queen, he tugged at his gray jacket and ruffled linen shirt, both a bit too snug for his wide plainsman shoulders.

Elena and Queen Tratal wound through the room and up the three stairs to join them atop the dais. The elv'in queen took her place at a delicate throne of silver, cushioned with midnight blue pillows. Elena followed to take the chair at the queen's right side, a matching throne but with more stern lines, clearly the king's seat. She settled into it uncomfortably. Er'ril and the others were positioned a dozen chairs away on Elena's wing of the table.

Er'ril caught Elena's attention as she sat down. Her green eyes, flecked with gold, showed clearly that she was scared and worried, but he noted the core of determination behind her gaze, too. She nodded to him, then turned back as the queen began to address the gathered audience.

"This is a fateful day." Queen Tratal's words were softly spoken but carried easily across the wide room. "Since our banishment from the shores of our ancient homelands, we have only been half a people. Our ancient king, King Belarion, was stolen from us—his wisdom, guidance, and love were lost in the mix of blood down the ages. And though we've grown beyond the need for grubbing the land and instead fashion castles in the sky, we can never forget what was stolen from us, what is ours by right of blood and heritage."

Queen Tratal motioned for Elena to stand. She obeyed, gliding to her feet. "Though King Belarion's bloodline was mixed with that of commoners, the iron in the royal blood can never be fully vanquished. Here stands the vessel for the return of our king. From her womb, King Belarion will be reborn to his people." Queen Tratal reached and lifted a slender glass of white wine. "Long live the king!"

Across the hall, celebrants raised their own glasses. The queen's words were carried and echoed across the room. *"Long live the king!"*

Er'ril scowled and was prodded from behind by a guard to take up his own glass. He downed his glass of wine in one gulp and slammed it back down upon the table, shattering the stem of the goblet. No one noticed. They were all too focused on the central dais. Only Mama Freda placed a restraining hand upon his elbow, cautioning him to be patient. Earlier, she had explained the details of *rhy'th lor*. He could only make his challenge after Elena's bridemate had been named—then he must state his own claim before the suitor sealed the engagement with a kiss upon Elena's cheek. After this gesture, no challenge could be made or accepted.

As the hall grew quiet again, Queen Tratal continued her speech. "On this auspicious night, with the moon silvering bright in the twilight skies, I will now seal the two halves of our people. With all here as witness, let it be known that Elena Morin'stal will be wed this night to my own sister's first son, Prince Typhon."

It was a well-rehearsed act. A tall slender man stood to the queen's left. There was no surprise on his dour face, nor delight. He wore a sickly pained expression as he lifted an arm in acknowledgment. He looked as if he were about to be fed naked to a pack of sniffers. Er'ril noted how a small-boned woman on his left touched his hand as he stood. Her eyes were full of regret and sorrow. He gave her fingers the barest squeeze, then released them. It seemed the prince had already given his heart to another. But with the royal princes spread thin—Meric off to the Northwall, Richald off to the South—the burden of uniting the two elv'in houses had fallen upon this young man's shoulders.

"I accept this offered hand of marriage," he said formally. "And will fill it with mine own."

Queen Tratal lifted her iron scepter, which scintillated with energy. "Let the offer be bound with a kiss so all may see the claim sealed. Then as the moon reaches its zenith, we will join these two in marriage. And by the dawn's light tomorrow, our two halves will be made whole upon their marriage bed."

Her words were greeted with more cheering. Prince Typhon slipped around his chair and stepped behind the queen's throne toward where Elena stood stiffly, her eyes wide and glassy.

Mama Freda nudged Er'ril. Now was the time.

Around the hall, the celebrants grew quiet, anticipating the kiss to come. Prince Typhon reached to Elena's gloved hand. The tall man leaned toward her cheek.

Before his lips could touch, Er'ril pounded his fist upon the hardwood table. Porcelain rattled, and wine spilled from neighboring cups. The crack of his knuckles echoed across the room. Gazes swung in his direction. Half bent toward Elena, Typhon glanced his way.

"By rite of *ry'th lor*," Er'ril bellowed, "I challenge this suitor for Elena's hand."

The low murmur in the hall went deathly quiet. Prince Typhon straightened, bewilderment in his eyes, but there was no confusion in Queen Tratal's gaze. Even from a dozen seats away, Er'ril felt the icy chill from the elv'in leader. Tratal's face was a mask of anger.

"You have no right to claim *ry'th lor*. It is elv'in law and does not apply to common folk of the lands below."

Er'ril was ready for this response. He had discussed the details at length with Mama Freda. "It is not your choice to deny my claim or not. Only the woman to be betrothed can dismiss the challenge and deny the claimant." Er'ril swung his gaze to Elena. "And by your own word, Elena is of elv'in heritage, so by your own elv'in law, she can make this judgment."

Er'ril noted Elena shift her feet and turn to face the queen. Though Elena's eyes glinted nervously, her words were hard and firm. "I accept the challenge for my hand by Er'ril of Standi."

By now, the queen's scepter spat tiny bolts of energy. Her thin lips had drained of color. She was trapped by her own laws and customs. "Elena may choose to accept the challenge, but I have the right to decide how the outcome will be judged."

Er'ril glanced to Mama Freda. She shrugged, equally in the dark about this statement.

"As ruler of Stormhaven, I declare that this challenge must be won only by blood. It will be a fight to the death."

Gasps arose from the gathered throng. Even Er'ril was taken aback by this turn of events. According to Mama Freda, the victor in the challenge merely had to make the other combatant submit, not kill him.

"By our oldest law, from the time of King Belarion himself, *ry'th lor* was decided by blood. So to win the hand of the king's heritage, I claim the old rites be followed. Only death will settle this claim." Queen Tratal turned to Elena. "Do you still accept this challenge?"

Elena's face had paled with the queen's words. She glanced up to Prince Typhon. He was young, lithe, and quick-eyed. Armed with a sword and dagger, the young elv'in lord would prove a formidable opponent. Even the prince looked little concerned about the challenge, his arms crossed, his face calm.

Only the young elv'in woman on the queen's side mirrored Elena's expression. Both women were frightened for their men.

"Do you accept Er'ril of Standi's claim for your hand?" Tratal repeated, a tiny smile beginning to form on her cold lips.

Elena turned to Er'ril, her face pained and terrified.

"Make your choice," the queen demanded.

TOL'CHUK SAT IN THE GALLEY OF THE *SUNCHASER*. HE WAS ALONE except for a single d'warf who worked at the small stone oven. Magnam was one of the smallest of the ten d'warf warriors. To him fell the more menial chores, like cooking their meals. But he did not seem to mind. He stirred a pot of stew with a long wooden ladle, a soft song bubbling from his lips. The language was unknown to Tol'chuk, but the deep tone and slow cadence whispered of old loss and ancient sorrows. It spoke to Tol'chuk's own spirit.

Atop the table, the large chunk of heartstone glowed mutely, merely reflecting the small flames from the galley's hearth. The shade of his father had told him he must take the Heart of his people back to where it was first mined—to Gul'gotha. But now they were all prisoners in the clouds. How could he hope to complete his journey?

Crouched beside the table, lost in his own pain, Tol'chuk failed to notice the small d'warf cook until a large bowl of stew was pushed in front of him, a wooden spoon stuck in the middle.

"Eat," Magnam said.

"I be not hungry," Tol'chuk mumbled politely, shifting slightly away.

The d'warf sighed and sat opposite from Tol'chuk. "You been staring at that bauble for days. It's time you started looking back out to the world." He used a thick finger to push the bowl toward Tol'chuk. "Even boulders like you must eat sometime."

Tol'chuk did not move.

"You can pine and mope just as well with a full belly."

Tol'chuk rolled a large amber eye in Magnam's direction.

The d'warf's face cracked with a soft smile. He reached for the jeweled stone, but his fingers hovered above its surface. "May I?"

Tol'chuk shrugged. What did it matter now? The stone was dead, poisoned by the Bane.

Magnam picked up the stone and held it up to the flames of a nearby lamp. He stared at it one way, then another. His eyes pinched with concentration. "Wonderful craftsmanship," the d'warf said, lowering the stone. "A master's work."

Tol'chuk shrugged.

Magnam sighed again, his gaze shifting to the untouched bowl of stew. "I might not have the skill to cut a stone of this quality, but I do make a tasty bowl of stew. It's the only real reason I was allowed to stay among Wennar's battalion. The taskmasters of the Nameless One don't coddle the small or weak-limbed. We're usually fed to his Dreadlords. I learned early on to concentrate on my strengths, not my weaknesses. An army travels on its stomach, and if you can fill it with tasty stews, you're less likely to become a tasty stew yourself."

The d'warf's easy manner slowly drew Tol'chuk out of his gloom.

Magnam continued. "I'll make a deal with you, Lord Boulder. You eat, and I'll tell you a story of d'warves and heartstones."

Tol'chuk stared warily. But curiosity made him reach for the bowl of stew. He picked up the spoon. "Tell me your story."

Magnam simply waited, eyeing the empty spoon.

Tol'chuk grumbled and scooped up a bit of potato and a chunk of beef. He started to speak around the mouthful of stew, demanding his story, but then the taste of the stew struck his senses. The beef melted on his tongue; the potatoes were delicate and savory with a thick creamy broth. Tol'chuk's eyes grew wide. He spooned up another mouthful, suddenly finding his hunger.

"So how's my stew, Lord Boulder?" Magnam asked with a raised eyebrow.

"Good."

Magnam settled back in his chair. "It'll be even better tomorrow. 'Twice-stewed is twice as good,' my ol' mammy always taught me." The small d'warf grew silent for a breath, his gaze on the past and distant memories.

Tol'chuk ate in silence.

Finally, Magnam stirred. "But I promised you a story, didn't I?"

Tol'chuk merely waved his spoon, too busy to speak.

The d'warf crossed his arms. "Do you know where heartstone first came from?"

His mouth full, Tol'chuk grunted his ignorance and shook his head.

"Well, the first piece of heartstone ever discovered was found by a d'warf—a fellow named Mimblywad Treedle. He was mining his claim off in the hinterlands of Gul'gotha, in a mountain named Gy'hallmanti. In the old tongue, this translates to 'the Peak of the Sorrowed Heart.' Many considered the old d'warf to be mad. Not only had the mountain been mined dry long ago, tales spoke of hauntings and ghosts in its tunnels. The last group of miners who had entered the mines some two centuries earlier had never returned, lost forever."

Tol'chuk slowed his eating, drawn into the tale.

"But ol' Mimblywad insisted he smelled fresh riches down in the lowest shafts of his mine. And mad or not, he was the keenest scenter of his time. It was said his nose could sniff out an opal in a pile of pig dung. So for moon after moon, he dug with pick and shovel. Neighboring homesteads reported the echoing sounds of his work both day and night. They also whispered of other noises, stranger sounds. But when they were asked for details, they would only shake their heads. Many moved away, leaving their claims unsold. After ten winters, the entire region around Gy'hallmanti was deserted, except for the lone Mimblywad Treedle."

"What happened?" Tol'chuk asked, his spoon forgotten for the moment.

Magnam grew dour and slowly shook his head. "Mimblywad would sometimes trek out of his tunnels for supplies. He would travel to trading stores, a wasted figure of bones and haunted eyes. He would talk to himself, mumbling angrily, as if arguing with someone only he could see. But addled as he was, he always seemed to come down from his mines with enough gold and bits of shattered rubies to buy more supplies and disappear back into his tunnels. He soon became a legend among our people. Ol' Mad Mimbly. Then for an entire winter, no one saw him. Most guessed he had finally died in the haunted tunnels of Gy'hallmanti, becoming just another ghost himself. But they were wrong."

Magnam took out a pipe from a pocket and filled it with bit of dried tobacco leaf. "More stew?"

Tol'chuk glanced to his bowl, finding it surprisingly empty. "No. I be fine. Tell me more of this Mad Mimbly."

Magnam lit his pipe and chewed on its end, speaking around the stem. "Some three winters later, ol' Mimbly comes down to the village of Tweentown, drawing a cart behind him like he were a mule. No one recognized the bent-backed, white-haired d'warf. His beard was wrapped around his waist, and his eyes shone with wormglow."

"Wormglow?"

Magnam nodded. "Wherever you find heartstone, you'll find the worms. Glowworms."

Tol'chuk remembered the Spirit Gate of his people, the arch of pure heartstone through which he had stepped to begin this journey so long ago. The tunnels leading to the Gate had been filled with worms that glowed the green of pond scum.

"No one knows what attracts the creatures, but if there's a vein of heartstone mined, within days you'll find the place crawling with the squirmy beasts. There are some who say they're actually birthed out of the heartstone itself."

Tol'chuk glanced to his own crystal. When first he had looked into the Heart, before its recent transformation, the Bane had appeared to be a black worm, a cousin to the tunnel's glowworms. Could there be some connection?

"Anyway, if you hang around the worms long enough, their glow creeps into your own eyes. Some say it lets you see not only this world but the *next*."

"The spirit world?"

"No, the future. Glimpses of what's to come." Magnam waved his pipe. "But that all makes no never mind. What ol' Mad Mimbly had in his cart was what drew everyone in Tweentown's attention. Piled atop his cart were gems never seen before. Redder than rubies, brighter than the finest cut diamonds." The d'warf pointed his pipe stem to the chunk of stone. "It were heartstone, the first ever mined."

"But how come it was never found before?"

Magnam shrugged. "I guess the mountains were finally ready to let them go. Miners say you'll never find a single jewel unless the Land herself wants you to find it."

"What did Mimbly say? Did he explain how he found them?"

"Ah, now there's the rub, Lord Boulder. He labored all those years, wearing his fingers to nubs—and what does he do when he finally strikes the motherlode of riches? He up and dies." Magnam clucked out a sad laugh and shook his head. "That very night, he falls dead on his bed in Tweentown."

Disappointment ached in Tol'chuk's breast. "He died?"

"In his sleep. Curled like a babe." Magnam sighed. "Fate can be cruel. But at least ol' Mimbly proved his nose. He had scented riches and found them at last. He was also the one to lend the new gem its name. He would let no one near his cart of jewels. He claimed it was the blood of the mountains, from the Land's very heart. Hence, its name—heartstone."

"Blood of the Land?"

"So he claimed, but he was addled after his years alone. Talking and hollering at invisible figments, swatting at the empty air. He claimed the stones were the Land's gift to our people, that it was all that could save them from the darkness to come. The jewels must be hidden away and protected. Everyone laughed at his babbling. Ol' Mad Mimbly." Magnam puffed out a perfect smoke ring and gave Tol'chuk a one-eyed stare. "But maybe he weren't as mad as we thought."

The d'warf kicked to his feet. "Best I return to my cooking," he mumbled.

"Wait. What did you mean, *'maybe he weren't as mad as we thought'*?"

Magnam nodded to the chunk of heartstone. "It guided you here, didn't it? After he died, his load was taken, spread throughout our kingdom, and crafted into thousands of objects. It was a jewel of such beauty that it could not be simply hidden away. For centuries, other miners tried to find ol' Mimbly's vein. But he must have mined it all himself. No other heartstone was ever found in Gy'hallmanti, not even a sliver. Occasionally a bit was found here and there across the lands, but never a strike like ol' Mimbly's."

Tol'chuk remembered his own tribe's secret: a towering arch of heartstone hidden deep in their homeland mountains. *The blood of the Land.* It had sent him forth on this journey. But according to the shade of his father, the Heart of his people had not come from this arch but from Gul'gotha, from these foreign lands. Realization slowly dawned in Tol'chuk. His words were a whisper. "No other large pieces were ever found in Gul'gotha?"

Magnam shook his head and crossed to his stove. "None. That's what makes heartstone so precious."

Stunned, Tol'chuk reached and took up his chunk of heartstone. If Magnam's story was true, there was only one place from which the Heart of his people could have come—from ol' Mad Mimbly's strike! Here was one of the very stones the ancient d'warf had mined. Tol'chuk squeezed the crystal, trying to sense its age. His father had assigned him to return the Heart to where it was first mined. He now had an answer. He stared back up at the d'warf. "The mountain of Gy'hallmanti—what else can you tell me of the place? Was nothing else ever found there?"

Magnam frowned, stirring his stew pot. "Now I didn't say that. After ol' Mimbly, many miners tried their hand at delving into Gy'hallmanti. They all went bust. But five centuries ago, a new strike was discovered."

"More heartstone?"

Magnam's face twisted into a pained scowl. "No, but like the heartstone Mimblywad discovered, it was a stone like no other. A stone the world had never seen before."

"What was it?"

Magnam returned to his stew. His voice hushed to a whisper. "Ebon'stone. They found ebon'stone, damn them all."

Ice crept into Tol'chuk's veins. His mind struggled to put this horror together. Heartstone, ebon'stone—both had been birthed from the same mines. What did it mean?

Magnam continued, this throat strained. "There is only one other thing that ever came forth from the tunnels of Gy'hallmanti."

"What?" Tol'chuk asked. His fingers clutched tight to the chunk of crystal, afraid of the answer.

"The Nameless One. From the endless tunnels of Gy'hall-manti, the Black Beast of Gul'gotha first walked our lands."

ELENA STARED AT ER'RIL. HE WAS DRESSED IN A GRAY SILK JACKET over a bright white shirt. His raven hair was combed back and tied into a tail. How could she ask him to risk his life in the challenge for her hand, especially with the odds so badly stacked against him? Prince Typhon was strong and hale, and armed with both sword and dagger against Er'ril's empty hand. What hope could there be for victory? If Elena accepted the claim of *ry'th lor*, she would be sentencing her liegeman to almost certain death. Yet if she refused, she would be married to Prince Typhon this night, and any hope for Alasea would die on her marriage bed.

"Make your choice, Elena," Queen Tratal demanded.

Elena refused to turn from Er'ril. Her eyes met his storm-gray ones. He stared hard at her, then his head nodded imperceptibly. His face showed no fear, no indecision. His eyes said he would win this fight. Elena drew strength from his gaze and stood straighter. She wiped her welling tears and turned to Queen Tratal.

Clenching her fists, Elena's words were harsh and sharply spoken. "It is upon your hands, Queen Tratal, that blood will be spilled this night. By your actions, you have doomed your nephew to his death. My liegeman will not fail me."

"Then you accept his challenge of *ry'th lor*?" The queen's voice snapped with anger.

Elena met her fury with her own. "You have given us no choice but to murder for the sake of our freedom. For this, I will never forgive you. I offer you this one moment to rescind your words. Put aside this claim of marriage, and we will part allies and friends. Insist on this course, and the blood of Prince Typhon will stain this hall's floor."

On the queen's other side, a thin elv'in woman stumbled to her feet. Her eyes, full of tears, were fixed upon the young prince. "Please, Queen Tratal . . . listen to the wit'ch."

Prince Typhon waved the woman back to her seat and hissed, "Mela, sit down. You shame me."

The woman would not be so easily cowed. She reached to Queen Tratal's sleeve. "I love him, my queen. I would give him up freely to this wit'ch for the sake of the kingdom, but not . . . not to his death. I could not live with that."

Queen Tratal snatched her sleeve from the woman's thin-fingered grip. "Begone from my side!" she snapped. She flicked her wrist to a guard. "Take Princess Mela to her room. She seems to have fallen ill."

"No!" the elv'in woman wailed. But two guards flanked her and took her arms. Mela fell limp in their grips, sobbing. Unperturbed, the stoic royal guards dragged the weeping woman from the hall.

Elena noticed the pained expression on Prince Typhon's face. He had taken a step in Mela's direction when she had first swooned, but a stern glance from the queen had frozen his steps.

The queen lifted her lightning scepter. "The claim of *ry'th lor* has been accepted. Let the way be cleared for the challengers to the hand of Elena Morin'stal."

Quickly, tables and chairs were pulled back from the foot of the raised dais. The celebrants now all stood, ringing a wide, empty space before the pair of thrones. Even the serving staff moved inside to cluster in corners or stand on chairs to view the coming battle.

Elena turned to Er'ril. Guards stripped him of his sword.

Queen Tratal lifted her voice to the crowded hall. "The challenger must meet the challenged with no weapon but the clothes on his back."

Elena's legs grew numb. Er'ril could not even don leathers to protect him. Only silk and linen. Yet despite the threat, Er'ril seemed little fazed. He merely stepped around the royal table and leaped to the cleared floor.

The elv'in queen raised her left arm. "The challenged will be allowed the traditional weapons to defend the hand of his bride-mate. Sword and dagger!"

Prince Typhon already had a sword strapped to his waist. He climbed off the dais to the other side of the floor. After shrugging out of his own jacket, he pulled free his sword and swept his thin blade in a deadly flourish before him, practicing, loosening his arms. The sword was a blur of silver. Polite clapping met this display of skill and swordsmanship.

Er'ril watched all this with dispassionate eyes.

Queen Tratal turned her head slightly in Elena's direction. Her voice was a whisper meant for Elena's ears only. "My blood is not so much ice as to refuse you one last chance, Elena. Dismiss this challenge and Er'ril will be spared."

Elena wanted desperately to take the queen's offer. What hope lay between honed steel and bare flesh? As if sensing her faltering heart, Er'ril turned to stare up at her. His eyes shone with pride and determination. All across the lands of Alasea and throughout the War of the Isles, he had been her protector and her champion. But since the war, Er'ril's role had drifted into the background. And she had sensed his ill ease at this new role. But no longer. Here was the old Er'ril, the man she had known during the long journey to this moment. As much as she feared for his life, she could not take this challenge from him.

"I will not decline the claim," Elena whispered back to the queen. "I will mourn the death of your kin."

The only evidence of the queen's anger was the flare of energy that burst along the iron scepter's length. "So be it."

Queen Tratal lifted both arms. "Let the strength of hearts now judge whose hand will be joined to Elena's this night! Prepare yourselves!"

Prince Typhon repeated his sword's flourish, moving now. He spun and twisted, weaving around him a deadly cloud of steel. More applause greeted his performance.

Er'ril watched for a moment, eyes narrowed, judging his opponent. Then he simply pulled out of his gray silk jacket and slowly stripped off the crisp shirt. Bare chested, he cracked the kinks from his neck and worked knots from his muscles. With hardly a concern, he wrapped his jacket around his left forearm, then twisted his shirt into a long whip. Once done, he simply stood still, staring across the way toward Prince Typhon.

The prince finished his bow to the audience, then faced his queen.

A long tense moment of silence stretched. Finally, Queen Tratal brought her scepter down. "Let the challenge begin!"

ER'RIL WAITED FOR HIS OPPONENT TO COME TO HIM. AROUND THE hall, the crowd cheered, and coins exchanged hands as bets were made. He forced it all away, focusing his full attention upon Prince Typhon. The elv'in swordsman crossed the polished pine floor with confidence, striding purposefully, the tip of his sword steady and aimed at Er'ril's heart.

"I will make your death clean," Typhon called as he approached. "I bear you no animosity."

Er'ril did not answer. His only response was the narrowing of his eyes. He studied his opponent's movements: how his swordpoint dropped when he led with his left leg, how he was easily distracted by the crowd—his gaze flitting to the side when a celebrant yelled his name. Typhon had probably never fought amid the chaos and screams of a true battlefield. Isolated as the elv'in were, it was unlikely the young prince had ever even killed a man.

The same could not be said of Er'ril. He had slogged through battlefields muddied with blood and muck. He'd had friends die at his side as he fought with sword or ax. The number slaughtered upon his sword were too many to count. Er'ril felt a twinge of pity for this young prince. Though he himself bore no edged weapon, he knew they were in fact evenly matched. And the lack of understanding in his opponent would be the elv'in's downfall.

Typhon paused when only two steps away. He steadied his sword. "I will honor your memory."

Er'ril tightened his grip on the rolled linen shirt. Typhon took a deep breath as he prepared for the fight. But unknown to the boy, the battle had already begun. Er'ril flicked his wrist and snapped the tip of the shirt at the prince's face.

Typhon, caught off guard, danced back.

Taking advantage, Er'ril leaped forward. He knocked the boy's sword aside with his jacket-wrapped left arm and spun past the youth. With a deft grab, he relieved the prince of the dagger at his belt and was away before Typhon could turn with his sword.

The young man's blade swept through empty air.

From a step away, Er'ril spun the dagger's hilt in his hand, testing its weight and grip.

The prince's eyes grew wider in surprise as he realized the dagger was now in Er'ril's possession. A twinge of concern entered Typhon's gaze—but not fear. The boy was still too green to know when to be properly scared.

The crowd around them grew hushed by the turn of events. From the corner of his eye, Er'ril saw Elena still standing beside the elv'in queen. From this distance, side by side, Er'ril recognized her elv'in blood: the high cheekbones; the long, graceful neck; eyes as bright as ice in sunlight. Elena met his gaze, a fist held at her throat with worry.

He did not have time to acknowledge her. With a hiss, Typhon leaped at him. Er'ril was barely able to parry the blade with his dagger. The elv'in moved with unnatural speed now, tapping into the elemental energies inherent in his family. His blade was a blur.

Er'ril danced back, reacting with pure instinct.

The attack continued.

Er'ril saw no opportunity to turn defense into offense. Though the young prince was green in actual battle, he was a skilled swordsman. He offered no break in which Er'ril could slip through with the dagger. Er'ril simply waited. He knew from Meric that this artificial speed taxed an elv'in. The boy could not maintain this level of swiftness forever.

Still, neither could Er'ril. The prince's sword sliced through his own defense, requiring Er'ril to block a fatal blow with his jacket-wrapped arm. The blade's edge sliced easily through the silk material, biting deep into the meat of Er'ril forearm. Hot blood immediately soaked through the ruined jacket and ran onto the floor.

Er'ril grimaced, not with pain but frustration. Did this boy never grow tired?

Around them, the crowd began to grow boisterous again. Stirred on by the crowd and whetted by the sight of Er'ril's bloody arm, Typhon fought more savagely—again proving his inexperience. He leaped at the wounded tiger, anticipating a kill, abandoning his art to attack with broad strokes.

Er'ril ducked under the sword and dove forward, driving his shoulder into the elvin's knee. Both men went down. Er'ril doubted the prince had much experience with simple brawling. Er'ril spun and found the prince had managed to keep his sword in his grip. Typhon roared, twisting, and hacked his sword at Er'ril.

But Er'ril was no longer there.

Er'ril rolled clear as the sword struck the pine planks with a *thunk* behind him. Before the prince could pull the sword away, Er'ril rolled back over the blade, laying atop it now, his dagger held between his chest and the sword's edge, pinning it to the planks. Typhon tried to yank free his trapped sword. Steel screamed on steel. Er'ril had only a moment. He slammed the elbow of his bloody arm into the prince's nose. Bones cracked. A cry of alarm burst from his opponent.

Er'ril next brought his elbow down upon the prince's fingers, crushing them against the hilt. The sword fell free as the prince abandoned his last weapon. Nose bloodied, he tried to roll away.

Er'ril followed, kicking the sword well away with the toe of his boot. Before the prince could gain his knees, Er'ril leaped onto his back and drove him back to the planks, knocking the air out of the boy's lungs. Now pinned under Er'ril's heavier weight and weaponless, the prince began to sob, gasping, sensing his death to come.

Er'ril grabbed a fistful of the young man's hair and yanked his head up, baring his neck toward the queen on her dais. Er'ril brought the dagger's sharp edge to the prince's throat. His own hot blood dribbled from his sliced arm, soaking the silver-blond hair of the defeated prince.

Er'ril turned to those gathered at the high table. The hall had grown silent. Er'ril stared hard at Queen Tratal. "I have defeated the suitor to Elena's hand in honest battle. I have bloodied your champion. Do you accept my claim upon Elena now, or must I slay the blood of your kin? Must this young one die because of your pride?"

Queen Tratal still held her scepter aloft, energy crackling along its length. Her eyes were ice, her face unreadable.

Elena spoke up. "By your own law, Er'ril is the victor here. Please release him of the need to slay Prince Typhon. I can tell the prince's heart has already been claimed by Princess Mela. Do not add sorrow atop sorrow."

The energies began to die along the length of the queen's scepter. "I cannot lose the king's line."

"And you will not. The king lives both in my brother and me—and will again in our future descendants. In exchange for the prince's life, I give my word and promise that sometime our two family lines will be joined. The two royal houses will be one again." Elena touched the queen's arm. "But not today . . . not this night."

The queen lowered her scepter. Energy faded from its red iron surface. She stared down at Er'ril. "By elv'in law, I declare the trial of *ry'th lor* to be ended. Er'ril of Standi is the victor. The hand of Elena Morin'stal is now claimed and sealed by blood."

Er'ril bowed his head, accepting his victory. He climbed from Prince Typhon's back and helped the young man stand. "Well fought," he whispered in the prince's ear.

Prince Typhon rubbed his neck where the dagger had been pressed and the fate of his life had hung. Er'ril tossed aside his dagger and offered his hand to the young elv'in. The prince stared blankly at Er'ril's open palm.

In the past, Er'ril had seen many a defeated man unable to accept his opponent's good graces, too prideful and angry.

But Typhon slowly lifted his good hand and took Er'ril's grip. He bowed his head. "It seems I've much still to learn."

Er'ril shook the man's hand. "As does every man."

Typhon released his hand and stepped aside. Er'ril moved toward the dais. The entire matter had yet to be completely resolved. He spoke for all the hall to hear. "With Elena's hand now free, I ask that you let us forego the marriage and allow us passage to Gul'gotha below."

Queen Tratal glanced down to Er'ril with confusion. "It seems you've misunderstood the trial of *ry'th lor*. You offered the challenge. Elena accepted it. You've proven the victor. As I said a moment ago, the seal has been forged in blood. It cannot be sundered."

"What do you mean?" Elena asked, mirroring Er'ril's own bewildered expression.

Queen Tratal stared back and forth between the two, then slowly sat down, shaking her head in defeat. "In the eyes of the elv'in, you're already *married*. You've just had your ceremony."

Elena turned, stunned, toward Er'ril.

Typhon clapped Er'ril on the shoulder. "Congratulations."

WITH DAWN NOT FAR AWAY, ELENA STOOD AT THE BALCONY OVERlooking the city of Stormhaven. She was still dressed in her bedclothes, unable to sleep. After the fight between Er'ril and Prince Typhon, the floors of the great hall had been quickly wiped of the combatants' blood, and the celebration of Elena's marriage had begun in earnest. Servants marched out course after course of food and wine: thick soups filled with onions and lentils, roasted quail wings in jellied orange sauce, salads made of a tumble of flower petals, breads rich in cinnamon and baked with raisins, fruits of every variety sculpted in shapes to delight, smoked duck curried with spices that burned the tongue, and finally velvety smooth chocolates accented with sips of port wine.

But the entire meal was just a long blur to Elena. After the fighting, Er'ril had been taken to the city's healers, along with Prince Typhon. Elena had yet to see him, even after the celebration ended and she was led to her rooms. Everyone assured her that Er'ril was fine and the healers of Stormhaven were the best. Her only consolation was that Mama Freda had gone with Er'ril. Elena trusted her skill, and as the party wound down to dancing and slow ballads played by minstrels in the balconies, Mama Freda had returned to report that Er'ril was mending well. "Dragon's blood will make short work of that little scratch on his arm." After passing the news, the old healer had left to return to Er'ril's bedside with the assurance that she and Tikal would watch over him.

As the party ended, Queen Tratal led Elena from the hall. Tratal had hardly spoken more than a word to her during the long night of celebration, merely picking at her food, nodding to those courtiers who attempted to engage her in conversation. But once free of the hall, Tratal had stopped Elena. "I will hold you to your word, Elena Morin'stal. One day, our two houses will be joined."

"You've waited countless generations," she had answered. "What is one or two more?"

Queen Tratal had just stared with those ice blue eyes.

Elena did not look away. "I will honor my word. There will come a day when our two houses are joined—of this I am sure—but it must never be by force. Only a hand freely given in love will unite the royal lines."

The queen had then sighed, her mask of ice momentarily melting away. Her voice softened. "Love . . . For one so young, it is so easily spoken. But do you even know your own heart, Elena?" With those cryptic words, Queen Tratal had drifted away, leaving Elena to her guards. The climb to the tower suite was long, and at the top, Elena found no rest.

The queen's words had nagged her. She was now married to Er'ril. And she did not know how she felt about it. On one hand, she knew it was merely a ceremonial act, and once free of the elv'in, it would mean nothing. But a part of her did not want it to mean nothing. She remembered the dance atop the tower, in Er'ril's arms. She had never felt safer. Yet at the same time, she did not want her hand won upon the point of a blade, not even by Er'ril. There was too much unspoken between them. Until those words could be voiced aloud, Elena would never feel married. She did not need roses, rings, and flowing gowns of silk and pearls—only a quiet moment with Er'ril, a moment when the heavy silence between them could finally be broken.

But the thought of such a meeting terrified her to the core of her spirit.

Queen Tratal was right. She was not ready to face the secret hidden in her own heart. Not now, not yet. The wit'ch and woman in her were carefully balanced on a knife's edge. It took all her spirit to define herself amid the powers raging in her blood. She lifted her hands to the stars. Even now the power sang in her blood, a chorus of wild energies that threatened to overwhelm. Like the city of Stormhaven imbedded in the heart of the raging storms, so Elena stood in the eye of her own power. Here no one could protect her, not even Er'ril. Her only wall against these wild forces was her own resolve and determination.

So how could she ever hope to share her heart with anyone? To open herself completely? That path she must not risk—not even for Er'ril.

Elena lowered her arms and leaned on the balcony's balustrade.

Far below, Stormhaven was a spread of tiny lights: homes, shops, narrow streets. Above, a sprinkling of stars, so quiet, so peaceful, blind to the storm beyond the walls. But from her vantage high in the royal spire, she watched the flares of lightning brighten the churning black clouds, a pool of energies beyond imagination. There was power enough there to lift cities into the skies—or to lay waste to the same. Life and death were all a matter of balance. Elena knew this only too well.

To the left, the storm's thunder grew louder, roaring now with the voice of giants. A sudden wind gusted forth to nip at the hems of her loose bedclothes. She shivered in the sudden cold. She wrapped her arms around her body and stepped back toward the open doorway and her bed beyond. Pausing at the threshold, she turned back to the dark storm. The hairs at the nape of her neck quivered.

Something was wrong.

From the left, a huge fireball burst from the storm's belly and arced high into the sky, like a meteor sailing back to the heavens. But it was not returning to the stars. It reached its zenith and began falling back downward—toward *Stormhaven*.

Trailing a fiery tail, the large flaming boulder crashed down into the city. The muffled crash seemed a small thing compared to the storm's thunder, but the devastation was anything but small. The boulder punched through the city and set fire to all around it. Elena saw a four-story building, lit by the flames, topple into the ragged hole.

Distantly the strike of hundreds of gongs sounded the alarm from the city's walls. Below, across the dark expanse, more lamps and lights flickered into existence as the city was shaken awake.

Elena again heard the telltale roar. She glanced up in time to see another flaming boulder belched forth from the storm—then another, and another.

From all directions, fiery arcs blazed across the night sky.

The door to her suite suddenly burst open behind her. Wennar and two of the elv'in guards tumbled inside the room.

"Stormhaven's under attack!" Wennar blurted out. "Come! We must reach the ships!"

Elena fled the balcony. "The others?"

"They're being gathered as we speak. Hurry, mistress."

"What's happening?"

Wennar shook his head. "We have no time to waste!"

Elena glanced back through the balcony doors. More and more flaming trails roared across the night sky. The strike of gongs became more strident. Distant explosions rumbled, shaking the ensconced wall lamps.

As Elena followed the d'warf toward the halls beyond, the floor canted under her feet, tilting abruptly. Caught off balance, Elena tumbled into Wennar's arms.

He grabbed her, holding her steady as the floors continued to list at an ever-steepening angle. His eyes were wide with fear.

"Stormhaven falls!"

14

ABOARD THE *SUNCHASER*, TOL'CHUK WOKE WITH THE FIRST EXPLO-
sion and was on his feet before the echoes had died down.
He tumbled out the door of his cabin. Up and down the lower
passageway, other doors banged open. Faces peered out in
confusion.

The d'warf Magnam tugged a shirt over his bare chest and
crossed to Tol'chuk. "What is going on?"

Crouched against the low beams, Tol'chuk shook his head.
Distantly a low roaring could be heard. "Something be wrong."
Confirming this, strident gongs began to clang. Tol'chuk turned
toward the door leading to the middeck just as it burst open.

A wild-eyed elv'in sailor waved them toward the open deck.
"Stormhaven is under attack!"

Tol'chuk hurried forward, leading the d'warves and elv'in
from their cabins. He clambered out to the open deck to find
the winds had picked up. Free of the passage, his keen nose immediately picked up a trace of smoke upon the sharp breezes.
Turning, he saw the source. A quarter league beyond the docks,
flames danced high into the night air.

Magnam stepped to his side, gawking not at the burning
city, but up at the sky. "What's bloody happening?"

Tol'chuk looked up. A score of fiery trails arced across the
night sky. He watched as one flaming boulder sailed past overhead and struck a steepled building, bounced off, then crashed
into a bridge, smashing it to splinters as new fires sprouted.

"Maybe the captain knows what's going on," Magnam said,
pointing toward the starboard rail.

Jerrick, temporary captain of the *Sunchaser*, stood with a
long spyglass fixed to one eye. The elder remained steady as

other flaming juggernauts struck the city, punching holes and setting homes and buildings ablaze. Tol'chuk followed the line of his spyglass toward the spires of the royal palace. With his keen og're eyes, he discerned a flicker from the highest tower: a mirrored signal.

Jerrick lowered his spyglass and turned to those gathered around the deck. His voice boomed for all to hear. "Cast off the mooring lines! Send word to the rest of the ships! Free the skiffs! We're to evacuate as many as we can from the fires!"

Elv'in sailors scurried to their posts. Ropes were tugged free and lines loosened. Sails tumbled down to snap in the steady wind. Along the harbor, other ships—both small and large— followed suit. A few drifted upward from their docks, their red iron keels glowing with energy.

By the rails, tarps were tugged from the smaller skiffs flanking the *Sunchaser*. Elv'in sailors scrambled to haul up the boats' short masts and loosen the skiffs' moorings.

After passing final orders to his crew, Jerrick crossed to Tol'chuk and the gathered d'warves. His eyes were worried, but his words were steady. "The word from the castle is to load you all into the *Sunchaser*'s lead skiff. I'm to take you to the palace to join your companions. The queen suspects the attack is not upon Stormhaven itself, but set against the wit'ch."

"What then?" Tol'chuk asked.

Jerrick shook his head. "I am to take you to the palace. Those were my orders." He led the way to the ship's stern. Beyond the rail, the largest of the skiffs was being readied. Sails bloomed from the short mast.

A splintering crash sounded off the port side. Tol'chuk watched a neighboring thick-bellied supply ship crack in half. A flaming boulder had struck its hull and arced over the tip of the *Sunchaser*'s masts. The heat of its passage burned like a passing sun. The damaged supply ship, its sails aflame, tumbled from the sky. In the fiery light, the small figures of sailors could be seen falling to their deaths.

Grim-faced, Jerrick waved Tol'chuk and the others onto the skiff. "Get aboard. We must be under way." As the d'warves clambered along the narrow gangway, the captain's eyes turned to his city now, aglow with scores of fires. The city itself began to tilt, sinking into the storm around it. Distant screams and shouts echoed out to them.

Tol'chuk crossed the short way onto the skiff. Jerrick followed last, his lips bloodless and tight. He waved a sailor from the boat's tiller and took the place himself. "I can manage on my own," Jerrick said. "Attend your duties on the *Sunchaser*. I've left the first mate in charge."

The elv'in sailor bowed, then scrambled back to the ship.

Once the last lines were loosened and the gangplank pulled in, the small skiff fell away from the *Sunchaser*. Its sails swelled, and it hove in a sharp turn toward the burning city, spiraling upward

By now, a good quarter of the city was ablaze. Smoke choked the skies. Tol'chuk watched as a flaming boulder exploded out from the city's center, punching through from below and shooting into the sky. Splintered wood cascaded upward, catching fire and showering back down upon the homes and buildings. New blazes blew into existence.

Numb, Tol'chuk settled to his haunches near the mast. The d'warves huddled in smaller groups in the cramped boat. Magnam scuttled over to join Tol'chuk. "So much for sneaking up on Gul'gotha unawares," he mumbled. "Someone knows we're here."

Now high enough, the skiff glided over the destruction below. Wafts of stinging smoke struck the small boat like rogue waves. Jerrick guided the craft with skill, shying from the worst flames and watching the sky for danger from above. Still the heat grew searing, and the smoky fumes watered the eyes and singed the nose.

Ahead, the spires of the royal palace drew nearer. Several of the towers listed like drunken sailors, threatening to topple at any moment. Tol'chuk glanced behind him.

Jerrick manned his post, his pale face smeared with soot and sweat. He, too, saw the danger, but maintained his stoicism, his sharp face fixed with determination. The captain's gaze flickered to the flash of a signal fire from one of the listing towers. The silver light flickered in code.

In response, Jerrick leaned his shoulder into the tiller, and the skiff swept around toward the threatened tower. "Your companions are in there," Jerrick said calmly, nodding forward.

Tol'chuk swallowed. The spire continued to tilt, falling slowly, as if the flow of time had slowed. They would not make it in time.

Jerrick tried to aim the skiff on a steady and swift course, but the fires wreaked havoc on the winds. The swirl of cold and hot air created pocket tempests. Jerrick was forced to cut back and forth, buffeted by errant gusts.

As the captain fought the tiller, a roar like a thousand raging dragons sounded below.

"Grab hold tight!" the captain bellowed.

Tol'chuk dug his claws into the rail as another boulder shot upward from below, passing no more than a stone's throw from the starboard side, a monstrous sun shooting past their tiny ship. D'warves scrambled away, crying out. The small skiff was pelted from below by splintered debris.

Tol'chuk turned forward in time to see a flaming section of a demolished house fly up in front of the skiff. It flipped end over end, throwing off burning shingles. Jerrick angled the skiff up and away and avoided a collision by less than a handspan.

But they did not pass the flying house unscathed. A handful of flaming shingles rained over the skiff. The d'warves kicked and swatted the fiery bits off the deck, but one shingle struck the sail, burning through it and setting the sailcloth aflame.

Tol'chuk shoved to his feet and patted at the flames, scorching the hair from his fingers and arms, but the fire spread quickly, eating away their only sail. Other flames spat up around the rails.

"The hull's on fire!" Jerrick yelled.

As Tol'chuk and the others fought the flames, the skiff went into a steep tumble down toward the burning city.

ELENA RACED WITH WENNAR DOWN THE SPIRALING STAIRS THAT led to the main keep of the elv'in palace. The steps were canted at a unnatural angle, as if this were all a fevered dream—but it was not. The air reeked of smoke. The heat was stifling in the tight stairwell. Screams echoed from afar. Through narrow windows in the tower, they caught passing glimpses of the destruction. Fires burned throughout the city. Whole sections were just cratered ruins.

"Not much farther!" Wennar wheezed.

Ahead a pair of elv'in guards led the way. They were to gather in the queen's audience chamber on the palace's lowest level.

Elena glanced out a window and spotted a few elv'in windships aloft over the ravaged city. Lamps lit their riggings, and ropes trailed down to rescue those most at risk.

Praying for the citizens of Stormhaven, Elena hurried after Wennar. As she ran, she pictured the face of the elv'in boy who had stolen a kiss from her cheek, his eyes full of life, full of joy. But now look what she had brought to his home: fire and death. Such was the fate of all who met her. And though the flames here were not lit by her own hand, they might as well have been. She was ultimately to blame for the destruction here. The dark forces of the Gul'gotha must have sensed her presence here.

"Thank the Sweet Mother," Wennar grumbled.

Elena glanced ahead. The stairwell's end came in sight. As a group, they rushed out of the slanted tower and into the main keep.

"This way!" one of the elv'in called.

In the main keep, the floors were still tilted, but it was now all downhill. They raced down the passage. Other elv'in crowded these lower halls, many still in their bedclothes like Elena, seeking refuge in the lower levels of the towers. Panic and fear were bright in their eyes. But that was not all. Elena caught the narrow-eyed glares and whispered curses as she was led past by the guards.

One thin man spat at her feet. "Begone, wit'ch!"

Wennar elbowed him aside and pushed Elena ahead. "Don't mind him, mistress."

Elena bit her lip.

But others took up the man's chant. *"Begone, wit'ch!"*

The noise drew other elv'in into the hall from neighboring passages. The guards were forced to bare their swords against the growing crowd. Their progress slowed. Behind them, the crowds now surged, pressing them from the rear.

"She's murdered us all!" a woman shrilled.

To the left, a dagger appeared in someone's hand. All Elena saw was a flash of silver. But Wennar was there, catching the attacker's wrist and breaking the thin bones with a loud crack. The man fell to his knees in pain, but Wennar kicked him aside after relieving him of his weapon.

Now armed, Wennar sheltered Elena in front of him, keeping her close to the backs of the guards. The double doors to the queen's private audience chamber lay ahead, but the way was packed with a swelling mob. They could not move forward.

"Kill the wit'ch!"

Wennar grunted as a piece of broken chair leg was thrown at his head, clouting him on his ear. His feet stumbled, but he kept his place. "We need to get clear of this passage."

Elena glanced to her ruby hands, ripe with power. Could she slay these panicked folk? Kill them so she might live? She clenched her fists. *Sweet Mother, do not make me do this.*

Then the doors to the audience chamber crashed open. All eyes swung around. Queen Tratal towered in the threshold. Though her form was clothed in a long shift and her hair fell loose to the small of her back, there was no mistaking that royalty stood before them. Her skin was as pale as fresh snow; her eyes blazed with ice-fire. All along her bare arms, blue cascades of energy shimmered. Even her hair was alive with power.

When she spoke, her voice rumbled with the threat of thunder. "What is the meaning of this?"

A man answered from down the hall, brave in his anonymity. "The wit'ch has brought this destruction upon us all! We must be avenged!" Murmurs of assent wafted through the crowd.

A dagger appeared in Queen Tratal's hand. She held it out toward the crowd. "Then kill *me*," she said, her words crackling down the hall. "It is I who brought Elena here against her will. If anyone is to blame for this night, it is your own queen. It is my pride that has brought ruin down upon us all."

Elena was close enough to see the tears in Tratal's eyes. The dagger trembled in the queen's fingers—not from fear, but agony and sorrow.

"Take this knife and plunge it into my own breast!"

The hall grew deathly silent. "No!" those nearest answered. The sorrow of their queen quickly spread outward. People fell to their knees, into each other's arms, sobbing. Like ice floes in spring, the crowd began to break up around them, falling away.

Tratal lowered the blade with a look of regret, almost as if she wished someone had taken up her challenge. Her eyes met Elena's, and the fire died in them. "Come," she said. "We've not much time."

Elena pushed past the guards and stepped around those weep-

ing on the slanted floor. Once at the queen's side, Elena touched
Tratal's bare arm, a silent gesture of sympathy.

Queen Tratal placed her hand gently atop Elena's. "I'm
sorry."

"Is there nothing I can do to help save your city?"

Tratal shook her head. "We'll take flight on our ships, save as
many as we can." The queen led Elena into her audience chamber. The room was deep and long. Its walls were draped in tapestries, and a throne of polished mahogany stood at one end. While
normally serving as a hall for the queen to settle disputes and
oversee her city, now it was a rallying point for the royal house-
hold. Elv'in of all ages and dress scurried about the room, preparing to evacuate the palace.

Elena stared at the organized confusion, frowning at a row of
elv'in elders bent over strange devices along the far wall. "What
of my friends?" she asked.

Tratal nodded across the chamber. Elena finally noticed Mama
Freda bandaging up Er'ril's arm. The plainsman sat atop a crate
of their gear. Even from across the room, Elena recognized the
Blood Diary in his lap; he guarded it even now.

Tratal led her toward them. "I've also sent for your companions on the *Sunchaser*. They should arrive at any moment with
one of the smaller skiffs. In the confusion, you should be able to
slip away as the city is pursued."

Er'ril spotted Elena and stood, trailing a length of ripped linen
from his left arm. "Elena, are you all right?"

"I'm fine," she answered, waving him back down. "Let Mama
Freda finish her work."

The old healer yanked on her length of bandage. "He's been
pulling at these reins since the first fireball, wanting to gallop to
your side."

Er'ril opened his mouth to protest, but Elena silenced him
with an upraised hand. She directed her next question back to
Queen Tratal. "These fireballs . . . do you know where they came
from? Or who attacks?"

Queen Tratal nodded to the four elv'in elders and their bronze
devices. "Come. We've not much time. But you should this see
yourself."

Elena and Wennar were led quickly across the room to the
four stations just behind the throne. The men sat upon high

stools before wooden columns sprouting bronze contraptions. They had their faces pressed to oval cutouts in the columns while their fingers manipulated bronze mechanisms.

As the queen approached with Elena, one of the elv'in straightened, pulling his face away from his station. "My queen," he said with a bob of his head. "I'm afraid we've discovered no safe path for the city."

Queen Tratal placed a hand on his shoulder. "Thank you, Germayn. You and the other farseers should attend to your own families. But first, could you show Elena what you've seen?"

He bobbed his head again. "Certainly, my queen." He hopped off his seat and patted the stool. "Sit, child."

Elena, her brow wrinkled with curiosity, climbed the seat. Wennar was offered another station. Once settled, the old elv'in coaxed the two to peer into the cutout in the column. The oval shape was a perfect fit for her face, the wooden edges worn smooth from ages of use. Within the column, Elena found only darkness, but sensed the column was hollow.

"Let me open a farseer channel," the elder said.

Elena heard the elv'in swivel the bronze controls. Queen Tratal spoke as he worked. "We've crystal eyes set on the city's underside to pierce the belly of the storm. Ancient architects of the city devised a complex of mirrors and prisms to allow us to spy upon the world below us."

"There we go," the elder mumbled. An echoing click sounded.

The interior of the dark column lit up, drawing a shocked gasp from Elena. A fiery view of a blasted landscape was reflected in a mirror tilted in front of her face. Elena instantly knew at what she was staring.

Wennar named it aloud, his voice strained. "Gul'gotha."

Below Stormhaven, a mountainous terrain spread in all directions. Even in the predawn darkness, the landscape was easy to discern. Sprinkled amidst the dark peaks glowed hundreds of volcanic cones. Crimson magma churned in their craters, some brighter than the midday sun. It was an infernal land of smoke, fire, and ash.

As she watched, one of the cones exploded forth with a fountain of lava. From the volcano's fiery throat, a large, flaming boulder coughed skyward. It was no random event. With her face pressed to the farseeing device, Elena saw other peaks cast out fireballs, all aiming in fiery arcs toward the city.

Elena pulled away, shocked, the blood draining from her face. "The Land itself is attacking the city."

"So it would seem," the queen said. "Scout ships and my far-seers had deemed the volcanos dormant. But once the city passed over it, the peaks began to erupt. Whether a foul hand directs the assault or whether it is some unnatural defense triggered by our presence, no one is able to say. All we know with certainty is that we've flown into this trap with no safe passage to escape it. Our only hope is for evacuation aboard our smaller, swifter ships."

Elena and Wennar climbed down from their stools. "Are there enough ships?" she asked.

Queen Tratal turned away, her pained expression answer enough.

Across the hall, near one of the narrow windows, an elv'in sentry with a spyglass called out to the queen, drawing all their attentions. "I've spotted Jerrick's skiff!" The young sentry turned, and Elena realized it was Prince Typhon, his nose bandaged. "But it's taken flame! It burns!"

Queen Tratal glanced down to Elena with concern.

"What is it?" Elena asked.

"It's your friends' boat," the queen said in a rush, hurrying toward Typhon. She yelled to her guards as she strode his way. "Open the Storm Gate!"

Elv'in scurried to obey, exposing long chains hidden behind narrow tapestries at the back corners of the room. As the chains were worked, old gears groaned overhead. The entire wall be-hind the throne began to rise, opening an expansive view across the city of Stormhaven.

As the monstrous gate winched open, smoke billowed into the hall. By now half of the city was aflame. Standing by the throne with the queen, Elena coughed and blinked against the fumes. Below, ships of all sizes drifted above the carnage. Rope ladders dangled down from the open hulls, crowded with fleeing townsfolk.

Elena glanced to Tratal. It was more than stinging smoke that drew tears from the queen's eyes. "What have I done?" Tratal moaned.

Prince Typhon stepped to their side. "There!" he said, pointing out into the maelstrom of smoke and fire. Off to the left, a tiny boat swept in a steep dive toward the palace. Its keel trailed smoke and flames. Its mast was a torch in the darkness. "They'll burn to cinders before they can reach here."

"No," Queen Tratal said firmly. "I may not be able to save my city, but I can rescue this one ship." She lifted her arms, eyes closing.

The young prince stepped away, drawing Elena with him. He stared back upon the queen with a mix of awe, love, and concern. "The queen weakens rapidly. All this horrible night, she has fought to bolster sections of the city, to keep the broken sections aloft long enough for ships to rescue as many as possible. But even here in the heart of the storm, her power is not limitless."

"Is there anything I can do to help?" Elena asked.

He shook his head. "She is mistress of the storm. This is her domain."

Er'ril, his arm bandaged from wrist to elbow, joined them. Mama Freda shadowed the plainsman with Tikal on her shoulder.

"I smell lightning in the air," Mama Freda whispered.

"It starts," Typhon said.

Elena glanced to him. "What?"

"The queen seeks the storm's heart."

Near the Storm Gate, Queen Tratal's arms crackled anew with blue energies. She gave a strangled gasp, and her hair blew into a nimbus around her. Rivulets of sweat trailed down her face as her skin grew translucent—but beneath her glassy skin was not bone. Instead, storm clouds churned amid flashes of lightning. She was becoming the storm itself.

As the queen stood, her limbs started to tremble. Prince Typhon rushed to her side, catching her as her legs gave out, holding her up. Suddenly Tratal's neck arched backward, and a scream ripped from her throat.

SINGED AND BLISTERED, TOL'CHUK CONTINUED TO BAT AT THE flames as the conflagration ate the last of the skiff's sails. It was hopeless. Flames raced along the rails. The deck burned underfoot. Tol'chuk bellowed his frustration.

Then, as if the skies themselves had heard his protests, an answering cry pierced the storm's thunder. Tol'chuk searched the skies. Far off to port, a stream of clouds broke over the city wall and raced toward their ship. Tendrils broke from its foremost edge, spreading outward. Tol'chuk's eyes grew wide. Lit by the fires below, the race of clouds looked like a giant's arm reaching out toward them, fingers spreading above.

The d'warves aboard the skiff stopped their attempts to stanch the many fires. "What new horror is this?" Magnam asked.

With a scream of winds, a spat of lightning danced among the giant's fingers. Thunder blasted, throwing them all to the deck.

Only Jerrick maintained his position, standing at his tiller, eyes filling with tears, face exposed to the winds. "My queen . . ."

Overhead, the clouds split open, and a downpour flooded over the burning ship, drenching, pelting, swirling. Near Tol'chuk, the burning mast hissed angrily as it was doused by rain.

Tol'chuk rolled to his feet. *Thank the Sweet Mother!*

"Look!" Magnam said, pointing toward the city wall.

Tol'chuk turned from the mast. Out beyond the towering wall, the storm clouds swirled, afire with lightning. At first, Tol'chuk failed to see what had caught the small d'warf's attention, but as his vision broadened, he began to discern a form hidden among the clouds.

No . . . not hidden in the clouds, but made of the storm itself.

He saw a woman crouching in the storm, with lightning for eyes, her arm reaching out over them, drenching their boat with life-saving rain.

From this distance, Tol'chuk recognized the pain and sorrow in her face. Even the thunder seemed to moan with the grief in her heart.

"Who is that?" Magnam asked.

Jerrick answered softly, sobbing, as he fell to his knees by the tiller. "My queen . . ."

ER'RIL WATCHED TRATAL FALL LIMP IN PRINCE TYPHON'S ARMS. He hurried forward with Elena at his side. "Let me help you," Er'ril said, bending down. He handed the Blood Diary to Elena, who clutched the book to her chest, her gaze fixed on the queen. "Let's get Her Highness away from this open gate."

Typhon nodded gratefully, his eyes wide with concern. Between the two of them, they were able to carry Queen Tratal to her throne. But Er'ril could have carried her on his own, even with his injured arm. Her body was as light as spun cotton.

Once the queen was settled in her cushioned chair, Mama Freda joined them and ran her hands over Tratal's body. "She's cold as the grave."

Typhon glanced between the queen's prone form and back to the open gate. Smoke continued to billow into the hall. Overhead, a fireball sailed past the top of the palace spires, smashing the highest levels to burning splinters, showering flaming debris across the gateway. The prince took a step toward the opening, but his gaze shifted back to the queen. His fists clenched in frustration. "I should help oversee the landing of Jerrick's skiff, but . . ."

"Go! I've enough help here. See to the boat!"

He nodded, relieved to have the decision taken from him, and raced to join the other elv'in at the gate.

"I should go help him," Wennar said. "It is my d'warves who are aboard the boat."

Elena nodded, giving him permission. Once he stepped away, she moved near the queen and Mama Freda. "What can I do to help?"

The healer fingered Tratal's throat. "The beat of her heart is faint. She is fading."

Elena held up one of her ruby hands. "What if I lent her some of my magick?"

Er'ril stepped closer to protest, but one look from Elena kept him quiet. Though he may now be her husband by elv'in law, she warned him that this was not a matter up for discussion. Er'ril bit his lip. Elena had lent her magick to others in the past to help bolster their spirits—once with her Uncle Bol as the old man's heart had failed, and once even with Er'ril when he had been poisoned by a goblin's dagger. But it was not without risk to Elena herself.

Mama Freda patted Elena's hand. "I don't believe your magick will help here, child. It is not her body that is fading, so much as her spirit. It is not sickness that casts the queen out, but her own will."

"But if I strengthen her body . . . ?"

Mama Freda shrugged. "I am no wit'ch. I cannot say."

Er'ril sighed and spoke. "If the queen is doomed, what harm could it do to try?"

Elena glanced to Er'ril with surprise. He maintained a fixed stare at Mama Freda. Though he might not like Elena's choice to risk herself for a queen who had betrayed them, he was still her liegeman. He would offer whatever advice and counsel that he possessed.

The old healer shrugged again. "As I said, I am no wit'ch."

Er'ril reached to his belt and pulled free a rose-handled dagger.

"My wit'ch's blade!"

Er'ril held out the dagger to Elena. "The queen had them return all our gear taken from the *Sunchaser*." He nodded to the stacked crates.

Elena passed the Diary to him in exchange for the dagger, but Er'ril kept his grip on the knife. He stared hard into Elena's eyes. "Be careful," he warned under his breath.

She nodded grimly at him as he relinquished the blade. Next, Elena knelt beside the throne. She took Queen Tratal's hand and bloodied a finger with the tip of the dagger. A drop of blood welled up on the queen's skin. Elena glanced nervously to Er'ril.

He touched her shoulder, striving to instill his own strength into her.

Taking a deep breath, Elena pierced one of her own ruby fingers. Against the dark crimson stain, it was hard to say if blood had been drawn, but Er'ril saw Elena stiffen slightly—not with pain, but with the release of her pent magick. Her eyes closed narrowly, lips parting. A breath escaped her throat.

She leaned closer to the queen, but before she could mix their blood, a loud crash echoed through the hall. The floorboards jarred. Elena grabbed the throne to keep from tumbling.

Behind the throne, Er'ril saw the cause of the interruption. A large boat had slammed broadside into the edge of the Storm Gate. Elv'in scurried at the opening, tossing ropes, shouting orders. Smoke and steam billowed from the beaten craft, but Er'ril spotted the large bulk of Tol'chuk near the stern.

Prince Typhon called out to them, hauling on a rope as the winds tore at the rocking boat. "The skiff is docked! We must load up your gear!"

Er'ril spotted Wennar already hurrying toward the crates. The d'warf could not handle the stack by himself. He stepped in the d'warf's direction, but stopped, hesitating.

"Go!" Elena said. "Get everything aboard. I will attempt this, then we must be off."

"We don't have much time."

"Then don't argue. Go!"

Er'ril paused a moment, locking eyes with Elena. She met his gaze. Her stony demeanor softened as she understood his consternation. "Go," she said softly but firmly. "I'll be fine."

Er'ril turned away. He had won her hand in marriage, but Elena was forever her own woman—and if truth be told, he would wish it no other way.

Tucking the Blood Diary inside his shirt, he hurried to join the others by the boat.

ALONE NOW WITH QUEEN TRATAL AND MAMA FREDA, ELENA returned to her duty. She lifted the queen's hand and positioned their two bloody fingers near one another. The dagger's slices still bled freshly from both wounds.

Mama Freda hovered at her shoulder. "Careful, child."

Elena barely heard the healer's words, turning her ear instead to the song of her own magick. After practicing her arts, Elena understood the flows of her own power, but in this matter, sending a part of her magick into another, control was critical. Too much energy and she could burn Queen Tratal into a smoking cinder.

Taking a steadying breath, Elena lowered her finger to the queen's.

Instantly Elena's mind snapped away, flowing down the blood link into the queen's prone form. Elena had done this before— with Uncle Bol, with Flint, with Er'ril—but nothing had prepared her for what she discovered inside Queen Tratal.

Storm winds tore at Elena's mind, threatening to tear her away from her own body. Elena struggled to hold her place, drawing more of her own energy to define herself in the maelstrom. Around her, dark clouds swirled; lightning flashed in silver streaks of fire. In that moment, Elena realized she was not inside Tratal—at least not in her body of flesh and blood.

Instead, she had entered the storm beyond the city. The queen and the storm had become one—and Elena had joined them.

She wrapped her magick around herself like a cloak, struggling to hold herself in place. She could not stay long. It was hard even now to discern the tenuous connection back to her body in the throne room. It was a mere thread in the whirlwind.

As she floated, anchoring herself in the storm, she sensed even fainter threads spreading in an infinite web around her, stretching out in all directions. The overall effect was one of interconnectivity. She knew what she was sensing out here in the middle of the storm. It was *life*—every living thing connected together in an endless web of energy and power. Elena longed to follow it outward. It called to her from countless throats. But even she did not have that much power. She would be lost in that infinite maze, a mote in the vastness of life.

So instead she concentrated on the one single thread near her—that which connected the storm to the queen's body.

As she did so, Elena felt eyes turning in her direction, a familiar icy stare. *Queen Tratal.* She must have sensed Elena's presence. Words formed in the howl of winds around her. "Go, child. This is my battle."

Elena recognized the figure of a woman, formed of clouds and energy, swirling around her. "You're dying," she yelled into the howling winds.

"So be it. Death is not an end, and by using my spirit to fuel the storm, giving myself fully to it, I can save more of my people."

Images formed in Elena's mind. A woman of clouds wrapped around the ravaged city, holding it to her breast, speeding it faster over the volcanic peaks, making the city a harder target. Elena understood. Queen Tratal intended to give her own life so more of her people might escape.

"I can help," Elena argued. "You do not have to spend all your life's energy. Use my magick!"

A tired smile formed in the clouds. "You are truly King Belarion's child." The thin thread back to the queen's body and the throne room blazed brighter. "But the path here is too fragile. Enough energy to make any difference would burn away this conduit, trapping you forever in this storm with me. I will not allow you to risk yourself."

Elena sensed the truth of her words. Even the bits of energy she used to define herself here threatened the weak connection. "But what of you?"

"Away, child. This is my battle."

Winds buffeted Elena, shoving her back along the thread. For a moment, she fought, refusing to give up. But the energy to resist frazzled the connection, thinning it to the faintest strand. Realizing the futility of her actions, she yielded to the storm, surrendering herself to the winds.

Elena felt herself pass through Queen Tratal's body. As she did so, she sensed the thin thread connecting the queen here to the storm snap away. Elena heard the last beat of Tratal's heart as she fell back into her own body.

Elena sagged, slumping backward, suddenly weak.

Mama Freda caught her. "You're safe, child . . . safe."

"The queen . . . ?" she asked faintly.

"Gone."

Elena grabbed the throne's arm to pull herself up. In the seat, she found Queen Tratal's shift crumpled on the cushions—but nothing more. Her body had vanished.

Typhon suddenly stumbled up to the other side of the throne, falling to his knees. He stared at the empty seat, tears running down his cheeks. He moaned. "She's given herself fully to the storm."

Elena nodded. "She means to use her energy to speed the city over the lands of Gul'gotha, to buy more time for her people to escape."

Wennar appeared behind Typhon. "Then we must hurry. We've already flown past the home mines of my people."

Mama Freda helped Elena to her feet.

"All the gear has been stowed," the d'warf captain added, stepping away. "We must be gone."

Typhon stood, wiping tears from his eyes. "I will captain the skiff myself. I know the queen's will in this matter—to get you safely to your destination."

From behind the prince, a tall elv'in man strode forward and rested a hand on the prince's shoulder. Er'ril was with him. Elena recognized the stern newcomer from the *Sunchaser*. It was Captain Jerrick. His face was smeared with soot, his hair and clothes soaked with rain. "No. I'll not allow it, Prince Typhon. Your place is here."

"But the queen's command . . ."

"The queen is no longer. And with her sons gone to the far corners of the world, you are the next in line to the throne. You must serve as regent until such a time as one of them returns."

Prince Typhon's eyes grew huge with horror.

Jerrick gripped his shoulder tighter. "You must lead our people from Stormhaven."

"I . . . I can't . . ."

"You will."

Elena understood his pain and shock—the sudden thrust of power, the burden of responsibility.

"Take your Lady Mela," Jerrick continued, "and lead as many away as you can. They are seeds cast to the wind. You must find them all a safe place to land."

"But what of Elena and her companions?"

"I will take them myself. That is my duty as ship's captain. Your duty is here."

Elena saw the young prince bow under the heavy mantle of leadership. For a moment, she thought he would break, but slowly he stood straighter. Pain and sorrow shadowed his eyes, but he nodded. "Take them to the skiff. I will see to our people."

Captain Jerrick nodded once, then lifted an arm to direct them to the ship. "We must hurry," he said.

Er'ril stepped beside Elena, putting a protective arm around her shoulders. "Are you all right?"

She leaned into him. "I'm fine." She glanced behind her to see Prince Typhon standing stiffly beside the empty mahogany throne. *He'll make a better leader than I,* she thought, and wished him strength for the hardships ahead.

At the gate, the winds had grown harsher. The small skiff bounced and rattled against its moorings. Elena saw that a burned hole in the sail had been hastily patched with a bit of tapestry ripped from the throne room's walls. A sailor with a long needle was repairing the last rent as their group reached the gangplank.

Captain Jerrick yelled into the storm's winds. "Clear off! Be ready to loose the moorings on my command!"

Elv'in scurried to obey, leaping from the rail or swinging on mooring ropes. Soon the deck was clear of all but Elena's party. The wit'ch crossed to join Tol'chuk, nodding to the gathered d'warves, who looked like a gaggle of drowned geese in their drenched clothes.

Elena moved to a spot near the stacked crates, seeking shelter against the wind. She was still dressed only in her nightclothes, but Er'ril joined her with a fur-lined cloak under each arm.

"This should could keep you warm until we can get to your packed clothes."

Teeth chattering, Elena accepted the cloak and wrapped its thickness around her. Warm gear was passed to the others. Soon they were all huddled under cloaks and blankets.

Captain Jerrick took his place near the skiff's tiller. "Ready to cast off!" he yelled to the elv'in manning the gate.

Knots were tugged loose, and the skiff lurched forward. Elena bumped into a neighboring crate.

"Keep low!" Jerrick ordered, his words directed at the skiff this time. The mast's boom swept by overhead, and the craft turned smartly in the wind. "It's going to get rough from here!"

Elena sighed. *Doesn't it always . . . ?*

The skiff circled out from the palace. By now, four of the building's twenty spires had fallen away, and another three burned, casting flames high into the air. Below, the city fared worse. Fully three-quarters of it was lost to the fires or destroyed by the rain of fireballs. But for the moment, there seemed a respite from the attacks. The night sky was empty of flaming juggernauts. It seemed Tratal's efforts had not been in vain. The elv'in queen must have succeeded in accelerating the city's flight—but for how long?

Overhead, other elv'in ships, crowded with peering faces, trundled past, many heading toward the walls of the ravaged city. A handful of others patrolled the lower city, searching out those still living, offering one last lifeline.

"What of those still in the palace?" Elena asked, glancing back to Jerrick.

"Stormhaven takes care of its own," he answered cryptically.

Elena turned to stare back at the retreating castle as the skiff drifted downward.

"Where are you heading?" Er'ril asked.

Jerrick pointed to the deck. "Straight down through the heart of the storm."

"Is that safe?" Er'ril said.

Jerrick wiped soot from his eyes. "Is anywhere safe?" he mumbled. But after Er'ril's expression darkened further, he added, "I'll get us through. Don't you worry. I've plied the storms since I was a boy."

Elena watched the elv'in citadel fade behind them, then gasped as all the remaining towers fell away like toppling sticks. "Oh, no! Prince Typhon . . . the others . . ."

But she need not have worried. A wondrous sight appeared. The walls of the central keep shed away, revealing the hidden heart of the castle. A gigantic ship rose from the wreckage of the palace, lifting atop an iron keel that glowed with the light of a rising sun. Slowly sails unfurled and caught the tempest's winds, billowing out. The ship hove gracefully away, leading the myriad scores of other ships, both large and small, away from the burning city.

Then the sight vanished as the skiff swept into the storm's edge.

"Hold tight!" Jerrick called out.

The bow end of the craft dipped steeply as the captain dove the skiff into the storm's depths under the city. Instantly winds tore at the craft. The sails whipped and snapped. Rains sluiced across the deck, soaking them to the bone. But Jerrick seemed little fazed by the bucking skiff. He manipulated his tiller, and energy danced along his hands as he touched his own magick.

As they fled through the clouds, lightning chased them. Thunder roared and pummeled the skiff. But the captain rode the storm's lines: coursing swiftly along downdrafts, banking steeply through eddies and rapids.

Elena held white-knuckled to the rail, while Er'ril did his best to shelter her. Overhead, the sail's patch began to tatter, its rent edge snapping in the winds. Jerrick's lips drew tighter, bloodlessly thin, but he continued to work his tiller.

Elena turned forward just as the skiff suddenly bucked, coming close to spilling end over end. Er'ril clutched hard to her as her knees lifted from the planks. Then the skiff slammed back to an even keel. She and Er'ril fell with a hard bump back to the deck.

"We're through," Jerrick said simply, as if they had been merely gliding along a calm stream.

Elena pushed up and was immediately struck by the heat.

After the endless chill, the air was stifling, reeking of sulfur and molten rock. She stared past the rail and saw the spread of dark peaks under them, aglow with the infernal light of volcanic cones. It was a sight to burn away her resolve. How could they hope to survive down there?

"A loathsome place indeed," Mama Freda mumbled.

"It wasn't always this way," Wennar said. "The land grew sick with volcanoes and quakes only after the Nameless One corrupted our people. It was once a green and hale place."

Searching below, Elena could never imagine that to be true. She turned her face away.

Overhead, swirling dark clouds swept past. Distantly, Elena saw bits of the hidden city fall through the storm's belly to litter the landscape below. Off to the side, a section of a building tumbled from the clouds, hit the peak of a mountain, and disintegrated into an explosion of broken planks. Elena stretched her neck and searched for escaping ships. There was no sign.

"Stormhaven slows," Jerrick said, noticing the direction of Elena's stare.

Elena realized he was correct. At the edges, the storm was fraying. Clouds drifted away. The queen's energy must be fading.

"Gul'gotha will again sense Stormhaven's passage," Jerrick said dourly. Punctuating his statement, a volcanic peak exploded a league away, belching out another fireball. The flaming shot of magma arced brilliantly, disappearing into the storm front with an immense hiss.

"The attack renews," Er'ril said.

The captain's face became lined with worry as he returned his attention to the skiff. "My people's ships and boats will not have enough time to escape safely."

As the skiff spun in a slow spiral toward the cursed landscape, Elena stood and tossed off her wet cloak. "I'll not let that happen." She slipped free her wit'ch's dagger.

"Elena . . ." Er'ril warned.

"If it's energy the storm needs, then it's energy I'll give it."

She sliced the meat of both thumbs, releasing coldfire from her left hand and wit'chfire from her right. Inside the swirling clouds, Tratal had warned her that passing magick into the queen's body would only burn away the tenuous tie between the woman and the storm, but Elena saw no such risk now. Tratal was gone from this world.

Elena studied the swirl of clouds. She did not know how much of Tratal still rode the storm, but there was one energy that the storm should be able to feed upon.

Lifting her right hand, Elena formed a fist and called for the power of the sun—touching its heat and fire. Energy built to a feverish blaze inside her clenched palm. Her hand grew to a bright ruby blaze. Elena next raised her left fist and summoned the magick of moonlight—cold and ice. Her fist grew to match the other; the only difference was a slight azure hue to the ruby glow.

Power sang in her blood and heart, rejoicing, crying for release. Elena was well-used to the song of the wit'ch and ignored the chorus of chaos and wild magicks. Instead she brought her two fists together, knuckles to knuckles. The trapped energy shook her very frame. Finally, when she could hold it no longer, she shoved her arms toward the sky, unfolding her fingers like an opening rose. A rage of energy blew skyward, a mix of wit'chfire and coldfire, the two becoming one in a blaze of *stormfire*.

Magick shrieked skyward, a tumble of ice and fire.

Elena gasped, her back arching as energy spasmed out of her.

Her stream of stormfire struck the storm and disappeared into it. Lightning radiated from the point of impact, like spokes on a wheel. But as she fed more and more of her power into the dark clouds, the lightning forked and forked again, becoming a blazing net of energy spreading through the entire bank of clouds.

"Elena!" Er'ril screamed into her ear, but she hardly heard him. Magick sang through her blood. "Elena! Look to the left!"

His words sank through the chorus of her power. Her gaze slowly turned, and she saw a fireball arcing directly at them. From the corner of her eye, she watched Jerrick fight his tiller. The captain must have been so fixed on her display that he had failed to notice the threat until it was too late. The boat could not move out of the path of the flaming boulder in time.

Though Elena should have felt terror, magick was too ripe in her. She rang with invincibility. Swinging her arms down from the skies, she separated her hands and flung a spray of pure coldfire at the magma ball, snuffing its flames and freezing it solid.

With hardly a thought, she followed next with a blinding lance of wit'chfire, striking the boulder when it was less than a dozen spans from the boat. The frozen ball of magma exploded with its touch, shattering into dust that plumed harmlessly over the skiff, coating them all.

Once done, Elena sagged to her knees, her magick spent. Er'ril was there, tossing her cloak back over her shoulders and hugging her tight.

"Get us down into the valleys!" Er'ril yelled. "We can't risk being shot at again."

Jerrick dove the skiff at a steep angle.

Elena sank into her knight's arms. Her bones felt like butter.

Er'ril squeezed and rubbed her arms. "The wards here must be attuned to magick, whether from the elemental energies or your own power."

"I was foolish," she mumbled. "I should have thought before acting."

"You were following your heart," Er'ril whispered.

Tol'chuk pointed behind the stern. "The woman in the clouds. She returns!"

Elena glanced skyward, staying in Er'ril's arms.

Above and behind them, the storm churned and roiled with lightning. But there was no mistaking the gigantic figure formed of clouds and framed by lightning.

"Queen Tratal . . ." Jerrick said, his voice cracking.

The elv'in woman floated along the tempest's belly.

As they watched, the storm grew thicker, its edges more substantial. The wide bank of clouds rolled more swiftly away from them, propelled upon unseen winds.

The figure in the clouds stared back down, a sad smile on her lips. Words swept toward them upon a gust of wind. "You've saved us." The words echoed and faded away. "Saved us all."

"Queen Tratal," Elena murmured.

"Godspeed, Elena Morin'stal." The woman dissolved back into the storm—but one final message whispered back to her: words only meant for Elena. "Remember your promise."

Elena stared as the storm streamed toward the dark horizon. "I will," she said firmly. And in her heart, she knew she spoke truly. In some distant time, some other place, the elv'in houses would be reunited again.

But not here, not now. That was another's story, not hers.

Elena leaned to the rail and stared below.

The skiff glided toward the blasted landscape of Gul'gotha: a maze of craggy red mountains, deep-clefted valleys, stunted trees, and blighted streams that glowed a sickly green.

This was *her* future.

Book Five

BROKEN CROWNS

15

MYCELLE KEPT A WARY WATCH ON THE DARK FOREST AROUND them, her breath billowing white before her. Nearby, Kral built a fire of deadfall wood to prepare their midday meal. Even the large mountain man's fingers shivered as he struck steel on flint. The days since leaving Castle Mryl and the Northwall had grown more frigid with every step. The skies, what could be seen of them, were now a blank slate of gray, and the night before, a gentle snow had sifted through the monstrous twisted branches. In the morning, the entire wood was dusted in white.

Mycelle stared around her. Normally a snow-cloaked forest held a certain calm beauty. But here in the Dire Fell, the sight was disheartening, like a frosted corpse, contorted by the ice.

The only warmth came from their own camp. Nee'lahn sat on a knobbed root of a tree and played her lute softly. The strings thrummed with hummingbirds and green leaves, ringing of soft-petaled flowers and long summer nights. It was no surprise that the Grim wraiths held back. It was the song of their True Glen, of the lost Lok'ai'hera. How it must pain them to be reminded of their past, here among the twisted boles and tortured branches of their ancient trees. Even Mycelle felt a twinge of the loss as she listened to the nyphai's gentle playing.

Meric stepped up to Mycelle. He rubbed his hands together, blowing on his bare fingers for warmth, but his eyes were on the sky. "It'll snow again tonight."

She nodded. The elv'in lord had a keen weather sense.

"We cannot keep going like this," he continued, moving nearer and lowering his voice. "If and when we pass this sick forest, the cold and winds will only grow worse. We need to find warmer gear for the road ahead."

315

"I know. I saw Mogweed eyeing Fardale earlier. He had a look in his eye like he wanted to skin his brother for his warm pelt." Mycelle frowned. They each had thick cloaks and leather boots to keep the worst of the chill away, but they would need furs and warmer bedrolls to reach Tor Amon and the Citadel of the Mountain Folk.

"If only the *Stormwing* could have crossed the Wall," Meric mumbled.

Mycelle sighed. It was a constant wish by them all. But shortly after escaping Castle Mryl, they had contacted Meric's ship through the use of Lord Tyrus' silver coin. Xin had reported that not only was the Northwall too tall to pass over, but even the breach in the wall was blocked by the monstrous trees. Any attempts they made to pass had triggered the forest to attack the ship with whipping, clawing branches, guided by wraiths perched in the trees' limbs. The *Stormwing* could not fly high enough to escape their assault.

"We'll manage," Mycelle said.

"I hope so," Meric said, and wandered back to the camp as Kral finally managed to coax the smoldering pile of dead leaves to take his flint's spark. Tiny flames sizzled up, drawing all their eyes.

The tiny snap of a twig sounded behind Mycelle. She whipped around, swords in both fists. A dark shape slinked from the scrubby brush. It was Fardale, returning from scouting the forest; the broken branch had been his way of warning her of his approach. His amber eyes glowed toward her. The image of an empty path appeared in her mind's eye, indicating the immediate region was clear of any wraiths.

"I'll tell Nee'lahn," she said. "Go warm yourself by the fire."

Tongue lolling, Fardale padded past her.

Mycelle watched the huge treewolf with a worried narrowing of her eyes. Since entering the forest, his sendings had grown rougher, his responses now curt and often unintelligible. It would not be long until Fardale was lost completely to his wolfish nature. According to Mogweed, the twins were little more than a moon away from settling into their current forms. Time was running out for them both—as well as it was for them all.

Working around the camp's periphery, Mycelle approached Nee'lahn. The small nyphai glanced up at her. Nee'lahn's eyes were haunted, shadowed with dark circles. Day and night, she had been forced to play her lute to keep the wraiths at bay. Only when the woods seemed clear could the woman take short naps. The burden was taking its toll.

Mycelle laid a hand on her shoulder. "Rest. Fardale says the woods around us are safe for the moment."

Nee'lahn nodded and eased her lute to her lap. She stretched her fingers, working free the knots and kinks from her cramped playing. Mycelle noticed her worn nails and the raw tips of her fingers. Nee'lahn searched through her pockets for the numb-weed balm.

"How are you faring?" Mycelle asked. "Will your fingers hold out until we reach the end of the forest?"

Nee'lahn stared dully at the forest around her. "It is not the playing that wears at me."

Mycelle understood. As much as her lute's song pained the Grim, so the dark wood drained Nee'lahn's own spirit. This had once been her home. Mycelle offered what consolation she could. "It won't be much longer. From my calculations, we should reach the far edge of the Fell in another two days."

Nee'lahn did not react. She only stared toward the north.

"Come. Let's get you some food." Mycelle helped her stand and guided her toward the growing fire. By now, Kral had managed to work up a solid blaze.

Once Nee'lahn was settled beside Mogweed at the fire, Mycelle returned to her sentry duty. With the lute's magick ended, the wood had to be closely watched against the encroachment of the Grim. During the first couple of days, any halt in the music had almost immediately resulted in their wailing assault. But now, several days deeper into the wood, the Grim were slower to respond. Either their numbers were not as great here or the music had by now succeeded in chasing the wraiths far from their path. Still, caution had to be taken. Eyes had to watch for shifting shadows, and ears had to remain pricked to the smallest sounds of the forest.

Mycelle nodded to Lord Tyrus on the camp's far side. The two would watch the forest during this break in the day's trek, circling around and around the camp until they were on the move again.

Mogweed came over with a tin plate of boiled roots mixed

with roasted snails. Mycelle ate on her feet, picking through the thin fare with her fingers. Hunting was poor in the Fell. Few creatures still lived among its twisted roots and haunted bowers: bony rabbits, burrowing moles, a few rangy birds. But at least the waters were fresh. Streams and brooks were frequent.

Mogweed kept pace with her for a few steps while she ate. The thin man eyed the forest with clear trepidation. "I heard you tell Nee'lahn that we should be out of this cursed woods in a couple of days. Is that so?"

"If my maps are accurate."

Mogweed chewed his lower lip, eyes narrowed. "And what then?" He lowered his voice. "Are we really going to try and sneak into Kral's old home up in the northern mountains? I heard him say that the snows up there never thaw, not even in the summer. And if the weather doesn't kill us, the d'warves surely will. It's not like we can surprise them. The encampment in Castle Mryl will surely send a bird reporting our escape."

Mycelle let the man drone on, then finally shrugged. "Who knows what we'll face up in the mountains? But I suspect d'warves and snow will be the least of our worries."

She could tell that her words did little to ease Mogweed's mind. His eyes grew wider as he obviously imagined the horrors ahead.

Mycelle sighed. "Don't fret so much about the future, Mogweed. It'll come whether you're ready or not. We'll deal with the cold as best we can. As for the d'warves, I imagine they'll think the wraiths have consumed the lot of us."

He nodded, appearing slightly relieved by this small bit of re-assurance as he stumbled back to the fire.

Mycelle shook her head. Despite her words, Mogweed's concern had set a seed of misgiving in her own breast. What were they going to do?

Finally, with the hole in their bellies somewhat filled, the party broke camp and moved out once again. Nee'lahn took up her lute, while Fardale patrolled the near woods. The remainder of the group trudged after them. Slowly more leagues passed under their boots. Few words were spoken.

Kral hung back, watching their back trail. But as the afternoon wore on, his post seemed unnecessary. No sign of the Grim threatened. Not even a distant wail was heard. Kral moved forward to join Mycelle.

"I don't like this quiet," he mumbled.

Mycelle nodded, then frowned as the small snake that roosted around her upper arm squirmed and tightened its grip. After traveling for so long with the large man, she had come to notice his presence often aggravated the tiny beast. She had always attributed this response to the man's strong elemental energies. The magick of deep caves and rock ran strong in Kral's blood. But then why didn't the snake respond to Meric or Lord Tyrus? Both were just as endowed in the Land's gifts. With no satisfactory answer, she pushed her misgivings aside and concentrated on the more immediate threat.

"The Grim have been growing less bold for the past few days," Mycelle said, staring out into the oddly silent forest. "Maybe at last Nee'lahn's music has succeeded in driving them fully away."

"What music?" Kral grumbled.

Mycelle opened her mouth to answer, then realized the mountain man was correct. The nyphai's lute had gone silent. Mycelle glanced forward and saw the small woman standing far ahead, frozen atop a slight rise in the land.

"Something's wrong," Mycelle said, and hurried forward.

Kral followed.

Mycelle closed the distance, collecting Meric and Tyrus en route. Neither of them had noticed Nee'lahn's lapse either. All afternoon, her music had been slowing and drifting lower. When it had finally stopped, no one but Kral seemed to have been aware.

As a group, they jogged forward. Nee'lahn continued to stare forward, the lute hanging limp in her fingers.

"What's wrong with her?" Tyrus whispered breathlessly as they reached the top of the hill. A light snow began to drift down from the gray skies. The sun was close to setting.

Mycelle glanced to the girl, then followed the line of her vision. In the hollow below, a small lake filled the lower lands, but what caught her eye was a huge tree on the lake's far side. Its bole, as thick around as a small cottage, stood straight as a sword, cutting up from the tangle of twisted trees around it. Its branches, though bare of leaves, splayed out in gentle terraces, like a hand offered to a tired traveler. It seemed so out of place among its tortured brethren.

"Nee'lahn?" Mycelle asked gently.

The nyphai's mouth moved, but no words came out. She licked her lips and tried again. "It's my tree." She turned finally toward Mycelle. Tears ran down her cheeks, streaming freely. Her voice became a sob. "It's . . . it's my home."

NEE'LAHN FELL TO HER KNEES. THE PAIN IN HER HEART WAS TOO much. She stared at her love, so tall, so stately. Though naked of its lush greenery and heavy violet flowers, Nee'lahn could never mistake its form. She had not thought to find her mate so untouched. It was as if it were only sleeping, not dead and lifeless. On her knees, she drank in the sight of her spirit tree. She had not even meant to cross near its resting place, knowing the pain it would cause, but her tired feet must have led her here, drawn to the only home she had ever known.

Mogweed stepped to her side. "It's so . . . so normal looking."

Nee'lahn wiped at her eyes. "I know. I don't understand . . . the Blight . . ." She waved an arm to encompass the rest of the forest.

"Come," Mycelle said gently, and helped her back to her feet. "Do you want to go closer?"

Nee'lahn covered her face with a hand. She wanted to run as lithe as a deer, but she did not know which way—toward her tree or away. It tore at her heart to see her love again. But she knew that as much as it pained her, she had to go on.

Clutching the lute to her breast, she nodded forward. "I . . . I must go."

Before a single step could be taken, Fardale came loping up the slope from the lake's edge, tongue lolling. His amber eyes glowed. Mycelle matched his gaze. After a moment, she turned to the others. "Fardale senses someone hiding ahead."

"One of the wraiths?" Tyrus asked.

"No . . . if I understand right, it's a man." Mycelle turned to Mogweed, clearly seeking to see if he understood his brother any better.

The small man shrugged. "He grows too close to the wolf," he mumbled under his breath. "I can barely understand him any longer."

"What's someone doing way out here?" Kral grumbled. He unhitched his ax and slowly pulled the snow leopard pelt off its iron blade. "Anyone who can survive among the Grim is surely tainted by the Dark Lord."

"Kral is right," Meric said, his eyes narrowed. "We must proceed with caution."

"Why proceed at all?" Mogweed said, stepping back. "Why not leave here, circle far around? Why invite danger?"

"Perhaps we should heed the shape-shifter," Tyrus said.

"And put an unknown enemy at our back?" Kral said. "I say we flush him out."

Nee'lahn swallowed hard. "Either way, I must go. Even if it's alone."

Gazes swung in her direction.

Before anyone else could speak, her lute began to play softly. Gentle notes wafted out and upward. Nee'lahn lifted the instrument in amazement. Her fingers were not touching the strings, yet the music began to grow fuller. A chorus flowed forth, bright as a summer moon, while around them the snow began to fall thicker. As soft as the falling flakes, the music floated over the lake.

Kral growled. "Quiet the cursed thing before it gives us away."

Nee'lahn pulled the lute away from him as he snatched at it. "No!"

Kral's warning proved too late anyway. As the music reached the far side, warm yellow light appeared, glowing forth from several small square openings in the tree's wide trunk.

Mogweed gasped and hid behind Kral.

"Windows," Meric said with amazement. "Someone's made a home inside your tree."

"Fardale's lurker," Tyrus commented, his family's fine sword in his grip.

"He must have heard the music," Mycelle said. "He's inviting us forward."

Kral squinted his eyes. "More likely inviting us into a trap."

"No, it's no trap." Nee'lahn stepped forward.

"How can you know that?" the mountain man gruffed.

"The music." Nee'lahn lifted her lute. "The wood rejoices. There can be no danger." And in her heart, she knew this to be true. She moved down into the hollow, meaning to follow the lake's edge.

She heard the elv'in whisper behind her. "I trust Nee'lahn. As corrupt as these woods may be now, they were once her home. Come. Let's see what mystery lies here."

As Nee'lahn reached the lake's edge, a bit of melancholy infused the lute's song. She understood why. Once this small lake had teemed with fish and tadpoles. Fireflies had lit the boughs that overhung the still waters, reflecting their beauty, while around its banks, flowers had always been in bloom. But now the lake was black and featureless, edged by dank algae and clinging weeds. So much beauty lost.

Nee'lahn turned her eyes to the overhanging limbs of her love. Only its branches still spread over the lake, shooting strong and straight from a trunk so thick around that thirty men couldn't join hands around it. New tears flowed on her cheeks. *Oh, my bonded, how proudly you still stand while all around you has fallen to grief and madness.*

As she led the others, she studied the lights that glowed forth from the trunk of her handsome tree. Though she should have felt anger at the violation of her beloved, the warm yellow glow cheered her heavy heart. A spark of life inside the dead. She found her feet hurrying.

The others followed.

Once they had reached the far side of the lake, a doorway swung open in the base of the tree, framed by the large roots, kneeing up from the soil. A figure stood bathed in the light. No threat was offered.

"We've been waiting so long for you," the figure at the door said in a gravelly voice.

Nee'lahn slowed as the lute's song faded away. "Who are you?"

The figure stepped clear of the door's brightness. It was a large man, dressed in simple rough-spun cotton. He was wide-shouldered, and though once clearly strong of limb, he was now gray-haired and leaned on a wooden crutch for support. "Have you forgotten me already, Nee'lahn?"

She shook her head. "Sir, I have no—"

He waved away her words with his crutch. "Och, it is of no matter. My eyes may have gone bad, but not my ears. All that matters is that I've not forgotten the voice of your lute. But then how could I?" He lifted a frail hand. "It's a voice I helped forge with mine own fingers."

Understanding struck Nee'lahn. "Rodricko?"

"Ah, the girl *does* remember the simple woodcutter."

She hurried forward, pausing a moment to recognize the man's sharp eyes and beaked nose that shadowed over a thick gray mustache. When last she had lain eyes on him, the mustache had been black as oil. The last fifteen winters had worn the man. Satisfied that it was indeed her old friend, she hugged him tight, holding her lute to the side.

Once done with their greeting, Nee'lahn pulled back. "Have you remained here, in the Fell, the entire time?"

He fingered his mustache, and the brightness in his eyes grew dark. He glanced from her lute to the twisted forest beyond. "Aye, lass."

"But why? How?" Nee'lahn tried to comprehend what had happened since she had left with her lute.

Mycelle stepped forward. She still had her swords bared. Nee'lahn realized Tyrus and Kral were armed as well. "Indeed. How have you managed to survive out here among the Grim without being consumed?"

Rodricko eyed their weapons. "Be at peace here, travelers. Sheathe your blades and come inside. If it's stories you ask, then it's tales I'll tell—but not before we get out of this snow and in front of a warm fire."

Nee'lahn cautiously reached and pushed Mycelle's blade down. "Rodricko can be trusted. It is he who carved my lute. He and his family have been friends of the nyphai for untold generations. They are as near to nyphai as any human can be."

Mycelle hesitated, then nodded. She swung her blades back into the crossed scabbards on her back. She waved the others to follow suit. Lord Tyrus slipped his Mrylian-steel sword away, and Kral slowly hitched his ax to his belt. Meric remained weaponless, arms across his chest. Mogweed hid in his shadow.

"Come inside," he urged them, holding the door open. "Just follow the stairs here to the room above."

Nee'lahn led the way, stepping reverently back inside her home tree. A mix of feelings swept through her as she mounted the winding stairs that led upward. The smell of wood oil and sweet camphors triggered a response that strummed through her as if she were a lute string herself. Old memories stirred. Joy and sorrow rang in chorus. The dust of the last fifteen winters' roads washed off her. Her hand rose and touched the bare wood, seeking the heartsong of the great tree. But she felt nothing there. It was empty. Her legs trembled, but the fingers of her other hand squeezed reassuringly around the neck of her lute. Here was where her tree's spirit now resided.

As she moved up the stairs, trailed by the group, Nee'lahn suddenly realized the path they were taking. The nyphai never made their homes inside their own trees. Instead, they built shelters and bridges among the branches. Only the bonded to a tree could enter inside the gentle giants, and it was a mingling of spirits, not a physical intrusion, like now.

She glanced behind her. Only once before had she entered her tree like this. Her eyes caught upon Rodricko's. He nodded and urged her onward.

Where she reached the head of the stairs, a large room opened up, encompassing the full diameter of the tree. A single thick pillar stood in the center of the floor, while around it the space was crammed with cabinets, chairs, and tables, all formed of the deeply whorled, rich wood. The woodwright had kept himself busy over the past fifteen years, making himself a cozy home here.

But Nee'lahn ignored all this. Instead, her eyes were drawn back to the central column, the true heart of her tree. She slowly circled it, searching until she found the spot in the column where a hollow had been carved from it. She held her lute up to it. The two shapes matched.

Rodricko stepped to her side. "Its true home."

She turned to him, glancing briefly around the room. "And I see you've made your own home here, inside my tree." A slightly accusatory tone crept into her voice.

"Like some burrowing worm," he said with a sad sigh. "Drilling and coring through a dead apple."

Nee'lahn touched his hand. "I'm sorry . . . I didn't mean to imply—"

"No, lass. It ain't natural. I've been among the nyphai too long not to feel the same way." He looked to his boots. "But after you left, the tree called to me."

"What?"

He shook his head. "Though its spirit had retreated into the lute, there was still magic in its root, enough to fuel a trace of its spirit. On the day you set off on your journey, I came here to gather my tools, and the tree spoke to me—well not rightly *spoke*, more a feeling inside my heart and head. It was not done with me yet."

"I don't understand."

He sighed. "Come by the fire, and I'll explain all." He leaned on his crutch and led the way toward the tall stone-lined hearth dug into one wall of the chamber.

Her friends were already gathered around it. Fardale lay sprawled before the hearth, almost laying in the flames, content, tail thumping slowly. The others stood, wary, ignoring the many wide chairs.

"Sit," Rodricko said. "Someone's got to use these chairs I've been whittling away these many long winters. Relax. I've warmed elderberry wine beside the fire. And afterward there are rooms and beds above."

Slowly the group settled to the chairs, and wine was passed from hand to hand, warming the chill from their bones.

Rodricko returned from a small pantry with cheeses and a platter of chestnuts for roasting on the hearth. "I promised you all my story," he said, shaking the pan of chestnuts as they popped and sizzled.

Mycelle nodded. "How did you survive out here when nothing else can?"

Rodricko groaned a bit as he stood, then settled to his own seat. "It's not a short tale I must speak, so let me start where all stories should start—at the beginning, with Cecelia."

"Cecelia?" Nee'lahn asked, shocked to hear the name of the ancient elder of the grove.

Mycelle set her mug of warm wine down. "Who is that?"

"Cecelia is the keeper of the True Glen," Rodricko said. "The eldest sister of the nyphai. She was bonded to the oldest tree of the grove, and when her tree began to twist and bend to the Blight, she herself was also tortured. Fevered dreams, delirium. It went on for three moons. But at last, when I was certain the end was near, she had a vision—of Lok'ai'hera sprouting to life in a lake of red fire. A fire born of magick. She bade me carve the heart from Nee'lahn's tree so that Nee'lahn might be free to search the lands of Alasea for this magickal cure to their doomed forest."

Nee'lahn stared into the fire. "It was Cecelia's prophecy that set me on my path." She raised her face to Rodricko. "But what of you? Why did you not leave? Your duty here was done."

"So I thought, but as I mentioned, the tree called to me, entreating me to one last task."

"But what of the Grim?" Kral asked.

"They do not bother coming near here. Nee'lahn's tree reminds them too much of what they lost. It stands straight and tall while all the rest lay twisted and tainted. The sight is too much for the wraiths to bear. So they stay away."

Mogweed knelt by the fire and checked the chestnuts. "But all this?" He nodded to the surroundings. "You have to have traveled to bring all this here. The chestnuts, the wine."

Rodricko nodded. "Twice each passing winter, I've journeyed to mountain hamlets for supplies. That is, until just recently."

Mogweed sat on his heels, eyes narrowed with suspicion. "Yet even on the woodland trails, the wraiths did not attack you?"

"I was still under the protection of the tree."

"How?" Mogweed squeaked.

Rodricko lifted the wooden crutch from where it rested between his legs and thumped it on the floor. "As Nee'lahn's lute was carved from its heart, I hewed a branch of this great tree as my walking stick." He pulled his hands away from the crutch's grip to reveal a single sprout of green near its apex.

Nee'lahn leaned closer. "Leaves!" A sprouted patch of tiny green leaves grew from the dead wood. Though each leaf was no longer than a fingernail, they were clearly koa'kona. "How . . . ?"

"A bit of magick and a bit of spirit keep it fresh."

Nee'lahn bent nearer, too—then she stared into the woodsman's eyes. "It draws off your own spirit."

"Magick alone was not enough." He lowered his cane back down.

No wonder the man had seemed to age so much since last she had seen him. "But why?" she asked. "What was so important?"

He met her gaze. "Hope."

"Hope for what?"

Rodricko leaned back and closed his eyes. "My family has served the True Glen for as far back as we can remember. It is our home, too. If there is a way to bring the Grove back, I would do anything, give up my own blood if necessary."

"But I still don't understand. What did my tree ask of you?"

He opened his eyes. "It's easier to show you." Rodricko struggled to his feet. "Come. The answer to all lies above."

Nee'lahn stood, biting back a twinge of misgiving.

The old woodwright crossed to a narrow, curved staircase. It led up to a landing above the hearth room. Without another word, he climbed the stairs with the rest trailing behind.

Nee'lahn heard Mogweed mumble, "I don't like this."

On the landing above, small rooms branched off. But Rodricko led the way to the innermost doorway. He rested a hand on the iron latch and glanced to Nee'lahn. His eyes were full of pain—and something else.

Her worries flared brighter.

"I'm sorry," he said, and pulled the door open. "You had better go in first."

Inside was another circular room, similar to the hearth chamber, only smaller. In this room, a central pillar also ran from floor to ceiling. And like the column below, this one had been carved. It contained a cubbyhole no larger than a pumpkin.

A soft gentle light wafted out from the opening.

Nee'lahn knew that faint purple light. It was the same glowing hue as given off by a blooming koa'kona. Alone, she moved nearer. Something rested inside the cubby.

Rodricko spoke behind her. "For almost a full winter, the tree had enough magick stored in its taproot and enough traces of residual spirit to keep its branches full of leaves . . . even flowers."

Nee'lahn glanced back to the doorway, where the woodwright leaned on his crutch. She recalled the day she had left her bonded, remembering it as clearly as if it were a moon ago instead of fifteen winters. Her tree had looked untouched.

With a feeling bordering on dread, she turned back to the carved cubby and what rested inside.

"The tree somehow knew it bloomed its last flowers," Rodricko said with a low voice. "It called out with its dying breath. One last time."

Nee'lahn barely heard his words, or the question asked by Mycelle.

"What do you mean?" the swordswoman asked.

"When a koa'kona is ready for its flowers to go to seed, it calls for another spirit, a kindred sister to leave her own tree briefly and mingle her spirit with its own, like a bee passing pollen from one flower to another. So Nee'lahn's tree called for someone to join with it."

"But there were no nyphai left," Mycelle said.

Rodricko lowered his voice. "Not true. Though the Grim are twisted, they are still nyphai. One came to the tree's call. It pushed past its own pain to respond to the tree's summons."

"Are you saying one of the Grim joined with Nee'lahn's tree?"

Rodricko's voice cracked. "It was Cecelia, the keeper. She was still fresh to the Blight and new to her madness. She came and shared her spirit so the tree's last flower could go to seed."

"Sweet Mother," Lord Tyrus said. "What happened?"

By now, Nee'lahn stared into the cubby. The answer lay within. A small babe lay cradled in the cubby. The source of the glow was easy to spot. It came from a plum-sized purple seed protruding from its lower belly, where a human baby's navel would be. She reached but was afraid to touch the seed or babe. *It germinated,* she realized with shock.

Rodricko continued. "A new nyphai was born from the fertile seed. Normally, the tree and its bonded would nurture the young sister until it was strong enough to plant her seed and grow another koa'kona tree, spreading the grove. But something . . . something went wrong here."

Nee'lahn saw that clearly enough. The germination from the seed looked to have proceeded naturally enough. All nyphai grew slowly from their seeds, like the trees themselves. And this young one, though appearing only an infant, was growing well for only fourteen winters. But Rodricko was most correct— *something was dreadfully wrong here*.

Rodricko continued. "I don't know what happened . . . or what it all means. Maybe it was due to the union with a Grim, a tainted and twisted spirit. I just don't know."

"What's wrong?" Mycelle asked.

Nee'lahn turned from the pillar, her legs swooning under her. "The new nyphai . . . it's a *boy*."

*   *   *

THE NEXT MORNING, KRAL CLIMBED DOWN THE STAIRS TO THE main hearth room. The scent of warm bread and the sizzle of pork flesh had drawn him from his goose-feather bed and quiet chamber. After almost half a winter on the road with only the hard forest floor as his bed and his rucksack as a pillow, he had slept soundly throughout the night and well into the late morning.

He stretched the kinks from his arms and entered the room. He was clearly the last to rise. The others were already seated around a wide table spread with breads, fruits, boiled eggs, and meats. He also noticed a stack of gear piled on the room's far side: fox-fur gloves, hooded cold-weather cloaks trimmed in ermine, even slabs of dried and smoked beef and hard cheeses.

Mycelle noticed his approach. The banded viper on her arm hissed at him, then settled back to its curled perch. "Kral, sit. Eat. We've much to discuss and plan."

He nodded, his nose filled with the scents of the table. His stomach grumbled appreciatively. He settled into his seat as Rodricko filled a stone mug with hot kaffee.

"I've done my best to put together warmer clothes and additional fodder for your trek from here," Rodricko explained. "But I don't know what good it will do. The snows are beginning to fall, and the upper passes of the Ice Trail will be impassable before much longer."

"We'll leave today," Mycelle said, "and set a hard pace. With your generous supplies, we can move faster and stretch each day's march a bit longer."

Mogweed groaned from across the table, but he remained otherwise silent. Kral could understand the man's consternation. A few more days here at this warm, well-stocked place would suit him, too. But he also understood the necessity not to delay. Mountain storms were unpredictable, especially this time of year. Blizzards, ice storms, and cold fogs were more likely with each day's delay.

"But how are we to travel the remainder of the Fell?" Meric asked, his thin fingers wrapped around his stone mug. "If Nee'lahn remains here with the child—"

"But she must," Rodricko interrupted. "The tree's seed has sustained the child until now but will not for much longer."

Nee'lahn glanced up from beside Mogweed. Her eyes were

shadowed and tired. Clearly she had not found her sleep as restful as Kral. She faced them. "The boy nears the age when he will separate from his birth seed. Afterward, he will need the tree's song and spirit to sustain him."

"So you must stay?" Tyrus asked.

"I have no choice. Boy or not, the foundling is the offspring of my beloved. I cannot abandon it. The song of the lute will help sustain the strange child while I care for him and protect him. I don't understand the significance of a male nyphai, or why this has come to be, but I must see it through." She stared around the table. "I'm sorry."

"I can take you through the woods," Rodricko said. He nudged his wooden crutch with its little sprout of leaves. "The fresh, untainted branch will be as much a bane to the Grim as Nee'lahn's lute. We should be safe."

Kral read doubt in the man's eyes. The short length of wood had protected the woodwright, but there was no guarantee its meager protection would extend to their party.

The others must have sensed the man's worry. A heavy silence grew around the table.

Distantly, a wailing echoed through the wood walls. A lonely sound that was soon joined by another . . . and another. As they sat stone still, the horrid chorus grew and swelled.

Kral smelled the sudden fear in their host. Rodricko's voice tremored as he settled his pitcher to the table. "They've never come so near."

Mycelle stood. "They must know we're here."

The others quickly gained their feet, and weapons were gathered.

"What are we to do?" Mogweed asked. "Will they attack?"

Rodricko crossed to a broad window that faced south. Kral and the others followed the woodwright. Beyond the window, the woods were bathed in early morning sunlight, but due to the perpetual cloud cover, it was wan and lifeless. Snow frosted the twisted branches of the surrounding trees, creating a stark landscape. Even the small lake was a black mirror.

As they watched, the shadows of the deeper woods stretched toward them, swallowing up the trees and snow, descending and sweeping into the hollow. It was as if a black fog were consuming the world.

"Wh-what is happening?" Mogweed asked, backing away, his fingers reaching for his brother.

Nee'lahn stood still. "The Grim gather. I've never seen its like."

Kral knew what she meant. The wraiths were generally solitary creatures, hunting the forest trails on their own. It was one of the reasons that the Northwall had withstood their numbers until now.

But as Kral stared out at the force gathering around the hollow, he understood how the great Wall had fallen. The Grim were now a unified force, a dark army. Kral remembered the ill'guard wraith who had possessed King Ry's dead body, animating it. Was this demoness the reason for the change in the Grim as a whole? If so, what control did she bear on these other wild, mindless creatures? How had she joined their madness to her own foul cause?

Outside, the wail of the wraiths grew to a fevered pitch.

The beast inside Kral stirred. How it wanted to howl along with the mad screams and cries, add its voice to the wild chorus. But Kral fought this urge. Now was not the time for Legion, not yet.

He closed his eyes and sent his beastly senses soaring. Touched by the Dark Lord, he felt a familiar thrill running through the gathered dark army. *She's out there,* he realized. The demoness herself led this force to their doorstep. She hid amid the wraiths, but she could not hide from another ill'guard. Kral understood who led this assault, but could not alert his companions without exposing himself.

Nee'lahn spoke up, drawing his attention back to the room. She lifted her lute. "I will go out to meet them."

Mycelle placed a hand on her shoulder. "I don't know if even your lute's song will be strong enough against such numbers."

"You will be a single note against a storm," Meric said. "Their chorus of wails will swamp the song of a single tree."

"I must try. We have no other means to drive them away."

"I will help," Rodricko said, lifting his crutch. "The bit of living spirit along with the lute's song may prevail."

"But we must all be ready," Nee'lahn said. "If I can drive a wedge through their forces, then you must be as fleet of foot as possible."

"What do you propose?" Lord Tyrus asked.

"Pack and stow the gear." She nodded to the stacks of warm clothes and food. "If Rodricko and I succeed in opening a breach, you all must take advantage and flee immediately."

"And you?" Mycelle asked.

Nee'lahn's eyes were haunted but determined. "I must stay and protect the child."

Mogweed shifted his feet, eyes darting everywhere, searching vainly for a means of escape. "Why not take the cursed child with you? If this tree is dead anyway, why do you need to stay here? We don't stand a chance in the woods on our own."

Nee'lahn opened her mouth to dismiss this thought, but Mycelle interrupted. "Mogweed's right. The child will always be in danger here. It is only two days' march out of the forest. If you could whisk him away . . ."

Rodricko agreed. "Perhaps you should heed their counsel, Nee'lahn."

"But I can't just—"

"This place is an empty tomb. As long as the child is at your side and you have the lute, he should remain safe." The wood-wright stared out at the gathering darkness. "Besides, the boy is close to ripening and dropping his seed. Perhaps it is best if that were not done here, in this Blighted soil. Maybe that's the reason you were all drawn here—to take the boy away."

"I . . . I don't know," Nee'lahn mumbled.

"Well, someone had better make a decision," Mogweed said, pointing to the windows. "Or it will be made for us."

Beyond the lake, no trees could be seen. A solid wall of darkness spread all around them.

Nee'lahn bit her lip, then turned to Mycelle. "Gather up the boy. Wrap him well against the cold. At his tender age, he's still susceptible to frost. You others grab as much gear as possible."

They all moved quickly, goaded by the rising howl of the wraiths. In moments, they were dressed in warm gear with packs of food and supplies on their backs. Mycelle had the additional burden of a child strapped to her chest. Encumbered as she was, she would be useless in a swordfight, but Kral knew it was not the point of a blade that would win freedom here.

He studied Nee'lahn as she held her lute in her arms, staring into the darkness. All their hopes were weighed upon this lone woman. Kral smelled the fear in her, but also her resolve and determination.

She must have sensed his gaze. She turned. "Let's get this done."

Kral nodded, turning away, but not before glancing one more time at the gathered horde. Again, he scented the Dark Lord's touch out there. The ill'guard demoness hid in that cloak of blackness, one wraith among many.

But to what purpose, what end?

NEE'LAHN WAS THE FIRST THROUGH THE DOOR. AFTER THE WARMTH inside, the sudden cold struck her like a fist. She gasped. It was an unnatural cold. As the wraiths drew the life from a victim, they now drew the warmth from the air.

She stepped away from the threshold and clear of the large tree roots. The lake lay ahead, rimmed in frost. Its edges had frozen overnight. Nee'lahn moved to its shore, facing the wall of blackness that circled the hollow, surrounding them. Closer, she saw that the wall whorled and churned as the massed wraiths writhed at the valley's edge.

"Sisters," she mumbled, praying. "Hear me and depart in peace."

As she lifted her lute, the group gathered behind her. Rodricko stood amongst them, his bit of living wood held out before him like a sword.

Taking a deep breath, Nee'lahn strummed her strings, and sweet notes spread into the gale of cries and screams. The music, though soft and sweet, fought through the cacophony. "Hear me, Sisters," she repeated, now singing forth with the lute's melody.

The notes swept across the cold water to strike the wall of darkness like a thousand arrows. Holes were rent through the solidness as individual wraiths wailed and fled. Glimpses of the snow-crowned forest peeked through the throng, but the tears did not last long. The holes quickly disappeared as the remaining Grim closed ranks.

Nee'lahn's eyes narrowed, suspicious of this action. *What was driving the wraiths forward? What was making them fight their natural urge to flee the touch of the True Glen?*

A sharp scream split the air. Nee'lahn swung around and saw

a wraith rip forth from the others and fly at her companions. It was a dark mist against the white snow.

Rodricko stepped forward, guarding the party with his crutch. Nee'lahn's fingers hesitated on her strings, fearful for her friends.

"Keep playing!" Mycelle urged, wincing against the railing screams. "Don't stop!"

Rodricko swept his bit of wood between him and the scrap of darkness. "Begone!" he yelled in the face of his enemy.

The bold wraith hesitated, then stabbed a stream of darkness toward the woodsman's chest. Rodricko danced back, surprisingly spry on his feeble legs. His stick sliced through the deadly shadow. Where it struck, light flared, the violet of blossoming koa'kona flowers. The wraith blew apart into ragged fragments. Its bits of shredded spirit fled back into the mass of wraiths.

Kral bellowed in triumph.

But Mycelle's eyes swung to Nee'lahn. "Play! Play if you want to live!"

Nee'lahn returned to her lute, strumming with renewed energy. The wall of wraiths squirmed in clear agony, screams chasing screams. Nee'lahn turned in a slow circle, casting her music in all directions.

"Hear the song of the True Glen," she sang softly as the music carried her words far, echoing out over the hollow. "Remember the spring shoots rising with the new sun . . . Remember the hills of a summer's night, aglow with blossoms . . . Remember autumn's display of brilliance and the endless rain of leaves, a warm blanket against the winter to come . . . Remember the winter's crisp breath when the sap runs slow and the stars shine like silver in the night sky. Remember it all. Remember the Glen. Remember life!"

Her words cast a spell on the wraiths. They began to flow and ebb to her music. The wail became less sharp, more mournful. Breaks in the wall grew all around them. Bits of darkness shot high in the air and away, crying in pain and sorrow.

"It's working," Meric said.

Nee'lahn continued to sing, now in the Old Tongue. She sang of flowers, and sunshine, and drops of morning dew, while the lute rang with woodsong and a call for communion. It was all too much, even for the strength of the gathered horde. More wraiths fled.

A pair tried again to attack the group, more in an attempt to stop the pain of her song than in true malice. But Rodricko quickly dispatched them.

Nee'lahn kept singing. Sensing victory, she let her voice grow in strength, but eventually she realized she did not sing alone. Another voice had crept in on hers, blending into her song so smoothly that Nee'lahn was not aware of it until it was too late. It came from the fraying wall of darkness. The new voice twisted Nee'lahn's song, subtly and skillfully, changing the bright to the dark.

"Dream of the sun's warm touch . . ." Nee'lahn sang.

". . . and the burn of an endless drought," the unseen singer chorused.

"Sing of petals soft with the first bloom . . ." Nee'lahn fought back.

". . . and worms that eat out the flower's tender heart."

Frowning, Nee'lahn struggled to chase the other off, singing more fiercely, ringing with the voice of the True Glen. But the parasitic voice would not let go, wrapping its song around her own, strangling it with whispers of dead wood and rotting roots. Slowly Nee'lahn realized she was outmatched. The singer was older, more experienced. The voice sang with the echoes of centuries.

Nee'lahn could not resist it. Her voice began to warp; her lute's music shook with disease and crumbling bark. All around the hollow, the wraiths regrouped, fortifying the dark wall.

"What's wrong?" Mycelle asked, moving nearer, clutching the small child to her chest.

"I don't know," Nee'lahn said, slowing her fingers on the lute's strings, struggling to think of a means to attack. "Something . . . something's out there . . . Something stronger than I . . ."

Kral moved to her other side. He growled. "It comes."

Mycelle glanced to him, then out to the gathered wraiths. A black cloud bloomed from the wall, a swirling formless fog. It drifted across the lake, slowly, laconically, as if it cared little for the small band of people or the music of the lute.

Nee'lahn and the others retreated from it.

Upon reaching the near shore, the cloud roiled inward on itself, fog becoming substance. The vague figure of a slender woman took shape on the frozen lake's edge. Silver energy traced her form. Her eyes opened.

Nee'lahn sensed here stood the singer who had so skillfully corrupted her song.

Fardale growled, baring his teeth, and Rodricko stepped forward, the branch held before him.

The dark woman smiled at the man's response. "A brave knight carved of wood," she said disdainfully. "The last protector of the True Glen." Yet despite her words, she held back.

"I know you," Nee'lahn said, recognizing the screechy voice and where she had heard it last. "You're the wraith who possessed King Ry."

The wraith's smile broadened, while growing colder at the same time. "Ah, yes . . . it was good to wear flesh again." She glanced to Lord Tyrus. "Even a moldy form as distasteful as that old man."

The Mrylian prince lunged forward, but he was blocked by Kral. "You've no weapon that can harm an ill'guard," the mountain man warned, holding fast to the prince's elbow.

The wraith ignored the men and swung her gaze back to Nee'lahn. "As you know me, so I know you, Nee'lahn." A laugh, empty of mirth, escaped the shadowy lips. "You caught me by surprise back at the castle. I had not been expecting you to pop out of the granite like that. But now I've had time to adjust to your presence. The Black Root has strengthened me against your pretty little song."

"You'll not have us," Nee'lahn warned. "I will fight with every spark of life in me."

This earned another laugh. "You've grown full of yourself, little one. But it is not you I want." The figure's gaze swung to the child held by Mycelle, then back to Nee'lahn. "I want the boy . . . *My* boy."

Nee'lahn jerked a step back. "Y-your boy?"

Again the laugh. "I thought you said you knew me, Nee'lahn." The smoky figure coalesced tighter, firming the vague form into someone familiar.

"Cecelia." Nee'lahn gasped, stunned.

Rodricko stepped forward. "The keeper of the Grove."

Nee'lahn moaned. No wonder her song had been thwarted. Before Cecelia's corruption, the elder's age had numbered in centuries. She was the wisest of the nyphai, full of knowledge and guile.

The wraith glanced down at the woodwright. "Are you still here?" She glided closer.

Rodricko swung his stave.

"No!" Nee'lahn called out.

The branch swept into the shadowed woman. Violet light again flared, but this time no harm was done to the wraith. Cecelia smiled, staring down at the wooden crutch imbedded in her chest. "Your tree's spirit cannot harm me. Our two spirits have mingled. We are one." A tendril of darkness swept out of the woman's chest to wrap lovingly around the branch.

"Get back, Rodricko!" Nee'lahn urged.

"I . . . I can't move . . ."

The wraith smiled. "I smell your spirit in the wood, brave knight. Has it been feeding on you? Such a cruel act, dragging out the inevitable so slowly. Let me show you the benevolence of the Dark One." The tendril spasmed on the branch, and Rodricko fell to his knees.

In less than a heartbeat, the woodwright's life was sucked through the branch and into the dread wraith. He shriveled with a scream on his lips, then tumbled dead to the snowy ground, a twisted, empty shell. The tree branch fell to cinders in his hand.

"A shame. So little life was left in him," the demoness whined, kicking aside the branch. "It did nothing but whet my appetite."

Nee'lahn felt her legs weaken. "Rodricko's family served you for generations. What have you become?"

Kral appeared at her side, holding her up. "Do not look for answers here. She is lost to the Black Heart, twisted to his will."

"Twisted?" The forest rang with her laughter and bitterness. "Look around you, man of the mountains. It was the Land itself that *twisted* my forest. The grief, the loss . . . it is unimaginable. And when Nee'lahn's dying tree summoned me, the pain grew a hundredfold. I could not stand it, touching the pure spirit with my taint." A mournful wail blew up into the sky.

Around Nee'lahn, her companions fell to their knees at the despairing cry. Only Nee'lahn remained standing.

Cecelia's keening moan slowly died away. She continued in a quieter voice. "In my weak and defenseless state, the Black Root found me. I let him do what he wished. What did it matter any longer? Afterward I was glad that I'd not fought. The Black Root's touch unwove what was tangled by the Land's curse. His fire returned my mind and revealed my true enemy."

"And what enemy is that?" Nee'lahn asked.

The wraith stared hard at her. "The *Land*, my dear! The cruel, harsh, unforgiving Land. The Black Root promised vengeance. I used my skills to gather the Grim to our mutual cause, to bring down the Northwall, to guard the paths up into the mountains. Nothing must interfere with his design."

Nee'lahn stood stunned.

Mycelle spoke up, still on her knees in the snow. "What does he plan to do?"

Cecelia's eyes shone with madness. "He'll make the Land wail as my sisters do. Twist it the same as my handsome forest."

After a stunned moment, Mycelle slowly stood. "And what of this child? What role does he play?"

This question seemed to shake the demoness. Her gaze fixed on the swaddled child held in the shape-shifter's arms. "He . . . he's mine."

Mycelle remained quiet, then whispered. "The Dark Lord doesn't know about your child, does he? You've kept a secret from your master."

The figure trembled. "He . . . he's mine," she repeated.

"Your last bit of purity," Mycelle pressed.

The edges of the shadow began to fray.

Nee'lahn stepped forward, sensing a weakness to probe. She tenderly stroked the lute's strings. The music wafted so gently that no human ear could hear it. She wove an ancient song—of birth and death, the cycle of life. Distracted, the wraith seemed unaware of it.

"Let us take the child from here," Mycelle urged. "Take him where the Blight can never touch him."

The wraith hesitated, becoming more cloud than woman. "There is no such place. Not until the Black Root destroys the Land. Only then will the boy be able to grow hale and straight."

Mycelle nodded her understanding. "Let us keep him safe until that day."

"He is safest with me. No harm will come to him."

"But how can you be so sure? Did you escape the Blight? Did

your sisters? The Dire Fell poses the most risk to the boy. His only safety lies in escaping here, as Nee'lahn did."

The black cloud swirled in indecision.

Nee'lahn continued to weave her song around the wraith, gently drawing out the motherly instincts of this tainted creature, holding tight to that seed of sanity buried deep inside.

"I can't . . . I can't part with him," the wraith moaned.

Mycelle persisted. "Would you rather the boy was raised on the wails of the Grim or the pure woodsong of Nee'lahn's lute? Which is more likely to leave the child hale? You've produced something new, something wondrous, something pure. Let us help you protect it."

Nee'lahn complemented Mycelle's words with her music. She wove the image of autumn leaves falling, crumbling back to soil and loam, feeding the next generation, preparing the forest floor for new sprouts. The cycle of life's sacrifice. The dead giving back to the living. The selfless act of love and birth.

Something finally broke inside the wraith. The dark cloud blew into the air, coursing over the lake. "Take the child," the wraith wailed. "Take my boy from here."

Her cry spread across the sky, shattering the wall of wraiths. As the ill'guard demoness flew through the forest, her sisters followed, only too glad to flee.

Nee'lahn crossed and knelt by Rodricko's body. She touched his cheek gently, wishing him a safe journey to the next world, and silently thanked him for all he had done. His sacrifice, as much as any, had brought this new life out of a dead forest.

Mycelle stepped near Nee'lahn, watching the darkness shred apart around them. "Cecelia is mad and not to be trusted. It took your music to sway her to her own nobler instincts."

Nee'lahn raised her eyebrows as she stood, surprised Mycelle had heard her lute.

"I have the ears of a shape-shifter," she explained. "I heard your song plying Cecelia's will. But we can't trust your enchantment holding for long, especially when she realizes where we're headed. She could turn back on us in a heartbeat."

"Then let us be gone far from here before that happens," Nee'lahn said, and slipped the lute over her shoulder. Her arms free, she took the child from Mycelle. Nee'lahn stared down into the tiny face, then back up at her tree, dead but still stately. Tears welled.

"Do you wish a moment to say good-bye to your home?"

Nee'lahn turned her back and stepped away, holding the child close. "This wood is no longer my home. Lok'ai'hera is dead. All that I love, I carry with me now."

16

MOGWEED'S LEGS ACHED, AND HIS LUNGS BURNED BOTH FROM THE cold and the air's thinness. He stared ahead at the narrow mountain trail. It wound up and up, higher and higher. For the six days since leaving the Dire Fell, the group had been continually climbing upward. There were only brief respites when the trail wound down into a short valley. Otherwise, for league after league, they climbed the granite peaks of Alasea's northernmost mountains.

But at least they had left the Grim behind in their twisted homeland. Here a forest of pine and redwood towered around them, boles as straight as arrows, limbs hanging heavy with snow.

It had been such a cheerful sight once they had climbed from the woods, but within a day's travel, they had come upon their first mountain hamlet. It had been torched. Singed chimneys stood amid burned and cracked timber, and heads had been staked in the town's central square—clear work of marauding d'warf raiders. Any hope of replenishing their supplies died as they tromped through the sacked hamlet. The only boon gleaned from the township was a scraggly, bone-thin pony found in the near woods.

After discovering the ruined hamlet, Kral had guided the group from the wide Ice Trail, deeming it unsafe. "After bringing down the Wall," Kral had said, "I'd wager the d'warves have cleared *all* the townships along the road here, fortifying the main approach to the Citadel. There'll be lookouts and guard posts all along the main pass. We'll be less likely to be spotted on the smaller, steeper back trails."

So the group had left the gentler, wider trails for the winding, cliff-hugging tracks. Near the head of the group, Nee'lahn rode the thin pony, nestled over the small child. She was the only one light enough for the small horse to carry. Mogweed scowled at the nyphai. He was not that much heavier than she was. Besides, the pony would have served them all better if it had been slaughtered and sun-cured. With the hamlets sacked, their supplies had dwindled rapidly.

At last, as the sun fell behind a ridge of snow-tipped peaks, Mycelle lifted an arm, signaling the end of the day's trek. "We'll set up camp near the stream," she called out, and pointed to where a creek chattered along a series of short falls off to the right.

"Thank the Sweet Mother," Mogweed mumbled. His thighs and calves were cramped knots. He stumbled away from the thin deer trail and followed the others to the flat shelf.

The camp was quickly assembled. After so long on the road, everyone knew their duties. Kral dug out a fire pit and cleared the dead pine needles from around the night's hearth. Bedrolls were laid out around it. Meric and Tyrus gathered wood and kindling, while Nee'lahn fetched water. Mogweed fished through the packs for their cooking gear and their dwindling fodder. He snatched a bit of hard cheese and popped it into his mouth, then pulled out some strips of dried mutton.

Mycelle stepped to Mogweed's side. He had to swallow his stolen tidbit quickly, but the woman's eyes were on the forest. "Have you seen any sign of your brother?"

Mogweed frowned. "No, not since last night."

"Fardale must be hunting wide off our trail. But I'd be happier knowing he was safe."

Mogweed straightened with a pan in hand. "He's safer in the wood than with us. Out there, he is just another lone forest creature."

"It's not the dangers of the forest that worry me." Mycelle glanced back to him. "It's his own will. The wolf inside draws close to claiming him completely."

"We've another moon at least before we settle."

Mycelle craned her neck toward the twilight skies. The moon hung full above. "I hope you're right." She stalked away.

A chill crept through Mogweed as he searched the surrounding forest. Where *was* Fardale? His brother had never disappeared for a full day before. And last night, before slinking off to hunt the dark forest, Fardale had turned to him, sending fuzzy images. They had made no sense. Even his eyes had not glowed as bright. Mycelle was right. The wolf was near to claiming him completely.

Mogweed, at least, wore a human form and was less prone to such urges. It was known that the wilder the beast, the quicker someone settled. Still, Mogweed could not dismiss that he had grown more and more comfortable in his current body. He recalled how at first his sallow and thin-limbed form had grated, how even wearing boots had chafed him with each step. But now, after so long, Mogweed wore his body with ease. In fact, he had grown to be possessive of it, and the fervency of his longings to melt from this flesh into another shape had dimmed. And even when he did crave to shape stronger legs or sprout a warmer pelt, it was always with the knowledge that he'd return to this same body.

Mogweed shivered. As much as he wanted to ignore these changes in perspective, he knew in his heart what it meant. He, too, was close to settling. The human in him threatened his true heritage. Even Mycelle understood Fardale better than he did. Not only were Fardale's sendings coarser, Mogweed's ability to receive was fading.

Mogweed stared up at the moon, full and bright in the darkening sky. *One more moon . . . then all is lost.*

"Quit stargazing," Kral grumbled, off to the side. "Get the cooking gear over here."

Mogweed turned and saw the mountain man had already managed to raise a small fire. With pots and pans in hand, Mogweed moved to Kral's side. The large man fed sticks into the flames, his black beard dripping as the ice melted from its dark curls.

"Where's that elv'in with some real wood?" Kral said. "I can't hold this flame without something more substantial to feed its hunger." The mountain man's eyes shone with a matching smolder.

Mogweed set his pots and pans down and stepped away, not turning his back. He had lived all his life in the deep forest, and even though he was close to settling, his woodland instincts were deeply instilled. He sensed something wild and savage in the tall man. And like Fardale, each day the beastly nature seemed to grow stronger, less hidden. Mogweed had assumed it was because they neared Tor Amon, the mountain folk's ancient homelands; perhaps that had Kral's old animosities burning brighter. But when near the man, as now, Mogweed was less sure of this explanation.

"I . . . I'll go look for Meric and Tyrus. Help them gather more wood."

"Make sure they each bring an armload," Kral growled, his eyes on the skies now. "We'll see snow tonight, and the cold will grow savage."

Mogweed nodded and moved away. He had no intention of looking for the others. That was not his chore. Besides, the woods had grown dark, and there was no way he was going to search for the others in those deep shadows. Instead, once out of direct sight of Kral, Mogweed slinked toward the river. He heard the voices of Nee'lahn and Mycelle. Moving on his toes, he crept close enough to overhear.

"How's little Rodricko doing?" Mycelle asked, referring to the nyphai male child. Nee'lahn had named the child after the old dead woodwright. Mycelle scooped a pail into the stream and hauled it out.

Nee'lahn took the pail from her with a shy smile. "The babe fares well and draws strength from my tree's spirit." With her free hand, Nee'lahn hitched the babe's sling higher, then touched her chest. "But he's not the only one. My own breasts have begun their swelling. They'll be ready to suckle by the time he drops his birth seed."

"And how much longer will that be?" Mycelle asked, picking up a second pail slopping with fresh water.

"It's hard to say. But no longer than a couple moons."

"So soon?"

Nee'lahn nodded. The two women moved in the direction of Mogweed's hiding spot. He scrambled behind a granite outcropping so as not to be seen, then followed them back to camp.

From his new vantage under the boughs of a redwood, Mog-weed spied upon the entire campsite. Meric and Tyrus had re-turned with ample wood, and Kral fed his fires. Nee'lahn placed her pail of water down nearby, then settled to a stone seat and gently rocked the babe in her arms.

Mycelle moved away from the flames and brought her pail to the tethered pony. It ignored the water and continued to tug on the scraggly patches of green grasses. Mycelle wiped her hands and stared up at the full moon. Even from his roost, Mogweed saw her sigh heavily, eye the camp, then slip off to the side.

Mogweed's lips thinned. He knew what she was about to do. He moved silently around, keeping Mycelle in sight. When he wanted, Mogweed could slip as silently through the woods as his wolfish brother.

Mycelle crossed back to the stream's edge, then tossed her cloak across a slab of flat granite. Next she worked off her swords' belts and unbuttoned her leathers. Shortly she stood only in her linen underclothes—then, oblivious to the cold, she shed even these, adding them to the pile of her garments. Once naked, she settled cross-legged atop her cloak.

Mogweed squirmed at the sight of her. He felt stirrings in his loins, a rush of heat, and licked his dry lips. His eyes wandered over her curves and her long, muscled legs. He hunkered down for a better look.

As she sat, it was easy to see that Mycelle was not completely naked. Twisted around her upper arm, she still wore the rainbow-banded snake, the paka'golo.

Mycelle glanced to the moon again, staring at it for a long moment.

As Mogweed had hoped, it was time—time once more for Mycelle to renew herself with the snake's poison. Carefully, My-celle teased the tiny paka'golo from its perch and onto her hand. It squirmed with clear agitation. It, too, sensed the moment had drawn near once again.

Mogweed swallowed in anticipation, his eyes fixed on what was to come.

Mycelle lifted the snake and brought it to her throat, craning her neck to bare the tender flesh at its crook. The paka'golo writhed in her fingers, its tiny tongue flickering. It drew back to strike, jaws opening, fangs unhinging to expose their lengths.

Mogweed did not see the serpent lash out. One moment it stood poised; then the next its jaws were fastened to Mycelle's throat. Mogweed watched the snake spasm as it pumped its poison into her.

Slowly the woman toppled backward limply, arms falling loosely to the side. Where the snake had struck, Mycelle's flesh melted as the poison spread. First her neck and shoulder dissolved into an amorphous shape, an amber-hued gel that flowed and churned. Then, as the poison spread outward, so did the transformation. Her naked form melted like a wax doll placed too near the flames.

Mogweed's fists clenched with both frustration and desire. Here was the true form of the si'lura. How he longed to melt himself and share with Mycelle. The man in him had responded to her naked form; now his si'luran half rang out with desire. Mogweed could barely contain himself. Sweat pebbled over his skin. His blood rushed, his heartbeat thudding heavy in his chest. But he was not the one to share this moment.

The paka'golo, floating atop the gelatinous amber mass of Mycelle, now sank into her depths, swimming through her, inside her. Through the translucency, Mogweed watched the snake sweep and contort in S-shaped waves. Mycelle's flesh seemed to ripple in response. Where the snake passed, the amber hues brightened. Soon her entire form glowed.

Once this was accomplished, the snake surfaced again, rising like a diver and floating atop Mycelle's body. Slowly the rippling and churning calmed, and a form began to reshape itself out of chaos. In a matter of moments, limbs were sculpted again, and a body of smooth curves re-formed.

Mycelle was reborn again. Her lips parted, and she gasped her first breath. With her chest heaving, she remained upon her cloak, eyes still closed as the transformation wound to completion. The paka'golo again perched upon her upper arm, coiling into place.

Mogweed trembled at the sight of her. Then something cold touched the flushed skin of his cheek. Mogweed yelled and tumbled backward, his arm raised in protection.

A large dark shape loomed over him. It took him a shuddering heartbeat to recognize his brother. Fardale settled to his haunches, tongue hanging loosely in wolfish amusement.

Mogweed sat up and cuffed his brother, but his blow was shaky.

"Who's out there?" a rasped voice called. It was Mycelle.

Mogweed cringed a moment, then scrambled to his feet. "It . . . it's just me! I've found Fardale." He moved forward as if he had just arrived. "I thought you'd like to know."

Pushing aside a branch, he found Mycelle already dressed in her linen underclothes. She nodded to him, eyes exhausted, then turned to her piled garments. "It's good to see you again, Fardale."

The treewolf growled in acknowledgment, then crossed to the stream and drank heartily.

Mycelle and Mogweed shared a glance. Both had noted Fardale's lack of mental greetings. He did not even try to communicate in the si'luran way any longer.

Muzzle still dripping, Fardale crossed to a bush and raised his leg. His hot stream steamed in the evening's cold.

Again Mycelle glanced to Mogweed, an eyebrow raised.

Mogweed stared in shock at his brother's casual action. Once done, Fardale lifted his nose, sniffed the air, then loped toward camp, clearly drawn by the scent of the night's stew pot.

Mycelle tugged on her leggings. "Fardale is close to full wolf. Are you sure you still have another moon's time before you both settle?"

Mogweed remembered his own response to Mycelle's naked form. He had wanted so desperately to take her like a man. Even now, he was glad his own cloak hid how much he still felt that way. "I . . . I don't know. No one's been cursed like us before."

Mycelle touched his shoulder, and Mogweed had to fight down a shudder of desire. "If there is a way to stop this, we'll find it."

Mogweed nodded and stepped away. He glanced at her snake as she retrieved her jerkin. His eyes narrowed as a sudden flare of frustrated anger burned through his desires. It was not fair that Mycelle had been given back her shape-shifting gifts by the serpent. She had *voluntarily* settled into her human form but was still given this second chance.

The snake seemed to sense his gaze and lifted its tiny head. Their eyes met. A tongue flickered out at him, tasting the air between them.

Mogweed's eyes narrowed, remembering the flow of Mycelle's flesh. For the thousandth time, he wondered if some clue to his own problem was not hidden under his own nose. The old healer, Mama Freda, had claimed that the snake was tied to Mycelle since her resurrection, and its magick was linked solely to her spirit. But what if that link were somehow broken? What if a *new* link could be forged?

Mycelle straightened and pulled into her jerkin. "We should get back to camp."

Mogweed nodded. He waited until she was fully dressed, then followed her down, watching her back.

As he strode, a new desire took hold of his heart: not the lusts of a man, but something darker. What if the link *could* be broken?

PERCHED IN THE LIMBS OF A MASSIVE REDWOOD, MERIC COUNTED the d'warves passing below. *Ten.* It was the second patrol the party had come upon as they neared Tor Amon. And like the other, this group had its guard down. The patrol's guttural laughter and loud voices had carried down the mountain pass, giving plenty of warning to Meric's group. Up here, the d'warves had grown lax. Then again, why shouldn't they? Between the Grim of the Fell and their own entrenched armies at Castle Mryl, what did they need to fear out here? Who could threaten them?

Meric lifted a hand and cupped his lips. He let out a piercing cry of an ice eagle. In response, Fardale burst from behind a holly bush and rushed the last d'warf in the party. He slashed the warrior's hamstring and was gone in a blur of shadowed fur. The wounded d'warf yelled and tumbled to his face. His fellow soldiers swung around.

With their attention diverted, Meric leaped from his perch and touched just enough of his wind magick to slow his fall to a graceful swoop. In his hands, a pair of crossbows hummed as their bolts shot free. One struck the eye of a d'warf; the other ripped through another's throat. Meric landed lightly in a pile of pine needles, tossing aside his bows and sweeping out his thin sword. He stabbed the closest d'warf, moving faster than an eye could follow.

Behind the party, Kral and Tyrus suddenly appeared—one dark as the forest's gloom, the other bright as a morning sun. The men rushed the unprotected rear guard with ax and sword. As they struck, Mycelle stepped from the trail's side to slice into the patrol's flank with her twin swords.

Caught by surprise, most fell with their weapons still sheathed. The slaughter was quick and savage. Kral cleaved through with his dire ax, blood and gore fountaining around him as he waded through the shattered patrol. Mycelle and Tyrus danced behind him, finishing off what the mountain man left in his wake.

Meric saw a d'warf break from the pack. This one was slimmer and longer legged than his companions. A runner, no more than a youngster. Eyes wild with terror, he raced back up the trail, clearly hoping to raise the alarm, hoping to live. Meric lowered his blade and shook his head.

As the d'warf fled up the deer trail, roots rose to tangle his feet. He crashed to his face, but to his credit, he rolled quickly back to his feet. But it was already too late. Fardale leaped silently out of the brush and tore out the young d'warf's throat.

Meric turned away as the wolf dispatched the runner.

Around him, the d'warf patrol lay torn upon the woodland trail, blood steaming in the cold morning air. A d'warf slowly tried to crawl away, moaning, his right arm cleaved off at the elbow. Tyrus stepped behind him and removed his head with a double-fisted blow of his sword. The Mrylian prince remained expressionless.

Nee'lahn stepped from the cover of a hawthorn bush, the babe in her arms. Mogweed came with her. Nee'lahn lifted an arm, and the roots that had tripped the d'warf runner sank back into the loamy soil. She stared at the slaughter with numb eyes. Finally, she turned away. "It's not right," she mumbled.

Kral searched through the dead, recovering satchels of foodstuffs, checking weapons. He straightened. His beard was soaked with blood, dripping. Meric winced. Nee'lahn had spoken truthfully: This was not right. He remembered the d'warf party accompanying Elena to Gul'gotha, the prisoners who had been freed of the Dark Lord's reign by the sight of the Try'sil hammer. This same party was no less tainted, bent to the will of the Black Beast of Gul'gotha. Was it right to kill them—he stared at the light in Kral's eyes—and to take so much pleasure from it?

Meric sighed and sheathed his weapon. What choice did they have? The Weirgate hidden at the Citadel had to be destroyed.

After hiding the bodies, the group gathered and continued up the trail. Fardale, tail in the air, swept ahead to scent out any further dangers.

The day stretched forever in the endless climb upward, but as the sun sank toward the shadowed western peaks, the party finally reached the height of the pass.

Meric was one of the first to reach the vantage point. A huge open valley stretched ahead, so wide the far peaks were barely discernable. Heavy mists hung in tattered shreds, bits of white against the dark pines. But all this was just a frame for the true wonder of the highland basin.

Below, all but filling the valley's bowl, was a gigantic mountain lake, midnight blue and as glassy as a mirror—*Tor Amon*.

Mogweed gasped as he stepped forward. "Sweet Mother."

Meric understood his surprise. Spanning the great lake of Tor Amon was a massive arch of granite. It crested over the waters, its legs rising from the waters themselves, its surfaces windscoured smooth. But its uppermost heights, its pinnacle, had been carved into a great castle of turrets, balustrades, and sweeping walls. Throughout the structure, torches glowed from windows and walls.

"The ancient home of the mountain folk," Kral said, his voice cracking, his eyes fixed on the high castle. "The Citadel of the Ice Throne."

"It's wondrous," Nee'lahn said, climbing off her scrawny pony.

The arch and castle not only climbed the skies, but were also reflected in the still waters of the lake below, creating the illusion of a continuous circle. It was indeed a wondrous sight—but not without a certain starkness. Below the arch, under the castle's battlements, hung massive icicles, formed from centuries of mists dripping from the stone and freezing in the thin, frigid air. They stretched toward the waters far below, their surfaces glinting in the last rays of sun like the icy fangs of some mountain beast.

Meric shivered, sensing the dark hunger flowing out from the place.

And he was not the only one. Tyrus scowled at the high castle. "It's out there. I can smell it."

"What?" Mycelle asked at his side.

"The griffin," the prince answered. "The Weirgate. Can't you feel it? A throbbing sickness, like a festering, feverish wound."

Meric nodded. "I sense it, too. A black hunger drawing off all life here. A hole in the fabric of the universe."

"I don't feel anything but the cold," Mogweed said, his teeth chattering.

"Neither do I," Mycelle said. "Are you sure?"

A small muffled wail startled them all. They swung around. The babe in Nee'lahn's arms cried, and its tiny limbs fought and kicked at its buntings. "The seed child feels it, too. As do I." She slipped back and sought to quiet the child.

Mycelle turned questioning eyes to Kral.

He nodded. "An evil worse than any d'warf has possessed the castle."

Mycelle glanced around the group. "But only the elementals feel it."

"What do you mean?" Meric asked.

"Mogweed and I sense nothing out of sorts. But all of you do." Her eyes narrowed as she returned to her study of the valley.

Meric pondered her words, then spoke. "Elena did mention that the Weirgates were tuned to magick and those who bore it. It has the capability of not only sucking magickal energies into its dark heart, but even people, if they are strongly enough imbued with magick."

"Like those with elemental gifts."

He nodded. "Er'ril was taken. Tyrus, too, briefly. And if we are to believe what was learned back at A'loa Glen, even the spirit of Chi himself is trapped inside."

"Then you're all the most at risk," Mycelle said. "If we are to destroy this gate, then only Mogweed, Fardale, and I can approach the griffin safely."

"But how will any of us destroy it?" Meric said, voicing a concern that had been nagging at him since the journey had begun. "If it can simply absorb our magick, how can we hope to fight it?"

Kral stepped forward as the sun finally sank away, a dark figure against the gloom. He hefted his ax in his hand. "All this chattering is not getting us a step closer. No matter what happens, I will find a way to carve this evil from the Citadel's heart. The Ice Throne will belong to the mountain folk again."

Mycelle sighed. "Kral is right. Nothing can be accomplished from here. We have no choice but to go on."

With the matter settled, the party headed down the trail leading into the valley. With the way downhill from here, Nee'lahn freed her pony, fearing it might be more a burden than an asset, and continued on foot. Meric helped her, taking her lute wrapped in its protective furs over his own shoulder.

After a bit, Mogweed slipped up to the head of the line, holding his cloak tight around his thin figure. He nodded ahead. "And has anyone considered how we're going to reach the castle? If it's guarded by d'warves and atop a peak of arched stone . . ."

"There is a way inside," Kral answered.

"What way?" Mogweed asked.

"The path by which my people fled the castle, five centuries ago."

SNOW AGAIN CAME WITH THE NIGHT, BLOWING AND GUSTING IN swirls around the party as they huddled in their cloaks and moved silently along the rocky beach. They hid in the shadows of the overhanging trees.

Kral led the way, his eyes narrowed, his beastly senses stretching outward. Full night had descended, and the lake waters were as black as oil. Kral stared at the white snow sweeping across the dark face of Tor Amon. Pausing, he sniffed the breeze. A storm was coming—a truc blizzard.

"We must increase our pace," he hissed to Mycelle behind him.

She grimaced. "It's more important to be cautious."

Kral stared out into the deeper forest that covered the valley floor. On the way to Tor Amon, they had come upon several d'warf encampments, but with their campfires, they were easy to spot and avoid. Even the occasional patrol was easily sidestepped, due to the d'warves' continued lax guard. Presently, the woods remained dark and silent.

"I suspect all our hens are nested for the night," he answered. "D'warves don't like the cold. They'll have their heads tucked tight tonight."

"Still, it pays to be cautious," Meric said, overhearing them. "We don't want to wake the whole henhouse."

"A storm is coming," Kral growled, angry. "A mountain killer."

Meric glanced across the lake to the north. "I sense it, too, but the blizzard might cover our approach."

Kral shook his head, icicles clinking in his frozen beard. "You might know the skies, elv'in. But you know nothing of the mountains. What comes this night will freeze you where you stand. We must be off the lake before it strikes."

"How much longer?"

Kral cocked his head. Already the winds were beginning to howl. "Not long."

Mycelle nodded forward. "Set the pace. We'll keep up."

As they continued, Mycelle drifted back to alert the others. Meric kept pace with Kral. After another league had passed under their feet, the snow began to fall thicker, now sticking in heavy flakes to the shoreline and tree limbs, accumulating quickly.

Meric spoke up, shaking snow from his cloak like a bird ruffling its feathers. "How much farther to this secret path into your mountain Citadel?"

"We near it now," Kral grumbled, not wishing to talk. With nightfall, the beast inside him grew in strength. It was difficult to ignore and harder to keep in check, especially with the dark magicks swirling throughout the valley.

"Where?" Meric persisted.

Kral pointed out into the water, to where the nearest leg of the arch swept out of the lake and climbed high into the sky. The base was as thick around as most castles. From here, a stout wooden bridge could be seen linking the shore to the arch's leg. Torches lit an iron door in a sheltered alcove. Kral knew it led to a long stair that wound up inside the stone arch to the distant castle above.

"The bridge is unguarded," Meric noted with surprise.

"The Citadel protects itself. It takes a strong man a half day to climb to the castle heights. None can sneak upon it unawares." Kral pointed to the tiny lights that dotted the sweeping leg of the arch. "Lookouts and guard posts line the stairs all the way to the top. What is the need to watch a single door?"

Meric nodded, but his eyes remained narrowed with worry.

As they continued, Kral stared out at the giant granite arch.

Now so close, Kral could sense both powers here—not only the dark power that thrilled through him, but also a deeper, more sonorous beat. Kral knew this voice. It was the call of the mountain roots, the deep vastness of stone. It vibrated up from below, chiming through the arch.

It was this same call that had first summoned the nomadic clans of the northern mountains, gathering the myriad Flames, the clans, to this place. It had taken his people a full century to mine out the tunnel that led to the arch's heights. The upper arch had originally been used as an ancient lookout for guarding the entire valley, a mutual means of defense when the lands were wild and wars frequent. But eventually the lookout's roost grew into a full castle and the many clans became one, united under the Senta Flame, Kral's own family clan.

But that was no more. Kral gripped his ax in an iron hold.

Five centuries ago, the d'warves had come, armed with dark magicks and accompanied by monsters of the foulest ilk. The clans had no defenses against such forces. His people were shattered into individual families and scattered throughout the mountains, nomads again.

Kral listened again to the deep call of the Citadel. The pain was almost too much to bear. Even the beast inside him cowered from it, retreating deep into his heart.

"How are we going to get up to the top without being seen?" Meric asked.

"By not going up," Kral answered, and turned to the dark waters of Tor Amon. The group gathered behind him. He tossed aside his winter cloak. "From here, I must go alone to see if the old path remains open."

"Go where?" Mycelle asked, joining them again.

Kral stripped out of his outerwear until he stood only in his linen underclothes. He ignored the cold breezes across his naked flesh. He held his ax for a moment, then reluctantly added it to his pile of discarded clothes. "Someone gather up my gear. Take it with you."

"Where?" Mycelle asked again, growing angry now. "Enough of these half answers. Speak straight."

Kral turned to her. "You and the others go ahead. Cross the wood bridge to the arch's iron entry. Hide in the door's shadows until I come for you."

"And where are you going?" Mogweed asked, shivering.

Kral turned again to the lake and pointed to the arch's reflection in the dark waters, lit by moonglow through the thickening clouds and the torchlight of the castle's heights. "I go to claim my birthright." He glanced back to Lord Tyrus. "As the Land gave your family the gift to melt stone into water and swim through it, so the Land had given my family the mirror to your magick: to turn water back to stone."

"I don't understand what—"

Kral ignored their confused expressions. It was simpler to show them—that is, if the Land still remembered his clan and the oaths spoken long ago. Before anyone else could speak, he dove into the frigid waters, diving for the reflection of the arch in the midnight waters, praying the Land had a long memory.

The water's cold struck him like a hammer to the chest. As his head crested back out of the water, he bit back a gasp and fought his muscles, which cramped from the water's icy grip. He kicked and swept his arms, swimming for the shimmering reflection of the archway.

He paused to glance behind him. The group stood stunned on the shoreline. He waved an arm angrily at them, and Mycelle quickly guided the others to gather his things and move toward the bridge farther down the shore.

Kral returned his attention back to his own responsibility. Kicking smoothly, he drove hard for the distant reflection, a fiery glinting on the waters from the Citadel's torches far overhead. As the cold sank through to his bones and his limbs grew leaden, Kral worried that he was on a fool's errand. This was surely madness.

But as he finally struggled into the fiery reflection of the castle, the waters grew warmer around him. At first, Kral thought it was merely his own exertion warming his muscles, but soon the waters grew much too warm to ignore.

Tears choked his throat. *The Land remembered . . .*

Fearing the miracle might disappear, Kral took a deep breath and dove into the depths. Under him, a glow spread deep into the water. Far below, he saw the fiery image of the Citadel reflected in the dark depths. He stared in wonder at the mirror image of his ancient homeland. Even a shimmering arch could be seen reflected in the watery depths, reaching up like welcoming stone arms. He remembered his first view of the valley: the archway spanning the lake, while at the same time, reflected in it, forming a complete circle.

Half stone, half illusion.

Invigorated by the sight, Kral kicked and drove for the closest leg of the ghostly arch. As he neared it, a twinge of doubt again flared. What was this folly? What was he doing? Surely it was just old family stories, old clan tales . . .

He reached a hand toward the shimmering reflection—and his fingers touched *stone*.

MYCELLE LED HER PARTY CAUTIOUSLY AROUND A GRANITE OUT-cropping. The bridge lay ahead. It appeared unwatched, but she held up a hand for silence as she listened, then waved Fardale forward to check the fringe forest for spies. They all huddled in the lee of the boulder, out of the worst of the fierce wind. Mycelle glanced around her. The others were all shivering, cloaks dusted with clinging snow. Kral had been most correct in his assessment of the weather. They needed shelter from this storm as soon as possible.

She stepped back around the boulder into the teeth of the snowstorm and searched for Kral. There was no sign of him. The waters had grown still again. Where was he? What was he up to? Her earlier misgivings flared. Since entering the valley, the tiny snake on her arm would hiss and squeeze with his approach, clearly agitated, offering some strange warning. Could Kral be fully trusted? For the thousandth time, she wished she still retained the gift of seeking, the ability to sense the elemental energy in another, but it was gone with her rebirth. In such matters, she was as blind as any other. Still, gift or not, something had changed in him, of this she was certain. But had they not all changed on this long journey?

Lord Tyrus touched her shoulder. "Fardale's back from his search."

Putting aside her suspicions, she nodded and followed the man back to the others. Nee'lahn huddled over her baby, while Mogweed leaned near Fardale.

"I can't understand you," Mogweed hissed at his brother.

Mycelle placed a hand on the thin man's shoulder. "Let me try."

Both Fardale and Mogweed glanced up at her. The amber glow in their eyes, once so bright, was now the barest glimmer. They were both close to settling.

Mycelle knelt before Fardale, placing a hand on his shoulder. "What did you find?"

A kaleidoscope of images swept across her mind's eye.

"Concentrate, Fardale."

A deep whine flowed from his throat, but the images slowed their spin: *Two d'warvish guards . . . hidden in a smoky alcove in a tumble of rocks . . . crouched around a small brazier of glowing coals.*

Mycelle straightened. "Spies watch the bridge from forest's edge." She turned back to the wolf. "Can you take us there?"

Fardale didn't bother to answer, just spun on a paw, ready to lead the way. Mycelle quickly nodded to Tyrus. "You come with me. Meric, you nock up a crossbow and watch over the others."

The elv'in nodded. Tyrus stepped to her side, his hand resting on his sword's hilt.

With a wave, Mycelle sent Fardale off, then she and Tyrus followed. They were all skilled at moving unseen, unheard. In a short time, Mycelle made out the weak glow of the makeshift camp shining from a tumble of boulders. It was a good vantage point: high enough to watch the bridge, but sheltered to keep the lookouts hidden.

With silent hand gestures, Mycelle passed instructions. Fardale flashed across the cave's entrance, making sure he was spotted, then dashed off again. A startled grumble erupted from the cave. One of the pair of d'warves bumbled to the entrance, weaving a bit on his feet, a wine flask gripped by its leather neck in his hand. It seemed the glowing coals were not enough to keep this bored pair warm.

The d'warf stumbled another step out to make sure the wolf was gone. Fardale had vanished, but not Tyrus. The tall prince stepped before the d'warf and drove his sword through the startled guard's neck. Blood sprayed across the white snow, matching the sloshing wine that flowed from the flask he dropped. Tyrus snatched the d'warf's cloak and tumbled him away from the alcove's opening. His crash was not silent.

"Did ye get the furry beast?" his companion called out, slurring in his d'warvish tongue. "I could use me some hot, bloody meat."

Mycelle kept her post on the opposite side of the shelter's opening. When the second d'warf stepped free, she drove both her swords through his chest, piercing his twin hearts. He fell back into the alcove, landing on his brazier and scattering coals around the rank space.

Tyrus stepped to her side, wiping his sword clean on a cloak stolen from the dead d'warf. He offered an edge to Mycelle so she could clean her own weapons. Once she was done, he handed the cloak to her. "Mayhap it would be best if you resumed your disguise as a d'warf. We may run into others."

Mycelle hesitated. She was more comfortable wearing her own form. Still, it was a wise precaution if they were entering a d'warf stronghold. As she slipped out of her own clothes, she likewise slipped out of her familiar form. She changed again into the d'warf huntress that she had imitated at Castle Mryl. Her body remembered the previous transformation and flowed easily into it. Legs bowed out and grew thick. Hair became ratted, and her face flattened and widened into the thick-browed visage of a d'warf. Once complete, she stole the outerwear of the d'warves and wrapped herself in the black cloak of the Gul'gothal soldiers.

Tyrus eyed her up and down, an amused expression on his face. It had been a long time since she had seen the man smile. She had forgotten how handsome he looked with that spark in his eye.

"What?" she asked.

He sheathed his sword and turned away. "You look better as a woman. Still, I was just wondering what it would be like to bed you . . . that flowing flesh and all. I'm sure it would be an interesting time."

Mycelle's eyes widened; a blush crept over the wide cheeks. Prince or not, it seemed there was still a bit of the pirate in him. She trudged after him in her new body, shocked at his words, yet oddly pleased at the same time.

When they reached the camp, Meric came close to peppering her with his crossbows until Tyrus waved him away. "It's Mycelle," he said. "We figured a bit of subterfuge may come in handy."

Meric lowered his bows. "If nothing else, it's certainly convincing."

Mycelle shoved forward in her bulky form and led the others around the boulder. "It should be safe to reach the arch now." She lumbered out to the bare stretch of rocky beach and leaned into the storm. The winds blowing off the lake had grown fiercer, howling now. The drifting snow sped almost horizontal to the ground. The party fought the storm and hurried to the bridge.

Across the wooden span, a single torch still glowed in the doorway alcove. The other had sputtered out, stanched by the wet winds. As a group, they hurried across and gathered in the cramped alcove. The single torch did little to warm the small space. Whirlwinds of snow continually swept into the tiny cubby.

Mycelle tested the iron door. It was locked and latched.

"What are we going to do?" Mogweed asked, eyes wide with fear.

Meric leaned against a wall. "Kral said to wait here for him, so we wait."

Mycelle had none of the elv'in's stoic patience. She drew out her sword and pounded its hilt on the door. Iron rang like a struck bell. "Stand back," she ordered. "If there's a d'warf guard, let him only see a d'warf at his door. And—"

The door crashed open. Mycelle fell backward.

A dark form filled the threshold, and a harsh voice barked out at them. "What are you all gawking at? Get your arses in here." The figure stepped forward into the torchlight. It was Kral, soaking wet and dripping. His sodden beard hung to the middle of his chest. "What took you so long?"

They all hurried inside. Kral, his teeth chattering from the cold, eyed Mycelle's new form as he dressed back into his own warmer clothes. Tyrus explained about the hidden spies in the rocks. "A good precaution," Kral said, nodding approvingly.

Mycelle searched around the entrance to the arch. A wide stairway carved from the stone itself wound upward. On its lowest step, a dead d'warf lay sprawled facedown upon the stair. Blood still flowed and dripped down the steps.

Kral noticed her attention. "It seems you were not the only ones to come upon a hidden watcher."

She nodded and turned away. But the tiny hairs at the back

of her neck quivered with warning. She tried to keep her stance and manner calm and disinterested. Something did not add up. Before Tyrus had spoken, Kral had recognized Mycelle in her d'warvish form. She had recognized the knowledge in his eyes and noticed the way he had sniffed at her like some woodland animal. And now the dead d'warf. How had Kral killed him? The guard's throat had been ripped out, sliced from ear to ear. But Kral had no weapon.

She studied him from the corner of her eye as he finished dressing and hitched his ax back to his belt. What unspoken game was being played here?

At her side, Mogweed craned his neck and searched the space. He asked the other concern in Mycelle's mind. "How did you get inside?"

The mountain man straightened, shoving his foot into his boot. "Let me show you." He pointed an arm. "Everyone on the stone stairs."

They obeyed, careful of the slick blood and dead body. Kral joined them on the lowest step. Mycelle watched him. His eyelids lowered, and his lips moved silently.

After a moment, he leaned closer, studying the stone floor. Whatever he saw seemed to satisfy him. He turned to the group. "Link hands, flesh to flesh. No one let go, no matter what happens."

Mycelle took Kral's hand herself, then reached to Tyrus. Nee'lahn bared her breast and tucked the child inside, skin to skin, then offered her free hand. The rest linked up.

At the line's end, Mogweed grabbed his brother's tail. "Ready," he squeaked out.

"Then let us go. The first step is dizzying, so hold tight." Kral made the last step, but never reached the floor. He seemed to fall, head over heel, tumbling, tugging Mycelle after him. Mycelle's first instinct was to let go, but she held firm, committed to this venture. She fell after him, feeling her stomach lurch sickeningly.

Then she found the floor back under her feet. She turned and saw the others gathered behind her. They were simply in the anteroom again. Nothing had changed.

"You can let go now," Kral said. "We've passed the threshold."

Meric touched his forehead, his face somewhat green. "What just happened?"

"We're right where we started from," Mogweed said.

"No." The mountain man pointed back to the staircase. "We're in the nether arch." Kral remounted the stairs. "We should hurry before a patrol finds the dead body of the guard."

Mycelle looked to the stair. The d'warf's body was gone. The stairs were clean of any blood. "What is going on?" she asked. "Where are we?"

Kral sighed. "I will explain as we climb." He started up the stairs. Once under way, Kral spoke. "We now walk in the reflection of the true arch—the mirror image that is cast upon the waters of Tor Amon. When walked by one of the royal family, illusion becomes substance."

"Water becomes stone," Tyrus muttered, repeating the mountain man's earlier words.

Kral nodded. "Lord Tyrus, the Land has granted my family a secret means of moving unseen through our arched home. We now walk behind the mirror of what is real."

Mycelle glanced out a passing arrow slit. The white snowstorm was gone. Only darkness lay beyond. Pausing, she reached a hand through the window and touched water.

"The lake," Kral explained, staring back at her. "As we climb these stairs, we are actually climbing into the depths of Tor Amon, following the reflection down into the waters." He pointed to a wider window up ahead, a lookout post. The windowsill and wall were wet, as were the steps. "I climbed from the lake through there, then came and fetched you."

"But why climb down . . . or up . . . or whatever to this watery castle? To what end?" Mycelle asked, wiping her damp hand.

"None will see us on this path. It is a way known only to the clans, a way that can only be opened by one of the Senta Flame. We are safe, and once we reach the castle, we can pass through the mirror and back into the true world—back into the castle—with no one the wiser."

Mycelle pondered his plan. If he spoke truthfully, it would certainly give them an advantage. "Can you move easily between the two planes—real and reflection?"

Kral growled his assent.

Mycelle nodded and waved him onward. Suspicions still rang

in her bones, but what choice did they have? The Griffin Weir-gate had to be challenged. She followed after the mountain man leading their party.

The climb grew into an endless trek. The stairs seemed to flow forever. Several times along the way, they came upon old bones tumbled in a landing's corner or sprawled across the steps. Kral's voice was a hoarse rasp. "The bones of the wounded. Many were too weak and died on the steps as the last survivors of the bloody war fled down this secret path, led by my ancestor. Here they remain forever, the last guardians of the Citadel."

In silence, as if walking a graveyard, the group continued up and up. Finally, exhausted and bone-tired, they reached the top of the stairs. A set of stone gates lay open. A wide echoing hall lay beyond, lit by netherlights, shimmering fiery glows.

"Reflections of the hall's torches in the true world," Kral explained, and led them through the wide gates.

Mycelle stepped forward. The hall was strangely empty, hollow, their steps echoing off the phantom walls. But at the same time, Mycelle seemed to sense the presence of others nearby. And she was not the only one to feel this way. The others darted glances around, as if spotting movement from the corner of an eye or hearing a whisper near an ear.

Holding back a shudder, Mycelle followed after Kral. "Where are we going?" she said in a hushed voice, afraid of being over-heard by the ghosts in the hall.

"To the throne room," Kral said. "If we are to start our search anywhere, it should be there."

Mycelle nodded. The mountain man increased his pace in his excitement. They left the entrance hall, climbed more stairs, and passed through a maze of tunneled corridors. Mycelle concentrated on remembering the way lest they get separated.

At last, they reached a wide hallway that ended at a towering, carved granite door. It stretched to the height of six mountain men and stood slightly ajar. Kral hurried forward.

"Wait!" Mycelle called, nerves jangling with warning.

But the mountain man was deaf to her. He slipped through the door and into the room beyond. Mycelle raced after him. "Keep up! He's our only way out of this stony reflection!"

Mycelle dashed through the door and into the cavernous

chamber beyond. Here, too, strange fiery netherlights lit the expansive floor of polished granite and vaulted ceilings. But in the room's center, an oily darkness stood, eating any light that reached it, a black whirlpool tipped on end. Its hungry eye stared back at them. Screams wailed up from its pit.

"Kral!" Tyrus yelled.

The mountain man knelt before the darkness—not in allegiance, but in terror. His hands and feet scrabbled for purchase, but it was clear he was being drawn, sucked toward the darkness. "I can't stop it!" he yelled. "It's drawing me out of the reflection and back to the real world!"

The group rushed forward, grabbing Kral's arms. But it was like trying to stop a ship from sinking. Kral's body dragged forward, hauling them all along like fishes on a line.

"We're not strong enough!" Tyrus said.

"But we can't lose him either!" Mycelle spat back. "He's the only one that can get us safely through the threshold and back to the real world!"

Kral's feet vanished into the oily whirlpool. "It's too late!" he cried.

Mycelle glanced to the others. "There is only one way to go from here. We stick together. Where Kral goes, we go!"

She reached a free hand to Nee'lahn. The nyphai took it. The others joined the link. Mogweed hesitated, glancing around the ghostly hall, then took Tyrus' hand. Nee'lahn grabbed Fardale's tail.

"Be ready!" Mycelle yelled.

As a group, they were tugged forward, tumbling into the dark void. Again there was the queer lurch. The world spun toe over heel, and then they were through.

Mycelle stared around her. The hall was the same as the one they had been in a moment before. But now instead of a whirling pool of darkness, she found them all collapsed before a monstrous stone statue of a winged black lion, its talons dug deep into the polished floor of the chamber, its fanged mouth open in a silent roar.

It was the Griffin Weirgate.

Beside it stood a tall, plain throne of silver granite: *the Ice Throne*. Seated upon the chair was a massive d'warf, white-haired and so wrinkled with age that it was difficult to make out his features.

The ancient one's hoary eyes stared down at Kral. "Ah, Brother," the ancient figure croaked, his dry lips cracking into a wide smile. "Be welcomed home. The Dark Master has missed you."

17

KRAL GAINED HIS FEET, TREMBLING WITH RAGE. TO EITHER SIDE, A mass of armored d'warves closed in on his stunned companions as they lay sprawled on the granite floor. From galleries high on the walls, archers bristled with arrows. It was an ambush, and he had led their group into it.

But guilt had no grip on his heart. Fury and rage burned out all other emotions. To see a d'warf seated on his family throne was too much for Kral's blood. He loosed the beast inside him, oblivious to all who witnessed it. He was past caring about secrets and allegiances. He had only one goal now—to destroy this d'warf king.

A roar burst from his throat as claws sprouted bloody from his fingertips. A snowy pelt shivered from his skin, and a muzzle of razored fangs grew forth from his face. Legion burst forth from the mountain man's clothes, shredding through the leathers, wearing the muscled and deadly form of the snow leopard.

With the heightened senses of the beast, he heard Mogweed gasp and scramble away.

"He's an ill'guard," Mycelle called out, tugging everyone back.

Deep inside, Kral registered the lack of surprise from the shape-shifter, but he ignored it for now. Instead, he turned his red eyes upon his true prey.

The ancient d'warf king also showed little surprise at Kral's transformation. A thin smile cracked his features. "So the kitten wants to play?"

D'warves closed ranks before the throne and attacked from all

sides, cleaving down with axes and swords. But Kral moved with
the speed and grace of the leopard, vanishing before any blade
could touch him. He was a white blur against the black granite.

From the corner of his eye, he saw his companions pinned
against the wall. Tyrus and Mycelle kept a wall of steel between
the attacking d'warves and the others, while Fardale shored up
any weak spots in their defense. Behind them, Meric's form
danced with blue energies, calling forth a flurry of winds to confound the aim of any arrows. Kral growled, acknowledging their
fierce hearts. But he knew they were doomed. The number of
d'warves was too great.

Dismissing them, he ripped out the throat of a d'warf in front
of him, and with a kick of a hind paw, tore open the stomach of
another. Imbued with dark magicks and armed with the natural
instincts of a forest cat, he was an unstoppable force. Slowly,
he worked toward the d'warf king seated on the Ice Throne. He
maintained a wary distance from the Weirgate. Kral knew it
had been the ebon'stone statue that had sucked him out of the
reflection—knew to fear its powers. Still, Kral would not accept
defeat, not until the last d'warf was slain in the Citadel.

With a wail, he dove into the line of d'warves before the
throne, shredding through them with teeth and claw. At last, the
way to the king lay open. Leopard muscles bunched under him,
ready to leap and claim his family's throne.

Still, the king did not move. He simply continued to smile,
meeting Kral's feral gaze with amused disinterest.

Kral's feline instincts thrilled with warning, suspicious. Why
was his prey not running?

"I know your secrets, Legion," the king said. "The Nameless
One has warned me of your special gifts—gifts you use to betray
him now." The ancient d'warf rubbed his crooked fingers along
the chair's granite arms. "Gifts to win back a throne."

A howl of red fury flowed from Kral's throat. He leaped with
all the muscles in his limbs—and still the d'warf king did not
flinch, but merely motioned with one hand.

Kral instantly knew his error. His body contorted in midair:
claws sank away, fur vanished in a breath, sharp teeth blunted.
Thrown off balance by the transformation, Kral's leap fell short
of his true target. He struck the steps that led to the Ice Throne,
shattering his collarbone as his shoulder hit.

Gasping, Kral rolled to his feet naked, a man again. The leopard was gone. He tried to touch the beast within, but nothing was there. He swung around as swords encircled him.

A d'warf warrior stood in the center of the chamber. In one hand, he held Kral's discarded ax—and in his other, the pelt of the snow leopard that had wrapped its iron head. He lifted the exposed weapon toward his king.

"You need a pelt to transform, don't you?" the d'warf king said behind him. "Without an animal's skin around your ax, you're nothing but a man."

The warrior tossed the leopard skin atop a torch borne by another d'warf. The fur caught flame. Clenching his fists, Kral watched any hope of winning burn away. He fell to his knees on the granite floor, defeated, hopeless.

The d'warf king cackled on the throne. "Do not despair, Brother. You've brought a bevy of elementals to my doorstep, additional kindling for the Dark Master's flame. Where you have failed, these will be made into unbending instruments."

Kral turned to see the ancient king creak up from his seat and step over to the monstrous winged statue. A wrinkled hand ran along the black stone, tracing one of the silvery veins in the rock with a fingertip. "You're also in time to see the Master's ultimate victory. As you've lost hope, so will all."

As d'warves ringed the group with ax and sword, Meric watched the game play out by the throne. He leaned closer to Lord Tyrus and Mycelle, who stood with their own weapons drawn. Both sustained bloody wounds from the recent skirmish. "We must not be captured," he said. "I've withstood one assault by the Dark Lord's twisting flame. I doubt I could withstand it again."

Nee'lahn agreed, clutching the babe tighter to her breast. "I'll not become like Cecelia. Neither will I allow the child to be taken."

"What are you saying?" Mycelle asked.

Tyrus answered. "The elv'in is right. All the elementals, myself included, must be slain. We cannot risk becoming tools of the Dark Lord."

Mycelle hissed back at them. "In my lifetime, I've poisoned

scores of elementals to keep them from the Dark Lord and called it a kindness. I understand your sentiment . . . but . . . but . . ."

Meric recognized the pain and guilt in her eyes.

"We can't lose hope. Not yet," she insisted. Turning, she muttered pained words only meant for herself, but Meric's sharp ears heard her. "Sweet Mother, don't ask me to do this. My hands are stained with enough blood."

Meric stepped back to Nee'lahn. "If she can't do this, we must."

Nee'lahn nodded.

Meric stared across the room crowded with d'warves. Overshadowed by the monstrous Weirgate, Kral was being trussed in iron shackles. What hope was there?

Nee'lahn touched his arm. "Hand me my lute."

Meric still had her instrument slung over his shoulder. He shrugged it off and peeled back its wrappings. "What are you planning?"

"The only thing I can to protect the baby." She pulled aside a bit of blanket from her seed child and exposed his small arm. In her other hand, a dagger appeared. Before Meric could stop her, she sliced the little one's palm.

The babe's scream echoed off the walls, drawing all eyes in their direction. Nee'lahn smeared her fingertips in the child's blood, then took the lute from Meric's stunned arms. Without pausing, as the child continued to wail, she strummed the lute's strings with her bloody fingers. Music and wailing wafted throughout the room, sailing out high windows and through open doorways.

"What are you doing?" Mycelle hissed back at her.

"Calling for those who would protect the child—calling to the one who would recognize his cries." Nee'lahn met Meric's gaze. "I'm calling for his mother."

Meric's eyes flew wide. She was summoning the Grim.

NEE'LAHN PLAYED HER LUTE WITH ALL THE ENERGY IN HER BODY, weaving the babe's sobs with chords of woodsong, striving to open a path to her sisters of the forest. "Come to me!" she sang in the ancient tongue. "Protect the child."

Tied to her music, she felt the song swell out and beyond. As she plied her strings, the lines of force in the room became apparent, scintillating in the air. Near the Griffin Weirgate, strains of magickal energy swirled in a tight vortex around the statue, unable to escape, eddying down into the black well. Nee'lahn sensed its sucking hunger, and for a moment, she sensed the malevolence at the heart of the griffin.

Reeling back in horror, she glided her music away from the Weirgate, but found she was unable. Hooked like a fish, she was trapped. Her music jarred to a stop, but it was too late. Lines of force now connected her to the Weirgate. She sensed that all that was elemental in her heart was being drawn into the statue.

"Nee'lahn," Meric said at her shoulder. "What's wrong?"

"The Weirgate," she gasped, weakening on her feet. The lute fell from her trembling fingers, but Meric caught it. "I touched it with my magick. I . . . I can't break free."

Meric caught her under the arms. "What can I do?"

She shook her head. The room began to grow dark. "I . . . I'm lost. Save the child . . ."

A darker shadow swept across her vision. Nee'lahn thought she was fading away—until a sibilant voice pierced through to her. "Is this how you protect my baby?"

Meric yanked her away.

The dark mist coalesced into the figure of Cecelia, the wraith ill'guard. "I will not let them harm my child—not even to avenge the Land's cruelty." Her words balanced between madness and grief. "Sisters, join me!"

From the chamber's shadowed corners, wraiths unfolded into the room, drawn forth upon the strands of Nee'lahn's music. The bits of darkness sailed free, flitting and flapping on unseen winds. Where they passed, screams arose. D'warves fell dead to the floor. Bodies tumbled from the galleries, crushing others.

And still the darkness continued to flow into the chamber. More and more of the Grim fell upon their prey. D'warves twisted and writhed on the floor. Across the hall, guards circled the throne, protecting their king.

Mycelle and Tyrus pulled closer to the others, backing from the wraith Cecelia.

Nee'lahn suddenly swooned to her knees, dragging Meric down with her.

"What's wrong?" Mycelle asked.

"She's dying," Meric answered, then faced Cecelia. "Can you stop this?"

Cecelia swung on Meric. "Why should I?"

Meric stood up and pointed to the griffin. "The statue is drawing Nee'lahn's power from her body, from her lute, from her spirit. Not only will she die, so will the last spirit of your trees. And with both gone, the babe will surely perish. If you love your child, if you love the future of your people, then stop what is happening to her."

Cecelia's darkness swelled out like a foul cloak. Her voice rose to a tortured scream. "I . . . I don't know if I can."

"Just try!"

Nee'lahn reached a hand and touched the baby's head, which peeked from his blankets. "Please . . ."

Cecelia stared down at her. A dark arm reached out. Nee'lahn was too weak to move away. An icy coldness brushed across her cheek. "You're so beautiful," the wraith whispered. "I ache to look upon you."

Nee'lahn had no words left. She pleaded with her eyes.

Cecelia turned away. "No matter the cost, I would rather my child grow as bright as you, than as dark as his mother."

The wraith swirled back into a dark cloud and shot up toward the vaulted ceiling, wailing the cry of the Grim. Around the chamber, the myriad shadows froze for a breath, ignoring their sprawled and twisted prey. As a group, they swept up to join their leader. The billowing darkness grew to fill the arched ceiling.

Throughout the room, d'warves cowered near the floor.

From the darkness, words sailed forth. "Sisters, it is time to end our suffering. We are not meant for this world."

Nee'lahn, tied to her sisters by bonds as old as her tree, understood what was about to happen. "No!" she struggled to yell, but her voice was a weak whisper. Her dry lips cracked, and blood dribbled down her chin. She was almost spent.

"Ride with me into the flames, Sisters! Allow us this one act of penance for all we've become, for all the sins of our past."

A howl rose from the gathered Grim.

Around Nee'lahn, her companions fell to their knees, palms pressed to their ears against the crushing noise. Even the d'warf king collapsed by his throne.

Despite the cries, Nee'lahn heard Cecelia's voice. "For the sake of Lok'ai'hera—for the sake of the last seed child— follow me!"

A bit of shadow broke from the flock and shot toward the statue. It hovered a moment. Nee'lahn sensed a gaze falling upon her from the dank mist. Words whispered in her ear. "Protect my child, little one." Then the shred of shadow shot at the statue, diving through the open jaws of the griffin with a scream. "Follow me!"

This final command of the last keeper of Lok'ai'hera could not be ignored by the Grim. A flow of shadows swept down from above in a continuous black waterfall.

"No!" the king of the d'warves yelled, gaining his feet. "Stop them!"

But who could stop a shadow? The Grim swept down the black maw of the beast. Its hungry throat swallowed them all, feeding, slaking upon their elemental energies, consuming them entirely.

"Stop!" the king yelled again.

Nee'lahn sensed the thin cord of power that linked her to the statue begin to burn away as the surge of energy swept through the Weirgate. As more Grim fled, wailing, into the griffin's maw, their flow of power sliced her free, tossing her back against the wall as the tether snapped. Gasping, she rolled to her knees. "They're sacrificing themselves!" she yelled as the last of the wraiths were swallowed away. "They're burning themselves away so I might live. All my sisters . . . gone . . ."

Meric touched her shoulder and whispered, "I think it's what they ultimately wanted: an end to their pain and a chance to secure a hope for the future."

Nee'lahn stood up, determined to honor their sacrifice.

Across the hall, the d'warf king glowered at the gathered party. An unearthly fire shone in his eyes. "You thought to destroy the griffin. But your efforts have only made the Weir stronger. I will burn you all upon the Master's altar and see the Land destroyed!"

Nee'lahn's eyes narrowed. The d'warf king had no understanding of the battle that had been won here. "Beware the Gate," she warned her companions. "Do not let your magick touch it."

One of the king's guards blew a horn, and the scattered d'warf forces slowly edged back into the throne room, wary of the dead bodies scattered across the floor.

Mycelle stepped forward, still in her d'warf form. "We'll only have this one chance. We attack now or be overwhelmed."

Tyrus stepped to her side. "What's your plan?"

"You all lead the attack against the d'warves. Leave the gate to me."

"What are you going to do?" Mogweed asked.

Mycelle's gaze fixed on the chained and defeated mountain man. "I have a plan." She turned to Lord Tyrus and spoke rapidly. "But I'll need Kral's ax." She pointed to where the weapon lay, clutched in the hands of a dead d'warf.

He nodded. "I'll fetch it." He set off across the floor, running low, sword at ready. But so far the d'warves were slow to regroup and offered little challenge.

As Meric stepped to Mycelle's side, a flash of movement caught Nee'lahn's eye. "Meric!" she yelled in warning.

The elv'in swung around, lifting an arm crackling with energy. But he was too slow to stop the arrow's flight.

The barb flew true, ripping through Mycelle's throat. Blood gouted from the wound as the swordswoman fell backward. She hit the floor, sliding, her blades clattering away.

Nee'lahn dove to her side, while Fardale joined Meric in raising a defense. Fierce winds blew a warding around them as the elv'in danced within the gale, sword in hand. At his side, Fardale ripped into any who drew too near. Even Mogweed recovered one of Mycelle's swords and knelt on the other side of the wounded woman.

"How is she?" Mogweed asked.

Mycelle struggled to sit up, but Nee'lahn held her down. "Don't move."

Mycelle opened her mouth to speak, but only blood flowed out. Mycelle clutched Nee'lahn's arm frantically, tugging her closer.

Nee'lahn leaned down.

Mycelle coughed to clear her throat, spraying Nee'lahn with gore, and managed to choke out a few hoarse words, waving toward the statue. "A sacrifice . . . like your sisters'." Blood again filled her throat, but she coughed. "The ax!"

Nee'lahn turned and saw Tyrus had recovered the mountain man's weapon. He was returning with it in hand. "It comes,"

Nee'lahn said. "But I don't understand what good it will do us."

Mycelle scrabbled with her other hand and slipped out a dagger. She pressed its hilt into Nee'lahn's hand and squeezed, struggling to get her to understand. Nee'lahn stared into the woman's pained and sorrowful eyes. Mycelle's lips moved, but no sound came out.

Still, Nee'lahn recognized the word she struggled to speak. *Shape-shifter . . .*

Nee'lahn's brow crinkled for a heartbeat. She stared at the dagger in her hand. Then her eyes widened with understanding and horror.

"Oh, Sweet Mother . . . no!"

MERIC HEARD NEE'LAHN'S OUTBURST. "HOW FARES MYCELLE?" he called back as he lashed out with a gale of winds, blowing away any who neared.

"Her wounds are mortal," Nee'lahn answered. "She dies."

Meric held his sword out in front of him. It was his fault. He had let his guard down, let the deadly arrow through. "What can we do to help her?"

Nee'lahn did not answer. He risked a glance over a shoulder. The nyphai held a dagger in her hand. He recognized it as Mycelle's. Nee'lahn leaned over the shape-shifter.

A growl drew his attention back around. Fardale pointed. Lord Tyrus returned, hacking through any who stood in his path. The man's eyes were lit with wildfire, the pirate shining through the prince.

Meric did what he could to help, blowing away any arrows aimed in the Mrylian lord's direction while maintaining the whirlwind around the others. Tyrus fought through the last of the d'warves, then dove forward.

Meric lowered his winds to allow the man inside, then cast them back up.

"How are you all doing?" Tyrus asked.

Meric opened his mouth to answer—then Tyrus saw Mycelle and dashed to her side, dropping Kral's ax.

"Mycelle!" He took her hand.

Backing a step, Meric closed his winds tighter. His magick

was not infinite. Eventually it would ebb away, and the winds with it. The d'warves must have sensed his already-weakening state and held back, waiting like wolves upon a wounded deer.

"Mother above!" Tyrus yelled. "What have you done?"

Meric turned as Tyrus elbowed Nee'lahn aside.

Meric now saw what the nyphai had been doing with Mycelle's dagger. Shocked, his winds whirled wildly.

Mycelle lay on her back, her belly and chest bare. Her chest still moved, and blood bubbled from her lips and nose. But from her rib cage down to her navel, her skin had been flayed loose by the dagger wielded by Nee'lahn. To Meric's horror, he realized the nyphai had been skinning the shape-shifter as he had guarded over them.

Knocked away, Nee'lahn still held the bloody dagger. "It's what she wanted," the nyphai mumbled. Only now did Meric see the tears running down Nee'lahn's face. "We can't win here on our own."

Mycelle reached out to the nyphai and nodded, her face a mask of agony. She was too weak to speak.

"I don't understand," Tyrus said. "What is going on?"

Nee'lahn pointed to the mountain man's ax. "She wants us to free Kral with her own skin."

With dawning horror, Meric now understood. He had heard the d'warf king's revelation of Kral's ill'guard nature. The mountain man's form was bent with a black magick that allowed him to assume the form of whatever beast's pelt wrapped his ax. Mycelle wanted to use her own skin to grant the mountain man the full gifts of the si'lura, the shape-shifters.

"But he's an ill'guard," Tyrus argued.

"And one who hates the d'warves' purpose here as much as we do," Meric said, gleaning Mycelle's goal. "Free him and he'll destroy all in his way."

"Including us," Tyrus said.

Mycelle motioned the Mrylian closer. He leaned his ear to her lips, then straightened, paler than a moment before.

"What did she say?" Mogweed asked on the far side, clutching one of Mycelle's swords.

"Prophecy," Tyrus said. " 'She who would give her blood to save the Western Reaches.' "

"What does that mean?" Meric asked.

"It is what I told her back in Port Rawl. I was sent there by my father's prophecies, to bring you all here: three shape-shifters and the woman who was both Dro and not Dro."

"Mycelle," Meric mumbled.

Tyrus took the shape-shifter's hand. "My father said her blood would be the key to saving the lands from corruption. She means to see this foretelling come true."

Everyone grew silent.

Tyrus held out his hand to Nee'lahn. She knew what he was asking for and placed the dagger's hilt in his palm.

He bent over Mycelle. "It was my father's prophecy."

MYCELLE SIGHED. SHE WAS FINALLY UNDERSTOOD.

As blood choked her throat, she closed her eyes, readying herself for the pain to come. It would only be a short time more. She prayed for forgiveness in these final moments. She had slain so many in the name of preserving Alasea. The faces of the hundreds of elementals murdered with her poison—some willingly, some without their knowledge—passed before her mind's eye: children, women, elders. So many. Tears flowed down her cheek—not from pain of her wounds, but from the hollowness of her heart.

"Mycelle . . ." Her name was whispered in her ear. She was too tired to open her eyes. She knew the voice. It was Lord Tyrus.

"Are you ready?"

She nodded, beyond worry of the dagger's bite.

"Mycelle . . ."

Be done with it already, she thought, flickering open her eyes.

Tyrus' face hovered over hers. He stared into her eyes. She was surprised to see the tears in his eyes. He was a hard man, a pirate who had slain thousands. His tears fell upon her face. "I release you from your duty. You've served our family well and long."

She felt a small bit of comfort from his words and smiled, closing her eyes again.

A flare of pain burned up from her belly as he worked the blade. She bit back a gasp, but found the prince's lips suddenly upon hers, pressing hard, holding back the pain with his touch.

Time stopped for just that brief moment, stretched beyond the pain and blood. She found herself sobbing.

"I love you," he whispered between their lips.

And in that final moment, she knew he spoke truly. The hollowness in her heart filled with warmth and love. Then, with the sweetest pang, the world let her free.

NEE'LAHN WATCHED TYRUS RISE FROM HIS EMBRACE OF MYCELLE. Her form had transformed while they had kissed, changing from the d'warfish figure back to the familiar long-limbed Dro. He pushed up, crying, and silently turned with a large swath of flayed skin in his hand.

Tyrus half crawled to Kral's discarded ax and cradled it in his lap. With his head hung, he wrapped the skin around the iron head of the weapon. "I'm sorry . . ." he muttered to no one.

Nee'lahn stood, giving him a moment of privacy.

"I think it's working," Meric said, staring across the throne hall.

Nee'lahn stared past the whirling wind and prayed Mycelle's sacrifice had not been in vain.

KRAL SLOUCHED NAKED IN HIS CHAINS, BLIND TO ALL AROUND HIM, deaf to the yelled orders. Some part of him knew the d'warves were grouping for a final assault on his old companions. But he found no part of him that cared. Any hope for freeing his ancestral home from the corruption here had died.

Then slowly, through the fog of his despair, he sensed a surge of energy, like a spark on dry tinder. Kral recognized this feeling. He rose with a growl to his feet while reaching outward to his ax.

Yes!

He felt the font of power, a new skin upon which to define the beast inside him. He touched the dark magick—and instantly recognized the skin that fueled the fire. *Si'luran . . . shape-shifter.* He glanced across the hall and saw his companions grouped together. Tyrus held his ax and stared back at him. The prince's eyes were bright with tears.

"Mycelle," he muttered to himself, understanding.

He stared down at the shackles that bound his wrists and

ankles. With a flow of flesh, he stepped free. Iron chains clattered to the ground.

The noise drew the eyes of the d'warf king, standing before the white granite throne. The squat creature's eyes grew wide as Kral stepped away from the chains.

"I'll have my throne now," Kral said coldly. He willed his body back to the shape of a snow leopard, fur spreading in a tingling wave, claws sprouting, injuries healing, muscles bunching into the lean and powerful form of a forest cat. He chose this form in honor of Mycelle. She had been Dro, and the leopard was their heraldic symbol. It was only fitting that the mountain cat of the deep north rip the evil from this place.

Before the king's guards could react, he leaped upon the old d'warf, tearing away an arm that was lifted in defense. The d'warf bellowed in pain and shock, tumbling back into the seat of the Ice Throne. "No! We serve the same master!"

Kral's lips pulled back in a feral grin, displaying long fangs.

"No!" the king cried.

Kral leaped again with a scream that roared throughout the hall and landed atop the d'warf, digging in his claws. The king cowered. Kral could smell his fear, hear the fluttering beat of his prey's twin hearts.

"Please . . ."

Snarling his victory, Kral ripped out the throat of the d'warf king. Hot blood sprayed the white granite. He tasted it on his tongue. His prey's mouth opened and closed as if drowning; then the light of life faded from his eyes.

Satisfied at last, Kral kicked aside the dead body and mounted his throne, crouched, muzzle bloodied. He stared around the hall, roaring again, claiming the Ice Throne for himself.

The remaining d'warves froze; then in a rush many fled, heartless with the loss of their king. Others, mostly the royal bodyguards, rushed forward with bloody vengeance in their eyes.

Kral met their charge, leaping and flying into their ranks. He used the full magick of the shape-shifter, flowing from one shape to another as he rolled through the axes and swords. He left a trail of broken and twitching bodies in his wake. He raced from one end of the hall to the other, no longer just satisfied with attacking those who threatened. He chased down fleeing d'warves, ripped out their hamstrings, then circled back to feed on their hearts.

Soon the granite floors were slick with blood. Nothing moved except the beast who stalked among the dead around the lone island of the living. A raging whirlwind protected these few. He lifted his muzzle and sniffed. The winds even kept their smells from him.

He edged toward these others, low to the ground, a growl flowing from his throat.

Once he neared, the winds died down. He found himself facing Tyrus. The Mrylian lord was flanked by Meric on one side and Nee'lahn on the other. Fardale and Mogweed hung back, near the sprawled body of Mycelle.

But Kral's eyes ignored them all. His eyes were focused on the ax.

Tyrus ignored his challenging growl and tore the shapeshifter skin from his ax. Once again, Kral felt the magick ripped from his control. Flesh flowed back to that of a man again. Kral pushed up and stood naked before them. He held out his arm. "My ax."

Tyrus lifted his sword between them. "First a promise, mountain man."

Kral lowered his arm. He knew he could not defeat Tyrus bare-handed against steel. "What?"

Tyrus swung his sword to encompass the room. "We've helped you win back your ancient throne and lands."

Kral stared at Mycelle's body. "I recognize your role. Ill' guard or not, I know the price in blood paid here. You're all free to leave. I'll not harm any of you."

"It is not our lives that we bargain for."

Mogweed squeaked behind him. "Not *all* we bargain for, that is."

Tyrus ignored the thin man. "I'll return the ax only if you swear to use it first on the griffin."

Kral glanced behind him. The monstrous black Weirgate still stood beside the Ice Throne. Its wings were spread wide, its jaw stretched in a silent howl of rage, revealing the black fangs. Kral stared at its red eyes. He could almost sense the Dark Lord staring back at him, raging at his betrayal, but he could not back down now. The Citadel would never be truly free, never be open to his people's clans until this monstrous statue was destroyed.

"I'll do as you ask," he said, turning back.

Nee'lahn stepped forward. "Be warned, Kral. Do not touch the statue yourself. It can tap into your elemental energy, draw the energy from your body."

"I understand." Again he held out his hand.

Tyrus still hesitated. "Swear it."

Kral sighed. "I swear on the Ice Throne and on my blood as a member of the Senta Flame."

Grudgingly satisfied, Tyrus dropped the ax and slid it across the bloody granite to Kral's feet.

Relieved, Kral bent and retrieved his weapon. He gripped the hickory handle. "What makes you believe I can succeed?"

Tyrus glanced to Mycelle, then back to Kral. "Prophecy."

Kral's eyes narrowed. He remembered the prophetic words of the prince's dead father. Mycelle was to give her blood, and he was to win back the crown of his people. Together, they held the key to true victory. He nodded and turned toward the waiting griffin.

"Let this end now."

MOGWEED WATCHED THE NAKED MAN STALK ACROSS THE HALL, holding the ax in his arms. All eyes were on what was to happen next. But Mogweed had his own concerns. He cared not about Weirgates and old thrones. He had started on this long road to find a cure to the curse that bound him and Fardale.

Prophecy.

It seemed that old King Ry's auguries were focused on this single night. Mycelle had died. Kral had won back his throne. But what of the prophecies surrounding the twin shape-shifters?

Two will come frozen; one will leave whole.

As the group watched Kral cross the throne hall, Mogweed turned his attention to Mycelle's body. He touched the edge of her cloak, pulling it back. Clearly Mycelle's prophecies had twined into Kral's future. So it made sense that the same might be true for the predictions about Mogweed and Fardale. The three predictions twining together—like a twisting snake.

Mogweed tugged the cloak from the dead woman's shoulders,

revealing the tiny striped viper. The paka'golo still lay snugged around her upper arm.

Here was the source of Mycelle's shape-shifting, and she had no further use for it. Why not make it his own?

Cautiously, he reached for the small viper. A tiny tongue flickered in his direction. He let the snake taste the tip of a finger with its tiny fork, then slowly drew back his hand. The paka'golo followed, uncoiling from its perch, stretching toward Mogweed's heat and scent.

It must know its prior master was dead.

The snake unwound and slid forward. Mogweed lowered his hand and shifted slightly forward, offering his palm.

The viper's belly touched his skin, sending a shiver over Mogweed's flesh. But he kept his arm still. The paka'golo slid up his palm, tongue flickering at the strange landscape. At last, its tail dropped from Mycelle's cooling flesh. With a tickling slither, it moved farther up Mogweed's arm. The tail wrapped itself around his fingers.

Mogweed allowed himself a thrill of excitement. It was accepting him.

He glanced up and found Fardale staring at him. The wolf's eyes glowed with the barest flicker of amber.

Sorry, Brother, Mogweed thought.

Then a sting like no other jerked Mogweed back. It was as if his hand had been thrust into the hottest flame. He opened his mouth but had no breath to scream. His chest was locked in pain. He stared down at his arm.

The open jaws of the paka'golo were locked onto his wrist. He watched its body spasm as it pumped its toxin into his veins.

Mogweed fell backward, shaking his arm. But the snake was latched by fangs and coiled around his wrist. The fiery burn spread up his arm.

Fardale leaped over Mycelle's body, coming to his aid.

Begging with his eyes, Mogweed held out his arm toward Fardale. Then the flesh of his limb began to melt. The pain was still there, but Mogweed stared in shock as the frozen flesh began to flow again like a true si'luran. He remembered spying upon Mycelle in the grove.

Sweet Mother, it's working!

Then Fardale was there, lunging and snapping at the snake with a flash of teeth. He managed to grab it by its tail.

"No!" Mogweed gasped out past the pain.

The snake's fangs released. It coiled around and struck Fardale on the tender flesh of his nose. The wolf howled.

Mogweed tried to grab up the paka'golo, but his flowing flesh would not obey. He struck Fardale in the nose as the wolf's muzzle melted with the magickal poison. Their two fleshes mixed.

Frightened, Mogweed tugged, but he found himself unable to free himself. The transforming poison continued to spread through both their bodies, both figures melding together.

Mogweed suddenly heard his brother's voice in his head, not in the wolfish images but plain words. *Brother, what have you done?*

He had no idea. He found himself dissolving away. The world grew dark around him, fading. He sensed he was not alone as he sank into the burning darkness. He had no mouth with which to speak. *Fardale, can you hear me?*

There was no answer. The darkness grew complete.

Mogweed cried out with his mind, pleading for salvation.

Then he heard voices in the distance, sounding as if they arose from down a hole.

"What's happened to them?"

"I don't know. It looks like they melted."

"Isn't that Mycelle's snake?"

"It's dead."

"What about Mogweed and Fardale?"

During this discourse, Mogweed tried to yell, struggling to let someone know he was alive. *But was he?* This last thought terrified him. He stretched toward the voices as they continued to speak, using them like a hook with which to draw himself out of the darkness.

"We have more important concerns," a stern voice said.

Mogweed recognized Tyrus. With each word, the voices grew louder and the darkness lighter. Mogweed continued to focus.

"Kral's almost reached the griffin," Tyrus continued.

"But we can't just leave them like this," Nee'lahn said.

"Wait," Meric interrupted. "Something's happening."

The darkness fell back away. Light flared again. Torchlight.

Mogweed opened his eyes. *He had eyes!* Hands rose to feel his face. He sat up and stared down at himself. He was back in his same body. He patted his form to make sure. Though he was naked and seated atop the clothes he had been wearing a moment ago, he was whole.

Conscious of the others' attention, Mogweed stood up, covering himself with his hands.

"What happened to your brother?" Nee'lahn asked.

Mogweed stared around him. Fardale was nowhere in sight.

"I watched you two melt together," Nee'lahn said. "One mass of flowing flesh."

"Two will become one," Mogweed whispered. He turned to the others. "The prophecy." He lifted an arm and concentrated. He felt the bone inside turn to warmed butter. He willed brownish fur to sprout along its length. "I can shape-shift again! I'm free of the curse!"

"And Fardale?" Meric asked.

Mogweed glanced around one more time. His brother was surely gone. He bit back a smile of triumph. *At last.* He was free of his brother.

Tyrus spoke from a few steps away. His eyes were on the far side of the hall. "Kral is ready."

Meric and Nee'lahn swung around.

Alone, Mogweed studied the small twisted snake lying on the floor.

Two will come frozen; one will leave whole.

Mogweed smiled. He was that one.

KRAL STOOD BEFORE THE GRIFFIN. THE TOWERING WEIRGATE loomed over him, wings spread wide. The lion's muzzle curled back from its curved fangs. Attuned to the dark magick, he felt the monstrous chunk of ebon'stone pulse with energy. He found his own heartbeat struggling to match. And deeper than his own heart, he felt the Dark Lord's brand upon him burn brighter, a black rune charred into the rock of his elemental spirit.

Kral hesitated, arms trembling. He tore his eyes from the griffin's ruby gaze and glanced to the white granite throne of his people. The blood of the d'warf king stained its pristine surface. Kral tightened his hold on the ax handle. He could not let this chance pass by. The Citadel, the ancestral home of his people, the throne of his own clan—it must be cleansed!

Stepping back, Kral raised the ax above him in a double-fisted grip. He knew his actions defied the very master who had granted him the power to win here, but he could not stop. He had crossed the line already, and there was no turning back. He made a silent prayer to himself. Once he was done here, he would do the bidding of the Dark Master. He would hunt down the wit'ch and burn her heart upon the Gul'gothal altar. He would pay back his debts in blood.

Kral turned once again to the griffin. He had been taught by his clan's elders: Look a victim in the eye. If you are strong enough to take his life, then do not shirk from seeing him. Kral did this now. He stared into the fiery gaze of the griffin and slammed his ax down between those ruby eyes with all the force and energy in his body.

His arms jarred with the impact, shattering a small bone in his right hand. The crystal ring of iron on stone echoed throughout the hall.

Kral cried out, falling back, not from the pain of his injured hand, but as something vital was ripped from the marrow of his bones. He lifted the ax, but all that lay in his grip was its hickory handle. The iron blade had split into shards upon impact with the Weirgate, while the ebon'stone statue remained unharmed.

Behind him, he heard Tyrus. "He failed. The mountain man failed."

Gasping, Kral stumbled another step back. The broken pieces of his ax head lay on the dark granite. He felt as shattered inside, but at the same time strangely free, as if rusted chains had fallen from his heart. He stared at the remains of his ax. The hidden fist of ebon'stone was nowhere to be seen.

What had happened?

Kral searched inside him. The black rune that had been forged upon his spirit was gone. He fell to his knees. "I'm free . . . truly free."

Where normally these words should have been shouted with joy, tears flowed down his face. The black rune was gone because the stone upon which it had been branded had vanished, too. He was empty. The Rock of his spirit had been sucked away, its elemental energy drawn fully into the Weir.

Kral knew from his battles with other ill'guard that without the fuel of an elemental fire, the dark magicks could not sustain. He touched his chest—both his elemental magick and the Dark Lord's taint were gone—leaving only this hollow husk behind. He covered his face and began to weep, unashamed of who might see. He had won his freedom but lost his heritage.

And to what end?

He stared back up at the statue. It was unharmed.

A shout rose behind him. "Kral! Beware the statue!"

Through the tears of despair, Kral watched the griffin lean toward him, wings spreading wider, black lips pulling back to further bare its fangs. He knew now what his efforts had succeeded in doing.

He had awoken the Black Beast of Gul'gotha.

Book Six

RUINS OF TULAR

18

JOACH WALKED TO WHERE THE SANDS ENDED AND THE DESERT LAKE began. He stared across the strange landscape. Though small boats sailed across its smooth surface, it was like no lake he'd ever seen before. Instead of blue waters, an endless sea of black glass spread to all horizons. Joach tapped his toe on the hard surface to make sure it was real. The lake was named *Aii'shan* by the tribes of the Southern Waste, "the Desert's Tears" in the common tongue. It stood between them and Tular.

"It's like a frozen sea," Sy-wen said behind him. Kast stood at her side. The pair wore desert robes and cloaks, hiding their outlander features.

Nearby, a small skiff loaded with bales and crates glided past with its sails full of the afternoon's breezes. It ran across the glass sea on a pair of sharpened steel runners, whisking past them with the slithery sound of its blades. In the distance, other ships could be seen plying the lake, crossing from village to village.

Kesla stepped up to Joach at the lake's edge. "We should continue on, if we are to reach Dallinskree by nightfall. The tithing caravan will leave at sunset."

He nodded, rubbing the stump of his right wrist against his hip. Phantom pains still plagued him. Though his hand had been bitten off by the foul creature of Greshym, Joach still felt an itching and burning in his lost fingers.

Behind them, Hunt stood beside one of the giant desert malluks. His ward, the child Sheeshon, sat perched on the shaggy beast's neck, one hand tugging on her mount's ear. "Klup, klup!" she called out, trying to imitate the drover's nickering call to get a stubborn malluk to move. The beast simply ignored her, huffing out its blubbery lips in an expression of exasperation.

Hunt patted her leg. "Leave the poor creature be, Sheeshon. It's tired."

As were they all, Joach thought. They had traveled the entire night to reach Aii'shan by morning and were still running short of time. The assembled children for this moon's blood tithing were due to depart from the town of Dallinskree that night, and they still had to cross the lake.

Atop the malluk, Sheeshon gave her mount's tufted ear a final tug, then settled back to her seat.

On the beast's other side, Richald hobbled forward, leaning on a wooden crutch. The elv'in's leg had healed rapidly. The recuperative powers of the elv'in, along with the medicinal magick of the desert healers, had mended the broken femur in less than half a moon. Still, Joach had tried convincing Richald to stay behind at the oasis of Oo'shal to attend his fellow elv'in, injured during the attack at Alcazar. But the prince had insisted on joining Joach on the journey to the Southwall. "I gave my word to see this through," he had said. "I will not dishonor it. Whatever strength or magick I possess, I will use to aid you in the battle to come."

Joach crossed to meet the elv'in now.

Richald wore a slightly pained expression. "Innsu returns," he said, and pointed an arm to the west.

In the distance, a small plume of sandy dust marked the approach of a malluk running at full speed. It was followed by another.

"He's not alone," Richald added needlessly.

The group gathered around, waiting to discover what Innsu had learned in the small lakeside village of Cassus. They had been traveling overland for the past half moon and had had little contact with any but a few nomadic tribesmen. They were anxious for news.

Joach stared at the stretch of dunes and endless sand. Kesla moved beside him. He heard her breathing, the rustle of her cloak. Again he found it hard to believe the old shaman's revelation that Kesla was no more than the Land's dream given shape and life, brought into being to draw him to the desert sands.

From the corner of his eye, Joach studied Kesla: her hair

shining like beaten gold in the bright sunlight, the deep bronze of her smooth skin, the twilight blue of her eyes. Even she did not know her true self. She thought herself as human as any other—and most times, he had the same problem himself.

Dream or not, he could not ignore or dismiss how his heart ached with the sight of her. Even now, he remembered the brief brush of her lips on his cheek as they fled Alcazar's keep. How he longed to explore that unspoken promise to its end. But he clenched his fist against such foolishness. She was not real.

At last, the clopping tread of the approaching malluks drew his attention forward. Innsu and the stranger drew their lumbering mounts up the low dune. Both beasts frothed and were damp with sweat. Innsu slid off his perch and landed lightly on his feet. The journeyman assassin shoved aside his cloak's cowl, his face tight with concern.

Kesla stepped up to him. "What's wrong?"

"Disaster," Innsu said, running a hand over his shaved head. "Word in Callus is that winged demons arrived this past night: pale, vicious creatures who scoured Dallinskree for every child. Any who resisted were slain."

"And the children?"

"They were taken, along with the tithing already gathered from the neighboring tribes."

"But why?" Kesla asked, her eyes wide with shock. "The pact . . ."

Innsu shook his head. "I don't know the full story. Only that every child was taken this morning, emptying the city. A caravan set out upon the point of a whip, heeled by demons."

Joach cleared his throat with a scowl. "For them to take so many young ones, something new must be afoot in Tular."

"But what?" Kesla asked.

"If only Shaman Parthus were here," Joach mumbled.

The elder of the desert tribes had remained at the oasis of Oo'shal, insisting that his presence was needed to help heal Alcazar and Guildmaster Belgan from the taint of the darkmage's occupation. But on the evening the group had set off into the desert, Parthus had pulled Joach aside. "I will watch for you in the dreaming sands. I will do what I can to help." And he had proved as good as his word. Every other night, the shaman had met Joach in the dream desert, instructing him in the art of sculpting dreams into reality.

Joach wished he could share the shaman's wisdom now. They had left the oasis so many days ago with a single plan in mind: to infiltrate this moon's tithing by posing Sheeshon as one of the sacrifices. Under cover of the tithing caravan, the group could have snuck to the very steps of Tular without raising suspicion. But with the children already under way . . .

"What are we to do now?" Kast asked. Sy-wen hung on his arm.

Innsu waved to the stranger, still seated on his malluk. "This is Fess a'Kalar, pilot of a skateboat in Cassus. He's willing to take us to the far side of Aii'shan. We might be able to intercept the caravan, overtake them as they travel the sands around the lake."

"For a price," the man said from his saddle, his voice dark.

Innsu nodded.

"What's this price?" Joach asked with suspicion.

The man shook back his hood. His black hair was cropped close to his head except for two locks hanging in front of his ears. His eyes were as black and hard as the lake at his back. "I will take you all to the far side of Aii'shan, but you must swear to bring back my young daughter."

Innsu explained. "His child was tithed this past moon."

The pilot turned away, but not before Joach saw the pain in his eyes.

Joach spoke up. "We'll do our best to free all the children."

"No," Fess a'Kalar said, turning back, his eyes sparking. "Innsu has already explained your plan to me: to hide under the cloaks of the children so you might sneak upon the ghouls unseen. I will not have my little Misha be a shield for your foolish attack."

"We will not risk the children," Joach said. "Their safety will be our foremost priority. This I swear."

"Besides," Innsu added, "the children are already doomed. Our presence will not add to their danger, but offer a chance of salvation. Once we reach the Southwall, we will send them fleeing under the protection of Hunt and the desert warriors."

The skateboat pilot appeared little swayed.

Kesla stepped forward. "Already a full legion of desert warriors is en route along Aii'shan's other shore. Once we've entered Tular, they'll lead a feinting attack on the Ruins. The ghouls will be too distracted to be concerned with the fleeing children."

Fess pulled his hood back up. "Misha is all that is left of my wife. She died three winters ago. I cannot lose Misha, too." He swung his malluk around. "I cannot."

Innsu turned to Joach and Kesla. "He was the only pilot willing to travel to Aii'shan's far side. It lies in the shadow of the Southwall. None will sail their boats so close to Tular."

Joach sighed and stepped forward to block the pilot's beast. "What would you have of us then?" he called up to the mounted rider.

The man's eyes almost glowed from inside his hood. "I would travel with you to meet the caravan. Once you've commandeered it, I want Misha freed before you continue on. With so many taken from Dallinskree, they will not miss one small child."

Joach considered the man's request. He glanced to Kesla. She gave him a barely perceptible nod. Joach returned his attention to Fess a'Kalar. Joach hated to be coerced in this matter when so much was at stake, but at the same time, he saw no harm in granting this man his demands. It was his child. It was his boat.

Joach answered the silent plea in the desert man's eyes. "So be it. We will free your daughter."

Fess bowed his head. Words—a prayer of thanks—flowed from the man's hood. *"Reliqai dou aan."*

Joach turned to the lake of black glass. The sun had climbed the sky to turn the lake's surface into a blinding glare. It was as if the world ended here. But Joach knew it did not. Beyond its far shore, the Basilisk Weirgate awaited them all. Standing on this shore, Joach could almost sense its baleful gaze. Even in the sweltering heat, Joach shivered under his cloak.

"So be it," he mumbled to himself.

As the sun sank toward the horizon, Greshym crouched within the shadow of the Southwall. He stared into the small pool of quicksilver and waved his hand over its mirrored surface, erasing the image of Joach and his allies. He used his staff to pull himself up. "So, boy, you still intend to put your head into the beast's jaws, do you?"

For the past few days, Greshym had been monitoring Joach's progress, plotting and planning. It was a simple thing to spy on the boy since the bonds between them went deeper than any suspected. The blood spell to open a window on Joach's doings was a simple thing—no more effort than reaching out and shaking a hand.

"Which is just as well." Greshym glanced up to the Southwall towering behind him. He cared not to draw the attention of what lurked inside Tular. He had made sure his hiding place was many leagues from the crumbled ruins and that any spells he cast were minor ones.

With the final pieces satisfactorily falling into place, Greshym allowed a small smile to crack his dry lips. Though he had been thwarted in Alcazar, the information he had gained was worth the loss. *The boy is a sculptor.* The shock of that revelation, more than any magickal assault, had sent him fleeing.

Greshym was well familiar with the magick of the dream. Long ago, he himself had been a member of the Hi'fai sect, a group devoted to studying prophecy and gleaning glimpses of the future through the art of dreaming. But since Ragnar'k, the stone dragon, had awoken and taken flesh, joining the wit'ch's fight, Greshym had considered the boy's elemental gift to be no threat. Now all that had changed.

Greshym turned his back on the black sea of glass and stumbled toward the wall of sandstone nearby. The revelation of Joach's true ability made a certain sense. Without a doubt, there was balance and symmetry in this.

But more than that—it was also a chance like no other.

Greshym approached the wall and heard telltale scrabbling and scraping coming from a narrow hole in the sandstone surface. He tapped his staff against the lip of the cave. The sounds stopped and a bulky shape backed out of the cubby. Its curled tail and hoofed hind feet came first, followed by its squat body and porcine head. Peaked ears swiveled in agitation and fear. "Mmmasster."

"Out of the way, Rukh." Greshym leaned down to peer into the hollow the animal had been digging. He frowned. It ended just a short way in.

The stump gnome must have smelled his displeasure. A stream of urine sprinkled into the desert as the creature groveled.

"Stone . . . hard," it pleaded and held up its gnarled hands. Its claws had been ground to nubs from digging at the sandstone. Blood dripped from the fingertips.

Greshym sighed and straightened. Why was he always plagued by beasts of such ill use? Greshym waved Rukh away. "Night comes. I'll be hungry with the moon's rise. Fetch something to eat."

"Yes, mmmaster." Rukh scurried out of his way.

Greshym bent to the hole, then turned and called back to the gnome. "And no more desert rats! Something with a bit of meat and blood!"

"Yes, mmmaster."

Greshym ducked and pushed into the sandstone cave. As soon as his head passed the threshold, Greshym could feel the power flowing through the Southwall. He had chosen this spot since it was upriver from Tular. Here, the Land's vein of power ran clean and untainted. Below Tular, the feeble, corrupted current would do him little good—not if he was to succeed in this first step.

Greshym reached the end of the excavated hole and slowly sat down, crossing his crooked legs in front of him and resting his staff on his knees. So near the heart of the true desert, the air almost glowed with energy, but Greshym knew it was just the sun setting, painting the desert in countless hues.

Settled, Greshym closed his eyes, waiting, patient. He touched the elemental gifts in his own body; they were long unused, almost forgotten, but still there. For any member of the Hi'fai sect, the dreaming was always just a breath away. Greshym sank into his trance, exhaling out the real world and willing himself into the dream desert.

Time drifted forward.

From a distance away, he sensed as stars began to shine and the moon's full glow climbed the skies. And still he waited.

Finally, Greshym felt a familiar tug and allowed himself to be drawn away from stars and moon. Night had come to the Wastes. The path to the dream desert opened, and Greshym flowed into it, ripe with power. He had tested entering the dream desert over the past several nights. From a long distance, he had spied upon Joach in the glowing sand, watching the boy practice his new talent.

But this night was different. He had no intention of merely

spying from a distance. This night he would take his first step on the path to ridding himself of this decrepit husk of a body, returning youth to his bent bones and ravaged flesh. And to take this step, he needed *power*.

Greshym opened his eyes. The cave had vanished around him. He now sat in the sands beside a bright silver river. He climbed slowly to his feet. The skies overhead were as blank as an empty slate, while around him the desert shone with a soft light. Greshym glanced back to the flat river. In its bright surface, he saw the Southwall reflected. He could even see the small cubby bored into its surface, so close he could reach out and touch it.

Smiling, Greshym leaned a hand over the great expanse of silver. The power here flowed like a raging river, but its surface was as still as a quiet pond. He passed his arm over the Southwall's reflection, resting his hand over the entrance to the tiny cave.

"Come to me," he whispered in the old desert tongue. As a member of the Hi'fai, Greshym had long ago studied the dreaming arts of the desert shamans. He knew their ancient tongue. He knew secrets lost to the ages. "Return to your master."

Slowly, a long thin object rose from the silver river. Once it was within reach, Greshym closed his fingers around his familiar staff. As flesh met petrified wood, the silver river turned momentarily black. As if sickened by its foul touch, the river shot the staff out with a blast. Greshym was knocked back by the force of the expulsion, landing hard in the soft sand, but he managed to maintain his grip on his prize. Relieved, Greshym hugged his staff to his chest for a few breaths before moving.

Finally, he rolled around and shoved to his legs. He still had one more chore to complete this night. Turning his back on the river, Greshym set out into the desert. He moved swiftly, casting out his elemental senses, honing in on a single target in this vast desert. So far, there was no sign. But after spying here these many nights, Greshym knew where to go.

With the boy taking sail this evening across the dead glass sea, Joach would be unable to enter the dream desert. Greshym could not pass up this chance. Leagues of sand vanished under him. In the distance, vague shapes arose from the sand as sleepers throughout the Wastes accidentally slipped into this plane.

Greshym ignored them all. He knew it would only sap his energy to give them attention. So he continued on toward the rendezvous.

As he neared the location, he sensed a ripple in the ever-present pressure of the desert's power, like a pebble dropped into a still pond. He hurried forward.

Ahead, a figure took shape in the sand, cross-legged, his head bowed. Greshym pounced upon the unsuspecting arrival. He swung his staff just as the man darted a glance in his direction.

Instincts made the newcomer attempt to block the blow, grabbing at Greshym's staff.

With a feral grin, Greshym allowed him to hold tight. "Well met, Shaman Parthus."

The elder's eyes shone with the glow of the dream desert. "Who are you?"

Greshym reached to the staff's power and felt his own dream image flow to match the shaman's, mirror images grasping the same length of petrified stone. "I'm you, of course."

Parthus attempted to shove aside the staff. But his eyes flew wide as he failed. The staff had hold of him. His eyes shone brighter. "You've brought something physical into the dream desert," the shaman said with horror.

"So it would seem. And if I remember correctly from the blasted texts of the ghoul Ashmara, on the dream plane, real objects can kill." Greshym touched his dark magicks and ignited the end of his staff.

Balefire blew forth to consume the shaman. Parthus attempted to flail backward, but he was anchored to the staff, unable to escape. His limbs caught fire and blazed brightly in the dimly glowing sands. The shaman's eyes turned beseechingly in his direction. *Why?* they pleaded.

Greshym only smiled. To forget one's past, foul or not, risked ruin. But Greshym had no interest in instructing this youngster any further. He fed a final burst of magick into the staff, and the man burst aflame. Around the pair, the sands blackened and melted, forming a molten pool. Greshym ignored it, floating atop its surface.

Once the shaman was nothing but a scorched skeleton clinging to the end of his staff, Greshym shook the bones off with disgust and stepped away. The smoldering remains sank into the molten sands of the dream desert. Greshym watched a moment, then turned away with a sigh.

Behind him, the blackened bit of sand faded away, erased by the endless desert sands. But he knew that in the middle of the oasis of Oo'shal, someone would soon discover the burned remains of Shaman Parthus, melted into a patch of black glass— what the tribesmen of the desert called *nightglass*, a miniature version of that great barren lake of Aii'shan.

As Greshym headed back over the sands to return to the silver river, he wondered if Joach was already sailing atop Aii'shan's midnight surface.

He smiled and glanced down at the form he had stolen from Shaman Parthus and laughed. No matter where Joach traveled now, when it was most important, he and Joach would meet again.

KESLA WALKED UP TO JOACH AS HE SAT ON A CRATE AND STARED out at the black lake of Aii'shan. She stepped to the rail. The night sky was clear, and stars shone both overhead and in the glassy surface of the surrounding sea. The wind remained swift over the smooth, hard surface, filling the sails of the skateboat and speeding them toward the rising full moon.

"How much longer?" Joach asked, not turning.

"The pilot says we'll reach the far side before the moon reaches its zenith." She glanced behind her. Fess a'Kalar stood by the tiller, face bare to the winds, his eyes on the stars and his sails. Up and down the boat, his four-man crew worked lines and cranked winches at his command.

Joach nodded. "Is everything prepared?"

"Kast and Sy-wen are ready to take flight as soon as we dock. Innsu and the tribesmen have their weapons sharpened, arrows fletched, and they are dressed in sand gear. Hunt and Richald oversee Sheeshon, who rests belowdecks." Kesla could not help but smile, even with the tension. "Hunt truly has a sweet voice when he sings her to sleep."

Joach glanced at her, a shadow of a smile on his face.

She settled beside him, sharing his crate. He made a motion to stand and move away, but she gripped his arm. "Stay . . . please."

After a pause, he sank back to his seat with a sigh.

Kesla remained silent, just appreciating this quiet moment.

Finally, she felt Joach relax beside her, leaning ever so slightly against her. She slid an arm smoothly around his back. Neither spoke; neither acknowledged the simple gesture.

As the boat glided across the lake, the whisper of its steel runners on the glass surface created a continual haunted music, echoing eerily across the night.

Finally Joach spoke. "Tell me about Aii'shan."

"What do you want to know?"

"Earlier you mentioned that the lake was formed during the ancient battle that first drove the ghouls from Tular, some magickal cataclysm that melted the sands to this black glass."

"Nightglass," she whispered, "like the dagger."

"Tell me more about this legend."

"It's not legend, but history. I've read books in Master Belgan's library—texts and scrolls stretching into the distant past of the Southern Wastes."

Joach glanced at her, their faces only a handspan apart. "You read?"

"Do you want to be pushed off this scow?" She smiled at him and stared into his eyes a moment. It was good to hear him tease. But there was a sadness in his gaze that she could not touch. It had been there since they had escaped Alcazar. He turned away. "So tell me about this place."

She sighed. "This region was once just desert, except for Ka'aloo at the foot of the Southwall, a sprawling trading port beside the desert's largest oasis. Silk merchants, spice traders, and dealers in wares would come from all over. Their tents would stretch for leagues into the sands around Ka'aloo."

"So what happened?"

"As the ghouls grew in power and perversity, fewer and fewer would make the trek, fearing for their lives. Tales began to spread of children disappearing, of strange cries echoing over the sands from Tular, of beasts that would come with the night to attack and pillage. So the flow of riches trickled away. This did not please the ghouls. They had grown to enjoy the varieties of wines, spices, and outlander wares at their doorstep. An order was sent out, demanding a certain tithe of goods be delivered to their representatives in Ka'aloo."

"The beginning of the tithing?"

Kesla nodded. "And as the ghouls grew ever more bold, so did their demands. Soon a tithing of blood was being demanded: cattle, malluks, goats . . . and . . . and eventually—"

"Children," Joach finished.

"Upon reaching manhood or with the first bleed of womanhood, the firstborn of every family was required to serve two winters in Tular. Most never returned. Those that did were crippled in the mind, unable to speak. Many had turned savage, more beast than man."

"Why did the tribes submit to them?"

"If a village or tribe refused, the basilisk was sent to them in the night and all were killed. Nothing could slay the beast. So as winters passed, slowly the tithing grew to be a custom of the Wastes, another harshness of the unforgiving desert."

"How horrible."

Kesla stared out at the glass sea. "Such was life under the ghouls."

"So what happened?"

"Occasionally there were assaults upon Tular, uprisings, but they were all beaten down and swallowed by the sands. None could resist the ghouls. Then one winter, a child was born whose eyes glowed with the shine of the dream desert." Kesla glanced to Joach to see if he understood.

He nodded.

"He was named *Shiron*, after the first star to rise each night. His family lived alone in the desert and immediately knew him to be special. It was said that hundreds of stars fell from the skies on the night he was born. Since the parents were isolated nomads and called no place home, they decided to risk defying the ghouls and keep their child hidden. It was only their own lives at risk. But soon, other tribes heard of the child and took up the family's cause. The family was spirited from tribe to tribe, from village to village. The child grew up to know the entire breadth and spread of the desert. All who laid eyes upon him knew he was the one to free them from the tyranny of the ghouls. Rumors spread of his ability to call water from the sands, to tame a sandstorm with the wave of his hand. All declared Shiron to be the chosen one, the child of the desert itself. Some questioned whether he had even been born of man and woman, but born out of the desert itself."

Joach suddenly stiffened beside her. She glanced to him, but he waved for her to continue, his expression slightly pained.

"So when he grew to manhood at the age of thirteen, no one in the desert wanted him tithed to Tular. Everyone whispered his name. But little happened in the desert of the Wastes that did not reach the ears of the ghouls. On the night of his passage from boy to man, the basilisk itself appeared in the sands outside the village where he was staying. It did not attack, but simply took up silent watch, warning all that the child must be taken to Tular. That night plans were made to whisk Shiron away, but the boy refused. Instead, after the celebrations of his passage to manhood, Shiron left the village and walked to where the basilisk was rooted. It is said that Shiron spoke to the ghouls through the beast and swore to bring himself to the Southwall."

"Why?"

"That's what the villagers asked him. They tried to convince him to flee, but Shiron left with the morning's light and made the long trek to the Wall. Each night of the journey, the basilisk would come to make sure he kept his promise, its baleful eye watching over the boy. But he did not try to run. He reached Ka'aloo in less than a quarter moon. There, with the moon shining as bright as it does this night, he found a ghoul named Ashmara waiting for him."

"Ashmara?"

"Every desert child's nightmare. It was said his skin was as pale as milk and his eyes glowed with red fires. He was the most corrupt of the ghouls, sick in his depravity and wild in his blood lusts. Some said his wickedness came with his birth. Born with skin that could not tolerate the sun's touch, eyes that could not withstand its brightness, he grew to hate the desert, only coming out at night to wreak his terror upon those that could walk the day."

"And this Shiron . . . did Ashmara take him to Tular?"

"No, in the center square of Ka'aloo, beside the pool of the oasis, Shiron finally refused and spat at the toes of the leader of Tular. He told Ashmara that from this day forward the reign of the ghouls would end, that his own blood would slay them all."

"What happened?"

Kesla turned from her study of the lake back to Joach. "Here is where texts vary on what happened. Some say Ashmara drew a dagger and attacked Shiron, while others say Shiron pulled a magickal sword from the sand and drove it through the ghoul but failed to kill him. But no matter the story, a great battle was fought between them. Dire magicks lit the night skies. Those in Ka'aloo fled into the desert with only the cloaks on their backs. The battle raged between Shiron and Ashmara throughout the entire night, and by sunrise, those that had returned found only a lake of steaming and running glass. *Aii'shan,* it was named—'the Desert's Tears.' It took a full moon's time for the lake to cool."

"And what of Shiron and Ashmara?"

Kesla shook her head. "Both were gone, consumed by their own magicks."

Joach stared at the smooth, dark lake. "And Tular?"

"Once word spread of Shiron, the tribes rose up once again. Not just a handful, as in the past, but the entire desert. Tular, though leaderless now, was not defenseless. The basilisk still lived, as did hordes of other wicked beasts. But Ashmara had been the strongest of Southwall's ghouls. With his loss, the others barely resisted the attack of the desert's tribes. A siege began that stretched for two winters." Kesla faced Joach. "Until one day, a woman came and instructed the artisans of the desert to sculpt a dagger from the glass of the lake."

"Sisa'kofa?"

She nodded. "The Wit'ch of Spirit and Stone. She spilled her own blood upon the blade, and on the night of the full moon, she walked naked into Tular and slew the basilisk. With the death of the ghouls' monster, the tide was turned. In less than a moon, Tular fell, the walls were pulled down, and the place was scoured of all living things. It became a cursed place avoided by all."

Joach sighed. "Until it all started over again."

Behind them, Fess a'Kalar called from the tiller. "We near the Southwall! Ready yourselves!"

Joach and Kesla both stood. Squinting her eyes, Kesla spotted where the gleam of the glass lake ended and the sands began once again. Beyond the sand, the far horizon lost its gentle curve as the stars of the night sky were sliced away by a straight, unyielding line. Though it was unseen, Kesla recognized the silhouette of the Southwall, dark and imposing.

Around her, the crew of the skateboat began to scurry in

preparation of beaching on the sands. Despite the activity, Kesla found her eyes fixed on the Wall. For a moment, two images lay atop each other. Ghostly in the moonlight, glimpses of pavilions and trees and a pool of midnight blue appeared around her.

"Ka'aloo," she mumbled.

"What was that?" Joach asked.

As the images faded away she shook her head and touched the nightglass dagger hidden under her cloak, seeking reassurance. It was just her imagination, the old stories come to life in her mind's eye. She turned her back on the lake, but she could not escape the feeling that for that brief moment she had been staring through Shiron's eyes, seeing ancient Ka'aloo as the boy must have seen it.

Joach touched her arm. "Is something wrong?"

She reached to his fingers and simply clutched them, fighting the sense of doom. "Let's get everyone ready. We've much to do before the dawn comes."

JOACH WAITED FOR THE SIGNAL. HE AND RICHALD LEANED THEIR backs against the outcropping of sandstone. Both of them were covered in cloaks that matched the sand and stone. Neither of them breathed. Across the shallow valley, Innsu hid with his ten warriors among the scrabble of rock. Between them, in the valley's center, Hunt and Kesla sat around a fire, with Sheeshon sleeping in a bedroll near the flames.

Bait for those that approached.

After disembarking from the skateboat, it had been difficult in the flat sands to find an adequate place to ambush the children's caravan without being seen. Even at night, the stars and setting moon were enough to cast the landscape in silver. But as much as it made their task difficult, it also made the approaching caravan easy to spot.

Even before the skateboat had beached, Kast had found the caravan with a spyglass. The long train trundled with wagons and mewling malluks, winding along the shores of Aii'shan as it headed toward Tular. Lamps swung from poles on both beast and wagon, a glowing snake splayed across the dark desert landscape. Kast had lowered his spyglass with a worried look. "I count six skal'tum stalking around the edges of the caravan."

With this dire news, they needed as much time as possible to ready the trap.

Fess a'Kalar had proven his skill as a pilot, gliding his ship well ahead of the caravan and finding a shelter in which to keep his boat hidden. Once landed, they had quickly set out and chosen this point along the shore road in which to set up their ambush. Framed by sandstone boulders, it offered plenty of shelter and deep shadows.

"Here comes the scout," Richald said, ducking down.

The heavy tread of an approaching malluk grew closer, coming from just over the next dune. Joach lay unmoving as the great beast shambled by. The musky scent of its passage swept over him. Once it was past, he shifted enough to watch the malluk crest the dune and head down the far side.

The rider called to those gathered around the fire. "Ho!"

Kesla acted surprised by the appearance of the scout. She stood quickly and spoke in the desert tongue. Joach did not understand it. The man was clearly questioning her, and she pointed an arm at Sheeshon bundled in her blankets. Joach knew what she was explaining to the man. She and her uncle were heading to Dallinskree with her niece, a tribute for this moon's tithing.

The scout stared around the small camp, clearly suspicious. Sheeshon awoke from all the noise and rubbed her eyes. Sleepy, she leaned closer to Hunt. He comforted her while motioning her to stay silent. It would ruin the ruse if Sheeshon should speak. Her Dre'rendi accent would certainly mark her as an outlander.

From his perch, the scout eyed the child. Joach prayed for him to rise to the bait. He seemed to sniff the air. The campsite had been ringed with malluk urine, a common warding against the sand sharks and other burrowing predators. Its strong musk also helped mask the presence of the hidden men. Fess a'Kalar had warned them that the guards for the caravan were desert outlaws who had been bought with gold for this foul duty. They were as cunning as they were savage.

Finally, the scout lifted a horn from his saddle and blew a long slow note, a signal that it was safe for the caravan to come forward.

The signal given, Hunt whipped back his cloak and swung

his hidden club. The man turned in time to take the brunt of the blow to the side of his face. He tumbled from his perch and struck the sand hard. Kesla flew to the malluk's side to keep it calm. Silently, Innsu slid from his hiding spot and raced to the mount and up into the high saddle.

Without a word, Innsu ambled the malluk to the crest of the hill, back in direct sight of the caravan. He lifted an arm and waved for the wagons to continue forward along the shore road. In the meantime, Kesla quickly bound and gagged the limp guard, then she and Hunt dragged him to where the desert warriors still lay hidden.

The plan was to allow the caravan to swing into the valley before beginning their attack. With the caravan's attention on the small roadside camp, Joach and his group would attack the flanks.

In the shallow valley, Kesla and Hunt returned to their positions around the campfire. Joach bit his lip against the tension. What occurred next depended on perfect timing and expert execution.

In short order, the forefront of the caravan wound over the rise and down into the valley. Malluks with solitary riders led the way; behind them came open wagons hauled by pairs of malluks. The wagon beds were loaded with baled hay and crates of goods sacked from Dallinskree. Behind them came cart after cart of barred cages. Inside, lit by torches, the scared, pale faces of children stared out at the surrounding sands. Their cries and sobbing echoed over the dunes. Flanking the children's wagons were outriders, scouts on leaner malluks.

But as Joach watched, the worst was yet to come. He saw the first skal'tum climb over the rise. Framed in firelight, it stood as tall as any malluk, and the folded wings on its back twitched as its black eyes stared across the valley. Joach prayed that the musk would continue to mask the hidden party. As the creature descended into the valley, its white flesh stood out starkly against the shadowed sands, like a corpse floating on a dark sea.

Joach held his breath as another of the beasts appeared, this time closer. It crawled along the sands on his side of the caravan, low, claws scrabbling on the rocks. It paused, perched like some winged carrion hunter atop a large boulder, no more than a stone's throw from Joach's position. It lifted its head and drank in the night's scents. Joach watched pale lips curl back, exposing its sharp fangs. Eyes, so dark that they appeared holes in a skull, gazed at the tiny camp below. A long, forked tongue slithered from its throat and tasted the air.

Muscles tensing, Joach studied the dark rocks on the valley's far side. The noises of the trundling caravan grew deafening to those who had been hiding in silence for so long. What was Innsu waiting for?

More of the caravan rode into the valley. Another two skal'tum appeared, one riding atop a cage of children who whimpered in mindless terror.

Below, a pair of outriders swept over to Kesla's campsite and slid from their saddles. The glint of ankle irons flashed in their hands.

Sweet Mother, what is taking them so long?

Joach's fingers wrapped around the sword hilt in his hand.

Finally a flicker of silver flashed from the dark rocks.

At last—*the signal!*

Joach tossed aside his cloak and burst into the open with Richald.

The skal'tum perched on the rock swung toward them and hissed, clearly surprised. Joach lifted his sword, and Richald raised his arms, shining bright with elemental power.

High-pitched laughter flowed from the skal'tum's throat. "Ssso the desert hides some ratsss." It wheezed, snapping its skeletal wings open. Clawed legs tensed as it prepared to leap. What did the monster have to fear? At night, the skal'tum were protected by dark magicks that made them impervious to swords and blades. In a burst, it hurled itself at them.

Joach rolled backward, and Richald scrambled to the side.

As it flew at them, a larger, darker shape flashed overhead, snatching the skal'tum in midair, like an eagle upon a sparrow. Then it was gone, leaving behind it a roar that deafened the entire valley. Ragnar'k had drawn first blood this night. The broken body of the skal'tum tumbled from the skies to crash atop a wagon, shattering its wheels with the impact.

The dragon's roar could strip the dark protections from the skal'tum, making them vulnerable. With the way clear, Joach hurried down the hill.

Below, a battle raged. Innsu and the desert warriors attacked the riders and drovers of the caravan with arrows and long, curved swords. Some outlaws, though caught by surprise, were quick to regroup, while others raced past Joach and offered no challenge. It seemed gold did not buy the most stalwart hearts.

Unimpeded, Joach ran down the slope to the campfire. Kesla and Hunt had already dispatched the two scouts and now guarded Sheeshon.

"What took you so long?" Hunt asked as Joach skidded to a stop.

Richald answered. "We were blocked by one of the Dark Lord's monsters."

"Ragnar'k killed it," Joach added, then scooped Sheeshon up under his free arm. He was no skilled swordsman, especially with his left arm. He had one duty this night: to whisk Sheeshon away from the fighting with Kesla. Hunt and Richald would join the battle.

Kesla led the way toward the rocks, while Richald and Hunt headed into the fighting. Joach glanced behind him. Across the way, he saw an outlaw lay a torch to one of the children's cages, clearly trying to divert the ambushers into rescuing the children. But before the wood could take the flame, the man collapsed, his back feathered with arrows. His torch fell to the sand and went dark.

Closer, a skal'tum fell from the sky to land, broken and bleeding, among the rocks. Joach glanced up. Ragnar'k continued to pick off the monsters while ensuring none escaped by wing to alert Tular.

Kesla suddenly tugged on his elbow. "Run!"

Joach swung around. A pair of wild-eyed malluks thundered toward them, dragging a smashed wagon behind. Joach ran with Sheeshon in his arms and managed by a single step to escape being trampled. They reached the rocks and climbed into their safe embrace to sit out the bloody storm.

In a shallow cave, they found Fess a'Kalar waiting. He sprang to his feet. "Did you find Misha?" he asked hopefully, looking to the bundled form in Joach's arms.

"Not yet," Kesla said. "We must first rid the caravan of outlaws and monsters; then we'll search for your daughter."

The skateboat pilot's face was pale with worry. "I saw those monsters." He hid his face in his hands. "My little Misha . . ."

Joach settled Sheeshon down. She sucked her thumb and stared wide-eyed at all around her. Joach placed a hand on the pilot's shoulder. "We'll get your daughter safely back into your arms."

Fess turned his face to hide his tears, then moved away. "I cannot sit idle and wait. I must offer what help I can." Fess stumbled away, a dagger in his hands.

"Don't." Joach stepped after him. "You don't have to fight."

The man stared at Joach, an incredulous look on his face. "It is my daughter out there."

Joach opened his mouth to argue, but found no words. He watched Fess disappear into the shadows. Joach turned away with a shake of his head. "Fess is no warrior."

Kesla nodded. "But he is a father." She pulled Sheeshon into her lap and gently cradled her, rocking ever so slightly.

Joach took up watch with his sword. Among the rocks, the sounds of battle were muted, but he could still hear the screams of terrified children. It was an awful sound. He could only imagine how much worse it must sound to the father of one of these children.

Kesla sighed behind him. "We might rescue the children from what awaits them in Tular, but we can't ever rescue them from this night."

Joach understood and remained silent. The horrors here would last a lifetime. Even Sheeshon stared wide-eyed into the night, cringing whenever the sounds of battle grew closer. Kesla met his gaze over her head.

Joach sought some way to distract the child. He ran a finger over his sword, slicing a tiny cut. He leaned over the floor of their little cave and squeezed a thick drop from his finger into the sand.

"What are you doing?" Kesla asked.

"Shhh . . ." Joach sat back and sighed out his breath, extending his senses. On the long trek to Aii'shan, Shaman Parthus had taught Joach how to pierce through the veil between the real and the dream desert by focusing on the magick in his blood.

Joach stared at the red drop resting atop the sand. As he watched, it slowly sank between the grains. Joach allowed his thoughts and a bit of his spirit to follow the blood down into the sand. From the corner of his eye, he noticed the rocks vanish and the dream desert open up around him, glowing softly into the distance. As he stared, the drop of blood grew brighter, becoming more real. Shaman Parthus had told him how one's attention could give substance to what was figment. Joach did that now, feeding a small bit of himself into the drop of blood and willing it to change.

Distantly he heard a small gasp from Kesla. Joach continued to work in silence, concentrating. Once done, Joach pulled himself back to the world of rocks and wind. At the entrance of the cave, a rose of sculpted sandstone stood mute watch. Joach waved a hand over it, touching the threads of power that still linked him to the dream desert. The rose's petals slowly bloomed open in the moonlight.

Joach heard Sheeshon giggle. He turned and saw her eyes bright upon his creation. "Pretty," she whispered, and reached out to it.

"Careful, honey," Kesla warned.

Joach waved to Sheeshon. "It's all right."

Sheeshon reached and plucked the rose from the sand. As the stem broke, the rose fell back to sand, falling away. She stared wide-eyed at the trick, then looked up at Joach with a twinge of guilt.

He patted her hand, dusting the silt from her fingers, then kissed their tips. "Don't worry, Sheeshon. Dreams aren't supposed to last forever."

She grinned at him, then snuggled against Kesla, who wrapped her arms around the girl.

Joach met Kesla's soft smile of appreciation. *Maybe dreams aren't supposed to last forever,* he thought as he stared at her, *but while they're here, maybe you should appreciate and cherish them.*

Slowly he sank back and joined Kesla. Together they watched over Sheeshon. And sometime during that long night, Joach found his fingers wrapped in Kesla's, the child guarded between them.

Finally, the scrape of heel on rock sounded. Joach jerked up, sword in hand. Hunt pushed forward. His cloak was stained in blood. He leaned on a rock. "Sheeshon?"

"She sleeps," Kesla said.

"Have we won?" Joach asked.

Hunt nodded. "The caravan is ours."

Joach and Kesla walked back out of the rocks, while Hunt picked up Sheeshon. She woke sleepily, smiled at Hunt, and hugged him tight around the neck. Joach noticed the hard man soften, saw the pain in his eyes mute. As a group, they continued back to the sand.

Joach stared at the carnage below. Both men and beasts lay bleeding in the sand. Across the valley, Ragnar'k landed and perched on the ridge. The moans and sobs filled the valley.

"The children are free," Hunt said.

Joach shook his head. These children would never be truly free after this night. He stared at a group of them cowering beside a broken wagon, bleeding, crying, and terrified.

"What about Misha, the pilot's daughter?" Kesla asked. "Was she found safe?"

"Yes," Hunt said.

Joach recognized the pang of sorrow in the Dre'rendi's voice and turned to face him.

Hunt hung his head. "Her father was killed. Fess attacked one of the skal'tum as it tore into a cartload of children. He died before Ragnar'k could come to his aid, but his death was not in vain. His attack managed to delay the monster long enough for the dragon to save the children."

Kesla turned away, a hand over her mouth.

Hunt continued. "One of the skateboat's crew has promised to take the child to her aunt and uncle."

Joach closed his eyes, taking a deep breath. He pictured the man's haunted face as he strode into the darkness.

Innsu strode up to them. "The outlaws have been either slain or driven into the sands. Once we regroup the caravan, we should be under way for Tular by daybreak."

Joach sheathed his sword. "No."

Eyes swung in his direction.

He faced them with a deep frown. "These children have suffered enough." He turned to Hunt. "I want you and the warriors to take all the children away from here. Now. Keep them safe."

Innsu protested. "But we'll need the caravan to hide our approach—"

"No. I won't hide behind these children. Fess a'Kalar spoke truly. We have no right to do this."

"But we saved them," Innsu continued to argue.

Joach laughed, but it was a pained sound even to his own ears. "We saved no one here." He moved away. "Hunt, gather the men and head out as soon as the sun rises."

"It will be done," Hunt said.

"Then what are we going to do when we reach Tular?" Innsu asked angrily.

Kesla answered. "We'll find a way inside without being seen. We're assassins, are we not?"

Her words shamed Innsu into silence.

Kesla strode to Joach's side.

He turned and stared into her twilight eyes and knew his decision was the right one—not because she represented the dream of the desert, but because her eyes glowed with the simple compassion and concern of a woman.

Joach bent down and kissed her deeply. He felt her flinch in surprise for a moment, then wilt into his embrace. They clung to each other, a simple acknowledgment of life—and maybe even of love.

19

AS TWILIGHT SPREAD OVER THE DESERT, SY-WEN RODE ATOP HER dragon, sweeping along the deep shadows of the Southwall. The immense sandstone structure stretched higher than Ragnar'k could fly, but its surface was far from smooth. Sections lay crumbled into a rocky scarp at the base, while countless sandstorms had pitted its face. In addition, old scars from ancient wars had burned the red rock black for large swaths. These signs of old battle grew in number as they swept toward the ruins of Tular.

We come to city, my bonded, Ragnar'k sent to her.

The dragon's vision was keener than hers. But she closed her eyes and shared his sight.

Ahead, it looked as if some giant had taken a hammer and

struck the Southwall a great blow. Boulders and huge chunks of sandstone lay jumbled at the base of the wall. The pile climbed halfway up the immense wall. Only as they swept closer did it become clear that the tumbled boulders were in fact once a great city. The remains of a half-circle curtain wall enclosed the debris. One watchtower still stood near the front, but its crenellated top had been worn by winds into a rough nub, and its base had been burned as black as the Aii'-shan sea. Within the walls, the remains of immense buildings and spires could be seen poking from the sandy dunes that had blown into the ruined city. It was as if the desert were trying to erase these scoured ruins.

"Keep to shadows, Ragnar'k," Sy-wen whispered into the wind, but she knew the dragon heard her thoughts. "We don't want to stir this nest."

Sy-wen studied the ruins of Tular. She saw no sign of movement, no sign that anything still occupied the city. But she also spotted the worn wagon trails that led through the broken gates and wound through the city. The trail of the old caravans crossed the city and disappeared into the yawning maw of a tunnel in the wall itself. From this height, Sy-wen could make out the carved figures of a man and a woman, done in relief at the tunnel's entrance, arms linked over the entrance in a clear gesture of welcome. Sy-wen imagined it was one of the last gentle images the children of the deserts ever saw before being swallowed away into the darkness.

She leaned closer to Ragnar'k to share the heat of the dragon, but still could not suppress a shudder.

The desert squirms, Ragnar'k said. He directed their shared sight below.

At first, Sy-wen did not understand what he meant—then she saw it, too. Around the base of the outer wall and stretching a good quarter league into the surrounding desert, the sands churned and roiled like living flesh. She silently urged the dragon to circle lower.

Tilting on a wing, Ragnar'k angled in a steep glide that swept them lower, almost to the heights of the tumbled ruins. As they coursed by, the source of the strange phenomenon became clear. The sands around Tular churned with the thrashing bodies of hundreds—no, thousands—of desert sharks. Sy-wen remembered the small school that had attacked them near the crash site of the *Eagle's Fury* and felt her limbs go cold.

There were so many. How could anyone hope to cross this treacherous moat?

She guided Ragnar'k up into the sky. No wonder there were no eyes on the walls. The sands themselves would shear the flesh from your bones if you dared approach without permission.

"Hurry. We must complete our duty and return."

Ragnar'k grunted his understanding and climbed higher and away. The two had been sent forth with the sun's setting to spy upon the ruins, to gain as much insight as possible into its defenses. Meanwhile, the others rested amid a crumbled section of the wall about three leagues from Tular.

But the reconnaissance of Tular was not her only duty.

After sending Hunt off with the children at dawn, the group had set a hard pace around the shores of Aii'shan, reaching the Southwall as the sun set. The plan was to enter Tular at midnight—but once inside, a distraction would be needed to buy them time to find the Basilisk Gate and destroy it.

The original plan had been to coordinate a simultaneous attack on Tular. Desert warriors, numbering over a thousand, marched around the far side of Aii'shan, approaching Tular from the opposite direction. Their forces would attack when the moon reached the highest point in the sky. It was Sy-wen's duty to play pigeon this night and deliver the detailed plan to the commander of the desert warriors.

Fires in the desert, Ragnar'k sent to her.

She turned her attention back outward. Far ahead, in the shadow of the Southwall, a hundred fires could be seen, spreading out as far as the shore of Aii'shan. It had to be the encamped desert forces. Ragnar'k sensed her urgency and swept more swiftly toward the gathered men.

But as they neared the site, what had appeared to be campfires were in fact massive bonfires. With Ragnar'k's keen vision, she could make out men staked within the flames, bodies contorted by the searing heat. By the glow of the bonfires, she spotted pale, winged creatures—skal'tum—and other strange beasts crawling among the dead. Desert scorpions the size of small dogs skittered atop the corpses. From the sands, snakes as thick around as her waist writhed up, bellies bulging with their swallowed prey. And here, too, sand sharks dove and gnashed in the blood-soaked sands. Throughout the carnage, rats and carrion birds feasted on all that was left, covering bodies from head to foot, fighting for a bite of flesh.

Without being told, Ragnar'k swung away and swept far out over Aii'shan on the way back to join their party. There would be no other attack on Tular. They were on their own this night. Wordlessly, Ragnar'k glided back in a wide circle as tears clouded Sy-wen's eyes. The image of the slaughter would live long in her heart, but she allowed it to steel her, too. The horror that roosted in Tular had to be destroyed.

In silence, they flew the final leagues and dove to land in the sands near where the group was hidden. Innsu rose from his hiding place, bow in hand. He whistled to the others.

From the rocks, Joach, Kesla, and Richald appeared. Sy-wen stared at their numbers. *Six.* How could so few win where a thousand warriors had failed?

Sometimes the smallest fish escapes between the teeth of the shark.

Sy-wen patted the neck of her large companion, hoping he was right.

Kesla must have sensed her despondency. "What's wrong? You're back much earlier than we expected you."

Sy-wen climbed from the dragon's neck. She sent her love to the great heart inside, then lifted her hand away. The magick reversed itself amid a flurry of scale and cloud, and Kast stood beside her once again. He stepped and wrapped an arm around her, pulling her tight.

"I'm sorry," he whispered in her ear.

She sank against him, needing his warmth and touch.

Kast faced the group. "The desert legion has been destroyed. Carrion eaters and worse feed upon the remains."

Innsu moved nearer with a cloak for Kast. "How could that be? They were a thousand of our fiercest warriors."

Sy-wen answered. "The evil here has grown stronger, fed on the blood of your own children." She explained in detail what she had seen, including the sharks encircling Tular. "It was as if the desert had turned against them."

Kesla's face paled in the rising moonlight. "Then how can we hope to succeed? If the desert is already corrupted, we've lost before we've even begun."

Sy-wen pushed out of Kast's arms. "No, if we lose heart, we give the evil power over *us*. We must not give up hope."

Joach stepped forward and touched Kesla's arm. "Sy-wen is right. We'll find a way."

KESLA KNELT IN THE SAND, UNMOVING. THE RUINS OF TULAR LAY A half league away, but it seemed much closer. The tumbled pile of sandstone filled the world ahead of her. With the moon full overhead, it was nearly as bright as day.

Kesla squinted and made out the line where the sharks roiled in the sand. She had spent half the night searching for some break in the ring of death, circling the entire curtain wall. It seemed impossible. They had considered having Ragnar'k ferry them over to the city, but judged this option only as a last choice, since the presence of a dragon flapping back and forth over the walls might draw more attention than they wanted.

Then, a short time ago, from out of the desert, a possible answer had appeared. Innsu had spied a single rider, racing atop a frothing malluk. From the black sash across his red desert robes, it was clearly an outlaw, most likely one of the cowards who had fled the caravan. Innsu had strung an arrow on his bow, meaning to take him out before he alerted Tular, but Joach had pushed his arm down.

"If he's heading to Tular," Joach had argued, "perhaps he can show us a way through the sharks."

They had all agreed it was worth the risk and had sent Kesla to spy upon him. She had sped after the rider on her lithe legs, sliding from shadow to shadow with her assassin-trained stealth.

She now knelt beside a boulder, no more than the length of five malluks from the rider. He had slowed his mount at the edge of the roiling sands. The road to the open gates ahead was blocked.

As Kesla spied, the outlaw tossed back his hood. His dark hair was unkempt, and a pale scar shaped like a spider blazed on his left cheek. From his cloak, he tugged out a small object. It hung from a braided cord around his neck. He slipped it over his head and held it at arm's length ahead of him. Kesla squinted but could not make out what swayed at the end of the cord. But whatever it was, it cast off a poisonous greenish light.

The rider lifted his object higher. Was it some signal to unseen eyes? But Kesla noticed his attention was not on the crumbled watchtowers flanking the city gates, but upon the sands ahead.

She heard him mumble a prayer of protection under his breath. But it was no spell, only a simple desert supplication taught all children.

The outlaw urged his mount another step forward, but it balked at the churning sands, its nostrils scenting the danger there. The rider took a whip to his mount and got it to take a small step forward. He again lifted his glowing talisman.

As the sick light spread over the deadly sands, the sharks fled from it, diving away with a frantic flip of their leathery tails. A path opened.

Encouraged and clearly relieved, the rider whipped the malluk again and slowly drove the beast forward. Ahead, the sharks fled from the glow of his talisman and extended a safe passage toward the waiting gates. The gait of the malluk increased as it sensed the sharks to either side. The lumbering beast shuffled forward while the sand sharks swept up behind it, closing in once again after the green light had passed.

Kesla squinted at the phenomenon. The outlaw's pendant must act as some protective ward, aglow with black magicks.

In his small island of safety, the outlaw continued to work his way toward Tular.

Kesla rose from her hiding spot and hurried forward. She knew she would have only this single chance. With a flick of her wrist, she loosed her climbing line and spun the trio of trisling hooks at the end of the braided silk rope.

She took careful aim, adding her own silent prayer, then cast out her line. The hooks flew as swift as any arrow, flying past the rump of the malluk. Once they reached her target, Kesla snapped her wrist. The hooks latched onto the cord from which the glowing talisman hung and snatched it from the outlaw's surprised fingers.

With her catch hooked, Kesla flung her arm backward and cartwheeled away, dragging the line back over her in a smooth arch. Rolling to her feet, she lifted a hand and caught the flying talisman in her palm. She shook free the trisling hooks and clutched the prize in her fingers.

Across the way, she saw the outlaw swing around in his saddle, a curse on his lips. Outlaw and assassin stared across at each other. Then the realization of the danger struck the rider as his mount suddenly reared, its neck stretched in a silent bellow of agony.

With the glowing protection gone, the sharks swamped back over the little island of security. The malluk's hind legs began to sink into the sand, devoured from below. The outlaw pulled his feet higher up in the saddle and scrambled away from the bloody sands. He crouched atop his mount's shoulder, his eyes wide with terror, his face pale.

At the last moment, he leaped from the beast's shoulder, aiming back for the road. But the malluk spasmed in death, throwing his balance. The man tumbled into the sands. Without a pause, he shot back to his feet, trying to spring away once again in a mad leap. But as he sailed upward, a monstrous bull shark shot out from the sand and caught him in midair, clamping his midsection and snapping him in half. Blood fountained as his severed torso flew. Other sharks burst up, snatching, biting, ripping. By the time his carcass landed, it was unrecognizable as a man. Behind him, his mount fared no better.

Kesla turned away, remembering the caravan of terrified children. She felt sorrow for the death of the poor, mindless malluk behind her; but for the outlaw, she felt nothing.

Kesla glanced down and stared at her glowing prize.

From the cord hung a large, serrated tooth of a sand shark.

JOACH FOLLOWED KESLA THROUGH THE GATES OF TULAR, CROUCHING in a watchtower's shadow. Joach studied the arrow slits and parapets for any sign of movement. Nothing. It was as if the city were as empty as it appeared. He squinted beyond the gates. The moon shone directly overhead, full and bright. The ruins of the ancient castle ahead were a mix of silver and shadow.

Behind him, the others hurried past the threshold, panting. Richald was last, leaning on his crutch. He glanced with a scowl as the sharks ate away the path behind them. Joach followed his gaze. The way back was again a sea of churning sand. "What now?" the elv'in asked.

"We forge on," Kesla said. She lowered her arm from which the stolen talisman hung and hid it back under her cloak.

Though the night was cool, everyone's faces shone with nervous sweat. The path through the sharks had frayed at their nerves—especially with the stripped bones of the malluk poking up from the sand. Innsu took the lead from here, running lightly on his toes as he guided them to the deeper shadows.

Weapons appeared in everyone's hands. Last night, the blades and arrowheads had been dipped in the blood of the skal'tum killed by Ragnar'k. By fouling their weapons, they had given the edges the ability to slice through the dark protections of the skal'tum, offering some defense against the monstrous beasts.

As they worked through the ruins, Kesla kept to Joach's side, while Kast and Sy-wen flanked Richald behind them. They all moved silently, watching for hand signals from Innsu to move from shelter to shelter.

Joach stared at the toppled spires and scorched walls. He could only imagine the old war that had wrested Tular from the ghouls. In his head, the boom of catapults and the strident wail of battle horns echoed. He pictured the flaming arcs of dire magicks, the screams of the dying. For a moment, he could almost smell the balefire in the air. Joach's fingers tightened on his sword's grip, remembering the thrill of magick coursing out from him, tied to his spirit and focused through a poi'wood staff. The stump of his wrist suddenly itched with the phantom memory of gripping Greshym's staff. He rubbed the smooth wrist on his hip with a pained expression, trying to erase the flare of desire.

Kesla glanced at his movement, her eyes asking if he was all right. He waved his sword tip forward.

With a worried nod, Kesla crept around the broken bust of a huge statue, lying on its side in the sand, half buried. Joach hurried under the gaze of its sand-scoured eye, unable to escape the feeling of being watched, studied like a scurrying bug. But as much as he searched, nothing threatened.

Slowly, as the moon crossed above them, they worked through the ruins without incident, aiming in a zigzagging pattern toward the opening in the Southwall that led into the inner chambers and tunnels. At last they found Innsu crouched on his ankles beside a low wall, his back against the stone.

He waited until they were all lined up beside him, then motioned around the corner of the wall. His voice was the whisper of sand over rock. "The way lies unguarded."

They all readied themselves, steeling their resolves.

"An open yard lies between us and the opening. We must move swiftly. I spy several openings in the wall's face."

"Watchers?" Kesla asked.

Innsu shrugged.

Richald half crawled toward them. "I can help. Sand lies thick all around. A slight breeze should cough up a bit of dusty cover."

"Could the magick alert those within?" Joach asked.

"Not if I ply the winds with care. The night winds are already sharp and gusty. It would not take much to guide its flow here for a brief moment."

Innsu shrugged again. "It's worth trying."

Joach nodded.

Richald leaned back against the sandstone wall, his eyelids lowering as he touched his power. A bit of elemental fire danced along his fingertips, but it was a weak trickle. "Be ready," Richald said. "On my word."

Kesla leaned a moment against Joach, a silent gesture of support. She raised her desert scarf across her mouth and nose. The others followed suit, waiting, tense.

"Now!" Richald whispered.

As a group, they rushed around the corner as a sudden gust raced through the ruins, coughing up a small sandstorm before it. Joach and the others disappeared within it. They ran toward the black tunnel entrance, sand stinging their eyes and winds whipping their cloaks.

Kast half carried the limping Richald with him.

Joach glanced up at the Southwall. Lost in the sandstorm, its heights were barely discernable. Ahead, a slightly darker shadow in the blank wall of swirling sand marked their goal. Innsu was first through, followed closely by Kesla.

At the entrance, Kesla spun around to urge the party forward, waving an arm. Joach urged his legs to move faster, his vision blurred by stinging tears. But he was not too blind to miss a pale shadow burst from deeper in the tunnel.

Innsu suddenly flew backward into the sandy yard, his curved sword sailing away. As the man landed on his back, Joach saw the bloody claw marks strafed across his chest.

Kesla dove out of the tunnel after him, moving with an assassin's speed.

Behind her, on her heels, skal'tum boiled out of the tunnel. The lead beast snatched at her but only caught her cloak. Kesla fought to shed her garment.

In the yard, Innsu rolled to his feet in the face of the onslaught. Daggers appeared in both hands, but he was too late to save himself. His body spasmed as the poison in the claw wounds struck his heart. His arms jerked as he fell. The daggers flew from the dead man's hands and buried themselves in the eyes of the skal'tum that clutched Kesla. The beast fell backward with a wail.

Kesla rolled free and raced to join Joach and the others gathered in the yard. "Innsu." She sobbed. But now was not the time for mourning.

From the tunnel, more skal'tum poured into the yard, while underfoot, monstrous scorpions shook free of their subterranean nests and danced toward the group, poisoned tails raised in threat.

"Behind!" Kast yelled.

Joach glanced over a shoulder and saw the sands roil and churn, driving toward them. It was the sand sharks again, closing off any retreat, driven to a thrashing fury.

A trap.

Sy-wen moved closer to Kast. "We can flee with Ragnar'k. Carry everyone away."

Joach backed away. What choice did they have? He began to nod when Richald threw down his crutch.

"No!" he said coldly, and shoved back the sleeves of the robe. "Flee now, and all is lost. I won't allow it." He jammed both arms toward the rushing monsters. Back arching, he drew upon all the energy in his body.

Energy cascaded brightly along his bared forearms, and a fierce gale slammed into the yard. Sand blew up with a scream of winds and struck the skal'tum with the force of a hammer. Beasts tumbled against the wall. Scorpions flew in the grip of whirlwinds and cracked against the unyielding stone.

"Run!" Richald said, driving his arms apart and blowing a way clear to the tunnel. "I can't hold this wind for long."

"Richald . . ." Joach began to argue, but he knew the elv'in was right. If any chance to destroy the Weirgate existed, it had to be now. Whatever evil had rooted here was already close to consuming the desert. He remembered his journey to the silver stream in the dream desert and the sight of the black whorl of disease consuming and spreading.

Richald met his eyes. The elv'in prince's face was hard and proud, but behind the sharp features, Joach saw the trembling strain as he reined the winds, and also a twinge of fear: a brave man who knew his death had come. "Go," Richald said between tight lips. " 'As long as we live, there's always hope.' "

Joach recognized his own words, spoken to Richald as the elv'in fought to hold his burning ship together. He understood the unspoken acknowledgment behind the prince's words. Richald would not lose heart this time. "Thank you, Richald."

The prince nodded, then turned his full attention forward, shoulders hunching as he fed all his power into a final gale of sandy winds. "Hurry!"

Joach led the way, bent against the winds that tugged at his cloak like a maddened dog. He rushed down the narrow path as scorpions and winged monsters fought the full assault of the wind. The tunnel ahead lay empty.

He dove into it and was followed quickly by the others. He stopped at the entrance and turned to face Richald. The elv'in's arms trembled. He stumbled backward.

Kesla grabbed Joach's sleeve and tugged out the shark tooth pendant to light the dark tunnel behind him. "We must be off, lose ourselves in these tunnels before they break free."

Joach frowned. Her plan was shortsighted. As soon as Richald was overwhelmed, the skal'tum would hunt them, scour the tunnels for their blood. Another plan was needed.

Joach shook free of Kesla and bared his forearm. He drew his sword across the flesh of his arm.

"What are you doing?" Kast asked, sheltering Sy-wen behind him.

Wincing at the sharp pain, Joach held out his arm and dribbled a solid trail of blood across the entrance. He intoned words to draw himself away, slipping into the dream desert, drawn easily by the amount of spilled blood.

As he concentrated on the red line in the sand, focusing his attention, a scorpion pounced to the tunnel's entrance. He barely saw it, lost between the dreaming and the real. The poisoned creature raced toward his leg, but before it could strike, a dagger impaled it between its stalked eyes, pinning it to the sand.

Kesla retrieved her weapon from its twitching body, then kicked it aside. "Hurry, Joach. Richald weakens."

Ahead, Joach saw a skal'tum scrabble out of the sandy gale, crouching. But its prey was not Joach.

"It's going for Richald!" Kast said.

Joach fought to keep his attention focused. A moment more. Then new movement caught his eye—not out in the courtyard of Tular, but in the dream desert itself. Someone rose from the sands off to his left. The visitor had been sitting near where the bright silver river wound through the empty sands. Even from the distance, Joach recognized the familiar figure. It was Shaman Parthus.

"Let me help you," Parthus said. The shaman stepped forward with the unnatural speed of this landscape, closing in swiftly, but Joach knew he had no more time.

Even as Parthus reached his side, Kesla cried out, "Richald!" Beyond the tunnel's entrance, the screaming winds died.

Joach snatched at the lines of power between the two worlds and fed his spirit into the dream sands. "Do my will!" he urged, and flung his arm high.

At his command, a wave of sand swept up to fill the tunnel's entrance, closing off the yard.

Though he had willed it, Joach still stumbled backward, stunned as he snapped back into the real world. Kast caught him, but Joach struggled back up. "We must hurry," he said, eyeing the sculpted structure. "I don't know how long this pile of sand will hold them back."

Kast touched the wall as Kesla held her glowing talisman higher. "It's not sand," the large man said. "It's rock."

Sy-wen ran her fingers along its surface. "Sandstone."

Joach felt the wall himself. It was solid. "Must be the flow of power here," he mumbled, remembering how the energy of Greshym's staff had transformed his first dream sculpture into rock—but he was not entirely convinced. He recalled the figure that had shared the dream desert and frowned. "Or maybe it was something Shaman Parthus did? He said he could help."

"Shaman Parthus?" Kesla glanced at him.

Joach shook his head. "It's not important. Let's find where they hid this cursed basilisk and end this horror."

Kesla nodded and turned with her talisman toward the dark tunnel, her face cast in a sickly green glow. "But where do we begin to search?"

GRESHYM KICKED RUKH OUT OF HIS WAY AS HE STALKED FROM HIS little cave out into the moonlight desert. "Curse that boy's rashness!" He thumped his staff into the sand. "He's going to get himself turned into fodder for those bloody beasts before he's served his purpose."

Leaning on his staff, Greshym sighed and shook his head. Deep inside, though, he was impressed with Joach's abilities. The boy grew quickly in skill. It had taken only a little of Greshym's dark magick to fortify Joach's sandstone wall. He would make a great sculptor one day—that is, if he lived long enough.

"Mmmaster," Rukh grumbled, nose close to the ground. "I kill meat."

Turning, Greshym eyed the gutted trio of burrow dogs. "Rodents. I'm burning away my energies waiting for that boy only to have him slip out of my grasp, and the gnome brings me burrow dogs." Rolling his eyes, Greshym held out his palm.

Rukh, ever obedient, rushed to fill his hand with one of the carcasses. Greshym sniffed at the bloody and raw meat, then glanced back to his tunneled cave. "It seems we are what we eat." He used the few teeth still rooted in his gums to tear the flesh from the tiny bones, chewing thoughtfully.

"But at least the boy's here, so close," Greshym said, wiping his lips on his sleeve. "And we know where he's heading." Filling his stomach with more meat, Greshym felt fueled enough for the final battle. The time of waiting and planning was over.

Tossing aside the bones, he swung back to the cave. "This time I'll be ready."

* * *

KESLA CREPT DOWN THE CORRIDOR, EARS PRICKED FOR ANY NOISES. With her assassin training, she could identify a mouse's pittering footfalls and tell you if it was a male or a female. But with the furtive whispers and sudden scrape of a boot heel on rock echoing from the others behind her, it was hard to concentrate. She cringed at their noises, sure it would attract whatever other monsters lurked in the darkness.

She held her shark tooth talisman higher, but it shed little light to guide their way from here. Three paths branched out from this hall. But which to take? Since entering the tunnels, the way had been a straight shot into the heart of the Southwall, but now a decision had to be made.

Kesla turned with her pendant in hand. "I don't know," she whispered. "I could explore each on my own and try to determine the best path."

"And how would you know?" Kast asked. "I doubt you'll come upon a sign with an arrow, saying *Basilisk lies this way*."

Kesla opened her mouth to argue, but Joach gripped her wrist and turned her to face him. "We stay together," he insisted. His eyes seemed to grow brighter in the gloom.

"Wait!" Sy-wen pointed to the shark's tooth.

Kesla glanced at it, not understanding.

Sy-wen took it from her, then quickly marched to each tunnel and held up the talisman. Upon reaching the third tunnel, it flared brighter. "I noticed it," Sy-wen explained, "when Joach turned Kesla around. For some reason, its light shines more boldly when pointed this way. This must be the correct path."

Kast frowned. "But the path to what? More sharks?"

"If it's somehow attuned to the monsters here," Kesla said, "Kast may be right."

"No," Joach said, "it grows in power as it nears the source of its energy—the Weirgate."

"How can you be so sure?" Kast asked.

"I can't, but what other choice do we have? We have one out of three odds of choosing the correct tunnel. I say we follow the magick."

Kast shrugged. "So let's follow the magick."

Kesla retrieved the pendant and set out down the side tunnel. The path from here was as convoluted as a fire ant's nest: tunnels twisting and turning, crossing and undercutting, passing through chambers both small and large. At one point, they were even forced to crawl. By now they were thoroughly lost. Kesla insisted she could find the way back, but when Kast kept asking, her answers became less and less assured.

"Follow the magick," Kast grumbled. "We might as well follow a blind rat."

"There's a light ahead," Sy-wen whispered, drawing them all to a halt.

Kesla closed her fist around the talisman. With the glow so close to her own eyes, she had missed it. She lowered the shark tooth into her cloak's pocket. Far ahead, past a turn in the tunnel, a fiery light flickered, casting a bloody tinge on the sandstone walls. As she stared, Kesla realized the glow was not *flickering*, but rather *pulsing*, like the beat of some massive heart.

The four glanced at each other. Then Joach moved forward, taking the lead. They proceeded slowly, stopping often to listen. Not a sound whispered. It was as if they had the entire Southwall to themselves.

Joach crept along the wall, sword pointed forward, until they reached the curve. He paused and motioned for the group to hang back while he went ahead to investigate. Once they had gathered, Joach took a deep breath, regripped his sword, and slipped around the corner.

Kesla leaned against the sandstone wall, biting her lip against the tension, imagining the horrors ahead.

Joach reappeared almost instantly. "The tunnel dead-ends into a chamber. It's empty." Relief was thick in his voice.

"The Weirgate?" Kast asked.

"It's there. The Basilisk Gate stands in the room's center." Joach swung around. "Let's go."

As a group, they hurried around the tunnel's turn and indeed a room lay at the passage's end. It was circular in shape, with four torches hanging on the wall. The flames seemed to ebb and flow, causing the pulsing glow.

Joach noticed her attention as they approached the room. "It must have something to do with the Weirgate."

Kesla nodded. His answer did not calm the tiny hairs on her arm from quivering. She had the oddest sensation of having walked this path before. It was as if an old memory were trying to surface with each step she took. She had a sudden urge to flee. Something waited for them in there—and it wasn't just the Weirgate.

Kesla reached the room's threshold and held back. She could not bear to move inside. She studied the chamber from her vantage.

In the room's center, a monstrous black sculpture rested atop the sandy floor. Its surface, rather than reflecting the firelight, seemed to eat the torches' glow. Even the room held a chill so unlike the desert, as if the black stone had sucked all the warmth from the space.

Kesla stared at the beast that had plagued their people both now and in ages past. It had the front parts of some foul carrion bird: sharp black beak, a ruffle of ebony feathers, and talons dug deep into the sand. But the rest of its body was that of a serpent, scaled and coiled behind it. It appeared bunched, as if it were poised and about to strike. Its ruby eyes glowed with a baleful light, seeming to stare only at her.

Joach turned from where he stood. "The nightglass dagger," he hissed. "Let us be done with this."

She swallowed hard, dreading to enter the room, but she knew she had no choice. It was a path she was born to walk. And as she stepped into the room, an old memory buried deep inside her swelled. She stumbled as images spun across her vision: swaying trees in the evening's breeze, the reflection of the moon on still water, a tumble of sandstone homes stacked like a child's toy blocks—and something else, something wrapped in a dark cloak moving toward her. She closed her eyes, gasping, suddenly dizzy. She never felt herself swoon, but found her knees striking the sand.

Joach was already at her side. "Kesla!"

She stared around her. Only a few spans from her knees, below the hooked beak of the basilisk, she spotted something she had missed. A pool of black glass, as if the monstrous beast had drooled blood into the sand at its feet. It was nightglass like her dagger, like the lake of Aii'shan. She felt herself grow weak at the sight of it. The small pool seemed more terrible than the beast that towered over it.

"The nightglass dagger," Joach urged.

She nodded, too weak to stand, and slipped the shard of glass from its sheath. She held it out to Joach. "Do it. I cannot . . .

Something . . . something . . ." She shook her head and could not make eye contact with Joach.

"It's all right," Joach said, taking the dagger.

"Hurry," Kast said somewhere behind her. "We don't know how long we'll be alone here."

Kesla knew the Dre'rendi warrior was mistaken. They were not alone now. She knew eyes spied on them, laughing eyes, the same eyes that had glowed from the dark-cloaked figure from her dream.

But Joach was not deterred by her misgivings. He rushed the statue with the dagger, aiming for its heart with the blade. With the weapon raised high, the vein of wit'ch blood glowed brightly through the dark glass.

Hurry, Joach, she silently prayed. *End this horror.*

Joach drew back with all the strength in his shoulder, then plunged the dagger into the beast with a shout of triumph.

Kesla heard a bright shattering sound, followed by a gasp from Joach.

He stepped away, glancing to her, then back to the basilisk. It was unharmed. The nightglass dagger lay in a thousand brilliant shards in the sand, half its length shattered. Joach held the jagged hilt in his hand, stunned.

Shock drove Kesla to her feet. "It failed!"

Joach stumbled away. "I don't understand."

As they all stared in silence, a tinkle of dark laughter rose from the basilisk. The torches dimmed, then blew brighter, flickering toward the ceiling.

"We must flee!" Kesla yelled, sensing the approach of the lurker.

They all raced for the door, but the sand would not let them escape. Sandstone claws grew out of the floor and grabbed their ankles, holding them tight.

Kast hacked at the stone with his sword, but the cleaved wounds healed as fast as they formed. Finally, another clawed hand rose from the sand and slapped the blade from his hand. Still, Kast was not to be beaten. He swung to his mate. "Sy-wen, the dragon."

She reached for him, fingers spreading to touch his seahawk tattoo. "I have need—"

Before she could make contact, her legs were yanked out from under her by the claws. She struck the sand hard and was dragged away by her ankles to the far side of the room. Once well out of reach, she was allowed to stand again.

Kast yelled to her. "Sy-wen!"

"I'm all right," she called back.

All the while, the laughter grew in volume, as if that which opposed them was amused by their efforts. Their attentions returned to focus on the basilisk. Kesla, closer than any of the others, realized the true source of the sick laughter. It was *not* the basilisk. The laughter rose from the small pool of nightglass at its feet.

Again a swirl of images rushed around her, dizzying her.

Words now rose from the black pool. "It struggles to remember."

Her vision blurred. It seemed as if a dark cloud were rising from the pool, mists on the water. But gasps behind her helped her focus. It was not an illusory figment. Something was rising from the pool in a haze of smoky mists—something cloaked, something dark.

Kesla remembered the brief image from a moment ago. *Moonlight on water, trees, and a black, cloaked figure coming toward her.*

Before her now, the cloaked figure grew more solid as it pulled fully into this world. She knew it was the same as in the dream.

He spoke from beneath his cowl, bending toward her, his deep voice full of mischief. "A girl, this time. How amusing. No wonder you hid from me for so long."

Kesla found herself answering. "I . . . I don't know what you're talking about."

The cloaked figure straightened. "Of course you don't. That is the way of the desert. It likes its little secrets."

"Who are you?"

The stranger shook back his dark hood to reveal a surprisingly handsome face. It was as if white ice had been carved by the most skilled artisan, framed by hair as white as newly fallen snow. Only his eyes burned with the fiercest red fire—and Kesla knew it was a fire more likely to burn with frost than with the heat of a true flame.

"Have you forgotten your old friend?" he offered gently. "Do you not know me?"

Kesla did indeed recognize the face, both from ancient texts and old stories. But it could not be. He was long dead.

"Come. Enough with these games. Name me as I name you."

"Ashmara," she whispered with a numb tongue. "The ghoul."

His bloodless lips smiled. "Now, Shiron, was that so hard?"

20

JOACH RECOGNIZED THE TWO NAMES FROM KESLA'S TALE OF Aii'shan, *Shiron and Ashmara:* the two combatants whose magickal battle had melted the sands below the Southwall into black glass.

Kesla stared in horror at the pale figure wrapped in a dark cloak of mists. "How . . . ?"

The figure waved a hand. "After our battle so long ago, my bones rested deep under the lake you've named Aii'shan, frozen in black glass. But when Tular was taken by the Burning Master, my shade was drawn back here, to guard over the new basilisk." He brushed his white fingers across the dark feathers of the monstrous statue, then turned to Kesla. "But it appears the desert sensed I had escaped its glass prison. It birthed another dream, breathing life again into another of its creations—another scion to bring its battle to Tular."

"I don't know what you're talking about."

Ashmara beckoned with a hand, and the sands under Kesla flowed, drawing her closer to him. Joach tried to grab her, reaching out instinctively with his right hand, but only a stump touched her cloak. Unable to escape, Kesla was dragged before the small black pool upon which Ashmara stood.

The shade bent and stared at her face. "You really *don't* know what you are, do you?" He straightened, laughing deep and long.

Kesla stared boldly at Ashmara, but Joach saw her shoulders

tremble. Was she more scared of the ghoul or of what the monster was about to reveal? He longed to protect her—but how? She had a right to know. His only regret was not telling her earlier. Maybe he could have spared her this pain, a pain Ashmara was clearly enjoying.

The shade smiled. "You are the desert's child, my dear. This age's Shiron, born again from the sands. Nothing more than a dream given substance. A clever desert mirage." He pointed to the sandy hands that gripped her ankles. "In truth, you have no more life than one of my creations."

Kesla shook her head. "It cannot be."

"Come now. In your heart, you know I speak truly. I can hear it in your voice."

Kesla swung away. "No . . ." She stared back at Joach for help.

He glanced down to the sand. "What he says is true, Kess. Shaman Parthus knew the truth from reading his bones." He glanced back up and saw the hurt and fear in her eyes.

"Wh-why?"

Joach knew there were so many questions behind that single choked word: Why had he not told her? Why had he kept this secret? Why had he made motions as if he loved her, a woman who was not real? Joach had no answers.

She covered her face and turned away.

A cruel laugh flowed from the shade of Ashmara. "It seems the desert never changes. Sending a child to do its battle." A sand-sculpted hand rose from the sand, picking up a shard of the shattered dagger in its fingers. "And it seems the desert never learns any new tricks. This stone basilisk is stronger than my old sand-sculpted original. Nightglass has no power over it."

Kesla lowered her hands, half sobbing. "If . . . if you are truly Ashmara, why are you doing this? How can you help poison the desert? As wicked as you were, these are still your lands."

Ashmara cocked his head. "There must be an echo in this room. You spoke the same words when we met last, attempting to appeal to my heart." He laughed again, a darkly cruel sound. "My bones are forever frozen in glass, put there by the desert itself when last we battled. Why should I care if it's destroyed?"

"Because it's still your home!" Kesla lunged out with a hidden dagger, moving as swift as a desert snake, stretching out from where she was held—but the blade merely passed harmlessly through the misty shade.

Ashmara simply smiled. "You don't seem to be having much luck with daggers this night." A spear of sand jutted out and knocked the blade from her hands. The dagger flew and buried itself in the sands. "Now let's end this once and for all. If you are so in love with your desert, then let me help you return to it." Ashmara waved a hand.

The sandy fists that held Kesla sank down into the floor, dragging her down with them.

"You buried me once," Ashmara said. "Now it's my turn to return the favor."

Kesla struggled to free herself, but to no avail. Her legs disappeared into the sand.

"We have to help her," Kast hissed, fighting to pry his own bonds with his sword.

But Joach did not move. He knew another course was necessary. He remembered the words of Shaman Parthus, that Kesla's mission to A'loa Glen may not have been solely to wet the nightglass dagger in his sister's blood, but also to draw him—another sculptor—to the desert. And now Joach knew why: he was brought here to fight Ashmara. One sculptor against another. But how could he hope to win here—a novice against a master? It was futile.

Still, Joach watched Kesla sink slowly into the sand and brought the jagged edge of the broken nightglass dagger to the stump of his right arm. He dug its tip deep, and blood flowed heavily into the sand at his feet. Joach winced, eyes closing, and sank with his blood into the dream desert.

The chamber walls around him grew misty. The glowing sands of the dream desert shone through them now. The two worlds merged, one atop the other. His blood flowed into both, bright as spilled wine.

Joach stared around at the dream landscape. Though the dunes in the distance glowed brightly, the sands under his feet were stained dark. He turned, and with his vision split between the real and the dream, he saw the basilisk statue perched atop the silver river, its talons dug deep into its substance.

In the dream desert, he watched the Land's energies slowly churn, sucked away into the whirling pit known as the Weir, the darkness feeding on this vein of power like some monstrous black leech. But that was not all he saw. He watched as the dark stain spread out from here into the desert, corrupting all it touched.

Joach suddenly understood the Dark Lord's goal here. The Gul'gothal monster must have grown tired of twisting the little bits of elemental power found in the Land's people. In the past, the Black Heart had used shards of ebon'stone as a focus in which to twist an elemental's energy, forging each one into an ill'guard. Now he plied the same dark magick on a much larger scale. Using the giant statues, he sought to corrupt the world's energy directly, to forge the very Land into an ill'guard creation—and he was close to succeeding!

A cry drew Joach's attention back to the real world. Kesla was waist-deep in the sand, fighting to hold herself up with her hands. But new pincers had risen from the sand, clamping on her wrists. Kesla writhed in their grip.

Again, with the two worlds merged, Joach was able to see the dark strands of power that linked Ashmara's sculpted creations to the dream desert: a tangled black web. Instead of a link by blood, Joach realized the power came from the Weir itself, arising from the black stain.

Joach cringed from the power here but knew their only chance to fight it lay in his own elemental blood. He concentrated on the spilled pool at his feet, touching the dreaming magick there. He lashed out with his own energy, slashing at the threads of power, severing them instantly.

In the real world, Joach watched with satisfaction as the sandy fists created by Ashmara fell away to plain sand. Kesla broke free and pushed from the sands. Ashmara grabbed for her, but his fingers had no substance. She rolled away from him.

Kast also broke free, rushing up to Sy-wen, who immediately placed her palm on his cheek. "I have need of you!"

Ashmara, initially startled by Joach's assault, was quick to realize the source of the new magick. His red eyes flared with anger as he swung to face Joach. "A sculptor!" The ghoul's arm shot up, and new sandy creations grew into existence—not only clawed hands, but also monstrous beasts, climbing right out of the sands.

Joach gasped at the play of power in the dream desert. Black threads twined and raced, feeding the new creations. Joach slashed at these, too, but he no longer had the advantage of surprise. Threads re-formed as quickly as he hacked at them. Still, Joach continued his assault. He had no choice.

In the chamber, Kesla dodged the sculpted creatures, moving across the sandy floor with the skill of an assassin.

Behind the basilisk, Ragnar'k had appeared with Sy-wen perched on his shoulder. The dragon ripped into the sandy beasts and hopped about the sand, making a difficult target.

Ashmara, his eyes glowing like two coals, crouched atop his black pool and cast out his attacks. He pointed to Joach. "Kill him!" he directed his new creations.

A beast, a muscled cross of a lion and a bear, scrabbled across the sands toward him.

Joach stepped back, but he had no way to defend himself, not while concentrating on fighting in the dream plane. He attempted to raise his own sculpted creature to battle the beast, but Ashmara's beast tore through his creation with no more effort than Sheeshon had used on his tiny rose. He was too untrained, his efforts too divided.

Kesla appeared at his side. "Give me the dagger," she said breathlessly.

"What?" he managed to squeak out.

She took the broken nightglass dagger from his fingers and swung around just as the lion creature leaped with a silent snarl. Kesla sliced through its throat as it lunged past. Its form dissolved back to sand, washing harmlessly over Joach.

Half crouched, Kesla lifted the nightglass dagger. "It might not work against the basilisk, but as in the past, it can slay dream beasts."

Understanding dawned in Joach. The basilisk of old had been a dream-sculpted creature, slain by the same dagger. So the dagger must, of course, work against *any* dream creation. Its shape did not matter.

Kesla slashed through a hand that tried to grab her. The sandy fingers crumbled away as she straightened.

In the dream desert, Joach watched the dark connection that linked the sculpture explode away with a flash of bright light. Joach remembered a similar sight, long ago, when Elena had tried to grab his poi'wood staff aboard Flint's ship. She had been thrown back with a similar blinding flash of light. The two magicks were deadly to each other: dark and light.

Kesla spun and planted the dagger into the eye of a monstrous snake. It fell away to sand. "Your sister's blood has proven as potent as Sisa'kofa's." She glanced over her shoulder. "I'll protect you. Do what you can to fight Ashmara."

He nodded.

Before she turned away, her eyes met his. "You should have told me."

He swallowed, knowing what she meant. "I . . . I couldn't."

"Why?" She stared hard at him, not allowing him to turn away from this question a second time.

He faced her and spoke rapidly lest he lose heart. "We're all just dust and ashes. What difference does it make if you come from sand? To me, you'll always be a woman." He turned away. "A woman I love."

Joach looked back to her, his heart in his throat. Tears welled in Kesla's eyes. Without a word, she whirled away and slashed the head off some twisted beast.

Joach returned to his own battle, leaving her to defend him. What had finally been admitted between them could never be acted upon unless they first won here. From the dream plane, Joach slashed the ghoul's cords of power. But even aided by Kesla's attacks, no real gains were made.

Ragnar'k tried to attack Ashmara, but the dragon had no more luck than Kesla's dagger. How could you kill a ghost?

As Joach continued his attack, he knew that this stalemate would end in their defeat. Even now, he felt himself weakening. His spirit was not endless. The nightglass dagger would also eventually exhaust its small supply of wit'ch blood. So while Ashmara tapped the bottomless well of the Weir, their energies were limited.

Unless some change tilted the balance, they would be defeated.

A voice spoke at Joach's shoulder—not in the real world but in the dream. "Maybe I can help."

Joach glanced behind him in surprise. The figure seemed to float within the stone of the Southwall, as the real world overlapped the dreamscape. His features were vague as Joach stood twixt the two planes, but he would know the thin man anywhere. "Shaman Parthus!"

Leaning on his old crutch, the elder smiled at Joach. "It seems you could use an extra hand."

GRESHYM ALLOWED A TRUE SMILE TO SHINE. JOACH SHOWED NO sign of suspecting the darkmage hidden behind the sun-bronzed face of the old shaman. He had hurried here once he'd felt the boy pierce the veil between the two planes. Timing was critical. He could not risk the ghoul killing the boy, at least not until he was done with Joach.

While crossing here, Greshym had used his dark arts to spy upon the first skirmishes of the two sculptors. Joach had some innate skill, but he was no match for a fiend with Ashmara's cunning. He now wished Shorkan had not been so skilled at drawing the shade here. Ashmara was a deadly warden, and one who might vanquish Greshym's one chance at regaining his youth.

"How can you help me?" the boy asked. "I thought you had no skill at sculpting."

Joach's form was misty and insubstantial, like the shimmers of heat seen floating above the desert at a distance.

"You are most correct," Greshym said, speaking with the voice of the shaman. "You hover between the dream desert and the world of substance and life. Only a true sculptor can travel that path."

"Then how can you help?"

"I can lend you my strength. Two are stronger than one."

Joach hesitated. "I'm not sure strength is the problem when fighting the shade of a dead man."

Greshym shook his head. "Ashmara can be defeated." He coaxed. "There are secrets I can teach you, from the old texts. Ways to defeat the ghoul."

Joach's form became more substantial as his interest grew, drawing nearer to Greshym in the dream desert. "What old ways?"

Greshym took a step back. For his spell to work, he needed the boy's spirit to enter the dream plane fully. Being no sculptor himself, even he could not reach Joach where he was now. Greshym beckoned with a wave. "It is not something that can be spoken in words. I must teach you, show you."

Joach's form grew crisper. "Then show me."

"I need you to pull yourself fully into the dream plane, where I can share with you." Greshym took another step back, invitingly.

Joach began to step toward him, then paused, almost taunting.

"What are you waiting for? Come to me, boy."

"You'd like that, wouldn't you, *Greshym*?" Joach's mask of naïve openness fell away. Under it was a face hard with suspicion.

Greshym frowned in surprise. He opened his mouth to argue, but the boy's eyes shone slyly. Joach would not be so easily tricked.

"Show yourself," Joach said. "Enough with these false faces. You tricked me once with Elena's form and now think to do so again?"

With an exasperated sigh, Greshym cast away the illusion of Shaman Parthus, returning to his own age-worn body. The small brown cane transformed into his gray stone staff. "Is this better?"

Joach scowled. "What did you do to Shaman Parthus?"

"I needed a new cloak to wear."

"So you killed him?"

Greshym shrugged. "But how did you know it was me?"

"You mentioned Ashmara. Shaman Parthus knew nothing of the ghoul's shade. He could not even see into the dream-sculpting plane. Your knowledge gave you away." Joach began to grow more insubstantial. "Now that you've been caught, begone with your tricks."

"Wait!"

Joach turned away. "We have nothing else to discuss."

Greshym knew he was about to lose the boy completely. If Joach returned to his battle, he was surely doomed. Ashmara would eventually wear the boy down and slay him. That must not happen. "I can tell you how to defeat him."

Joach glanced back, eyes narrowed. "And trust you?"

"It is not *my* trust that will matter, but *yours*."

Joach turned around. "How is that?"

"I offer you a trade. I'll give you the secret to defeating Ashmara, in exchange for your promise to return here to the dream desert."

"Why do you want me there?"

Greshym smiled slyly. "I'm only selling one secret here. But I promise you this: if you honor your word, I will not kill you, trap you, or darken your spirit in any manner. This I swear."

"As if your word has any value," Joach mumbled, but he did not turn away.

"Take my offer or leave it." Greshym gripped his staff tighter. "Save your friends . . . or die here. It's no matter to me.

Joach hesitated. His one hand formed a fist. "Tell me," he said with a tight voice.

"First swear on your sister's life that you'll return here to me."

Joach bit his lip, then reluctantly nodded. "I so swear. But only if your secret truly helps us in defeating Ashmara."

Greshym grinned, relaxing. "Oh, don't worry. If I'm wrong, Ashmara will kill you all."

"Tell me," Joach snapped. "What's the ghoul's secret?"

Shrugging, Greshym used his staff to draw a circle in the dark sand around his feet. "Have you not noticed how Ashmara never steps from his little black glass island?"

Joach's eyes glinted. "What of it?"

"It is his physical link to this plane." Greshym smudged out the scrawled line with the staff's butt end. "Shatter it, and the shade will again be imprisoned with his bones under Aii'shan."

Joach's surprise dissolved the veil between them. He almost snapped fully into the dreamscape, but at the last moment, he drew away again. "It is that simple?"

"Most magick is," Greshym said with a disappointed sneer.

"You'd better not be lying." Joach turned and grew misty again.

Greshym leaned heavily on his staff and called out to Joach. "Be careful, boy. Don't get yourself killed."

SPINNING, KESLA JABBED THE JAGGED END OF THE NIGHTGLASS dagger into the back of a sand-sculpted scorpion, then whirled on her heel to slice the throat of a clawed salamander. Forms blew away into puffs of sand around her. She leaped and rolled as a spike of sandstone shot upward under her.

Gasping, she crouched. She had been trained to run for leagues through a midday desert, but this constant assault wore on her. She had to protect both herself and Joach.

Her only allies were Sy-wen and her dragon. Ragnar'k roared through the chamber, keeping Ashmara busy. Its wings shattered creatures on all sides, while silver-clawed talons ripped through the sand.

But still, the pale ghoul stood on his little pool of nightglass, wrapped in his cloak of dark mists. He seemed little worn by the battle here. In fact, his amusement had grown and he laughed often as he forced Kesla through her paces.

He's playing with us, Kesla realized, *like a cat with a mouse.* She was sure the ghoul could call all manner of real beasts to harry them: the skal'tum, the burrowing black scorpions, sand sharks. But he didn't. He continued to chase them with his dream-sculpted creations, enjoying the challenge, amused by their efforts, immune to any direct assault himself.

"Kesla," Joach said behind her.

She spun and raked a sand serpent's belly. "What?"

He spoke rapidly, while motioning her closer. "I know a way to destroy Ashmara."

"How?"

"The pool of glass under his feet. Destroy it, and his shade will be drawn back to Aii'shan."

"Are you sure?"

He hesitated, then spoke. "No, but it's worth attempting."

"How do we destroy it?"

"I don't know." Joach frowned. "Try using the nightglass dagger."

She nodded. It made a certain sense. The ghoul had remained atop the circle of dark glass. He seemed unable to leave it. "I'll try. But you'll have to defend yourself from here."

"Don't worry about me. I've sent a message to Ragnar'k. He and Sy-wen will keep guard. Just shatter the pool."

Kesla glanced to his face. Their eyes met briefly. So much was still unspoken between them. She spun away before anything else could be said. She slashed and hacked her way through the sand beasts, dropping, rolling, whirling on hand or foot.

She noted Ashmara's attention turn toward her. His red eyes glowed in his pale face. The attacks on her grew fiercer. Her momentum forward slowed. She was fought to a standstill. Did the ghoul sense her new knowledge?

"You move well," Ashmara said from a few paces away.

"Much better than that sallow-limbed thing that met me in Ka'aloo."

Kesla kicked out, bouncing off one sand-sculpted creature and impaling another. The creatures attacked from all sides, a blur of claws and teeth. "It was Shiron that killed you last time, ghoul!" Kesla called back at him.

"No," he answered, his voice bitter. "It was my own foolishness and desire that doomed me. Shiron claimed his blood could cleanse Tular—and I believed him. I could not let the boy escape. I cast out my magick recklessly, drawing off the shared energy of the other sculptors in Tular. But the desert protected the boy. Instead of harming Shiron, our magicks washed over and through him, burning the desert around us, melting it to glass. Only when it was too late did I realize my mistake. I had cast my magick so far and wide that I could not escape the molten desert. My physical form sank into the glass, while my spirit was held tight by Shiron in the dream desert. I could not escape."

Kesla continued to slash and jab with her broken dagger.

All amusement had seeped out of the ghoul with the telling of his tale. "But I will have my victory, my revenge." He glanced over his shoulder at the looming basilisk. "I will see the entire Southern Wastes destroyed."

With the attention of the ghoul momentarily distracted, Kesla leaped atop the back of a scorpion, dodged its sandstone tail, and dove at Ashmara.

He swung around, instinctively lifting an arm in warning, but Kesla flew through his form as if it were air and crashed to the hard nightglass surface.

Ashmara laughed, lowering his arm with a shake of his head. "Still trying to slay the dead?"

Reaching out, Kesla lifted her arm and slammed her dagger into the center of the black pool. Glass fractured in a loud tinkling shatter. Pain flared in her hand. She stared down. The nightglass dagger had shattered completely away. The black pool beneath remained unharmed, not even scratched.

A sinking feeling of despair welled in her chest. "No." She moaned. Not only had she failed, but she had destroyed their only means of slaying the ghoul's dream beasts.

Laughter wafted down from atop her.

Kesla lifted her hand. A chunk of broken nightglass was

pierced through her right palm. She yanked it out, and blood flowed freely from the wound. Though hopeless, she pushed off the hard glass surface, ready to fight with the last breath in her body.

The ghoul's taunting voice seemed to whisper at her ear. "I've enough of this game-playing. It is time to end this." Triumphant laughter flowed.

Kesla shoved up, ready to spring away, but her balance was thrown off as her left hand sank into the loose sand.

The ghoul's laughter cut off abruptly with a sharp cry.

Staring down, Kesla saw that her left hand had melted through the black glass to the soft sand beneath. She lifted and studied her wounded palm. Blood flowed thickly down her wrist. She remembered Ashmara's story: *Shiron claimed his blood could cleanse Tular*.

Understanding dawned in her. Again whispery images of swaying palms and blue waters grew around her. She glanced up and saw the look of horror in Ashmara's red eyes.

"Please . . . don't . . ."

Kesla leaned back to the nightglass pool and swept her bloody hand over its surface. Where her blood touched, the hard glass slowly dissolved back to plain sand.

A howl of agony and terror rose from Ashmara. "No, don't send me back!"

Kesla ignored his screams as surely as he had ignored the terrified cries of all the children bloodied at his feet. She scrubbed her blood across the entire surface. Once the entire pool was covered, she rolled away. Her blood bubbled on the hard surface, transforming glass back to sand.

Standing, Kesla stepped back. Like the glass, the pale face of Ashmara was eaten away. He had no mouth with which to scream, but his eyes shone with agony and despair; then those, too, were consumed by the magick in Kesla's blood.

Soon only empty sand lay before her.

Kesla clenched her bloody fist. *Magick of the desert*. She could no longer hide from the truth spoken from the lips of the ghoul. She was not a woman, only some construct of the desert, a magickal tool used to stab at the evil in Tular.

Though victorious, tears rose in her eyes.

*   *   *

JOACH HURRIED TO KESLA'S SIDE. HE DID NOT NEED THE TEARS TO recognize the grief in her eyes. "What's wrong?" he asked.

She shook her head and stepped away from him.

Before he could question her further, Sy-wen called to them. She hopped from her dragon's neck, and Ragnar'k roiled back down into the naked figure of Kast. "What happened?" Sy-wen asked. "How were you able to drive off the ghoul's shade?"

Kast pulled the shreds of his cloak from the sand and joined them.

Joach explained about his visit with Greshym in the dream desert and about the darkmage's revelation.

"Why was the fiend so helpful?" Kast asked with clear suspicion.

"I made a pact with him," Joach said. "I promised I'd return to the dream desert."

"It's surely a trap," Sy-wen said.

Joach nodded. "No doubt."

"And what of your promise?" Kast asked.

"I'll honor my word," Joach said. "I'll return to the dream desert, but I never promised *when* I'd return. Certainly not today, certainly not tomorrow, maybe not for many, many winters."

Kast grinned. "The darkmage will be waiting a long time."

Joach shrugged. "He's lived five centuries. What's a few more decades?"

Sy-wen glanced over to Kesla, who still stood near where the black glass pool had been. "But what of her trick? Did Greshym reveal that, too?"

"No." Joach stepped toward Kesla and touched her shoulder gently. "What happened here?"

She finally turned, wiping at her eyes. Her voice was as shattered as the nightglass dagger. "The ghoul and Shaman Parthus were right. I'm not real." She shrugged away from his hand. "Like Shiron, my blood contains the magick of the desert, potent enough to heal what's corrupted."

"But you are real," Joach said, reaching out and clutching her arm. He squeezed her wrist. "You're flesh and blood. What does it matter if you weren't born of a man and a woman?"

She stared up at him, fresh tears in her eyes. "It matters to me." She reached down and peeled away his fingers. "And it will to you . . . eventually."

"Never," he said. He sought some way to ease the despair in her voice.

But she had already moved away, stepping toward the basilisk. "I now know how to destroy the Weirgate. My blood will rid the sands of its evil." She stood before the large carved stone, staring up at its baleful red eyes. "I know my role here."

Joach hurried toward her. "Kesla, don't. The Weirgates—"

She lifted her bloody hand and placed it against the feathered stone breast of the basilisk. Her hand sank into its form as if it were only shadow, not solid rock.

"Kesla!"

She glanced over her shoulder, her face a mix of shock and horror. "Joach!"

He leaped at her, grabbing for her cloak. His fingers twisted in the heavy cloth. But Kesla fell forward anyway, as if yanked by the arm. She tumbled into the Weirgate and was gone. Her scream trailed back out, fading farther and farther away, as if sailing down some bottomless well.

Joach still held her cloak in his grip. The rest of her clothes lay in a crumpled pile at the bottom of the statue. He threw aside her cloak and reached to the stone, ready to go after her. But his palm found only cold stone. He ran his fingers over it, searching for a way inside.

The basilisk just stared down at him, cold and menacing.

She was gone.

Joach sank to his knees in the sand. "Kesla!"

A slithering sound of shifting sands drew his attention back up. Sy-wen gasped. Joach watched the ebon'stone serpent slowly begin to uncoil, stretching and curling in the sand. Ruby eyes fueled by darkfire turned in Joach's direction.

The basilisk of Tular lived again.

Book Seven

GUL'GOTHA

21

WITH THE SUN SETTING AT HIS BACK, ER'RIL STOOD AT AN OUT-
cropping overlooking the gorge. Deep below, molten rock
flowed like a river. Even from this height, Er'ril's face grew hot
as he glanced north and south. The gorge extended leagues in
both directions. The d'warf kingdom lay only a short distance
ahead, but there was no way forward from here.

Scouts had been sent in both directions, searching for some
way across. While waiting for their return, the group had set up a
night camp.

Er'ril frowned and headed down the short slope, fleeing from
the heat of the gorge. Since beaching the elv'in skiff in these
lands six days ago, the overland trek had been arduous and
fraught with pitfalls: poisonous rivers, winds tainted by deadly
smokes, barren stretches without a single blade of grass. And now
this impassable molten valley. Er'ril stared around him. Mountains spread in all directions, jagged peaks and clefted gorges. It
was as if they camped inside the fanged mouth of some monstrous beast.

As Er'ril approached the camp, he saw Elena kneeling with
Tol'chuk and Mama Freda. The elder was busy changing the
dressings on the elv'in captain's leg, while Tol'chuk held the
feverish man in place. Elena hovered over them both, worried.
Two days ago, Jerrick had stumbled too near a tigersfang bush. It
had lashed out at him with its vines, lancing his leg with its
finger-length thorns. Wennar had axed the trapped man free, but
his wounds had continued to fester.

"How's Jerrick?" Er'ril asked as he stepped into camp.

Mama Freda wiped her forehead. "The willow bark tea is not
strong enough to break through the poison's hold." She placed

her fingers on the elv'in's wrist and shook her head. "I don't think he'll last till morning." Her voice quavered at this last pronouncement, and her fingers lingered on the captain's hand. Mama Freda and Jerrick, both gray-haired elders, had grown closer on the long march here.

Er'ril frowned. *So much death.* If Jerrick died this night, he would be the third member of the party to fall on the six-day trek to reach this point. They had lost a d'warf scout to a fireworm and another who had stepped on a horned toad buried in the red dirt. The first had died immediately, but the other had screamed for half a day before succumbing to the poisons in the toad.

And now Jerrick . . .

"Maybe my magick can help?" Elena asked for the hundredth time, hands wringing together.

"No," Er'ril said sternly, joining them. "We know this land is attuned to magick. It's dangerous enough without awakening it further."

"But—"

Mama Freda interrupted. "Er'ril is right. Your magick couldn't save him anyway. It would only prolong his suffering." Finished with his wraps, she sat back on her heels, frustrated and worried.

Jerrick's writhing slowed.

Tol'chuk mopped the elv'in's brow with a damp cloth.

The old healer sighed. Tikal, perched on her shoulder, pressed against her cheek. The pet only left her side to relieve itself. Otherwise, it seemed unwilling even to touch this poisoned land. "If only I knew these lands better," Mama Freda said quietly, "I might be able to find a local cure. But I've never seen such a variety of sick creatures and plants."

Wennar spoke as he approached out of the twilight gloom. "None of these ill creatures existed until the Nameless One stepped out of our ancient mines." He glanced around him. "These very mountains were once covered in pine and redwoods; their bowers were full of deer, rabbits, foxes, and badgers."

Er'ril stared at the surrounding landscape as night descended. It was hard to believe Wennar. How could this land have grown so corrupted?

Elena sat atop a smooth stone by the campfire. "If we don't stop these Weirgates, the entire world could become like this."

"But how do we continue from here?" Er'ril glanced over his

shoulder. The eastern skies glowed from the fires of the nearby molten gorge.

"We'll have to hope my scouts find some answer," Wennar said.

Pairs had been sent out, two in each direction, armed with spyglasses. They were to climb the neighboring peaks to look for some end to the gorge, some way around it.

Er'ril glanced around the campfire. With the scouts gone, there were just Wennar and another six d'warves—too few to thwart any real danger. He did not like the odds here. Besides their dwindling numbers, the entire party had grown bone-tired. Many had developed illnesses from the sick air and tainted waters: coughs, fevers, and stomach cramps. But the d'warves seemed to fare the worst: not just from illness, but also from their despairing hearts. They spoke little, just staring numbly at their ravaged homelands.

Elena cleared her throat and pointed up. "A full moon rises this night."

Er'ril turned his attention back to her. He saw the light in her eyes and could guess the intent behind her comment. "You want to risk opening the Blood Diary?"

"If we're to succeed," she said softly, "we'll need every resource available to us."

"But your magick—?" Er'ril started.

"I need cast no magick to bring the spirit of Cho out of the book. The power is inherent in the book, wrapped in the ancient spell your brother cast. It should do nothing to alert whatever wards lie here."

"We don't know that. Perhaps it would be best if we wait until the scouts return."

As if hearing him, a scuffle of rocks sounded. Everyone was immediately on their feet. One of the camp's sentries called out into the darkness and was answered in the d'warvish tongue.

Soon a pair of ragged d'warves stumbled into camp. But they were not alone. Trussed up in ropes and slung between them was a strange purple-skinned creature with bright yellow eyes. It looked somewhat like a frog, especially with its splayed fingers and toes, each digit ending in a little muscular sucker.

"What is that?" Elena asked, bending closer.

Er'ril pushed her slightly back, wary of this creature.

One of the scouts shook his head. "We climbed a ridge and were searching the gorge to the north. It stretches and curves all the way to the horizon. There is no way across in that direction."

Er'ril suppressed a groan.

"But what be this creature?" Tol'chuk asked, pushing up into the firelight. "Can we eat it?"

The purple creature spotted the large og're and began to tremble all over, its yellow eyes wild. It tried to squirm away. "No," it suddenly squeaked from its wide, blubbery lips. "Please, no eat poor Greegrell."

"It talks!" Elena said.

One of its captors shook it. "Quiet down, you stinkin' pile of horse dung."

The creature cowered and whined; its trembling grew more violent.

Elena frowned and moved forward, pushing aside Er'ril's hand. She knelt by the trussed-up creature and placed a palm on its arm. "Shh, it's all right. We're not going to hurt you."

"We caught him trying to steal our spyglass. I set it down on a rock for a moment, but when I turned around, this little bugger was hopping away with it in his grubby little paws."

"It nice thing . . . shiny," the creature whined.

"We only caught it by a well-aimed throw of a stone," the scout finished.

Er'ril rolled his eyes. "What is it?"

Wennar answered. "It's a vorg. I've heard of their foul ilk. They have a crude intelligence, a half notch above goblins. The creatures used to plague miners: stealing tools, defiling shafts with their droppings, even bringing down rockfalls to trap d'warves."

Behind them, Jerrick groaned, thrashing again.

Mama Freda backed to his side. "I'll heat up some more willow bark tea."

The vorg stretched its neck high, attempting to peer over Elena's head. Large yellow eyes blinked at the elv'in. Its slitted nostrils twitched. "Bad pointy poke," he said, following with a slight roaring sound deep in his throat, mimicking the sound of a striking tigersfang bush.

Elena met Er'ril's startled gaze.

Er'ril lowered himself next to the beast. "How do you know what happened to him?" he asked sternly, pointing to Jerrick.

The vorg cringed back from his tone.

Mama Freda spoke up. "If this creature knows about the tigersfang, maybe he knows a cure."

Elena edged Er'ril back, then faced the creature. "Greegrell," she said softly and patted the vorg's hand, "do you know how to help this man?" She nodded back to the elv'in captain.

The vorg relaxed, leaning slightly nearer to Elena. "Greegrell knows."

"You'll show me?"

The toadish creature nodded.

Elena waved for the two scouts to free the vorg's rope.

Wennar stepped forward and kept the scouts from obeying. "My lady, do not trust a vorg. They're full of mischief."

Sighing, Elena stood up. "If we don't try, we're certain to lose Jerrick. Keep a lead on the vorg if you like, but let's see what it knows."

Wennar nodded and secured a loop of rope around the vorg's scrawny neck, then allowed its limbs to be untied. "Show us," Wennar said, motioning as if he was going to kick the creature.

Elena frowned at him. "Let me take him."

Before she could reach the lead, Er'ril took the rope. "You mind the vorg. I'll mind the tether."

She nodded and touched Greegrell's shoulder. "Go on, little one. Show us what can help him."

The vorg whined and hopped forward on its muscular hindlegs; its small forelimbs never touched the ground. "Come, come, come," it mumbled with each leap. It headed away from the camp and out into the cooling night.

The vorg would leap, sniff with his nose up in the air, then move farther. Elena kept to its side, while Er'ril followed, flanked by Wennar and followed by Tol'chuk and Mama Freda. The creature worked his way down a short, scrubby slope, slipping from rock to rock, stopping at last by a pool of brackish water, thick with a greenish-glowing algae.

Greegrell bent down, leaning on one splayed hand.

"Will this help?" Elena asked.

Mama Freda hobbled up and peered at the pool. "Different algae do have remarkable healing properties."

Elena glanced to the vorg, who still leaned beside the pool. "Can this cure—?"

Suddenly the vorg twisted, and the rock under its hand shot out and cracked Er'ril in the knuckles. The rope dropped from his jarred fingers, and the vorg was off. It bounced into Elena, then away, leaping and careening from rock to rock and up a cliff face. Its suckered feet gave it amazing agility.

Caught by surprise, none were able to snag the rope or the vorg. It clambered to the top of the cliff, then turned back to them. Its dark form was limned against the rising full moon. "Sorry. Greegrell sorry," it called back to them. "Green good. Green good for bad poke." It waved its arm, something glinting in its grip, and vanished.

Elena patted her waist, then swore loudly.

"What?" Er'ril asked.

"It stole my dagger." She turned to him, cheeks reddening both from anger and embarrassment. "My wit'ch dagger."

"Curse the little thief," Wennar grumbled.

"No." Mama Freda straightened by the pool, straining a fistful of the brackish algae. "It was a trade. His secret in exchange for Elena's dagger."

Elena shook her head. "I guess if the algae can truly cure Jerrick, then it was a cheap price."

Mama Freda smiled gratefully.

They all stood for a moment more, feeling foolish, outwitted by the purple-skinned vorg, then headed back to camp. There they found the second pair of scouts talking around the fire.

"What did you find?" Wennar asked them.

Their report was just as grim as the first team's. The gorge spread with no end and with no way to bridge it.

Er'ril turned to Elena. "Maybe you had better consult the Blood Diary."

ELENA SAT ALONE ON A ROCK, THE BLOOD DIARY OPEN ON HER LAP. The full moon floated high in the hazy night sky, while around her spread the red, craggy mountains of central Gul'gotha. A short distance behind her, the others were gathered at the campfire, but Elena could feel the plainsman's eye on her, ever watchful, but keeping a respectful distance.

She tugged her jacket, lined warmly with rabbit fur, tighter around her body and scowled as the apparition of Aunt Fila floated before her. They had been conversing for some time: Elena detailing the story of their journey here while Fila interrupted with questions. The course of the conversation was not going as Elena had hoped.

"So you're married?" Aunt Fila asked with a laugh. "To Er'ril?"

Blushing, Elena stared down into the book, now an open window into the starry Void. "I'm married in the eyes of the elv'in *only*," she explained again. "It wasn't exactly a mutual exchange of vows."

"Well, with that royal blood in your veins, you're certainly part elv'in. So I guess that makes you at least half married." Aunt Fila smiled warmly, taking the sting from her teasing.

The subject was a tender one. While traveling here, Er'ril had been overly formal with her, unusually awkward. Whenever she had tried to glancingly broach the subject or make some light remark about it, he would find some other task to occupy his time: building a fire, hunting for grouse, or checking with the d'warf scouts who watched the trails ahead.

"Enough about my marital status," Elena said, exasperated by the focus of her aunt's attention. "I need your counsel on more important concerns."

Aunt Fila smiled. "Fine, my dear. What is it?"

Elena sighed. "We've almost reached the valley of the d'warves, but we can't find a way past a deep gorge. A molten river flows through it with no way across."

Aunt Fila's shimmering face grew more sober. "What about the elv'in's skiff?"

Elena glanced down to the camp. "We considered going back for it. But we came close to crashing the boat to get as close to here as we did. Besides, the captain is gravely ill, poisoned by one of the foul plants here. We need some other answer."

"So you want to know if Cho has some magick to carry you all over to the other side."

Elena nodded.

"I'll allow her through, but I suspect she'll not be much help."

"We'll take whatever help she can supply."

Aunt Fila smiled, then closed her eyes. When next she opened them, Elena knew she was gone. Though the face was the same, the warmth had vanished from the figure, and in her aunt's eyes now shone the Void of the book: cold, distant, dispassionate.

"Cho, we seek your guidance," Elena said softly.

The figure seemed not to hear her, glancing over a shoulder. *"I sense Chi is near."* The voice was as icy as her eyes.

Elena followed Cho's gaze. It aimed toward the d'warf kingdoms beyond the gorge. "We believe in that direction lies one of the Weirgates—one of the black shackles that holds your brother trapped. It must be destroyed if—"

"The pain," Cho interrupted. *"I can sense his agony."* The figure turned back, and Elena recognized a bit of human warmth in her sorrowful expression.

"We will find a way to help him, to free him," Elena said. "This I swear, but first we must find a way across the flaming gorge." She explained quickly about what blocked their path.

"Fire can be fought with ice," Cho said. *"Thus it has always been. Stars burn and the Void freezes."*

Elena frowned. She needed clearer answers. "Surely there is a bit of magick you can teach me to bring us past this gorge."

"Come to me," Cho said, and waved a moonstone hand in her direction.

Elena hesitated, then stood, carrying the book.

"You have known me, touched me, shared my spirit. I am the ice of the Void, the flame of the Star, and the storm that rages between." Cho stared hard at Elena as she approached. *"But I am also the Spirit that walks unseen."*

Elena knew she was referring to the various aspects of her magick: coldfire, wit'ch fire, stormfire, and ghostfire. "I understand."

Cho held out her arms. *"Understand more."*

Elena's hands, bright with ruby magick, rose toward the figure, unbidden, uncontrolled. It was as if some unseen force had gripped her wrists. The Blood Diary slipped from her hands. Gasping, she tried to resist the pull, but failed.

Her hands drew into and through the ghostly figure of Cho, passing as far as her upper arms. Elena gasped as she felt the familiar surge of renewing. But she was already ripe with power. Frightened by the strangeness, Elena dug her heels into the rock and leaned against the tidal pull coming from Cho. *What was happening?*

Elena fell back as the control of her limbs returned to her.

She fell hard on her backside, wisps of smoke trailing around her. She coughed and lifted her arms. The sleeves of her jacket had been burned away; the edges still glowed and smoked in the cooling evening. But it wasn't the state of her jacket that made Elena cry out. Both arms, from her shoulders on down, whorled with blood magicks.

Elena scrambled to her feet. "What have you done?"

She heard footsteps behind her. "What's wrong?" It was Er'ril.

Instinctively, Elena tried to hide her transformation, lowering her arms out of sight. But her smoking jacket drew Er'ril's eyes. He came around and saw her arms, his eyes wide with shock. "Elena . . . ?"

"I don't know what just happened," she mumbled, eyes turning accusingly toward the apparition of Cho.

"The bridge is open," Cho said, as if this were explanation enough.

Er'ril moved to Elena's side. "Why have you done this?" he asked.

"Fire can be fought with ice." Cho glanced over again to the glowing eastern skies.

Elena's shock had faded enough for her to sense the magick in her arms. "It's coldfire," she mumbled. "It's all coldfire. Both arms."

Er'ril glanced up to her as he retrieved the Blood Diary from the dusty ground. "What do you mean?"

"My right fist was renewed by the sun. Ripe with wit'chfire. Not only has the amount of magick more than trebled, but Cho has transformed my fistful of sun magick back to the moon." Elena stared at Cho. "I don't understand."

"Maybe we should talk to your aunt," Er'ril said. "She may be able to translate the spirit's meaning for us."

Elena nodded. "Cho, I'd like to speak to Aunt Fila again."

The figure turned back and nodded. *"The one called Fila waits."*

The transformation was immediate, as if a flame had swept into the moonstone sculpture. "Elena, I'm sorry. I didn't know Cho would do that."

Elena lifted her arms. "What did she do?"

"The bridge is open," Fila said, repeating Cho's earlier words. "In the past, Sisa'kofa could only link a small part of her body, her hands, through the meager connection of refracted light—but now the Blood Diary exists. It's a portal to Cho, a direct well to the source of its nearly infinite power. When Cho chose you, a descendant of Sisa'kofa, she attuned herself to your spirit as surely as she is tuned to mine now. As she shares with me, so she can with you."

Elena rubbed her wrists, remembering the lack of control. It *was* as if something had taken control of her. This thought frightened her more than the well of power coursing through her veins.

Aunt Fila must have sensed her distress. "I know this is disconcerting. It was the same for me when I first merged with Cho in the spirit plane, opening the bridge to the book. But it is not without its advantages. When the moon is full and the diary open, all Cho's magicks are available—all forms, all depths. During these times, there are almost no restrictions to your magick. You become, in fact, Cho."

Elena's eyes grew wide. She knew that her aunt was trying to comfort her, but this revelation terrified her. She began to shiver uncontrollably, as if the coldfire in her limbs chilled her.

Er'ril was suddenly there, putting his arm around her and pulling her tight against him. She melted into his warmth, needing his touch. "This much power . . ." he said. "It risks burning her spirit away."

"Indeed it does," Fila said. "But I trust both Elena's heart and your strength, plainsman." She stared at them with an amused glint in her eyes. "And I don't think it was just chance that the elv'in people joined you two in marriage. I believe there was more significance in that gesture than either of you understand—or are willing to admit."

Er'ril stiffened beside Elena. He gave her a final squeeze, then awkwardly extracted himself, clearing his throat. "About . . . about this coldfire business," he said, changing the subject. "How can this help us cross the river of molten rock?"

Aunt Fila frowned. "I'm not entirely sure. Cho sees things on a larger scale than you or I. She moves between worlds. It's hard for her, I think, to fully understand details. To her, it is fire that blocks you, so she grants Elena ice."

Elena rubbed her arms, sensing the coldfire beneath the ruby flesh. "Lots of ice."

Aunt Fila shrugged. "If there is an answer to crossing this gorge, I'd say to attempt it this very night. You only have another two evenings when the moon will be full enough to open the Blood Diary. Don't waste them sitting here."

Elena nodded. "I'll try."

"Then Cho and I should return to the book. We must ration this moon's magick so it lasts all three nights."

Elena bit her lip. She did not want Aunt Fila to leave.

The apparition drew nearer to her. Her words were whispered for Elena only. "You'll be fine, my dear. But remember what I said. Share your burden. You've a figure of Standish iron at your back. Lean on his support."

With these final words, Aunt Fila swirled away, returning to the open book held by Er'ril. With the glowing apparition gone and the book closed, the night seemed darker, more empty. Just Er'ril and Elena.

"What did Aunt Fila say at the end?" Er'ril asked, holding out the diary.

Elena accepted the book, her fingers brushing his. "Just to keep warm."

ON WATCH, TOL'CHUK CROUCHED AT THE EDGE OF THE GORGE, staring across the molten valley. The heat from below wafted like the breath of a fiery beast, but Tol'chuk did not seek the shelter of the cooler shadows. Beyond the lava river was the d'warf kingdom, and though he did not have the Heart of his people to guide him, Tol'chuk knew his goal lay out there. After hearing the tale of Mimblywad Treedle and the mines of Gy'hallmanti, Tol'chuk knew he had to reach those ancient tunnels. He had to honor the final plea from his father: to return the Heart to where it had been first mined.

But why? What was so important? How could any of this help rid the Bane's curse from his people? And what did any of this have to do with his ancestor, the Oathbreaker, the great betrayer of the Land?

A rattle of rock alerted Tol'chuk to someone approaching. He glanced to the moon. It was too soon to be relieved. Maybe Elena had finished speaking to the spirits in the book. He prayed she had learned some way to cross this gorge. All his hopes depended on it.

Out of the darkness, a small shape hobbled forward, breathing hard. A voice called out to him. "Lord Boulder, I see you've found a warm spot to wile away the night. Who needs a campfire when we have this impassable hearth to keep the chill from our bones?"

Tol'chuk sighed. It was Magnam, the smallest of the d'warf party. "What be wrong?"

Magnam shuffled up to join him, scowling at the gorge. "For once in this cursed land, nothing. As a matter of fact, that little frog-faced vorg was as good as his trade. The old healer says the captain rests well after applying that smelly poultice, and his fever seems to have broken, too. She's drying the remainder of that green pond scum by the hearth."

"It be good to hear Jerrick fares better."

"Yes, I can tell from that grumbled tone that inside, you're cartwheeling with delight."

Tol'chuk turned his back on the d'warf. "What do you want?"

Magnam passed over a satchel. "A bit of warm meat and scrawny turnips."

Tol'chuk grunted.

"You're welcome," Magnam said, settling beside him uninvited.

Tol'chuk ignored the food and his guest and continued his study of the gorge.

"So do you want to talk about it?" Magnam asked.

"About what?" Tol'chuk grumbled.

"Ever since we've set up camp, you've been as antsy as a pig in a field of nettles," he said. "I came out here to make sure you weren't trying to swim across the river by yourself."

Tol'chuk scowled at the annoying little d'warf.

Magnam shrugged and leaned back on his hands. "I've been studying the maps. It's just over yonder, if you want to know."

"What?"

"Gy'hallmanti. Old Mad Mimblywad's mountain."

Tol'chuk sat up straighter. "Where?"

"Do you promise not to go leaping off this cliff and wading through that fiery river?"

"Where?" he asked again.

Magnam sighed and lifted an arm. "Just beyond that jagged point. Do you see that mountain shaped like a crooked fang?"

Tol'chuk peered past the glare of the gorge. It was hard to miss. It was one of the tallest peaks, stretching high into the sky. The moon seemed to teeter atop its pointed summit. At last, there stood Gy'hallmanti, "the Peak of the Sorrowed Heart," the birthplace of both heartstone and ebon'stone, and the cradle from which the Dark Lord first walked these lands.

Tol'chuk stepped toward the cliff's edge.

Magnam frowned. "Remember your promise. No leaping to a fiery death."

Before Tol'chuk could respond, voices arose behind them—many voices, excited and talking rapidly. He turned and saw most of their party hiking up the slope toward them. In the lead were Elena and Er'ril.

"I think you should consider this more fully," Er'ril said.

"The moon is near setting for the night," Elena answered. "We've argued long enough. I say we attempt this now."

"But it's untested magick. You've never tried to harness this much energy. Maybe you should start a little slower."

The pair climbed up to Tol'chuk's watchpost, followed by Wennar and four other d'warves. Tol'chuk imagined Mama Freda was still overseeing Jerrick.

As Elena stepped fully into view, Tol'chuk immediately saw the change.

Magnam did, too. The d'warf gasped. "Sweet Mother, the lass is red all the way up to her pretty little chin."

"What happened?" Tol'chuk asked as the party drew abreast.

"Coldfire," Er'ril said with a scowl. "Enough, Elena believes, to freeze a path across the river."

"Why else would Cho grant me such a font of power," Elena said, "unless it was to use the coldfire against the molten rock? You heard what Cho said: ice against fire."

Tol'chuk sensed this argument had been going on for quite some time.

Magnam grumbled under his breath and shook his head. "That's why I never got married."

Elena stepped to the cliff's edge. "Power is power. I'll unleash enough as a test. If it appears to be working, I'll freeze as much of the river as I can until the magick ebbs, then renew while the moon is still up."

Er'ril shook his head, clearly accepting her judgment under protest.

Elena nodded, as if satisfied, and turned back to the gorge. She reached to her belt and found her scabbard empty, clearly forgetting the vorg's theft. Sighing, she turned to Er'ril. "Slice my palms."

The plainsman's eyes grew round. He backed a step.

Magnam stepped forward, offering his own dagger, hilt first. "My lady."

She accepted the weapon. "Thank you."

As the others looked on, Elena closed her eyes and took a deep breath, obviously centering herself. Her hands began to glow, rising quickly to a blinding hue.

"Careful," Er'ril said.

Elena took another breath.

Sharing the cliff's edge, Tol'chuk saw her lips tighten as she forced the brightness back to a deep, rich glow. Once ready, she took the blade's edge to her palms, slicing one, then the other. Wincing, she reached both hands over the yawning gorge. Slowly, the red glow of her hands developed an azure hue. Blood dribbled from her palms and fell down into the gorge.

Tol'chuk's sharp eyes followed the rain of drops until they disappeared into the fiery abyss. The reaction was almost immediate. The molten river exploded upward in a crown of fire, as if a boulder had crashed down from the cliffs. Near the edge, Tol'chuk suddenly remembered the attack on Stormhaven, how this corrupt land reacted to the touch of magicks. "Stop!" he yelled, and moved toward Elena.

But it was already too late.

From the molten river, a mighty bird shot forth, formed of molten rock and trailing flames. As it flew upward, its wings snapped wide, stretching from one side of the river to the other. Bits of molten rock were thrown from its fiery pinions, raining all around them.

One of the d'warves screamed as he was struck in the face by a gob of lava. He fell backward, his hair on fire, and was dead before he hit the ground. Mayhem ensued as everyone sought cover. Both Tol'chuk and Er'ril dove for Elena, who still stood at the cliff's edge.

But neither reached her side. Elena's arms shot upward, and both defenders were blown backward on icy gusts. Tol'chuk rolled to his feet, his skin half frozen.

Nearby, Er'ril screamed, *"Elena!"*

The firebird climbed above the canyon's rim. Tol'chuk watched as a fiery talon snatched Elena from the cliff's edge and flew into the air.

ELENA'S FORM RANG WITH POWER. THE HEAT OF THE FIREBIRD'S talons could not penetrate her cocoon of coldfire. The ice spell had snapped around her spontaneously, the wit'ch power instinctively protecting its host. Not even Elena's clothes were singed by the molten talons' grip.

A trace of fear edged through Elena's heart, but her wild magick thrummed in her veins, singing with immense energy. She stared up as the bird arced into the night sky. It was a dread sight: a molten statue flowing with the fire of the world's core.

The creature's head cocked backward to study its captured prey. Flaming eyes stared down at her, clearly wondering why she had not been burned to a cinder in its grip. Its beak opened, and a gale of fire erupted. Elena's arms sprang up and cast a shield of pure ice magick before her, blocking the fire from ever reaching her.

Again it was an instinctive response, the wit'ch reacting without forethought. With so much magick flowing inside her, Elena had little control. She was but the tiller of a boat in a raging sea. This, more than anything, scared her. She had never felt so helpless. She fought against this chorus of the wild magick, this call of the wit'ch. But it was too strong. She was losing herself inside the magick.

She began to fall away.

"Er'ril," she moaned, knowing how much she would lose if she succumbed. Memories filled her: their single dance atop the tower at midnight, his strong arms holding her safe, the scent of his neck as she leaned against him. The woman inside her grew in strength with these thoughts and helped define her as a creature of flesh, blood, and human desire. She was not just a vessel of wild magicks and otherworldly senses, but a woman with a heart and a will. Elena fought for her spirit, shoving back the wit'ch in her.

As she did so, a realization struck her. She suddenly knew the true name of the wit'ch inside her. With this font of power instilled in her, Elena saw more clearly what had been sharing her body. Aunt Fila had all but told her.

You become Cho.

Elena now understood. It wasn't just wild magick and her own baser desires that had sought to overwhelm her, but also a sliver of Cho's spirit, the spirit of a creature from the Void who had never walked a world, never worn flesh, never shared her heart with another.

Knowing this, Elena found it easier to draw herself out of the Void. She concentrated on her own body, her own flesh, her own blood: the beat of her heart, the ache in her legs, the hunger in her belly. But she reached even deeper. She remembered how this same body, a form aged by magick into the fullness of womanhood, reacted to Er'ril. She used this power now, a magick all its own, remembering how her skin flushed when Er'ril glanced at her, the surge of heat through her core when he was near, and the longing ache deep inside whenever he brushed against her.

She wrapped all these sensations around her. As the ice shell protected her from the firebird's talons, so too did these sensual feelings insulate her from the wit'ch. She found a way back into her own body, back to the fight.

And as she did so, the world shattered with a scream.

Elena glanced up. The firebird had abandoned its attempt to burn through her shield and now roared in frustration. It swooped over the river now, wings spread from one side to the other. Elena felt the talons loosening, meaning to drop her into the river below.

Elena tensed and reached out. She was done reacting with just a wit'ch's instinct. She took both hands, flaming with coldfire, and grabbed the claw that was holding her, refusing to be dropped into the river. She fed ice into the talon, and molten rock froze into solid stone.

The firebird screeched and attempted to shake Elena free, but she was now locked in stone, and though jarred and tossed, she remained secure in its rocky grip.

Screaming again, the gigantic creature turned on a wing and swept back toward the gorge, gliding lower. The river swelled below them as the firebird aimed for it. The desire of the creature was obvious: it intended to dive back into its molten den.

Elena studied the landscape below as a plan came to mind. She had to time this perfectly. She raised her arms and surged all the energy in her body up into her clenched fists, stanching the flow from escaping, building it to a raging force. Her hands grew as bright as cold suns. Her arms trembled with the pent energy, and the wit'ch in her screamed for release, but Elena held back, waiting until the right moment.

The firebird swept lower, almost to the rim of the gorge. Elena tensed. She felt, more than saw, the beast begin to tuck its wings for the final dive into the river below.

Now!

With a gasp, she opened her fists and released the twin fonts of pure coldfire. Her body arched backward in the bird's stone grip as the magick ripped from her spirit. The backlash of hoarfrost blinded her, but she did not pause. She cast every bit of energy out of her body and thrust it at the firebird. Long ago, in the mountains of the Teeth, she had frozen an entire forest with only a fistful of coldfire. Now a greater miracle was needed.

A twinge of doubt grew as the last bit of magick escaped her body—then Elena was slammed forward. Her head struck the stone edge of the firebird's claw. Her arms fell limp, and darkness swept over her.

ER'RIL RAN ALONG THE GORGE'S EDGE. A MOMENT AGO, THE FIREbird had disappeared into a cloud of ice. Its piercing scream had shattered the night. When next he had seen it, the firebird had plunged out of the cloud, its flames doused and no longer molten. The bird was a plummeting sculpture of frozen rock. With stone wings spread wide, it crashed at a gliding angle into the gorge. But rather than plunging into the molten river, it was stopped by its own monstrous wingspan. The stone bird had jammed itself into the gorge only a few spans down from the rim of the molten canyon, imbedding itself in place, becoming a stone bridge across the gorge.

Er'ril stumbled to a stop at the cliff's edge, staring down at the crashed bird. *Elena!* He fell to his knees, searching. Then he spotted movement from under the bird: a pale arm moving weakly. Elena hung limply in one of the stone talons—but she was alive!

Tol'chuk appeared behind him, as did Wennar.

Er'ril turned. "Get the climbing ropes."

In short order, d'warves were scrambling down the slope and atop the stone wing of the bird. Er'ril was lowered to the talon in a rope sling. The heat rising from below made it hard to breathe, searing his lungs. He swung to where Elena slouched in the claw's grip. Once there, he anchored his legs against a stone claw and waved a pinch of herbs supplied by Mama Freda under Elena's nose.

Her head jerked back from the smell, and her eyes blinked open. She startled for a moment and struggled away from him.

He grabbed her arm.

Elena's eyes widened as full consciousness returned. "Er'ril?"

He smiled at her. "Next time, let's practice that maneuver first."

She stared up at the stone bird, then back at him. Suddenly she leaned forward and wrapped her arms around his neck.

Thinking her frightened, he tried to console her. "Don't fear, Elena. I'll get you out of here safely."

She tightened her grip and whispered in his ear. "You've already saved me."

22

CARRYING THE D'WARF HAMMER ON HIS SHOULDER, TOL'CHUK trudged up the face of the high ridge with Magnam at his side. The mountains on this side of the gorge were even more desolate, covered in scrub bushes and twisted trees, red rocks and yellow lichen. Around them, hundreds of steaming vents cast noxious gases into the midday sky. Overhead, the sun was a pale shadow in the greenish haze.

But at least they were past the gorge.

In the early morning light, scouts had cautiously traversed the stone bird, reaching the far side safely. The others had quickly followed, not trusting the bridge's stability. As they crossed, little rocks had fallen from the cliff faces to rattle across the stone surface, making them all cringe and sweat. But they had made it safely and had rested briefly before setting out into the mountains again.

Even Jerrick fared better today. His fever had broken overnight, and he had refused to ride the makeshift sling this morning. He hobbled ahead of Tol'chuk with the use of a staff hewn from one of the stunted trees. The party was spread out up the slope of the steep ridge, moving slowly along a thin, zigzagging trail. Tol'chuk and Magnam were the last in line.

"Dragonback," Magnam mumbled.

Tol'chuk glanced questioningly at him.

The small d'warf swept an arm before him. "It's named Dragonback Ridge. Beyond here lies the d'warf kingdom. It is said the ridge circles all our lands, a jagged crown of rock."

Tol'chuk glanced up. The ridge's heights were indeed jagged, but rather than a crown or a dragon's back, they reminded the og're of the fangs of some beast.

As he craned his neck up, Tol'chuk's nose caught a familiar scent. In the dark caves of his homelands, the sense of smell was sharp in all og'res. He sniffed, then spun around, catching a brief glimpse of something darting behind a boulder.

"Show yourself!" Tol'chuk bellowed, lifting his hammer.

Magnam stopped, as did Jerrick. Farther up the slope, faces turned in his direction.

"What is it?" Magnam asked.

Tol'chuk held up a clawed hand for silence.

Slowly, from behind the boulder, a small face peered out: bulbous yellow eyes; flat-splayed nose; and wide, blubbery lips. The purple creature edged from its hiding place, hands held up, offering the stolen silver dagger. "Shiny. Greegrell give shiny back."

Magnam scowled. "The vorg again. Great. As if our ancient homelands weren't fouled enough."

It edged up the slope, head low to the ground, bent in a clear posture of someone waiting to be beaten. "Give shiny back," it mumbled, sinking lower and lower as it crept forward.

"Don't trust that purple-skinned imp," Magnam said.

Jerrick slipped beside them, leaning heavily on his staff. "Is this the creature that saved my life?"

"Yes," Tol'chuk said, not moving his eyes from the quivering vorg.

Jerrick bowed deeply before the creature. "Thank you for your help. I am in your debt."

Greegrell did not seem to understand. Its trembling grew worse. It set down the dagger and scrambled back a few steps.

"Do not fear," Jerrick said, moving nearer and retrieving the knife. He slipped it into his belt, then offered his open palm to the vorg. "What do you ask of us? I will see if it can be granted."

The vorg's yellow eyes shifted from Jerrick to Tol'chuk, then higher up the slope. From the scuff of boots on rock, the group was hurrying down here; the purple vorg scooted back. "Greegrell no mean bad. I give shiny back." It pointed behind him. "You make good rock over . . . over . . ." It made a sound like the sizzle and pop of the molten river. "Greegrell now go home."

By now, the others were gathered at Tol'chuk's back.

Mama Freda spoke. "He's trading back the knife for the use of the bridge we built."

Elena moved forward. "But what does it mean about going home?"

The vorg must have heard her. It patted the ground with its hand. "Greegrell home."

"But how could that be?" Er'ril asked.

Elena moved slowly toward the beast, bent low. "Greegrell, how could this be your home? You were on the far side of the fire river."

The vorg edged into her shadow, still cowering. "I go hunt. Leave caves. Go far for snipsnip leaves." It shifted and revealed a flapped pouch on its belly, exposing a handful of leaves edged with red. "Make better bad belly. Many sick, sick, sick."

"He was hunting for medicinal herbs," Mama Freda said with shock in her voice. "He must be his tribe's healer."

Elena frowned back at them, then knelt on the rock. "What happened?"

The vorg shook his head, cringing lower. "Then bad, bad, booming bad." It made sounds of whistling explosions. "Sky angry. Boom. Trees fall from sky, burn, burn, burn."

"The attack on Stormhaven," Jerrick mumbled.

"Greegrell hide." It covered its head with its hands. "Bad booming stop and Greegrell go look." It mimicked peeking from under its arms. "Greegrell run home, fast, fast, fast. Then find—" It glanced to Elena. "—fire river. Bad burning bad. No go home."

Elena straightened. "So the gorge formed when the Land attacked Stormhaven, and it kept him from returning home."

"A second level of defense," Er'ril said. "It means to protect what is hidden here."

"The Weirgate," Elena mumbled, and turned back. "Maybe the vorg knows something about the manticore."

"Ask it." Er'ril leaned nearer.

Elena nodded. "Greegrell, do you know of a great black stone? It has a body like . . . like . . ." She pointed to Tol'chuk. "Like an og're but with the tail of a scorpion."

The vorg scrunched up its face, clearly not understanding.

Elena sat back on her heels and sighed.

Wennar spoke behind them. "Vorgs only have a small intelligence, just enough for mischief."

Tol'chuk turned to the d'warf leader. "Scorpions . . . be they native to these lands?"

Now it was Wennar's turn to squint his eyes. "No, now that you mention it. I don't believe so."

"Then how can this creature know what Elena asks?" Tol'chuk stepped forward, reaching to his thigh pouch. He pulled out his chunk of heartstone. It glinted dully in the weak light.

The vorg's eyes grew huge at the sight of the jewel.

Leaning on the d'warf hammer, Tol'chuk bent down beside the vorg. He held the jewel up to the sun and pointed at it. "Greegrell, have you seen something that looks like the black creature inside the stone?"

Greegrell did not seem to hear him. Splayed hands drifted up toward the bright jewel. "Pretty, shiny, pretty."

Tol'chuk shifted the stone higher, beyond the reach of the vorg's sucker-tipped fingers. "No. Look inside the crystal."

Reluctantly, the vorg lowered its hands and stretched its long neck, cocking its toadish head and peering at the heartstone. "Shiny, pretty," it continued to whine.

Then the vorg froze, and a choking sound strangled out.

Its eyes twitched between Tol'chuk and the stone. A flash of recognition flared. Then it cringed, scuttling backward. Its eyes were wide with terror. It made a warding gesture with both hands. "Bad, bad, nasty bad."

Elena turned to Tol'chuk. "It knows."

He nodded and stared hard at the cowering vorg. "Where, Greegrell? Where is nasty bad place?"

The vorg covered its head with both arms and pressed its face against the rocky ground. "No, no, no. Bad no go. Nasty black darkness bad."

Elena slid closer and gently touched its trembling skin. "Please, Greegrell, tell us."

The vorg pointed a purple arm. Tol'chuk turned to see where he pointed. It was the same peak Magnam had mentioned in his stories. "Gy'hallmanti," Tol'chuk mumbled.

The vorg jerked with the mention of the name and ducked farther down.

Magnam frowned at Tol'chuk's side. "It recognizes the ancient name of our mine."

Tol'chuk gripped his heartstone harder. "Great evil has a way of surviving through the ages."

Er'ril turned to stare at the dread peak. "At least it confirms that the Manticore Gate is here."

"Can you take us there?" Elena asked the vorg.

It squeaked. "No go. Bad nasty."

"Please," Elena whispered.

Greegrell just quaked and quivered.

Mama Freda hobbled next to Tol'chuk. "Maybe a trade," she suggested. "The vorg seems to like to barter."

Elena turned to Jerrick. "My dagger."

The elv'in nodded and handed back the blade. Elena held the knife toward the creature. She turned it back and forth so it reflected the sunlight. "Greegrell . . ."

The vorg glanced up, drawn by the flashing blade. It sat up straighter. "Shiny good." A finger raised toward the dagger.

"Yes. It can be yours if you take us to the bad nasty place. Show us where the night stone lies."

Greegrell's hand snapped away. "No go."

"The dagger's not tempting enough," Er'ril said. He palmed the hilt of his sheathed sword. "But I've a span of steel that might goad him to cooperate."

"We'll not force him," Elena said. "We have no right." She sighed and wrinkled her brow.

Tol'chuk had an idea. He joined Elena and held out the Heart of his people. The stone glowed ruby in the light, refracting the sun's brilliance. "Greegrell. Show us to the bad dark place. You don't have to go there yourself. Show us and I'll give you this stone."

The vorg raised its head. Yellow eyes fixed on the chunk of heartstone. A tongue came out to lick its thick lips. "Shiny bright . . . Fetch many mates."

"Ah," Magnam said, "no wonder he wants our shiny things."

Greegrell stared at the heartstone, then squinted at Tol'chuk. "Show? No go."

"You need only take us to where it lies."

The vorg leaned toward the heartstone, sniffing at it. One eye narrowed. It seemed unable to decide.

Tol'chuk started to shove the heartstone back in its pouch, but Greegrell's arm sprang out. The suckered tips of its fingers clung to the stone surface.

"It seems the vorg's not done bargaining yet," Magnam scoffed.

Greegrell looked up at Tol'chuk. "I take you. Quick, fast, fast, fast."

Tol'chuk extracted his stone back from the vorg. "Only once you take us."

The vorg sagged, but bobbed its head.

With the matter decided, the party took off once again, climbing the switchbacks toward the heights of Dragonback Ridge. Greegrell led the way, scampering and hopping up the slope, impatient with their pace. The vorg also proved skilled at ferreting out hidden dangers along their paths. Even Wennar stopped complaining after Greegrell blocked the d'warf from stepping into the subterranean burrow of a spiderwasp.

Still, even with the vorg's help, it took until the sun was low in the sky to reach the top of the ridge. The party stared at the wasteland ahead.

Magnam wiped at his eyes.

Spreading to the horizon were barren peaks and valleys. A few small hollows showed signs of green life, but the remainder of the landscape was pitted red rock and wind-blasted stone. The ancient mines could be seen from here, countless black holes riddling the bare mountains, making their slopes appear pocked with disease. Dry streambeds crisscrossed the region like old battle scars, and the peaks themselves, bare of any vegetation, had been eroded by storms and scoured by winds into twisted shapes. It was as if the entire kingdom had been reduced to its bones and left to the elements. Tol'chuk had never seen a more desolate place.

"I can smell the disease here," Mama Freda said, her pet tamrink cowering on her shoulder. "It's as if all the living energy of this place has been drained away."

"Welcome to our home," Wennar said sourly, turning away.

Elena moved to his side and placed a hand on his shoulder. "This is the Dark Lord's doing. His touch has poisoned your land, but it can be brought back to life. As long as there is blood in your veins, you can heal your kingdom."

Wennar nodded, but his eyes appeared hopeless.

After a short rest, the party moved on, led by the vorg. It hurried them down a steep slope of loose stone. Jerrick took a tumble on the sliding shale. Er'ril caught him and helped the captain down the remainder of the slope. The elv'in was weakening from the long day of hiking, but he refused to return to his sling and slow them down. Mama Freda hovered alongside him.

Luckily, once into the valley, their way became mostly flat, the going easier for all. They followed a dry streambed past steep cliffs and broken scree. Around them, nothing moved. Nothing made a sound. Their footsteps sounded loud to Tol'chuk's ears. He sniffed. Even the air was dead here.

By now, the deep gloom of twilight had set in.

"Maybe we should stop for the night," Elena said. "The moon will rise soon."

Greegrell heard her. "No, not far." The vorg pointed its arm frantically forward.

"He's been saying that," Jerrick complained, "for the past two leagues."

Tol'chuk grumbled deep in his throat. "Perhaps we should heed the vorg. We be not alone out here." He nodded to where a few distant mines glowed with firelight. "The sooner we be done here the better."

No one argued; the pace even increased.

The night slowly wore on, and the moon crept up from the horizon. This was the second night of its fullness, when the moon was most bright. Elena pulled out the Blood Diary, and the gilt rose on its cover glowed with a brilliant light.

"Pretty, shiny," Greegrell said, mesmerized by the book.

"How much farther?" Er'ril asked, redirecting the vorg's attention.

Greegrell pointed forward as the streambed rounded a short peak.

Ahead, no more than a league, the mountain climbed into the sky. It towered higher than any of the nearby peaks, a black shadow against the stars. Even its silhouette stirred dread in Tol'chuk's heart. Here was where the Heart of his people had been mined, and from whose dark throat the Black Heart had entered this world.

"Gy'hallmanti," Magnam mumbled.

The vorg urged them along. "Quick, fast, fast."

Er'ril kept to Elena's side, while Wennar maintained her flank.

The party continued onward, following the riverbed as it wound through an ever-narrowing defile. Soon sheer cliff faces rose on both sides. Tol'chuk began to grow uneasy. His eyes studied the ridges for movement. His skin began to itch with warning—but nothing moved.

The party closed ranks and proceeded more cautiously.

Ahead, the dark shape of Gy'hallmanti filled the sky, a monstrous black hole. The moon climbed toward its highest point, but still failed to shine upon the peak's dark slopes. Tol'chuk understood how the mountain had gained its reputation. It was all shadow, no substance.

Tol'chuk tore his eyes from the sight. It seemed to sap his will.

At last, after another tense quarter league, the cliffs fell away to either side. The roots to the great mountain lay before them, spread to either side, as if a dark-cloaked figure were kneeling before them. Tol'chuk could almost feel the eyes of this black stranger staring down at him. He feared looking up, afraid of what he might see.

The dry streambed led between the roots of the mountain to a hole in its side. Long ago, a deep spring must have once fed this waterway, but now it was all dust and dry rock, as dead as the peak itself.

"Does the Manticore Gate lie within?" Elena asked with clear dread.

The vorg pointed not toward the opening from which the old river flowed, but up toward the face of the mountain.

"Maybe he means one of the old mine shafts," Magnam said. "The ancient peak is hollowed with old tunnels and pits."

"If so," Er'ril said, "we could spend an entire winter searching for where the manticore is hidden."

But the vorg pointed its arm more vigorously. "Bad nasty dark!"

"Show us," Tol'chuk said. "Where?"

Greegrell sighed and pointed both arms, spreading them wide.

Er'ril scowled. "He must not know, or doesn't under—" Then the plainsman's voice cut out. "Sweet Mother above!"

In the sky, the moon moved a fraction higher, now poised above the very tip of the jagged peak. Moonshine flowed down the face of the mountain like a rush of silver water, washing away the shadows to reveal the peak at last—or what had become of it.

This entire face of Gy'hallmanti had been worked and carved, hollowed out and chipped, to form a towering granite figure. The detail must have been the work of countless masters slaving for decades: the strain in the figure's face, the muscles bunching with both triumph and pain, the lines of anger around the eyes. It seemed as if the subject were climbing out of the bulk of the mountain, one arm stretched toward the sky, one leg still sunk in the rock. Behind its massive shoulders, its scorpion tail arched over its back, poised to strike.

"The manticore," Elena gasped.

No one spoke for several heartbeats, too stunned by the sight.

"But it's carved of granite," Er'ril said. "Not ebon'stone."

"No, you're wrong," Elena said, and pointed toward the outstretched arm of the figure. In its clawed grip lay a boulder as big as a small cottage. Its oily surfaces shunned even the moon's brightness. It was as if the figure clutched living shadow, waiting to be molded into something sinister. Even looking at it chilled one's blood. "There lies the true heart of this statue—*ebon'stone*. The first of the four Weirgates."

As the others stared in awe, Tol'chuk dropped the d'warf

hammer into the dirt. He fumbled to his thigh pouch and removed the Heart of his people. His fingers ran over its surfaces, dreading what he would find, but already knowing the truth. He had carried the Heart across all the lands of Alasea. He knew every facet, every chink as if it were his own face.

Tol'chuk stared up, unable now to turn away. He now knew the source of the dread that had clamped around his heart. Deep inside, a part of him must have known it all along.

Magnam spoke, pointing toward the sculpture. "The depiction of the manticore climbing forth from Gy'hallmanti. It must represent the Nameless One's rise from the heart of the mountain. We may be the first in centuries to peer upon the face of the Nameless One."

Tol'chuk's legs weakened, and he fell to one knee. He held up the Heart of his people toward the ebon'stone boulder, praying the two were not the same. His prayer was shattered as he lifted it high.

They were an exact match. But that was not the worst—not by far.

Nearby, the vorg was the first to realize the horrible truth. The toady creature stared at Tol'chuk, then back up at the manticore statue. Its eyes flicked back and forth, then grew huge. It squeaked and backed away from him, trembling with terror; then it fled back down the narrow defile.

The others turned to see Greegrell scramble away.

Lowering his arm, Tol'chuk slumped in despair. There had been so many hints: The Triad choosing him for this mission. The shape of the Bane in the stone. And deep in the cellars below Shadowbrook, the d'warf lord who had tortured Meric and Kral had fled from Tol'chuk in terror—just as the vorg did now. But it wasn't only fear in their eyes, but also something worse: *recognition*.

Tol'chuk opened his eyes.

Slowly, one at a time, their faces paled with dawning realization. Heads turned to the manticore, then back to Tol'chuk.

Elena was the first to state it aloud. "The carving . . . the face and body of the creature . . . it's Tol'chuk."

Magnam backed a step. "The Nameless One."

Dropping his heartstone, Tol'chuk covered his face with his

hands. "Our people call him by a different name. Not Dark Lord, not Black Heart, not Black Beast . . ."

"What name then?" Magnam asked.

Tol'chuk dropped his hands, hot tears flowing down his face. *"Oathbreaker."* He sagged to the ground, crushed under the realization of his true heritage. "He betrayed the trust of the Land and cursed my people. His blood runs in my veins."

Elena moved up to him. "But he is not you."

"It does not matter." Tol'chuk glanced up to the statue. "The stone does not lie. I am the last born of the Dark Lord."

ELENA PUSHED ASIDE HER SHOCK. SHE RECOGNIZED THE GRIEF, guilt, and despair in Tol'chuk's face. She had felt similar emotions when confronted with her own heritage. She went to Tol'chuk and gently touched the crown of his head. "A heart is stronger than one's blood, and you've proven your heart in countless battles. You're no monster."

Tol'chuk would not look up, only mumble. He reached and squeezed the chunk of heartstone. "I've failed my people. The Heart died in my care. I be no better than the Oathbreaker."

Magnam moved closer and shrugged. "Better or worse, what does it matter? At least you scared the vorg off." He placed his fists on his hips and searched around. "So we're here . . . Now what?"

Elena knelt beside Tol'chuk. "We go on. We destroy the Gate as planned."

Er'ril stood behind her. "We *all* go on. You were sent by your Triad, guided by the Heart of your people. Both elders and spirits judged you the best one to right the wrong of your ancestor. Whether you name him Oathbreaker or Dark Lord, you don't have to accept his name as your own. You can forge your own future."

Tol'chuk finally lifted his head.

Elena stared him in the eye, urging him up. "We'll stand by your side."

"Or at least behind your back," Magnam added with a snort.

Tol'chuk pushed up, wiping his nose on his forearm.

Wennar moved forward and lifted the Try'sil from the dirt. He offered Tol'chuk the rune-carved handle.

Tol'chuk shook his head. "I be not worthy."

Wennar thrust the hammer farther forward. "Long ago, the hammer was used to shape ebon'stone and doomed our lands at the hands of the Nameless One. Use it now to free us. Destroy what has been wrought in his cursed name."

Tol'chuk lifted his arm and gripped the handle. "I will try."

Wennar nodded and stepped away.

Jerrick hobbled up to them. His face shone with a returning fever. The day's exertion had worn the captain's health. "If we mean to continue this night, we should move on."

With the matter decided, Er'ril led the way with Wennar. Elena kept beside Tol'chuk, sensing the og're needed support. It seemed their two lives were intertwined by more than just a chance meeting long ago in the highland forests of Winter's Eyrie. Their twin stories stretched back generations—hers to the wit'ch Sisa'kofa, and his to the Dark Lord himself.

"We're not our pasts," she said softly to the night.

Tol'chuk nodded. "I know this in my head, but it be hard to convince my heart."

"Then trust those around you," she said. "Trust me."

The og're turned in her direction.

She met his gaze. "I know in *my* heart that you are a spirit of goodness and honor. I will never doubt otherwise."

He swallowed hard and turned away, his voice a whisper. "Thank you."

The group continued in silence. Four d'warf scouts fanned out to survey the empty stretch of bare rock that led to the mountain. The party seemed small as it fell under the shadow of the manticore.

Elena craned her neck. The statue towered above them.

Jerrick spoke at her shoulder. "We'll need to find a way up onto that arm. I almost wish that sticky-fingered vorg were still here."

"No need," Mama Freda said. "Tikal is just as agile and has sharper eyes. He may be able to hunt a way to the top."

But as they neared the mountain's base, they discovered neither of the creatures' skills would be needed. Carved into the granite, a steep stair led up the mountain's face toward the statue.

"An old work trail," Wennar guessed. "Crude, narrow, meant for the sculptors as they labored here."

A d'warf scout stood a few steps away, a spyglass fixed to his eye. "It's too dark to say with good certainty, but the stairs do seem to climb all the way up."

"Then let's go," Elena said.

Wennar led the way. The stairs were only wide enough for a single d'warf, but two people could walk abreast. Elena now marched with Er'ril, Tol'chuk on the step behind them. Jerrick had attempted to keep up, but it was soon evident the elv'in captain was too weak and worn from his recent fevers to continue. His pale face glistened with fever sweat, and his breath had grown ragged. A short way up the cliff face, they abandoned him on the steps in the care of Mama Freda.

"Tikal and I will watch over him. You all continue on."

Elena was loath to leave the two elders alone and ordered three of the d'warves to watch over them. "They can also guard our back trail," she added before Mama Freda could protest.

With their numbers lighter, they set a harder pace. Elena's last view of Mama Freda and Jerrick was of the old woman taking the captain's hand. The sight buoyed her spirit. Even in this cursed land, a bit of love could grow.

With this thought held in her heart, she continued up the long staircase with Er'ril at her side. The d'warf scout had proven to have good eyes. The steps climbed to a tunnel near the base of the statue, where the leg of the og're stretched out of the mountainside.

Elena tugged a glove from her right hand and nicked a fingertip with the tip of her wit'ch dagger. They had no torches and had to risk a bit of magick to light their path. She cast free the tiniest thread of wit'ch fire and wove it around and around like a skein of yarn, forming a ball of fire. It floated just above her fingers. Lifting it high, she stepped to the tunnel. The fiery light revealed a spiraling staircase leading up.

"More steps." She glanced over a shoulder.

Wennar took the lead again. His long shadow, reflected in the firelight, stretched upward. They followed again.

Elena wove a spell to keep the ball of wit'ch fire floating above her head, attached by the thinnest thread of magick to her right hand.

Er'ril marched beside her. Their climb slowed as side tunnels branched off periodically. The party approached each with caution, fearing attack from unknown monsters. But each passage proved empty, with only the wind moaning through the dark throats.

"Where are the defenders?" Elena finally asked.

"In this desolate land, what is the need?" Er'ril said. "It seems this land protects itself with its fireballs, poisons, and ill creatures. Besides, considering the vorg's reaction to this place, I doubt any will near it." But even his own explanation did not seem to satisfy the plainsman. He kept a tight grip on his sword and studied every shadow ahead.

The others, too, grew more wary with each step. The climb seemed endless. But at last they reached a cavernous side tunnel. It gaped so wide that the entire party could have walked abreast.

Elena stared down the passage. "Are we high enough to have reached the arm of the statue?"

"I think so, my lady," Wennar said. "I'll go see."

Elena detached a thumb-sized ball of fire from her own sphere and sent it sailing down the tunnel. "To light your way."

Wennar nodded, then departed with one of the d'warf scouts, disappearing into the darkness. The remainder of the party rested on the stair, the globe of fire floating above them all. Elena leaned against Er'ril. He put his arm around her.

"How are you holding up?" he asked, and nodded to the fireball. "Is it sapping much of your strength?"

She shook her head. "It's but a drop." After the events at the gorge, Elena had renewed both fists: one in sunlight, one in moonlight. She rested her head on his shoulder and closed her eyes, sharing his warmth and breath.

For a moment, as they waited, exhausted and worn, Elena dozed off in his arms—but it was a short respite. A horrible scream shattered out from the cavernous tunnel. They all jerked to their feet, but the cry was sliced from the air. Distantly, the strike of iron on stone reached them.

"It seems we aren't the only ones here," Magnam said.

Elena stepped toward the tunnel, but Er'ril had a hand clamped on her shoulder. She turned to him. "We have no choice but to go on. The fate of Alasea lies in destroying the Weirgate here." She fed more energy into the small fireball, no longer worrying about keeping her magick hidden. It swelled out and shone deep into the tunnel.

She cast the fireball ahead and followed it. "We cannot turn back now."

A bellow of rage echoed down the hall toward them.

"It's Wennar," Tol'chuk said. "He's still alive."

"But for how long?" Elena asked.

They ran at a fast trot, the ball of fire rolling across the roof of the tunnel ahead of them. It lit the passage for some distance.

"Up ahead!" Er'ril warned.

Elena saw it, too. Moonlight flowed from around the curve ahead, signaling the end of the tunnel.

Their pace slowed to a more cautious approach. Er'ril led the way, flanked by a pair of d'warves on each side. Tol'chuk kept near Elena's shoulder, the d'warf hammer ready for battle.

They rounded the corner and saw a sight born of nightmares. The tunnel did indeed end ahead, but it was not open. Something blocked the passage. At first Elena thought it was a huge spider crouched in a web across the opening, but as her ball of wit'ch fire rolled forward, the true horror revealed itself.

It wasn't a monstrous spider, but something much worse.

Lodged in the opening and held in place by ten articulated legs was a single creature. Its main body hung in the opening, gray and glistening, like a netherworld slug, striped in slashes of black and red. But mostly it was all mouth: a black maw that writhed with poisoned tentacles. A tangle of stalked eyes as black as polished obsidian waved above the razor-lined mouth.

Elena knew this creature. She had battled one in the highland forests of her home after it had killed her Uncle Bol. It was a mul'gothra, one of the birth queens of the skal'tum. Elena watched its thick gray body convulse in a violent spasm, and something green and steaming squeezed from its lower belly and fell with a wet *plop* to the tunnel's floor.

The queen was in the middle of birthing.

The object roiled on the stone, steaming a noxious green cloud; then damp wings unfolded and claws sprouted as it scrabbled to stand on its own. A new skal'tum was born into the world.

Above its newborn, the creature hissed, belching out a flurry of suckered tentacles at the lone combatant before it.

Wennar.

But the d'warf ignored the looming creature. He was out of

reach of its tentacles and had more immediate concerns as he danced with an ax in one hand and a sword in the other.

A pack of newborn skal'tum surrounded him.

Dripping with fetid slime, the bony beasts raked at him with claws and hissed like a pit of snakes. His blades bounced off them harmlessly as dark magicks protected their flesh. All he could do was keep them at bay. Newborn skal'tum were impervious to most harm until they had their first kill.

Behind Wennar, the mul'gothra continued to push more of its abominable children into the world, its belly churning and spasming.

"Free him," Elena said, waving an arm to Er'ril and the d'warves. "Get him out of harm's way." She pulled her dagger from its sheath.

Er'ril hesitated for a moment, met her eyes, then nodded. He and the remaining d'warves ran to Wennar's rescue. Tol'chuk kept to Elena's side, protecting her back.

Elena drew a line of fire across each palm with the sharp tip of her silver blade and rallied the magick in both fists. Across the way, the sudden appearance of new foes startled the immature skal'tum. Most scurried away toward their mother, while the few that remained were beaten back by the larger force.

Free, Wennar sagged toward the ground, but he was caught by two of his fellow d'warves. He was dragged away as Er'ril and the others guarded their retreat.

Wennar gasped as they returned to Elena's side. "I didn't see it until it was too late."

Lost to her magicks, Elena barely heard him. Energy surged through her. She stepped forward and raised her arms. Lacing her fingers together, she merged fire and ice, building up the storm between her palms.

Across the way, the skal'tum regrouped, gaining courage from their numbers. They hissed and clambered. Tiny wings snapped and beat at the air, but they were still too young to fly.

Elena stepped toward them. "Stay back," she warned her companions.

Moving slowly, building her storm to a trembling that raged between her palms, Elena edged closer. Beyond the pregnant mul'gothra, limned in moonlight, Elena saw the outstretched arm of the manticore statue and the shadowy chunk of ebon'stone.

She almost looked away, but a flash of movement caught her eye. Out on the granite arm, she spotted three other skal'tum, newborns like those huddled under their mother, scrabbling toward the ebon'stone boulder. Curious and concerned, she hesitated, watching.

The first newborn reached the stone. It appeared frightened, cowering back, but it seemed unable to stop its legs. It reached the stone and with a screech, fell into it, as if diving down a black well, and was gone. She heard its small cry of terror fade away. The others followed.

Elena's attention swung back to the mul'gothra. She suddenly understood what the creature was doing here, what they had interrupted. The mul'gothra, when ripe with offspring, must be drawn to this place like a moth to a black flame. They then used this high perch to hatch their foul offspring, feeding them through the Weir to be bent and enslaved to the Dark Lord. Here was the source of the Black Heart's endless winged armies—the Manticore Gate.

More than ever, Elena knew it had to be destroyed.

"What are you waiting for?" Er'ril said behind her, stepping in her direction.

"Stand back," she repeated, and pointed her arms at the gathered skal'tum. She bloomed open her fingers and cast out a raging torrent of ice and fire. Lightning crackled, and winds screamed in fury. Elena swept her stormfire across the floor of the tunnel, keeping its focus tight to rip through the extra protections of these newborn demons.

Deep inside her, she felt her magick strike the gathered skal'tum. She sensed their sharp flames of life snuff out, one after the other, buffeted and blown away by the rage of her magick.

The wit'ch in her sang with each death, much louder than usual, harder to resist, as if the veil had thinned between wit'ch and woman. Elena fought to keep her focus, to maintain her control. But something had changed inside her, something following her intimate sharing with Cho last night. The wit'ch in her had grown stronger, wailing its wild lusts, buffeting against her inner shields.

Standing in the eye of her raging magicks, Elena again sensed the tenuous connection of all life, especially the ties among those in the room. She felt the flickers of energy from her companions and tasted the raging fire of the mul'gothra.

Across the tunnel, the wit'ch continued to consume the tiny flames of the newborns—but Elena knew, if left unchecked, the wit'ch would never be satisfied with such a small feast. It wanted to burn all away—not just the mul'gothra, but also her companions. It did not discriminate. It wanted everything, even Elena herself.

Cringing against such lusts, Elena reined in her magick. Slowly the fire died in her hands. The mad chorus of the wit'ch faded, replaced by the mewling cry of the mul'gothra.

Elena's eyes refocused here. She saw the smoldering and burned bodies of the skal'tum. Only a single newborn remained, cowering under the belly of its mother. Its sibilant hiss had turned to a plaintive wail. The mul'gothra lowered itself over its last offspring, continuing a piping mewl of pain and sorrow. It drew its tentacles gently around the newborn and pulled it closer, protecting its child.

Er'ril stepped to Elena's side. "Why did you stop? Finish it off."

Elena bit her lip, then spoke. "I . . . I can't." She had seen the tiny flames of the slain beasts. Life was life—and this mother only wanted to protect its offspring. The mul'gothra here was as much a slave as any other. It did not want to feed its offspring to the Weirgate, but it had no other choice. Dark magick had bent its instincts to this unnatural purpose.

Stepping toward the monster, Elena waved her hand. "Go! Take your child and leave!"

The mul'gothra hissed at her motions, cringing down over her child, but when Elena did not attack, it mewled again, frightened and confused.

Elena waved her arm. "Begone!"

Thousands of orbed eyes watched her, studying her—then in a flurry of movement, its legs jerked, and the mul'gothra shot out of the tunnel and into the air, carrying the child in its tentacles. Huge wings snapped open to catch the late night's breezes. It swung once in a tight circle, then shot out over the jagged mountains and was gone.

"Why did you let it go?" Er'ril asked.

Elena shook her head. "I needed to." She moved ahead. "Let's finish this."

As a group, they climbed through the burned remains of the skal'tum and out into the night. Elena took a deep breath, clearing her lungs of the reek of charred flesh. The granite arm of the statue stretched ahead, a wide bridge that led to the massive chunk of ebon'stone resting in its palm.

Tol'chuk took the lead this time, the Try'sil hammer in hand. Elena followed with Er'ril.

She stared down. The arm's upper surface was flat and easy to cross. She could only imagine the long litany of horrors that had transpired here. Ahead, Tol'chuk reached the arm's wrist and paused. Before him lay the stone hand. Clawed fingers circled the ebon'stone like beastly pillars.

Elena stepped to Tol'chuk's side. "You can do this."

He nodded. "I can." Then he turned and climbed atop the stone palm, lifting the hammer high. "This is for my father's spirit!" Tol'chuk slammed the hammer down with all the strength in his og're shoulders.

But the blow never struck. The iron head fell into the stone as if the boulder were merely cloud. Tol'chuk, thrown off balance, fell forward and struck the side of the stone. On his knees, he twisted around and lifted his arm. He gripped only the rune-carved handle. The hammer itself was gone.

Behind her, Wennar fell to the stone and wailed. "The Try'sil!"

Elena stared at the unharmed stone. What had just happened? The hammer had been used to sculpt the cursed stone. It had been destined to be returned here and free the d'warves from the Dark Lord's yoke. Why had it failed?

For just a moment, Elena felt a twinge of suspicion of Tol'chuk. But she forced such thoughts away. It was impossible. The og're had saved her life many times, had served the Land with all his heart.

But Wennar did not know Tol'chuk as well. The d'warf burst to his feet, pointing an arm. "You! You did this! You've doomed our people just like your cursed ancestor!"

Tol'chuk covered his face.

Elena raised an arm between them as Wennar made a lunge toward Tol'chuk. "No! It's not his fault!"

"Then whose?" Wennar asked, his face almost purple.

Er'ril answered, moving to Tol'chuk's side. "We're all at fault."

Wennar blustered, but Magnam placed a restraining hand on his leader's arm. "Listen to him."

Er'ril turned to face them. "We failed because we're all victims of prophecy. We assumed we knew their import, but we were all obviously blinded by our own hopes." He glanced over his shoulder to the chunk of black rock. "I've traveled through the Weir before. It's a lodestone for elemental magick. Anything—objects or people—ripe enough in power will be drawn into its black heart."

"The Try'sil . . ." Wennar moaned.

"It was rich with the wind magick of the elv'in. We should have never let it near the Gate, but we were blinded by our faith in prophecy. And if there is one thing I've learned from my brother, placing one's full faith in prophecy can be damning."

Tol'chuk climbed to his feet. "Then what can we do? How do we destroy it?"

Elena spoke up, her voice full of dread. She glanced to the moon. It was low in the sky, close to setting. "I must consult the Blood Diary. It was Chi who fell into the Weirgates long ago and fused the four into this well of dire magicks. Cho, his sister spirit, may have some answers."

Er'ril nodded. "But back well away. I don't want you or that book near this stone."

Without arguing, Elena stepped farther down the wide arm.

Er'ril positioned a wall of d'warves between her and the ebon'stone boulder. He then joined her as she pulled the book free. Glancing up, she found his eyes on hers. Er'ril reached and clasped his hands over hers as they held the book between them. "You're trembling," he whispered.

"Just the cold." Elena turned away and tried to pull her hands free.

But she could not free her hand. The plainsman could turn to stubborn Standish iron when he wanted. "I don't know what is troubling you, what happened back in that tunnel to frighten you, but know this, Elena. I'm your liegeman. I'll always be at your side. My strength is yours to call upon."

She felt that strength now. The warmth of his palms calmed

her trembling. She leaned toward him, and he drew her in, hugging her. "I may not have faith in prophecy," he whispered into her hair. "But I have faith in you."

She fought back tears and huddled in his embrace. After a moment more, she took a deep, centering breath and stood straighter. He let her go, but she still felt his warmth wrapped around her. It was enough.

She turned away and opened the Blood Diary.

ER'RIL WATCHED ELENA TURN AWAY AND CLENCHED A FIST, worried for her. Though he did not see her open the book, he knew when its cover had been cracked. A blast of light exploded forth, and Elena flew backward into his arms.

He held her. Over her shoulder, he watched the flare of light empty out of the pages of the book and shoot skyward. He caught a peek into the Void: stars, and ribbons of glowing gases, and the edge of a blinding sun. Then a cry arose from the swirl of light overhead. It took on the form of a woman sailing high into the air.

"Chi!" The name was yelled like a striking bell, piercing the night and echoing off the surrounding peaks.

Holding the book, Elena stepped forward. "Cho! Calm yourself."

"I hear him!" Her voice became a wail. *"He cries and screams for me."*

The apparition swept down and along the arm, passing through the line of d'warves. It aimed for the ebon'stone boulder. Tol'chuk stood, raising to his full height, arms up, blocking Cho's way. But like the d'warves, she swept through his body and into the stone.

"No!" Elena gasped.

But the stone had no more effect on Cho than Tol'chuk's body had. The shining apparition shot out the other side, arced back around, then dove through again and again. *"He screams and screams. I must go to him!"*

Cho continued to dart back and forth through the stone, like a glowing will-o'-the-wisp. *"I can hear him! He is so close."*

Elena glanced at the sky. Er'ril knew what held her attention. *The moon.* It was near to setting. They were about to lose this night.

"Cho!" Elena called again. "You cannot reach Chi. You have no substance here. Listen to me!"

The sailing figure sobbed and slowed, hovering above the black stone. *"He needs me."*

Elena passed the Blood Diary to Er'ril. "I must calm her," she whispered to Er'ril. "Guard the book."

Next, she raised her arms. "I know, Cho. I once lost my brother. I understand the pain. But I need your guidance. I am your vessel in this world, your physical connection to this plane."

Cho drifted from the rock and settled to the stone palm. One hand reached back and touched the rock, passing through its substance. She was obviously loath to leave her brother's side. *"It is only together that we can free my brother."*

Elena relaxed. "Exactly. Together."

Cho turned in her direction. Eyes full of the Void stared back, cold and with an intelligence unlike any on this world. Then, for the briefest moment, Er'ril saw the flash of something human bchind those eyes. It was Fila. The apparition's lips moved. "No! Elena, no! You must not—"

Fila vanished, swept back into the Void. Only Cho was there.

Elena tensed, moving back into Er'ril's shadow. She glanced at him, confused. *What had Fila been warning?* she seemed to ask.

"Together . . ." Cho echoed.

Er'ril saw some seed of understanding—and terror—dawn in Elena's eyes. She swung back around as Cho dove forward, sweeping through Tol'chuk, through the d'warves, too fast to follow, like a reflection of moonshine off water.

"Break the bridge!" Elena yelled. "Close the book!"

Er'ril attempted to obey, but he was too slow. The spirit struck Elena, folding in, around, and through her. Er'ril was blasted back in a searing explosion of magick. Flying, he landed on his back and slid along the arm, keeping his fingers locked on the Blood Diary.

He sat up, his eyebrows smoldering from the brush of wit'chfire.

Down the granite arm, he stared at what remained of Elena. She still stood where she had a moment ago, but all her clothes had been burned from her body. Even her hair had been singed away. She stood naked to the night. From toes to scalp, her skin whorled with crimson magick, a ruby statue sculpted in the shape of woman.

Slowly, she began to step forward, toward the ebon'stone.

In her wake, a glowing mist formed, swirling down into the familiar form of the book's spirit, but it was less distinct, blurring at the edges. "Elena . . ." From the pain in the voice, Er'ril knew it was Fila rather than Cho.

Er'ril hurried forward.

The apparition lifted an arm. "No, Er'ril, stay back." She raised her voice. "All of you. Stand aside. Do not try and stop her! She can kill with a touch."

Though Er'ril could easily have walked through Fila's ghostly image, he held back. "What has happened to her?"

"Cho will not be stopped. She has heard her brother's tortured screams and must go to him."

"And Elena?"

"The girl was right. The only way Cho can effect any change in this plane is through Elena. Cho has merged almost all her spirit into the girl."

"Then she's taken over Elena's body?"

"No, Cho is in the Void. Elena still exists somewhere inside there, but the sudden surge of immense energies has unmoored her. She is lost to the desires of Cho, unable to break free, and her body responds. The only question is if Elena's strong enough to fight back to her own self."

Er'ril made a move forward, determined to help.

"No, Er'ril. Any interference could doom her."

Ahead, Er'ril watched Elena pass Tol'chuk and step up to the ebon'stone boulder. She stopped before it, ruby against black stone. Her neck craned, studying the ebon'stone as if she had never seen it before.

Elena, he prayed, *move back.*

Cocking her head, she reached forward.

"No!" Er'ril yelled. "Elena, stop!"

Without a look back, she stepped through the Weirgate and vanished.

23

STILL DAZED BY CHO'S ASSAULT, ELENA FOUND HERSELF WITHOUT any bearing. A part of her, as distant as an echo, felt her body carried forward and through the Weirgate. But it felt unnatural, like a dream after waking, hard to grasp and easily forgotten. Energy of unfathomable depths surged through her. The wit'ch thrummed in every fiber of her body, singing, wailing, crying out. It was a chorus of wild power and passions.

Her own spirit was but a mote in this frenzied storm.

Elena resisted the raging current. *I must not lose myself.* She forced her mind to stop its panicked attempts to fight against the tidal forces inside her. Instead, she pulled herself inward, using the swirl of these foreign energies to draw herself down to a single flickering flame of intense brilliance, a beacon in the dark storm. From this island of security, she fortified herself.

Once steady, she slowly extended her perceptions outward, riding the currents of power this time, rather than fighting. She first became aware of her own heartbeat, slow and steady. This helped reassure her. She was still alive.

Reaching farther, she followed her blood as it fanned throughout her body. As she did so, the sense of her limbs returned: bone, muscle, sinew. It was as if she were rebuilding herself from the inside out, incorporating Cho's power in each bit, redefining herself in this new context. With care, she stretched farther and steadily rediscovered her senses.

The wit'ch's mad song dimmed as Elena now listened through her own ears. A great silence blanketed her. It was not so much an absence of sound as an unsettling pressure—like diving into a lake. Just the pressure and the quiet.

But Elena knew this was no mountain lake.

This was the Weir.

Floating in this strange otherworld, Elena kept her eyes closed, fearing what she might see. *Cho, what have you done?*

Tentatively, Elena reached out with her other senses. She smelled no scent, tasted nothing in the air. The only sensation she did discover was a tingling burn that seemed to paint her entire body. She willed her arms to move and was surprised to discover control had returned to her limbs. As she swept her arms, struggling for anything solid, the burning grew worse from hands to shoulder, almost painful.

Swallowing back her fear, Elena risked opening her eyes—staring for the first time into the strange landscape of the Weir.

Around her was a swirling dense darkness, like a midnight sea—only this had the feel of something living. It caressed against her, but where it touched, her ruby skin flared brighter. As a matter of fact, her entire form burned like a tiny crimson flame in the darkness.

She studied herself and moved her arms through the substance of the Weir. Her skin flashed brighter. Elena understood. *Cho's magick is protecting me, suiting me in ruby armor against the touch of the Weir.*

With this realization, Elena stared around her. She turned and caught a flicker of movement. With a kick of her legs, she moved nearer, cautiously. The darkness seemed to clear, and she saw a surprising tableau: Er'ril and the others stood a short distance away, staring back at her. It was as if she were staring at them through a dark glass. She swam closer, her hands reaching forward. But her fingers ran into a solid barrier. She pressed against it. The group did not seem to see her

Muffled words reached her. "How do we know she still lives?" Er'ril asked.

The ghostly form of Aunt Fila stood behind his shoulder. "Because I'm still here. If Elena dies, so does the magick of the book. I would not be here if the bridge were severed."

Er'ril glanced to the sky. "But the moon is setting. What then?" Fila only shook her head.

Elena tried to beat against the barrier, but it did no good. She was locked into the ebon'stone Weirgate. "Er'ril!"

No one heard her.

She tried louder. *"Er'ril!"*

Tol'chuk jerked in her direction. He was closest to the stone. *"Tol'chuk! Can you hear me?"*

He leaned closer, placing a hand on the rock. "Elena?"

"Yes!" She almost wept with relief.

The og're glanced over his shoulder and bellowed, "It's her! Elena!"

Er'ril hurried forward and pressed his hands against the rock, trying to find a way through, risking the Weir to come to her aid. But he no longer had magick in his blood. The Gate would not open for him

"Er'ril, I'm safe! Cho's magick is protecting me."

"Then leave while you still can!"

She beat a ruby fist against the barrier. "I can't!"

Er'ril shoved harder, shoulders bunching. But it did no good.

Elena reached up and placed her hand over his, their palms separated by the magick of the Weirgate. "There must be another way out," she called. "Or a clue to destroying the Gates. I must go look."

"Elena! No! We'll find a way to get you out."

Elena lifted her palm from his and drifted back. "I'm sorry. I must try. Too much depends on it." And she knew this was true. Whether it was her own intuition or something gifted from Cho, Elena sensed an urgency to move on.

She pushed from the glass wall. The dark sea of the Weir swept back over the glass and swallowed the view of the others. Elena twisted around and delved deeper into the heart of the Weir.

The living darkness again surrounded her, featureless and forever. As she swam, Elena worried she would not even be able to find her way back. What if she never escaped here? How long would the ruby magick protect her? Her heart began to grow louder in her ears. A twinge of panic set in—but as she continued forward, she realized the pounding in her ears was not her own heart, but something beyond herself.

She paused, hanging in the dark sea, and concentrated on the source. She did not know what lay ahead, but it was better than the endless blank expanse. It was *something*.

She slowly swam forward again, aiming for the source of the deep, sonorous beat. After what seemed an endless time, she noticed the darkness grew lighter ahead, almost as if she were coming to another window to the real world. She kicked her legs more vigorously, creating a burn along her skin as the ruby magick flared brighter. Ignoring the pain, Elena sped faster.

The darkness continued to part until a white flame appeared ahead, floating in the black ether. It flared and dimmed in step to the thunderous beat.

Elena swept to a stop before it.

She knew what she was looking at. *"Chi,"* she said aloud.

But speaking the name caused no change. The light continued to ebb and flow like a living heart of white flame. Elena's face, chest, and legs burned brighter with each beat, the two opposing magicks igniting against one another, like a match set to oil.

Elena finally understood. She swung around. The living sea through which she had swum and continued to float now . . . it was all one entity. It was *all* Chi.

Spinning in place, Elena was overwhelmed by the immensity. If only she could speak to him, as she did to Cho. But she had no bridge to this spirit. She settled to a stop, drifting closer to the center of the Weir, the heart of Chi. How could she ever hope to free him? How did you destroy the Gates that bound him here, especially when the stone statues were tied to such a bottomless well of energy? It was a riddle she could not solve alone.

Cho, she silently prayed, *if you know some way to communicate with your brother, help me.*

Elena expected no answer. Cho was not truly inside her, just the spirit's energy. In some ways, Elena was like the Weir herself: a vessel full of power and energy. But unlike the Weir, she did not hold Cho's true heart inside her. It was still somewhere out in the Void.

Elena stared around her, wishing she had a better understanding of Cho and Chi, of the flows of power here. Then an idea formed. She did not know if it would help. *A spell*—one of the first magicks she had ever learned, one born of her own blood.

Raising a hand, Elena placed her forefinger between her teeth and bit into the skin at its edge. She tasted blood on her tongue, and as she pulled her finger free, a ruby radiance flamed forth from its tip. Craning her neck back, she squeezed her injured hand and dribbled a drop of fiery blood into each eye. The pain was almost too much. She gasped and clamped a hand over her eyes. It had never stung like this in the past.

Slowly, the pain dulled to a scratchy burn, and Elena risked opening her eyelids. She held her breath, fearing she had blinded herself. But she was fine. The sting had just been the Weir reacting to her magick.

She stared around. A new landscape opened, revealed by the magickal sight imbued in her blood. The sea of the Weir was still dark, but now it was veined with glowing lines of silver. Elena could not help but be struck by the similarity to ebon'stone: a black rock streaked with silver.

But these veins were not silver ore. Elena recognized the sheen to this power. She had seen it in Mycelle, Kral, and many others. It was elemental energy. Elena gaped around her. There was so much of it. The lines flowed under, around, and over her.

As she stared, the silver lines grew more substantial. She began to see a pattern stretching away into the darkness of the Weir. A far way off, the veins seemed to fuse and join, forming ever-thicker arteries. It was as if she were deep underground, tangled in the roots of a silver tree and looking up toward where the rootlets became thicker roots, which in turn became the trunk itself.

She glanced around and realized there were four trees, one growing in each direction of the compass. Elena knew this had to be significant.

Four Weirgates, four ebon'stones statues, four elemental fonts.

She approached the nearest, the one heading in the direction from which she came. She reached to the nearest vein and touched the silvery sheen. But nothing happened. Her hand passed through it without harm to either.

Then Elena had another idea. Her blood had opened her special sight. Could it do more? She brought her bitten finger, still blazing with blood, to the same vein.

As her finger touched it, her mind was torn away. She found herself staring back at Er'ril and the others, as if she again hung before the dark glass window. "There must be a way to free her," Er'ril said.

Surprised, her finger broke contact. And she found herself back beside the flaming heart. It was a direct conduit to the Manticore Weirgate.

Elena glanced around her. She drifted around the giant flame to the neighboring tree's roots and touched one of its rootlets.

Her mind again snapped away. She found herself staring at a

dark room. A brazier of red coals lay open on the floor before her, covered with a grate ornamented with twisted beasts and fantastic creatures. The iron of the grate glowed a fiery red. Beyond the coals, she sensed tiers rising up the room's walls: an amphitheater of some sort. She sensed eyes back there, spectators in the shadows.

Then movement drew her gaze closer. A cowled figure approached, guiding a naked, towheaded child of about four by one hand. The dark figure tossed aside his cowl to reveal a blasted and ruined face. It was as if someone had melted his features, then froze them in place. Elena gasped with recognition. It was Shorkan, leader of the Black Heart's darkmages, and Er'ril's brother.

Elena now knew she must be staring through the Wyvern Weirgate, the statue whisked away by Shorkan as he fled A'loa Glen.

Shorkan moved nearer the brazier. "On this black night, the Master's plan to break the Land upon his forge will come to fruition. As the moon sets, so will the hope of all the world. Let us praise the Black Heart!"

Voices cried from the dark galleries. "Praise the Black Heart!"

Shorkan whipped up an arm, revealing a jagged, curved dagger. "A sacrifice in his honor! An innocent heart cast upon his flames!"

Elena's gaze swung back to the cowering little boy. "No!" she cried out.

Ahead, Shorkan paused, his head cocking with suspicion. He seemed to lean toward her, eyes narrowed.

Elena froze. Could he see her? Sense her?

After a moment, Shorkan shook his head and straightened. Clearing his throat, he lifted the blade high again. "Praise the Black Heart!" The dagger slashed down.

Elena jerked her hand away. She could not watch.

She glided away from this foul tree, less sure, fearing she might have given her trespass away. As she slid around the flaming heart of the Weir toward the next elemental tree, she pondered Shorkan's words: *to break the Land upon his forge*.

She stared around at the flows of elemental energy that led from the Gates to here and began to understand. These were not so much *trees* of energy as rivers spilling through the gates and spreading into a thousand streams. The Gates were sucking vast fonts of energy into the Weir.

Her eyes grew wide. She now knew why the ebon'stone statues had been placed so carefully. Across the lands, there were points where the Land's elemental powers flowed stronger. She had learned this from Cassa Dar in the swamps of the Drowned Lands. The Dark Lord had tried to destroy such an artery long ago, a silver river of the Land's energy under Castle Drakk. But there were many others throughout the world.

Clearly the Black Heart had not given up on his desire to harm the Land. He must have positioned the Weirgates at four of the world's pulse points. But why? To tap the energy? Or was there a darker purpose?

Shorkan's words echoed in her head: *to break the Land upon his forge . . .*

Elena gasped with sudden insight and horror. The Dark Lord broke individual elementals by using slivers of ebon'stone to draw off their energy and corrupt it, twisting the bearer in turn, too. This was also the Black Heart's plan here—but not just to corrupt a single person or even a single land.

He meant to corrupt the entire *world*! By placing his monstrous Weirgates at key points around the globe and tapping into the planet's energy, he was going to forge the world into *one* monstrous ill'guard.

And if Shorkan spoke truly, this transformation was to occur this very night. Elena swam forward toward the neighboring nexus of elemental energy. Whether the Gates could be broken or not, a more immediate danger faced them all. If the Dark Lord succeeded, then they were all doomed.

Elena brought her flaming finger to a silver rootlet and touched it. She found herself staring into a gray granite room covered with dead bodies. *D'warves,* she realized, *scores of them.* The view shifted slightly, as if the window through which she peered were moving. It made no sense. Then the window turned, and she found herself staring at a familiar, shaggy, black-bearded face.

"Kral!" she yelled.

The mountain man fled backward in shock.

Behind him, Elena spotted other faces: Mogweed, Meric, and a sandy-haired man she did not know. And standing among them was a sight that made no sense: *Nee'lahn.*

Meric stepped up beside Kral, though a little warily. "Elena? Are you inside the griffin?"

"I'm in the Weir! We don't have much time! You must find a way to break the Gate's connection to its elemental source! Can you do this?

Meric shook his head. "We've tried everything. The Griffin Gate now defends itself, coming to life, attacking any who near it."

Elena thought quickly. *It must be nearing the time of transformation.* "Don't worry about destroying the griffin! Find a way to separate the stone beast from the elemental connection upon which it's feeding! Now! This night! Before is all lost!"

Meric frowned. "We don't know how."

Kral elbowed Meric away. "I do."

Meric tried to interrupt, but Kral faced Elena. "I will do this. Trust me."

Elena sighed with relief. "I must check the other Gates."

He nodded and lifted an arm. "I'm sorry, Elena."

Her finger lifted from the silver vein as these last words were spoken. She did not understand their exact import, but she did not have time to return and ask Kral. She didn't know how many of the Weirgates must be broken to thwart the Dark Lord's ambition, but she knew the surest course was to eliminate as many as possible.

She kicked and paddled over to the last of the silver flows, calculating in her head. The only Weirgate left was the basilisk, somewhere in the Southern Wastes. She slid up to the nearest shining branch and touched her finger to it.

A new view opened before her mind's eye: a sandy-floored chamber in a cavernous room. She almost cried in relief. Sy-wen sat atop Ragnar'k. At least some of the desert team had reached the Basilisk Weirgate. The view swung around. Clearly this Gate had come to life, too. A third combatant was revealed.

"Joach!" she shouted.

The call of his name startled her brother. "Kesla?" He stumbled back, falling on his backside.

"No, it's your sister!"

Sy-wen shifted her dragon back into view. "Elena?"

"I don't have much time!" She rapidly repeated everything

she had told Kral. "Can you find a way to break the Weirgate's connection to the Land?"

"I don't see how," Sy-wen answered. "Not even Ragnar'k can near that monster."

Elena saw the long gash on the dragon's chest, dripping with blood. She turned to the other party in the room. "Joach, do you know some way? Even a dark spell learned from the time you had Greshym's staff."

Her brother's head had remained bowed during her explanation. He raised it now. His eyes held a lost, hopeless look. "I think I do."

"You must try," she urged. "Or all the world is doomed."

Joach nodded, turning away, his voice pained. "Go. I know my duty."

Elena longed to reach through to him, to hold and comfort her brother, but instead, she pulled her hand back, and the sight vanished. *Comfort must come another day.* Elena floated in place. She had done all she could here. The rest was up to the others.

Elena kicked and swam back to the original silver river, then followed its course home. She had no idea how to accomplish what she had asked of the others. The Manticore Gate seemed invincible. She pondered her options, but she still had no answer by the time she reached the black glass barrier. She had secretly hoped that a way would reopen for her now. But as she swam up and pressed her hands against its surface, it was as impervious as ever.

With her spellcast eyesight, she now saw the flow of elemental energy piping up from the mountain and through the arm to the ebon'stone boulder. It seemed hopeless. There was no way to move the ebon'stone boulder or break the stone arm off. With so few here, it would take several moons to hack through this stone arm. If only she were free of the stone, she could attack with her magick.

Elena called to the others—they were still gathered near the stone—and told them all she had learned.

Aunt Fila drifted closer. "So we must either break the Gate or sever its connection?"

Elena nodded, then realized no one could see her. "Yes. It must be done this night, or the entire world will be corrupted."

Er'ril shook his head, looking all around. "I don't see how we can succeed."

"What of your magick, my dear?" Aunt Fila asked.

Elena had already tried freshening her finger wound and using the magick to shatter through, but this attempt had failed, too. The Weir was too large, and she was too small.

"It won't damage the stone," she answered in a tired voice.

"That's not what I was asking," Fila said. "I was talking about Cho's magick that's protecting you. It's not inexhaustible."

Elena stared down at her limbs, noticing for the first time how much less her skin glowed. She lifted her arms. Her magickal armor was rapidly thinning. She stared out into the dark Weir.

She knew once her magick was gone, so was her life.

WRAPPED ONLY IN A CLOAK, KRAL STARED AT THE CIRCLE OF FACES. They were fewer in number than when they had entered the throne room. Fardale had vanished, and Mycelle lay cold on the stone, covered in Tyrus' cloak, the family sigil of a striking snow leopard blazed on top. As Kral stared, he could read the distrust in their eyes, and he had no answer to their silent accusations, no way to ask for their trust.

"How do we know you're not still a pawn of the Dark Lord?" Meric finally asked. He pointed to the griffin, poised by the Ice Throne, its ebon'stone nails dug deep into the granite of the Citadel's arch. Now wakened, there was no safe way to approach the beast. Any who neared was threatened with talons and fang. Meric continued. "You attack the griffin, fail, and it comes to life. How do we know you didn't plan this?"

Kral hung his head, his fingers in his beard. "You can't."

Nee'lahn stepped to him, staring him hard in the face. She held her baby in her arms, rocking. "I don't know," she said.

Mogweed hung back. "I say we just leave. Strike out now while we still can."

"You're free to run," Tyrus said, nodding to the open door. "You've regained your shape-shifting abilities. Go. Take your chances with the d'warves out there waiting to avenge their slain king."

Mogweed scowled but did not take up the man's offer.

Tyrus held his family's sword pointed at Kral's heart. "I, for one, don't mean to leave until we do what your young wit'ch asked of us. We need to break this griffin's hold on the north." He glanced to Meric. "And I don't care a broken copper if this man is tainted or not. As a pirate of Port Rawl, I've fought beside cutthroats and brigands, and if I've learned one thing, it's that as long as a man's goal is the same as yours, then welcome him to your side, noble or not, tainted or not."

Meric seemed about to object, but Tyrus held up his free hand and continued. "I know Kral wants to rid the north of this evil as much as I. We are both men of stone—two sides of the same coin. I'm the granite wall. He's the mountain's root. If he says he can rid us of this cursed beast, then I say we give him our full support."

A silence descended after this speech. Then Nee'lahn finally nodded. "I think Lord Tyrus speaks wisely."

Meric sighed and shrugged. "I guess we don't have much choice. Sunrise is not far off, and he's the only one with a plan." Meric stepped forward, knocking aside Tyrus' blade, and offered his hand to the mountain man.

Kral hesitated, then took it. "I'll not betray anyone. Never again."

"What is this plan of yours?" Tyrus asked, his sword still unsheathed but no longer pointed at Kral's chest.

The mountain man straightened and faced them. "It was King Ry's prophecy."

"My father?" Tyrus exclaimed.

Kral turned to the hall, his eyes on the Ice Throne. "He predicted our victory in winning back my family's throne."

"Yes, so?"

"But have you forgotten the other part of the prophecy, words you told me on the docks of Port Rawl?"

Tyrus shook his head.

"You said I'd win back my throne, but I'd wear a broken crown."

"I still don't understand."

Kral held back the pain in his heart. He was free of the ill'guard curse, but not of his own guilt and shame. Losing his elemental powers was a small price, hardly enough to wash away the deaths, the betrayals, and the countless lies upon his tongue. Though the Dark Lord's taint was gone, Kral would be forever damned in his own eyes. He could still remember the rush of the chase, the taste of hot blood on his tongue, and the rip of life from a body. And free or not, a small part of him still thrilled to it.

Kral closed his eyes and swallowed. "There is another prophecy among my own people. I told it to Er'ril when first we met in Winterfell."

"I remember," Nee'lahn said. "You told us that the appearance of Er'ril, the Wandering Knight of legends, would mark the doom of your clans."

Kral turned to Nee'lahn, tears in his eyes. "Even then I was a coward. I didn't tell you all. My distress at that moment was not all for my people's future, but also for myself. The prophecy predicted that *whoever* met the Wandering Knight would bring about this doom."

Tyrus frowned. "I still don't understand the point. Broken crowns, prophecies of doom . . . what does it mean?"

Kral glanced one last time at his family throne. "By my own hand, I must break the crown of our people."

"What crown?" Mogweed asked. "Where's it hidden?"

Kral turned. "Our kings have never worn a crown. We have only the Ice Throne. The true crown of our people is here. You are standing in it. It is the arch rising from the waters of Tor Amon and reflected back in it—a circlet of granite and illusion. That is our crown."

"And you can break it?" Tyrus asked. "Bring down this arch?"

Kral nodded. "There is only one way."

Nee'lahn spoke up. "And if you succeed, then the Griffin Gate will be severed from the font of elemental energy rising here."

Kral bowed his head. "So I pray. May this one act help in some small way in salvaging my family's honor."

"Then let's do it," Tyrus said. "How do we begin?"

Kral searched their faces. "We must first return to the arch's reflection." He turned his back on the Ice Throne and stepped to the far wall. "Here is where we came in; here is where we must leave."

"Can you still open the way?" Nee'lahn asked. "If your elemental power is gone . . ."

"It is the arch's energy that drives the transition. It is only my royal blood that is the key. And elemental energy or not, I am still Kral a'Darvun of the Senta Flame." He held out his hand for them to link up.

It gave him a small bit of solace when Nee'lahn took his hand without a second glance. The rest linked flesh to flesh.

"Are you ready?"

"Get on with it," Mogweed snapped.

Kral nodded, then turned to the wall, closed his eyes, and took a step of faith. For a moment, he feared the arch would reject him, but ever loyal to his family, it opened the way. Kral felt the familiar, head-over-toes disorientation; then they were through.

The same throne room lay before them again, but the bodies of the dead were gone. Shimmers marked the torches' positions in the real world, creating a dim glow. Across the chamber, the mirror image of the Ice Throne stood tall, and beside it, the black whorling vortex that marked the griffin's shadow. Only now the black well had grown larger.

"What now?" Tyrus asked. "What do you want us to do?"

Kral walked toward the Ice Throne, keeping a wary distance from the vortex even though he no longer was an elemental. "I want you all to escape."

He reached the throne and sat down in it.

Tyrus stepped toward him. "I don't understand."

Kral pointed to the stairs. "Go down the way we came up. It should lead you back to the foot of the arch."

"But we can't leave the reflection on our own," Nee'lahn said. "Not without you."

"Yes, you can. When the crown breaks, so will the magick. You may get your feet wet, but you'll be free."

"And you?" Nee'lahn asked.

Tyrus answered instead. "He will win his throne but wear a broken crown."

Kral nodded. "Go . . . while you still can." As they made to move away, Kral remembered one last thing. "I'll need a blade— something with a fine edge."

Nee'lahn slipped a dagger from her belt, but Tyrus stayed her hand and unsheathed his own family sword. He crossed with care and offered Kral the hilt.

"I can't take your sword. Any blade will do."

Tyrus held the weapon at arm's length. "It is for the honor of my people. They're all gone. Mycelle was the last Dro warrior, and I'm the last of my line. Take my sword and accept a promise from me. Though this act will doom your people from ever returning to their ancestral home, I promise to seek your scattered clans and offer Castle Mryl as their new home. One granite castle for another." He pushed the sword closer. "A pact sworn in blood."

Kral did not wipe the tears that flowed down his cheek and into his beard. He simply took the length of fine Mrylian steel in his palms. "Thank you, King Tyrus. May I be the first of my people to swear allegiance to you."

"I accept your word with honor." Tyrus bowed, then led the group toward the stairs.

Kral did not watch them leave. It was too painful. Instead, he stared at the handsome sword and closed his fingers around it, the ache in his heart suddenly lighter. He had a long wait in this cold seat.

He listened to the footsteps of his friends fade to echoes, then away. And still he waited. He needed to give the others as much time as possible to climb out of the depths of Tor Amon.

Yet he did not have forever. The edges of the black vortex continued to expand, stretching toward the neighboring throne. Kral knew he would have to act before that darkness reached the white granite. He could not risk losing this chance.

As he watched the shadows encroach, a frightening sight took shape in the center of the vortex. The griffin began to push out of the whorling eye of the pool, as if it were merging between the two planes. Kral knew this was a bad sign. The corruption was beginning to wear through the veil between reality and reflection.

He stared, mesmerized, as the griffin grew more solid in form: wings, claws, the bulk of the lion, and jaws that seemed ready to swallow the world.

Kral knew he could wait no longer. "Godspeed, my friends." He grabbed the steel sword in his bare fingers and slid his hands down the blade, slicing palms and fingers to the bone, wetting the blade with his own blood.

Once done, Kral tilted his hands up and allowed his royal blood to pool in his palms. As he did so, he watched the griffin's wings begin to spread. Centuries ago, Kral's ancestor, defeated by the Dark Lord's forces, had not been brave enough to destroy the Citadel. But where his ancestor had faltered, he would not. Ready, Kral slapped his bloody hands on the arms of the throne.

Immediately, the ground trembled. A great quake shook upward, seeming to rise from the throne itself. Kral held tight to the arms of his throne, bearing final witness to the end of the Citadel.

Off to the side, he noticed the strange change in the griffin, but he was beyond such mysteries any longer and entering a greater one.

He turned his gaze upward, toward the world.

"To'bak nori sull corum!" he called to his friends with all the breath in his lungs and closed his eyes at last.

Until the roads wind us back home, you'll always be in my heart.

LOCKED WITHIN THE SOUTHWALL, JOACH KNEW HE HAD NO OTHER choice. He had to return to the dream desert.

"But Greshym is waiting for you down there," Sy-wen argued. She stood beside her dragon, one hand touching his scaled flank to keep Ragnar'k from reverting back to Kast. They needed the dragon's strength if any of the monsters attempted to attack from the tunnels beyond the basilisk's chamber.

Joach stared at the ebon'stone statue. No longer threatened, the basilisk had grown quiet again, coiled in place on the sand, content with its single meal. Joach turned away as tears threatened to rise. *Kesla . . .*

"What do you hope to accomplish?" Sy-wen asked. "You've already tried attacking the Weirgate with your dream-sculpted creatures, but they just fell to sand with the basilisk's touch. What more can you do?"

Joach had indeed thrown all his raw skill and power into sculpting something with which to attack the ebon'stone statue, but his forms were not strong enough. He needed to transform sand into stone—and he knew only one person with enough dark magick to accomplish this.

"I must go to Greshym. He may hold the key to destroying the Weirgate."

"But he's a creature of the Dark Lord. How can you trust him?"

"Because I have something he wants."

"What?"

Joach shook his head. Here was the crux of his own concern. What *did* the darkmage want with him in the desert? "I don't know," he mumbled. "But he's our only hope."

"A very dark hope." Sy-wen sighed. In her eyes, he saw that she grew resigned to his plan. What other choice did they have? The night wore thin, and daybreak was not far off. If they were to save the deserts, the risk had to be taken.

Joach stepped into the open sand. "Keep a watch on the basilisk."

"Be careful," Sy-wen said. "And wary!"

Joach nodded and slipped a dagger from his belt. He slit his thumb, then held his wounded hand over the sand. Bright red drops fell and spattered into the sand. Joach closed his eyes, linking to the dreaming magick in his blood, and fell back away toward the dream desert.

Be careful . . . and wary!

He would be both. Joach pulled up short from fully entering the glowing desert of the dream. He hovered in the shadow between the real and the dream, where only true sculptors could walk. He saw Greshym waiting in the sands, his arms crossed, leaning on his staff.

"I see you, boy. Have you come to honor your word?"

"No, the bargaining is not yet finished."

Greshym unfolded his arms. "What bargaining? You swore an oath."

"I swore I'd return to the desert, but I didn't say *when*."

Greshym's one good eye narrowed. "It seems I taught you deceit too well." The darkmage leaned forward. "What do you bargain for now? I've watched your little battle with the basilisk. Now you seek more answers? Must I do all your work for you?"

Joach clenched his single fist. "All I ask is that you lend me your staff. Give me access to its dark magick so I might sculpt an arrow strong enough to shatter the basilisk."

"You want this?" Greshym held up his length of petrified wood.

Joach stared at it, sensing the flow of dark energies. Already attuned to that tempting song, Joach knew the staff was not just dream, but real. Greshym had somehow brought its physical form into the dream desert with him.

"If you want my staff," Greshym said, stepping away, "you're going to have to come get it."

Joach had expected nothing less of the darkmage. "And if I do, you'll allow me to leave with it."

"I wouldn't have it any other way. The staff is yours."

Sighing, Joach closed his eyes. He knew it was a trap, but he would have to risk it. In his mind's eye, the length of petrified wood shone as a bright beacon. He *must* have the staff. Ever since first laying eyes on it, Joach had been fighting his lust for its touch. Now he used that sickness to give him the courage to step through the veil and into the dream desert.

Joach shifted and felt sand under his feet. He opened his eyes and stared back at Greshym. "I'm here. I have met my end of the bargain."

"I hear such anger in your voice, boy. Don't you trust me?"

"You swore to relinquish the staff."

"It is yours." Greshym held up the magickal length of wood. The darkmage's hoary eyes glinted with amusement and something darker, feral: a black hunger.

Joach knew this was the trap, but he could not help reaching for the staff. His arm rose, and his fingers reached. In his mind, he reconciled the decision as necessity, but in his heart, lusts and anger merged to a burning flame of desire. He had watched Kesla die, her tiny flame of magick swallowed into the bottomless well of the Weir. He would see the basilisk destroyed, no matter the cost!

His fingers wrapped around the petrified wood, and images flashed across his mind: *Shaman Parthus grabbing the same staff, Greshym's form molding to mimic the elder.*

Joach felt a jolt through his body. His vision grew dark. He felt the sands swirl around him in a whirling cyclone. His senses spun. Joach fought against a strange pull and dragged his awareness to the forefront. He and Greshym spun within a sandy cyclone, linked by the length of magickal wood—Greshym at one end, Joach at the other. Flames of darkfire raged along the staff's length.

As the twister spun faster, the darkmage's laugh grew stronger. Drawn out by the force of sandy cyclone, Joach felt something vital pull from his body. He gasped. Across the way, the form of Greshym blurred. They spun so fast now that Joach's image seemed to overlap Greshym's, the two blending together. As he watched in horror, a savage jolt suddenly ripped through Joach's body.

He screamed—and it was over.

Joach stood again in the sand, holding the staff in his grip, weak and dizzy.

Greshym stood across from him, but the darkmage had changed. His skin was smooth; his brown eyes were bright and clear; and his hair—a thick, rich copper—trailed to his shoulders. The darkmage straightened, unbending the crook in his spine. A laugh, full of vigor and substance, flowed from him. "Thank you, Joach." He released his grip on the petrified wood. "As promised, the staff—and all the magick in it—is yours!"

"What—?" Joach lifted his prize. The wood was gripped by a hand he did not recognize—a withered and bony thing lined by purplish vessels. He looked down at himself. His legs shook, thin as reeds now. He planted the staff into the sand to keep from falling over. "What have you done?" His voice cracked.

"A small price to save your world," Greshym said. "I have not slain you or corrupted you, just stolen your youth!" The darkmage waved a hand, and the mirage of a mirror appeared. Joach found himself staring at a bent-backed elder leaning heavily on a staff, his white hair trailing to his waist, his face wrinkled and splotched. But Joach knew this was no stranger. Green eyes—eyes he knew—stared back at him from the mirror.

"An illusion," Joach said, disbelieving. "Like Shaman Parthus."

"No, I'm afraid the shaman was just an ordinary dreamer, dealing with illusion. But you are a sculptor. Changes wrought with your magick are *real*. The youth I stole from you is permanent."

Joach sensed the truth to Greshym's words. He pointed the staff at the darkmage. "Undo it!"

Greshym stepped back. He held a hand up, not to ward against Joach's threat, but to admire the beauty of his own youth. "It's simply wonderful. Youth, more than gold or power, is the truest treasure in life."

Joach reached for the dark energies in the staff. Though he may have aged, he could still wield magick. He raised the weapon, but to his horror, he found the wood empty.

Greshym smiled sadly at him. "I told you I'd give you the staff, Joach, and any magick it contained, but I'm afraid my little spell was quite a drain on energy. I needed *all* its magick to wreak this transformation."

"You tricked me."

Greshym waved his hand dismissively. "I played to your own base desires. You didn't come here to save your world. That was just an excuse. You came because you lusted for the staff and its dark magick."

Joach's legs trembled. He wanted to rail against Greshym's words, but he didn't have the strength to put up a false face. Deep in his heart, Joach knew the darkmage spoke truthfully. He hung his head.

Greshym sighed. "I do feel like I've sorely used you. So let me grant you this additional boon—for free, from the generosity of my youthful heart."

Joach glanced up.

Greshym waved an arm. "The answer to your problem is here. It does not require black magick, only your own, Joach. You've always been the answer—you and that bit of a dream shaped like a girl."

Joach closed his eyes. "Kesla is gone, consumed by the Weir."

"Oh, come now, since when can a dream be destroyed? Did the original Shiron die after the battle with Ashmara? As long as the desert lives, so does the dream."

Joach drew himself up on his staff, hope flaring.

"You're a sculptor. This is the dream desert. Draw this girl back to the sands."

Joach blinked. "I can do that?"

Greshym rolled his eye. "Oh, how I'd love to train you. You're so unmolded." He then sighed and spoke more soberly. "Of course you can resurrect her . . . if you concentrate hard enough."

Joach remembered Shaman Parthus' warning about the figments of the desert: *if you stare too long, they can become real.* He faced Greshym. "But how can bringing Kesla back help? She failed last time."

Greshym stared at him for a long time. "I think I've told you enough. If you want to savor a victory here, then figure out the rest by yourself." The darkmage stepped away, lifting an arm, ready to depart.

"Wait!"

"Look around you, Joach; look around you." Then he was gone.

Joach felt the ember of hope burn away. What good would resurrecting Kesla accomplish? She was dream. If the desert died, so did she, and Joach could not bear to watch her die a second time.

He leaned on his staff and searched the desert. Underfoot, the sands were black with the stain of the basilisk. He stared out and saw the darkness spreading farther and farther into the glowing desert. It was close to being entirely consumed. Joach turned away and stared at his toes, defeated.

Then realization dawned inside him, burning away all emotions, hollowing him out, leaving only cold horror. He fell to his knees. Somewhere far away, he heard harsh laughter.

Curse you, Greshym.

Joach now understood the role Kesla and he were meant to play. He dropped the staff across his knees and covered his face with one hand. What was asked was too hard. Not this price.

Rocking in the sand, Joach knew he had no choice, but he could not bring himself to start. He shut out everything and pictured Kesla's violet eyes—the same shade as an oasis pool at midnight—and imagined her skin, as soft as the finest sand and the color of burnt copper. He remembered her lips, so soft against his, her touch so gentle and warm, her curves so inviting to melt into. He touched the love in his own heart, still fresh, still raw from its recent loss. He knew his love had been shared.

"Sir?" a voice spoke before him.

Joach jerked back and saw a sight that quaked his being. Kesla stood before him, leaning over, an arm outstretched.

"Can you tell me where I am?" Kesla stared around the blackened landscape. "I've lost my friends." She touched her forehead. "We were in the Southwall."

Joach used his staff to regain his feet. "Kesla."

Her name spoken by a stranger clearly startled her. "Sir, do I know you?"

Joach smiled sadly at the wary glint to her eyes. No matter the circumstance, it was wonderful to see her again. He stared and willed all his love toward her.

Take all my love from me, he prayed, *or I won't have the strength to do what I must.*

Concentrating with all his heart, he felt a part of his spirit drain out of him, giving substance to what his pained imaginings had wrought. He sent everything in him toward the figment of his love. As he did so, she seemed to grow more solid, more detailed. He saw the sweat that beaded her brow, the scared tension in her stance; then he saw a glint of recognition. She stepped nearer, staring back into his eyes.

"Joach?"

He closed his eyes to hold back the tears. "No," he said with a hoarse choke. He did not want her to know him.

"It is you!" Kesla closed the space between them. He felt the warmth of her presence.

He opened his eyes, and tears flowed down his face, hot and burning. "Kesla . . ."

She leaned into him, reaching her arms around him, pressing her soft cheek against his. "Oh, Joach, I thought I had lost you!"

Joach stared over her shoulder to the spreading black stain of corruption. Kesla loved the desert.

Still, Joach hesitated. He pulled back and stared into her eyes one last time. "I love you, Kess. I always will."

She smiled and hugged him back to her, tight and forever. "I love you, too."

Joach closed his eyes and willed the blade to appear in his hand: a long dagger, with an edge so fine it sliced without pain. In this dreamscape, anything was possible. Joach held Kesla tight, willing a lifetime of love into her—then drove the blade through her heart.

He felt a small gasp escape her, and her grip tightened on him. He held her tight. Blood poured over the blade's hilt, over his hand, and drained into the black sand at their feet.

"Joach . . . ?"

"Shush, my love. It's only a dream."

Joach kept his eyes closed, holding her as she slowly sagged against him. Tears flowed until he felt her last breath on his cheek, and still he did not release her. He stood for an untold length of time, then finally opened his eyes.

The pool of blood at his feet had washed away the stain from the sands. Like the black pool upon which Ashmara had stood, the darkness here was vanquished by the purity of Kesla's blood. Under him, the sands glowed bright again, and as he watched, the miracle spread, cleansing the sand in all directions, driving the basilisk's touch from the elemental desert.

Joach, too heavy of heart to stand any longer, sagged to the ground, cradling Kesla's limp form in his lap. He brushed back a strand of hair from her face and wept.

"You did it, Kesla. You saved your desert."

24

CROUCHED ON THE STONE ARM OF THE MANTICORE, TOL'CHUK stared at the skies. The moon had almost set; only its edge still gleamed above the jagged horizon. Closer, the ghostly apparition from the book had grown hazy, weakening with the moon's departure.

"We must hurry!" Fila said.

Er'ril stood before the ebon'stone boulder. His face was ruddy from exertion, his forehead slick with sweat. He raised the ax once more and drove it down upon the boulder. Iron rang brightly against the stone, but it did no harm. Er'ril hefted the ax again, its edge now chipped and dulled from his previous assaults.

"It's no use," Wennar said. "Only the Try'sil could hope to shatter it." The d'warf glanced accusingly in Tol'chuk's direction.

Tol'chuk looked down.

"Elena!" Er'ril called.

"I'm still here," she answered, her voice floating out of the stone. "But I don't know for how much longer. The magickal protection wears thin. Already I feel the pull of the Weir. Once Cho's magick dies, I won't be able to stop it from claiming me."

Tol'chuk closed his eyes. There had to be an answer. Er'ril had spent his brute force, Fila had sought an answer in the spiritual plane, and Wennar had simply accepted defeat. What role did he play? The Heart of his people had guided him to the wit'ch. His father's shade had pointed him to Gul'gotha, and the Bane had led him to the Manticore Weirgate.

And now Tol'chuk sat on his haunches—useless. What was he supposed to do? He had all these fragmented bits, and he knew some answer lay among them, but only if he could fit them into proper order.

He clenched a clawed fist in frustration. He wore the face of the Dark Lord, proof of his cursed lineage. This thought kept him from being able to think clearly. It blanketed him with a sense of doom. He thrust it back now. He would not accept such a fate.

Reaching to his thigh pouch, Tol'chuk ripped it open and tore out the chunk of heartstone. He held it up to the moon's light, staring at the black Bane hidden inside the ruby stone. *What be the meaning? Why has the Land cursed my people? Why has it led me here?*

Elena's voice called from the stone. "Er'ril, I can't hold on . . ." Her voice faded.

"Elena!" Er'ril called.

Tol'chuk turned, knowing all was about to be lost. He gripped the heartstone and stared at the boulder. A seed of realization struck him. The Heart of his people was a ruby stone holding something black at its heart, and the Weirgate, with Elena inside, was a black stone holding something ruby. The symmetry had to have meaning. But what? What was the Land's purpose in putting the Bane in the stone? Why have it feed on his people's spirits and leave the stone dead and without magick?

Tol'chuk blinked, then burst to his feet. *"Without magick!"* he yelled.

Er'ril glanced over his shoulder.

Tol'chuck lifted the Heart of his people. "It be without magick! The Bane killed it!"

Er'ril frowned, wiping his brow.

Tol'chuck rushed forward. "The Land did not curse our people! It gave us the tool to avenge my ancestor's betrayal!" He recalled the tale of Mad Mimbly, the miner who had first discovered heartstone. In his ramblings, the d'warf had claimed that only *heartstone* held the power to defeat the coming darkness.

Er'ril moved to block him, but Tol'chuk let his sudden surety guide him. He knocked Er'ril aside.

"Help me!" Elena called, her voice a faint whisper trailing away.

Tol'chuk raised his chunk of heartstone over his head. "Without magick, the Weir has no hold over the Heart!" With all the strength in his og're shoulders, Tol'chuk slammed the heartstone into the black boulder.

The resulting explosion flung him back, slamming him into Er'ril and sending them both tumbling. A scream pierced the night, echoing out into the mountains.

Tol'chuk sat up. Atop the stone palm, the boulder lay in a shattered ruin. But it was no longer ebon'stone. Piled and broken atop the palm was pure *heartstone*.

Er'ril jumped to his feet and rushed to the piled debris, climbing and kicking his way through ruby rubble. "Elena!"

Tol'chuk lifted his hand. The Heart was still gripped in his claws, unharmed. He lifted the jewel, and it burst into a blazing glow. Startled, Tol'chuk almost bobbled it from his fingers, but then gripped tighter. It had been restored! He lifted it higher. Even the Bane had vanished!

"Elena!" Er'ril's tortured scream drew him from the stone.

The plainsman crouched amid the ruby rubble. He bent and lifted a pale figure from out of the debris. It was Elena. Er'ril turned and faced them. She hung limp in his arms.

"She's dead!"

MERIC STOOD AT THE EDGE OF TOR AMON. HE HAD KEPT HIS VIGIL all night, searching the dark lake for any sign of Kral. Earlier, the snowstorm had blown itself out, except for occasional gusts that carried a few flakes. But he had refused to leave the lake until dawn. He had to be sure.

The lake's surface had settled back to its placid, glassy sheen, snow banked high along its sides. The only evidence of the great arch was a few shattered chunks of broken granite poking above the water.

The fall of the Citadel had been sudden and rapid.

After leaving Kral's side, he and the others had fled down the stairs, just reaching the base when a violent quake shook the entire structure. Kral's last words had proven true. With the shattering of the arch, the group had been tossed back to the real world. Free, they had raced across the narrow bridge to the forests beyond, fleeing the huge waves that washed the shores as massive chunks of granite crashed into the deep lake.

The others—Mogweed, Nee'lahn, and Tyrus—were hidden in a nearby cave, warming by a strong fire. Meric glanced over his shoulder and made out the small glow of their hearth. He also noticed the eastern skies had paled, stars vanishing with the approach of dawn.

The plan was to head out with the rising sun, to escape over the pass before another storm came and closed the upper mountains completely. Earlier, Tyrus had used his silver coin and contacted Xin aboard the *Stormwing*. The ship would meet them beyond the Northwall, though there seemed to be some problem with the *Stormwing* that Xin couldn't fully explain—adding another reason not to delay here.

It left little time to mourn lost friends.

Sighing, Meric surveyed the lake one last time and headed back to the small camp. He trudged through the snow. At least there was no sign of d'warves. They must have all fled in a panic with the collapse of the Citadel.

Meric climbed up the icy slope to the cave, drawn to the warmth and light.

Tyrus stood guard near the entrance. He did not even bother asking if Meric had spotted any sign of Kral. "It was a fool's errand," the man had stated earlier. "The mountain man is gone."

Meric could not fault Tyrus' assessment, but the prince had not shared the cellar under Shadowbrook with the mountain man. Both Kral and Meric had been tortured by the d'warf lord Torwren. Kral had come to rescue Meric, but the mountain man had ended up paying the ultimate price, while Meric had escaped with nothing but burns and bad dreams. Meric owed Kral. Guilt had forced Meric to search for a sign of the man, for some slim chance.

But at the end, Tyrus was right. *It was a fool's errand.*

Nee'lahn looked with sympathy upon him. "I will write a song of him," she said softly. "Of his sacrifice. He'll live on in my music."

Meric smiled weakly. "Someday you'll have to play it at Castle

Mryl—for Kral's people, when they return from their centuries of wandering."

She nodded. The babe in her arms slept soundly after the long, loud night.

Meric settled to a seat next to Mogweed. "So I expect you'll be returning to the forests of the Western Reaches."

Mogweed shrugged, staring sullenly into the flame.

Settling to a cup of weak tea, Meric warmed his chilled bones. Slowly the skies continued to brighten, and after a while, Tyrus called for them to prepare for the day's march.

Meric stretched his legs and shouldered his pack. He stared as the sun's first rays pierced the horizon. At his side, Mogweed suddenly collapsed, a fist clutched to his chest. Meric was closest and hurried to his aid.

Mogweed was down on his hands and knees.

Meric reached for him. "Mogweed . . . ?"

A growl escaped the man, feral and wild. The man shoved back and rose. "I'm not Mogweed."

"Then who—?"

The man turned to the rising sun. "Fardale." Though the man's face was the same, there was no doubt a change had occurred. This man carried himself differently. His eyes were sharp and quick.

Nee'lahn and Tyrus joined him.

"Fardale? How?"

The man scowled. "More of my brother's mischief. Mycelle's snake. It's fused us in some strange manner."

"And Mogweed?"

Fardale wiped his hands on his shirt in disgust. "Though I can't feel him, he's still in there, where I was a moment ago: locked in a prison without bars, watching all transpire while you're held helpless."

"But what made the switch occur?" Nee'lahn asked.

"I had no control of it; neither did Mogweed."

Meric spoke up. "Mycelle's paka'golo was attuned to the moon. And you appeared with the first glint of the sun. Hmm . . . I wonder . . ."

Fardale stared at him, clearly not understanding.

Meric glanced to the rising sun. "I suspect that during the day you'll control this body, but at night, Mogweed will take over again."

Fardale's expression grew ill. "If true, I must find a way to break this spell."

"And I'm sure Mogweed will feel the same way." Meric snorted. "I guess you'll both be staying with us a little longer."

Tyrus shook his head and stomped away. "Then let's be off. We've a long road ahead of us."

JOACH STAYED WITH KESLA'S BODY UNTIL THE SUN ROSE IN THE REAL world and the dream desert dissolved around him, stealing Kesla from his lap. Joach found himself back in the chamber of the basilisk.

Sy-wen crouched on one side of him, Kast on the other. His transformation must have frightened them into releasing Ragnar'k for the moment.

"Are you all right, Joach?" Sy-wen asked.

"You aged a hundred winters right before our eyes." Kast stepped aside.

Joach caught his first sight of the basilisk. He frowned. It still bore the same shape: a feathered serpent with the head of some foul carrion bird. But it was no longer sculpted of black ebon'stone. It now glowed with a soft ruby light, reflecting the torchlight.

"Heartstone," Joach mumbled.

Kast straightened and glanced to the statue. "It happened not long after you aged." He turned back to Joach. "What happened?"

Joach shook his head. He held an arm up for the Bloodrider's help in climbing to his old legs. Bones creaked, and flares of pain lanced his joints; but he bit against the pain and stood. He took a step and tripped over something in the sand.

He glanced down.

"What's that?" Sy-wen asked, and reached for it.

"Don't!" Joach snapped harshly, frightening her back with his tone. Assisted by Kast, he bent down and retrieved the length of wood. "It's mine."

Joach had paid a high price for his prize. He was not about to give it up. He lifted the staff from the sand and leaned on it, not even hearing his own sigh of relief. With care, he hobbled toward the statue.

"Be cautious," Sy-wen warned.

With his back toward them, Joach lifted a corner of his lip in a silent snarl. His fingers sensed the small amount of dark energy coursing through the wood. Empty before, the petrified wood must have absorbed the power from the black sands after he'd tossed the staff aside. Joach lifted it now and pointed it at the statue.

"Joach!" Sy-wen called with warning.

He ignored her. He reached to the magick in the staff and spoke the spell of balefire, a spell as familiar as his own name. His lips grew cold, and the tip of the staff bloomed black. He finished the last words, and a spear of darkness shot out and struck the bright stone, shattering the basilisk and spraying the far wall with thousands of ruby shards.

Joach lowered his staff and leaned on it as he turned.

"What happened to you?" Kast asked again.

Joach simply nodded toward the tunnel leading out of the chamber. "I'm done with deserts."

ATOP THE PALM OF THE MANTICORE, ER'RIL STUMBLED OUT OF THE shards of broken stone and carried Elena free. Weak with shock, he fell to his knees before the apparition of Fila, holding Elena's body in his arms. "She doesn't breathe," he struggled out, his throat clamped tight. "I feel no heartbeat."

Fila knelt in front of him. Her hands reached and passed through Elena's form. "No, Er'ril, she's still alive, only weakly so. The Weir has touched her and driven her far."

Er'ril sagged with relief. "She'll live. She'll recover. The healing properties of the Blood Diary . . ."

Fila frowned and glanced to where the book lay open on the granite arm. "I'm not so sure. This is no bleeding wound or sick bowel. Her injuries go much deeper. Displaced so recently by Cho's merging, Elena was especially fragile, her ties to herself weak. The Weir may have permanently ripped her from her moorings."

"Elena's strong," Er'ril began. "She'll fight back."

"I don't know if that is something she can do alone." Fila

stared back at him. "There are bonds between you two that go unspoken."

Er'ril closed his eyes, hiding his shame.

"With her own tethers burst, she needs those bonds now. Your bonds. Something to help her find her way back."

"I don't understand." Er'ril lifted his face.

Fila shook her head. "Men," she sighed. "You must—"

In a whisk of light, Fila vanished. Er'ril turned to the book. It was still open, but the Void was gone, replaced by plain, blank white pages. He glanced to the sky. The moon had set, ending the book's magick for this night.

Er'ril was alone with Elena. He swung to Magnam. "Go fetch Mama Freda."

The d'warf nodded and dashed away.

Tol'chuk appeared at his shoulder. "The healer will never arrive in time." The og're knelt beside Er'ril. "And what ails her won't be cured with herbs."

Er'ril did not answer Tol'chuk. He knew the og're spoke the truth. He simply nodded and waved the og're away.

Er'ril bent over her body. *There are bonds between you that go unspoken.* He touched her face, not caring who saw. Something deep inside him finally broke. The Standish iron in his heart melted, running hot through his blood. He could not hide his feelings any longer. He yielded to his grief. Tears flowed and fell from his cheek to hers. His throat choked as he leaned closer. "If you can hear me, Elena, come to me."

He bent and allowed his lips to brush against hers. "Hear me; come back to me." As he hovered over her, he felt the slightest brush of breath flow between her lips, the barest flutter.

She needs those bonds now. Your bonds.

He lifted Elena in his arms, wrapping her tight to him. He hesitated, then pressed his lips to hers. She was so cold, but he did not pull away. He warmed her with his breath, with his touch, with his tears. "Come back to me," he whispered between their lips.

SHE HUNG IN DARKNESS, LOLLING, WITHOUT A NAME, WITHOUT substance. She had no knowledge of a past or a future, just the endless moment of now, hanging in the cold abyss of nothingness.

Then a single word rang through to her. *"Elena."*

It held no meaning.

She ignored it.

But soon a wave of warmth wafted through the darkness. And more meaningless words. *"Come to me."*

She pushed these aside, still far from understanding, and followed the river of warmth. A basic instinct: to warm oneself. She swept along and found the cold fall away from her. It was good.

As she sailed toward this pleasure, additional feelings swelled into existence, substance forming out of darkness. She allowed these new sensations to wrap around her, to become her. She learned she had an outer being, defined spaces—and she was rewarded. Warmth turned to heat, and it pressed against her, bright and hot.

In this moment, one word crystallized—not a name, but a word she fought to understand.

Iron.

She wanted more of it. She wrapped it around herself. She pulled it closer and allowed it to move through her. With each touch, she understood more of herself: lips, skin, touch, moisture, breath, heat, and a scent that was musky and familiar.

"Elena." That word again flowed to her.

She felt her newfound lips moving. "Er'ril . . ."

The heat around her surged stronger, everywhere, all around her. Encouraged, she repeated the name. It was a *name*! "Er'ril . . ." She wanted to say more but could find no other words. She needed words! Panic allowed the coldness to seep back in—but then he was there, calling to her, touching her, warming her.

"Elena, come to me."

"Yes." She spotted a brightness in the dark abyss and fled toward it. The voice came from there. *Er'ril.*

She dove into and through the light. Words and memories flooded—too much, too bright, too fast. Darkness threatened at the corners.

"Elena, come back to me."

And with a final spasm of light, sound, and memory, she did.

Elena opened her eyes, knowing who she was again. She found herself wrapped in strong arms, being kissed. Startled, she broke away.

Staring up, she found Er'ril, his eyes full of tears and something much deeper. "I love you, Elena," he said, his voice hushed and pained.

Elena met his eyes and reached a trembling hand to touch her own lips.

The shine in Er'ril's eyes dimmed. "I . . . I'm sorry."

He moved to release her, but she placed a hand on his shoulder and leaned up to him. She kissed the lips that had saved her, tasting the salt of his tears. "No," she whispered, and melted into him.

He closed his arms around her.

Here was where she belonged.

25

ELENA HURRIED DOWN THE HALL, THE HEM OF HER GREEN DRESS sweeping through the rushes that lined the castle's stone floor. She was late. The others should already be gathering in the Grand Courtyard.

She passed a mirror and brought a hand to her hair. After being burned away by Cho's assault, her fiery curls had grown out to the length of four fingers. But they were still as short as a boy's. She sighed. Mama Freda had done her best. Two combs of silver and pearl and her dress's high neckline detracted from her boyish hair. She looked at least presentable for the ceremony.

At last, she reached the restored glass-and-gilt doors that opened to the courtyard. Two d'warves armed with pikes stood sentry, but upon seeing her, they moved from their positions to open the tall double doors. Elena stared as morning sunlight poured through the panes depicting two roses twined together, the petals of heartstone, the leaves of emerald.

As the doors opened, the Grand Courtyard spread before her in all its spring beauty. While she had been away, the repairs on A'loa Glen's castle had continued. In the yard, there was little evidence of the recent war.

Beds of roses and snow-white poppies filled the space, while rows of trimmed holly bushes lined paths of crushed white stone. Along the wall, saplings of dogwood were in bloom, their soft petals drifting on gentle sea breezes. Even the walls had been repaired, and veins of green ivy already climbed their surfaces. The only clear sign of the War of the Isles was the eastern tower called the Broken Spear. Scaffolding and piled bricks encircled its ruins as work continued.

Elena crossed through the doors to the steps. A small group gathered in the central circle of the courtyard. Er'ril noticed her and raised a hand in greeting, but she knew that exasperated set to his lips: she was late for the ceremony.

Hiding her smile, she climbed down the stairs, lifting the skirted edge of her dress, and headed across the crushed stone paths. This was the first time everyone had gathered in one place since Meric's group had returned from the north. The party that had sought the Griffin Gate was the last to arrive back at A'loa Glen, coming almost two moons after Elena had returned and one moon since Joach had.

But everyone was here . . . finally.

As Elena crossed toward them, she remembered her own journey back. She had left A'loa Glen in early winter and had returned with the first buds of spring. The return journey had been arduous. With the Manticore Gate destroyed, they had set off overland back to Jerrick's skiff. The going was slowed by their injuries and their load of heartstone from the broken Gate. Tol'chuk had insisted they haul it out with them. "Mad Mimbly claimed it could destroy the darkness," he had said. Elena hadn't argued. The og're and his heartstone had saved her.

Still, loaded or not, the true delay in reaching A'loa Glen had proven more ominous. Upon reaching Jerrick's skiff, it was discovered that the elv'in had a harder time controlling his small boat. They had to make short hops with rest breaks in between, slowing their progress. There was no way they could cross the Great Ocean in such a state, so they worked their way overland to the coastal township of Banal and hired an ordinary ship with a few pieces of heartstone.

At first, Elena had attributed Jerrick's weakness to his recent poisoning, but upon reaching A'loa Glen, she had learned it was a generalized ailment. A good part of the remaining elv'in fleet now rested atop the sea. And this malaise was not limited to the elv'in. All those with elemental gifts found it harder to touch their inner magick and exhausted more quickly. It seemed that, though the destruction of the three Weirgates had managed to thwart the Dark Lord's design, damage had still been done. The Land had been weakened by the near-fatal assault, crippling the magickal gifts of all elementals.

Yet, despite this, one significant gain had been made.

As Elena reached the central circle of the courtyard, she spotted Wennar, outfitted in polished armor, with Magnam at his side. The breaking of the Manticore Gate had freed their people, shattering the Dark Lord's yoke upon them. Meric had returned with several d'warves in tow. He had met these stragglers on his return journey, and he promised that legions more were already en route to help bolster A'loa Glen.

All in all, it was a bittersweet and costly victory. The Dark Lord had been thwarted, but Chi remained a prisoner, shackled by the last remaining Weirgate. And in addition, many good friends had given their blood to protect the Land: Mycelle, Kral, Richald, Queen Tratal. The list stretched even longer, with losses among the d'warves, the elv'in, and the desert folk.

Then again, it seemed no one who had ventured out on these journeys had returned unscathed. She stared around the circle of friends gathered here.

Meric stood on the far side. His eyes were still haunted, grieving for the loss of his mother and brother. Each day he sent birds out, seeking some word of what had become of the refugees of his shattered home. But none ever returned. The fate of the denizens of Stormhaven remained unknown.

Beside the elv'in stood Lord Tyrus, dressed in black finery, both prince and pirate. He had offered her his allegiance and had already succeeded in rallying a rather unsavory lot from Port Rawl. The prince refused to return to his empty castle in the Northwall until the Dark Lord was defeated. "The Grim wraiths are gone from the Fell, but Mryl will never truly be secure until the Black Beast is driven from our shores," he had told Elena.

At the prince's shoulder, Fardale wore Mogweed's face. Elena had learned of their strange transformation, two sharing one body. The "pair" made her uncomfortable. She always sensed the extra eyes staring out of the amber glow. Still, they had proven their loyalty. The two were simply wounded like so many others, and Elena would do her best to seek a cure. In turn, they had pledged their shape-shifting talents to her cause.

Crossing the stones, Elena stepped beside Er'ril. The back of her hand brushed his, and their fingers instinctively sought one another, wrapping and twining together. Er'ril squeezed her hand. On the long journey here, they had both decided to take their relationship slowly, one step at a time. They had not shared a bed, but only tentatively sought to know each other in the quiet hours alone. And for now, that was enough.

"You're late, wife," he whispered teasingly.

"And you don't have layers of petticoats and fancy dress to attend to, husband." Elena hid her smile while shifting an imaginary lock of hair from her face.

Er'ril nodded to a shaded corner of the courtyard. A figure sat upon a bench staring toward them. "It's good to see Joach abandon his books and scrolls for a short time."

Elena's smile dimmed. Of all those who had returned from the various lands of Alasea, Joach was the most changed—not just physically aged, but also harmed in unseen ways. She had heard the tale of Kesla's death from Sy-wen. Deep inside, her brother's heart had been wounded past repair. Upon returning, Joach had been clearly happy and relieved to see his sister safe and alive, but otherwise he kept to himself, locked in the castle's library, reading ancient texts for spells that might cure him. Some nights Elena had spied him in the training yards, practicing some arcane magick.

Er'ril scowled. "I just wish he'd left that cursed staff in his rooms. It shouldn't be here."

Elena agreed. The sight of it made her stomach churn: its petrified wood was the gray of a corpse, and the tiny green crystals imbedded along its length reminded her of pus from a festering wound. It was a corrupt instrument, and she wished Joach would simply destroy it. But she also understood her brother's obsession. The staff had stolen his youth, so it might still hold the answer to returning it.

Er'ril sighed and returned his attention forward. "The staff, the age-ravaged body, even the stumped wrist—it's as if he's becoming the same darkmage he despises."

Despite the day's warmth, Elena shivered.

Er'ril glanced to her. "I'm sorry. This is a joyous moment and shouldn't be marred by such dark thoughts." He pulled her closer to his side. "Such matters can wait till another day."

She leaned against him. "Where's Nee'lahn anyway? I thought I was the late one."

Er'ril straightened. "We were waiting on you." He raised his other arm, signaling Kast, who stood a few paces off with his mate Sy-wen.

The Bloodrider lifted a horn to his lips and blew a single long note. It was a bright and triumphant sound that echoed far out to sea and served to drive away the bit of melancholy from Elena's heart.

Rising on her toes, Elena craned for a better view as the small western gate of the courtyard swung open. Tol'chuk stepped forth, leading the diminutive form of Nee'lahn.

The og're wore a huge grin. It was one of Tol'chuk's last acts before leaving for his homelands in the mountains. He would be returning the Heart of his people and seeking the counsel of the Triad. There was a mystery yet to be solved: the strange connection between ebon'stone and heartstone. The two crystals—one bright, one dark—had been mined from the same mountain. There was some dark link between the two, and even the spirits of the Blood Diary sensed an answer must be sought out. Tol'chuk hoped his own tribal elders might hold some piece to this ancient puzzle.

But even this mystery could wait. Today, Tol'chuk had been granted the honor to lead Nee'lahn forward, a giant leading a child.

Nee'lahn stepped to the crushed white stones, dressed in flowing silks that seemed to catch the breeze with each step, a petal in the wind.

As Tol'chuk led her, so Nee'lahn led another small figure. Her fingers gripped the hand of a child. The boy appeared no older than three, but Elena knew that the nyphai did not age like humans. When his seed was still attached to his belly, dormant and waiting, he had appeared no more than a babe. But a moon ago, when Nee'lahn had first set foot upon the shores of A'loa Glen, the child had shed his seed. From that moment on, he had grown rapidly, from babe to toddling child in only a single moon.

Upon landing here, Nee'lahn had taken the dropping of the

boy's seed as a harbinger of hope—and on this spring day, she was responding in kind, taking a chance.

Nee'lahn led the boy to the circle of spectators. Once there, she took her place and guided the boy ahead of her. "Go on, Rodricko. You know what to do."

He glanced up to the nyphai's face. His eyes were the same violet as Nee'lahn's, and his hair the same color of warm honey. "Yes, Mama." He let go of her hand and ventured out into the center of the circle.

The boy glanced at those gathered around him. He bit his lower lip, clearly shy of so many faces peering down at him. But he did not falter. He crossed to where stone ended and freshly turned loam began. Along with the repair of the courtyard, the blasted root of the old koa'kona tree had been dug up from the central yard, and clean soil had been hauled in to fill the space. Nothing had been sown here by the gardeners. It was as if they had innately known that only one thing could be planted in this particular place.

Another koa'kona.

Little Rodricko, named after the caretaker of Nee'lahn's own tree, stepped from the stone to the soft loam with a large seed clutched in his tiny hand. It was the seed from which he had been born, and now he was returning it to the soil.

He dropped to his knees, put the seed aside, and began to dig a hole. Once it was as deep as his own elbow, he straightened and grabbed up his seed. He glanced over his shoulder to Nee'lahn, who smiled proudly at his efforts. She gave him a small nod.

The child dropped the seed into the hole and slowly pulled handfuls of soil over it. Elena heard him sniff and wipe at his eyes. After being joined for so long—boy and seed together— this was certainly a difficult act, a rite of passage for the boy.

Once done, he climbed back to his feet. He stared down at his handiwork.

Nee'lahn coaxed him gently. "Go on, Rodricko. Try."

The boy turned to his mother, tears glimmering in his eyes.

"Go on, my love."

He nodded and swung back, lifting a hand over the newly filled hole.

Elena held her breath, as did everyone else. Nee'lahn clutched both her hands to her neck, clearly praying. The original koa'kona had died here, its roots drowned in saltwater when the island sank. Er'ril had warned Nee'lahn that this was not fit ground to plant the first new koa'kona. But Nee'lahn had been sure the boy's seed-dropping on this shore was a sign. "A male has never been born to my people," the nyphai had explained. "The boy is special, so certainly his tree must be unique. Maybe it will thrive where another could not."

The boy continued to stand with his hand over his planted seed. Slowly, a slight greenish glow seemed to flow over the boy, as if the sunlight overhead were filtering through unseen leaves.

Nee'lahn made a small sound—half sob, half sigh of joy.

From the soil between the boy's toes, a small green shoot wriggled up and climbed into the sunshine. It was bright and healthy and pure.

"It's rooting," Er'ril said, turning to her, his eyes huge with amazement.

She reached an arm around his waist and hugged him.

A cheer arose from the others. The little boy turned in a slow circle, a wide smile on his little face. Nee'lahn rushed forward and scooped him in her arms, kissing his cheek.

Elena watched Nee'lahn with the boy and sank deeper into Er'ril's arms. She stared at the little green shoot poking from the dark soil. It stood for so much: life from death, a new cycle beginning. Tears rose to her eyes.

"What's wrong?" Er'ril asked.

She could not answer. Her heart was too full. She glanced to the others, wounded but somehow surviving, celebrating. To her, to all of them, the green sprig represented one other thing.

Hope.

AND HERE I'LL END THIS SECTION OF ELENA'S TALE, ON A MOMENT of hope, balanced on the tender leaves of new growth. All that remains is one last chapter, one last battle, one last chance. From here, all that has been hidden will be revealed. Truths will burn, lies will heal, and hearts will be broken upon a single word.

So enjoy this one scintillating moment in time. Savor it like the crystalline drop of the finest wine on the tongue. But know this: nothing lasts forever.

Not wine, not hope, not love . . . not even a wit'ch.

Read on for a sneak peek at

Wit'ch Star

SEATED ON THE ROSETHORN THRONE, ELENA STUDIED THE RIDDLE before her. The small stranger, dressed in a patchwork of silks and linens, appeared just a boy with his smooth and unlined face—but he was clearly no youngster. His manner was too calm under the gazes of those gathered in the Great Hall. His eyes glinted with sarcastic amusement, bitter and road-worn. And the set of his lips, shadowing a smile, remained both hard and cold.

Elena felt a twinge of unease near the man, despite his illusion of innocence.

The stranger dropped to one knee before her, sweeping off his foppish hat. Scores of bells—tin, silver, gold, and copper, sewn throughout his clothes—jangled brightly.

A taller figure stepped to the tiny man's side—Prince Tylamon Royson, lord of Castle Mryl to the north. The prince-turned-pirate had forgone his usual finery and wore scuffed boots and a salt-scarred black cloak. His cheeks were ruddy, and his sandy hair unkempt. He had arrived at the island's docks with the rising sun, requesting immediate audience with Elena and the war council.

The prince bowed to one knee, then motioned to the stranger. "May I present Harlequin Quail? He has come far, with news you should hear."

Elena motioned for them both to stand. "Rise, Lord Tyrus. Be welcome." She studied the newcomer as he rose to his feet amid another chorus of jingling. The man had indeed come from afar. His face was oddly complexioned: a paleness that bordered on blue, as if he were forever suffocating. But it was the hue of his eyes that was the most striking—a shining gold, full of a wry slyness.

518

"I'm sorry for disturbing you so early on this summer morn-ing," Lord Tyrus intoned formally, straightening his disheveled cloak as if noticing for the first time his sorry state.

Er'ril, Elena's liegeman and husband, spoke from his station beside the throne. "What is this urgency, Lord Tyrus? We have no time for fools and jesters."

Elena did not have to glance to the side to know the Standi plainsman wore his usual hard scowl. She had seen it often enough over the last two moons as sour tidings had been flow-ing into Alasea: supply chains to the island cut off by monsters and strange weather; townships struck by fires and plagues; ill-shaped beasts roaming the countryside.

But the worst tidings struck closer to home.

Elementals, those rare folk tuned to the Land's energy, were succumbing to some dread malaise. The mer'ai were losing their sea sense and their link to their dragons; the elv'in ships could not fly as high or far; and now Nee'lahn reported that the voice of her lute was growing weaker as the tree spirit faded in-side. Clearly whatever damage had been inflicted upon the Land by the Weirgates was continuing its onslaught. Elemental magicks waned as if from a bleeding wound.

As a consequence, the press of dwindling time weighed upon them all. If they were to act against the Gul'gotha, it must be soon—before their own forces weakened further, before the gifts of the Land faded completely away. But their armies were spread wide. As matters stood, the campaign against the Dark Lord's stronghold, the volcanic Blackhall, could begin no sooner than next spring. Er'ril said it would take until midwin-ter to position all their armies; and an assault upon the island then, when the northern seas were beset with savage storms, would give the advantage to Blackhall.

So spring at the earliest, when the winter storms died away.

Elena had begun to doubt whether they'd be ready even then. Their forces were far from prepared. So much was still unknown. Tol'chuk had yet to return from his own lands; gone these past two moons with Fardale and a handful of others, he sought to question his og're elders about the link between heartstone and ebon'stone. Many of the elv'in scoutships had not returned from reconnaissance over Blackhall. The d'warf army, led by Wennar, had sent crows with news that their forces yet gathered near Penryn. The d'warf captain wanted more time to rally his people. But time was short for all of them.

And now this urgent news from afar.

Lord Tyrus turned to his companion. "Harlequin, tell them what you've learned."

The tiny figure nodded. "I come with tidings both bright and grim." A coin appeared in his hand as if conjured from nothing. With the flick of a wrist, he tossed it high into the air. Torchlight glinted off gold.

Elena's gaze tracked the coin's flight as it danced among the rafters, then fell.

She startled back on her throne upon finding the strange man now toe-to-toe before her, leaning in. He had crossed the distance in a heartbeat, silent despite the hundred bells he wore.

Even Er'ril was caught by surprise. With a roar, he swept out his sword and bared it between queen and jester. "What trick is this?"

As answer, the man caught the falling coin in an outstretched palm, winked salaciously at Elena, then backed down the two steps, again jangling with a chorus of bells.

Lord Tyrus spoke up, a cold smile on his face. "Be not fooled by Harlequin's motley appearance. For these past ten winters, he has been my master spy, in service to the Pirate Guild of Port Rawl. There are no better eyes and ears to sneak upon others unaware."

Elena straightened in her seat. "So it would seem."

Er'ril pulled back his sword but did not sheathe it. "Enough tricks. If he comes with information, let's hear it."

"As the iron man asks, so it shall be." Harlequin held up his gold coin to the flash of torchlight. "First the bright news. You've cut the Black Heart a deeper wound than even you suspect by the destruction of his black statues. He's lost his precious d'warf army and is left with only men and monsters to defend his volcanic lair."

Tyrus interrupted. "Harlequin has spent the last half winter scouting the edges of Blackhall. He's prepared charts and logs of the Dark Lord's forces and strengths."

"How did he come by these?" Er'ril grumbled.

Harlequin stared brazenly back. "From under the nose of the Dark Lord's own lieutenant. A brother of yours, is he not?"

Elena glanced to Er'ril and saw the anger in his eye.

"He is *not* my brother," her liegeman said coldly.

Elena spoke into the tension. "You were inside Blackhall itself?"

Harlequin's mask of amusement cracked. Elena spotted a glimpse of something pained and darker beyond. "Aye," he whispered. "I've walked its monstrous halls and shadowed rooms—and pray I never do so again."

Elena leaned forward. "And you mentioned grim news, Master Quail?"

"Grim news indeed." Harlequin lifted his arm and opened the fingers that had clenched around the gold coin. Upon his palm now rested a lump of coal. "If you wish to defeat the Black Heart, it must be done by Midsummer Eve."

Elena frowned. "In one moon's time?"

"Impossible," Er'ril scoffed.

Harlequin fixed Elena with those strange gold eyes. "If you don't stop the Black Beast by the next full moon, you will all be dead."

MERIC RAN THE LENGTH OF THE STORMWING. HIS FEET FLEW across the familiar planks, hurdling balustrades and leaping decks. His eyes remained fixed to the skies. Through the morning mists, a dark speck was visible high overhead, plummeting gracelessly out of the sky. It was one of the elv'in scoutships, returning from the lands and seas around the volcanic island of Blackhall.

Something was wrong.

Reaching the prow of his own ship, Meric lifted both arms and cast out his powers. A surge of energy billowed through his form and into the sky, racing upward to flow into the empty well that was the other's boat's iron keel. Meric fed his power, but the plummeting ship continued its dive toward the waters around A'loa Glen.

As he fought the inevitable, Meric felt the weight of the other ship upon his own shoulders. He was driven to one knee as the *Stormwing*, drained of its own magickal energies, began to drift lower toward the docks.

Gasping in his exertions, Meric refused to relent. *Mother above, help me!*

He now saw with two sets of eyes: a pair looking up and a pair looking down. Linked between the two ships, he felt the weak beat of the ship's captain, *Frelisha*—a second cousin to his mother. She was barely alive. She must have drained all her energies to bring the ship even this close to home.

Below, Meric whispered into the wind. "Do not give up, Cousin."

He was heard. Through his magickal connection, the last words of the captain reached him. "We are betrayed!"

With this final utterance, the heartbeat held between Meric's upraised hands fluttered once more, then stopped forever.

"No!" Meric fell to his other knee.

A moment later, a huge shadow shot past the starboard rail. The explosion of wood and blast of water nearby were a distant echo. Meric slumped to his planks, head hanging. As alarm bells clanged along the docks and shouts rose in a chorus of panic, one word whispered from his lips: "Betrayed . . ."

SEATED IN THE GRAND COURTYARD OF THE CASTLE KEEP, NEE'LAHN watched the children pause in their play as bells rang along the docks beyond the stone walls. Her own fingers stopped in midstrum on the strings of her lute.

Something had happened at the docks.

A few steps away, little Rodricko lowered his stick, a pretend sword, and glanced to his mother. His opponent in this playful sparring match—the Dre'rendi child Sheeshon—cocked her head at the noise, her own fake sword forgotten.

Nee'lahn rolled to her knees and swung her lute over a shoulder, bumping the thin trunk of the koa'kona behind her. Leaves shook overhead. The fragile sapling was thin-limbed and topheavy with summer leaves—not unlike the male child that was its bonded twin.

"Rodricko, come away," Nee'lahn said, reaching out to the boy. Rodricko was all limbs and awkwardness. *Thank the Mother, his initial growth surge is about over.* Both tree and boy would grow into their forms more gradually from here.

"Sheeshon, you too," Nee'lahn added. "Let's see if the kitchens are ready with your porridge."

As Nee'lahn straightened, she dug her bare toes into the rich loam at the base of the tree and took strength from the energy in the soil. She readied herself to enter the stone halls of the castle. Reluctant to leave, she drew the strength of root deep inside her.

Around them, the gardens of the Grand Courtyard were in the full bloom of summer. Tiny white flowers garlanded the ivy-encrusted walls. The dogwoods stood amid cloaks of fallen petals. Red berries dotted the trimmed bushes that lined the crushed white-gravel paths. Most glorious of all were the hundreds of rosebushes, newly planted last fall. They had blossomed into a riot of colors: blushing pinks, dusky purples, honeyed yellows. Even the sea breezes were given color and substance by their sweet fragrances.

But it was more than beauty that held her here, for only in this courtyard were her past, present, and future gathered in one place: the lute that held the heart of her own beloved, the sapling that sprang from the seed of her bonded, and the boy who represented all the hopes of the nyphai people.

Sighing, Nee'lahn tousled the mop of sun-bleached curls atop Rodricko's head and took the boy's hand. So much hope in such a little package.

Sheeshon reached to take Rodricko's other hand, the webbed folds between the Dre'rendi girl's fingers marking her as a link between the seafaring Bloodriders and the ocean-dwelling mer'ai. Rodricko joined hands with her. Over the past moons, the two children, alike in their uniqueness, had become all but inseparable.

"Let's see if the kitchens are ready," Nee'lahn said, turning.

She stepped away, but Rodricko seemed to have taken root in the soil. "Mama, what about the bud song? You promised I could try."

Nee'lahn opened her mouth to object. She was anxious to learn what had arisen at the docks, but already the alarm bells were echoing away.

"You promised," Rodricko repeated.

Nee'lahn frowned, then glanced to the tree. She had promised. It was indeed time he learned his own song, but she was hesitant, reluctant to let Rodricko go.

"I'm old enough. And this night the moon is full!"

Nee'lahn found no way to object. Traditionally among the

nyphai, the first full moon of summer was when the young bonded with their new trees, when babe and seed became woman and tree.

"Are you sure you're ready, Rodricko?"

"He's ready," Sheeshon answered, her small eyes surprisingly certain. Nee'lahn had heard the child was rich in sea magicks, an ability to sense beyond the horizons to what's to come. The *rajor maga*, it was termed by the Dre'rendi.

"Please, Mama," Rodricko begged.

The dock bells had gone silent.

"You may try the bud song; then it's off to the kitchens before the cook gets angry."

Rodricko's face brightened like a sun coming through the clouds. He turned to Sheeshon. "Come on. I have to get ready."

Sheeshon, always the more sober child, frowned. "You must hurry, if we have to finish before the kitchen closes."

Nee'lahn nodded. "Go ahead, but don't be disappointed if you fail. Maybe next summer . . ."

Rodricko nodded, though clearly deaf to her words. He crossed to the tree and knelt on limbs nearly as thin as the sapling's branches. Now would be the moment when all the fates would either come together or fall into disarray, for Rodricko was the first male nyphai. Both sapling and boy were unique, the result of the union of Nee'lahn's tree and the twisted Grim wraith Cecelia. Who knew if the ancient rites, songs, and patterns of growth would hold true here?

Nee'lahn held her breath.

Rodricko touched the tree's bark, drawing a fingernail down through the thin outer coating. A droplet of sap flowed, and the sapling's treesong rose up from its deep thrum and quested out for Rodricko. Nee'lahn listened with both ears and heart. The boy was either attuned to the song, or he would be rebuffed. She was not sure which she hoped. A part of her wanted him to fail. She had been given so little time with him, less than a single winter . . .

Rodricko used a rose thorn to prick a finger, drawing blood. He reached his wounded finger toward the flow of sap.

"Sing," she whispered. "Let the tree hear your heart."

He glanced over his shoulder toward her, his eyes shining with his fear. The boy sensed the weight of the moment.

Sing, she willed to him silently.

And he did. His lips parted, and as he exhaled, the sweetest notes flowed forth. His voice was so bright that the sun seemed to grow pale in comparison. The world grew dark around the edges, as if night had come early, but around the sapling, a pool of luminescence grew brighter and brighter.

In response, the sapling's own song swelled, like a flower drawn to the sun. At first tentatively, then more fully, boy and sapling became transfixed in treesong.

At that moment, Nee'lahn knew the boy would succeed. Tears flowed down her cheeks with both relief and loss. There was no turning back. Nee'lahn could feel the surge of elemental magick from the boy and tree, one feeding on the other, building until it was impossible to say where one began and the other ended.

Two songs became one.

Nee'lahn found herself on her knees without realizing she had moved. Treesong filled the world. She had never heard such a chorus before.

She craned up at the thin branches; she knew what would come next. Leaves began to shake as if from a strong breeze. Each branch tip throbbed with treesong and elemental energy. And still tree and boy sang in harmony, voices louder, strained, beautiful, expectant.

With nowhere else to go, the magick trapped in the tips of each branch had only one course left to follow.

From the end of each tiny branch, buds pushed from stems, growing from magick and blood: petaled expressions of the treesong brought to existence by the union of boy and sapling.

He—they—had done it.

A gasp escaped from Rodricko, both joy and pain.

Slowly the treesong faded, as if draining down a well, exhausted. The summer sun returned to the courtyard.

Rodricko turned, his small face shining with joy and pride. "I did it, Mama." His voice was now deeper, richer, almost a man's voice. But he was no man. She heard the lilt of magick behind his voice. He was nyphai. He turned back to his tree. "We are now one."

Nee'lahn remained silent, her gaze fixed on the tree. *What have we done?* she thought silently. *Sweet Mother, what have we done?*

Hanging from the tips of each branch were indeed the buds of new union. They would open for the first time this evening with the rising of the summer's first moon. But Rodricko's flowers were not the bright violet of the nyphai, jewels among the greenery. Instead, from each tip hung buds the color of clotted blood, black and bruised—the same night shade as the Grim wraiths.

Nee'lahn covered her face and began to sob.

"Mama," Rodricko spoke at her side, "what's wrong?"

DEEP BELOW THE GRAND COURTYARD, JOACH SLOUCHED ALONG A narrow tunnel. It had taken him a full moon's time to find this hidden path. Much of the secret tunnel system under the Edifice had fallen to ruin, destroyed during the awakening of Ragnar'k from his stony sleep. Joach remembered that day: his own harrowing escape from Greshym's enthrallment, his flight with Brother Moris, the battle at the heart of the island. Though less than two winters had passed, it now seemed like ages. He was an old man, his youth stolen from him.

Joach rested, leaning heavily upon his stone staff, a length of petrified gray wood impregnated with green crystals. The end of the stave glowed with a sickly aether, lighting his way. It was the only bit of dark magick left in the dread thing.

His fingers tightened on the staff, sensing the feeble trickle of power remaining. He had struck a bad bargain with Greshym for this length of petrified wood. It had cost Joach his youth, leaving him a wrinkled and brittle version of himself. Standing now deep underground, Joach felt the weight of rock overhead press upon his thin shoulders. His heart pounded in his ears. It had taken him all morning to climb the long-hidden stair to reach here.

"Only a little way more," he promised himself.

Fueled by determination, he continued, praying the chamber he sought was still intact. As he reached the tunnel's end, he used the stump of his right wrist to shove aside a tangle of withered roots hanging across the threshold. They crumbled away at his touch.

He lifted his staff forward.

Beyond, a cavernous chamber opened.

Joach wheezed with relief, and limped past the threshold. Overhead, roots and fibrous stragglers hung like swamp moss, yellow and brittle. Rodricko's thin sapling, above, had yet to send its young roots down into this cavernous tomb. Here death still reigned.

Joach found a certain solace in that gloomy realization. Beyond the castle walls, the summer days were too bright, too green, too full of rebirth. He preferred the shadows.

Exhausted, knees complaining, he advanced. The chamber floor was strewn with boulders and the moldering corpses of the dead. Tiny furred and scaled creatures scurried from his staff's sickly light. Joach ignored the scavengers and lifted his staff. Old scars marked the walls, from the swaths of the balefire wielded by Shorkan and Greshym during the battle. They looked like some ancient writing in charcoal.

If only he could understand it . . .

Joach sighed. So much remained closed to him. He had spent the past two moons holed up in the libraries and nooks, poring over texts, scrolls, and manuscripts. If he ever hoped to regain his youth, he needed to understand the magick that had stolen it. But he was a mere apprentice to the black arts, far from true understanding. He had only managed to glean one clue: *Ragnar'k.*

Before joining with Kast, the dragon had slumbered in stone at the heart of the island for untold ages, growing rich with the elemental magick of the dream, imbuing the rocks and crystals here with its energies. Any hope of regaining his own youth lay in the mystery of the dreaming magick. Joach had lost his youth in the dream desert—his youth and one other thing.

He closed his eyes, again feeling the flow of blood across his hand, the slightest gasp in his ear. "Kesla," he whispered out to the cavern of the dead. She too had been like Ragnar'k, a creature of dream.

If all his pain arose out of dream landscape, perhaps his cure lay there, too. This frail hope had finally driven him down into the bowels of the island.

He had a plan.

Using his staff as a crutch, Joach limped over bones and around boulders. Though Ragnar'k was long gone, the dragon had slept in this chamber for so long that every stone, every bit of broken crystal, had been imbued with its magick. Joach planned to tap this elemental power.

Like Greshym, Joach was a dreamweaver. But unlike the darkmage, Joach was also a dream *sculptor*, with the ability to craft substance out of dream. If Joach hoped to take on Greshym and steal back his youth, he would need to hone his skill. But to do that, he first needed energy. He needed the power of the dream.

Joach crossed to the center of the half-collapsed chamber and slowly turned in a circle, studying the room. He sensed the abundance of energy here. Satisfied, he shifted his staff to the crook of his stumped right arm and slipped out a dagger. Clenching the hilt between his teeth, he sliced his left palm. As the blood welled, he spat out the dagger and lifted his wounded hand. Squeezing a fist, he dribbled blood onto the stone floor. Drops splattered at his feet.

Ready, Joach let his eyes drift half closed, slipping into the dream state. The dark chamber grew fitfully brighter, as swaths of rock and wall took on the soft luminescence of residual energies—echoes of the dragon's dream.

A smile formed on Joach's thin lips.

Reaching out with the magick in his own blood, he tied the energies to himself, weaving it all together as was his birthright. Once all was secure, Joach grabbed up his staff again with his bloodied left hand. He lifted the weapon and again slowly turned in a circle, drawing the magick into the staff. He turned and turned, dizzying himself, but did not stop until every dreg of magick was siphoned into the length of stony wood, weaving stone and magick together.

As he worked, the staff grew cold to the touch, trembling with pent-up power. The crystals along the staff's length glowed with brilliance, flaring brighter, even as the cavern grew dimmer.

Soon there was nothing but darkness around Joach.

Satisfied, he lowered the staff and leaned upon it, his legs wobbling and weak. He stared at his crutch. The green crystals there gleamed with a sharp radiance. Joach's shoulders shook with relief. He had done it! He had bound the energy to the staff.

All that was left was to bind the staff to *him*, to give him the skill to wield it to its fullest extent. Dreamweaving alone could not do the binding that he needed. A deeper connection was necessary, and he knew a way—an old spell, and one that came with a high cost, as did all things powerful. But what were a few more winters lost, when so many more had already been stolen from him? Besides, he had been involved in this same spell before, when it had been cast by Elena and forged upon Greshym's old staff. So why not once more? Why not cast by his own hand, and forged upon this new staff, now ripe with dream energies?

To challenge Greshym, he needed a mighty weapon and the skill to use it. There was only one way to quickly gain such skill.

He must forge the staff into a *blood weapon*.

Joach prepared himself, concentrating on the red dribble trailing down the staff's surface. It was not a particularly difficult spell, simpler really than calling forth balefire. It was the cost that gave him pause. He remembered Elena's sudden aging.

But it was too late to look back. Before he could balk, Joach released the spell in a flow of words and will.

The effect was immediate. He felt something vital rip from him and pass through his blood into the staff.

Gasping, he fell to his knees. His vision blurred, but he refused to give himself over to the darkness. He breathed deeply, sucking in air like a drowning man. Finally his vision cleared. The room slowed its spin.

Joach pulled the staff across his knees, and stared at the hand that gripped the wood. As with his sister before him, the spell had aged him instantly. His fingernails had grown out and curled; his skin had crumpled. Had his sacrifice of winters been worth it?

He lifted the staff. The gray wood was now as white as snow. The green crystals, aglow with dream energies, stood out starkly, like the crimson streaks flowing from the withered hand that held it. With each thud of his heart, the streaks flowed farther down the shaft, fusing staff and body, forging weapon to wielder.

Joach hauled himself to his feet. When Elena had forged Greshym's old staff, Joach had become a skilled warrior with the weapon. Would the same hold true here? Had the fusion granted him, as he hoped, the ability to wield the dream magicks now woven to the staff?

Shaking back the sleeve of his cloak, Joach exposed the stump of his right arm, his hand lost to the blood lust of Greshym's beast. If Joach could mend that injury, then perhaps there was hope—not only for himself, but for them all. A mighty war was coming, and Joach did not want to remain behind with the children and the feeble.

He reached out to the staff. As his severed wrist touched the petrified wood, Joach willed his magick—not weaving this time, but *sculpting*.

From the stump of his wrist, a phantom hand bloomed out in wisps and tendrils. Ghostly fingers stretched and gripped the staff. Joach's legs shook, but he used his blood connection with the staff to draw upon the dream energies. Slowly the spirit hand grew solid, gaining substance from his focus and attention. Fingers that had once been ghostly became whole. Joach felt the grain of the staff's wood, the sharp edges of the crystalline stone.

He lifted the staff with his dream-sculpted hand and held it aloft. Blood continued to feed the staff through his conjured hand.

Dream had indeed become substance!

Power thrilled through him. Dark magick and dream energies, now fused, were his to command! He pictured a girl with eyes the color of twilight, and his lips moved in a silent vow of vengeance. He would find Greshym and make him pay for his theft, make them all pay for what Joach had lost among the sands.

Joach lowered the staff, then wrapped his sliced palm and took the staff back up in his gloved grip, severing the connection between flesh and petrified wood. As the blood drained out of the white wood, its length grew gray again. For now, he would keep his new blood weapon a secret.

Joach raised his right arm and stared at the sculpted hand, formed out of elemental energy. It would not do to let this be seen yet, either. There would be too many questions . . . and besides, it drained his precious energies. He waved the hand through the air and unbound the pattern, and like a snuffed candle, the hand wisped out of existence, back to just dream.

Using his staff as a crutch, Joach headed out of the cavern.

There would come a time to reveal his secret. But for now he would keep the knowledge close to his aching heart, next to the memory of a tawny-haired girl with the softest of lips.